AUSTRALIAN

The Workingman's Paradise

For Uncle Jack
   Just got copies from the printer
today — 18 xii 80 — in time to
miss the Christmas market! I
think you might find it
interesting — & Lane himself
a type familiar to you — he's
an amazing character — eventually
I will finish a full length study
of him — This is just a
part of his life. W.R very
best wishes for Christmas
1980, Michael.

AUSTRALIAN LITERARY REPRINTS

General Editor: G. A. Wilkes
Challis Professor of English Literature
University of Sydney

———————

Rolf Boldrewood: *The Miner's Right* (1890)
with an Introduction by R. G. Geering

C. J. Brennan: *Poems* [1913]
with an Introduction by G. A. Wilkes

Marcus Clarke: *Old Tales of a Young Country* (1871)
with an Introduction by Joan Poole
(out of print)

Frank Fowler: *Southern Lights and Shadows* (1859)
with an Introduction by R. G. Geering

Henry Kingsley: *The Hillyars and the Burtons* (1865)
with an Introduction by Leonie Kramer

'John Miller' (William Lane): *The Workingman's Paradise* (1892)
with an Introduction by Michael Wilding

Catherine Helen Spence: *Gathered In* (1881-2)
with an Introduction by B. L. Waters and G. A. Wilkes
(out of print)

Charles Tompson: *Wild Notes, from the Lyre of a Native Minstrel* (1826)
with an Introduction by G. A. Wilkes and G. A. Turnbull

WILLIAM LANE

Chairman of the New Australia Co-operative Settlement
Association and first editor of *The Worker*, the journal of the
Associated Workers of Queensland, published in Brisbane at one
penny. Reproduced from the front page of Volume 4, Number
116, 22 July 1893.

The Workingman's Paradise

AN AUSTRALIAN LABOUR NOVEL

by

'John Miller'

(William Lane)

WITH AN INTRODUCTION BY

Michael Wilding

SYDNEY UNIVERSITY PRESS

SYDNEY UNIVERSITY PRESS
Press Building, University of Sydney

UNITED KINGDOM, EUROPE, MIDDLE EAST, AFRICA
Eurospan Limited, 3 Henrietta Street
London WC2E 8LU

NORTH AND SOUTH AMERICA
International Scholarly Book Services, Inc.
Forest Grove, Oregon

National Library of Australia Cataloguing-in-Publication data

Lane, William, 1861-1917.
The workingman's paradise.

(Australian literary reprints)
Facsimile reprint. Originally published, Brisbane:
Edwards, Dunlop & Co. and Worker Board of Trustees,
1892.
ISBN 0 424 00057 1

I. Title. (Series)

A823'.2

First published 1892
by Edwards, Dunlop & Co., Sydney, Brisbane and London
and the Worker Board of Trustees, Brisbane

Facsimile edition 1980 by Sydney University Press
Introduction © Sydney University Press 1980

Printed in Australia
by Southwood Press Pty Limited, Marrickville, N.S.W.

CONTENTS

ILLUSTRATIONS

INTRODUCTION

William Lane was born in Bristol, England on 6 September 1861, and died in Auckland, New Zealand on 26 August 1917. He was the eldest of five sons and one daughter. His brother John, next in age, recalled that the family

> sprung from peasant blood of County Cork and County Gloucester. Lane combined the sturdy persistence and love of adventure of the West Saxon, with the warm-hearted idealism and brilliance of the Celt. His English mother's Puritan influence remained with him throughout his life; and the evils of drink bitterly felt by him in childhood, made him a life-long enemy of alcohol.[1]

His father, as the youngest brother, E. H. Lane, put it 'had emerged from a peasant environment in Ireland to that of a humble member of the petty bourgeoisie',[2] an Irish protestant of strong conservative politics; a landscape gardener, he had at one time employed twenty workmen but had been proletarianized into poverty and alcoholism. John Lane records of William that

> before he was 16 he struck out for himself, and migrated to America, landing in New York, penniless, friendless and unknown. He worked at odd jobs in town and country; as shop boy in stores, as handy boy on farms, and, finally, after varied

1. John Lane, 'William Lane's Task', *Daily Mail* (Brisbane), 17 February 1930. This was the first of a five part series written for the *Mail* by John Lane about his brother and the New Australia movement. An earlier account by John Lane, delivered as a lecture to the Brisbane Workers' Educational Association, appeared in three parts in the *Daily Standard* (Brisbane), 9, 10 and 12 May 1924.
2. E. H. Lane ('Jack Cade'), *Dawn to Dusk: Reminiscences of a Rebel*, William Brooks, Brisbane 1939, p.6.

experience in the United States and Canada, became printer's devil on a Detroit newspaper, where he worked up to be compositor, and then a reporter, in which he found his vocation. While doing press work in Detroit he married an American-bred grand-daughter of a Scotch professor.[3]

Her name was Anne McQuire. William 'never took kindly to American ways and manners' according to John, and in 1885 emigrated to Australia, where his brothers Ernie and Frank had arrived the previous year. Settling in Brisbane he found work as a journalist for *Figaro*, the *Telegraph*, the *Courier* and the *Observer*. He wrote under various pseudonyms, one of which, 'John Miller', he used for *The Workingman's Paradise*. The name derives from the opening chapter of William Morris's Marxist romance, *A Dream of John Ball* (1887), part of the password of the revolutionaries of John Ball's Peasant Revolt of 1381: 'John the Miller, hath y-ground small, small, small'. The correct reply was 'The king's son of heaven shall pay for all'.[4] It was the appropriate pseudonym for Lane's mystical, religious communism.

Together with a compositor friend Alfred Walker, Lane established *The Boomerang* (19 November 1887), a weekly labour-liberal paper: 'A Live Newspaper — Born of the Soil'. From reporting on labour issues, Lane became increasingly involved in the trade union movement. He was one of those advocating the 'New Unionism' — the extension of the union movement into non-skilled, non-craft, non-trade areas to form a united body of the working class.

3. *Daily Mail* (Brisbane), 17 February 1930.
4. *A Dream of John Ball* in A. L. Morton (ed.), *Three Works by William Morris*, Seven Seas, Berlin 1968, p.40. *The Worker* (Brisbane), II, 26, 13 June 1891, p.7 identifies Lane's pseudonyms: ' "Sketcher," "Bystander" mostly . . . "John Miller." '

'He felt that if only the working classes could be got to understand the why and wherefore of things, then, and then only, would it be possible to change living conditions, so that life for all would be worth living', wrote John Lane.[5] He was chief architect of the Queensland Australian Labour Federation (ALF), planned as the spearhead of a federal organization of unions.

The Boomerang ran into financial difficulties and came under pressure from advertisers restricting editorial freedom. Lane resigned. The ALF established a new paper, *The Worker*, and Lane was appointed editor. The first issue appeared on 1 March 1890 and having been boycotted by the newsboys, was sold along the line of the Eight-Hour-Day procession by volunteers. In 1891 government hostility to *The Worker* and fear of its influence resulted in the imposition of a postage charge on all newspapers, previously carried free, raising *The Worker's* subscription from two shillings to three shillings a year.[6]

Through *The Worker*'s columns Lane attempted to direct the union movement beyond the specific concern of wages and employment into a wider political programme of socialism. 'Lane's role was to wed the labour movement in Queensland to the socialist ideal', Robin Gollan wrote; as a consequence, from 1887-93, Lane 'occupied a position of leadership that has rarely been equalled in the history of Australian radicalism'.[7] 'When future historians ever

5.   *Daily Mail* (Brisbane), 17 February 1930.
6.   B. J. Guyatt, 'The Publicists — The Labour Press 1880-1915' in D. J. Murphy, R. B. Joyce and Colin A. Hughes (eds), *Prelude to Power: The Rise of the Labour Party in Queensland 1885-1915*, Jacaranda, Brisbane 1970, pp.248-50. *The Worker* (Brisbane), II, 42, 9 January 1892, p.1.
7.   Robin Gollan, *Radical and Working Class Politics: A Study of Eastern Australia 1850-1910*, Melbourne University Press, 1960, pp.124, 105.

undertake the task of analysing and assigning the causes and effects and course of the phenomenon of Australian Socialism', A. St Ledger wrote in 1909, 'Lane's writings in *The Worker* will be found the *fons et origo* from which all further and subsequent explorations must begin'.[8] Lane's journalism of this period has never been collected, but four examples of his work are reprinted in Manning Clark's *Select Documents in Australian History 1851-1900*.[9]

The newly organized unions were immediately tested in the financial crisis of 1890-3. The employers organized amongst themselves and a succession of strikes ensued. 'Writers on the period agree substantially that the aim of the employers was to break the unions'.[10] The first part of *The Workingman's Paradise*, Lane points out in the preface, covers two days 'during the summer of 1888-9'; the second part is set 'at the commencement of the Queensland bush strike excitement in 1891' (p. iii). The novel begins, that is, with the union movement untested; between parts one and two came the maritime strike; and the novel ends with the beginning of the shearers' strike. These political confrontations are the off-stage determinants of the characters' political consciousness; they are a major unwritten, but present, component of the novel. The events occur off-stage, but they are also assumed to be known, so vast, so public. Robin Gollan indicates the strikes' significance as mass action, mythic confrontation.

The Maritime Strike began in August 1890, and soon involved transport workers, miners and shearers in the eastern

---

8. A. St Ledger, *Australian Socialism: An Historical Sketch of its Origin and Developments*, Macmillan, London 1909, p.14.
9. Manning Clark, *Select Documents in Australian History: Volume II, 1851-1900*, Angus and Robertson, Sydney 1955, pp.564-73, 778-81.
10. Gollan, *Radical and Working Class Politics*, p.131.

colonies, South Australia and New Zealand for periods of a fortnight to two months. The whole of the trade union movement was involved financially, and many workers not on strike were thrown out of work. The issues were, on the union side, "the recognition of unionism", by which they meant the exclusive right of the unions to negotiate working conditions in industry. On the employers' side the issue was "freedom of contract", the right of employers to engage unionists or non-unionists, to work under union conditions or under conditions agreed to by individual employees. The strike was fought with great bitterness and as it progressed became open class warfare. The large numbers involved, and the mass demonstrations, such as the fifty thousand in Flinders Park, Melbourne, and the procession a mile and a half long through the streets of Sydney were quite different from anything that had previously occurred in the history of Australian unionism. In fact, the strike became a mass movement in support of specific trade union demands, but also implicitly, and in part consciously, a political movement in support of vaguely defined political objectives. The unions were defeated by lack of funds, by the employment of non-union labour and by the lack of a definite political objective.[11]

The shearers' strike began in the first week of January 1891 when unionists refused to sign the pastoralists' contract of 1890, which, after the defeat of the Maritime strike, disavowed the principle of the closed shop. The agreement also reduced the rates for labourers in the shearing sheds, sometimes by upwards of thirty-three per cent; the labourers constituted sixty per cent of the employees on the stations.[12] Gollan records:

11.   R. Gollan, 'The Trade Unions and Labour Parties, 1890-4', *Historical Studies Australia and New Zealand*, VII, November 1955, p.22.

12.   D. J. Murphy, 'Queensland' in D. J. Murphy (ed.), *Labor in Politics; the State Labor Parties in Australia 1880-1920*, University of Queensland Press, 1975, p.144.

The Shearers' Strike was contested with even greater bitterness than had been the Maritime Strike. The issues were
essentially the same, the "recognition of unionism" and
"freedom of contract". But in Queensland, partly as a consequence of the socialist opinions of the union leadership, and
partly because of the only thinly disguised partisanship of the
government, from the first the strike was pictured by
unionists as resistance to an attack on unionism by a combination of pastoralists and government.[13]

There were some 500 unionists camped near Clermont,
and 1,000 at Barcaldine. By the third week in February
1891, 107 police, 140 special constables (mostly pastoralists
and their employees) and 151 military were in the Clermont
district. By the end of March there were 29 officers and 509
men based in Barcaldine.[14] Altogether the Queensland
Defence Force provided 1,357 men, 85 officers, 765 horses,
3 nine-pounder guns and 2 Nordenfelt machine guns 'for
special service in aid of civil power', Colonel Drury's report
records.[15] 'With the systematic arrest of union leaders in
late March and early April, including the members of the
strike committee, it was made much clearer that the strikers
were likely to lose'.[16] Non-union labour was shipped into
Queensland under armed guard. On 10 June the ALF
executive asked the camps to consider calling off the strike
as funds were now exhausted. There was no formal ending
to the Queensland strike, but few held out beyond this date.
The criminal statistics return for 1891 records 25 arrests for
conspiracy, 100 for intimidation and 36 for riot and breach

13. *Historical Studies*, VII, p.32.
14. H. Kenway, 'The Pastoral Strikes of 1891 and 1894' in Murphy,
     Joyce and Hughes (eds), *Prelude to Power*, pp.114, 116.
15. E. R. Drury, *Special Service by Corps of the Queensland Defence
     Force*, James C. Beal, Government Printer, Brisbane 1891, pp.1, 7.
16. Kenway, *Prelude to Power*, p.117.

of the peace. Unionists comprised almost all of these arrests. 'These were not the total range of charges brought against unionists, but in these three categories 82 out of the 86 men convicted were imprisoned for terms of upwards of three months in the case of intimidation, and of three years for conspiracy.'[17]

The leaders of the Barcaldine and Clermont Strike Committee were arrested on charges of 'unlawful assembly, riot and tumult'.[18] They were acquitted, but the government prosecuted again under an 1825 conspiracy act, still in force in Queensland though repealed in England. Judge Harding gaoled twelve of the unionists for three years imprisonment each; Harding's attacks on the police for failing to fire on assembled unionists, his bullying of the jury for three days until it came up with a verdict of guilty, and his contemptuous refusal to consider the jury's recommendation of clemency, made the trials notorious. William Lane wrote *The Workingman's Paradise* to raise funds for the families of the imprisoned unionists, and to draw out the socialist message of the strike. Alec Forrester, one of the twelve gaoled for conspiracy, recited extracts from the novel in St Helena prison and was sentenced to seven days on bread and water for his troubles.[19]

The first recorded use of the phrase 'the Workingman's Paradise' is in Henry Kingsley's novel, *The Recollections of*

---

17. Ibid., p.118.
18. Clement Semmler, 'Some Notes on the Literature of the Shearers' Strikes of 1891 and 1894', *Australian Quarterly*, XLI, December 1969, p.81.
19. Gavin Souter, *A Peculiar People: The Australians in Paraguay*, Angus and Robertson, Sydney 1968, pp.12-13, 122.

Geoffry Hamlyn (1859): 'Australia, that Workingman's
Paradise'.[20] Lane uses the phrase with bitter irony for his
title. The phrase was turned ironically against him in the
British Government's Foreign Office report on New
Australia: 'New Australia was anything but a workingman's
paradise'.[21] It is a resounding phrase; and it is the exposure
of the ideology embodied in the phrase that is Lane's
subject in his novel, an exposure effected by revealing the
economic and social realities of the workers' life in this
antipodean paradise.

The Workingman's Paradise does not deal with the detail
of the shearers' strike. There was a considerable response to
the strike in the writing of the time, as Clement Semmler
has shown; and Lane appears as a character in Vance
Palmer's play about the events, *Hail Tomorrow!* (1947).[22]
But when Lane wrote, the strike had been defeated. He was
concerned to widen the issues from a specific defeat into a
socialist analysis of the society that generated the confrontation. His intention was to expound the basic ideas of
socialism and communism in a readable and accessible
form, to raise his readers' consciousness for the next round
in the battle.

The novel's protagonist, Ned Hawkins, begins with a
very moderate position. ' "We only want what's fair", he

20. G. A. Wilkes, *A Dictionary of Australian Colloquialisms*, Sydney
     University Press, 1978, p.365.
21. *Paraguay: Report on the "New Australia" Colony in Paraguay*,
     Foreign Office Miscellaneous Series of Reports on Subjects of
     General and Commercial Interests, No. 358, Her Majesty's
     Stationery Office, London 1895, p.6.
22. Vance Palmer, *Hail Tomorrow!*, Angus and Robertson, Sydney
     1947. See also Vivian Smith, 'Australia of the Spirit: Some Aspects
     of the Work of Vance and Nettie Palmer, 1938-48' in Leon Cantrell
     (ed.), *Bards, Bohemians and Bookmen: Essays in Australian
     Literature*, University of Queensland Press, 1976, pp.241-4.

said. "We're not going to do anything wild." ' His naivety appals Nellie Lawton, the girl he comes down from Queensland to visit.

> How dared he talk as he did about only wanting what was fair, she thought! How had he the heart to care only for himself and his mates while in these city slums such misery brooded! And then it shot through her that he did not know. With a rapidity, characteristic of herself, she made up her mind to teach him. (p.10)

And the novel consists of Nellie's opening Ned's eyes to the social conditions of Sydney, and directing his unionism into a committed socialism. 'The evolution of Ned was the evolution of Lane and of the workers of Queensland', Lloyd Ross remarked.[23] And the political education of Ned is Lane's political education of his readers.

Lane's base had been Queensland, Brisbane in particular, but he was a frequent visitor to Sydney and he set the novel in Sydney because the aftermath of the shearers' strike had made it 'not thought desirable, for various reasons, to aggravate by a local plot the soreness existing in Queensland' (p.iii).

Marcus Clarke in his 'Lower Bohemia'[24] series and John Stanley James in 'The Vagabond Papers'[25] had produced earlier exposes of Melbourne in the Mayhew tradition.

23. Lloyd Ross, *William Lane and the Australian Labor Movement*, Sydney 1935, reissued Hale and Iremonger, Sydney 1980, p.88.

24. 'Lower Bohemia' by "the Peripatetic Philosopher", *The Australasian*, in six parts, 12 June - 21 August 1869; reprinted in L. T. Hergenhan (ed.), *A Colonial City, High and Low Life, Selected Journalism of Marcus Clarke*, University of Queensland Press, 1972, pp.132-73.

25. *The Vagabond Papers*, 5 volumes, George Robertson, Melbourne 1877-78. Selection: John Stanley James, *The Vagabond Papers*, Michael Cannon (ed.), Melbourne University Press, 1969.

Lane continued the mode in articles he wrote for the *Observer* and *Boomerang* under the name 'Sketcher', 'gradually taking up the task of exposing glaring cases of social injustice — over-crowded slums, sweated labour, and the long hours of shop assistants, waitresses, and tramway men'.[26] He was able to draw on these detailed accounts of inner-city living for the novel. The lack of any specifically industrial material indicates the Brisbane basis of his explorations; Brisbane did not have Sydney's industries, and this makes the novel present a somewhat distorted picture of working-class life in Sydney. The stress is on the housing, the living conditions, on cottage industries and on domestic and service employment. Ned, of course, is a bushman, a shearer, not an industrial worker: he was one of 'the genuine western men, strong, tall, brave, kind-hearted men, the best men in the whole world and the tenderest'[27] that Lane knew and in whom he put his faith, rather than one of the industrial proletariat.

Ned comes down to Sydney and suggests he and Nellie go to visit some of the typical attractive leisure spots — 'to Manly or Bondi or Watson's Bay'. Nellie suggests they 'see a little bit of real Sydney' (p.13). So they see the slum housing; they see Mrs Somerville slaving in the cottage garment industry; they go to 'a fashionable Sydney restaurant' (p.23) where Nellie cross-questions the waitress about work conditions. They end up with 'Saturday Night in Paddy's Market', a chapter Leon Cantrell includes in his anthology *The 1890s*, arguing that

> The most frequent picture of city life in Australian writing of the period stresses this poverty of the down and outs . . .

26. *Daily Mail* (Brisbane), 17 February 1930.
27. *New Australia*, I, 2, 17 December 1892, p.3.

Though William Lane's novel *The Workingman's Paradise* deals with the breaking of the strikes, it makes an impassioned plea for a socialist future where the distress and suffering we see in "Saturday Night in Paddy's Market" will be swept aside.[28]

Other commentators have stressed Lane's English literary sources. Graeme Davison notes the influence of James Thomson's 'City of Dreadful Night' (1874),[29] whose mode had been followed in Australia by the 'Arnoldian Socialist' Francis Adams, a friend and fellow journalist of Lane's in Brisbane. John Docker points to Charles Kingsley's *Alton Locke* (1850):

> The tradition of seeing the urban landscape as the location of squalor and bitter class experience, equivalent to the "industrial tradition", can certainly be witnessed in Lane's *The Workingman's Paradise*, and the evocation of "Saturday Night in Paddy's Market" by Lane bears a remarkable similarity to a disgusted description of a Saturday night street market scene in working-class London in chapter eight of Kingsley's *Alton Locke*. Yet both of these scenes, intended to typify working-class life in London and Sydney, can be contrasted to the chapter in Louis Stone's *Jonah* (1911) which almost enviously evokes the pleasurable shopping and eating of the Saturday night crowd at Paddy's Market.[30]

Kingsley's street-market is discussed in P. J. Keating's *The Working Classes in Victorian Fiction*:

28. Leon Cantrell (ed.), *The 1890s*, University of Queensland Press, 1977, p.30.
29. Graeme Davison, 'Sydney and the Bush: An Urban Context for the Australian Legend', *Historical Studies*, XVIII, November 1978, p.202.
30. John Docker, 'The Politics of Criticism: Leon Cantrell and the Gloom Thesis', *New Literature Review*, 6, 1979, pp.30-1. Lane published an excerpt from *Alton Locke* on 'the start of the infamous sweating system' in *The Worker* (Brisbane), I, 5, 1 July 1890, p.9.

Kingsley's sole intention is to describe to the reader the horrors of working-class life; to recreate the feeling of repulsion experienced by himself . . . he makes no attempt whatsoever to present it from a working-class viewpoint . . . This kind of slum description is the most common in Victorian fiction before the eighties. They are not incidental but hold a central place in the novels, in that they are being used to grip the reader and stir his conscience. Almost everything else that happens in the novel depends upon such scenes for its vitality.[31]

But Lane had a political, didactic purpose. He was not recoiling in disgust, but analytically presenting the market, as Brian Kiernan points out, as 'the focus for the critical depiction of Sydney' with 'Sydney as the centre of the exploitative capitalism that is dominating the whole continent'.[32]

After the market, Nellie takes Ned to visit a group of intellectuals, bourgeois bohemians interested in the labour movement. The episode has been variously interpreted. Graeme Davison finds that 'the salon conversation of his radical intellectuals (Geisner, the Strattons) exposes, even as Lane himself attempts to repair, their fragile alliance with the working classes'.[33] Whereas John Docker, countering Cantrell's 'Gloom Thesis' argues 'the novel in these sections can be seen as offering a glowing account of Sydney's early nineties radical intellectual life': 'the house is surrounded by a leafy garden, and the inner spirit of the household is shown as at one with the natural world of the

31. P. J. Keating, *The Working Classes in Victorian Fiction*, Routledge and Kegan Paul, London 1971, p.20.

32. Brian Kiernan, 'Sydney or the Bush: Some Literary Images of Sydney' in Jill Roe (ed.), *Twentieth Century Sydney: Studies in Urban and Social History*, Hale and Iremonger, Sydney 1980, p. 151.

33. *Historical Studies*, XVIII, p.205.

harbour'.[34] The opposed responses are not accidental. Lane saw the contradictions: they were the dialectic of his argument, from which Ned's final commitment to the working-class movement through radical action issues.

Joseph Jones singled out the Stratton episode as the most successful part of the novel, which otherwise he found flawed:

> Stagey, sentimental and exhortative by turns, it has more than its share of technical faults but it does nevertheless dramatize the perfervid attitudes of the day, most successfully in a long "Medley of Conversation" held in the home of a middle-class Sydney family named Stratton.[35]

But when Lane was 'stagey' he was consciously stagey; he was a self-aware writer. After leaving the Strattons Nellie takes Ned through the Domain where the homeless sleep out. Here, in answer to Ned's queries as to 'What is Socialism?' Nellie kisses a sleeping prostitute on the cheek.

> 'This is Socialism.' And bending down again she kissed the poor outcast harlot a second time . . . Perhaps if he had been less natural himself the girl's passionate declaration of fellowship with all who are wronged and oppressed — for so he interpreted it by the light of his own thoughts — might have struck him as a little bit stagey. Being natural, he took it for what it was, an outburst of genuine feeling. (p.100)

Joseph Jones' 'stagey' is a reaction Lane has taken into account: he accommodates, absorbs and situates it.

Arthur Rae, a member of the New South Wales Legislative Assembly, and a vice-chairman of the New Australia

---

34. *New Literature Review*, 6, p.30.
35. Joseph Jones, *Radical Cousins: Nineteenth Century American and Australian Writers*, University of Queensland Press, 1976, p.82.

Association, had a more practical complaint about the episode.

> "Ah! Will," said Rae, "You didn't complete the picture. When the prostitute woke up she wouldn't know that she had been kissed by a girl. Nellie should have left half a crown in her hand — that would have been practical Socialism!"[36]

Robert Louis Stevenson, who visited Sydney four times between 1890 and 1893, described the plight of the homeless sleeping out in Sydney's Domain in *The Wrecker*.

> The long day and longer night he spent in the Domain, now on a bench, now on the grass under a Norfolk pine, the companion of perhaps the lowest class on earth, the Larrikins of Sydney. Morning after morning, the dawn behind the light-house recalled him from slumber; and he would stand and gaze upon the changing east, the fading lenses, the smokeless city, and the many-armed and many masted harbour growing slowly clear under his eyes. His bed-fellows (so to call them) were less active: they lay sprawled upon the grass and benches, the dingy men, the frowsty women, prolonging their late repose . . . Yes, it's a queer place, where the dowagers and the kids walk all day, and at night you can hear people bawling for help as if it was the Forest of Bondy, with the lights of a great town all round, and parties spinning through in cabs from Government House and dinner with my lord![37]

When Ned sleeps in the Domain there is no prolonging any late repose. A grinning gorilla-faced constable kicks him in the ribs and threatens to run him in for indecent exposure.

Ned's rude awakening occurs in part two of the novel. Between the two parts came the defeat of the Maritime

36.   E. H. Lane, *Dawn to Dusk*, p.48.
37.   Robert Louis Stevenson and Lloyd Osbourne, *The Wrecker* (1892); quoted in John Douglas Pringle, 'R.L.S. in Sydney' in Pringle, *On Second Thoughts*, Angus and Robertson, Sydney 1971, p.63.

Strike, the worsening of the situation of the working class. The baby born in the first chapter of part one, dies in the first chapter of part two. Marcus Clarke had complained that 'the success of the "dying children" urged Dickens to extremes. Every book must have a dying child, and the trick becomes wearisome'.[38] But Clarke used the theme himself in *His Natural Life* and in the story of the child dying in the bush, 'Pretty Dick'. The child's bush death became a familiar theme in Australian fiction and painting. Lane shifts it back to the Dickensian urban milieu. But to see this as primarily a 'literary' topic and as sentimental or melodramatic, is to refuse to recognize the reality of nineteenth-century experience. Humphrey Osmond remarks

> I am pretty sure no modern author has to remind himself not to introduce that incomparable tear-jerker, the dying child. Unlike the Victorian author, who could be certain of a large and deeply involved readership who had experienced the loss of brothers and sisters in the home, and who had lost a child or two as parents themselves, the modern author cannot expect such a predictable response.[39]

With Lane, the death of the child is firmly related to the slum housing conditions and working-class poverty. Capitalism is the cause of 'The Slaughter of an Innocent'.

Between the two parts Ned's consciousness has changed — through the experience of the Maritime Strike, in which the Queensland shearers were involved for one week in September 1890, and through the education from Nellie and Geisner. In Part I Nellie seizes every opportunity to

38. Marcus Clarke, 'Charles Dickens', *Argus* (Melbourne), 8 July 1870, p.7; reprinted in Michael Wilding (ed.), *Marcus Clarke*, University of Queensland Press, 1976, p.633.
39. 'The Dying Child', *Notes and Furphies*, 4, April 1980, p.11.

propagandize. By Part II Ned similarly recruits the unemployed youth in the cheap lodging house. The capitalist Strong, whose appearance Ned likes in Part I, is encountered in Part II and revealed as the intransigent, unscrupulous power worshipper. The individual episodes of the novel have the force of illustrative vignettes; but they are all part of an ongoing dynamic, a process of revelation and commitment. And it is all situated in Sydney and around the harbour: 'the most beautiful spot I know,' says Geisner, in a context of a world in which 'all countries are beautiful in their way' (p.105). The beauty is there, the setting for what could become a just society, a paradise.

The progressive stages of Lane's own political development all find their place in *The Workingman's Paradise*. John recalls that when he and William sailed to Australia on the Quetta in 1885, William 'had bought for study on shipboard a collection of books on political economy, including Karl Marx's *Capital*, Adam Smith's *Wealth of Nations*, and Henry George's *Progress and Poverty*'.[40]

The first English translation of *Capital* did not appear until 1887. William may have possessed it untranslated, or John may have placed Will's certain later acquaintance with *Capital* back in time a little. William certainly arrived in Brisbane radicalized. Ernie Lane recalls

> to my horror I discovered that Will had evolved into a radical or worse. When he had left England for America some years before he had given me as a parting gift a Church of England prayer book in the fly leaf of which he had written "Fear God and Honour the King." That was the very foundation of our material and spiritual life. I reminded him of this. He had forgotten, and I said sadly, "Don't you believe that now?" He

40. *Dawn to Dusk*, p.7.

laughed and replied "No! And you won't some day when you know better."[41]

Ten years in the U.S.A. had had a profound radicalizing effect on William. He arrived in time to experience the Great Upheaval of 1877, the wave of general strikes that were, as President Hayes recorded in his diary, 'put down by force,' and in which more than a hundred strikers and onlookers were killed by police and troops.[42] Henry George and Edward Bellamy, both Americans, were influences on his social thinking until he discovered Marx. And Lloyd Churchward notes that

> William Lane had spent some time in Detroit before he settled in Brisbane and he had a high regard for the achievement of the Knights of Labor in the United States before he joined the Sydney-based Eureka Assembly of the Knights of Labor in 1891.[43]

The Knights of Labor had been founded in 1869. 'It combined the functions of a trade union with an opposition to the wage system as a whole, and originally had a deep religious strain as well.'[44] Unlike the traditional trade unions of that time, which generally represented only the highly-skilled craftsmen and were concerned to maintain their comparatively privileged position in the labour force, 'the one great sentiment embodied in the Knights of Labor was the idea of solidarity among all workers, whether white or black, skilled or unskilled, men or women'.[45] The

42. Jeremy Brecher, *Strike!*, Straight Arrow, San Francisco 1972, p.21; Robert V. Bruce, *1877: Year of Violence*, Bobbs-Merrill, New York 1959, p.315.

43. Lloyd Churchward, *Australia and America 1788-1972*, Apcol, Sydney 1979, p.116.

44. Brecher, *Strike!*, p.28.

45. Ibid., p.28.

Knights were opposed to strike action; strikes distracted from the programme of creating producers' co-operatives and of controlling monopoly through government, and strikes threatened to generate revolutionary disorder. But it was the Knights of Labor's success in the 1885 Railroad Workers Strike against the railway 'king' Jay Gould, that resulted in the rapid growth of their organization — from 71,326 members in July 1884 to 729,677 members by July 1886. An organizer was sent to Australia in 1888,[46] and, Churchward notes, 'William Lane, in particular, quoted freely in the *Boomerang* during 1888-90 from *United Labor*, the journal of the Knights of Labor, printed in Philadelphia'.[47]

Henry George's *Progress and Poverty* which Will brought with him to Australia, had already been serialized in a Sydney newspaper in 1879, the year of its publication in the U.S.A. And, as Churchward points out, land taxation and land nationalization theories were already widespread in England and America before George's book. T. A. Coghlan's *Wealth and Progress of New South Wales*

revealed that while 212,639 selections were sold in New South Wales over twelve years, 1876-88, individual holdings of one acre upwards had increased only from 39,639 to 46,142. In 1889 580 persons held 25 million acres comprising 53 per cent. of the alienated land of New South Wales. These facts caused the early Australian interest in progressive land taxation.[48]

Land nationalization leagues were widely established

46.   Joe Harris, *The Bitter Fight: a Pictorial History of the Australian Labor Movement*, University of Queensland Press, 1970, pp.61-2.
47.   L. G. Churchward, 'The American Influence on the Australian Labour Movement', *Historical Studies Australia and New Zealand*, V, November 1952, pp.263-4.
48.   Ibid., p.260.

through eastern Australia in 1887. Lane wrote in *The Boomerang*

> Land nationalization would do more in a single day than protection will do in a century towards adjusting and keeping perpetually adjusted that distribution of wealth, the present mismanagement of which is the cause of all poverty, nearly all crime, and most vice.[49]

In 1890 Henry George lectured in Australia, expounding his 'single tax' programme, and attracted a considerable following. The novelist Catherine Spence was active in the single-tax movement in South Australia, and the poet and story writer John Farrell in N.S.W. Churchward argues that

> the influence of Henry George on the Australian Labour movement was a general rather than a specific one. No part of the Labour movement accepted the panacea of the 'single tax' but George's books and his visit to Australia in 1890 did much to popularise the principle of the taxation of unimproved land values and partly explains the prominence of this principle in the early Labour Party platforms. More generally still his visit in 1890 helped arouse the sections of the middle class to the claims of labour and served to strengthen the optimism of the workers which was so marked in the early strike struggles of 1890.[50]

In *The Workingman's Paradise* Geisner explains to Ned

> George's is a scheme by which it is proposed to make employers compete so fiercely among one another that the

---

49. *William Lane and the Australian Labor Movement*, p.57. 'The entire Abolition of the Private Ownership of Land' was one of the declared political policies of *The Bulletin*, 17 June 1893. See Russel Ward, *The Australian Legend*, 2nd edn, Oxford University Press, Melbourne 1966, p.225.
50. *Historical Studies*, V, p.263.

workman will have it all his own way. It works this way. You tax the landowner until it doesn't pay him to have unused land. He must either throw it up or get it used somehow and the demand for labour thus created is to lift wages and put the actual workers in what George evidently considers a satisfactory position. (p.110)

George's *Social Problems* was the second work discussed by Lane in his 'Books Well Worth Reading' series in *The Worker*.[51] Although he found *Progress and Poverty* 'a wearisome book for all its brilliant writing and repeated outbursts of intensest passion', and *Freetrade and Protection* 'a mere piece of special pleading', he declared that 'George is the man who, most of all the English writers — writers of English — has clothed the dry bones of political economy with the flesh of humanity and the blood of passionate sympathy'. He recommends *Social Problems*, defining its limitations at the same time that he acknowledges its propagandistic strengths.

> It is readable from beginning to end. It is short. It is George at his very best, that phase of George which all who seek better things love and admire and respect. Every man and woman who can read can wade through it easily and if they do so they will feel, when they put it down, that they are better and truer and nobler than when they picked it up.
>
> George may be out on interest. He may be wrong in maintaining that population, the illimitable quantity, cannot get to the limits of land the limitable quantity. He may be not quite logical in assuming that competition is a great thing. But he is a great man and a good man and "Social Problems" is *his* book.

The last issue of *The Worker* that Lane edited, 30 July

---

51. J. M., 'Books Well Worth Reading. II. George's "Social Problems" ', *The Worker* (Brisbane), I, 2, 1 April 1890, p.14.

1892, carried on its front page Karl Marx's letter of 1881 on Henry George and his theories: 'the man is a back number'. Geisner's view is similar and he explains to Ned the inadequacies of the 'Single Tax' proposal:

> The capitalists, who alone can really use land remember, for the farmer, the squatter, the shopkeeper, the manufacturer, the merchant, are nowadays really only managers for banks and mortgage companies, will soon arrange a way of fixing the values of land to suit themselves. But apart from that, I object to the Single Tax idea from the social point of view. It is competitive. It means that we are still to go on buying in the cheapest market and selling in the dearest. It is tinged with that hideous Free Trade spirit of England, by which cotton kings became millionaires while cotton spinners were treated far worse than any chattel slaves. (p.111)

Lane presents the Single Taxers amongst the Sunday afternoon speakers in the Domain. There was 'a vigorous iconoclast, who from the top of a kitchen chair laid down the Law of the Universe as revealed by one Clifford' and 'a wild-eyed religionary' who had been enabled 'to foretell exactly the date of the Second Coming of Christ. Then came the Single Tax platform' (p. 120).

It is not an utterly hostile placing. The iconoclastic puritans of the English revolution, the millenarian visionaries, were the transmitters of a radical consciousness as much as the Single Taxers. They were all progenitors of socialism. W. K. Hancock remarked of the 1890s, 'the waters were turbulently Marxian; but Lane was at heart an English Puritan, a spiritual descendant of Winstanley and the digger-communists of seventeenth-century Sussex'.[52] The communism of the radicals of the English revolution (not confined to Sussex) was transmitted into the nineteenth

---

52.   W. K. Hancock, *Australia*, Benn, London 1930, p.200.

century through radical, independent religious groups. At the Strattons, Ford tells of his childhood in the west of England and how his elder brother

> took to going to the Ranters' meetings instead of to church. My mother and father used to tie him up on Saturday nights and march him to church on Sunday like a young criminal going to gaol . . . It was the deadliest of all sins, you know, to go to the Ranters. (pp. 80-1)

In the end the whole family went.

The Ranters were an anarcho-communist sect, adherents of the medieval doctrine of the Free Spirit. Norman Cohn has explored their European connexions in *The Pursuit of the Millenium*. A. L. Morton and Christopher Hill have traced their role during the English revolution, and Jack Lindsay has indicated the transmission of their beliefs into Blake's milieu.[53] Their beliefs were straightforward. 'The true communion amongst men is to have all things common and to call nothing one hath one's own', Abiezer Coppe wrote. God, 'that mighty Leveller' will 'overturn, overturn, overturn'. 'Who are the oppressors but the nobility and gentry?', asked Lawrence Clarkson.[54]

Lane continually refers back to the English revolution. The recurrent paradise image of the novel's title, with Ned as Adam, Nellie as Eve, and Geisner as Satan, associates

53.   Norman Cohn, *The Pursuit of the Millenium*, Secker and Warburg, London 1957; A. L. Morton, *The World of the Ranters*, Lawrence and Wishart, London 1970; Christopher Hill, *The World Turned Upside Down: Radical Ideas During the English Revolution*, Penguin, Harmondsworth 1975; Jack Lindsay, *William Blake: His Life and Work*, Constable, London 1978, pp.48-50, 277-80.
54.   Abiezer Coppe, *A Fiery Flying Roll* (1649), and Lawrence Clarkson, *A Generall Charge or Impeachment of High Treason, in the Name of Justice Equity, against the Communality of England* (1647) quoted in Hill, *The World Turned Upside Down* (1975), pp.212, 210, 214.

him with that seventeenth century focus on Eden for radical propaganda that we find in Winstanley's *True Leveller's Standard* and Milton's *Paradise Lost*. In the tradition of the Ranters and Blake, the conventional story is inverted. Geisner's temptation is the positive force of Socialism. As for Nellie, 'For that kiss Ned gave himself into the hands of a fanaticism, eating of the fruit of the Tree of Knowledge, striving to become as a god knowing good from evil' (p.100). Lane also shares the doctrine of the Norman Yoke, which Christopher Hill has shown was a central myth of the Cromwellian revolutionary period.

> Before 1066 the Anglo-Saxon inhabitants of this country lived as free and equal citizens, governing themselves through representative institutions. The Norman Conquest deprived them of this liberty, and established the tyranny of an alien King and landlords. But the people did not forget the rights they had lost. They fought continuously to recover them.[55]

Writing in *The Worker* the week the shearers' strike was called off Lane declared:

> Class governance is a usurpation, a tyranny which has its roots in the ages when armed robbers, military castes, ground the peaceful tillers of the soil into slavery. Our parliamentary system, of which the very opponents of one-man-one-vote profess to be so proud, is only a degenerated survival of the assembly at which in primitive times our Teutonic forefathers gathered, free and equal, to make for themselves laws for their common governance.[56]

John Lane recalled how William would announce 'we

---

55. Christopher Hill, *Puritanism and Revolution: Studies in the Interpretation of the English Revolution of the Seventeenth Century*, Secker and Warburg, London 1958, p.57.
56. John Miller, 'One-Man-One-Vote', *The Worker* (Brisbane), II, 26, 13 June 1891, p.5, reprinted in Clark, *Select Documents*, p.569.

Germanic people came into history as Communists. From our communal village we drew the strength which broke Rome down, and the energy which even yet lets us live'.[57] Southern England was always thought to be more Norman than the Midlands, West and North. Lane wrote in the *Boomerang,*

> Australia is not a sect or a section, it is not a caste or a class, or a creed, is not to be a Southern England nor yet another United States. Australia is the whole white people of this great continent.[58]

The stress on the Aryan tradition, the Germanic heritage, the Anglo-Saxon, provided, too, an ideology for the racism of the early socialists.[59]

Humphrey McQueen has called Lane 'a fanatical racist'.[60] Certainly racism is a major component of his thinking. In *The Workingman's Paradise* Nellie recalls Ned telling her that the 'squatters were mostly selfish brutes who preferred Chinese to their own colour and would stop at no trick to beat the men out of a few shillings' (p.10). Lane correctly saw that the pastoralists were eager to import Chinese or kanaka indentured labour as a way of undercutting and destroying the unions. Lane's first novel, *White or Yellow? A story of the Race-war of A.D. 1908* by 'Sketcher',[61] predicted an alliance of the pastoralists of the Queensland establishment and Asian capital. The alliance

57.   *Daily Mail* (Brisbane), 18 February 1930.
58.   *The Boomerang,* 19 November 1887.
59.   Cf. Philip S. Foner (ed.), *Jack London: American Rebel,* Citadel, New York 1964, p.36.
60.   Humphrey McQueen, *A New Britannia: an Argument Concerning the Social Origins of Australian Radicalism and Nationalism,* Penguin, Ringwood 1970, p.51.
61.   Serialized in twelve episodes in *The Boomerang,* 18 February - 5 May 1888.

is destroyed by white, working-class unionists taking up arms and fighting. The Chinese are driven up to the northern tip of Queensland and then deported. The economic predictions may yet come true; but over and above that there is a racism. Instead of seeing the Chinese or kanakas as equally oppressed peoples and forging an alliance with them, Lane believed that blacks and orientals were inferior races, decadent, doomed to extinction. Though in his pessimistic projections of industrial capitalism, he speculated that perhaps in the decadence of these last days of capitalism, the Chinese were destined to survive better than the Celtic-Saxon Aryan. Nellie speculates

> this yellow man and such men as he were watching them all slowly going down lower and lower, were waiting to leap upon them in their last helplessness and enslave them all as white girls were sometimes enslaved, even already, in those filthy opium joints whose stench nauseated the hurrying passers by. Perhaps under all their meekness these Chinese were braver, more stubborn, more vigorous, and it was doomed that they should conquer at last and rule in the land where they had been treated as outcasts and intruders. (p.9)

Lane wrote about the opium dens and the gambling joints in his 'Daylight and Dark' series in *The Boomerang*. He tried opium and noticed that

> the world seemed to move back a peg or two and that it seemed as though there was getting to be nothing but friendliness in it and that the jarrings of life were getting covered with india-rubber shields. . . . I noticed mostly that I began to hate less these calm-faced impassive invaders of our civilization and to feel less intensely against their abominable habits . . . And then I recollected seeing a year ago in this very same place and at much the same time of day a bloated-faced, fair-haired white girl, hardly 20, who was lying insensate with the poppy-drug in the midst of these smooth-faced and

heartless yellow men . . . And then I wanted to kick the lamp over and burn down this joint and all the other joints and with it every one of these yellow devils who, with mask-like faces and fawning guise and patient, plodding ways and superb organization, have come here and rooted themselves here and brought with them all their virtues and all their vices and who threaten us with this frightful habit which will wreck the manliness of our men and the womanliness of our women, and will bury our nationality in a deadly slough of sloth and deceit and filth and immoralities from which the vigorous white race man now shrinks in horror.[62]

An intractable hostility to the Chinese and to their use of opium was another feature of the American Labor movement that Lane brought with him to Australia. 'At its first meeting in 1881, the first act of the Federation of Organized Trades and Labor Unions was to condemn Chinese cigarmakers of California and to urge that only union-label cigars be bought.'[63] The Federation became the American Federation of Labor in 1886 and its founding president, Samuel Gompers, led the campaign against the Chinese until his death in 1924. The Chinese were seen as a threat to organized labor since they were held to work harder for longer hours at lower wages than white workers, and their opium usage was held to help them work harder for less. The labor unions' campaign against the Chinese resulted in legislation prohibiting the importing of opium by Chinese to the U.S.A. in 1887, the Chinese Exclusion Act barring the further immigration of Chinese into the U.S.A. in 1889, and the restriction of the manufacture of smoking opium to American citizens in 1890.[64] Concerted

62. *The Boomerang*, 21 January 1888, p.8.
63. Thomas Szasz, *Ceremonial Chemistry: The Ritual Persecution of Drugs, Addicts, And Pushers*, Anchor/Doubleday, New York 1975, p.72,
64. Ibid., pp.71-5.

anti-opium campaigns, directed against the Chinese, began in Melbourne and Sydney in 1890.

When Lane established his communist settlements in Paraguay in 1893, he was adamant that there should be no contact with the native *guarani*. Of course there was contact. When Mary Gilmore left the Cosme settlement in 1900 she explained 'ostensibly we left because of the climate, actually because (a) we feared, if not in this, in a later generation, the admixture of the native' and (b) because it was no longer operating communistically.[65] The fear of interbreeding, the sex-fear is exploited by Lane in his Lucinda Sharpe column.

Lane's racism is blatant; but it is important to realize it was a racism shared widely by his fellow communists and socialists. McQueen notes:

> What Lane was fond of calling "the piebald issue" dominated the thinking of the Labor Party to such an extent that when the Objectives of the Federal Labor Party were adopted in 1905:
>
>> the cultivation of an Australian sentiment based on the maintenance of racial purity and the development in Australia of an enlightened and self-reliant community
>
> took precedence over:
>
>> the securing of the full results of their industry to all producers by the collective ownership of monopolies and the extension of the industrial and economic functions of the state and the municipality.

---

65. Mary Gilmore, 'Colonia Cosme', *Daily Telegraph* (Sydney), 5, 6 and 7 November 1902, reprinted in Charles Higham and Michael Wilding (eds), *Australians Abroad*, Cheshire, Melbourne 1967, p.77.

In other words, the Labor Party was racist before it was socialist.[66]

In this context it is a mistake to see Lane as in any way exceptional in his racism. It is a contradiction that was endemic to the labour movement. Lane recognized the economic advantages to the capitalists in using cheap coloured labour; he failed to realize that a racist reponse merely supported the capitalists in dividing the working classes.

In 1887, recalled Ernie Lane,

> My brother started a Bellamy society. *Looking Backward* was just then in the boom. We met regularly on the closed-in balcony of George Marchant's hop beer factory in Bowen Street [Brisbane], and there were about a dozen of us used to attend.[67]

Lane began serializing Edward Bellamy's utopian novel *Looking Backward 2000-1887* (1887) in the first issue of *The Worker*,[68] and he discussed it in the first of his 'Books Well Worth Reading' series in the same issue. 'It has won rich men to the side of State Socialism, and has moved the masses as no book dealing with political-economic topics

66. *A New Britannia*, pp.52-3. On Lane and racism, see also Gollan, *Radical and Working Class Politics*, pp.116-18; Ray Markey, 'Populist Politics' in Ann Curthoys and Andrew Markus (eds), *Who Are Our Enemies? Racism and the Australian Working Class*, Hale and Iremonger, Sydney 1978, pp.66-79; Andrew Markus, 'White Australia? Socialists and Anarchists', *Arena*, 32-3, 1973, pp.80-9.

67. *Dawn to Dusk*, p.12. On Bellamy see also *Radical and Working Class Politics*, pp.121-4; S. E. Bowman (ed.), *Edward Bellamy Abroad*, Twayne, New York 1962; *William Lane and the Australian Labor Movement*, pp.116-19.

68. *The Worker* (Brisbane), I, 1, 1 March 1890, pp.12-13. The novel was somewhat abridged for serialization.

ever moved them before,' Lane wrote.[69] Bellamy's vision of
the year AD 2000 was one of 'all change.'

> Industry has readjusted itself to the age of machinery;
> competition has been swept away by natural process; the state
> has absorbed all the means of production and distribution;
> equality of wealth reins supreme, and in this equality in-
> dividualism finds unlimited scope, and the ablest lead, and the
> weak are happy with the strong. Woman, too, has won her
> equality, and shares fully with man in the abounding wealth
> and marvellous opportunities of a great community, where all
> are workers, and where no man robs another, where crime is
> unknown and immorality unthought of, where the dreaming
> of the good and great is realised at last . . .[70]

An immensely influential work for the labour movement,
Bellamy's novel lies behind the portrayal of Australia in
The Workingman's Paradise. Sydney in its slums, its
poverty, its inequalities and its exploitation is the counter-
type of Bellamy's utopian city.

Bellamy's industrial army of socialism may have been in
the background of the New Australia movement. The first
issue of the journal, *New Australia* asked 'DO YOU
BELIEVE'

> That there is intelligence enough and power of organization
> enough among the workers to enable them of their own free
> will to organize the present conditions of industry and to give
> the world an example of a peaceful and *self-sustaining* in-
> dustrial community in which there are none but workers in
> which all are equal?

'IF YOU DO, JOIN THE "NEW AUSTRALIA"

69. M., 'Books Well Worth Reading. 1 — Bellamy's "Looking
     Backward" ', *The Worker* (Brisbane), I, 1, 1 March 1890, p.14.
70. Ibid. p.14.

MOVEMENT.'[71] But the industrial model was never developed in New Australia or Colonia Cosme. 'Socialists whose conception of the truer life is a *Looking Backward* city have no place with us,' John Lane wrote in 1900.[72] *Cosme Monthly* declared 'The life within reach of our outstretched hands is the heaven of which William Morris dreamed and Sir Thomas More saw afar off.'[73]

Looking Backward postulated that socialism would be established with absolutely no violence, by the natural process of take-overs and monopolization, culminating in one big, state monopoly. The final episode appeared in *The Worker* for 13 December 1890. The next issue, 10 January 1891, carried the first reports of the beginnings of the shearers' strike. Events undercut Bellamy's theory of social change. The defeat of the maritime strike of 1890 and of the shearers' strike of 1891 made it quite clear to Lane that monopoly capital was not going to happily surrender its power and wealth to a socialist ideal. In his earlier political writings he had preached moderation and co-operation;[74] but it became clearer than ever before, that any thought of co-operation now with capital was absurd. Lane introduces into his novel the 'managing director of the Great Southern Mortgage Agency, a big concern that owns hundreds and hundreds of stations. At least, the squatters own the stations and the Agency owns the squatters, and he as good as owns the Agency' (p.26). Historians have calculated that by 1890 about half the pastoralists of N.S.W. were mortgaged

71. *New Australia*, I, 1, 19 November 1892, p.3.
72. John Lane, letter to *British Socialist News*, 3 August 1900; MS copy in John Lane's letter book, folio 22, Hilda Lane papers, Fisher Library, University of Sydney.
73. *Cosme Monthly*, October 1900, p.1.
74. See *Radical and Working Class Politics*, p.126; *William Lane and the Australian Labor Movement*, p.81.

clients of banks or other financing agencies.[75] Strong, the managing director, 'is Capitalism personified' (p.207). His encounter with Ned at the novel's end is a precursor of Wickson's encounter with Ernest Everhard in Jack London's *The Iron Heel* (1907) and of Winston's encounter with O'Brien in Orwell's *Nineteen Eighty-four* (1949).[76] Strong sums up the unrelenting, unbending attitude of capital, the imperative of *power:*

> "Rich!" sneered Strong. "What is rich? It is Power that is worth having and to have power one must control capital. In your wildest ranting of the power of the capitalist you have hardly touched the fringe of the power he has." (p.204)

Ned initially has had a sort of admiration for the abstemious disciplined Strong. He even shakes hands with Strong after the encounter as they both declare 'war' (p.205). But any sentimentalism about Strong as the noble gentleman warrior is immediately dispelled as Strong, having shaken Ned's hand, sends a coded telegram to arrange for Ned's arrest on his way back to Queensland. Power, not honour, is Strong's characteristic.

Bellamy, rejecting violent revolution, argued that the nineteenth-century anarchists 'were paid by the great monopolies to wave the red flag and talk about burning, sacking, and blowing people up, in order, by alarming the timid, to head off any real reforms'.[77] Lane was to have his

75. F. S. Piggin, 'New South Wales Pastoralists and the Strikes of 1890 and 1891', *Historical Studies*, XIV, April 1971, p.547.

76. Jack London, *The Iron Heel*, Journeyman, London 1976, p.63; George Orwell, *Nineteen Eighty-four*, Penguin, Harmondsworth 1961, p.211; see Michael Wilding, *Political Fictions*, Routledge and Kegan Paul, London 1980, pp.114-15, 239-41.

77. Edward Bellamy, *Looking Backward 2000 - 1887* (1887), The Riverside Library edition, Houghton Mifflin, Boston, n.d., p.252. Chapter XXIV, containing this discussion, was one of the chapters omitted from *The Worker's* abridged serialization.

own experience of agents-provocateurs in Paraguay; they were not a concept foreign to his world. But he rejects utterly Bellamy's identifying the anarchists with the instruments of repression. Nellie introduces Ned to the amiable anarchist Sim, one of 'the dynamiters' (p.40) as she calls him, at Paddy's Market. Sim announces, 'Jones vows that there is only one way to cure things and that is to destroy the rule of Force' (p.41). Ned's education is continued by Geisner. ' "The Anarchist ideal is the highest and noblest of all human ideals ... Anarchical Communism, that is men working as mates and sharing with one another of their own free will, is the highest conceivable form of Socialism in industry." ' (p.112) Though Geisner himself is not an anarchist but a communist. He explains

> I freely admit it is the only form of Socialism possible among true Socialists. But the world is full of mentally and morally and socially diseased people who, I believe, must go through the school of State Socialism before, as a great mass, they are true Socialists and fit for voluntary Socialism. Unionism is the drill for Socialism and Socialism is the drill for Anarchy and Anarchy is that free ground whereon true Socialists and true Individualist meets as friends and mates, all enmity between them absorbed by the development of an all-dominant Humanity. (pp.112-13)

Geisner recognizes the idealism of the anarchists. But his own programme is a conventional communist programme, accepting the necessity for the period of state socialism, the transitional stage before the withering away of the state.

The extent of Lane's knowledge of and commitment to Marxism has always been a matter of dispute. As Lloyd Ross remarked, 'Considerable time could be spent in showing the contradictory views held by Lane at different times on the reforms to be advocated and in showing the inconsistency between his Socialistic drive and his immediate steps'.[78] A. St Ledger, a Queensland senator, had no doubt about Lane's revolutionary Marxism: in *The Worker* leaders Lane 'endorsed all that Karl Marx had written against capitalism'[79] wrote St Ledger in 1909. 'The A.L.F. under his guidance founded a library of Socialistic literature, in which Bellamy and Marx were the Bible and Shakespeare to its new recruits. Thousands of leaflets were distributed to all its branches.'[80] Lloyd Ross argued that 'Marx certainly influenced him less than had Bellamy'.[81] Henry Mayer mentions Lane only in passing, as a teetotaller, in *Marx, Engels and Australia*.[82] Bruce Mansfield does not mention Lane in 'The Socialism of William Morris: England and Australia'.[83] Grant Hannan[84] and Humphrey McQueen[85] have denied that he was a Marxist at all.

Lane discussed Marx in his *Worker* series, 'Books Well Worth Reading'.[86]

Karl Marx is the father of modern Socialism, that is to say he is the man who in his famous work "Das Kapital" first

78. *William Lane and the Australian Labor Movement*, pp.156-7.
79. *Australian Socialism*, p.24.
80. Ibid., p.35.
81. *William Lane and the Australian Labor Movement*, p.90.
82. Henry Mayer, *Marx, Engels and Australia*, Cheshire, Melbourne 1964, p.63.
83. Bruce Mansfield, 'The Socialism of William Morris: England and Australia', *Historical Studies Australia and New Zealand*, VII, November 1956, pp.271-90.
84. G. Hannan, 'William Lane — Mateship to Utopia' in Murphy, Joyce and Hughes (eds), *Prelude to Power*, pp.181-6.
85. *A New Britannia*, pp.191-3.
86. J.M., 'Books Well Worth Reading. Karl Marx Father of Modern Socialism', *The Worker* (Brisbane), I, 5, 1 July 1890, p.6. Quotations in this paragraph are all from this article.

systematized into the nationalization of land and machinery the previously crude theories that somehow or other every man must get what he produces in order to be not a slave. He reaches the bed-rock principle that "interest is usury and usury is robbery" and propounds in scientific and convincing method the economic truths which now begin to win recognition throughout the civilized world. For we workers are all Socialists nowadays, though some of us are so ignorant that we don't know it. We follow Marx in the contention that Labour's rightful share of Production is *all*.

But Marx is a recondite writer, a man who reasons algebraically and with pitiless disregard for the dryness of mathematical demonstration.

The difficulty of Marx's work meant that 'to the every day man, Marx is unreadable'. For the immediate propagandist work of converting the union movement to socialism, Lane had found the works of Bellamy and Henry George more accessible: Bellamy, George and Olive Schreiner were discussed in 'Books Well Worth Reading' before Marx. Moreover, copies of *Capital* were hard to acquire, 'so, very few have got copies and it is very dear'; neither *Boomerang* nor *Bulletin* could direct Twomey, a Charters Towers radical, to a copy when he inquired. Though he did acquire a copy — as did Queensland premier Griffith and *Worker* Secretary Seymour. Lane remarked, 'There are probably others in Queensland but not many, though with Socialism becoming fashionable it may soon expect to be bought for ornament if not for use. I doubt if there are a thousand men who have Marx at their finger's ends in the whole world.' But though like William Morris, Lane stressed the difficulty of reading Marx, he also, like Morris, recognized that *Capital* was the basic text of socialism.

Yet Marx sways the world. From his epoch-making work all modern economic writers draw as from a well of learning, pure and undefiled. There, "Das Kapital" — "Capital" — is laid out on the dissecting table of enquiry; its very marrow is laid bare by his piercing intellect. From the time when he safely gave his two immortal volumes to the thinkers the cause of the toilers was won. With the divinity stripped off that had cloaked "Property", with the brand of theft stamped indelibly upon the exactions of Capitalism, with Labour set up on high as the sole producer of all the wealth which was and is and can be, and all done with the cold logic of a matchless logician — it was only a question of years till to the masses below the truths acquired by the genius on the mountain tops would waft slowly down. It is mainly because of Marx that the world sees its way to a remedy for the social ills that oppress us — and Marx, *also*, was a Jew.

Lane was also in communication with the Morris circle. John Lane recalls

> One of the most highly-placed educationalists then in Queensland was a friend and correspondent of William Morris, the English socialist, poet, and reformer. He used to meet Lane in secret, and with him discuss politics and literature.[87]

Another contact was A. G. Yewen, as E. H. Lane recalls:

> A personal friend of William Morris, Yewen assisted him to form the Socialist League (1884) in a breakaway from the S.D.F. [Social Democratic Federation], whose high priest was H. M. Hyndman . . . Owing to ill health Yewen was ordered to go to Australia. He had a letter to W. Lane in Brisbane and Will sent him up to Umbiram, Darling Downs, where my brother John was school teacher. Yewen stayed with John for six months and in improved health, went to Sydney. There he threw himself into the work of the Australian Socialist League, of which McNamara was secretary.[88]

87.   *Daily Mail* (Brisbane), 17 February 1930.
88.   *Dawn to Dusk*, p.13.

Yewen, W. A. Holman and Henry Lawson later got painting work in Sydney through another former member of the SDF, G. Chandler.[89]

Marxist ideas were current. The English socialist writer, Francis Adams, a friend of Lane's in Brisbane, addressed a sonnet to Marx: 'We praise you, worker, thinker, poet, seer!'. And Lane persuaded Sir Samuel Griffith,[90] the then premier of Queensland, to contribute to the Christmas 1888 issue of *Boomerang*. Griffith wrote an exposition of Marx's theory of surplus value. 'There are only two sources of wealth; the gifts or products of nature and human labour', Griffith began.

> In order that additional wealth of capital might come into existence, labor must be applied to raw material in such a manner that the value of the resulting product is greater than the value of the raw material together with that of the things consumed in the process of production . . . Such new value created should, however, belong not to the employer nor to the owner of the raw material, but to the labourer himself. In practice, the employer expropriated a large proportion of the new value created; hence arises the unequal distribution of wealth within the community.[91]

In *The Workingman's Paradise* Geisner explains to Ned how the employer expropriates the new value created. The worker

> must bargain for the owner of machinery to take the product of his labour for a certain price which of course isn't its full

89.   Ibid., p.21.
90.   Griffith later reneged on his socialist sympathies and Lane singles him out for attack in *The Workingman's Paradise*, pp.143-4, 148-9. See *William Lane and the Australian Labor Movement*, pp.150-1.
91.   *The Boomerang*, December 1888.

value at all but the price at which, owing to his necessities, he is compelled to sell his labour. (p.107)[92]

And, as Marx points out in *Capital*

> The fact that half a day's labour is necessary to keep the labourer alive during 24 hours, does not in any way prevent him from working a whole day. Therefore, the value of labour-power, and the value which that labour-power creates in the labour process, are two entirely different magnitudes: and this difference of the two values was what the capitalist had in view, when he was purchasing the labour-power. . . . The seller of labour-power, like the seller of any other commodity, realises its exchange-value, and parts with its use-value. He cannot take the one without giving the other. . . . The owner of the money has paid the value of a day's labour power; his, therefore, is the use of it for a day; a day's labour belongs to him . . . The daily sustenance of labour-power costs only half a day's labour, while on the other hand the very same labour-power can work during a whole day . . . consequently the value which its use during one day creates, is double what he pays for that use.[93]

A reading of *The Workingman's Paradise* in the context of *Capital* and *The Manifesto of the Communist Party* indicates the extent to which Lane used his novel to expound some of the basic principles of Marxism.

Geisner explains to Ned that unionism is no answer to the system.

How can you get what you want by unionism? The evil is in

92. The 1948 edition of *The Workingman's Paradise* (Cosme Publishing, Sydney, p.113) reads: 'must bargain with the owner of machinery to take his labour power for a certain price, which, of course, isn't it's full value at all. . .'

93. Karl Marx, *Capital*, Volume I, translated by Samuel Moore and Edward Aveling (1887) and edited by Frederick Engels, Progress Publishers, Moscow 1978, p.188.

having to ask another man for work at all — in not being able to work for yourself. Unionism, so far, only says that if this other man does employ you he shall not take advantage of your necessity by paying you less than the wage which you and your fellow workmen have agreed to hold out for. You must destroy the system which makes it necessary for you to work for the profit of another man, and keeps you idle when he can't get a profit out of you. The whole wage system must be utterly done away with. (p.108)

The Communist Manifesto is in the background here:

The essential condition for the existence, and for the sway of the bourgeois class, is the formation and augmentation of capital; the condition for capital is wage labour. Wage labour rests exclusively on competition between the labourers.[94]

Competition amongst wage labourers is inevitable under the capitalist system. Geisner points out

The fits of industrial briskness and idleness which occur in all countries are enough to account for the continual tendency of wages [to keep] to a bare living amount for those working, as many of those not working stand hungrily by to jump into their places if they get rebellious or attempt to prevent wages going down. (p.108)[95]

These 'fits' are the 'epidemic of overproduction' as the *Manifesto* calls them.[96] Engels explains them in *Socialism Utopian and Scientific*.

Since 1825, when the first general crisis erupted, the whole

---

94. Karl Marx and Frederick Engels, *Manifesto of the Communist Party*, translated by Samuel Moore (1888), Progress Publishers, Moscow 1973, p.60.

95. The 1948 edition of *The Workingman's Paradise* adds the words 'to keep' (p.114).

96. *Manifesto*, p.50.

industrial and commercial world, production and exchange among all civilized peoples and their more or less barbarian appendages, have broken down about once every ten years. Trade comes to a standstill, markets are glutted, products lie around in piles as massive as they are unsalable, hard cash disappears, credit vanishes, factories are idle, the working masses lack the means of subsistence because they have produced too much of them, bankruptcy follows upon bankruptcy, forced sale upon forced sale.[97]

From the increasing pool of the unemployed, strike breakers and non-union labour are recruited by the Queensland pastoralists. Nellie reflects on how 'the scum of southern towns and the sifted blacklegs of southern "estates" were to be drafted in hordes to Queensland to break down the unionism that alone protected the bushman'. (p.132) The *Manifesto* has already provided the analysis of this process, together with the term 'scum':

> The "dangerous class", the social scum, that passively rotting mass thrown off by the lowest layers of the old society may, here and there, be swept into the movement by a proletarian revolution; its conditions of life, however, prepare it far more for the part of a bribed tool of reactionary intrigues.[98]

Lane presents such a 'bribed tool of reactionary intrigue' in the anonymous 'burly man of unmistakably bush appearance, modified both in voice and dress by considerable contact with the towns' (p.195). Strong hires him to 'start another union against the present one' (p.196) — a tactic the pastoralists did indeed employ, just as the CIA did fifty years later.[99] Lane's suspicion of the urban proletariat and

97. Frederick Engels, *Socialism: Utopian and Scientific*, Foreign Languages Publishing House, Peking 1975, p.86.
98. *Manifesto*, p.57.
99. Fred Hirsch and Richard Fletcher, *CIA and the Labour Movement*, Spokesman, Nottingham 1977.

lumpenproletariat and his preference for the bushmen had
its Marxian analysis behind it.

Geisner elucidates the developing monopoly stage of
capitalism. 'It takes more and more capital for a man to start
for himself. This is a necessary result of increasing
mechanical powers and of the economy of big businesses as
compared to small ones' (p.107). As the *Manifesto* put it

> The lower strata of the middle class . . . sink gradually into
> the proletariat, partly because their diminutive capital does
> not suffice for the scale on which Modern Industry is carried
> on, and is swamped in the competition with the large
> capitalists, partly because their specialized skill is rendered
> worthless by new methods of production.[100]

Geisner explains the proletarianization of the lower middle
classes to Ned; 'more and more go round asking for work as
what we call civilisation progresses, that is as population
increases and the industrial life becomes more complicated.
. . . This system operates for the extension of its own worst
feature, the degradation of the working masses' (p.107).

It is not only in Geisner's dialogue with Ned that
Marxism is expounded. The language of a Marxist mode of
thinking runs through the novel — capital, capitalists,
working masses, labour, even scum. And the *leitmotiv* of
prostitution has its specific Marxist resonance. Marx
concluded volume I of *Capital* with an examination of 'The
Modern Theory of Colonisation'. Prostitution is specified
as one of the direct consequences of the capitalist exploitation of Australia.

> The shameless lavishing of uncultivated colonial land on
> aristocrats and capitalists by the Government, so loudly

100. *Manifesto*, p.53.

denounced even by Wakefield, has produced, especially in Australia, in conjunction with the stream of men that the gold-diggings attract, and with the competition that the importation of English commodities causes even to the smallest artisan, an ample "relative surplus labouring population," so that almost every mail brings the Job's news of a "glut of the Australian labour-market," and prostitution in some places there flourishes as wantonly as in the London Haymarket.[101]

When Nellie takes Ned around Sydney they encounter the prostitutes near Town Hall, the recognized beat in the 1890s: 'the sad sisterhood were out in force where the bright gas-jets of the better-class shops illuminated the pavement, swaggering it mostly where the kerbs were lined with young fellows' (p.39).

This realistic observation also has its iconographical significance. The *Communist Manifesto* declares

On what foundation is the present family, the bourgeois family, based? On capital, on private gain. In its completely developed form this family exists only among the bourgeoisie. But this state of things finds its complement in the practical absence of the family among the proletarians, and in public prostitution.[102]

It is self-evident that the abolition of the present system of production must bring with it the abolition of the community of women springing from that system, i.e. of prostitution both public and private.[103]

Prostitution turns up metaphorically at the Strattons in a discussion of journalism under capitalism. ' "Why, we're nothing but literary prostitutes," said George,

101. *Capital*, I, p.724.
102. *Manifesto*, p.68.
103. *Manifesto*, p.71.

energetically. "We just write now what we're told, selling our brains as women on the streets do their bodies" ' (p.87). It is a traditional analogy, but it takes on a force here from the literal prostitution shown before and after the Stratton episode. On the way back from the Strattons there is the episode in which Nellie 'kissed the sleeping harlot on the cheek' (p.100). The Victorian fear that venereal diseases were transmitted by such contact as kissing provides the frisson of horror here for Nellie's gesture. Later, in Nellie's account of the fate of her sister, prostitution is never named but it is implied throughout the story. This episode, 'Nellie's Sister', appeared separately, before book publication, in the Christmas issue of the *Worker* for 1891.[104] Part of a realistic portrayal of urban life, prostitution, as the stress on it in the *Communist Manifesto* makes clear, is one of the central expressive emblems of industrial capitalist society.

Lane was one of the major advocates of women's rights in the Australian labour movement, and one of those pressing for womanhood suffrage. He wrote a weekly letter in *Boomerang* and later in *The Worker* about women's issues, under the name of 'Lucinda Sharpe', supposedly an American woman resident in Queensland. He adopted the pseudonym 'A Mother of the People' in *The Worker* and *New Australia*. These female impersonations have led P. J. Bruce to speculate on Lane's 'androgynous nature', and he notes, too, the recurrence of the 'idealized mother figure' in Lane's writings.[105] But Freudian interpretations cannot

---

104. *The Worker* (Brisbane), II, 41, 26 December 1891, pp.2-3. A footnote states, 'Being part of Chapter IV., Part II, of "The Working Man's Paradise," now in press and to be published on behalf of the Union Prisoners' Defence Fund'.

105. P. J. Bruce, 'William Lane: Personality and Politics,' unpublished BA thesis, University of Adelaide, 1970, pp.48n., 37.

depoliticize Lane's radical vision. Geisner tells Ned of the

> two great reforms which must come if Humanity is to
> progress. . . . One reform is the Reorganization of Industry.
> The other is the Recognition of Woman's Equality. These two
> are the practical steps by which we move up to the socialistic
> idea. (p.123)

The women's issue is of central significance in *The Workingman's Paradise*. As Geisner stresses, it is a practical and a political issue. Nellie expounds the women's movement at the Strattons. The tour she gives Ned is one that emphasizes the situation of women — the struggle of the housewife and the mother in the slums, the exploitation of women workers in the garment trade, in restaurants, and in prostitution. Lane is in advance of most of his contemporaries in his awareness of and stress on the women's issue. And he recognizes that it was for women to determine their future role in society, not for men to interfere yet again. As Nellie points out ' "What women really want is to be left to find their own sphere, for whenever a man starts to find it for them he always manages to find something else. . . . You can't raise free men from slave women." (pp.72-3). And just as she educates Ned in socialism, so she educates him in the women's movement, so that he 'began to dimly understand how it touched the Labour movement' (p.75). It is in the combination of the reorganization of industry and the women's movement that Lane sees the achievement of socialism. It is a radical, working-class women's movement that Lane stresses, a women's movement committed to the socialist ideal.

As the 'Leading Australian Woman Critic' who reviewed the novel for *The Worker* stressed

The author has recognised the fact that in woman's pulse

throbs the secret of a nation's redemption or its degradation and his book, man-written though it be, is essentially a woman's book proclaiming aloud the gospel of redemption for her who shall thereby redeem the world.

And it is to women that the book will chiefly appeal. There are magnificent passages in it which will wring every fibre of a true woman's nature; passages where the writer plays on the chords of slumbering maternity with the touch of inspired genius, where he reveals to woman her own love-nature and love-power as she herself seldom sees it.[106]

And the revolution? Lane was writing his novel after the defeat of the unions, the gaoling of strike leaders, and the mobilization of troops. The expression of revolutionary sentiments had to be carefully done. But revolution was what Lane expressed. Geisner warns Ned

"there are two Socialisms. There is a socialism with a little 's' which is simply an attempt to stave off the true Socialism. This small, narrow socialism means only the state regulation of the distribution of wealth. It has as its advocates politicians who seek to modify the robbery of the workers, to ameliorate the horrors of the competitive system, only in order to prevent the upheaval which such men recognise to be inevitable if things keep on unchanged." (p.114)

Ned pledges 'to be a Socialist of the right sort' and Geisner continues

"It can only come by the utter sweeping away of competition, and that can only come by the development of the socialistic idea in men's hearts . . . Year after year the number of men

---

106. 'The Workingman's Paradise. What a Leading Australian Woman Critic Says About It', *The Worker* (Brisbane), III, 49, 9 April 1892, p.3. The reviewer is not identified as other than 'a Sydney woman writer who is recognised as one of the ablest art critics on the continent'.

and women who hold Socialism as a religion is growing. And when they are enough you will see this Old Order melt away like a dream and the New Order replace it. That which appears so impregnable will pass away in a moment. So!" He blew a cloud of smoke and watched it disappear circling upwards. (pp.115-16)

The puff of smoke illustrating the classic Marxist spiral ascent suggests the ease of the melting away; but it suggests too the smoke of gunfire. And when Geisner talks of the role of the unions, it is in military terms: 'drill, organisation, drill' (p.117).

Lane's position on armed revolution has been misrepresented by historians. McQueen, having noted that 'Lane's *Boomerang* was often criticized for its militaristic utterances by the Sydney anarchist S. A. Rosa'[107] nonetheless later refers to Lane's 'rejection of violence'.[108] McQueen selectively quotes from Lane's *Worker* editorial at the height of the shearers' strike: 'tolerate still, not because rebellion, i.e. armed resistance to established authority is wrong . . . but because we should endure to the utmost for the sake of humanity which shrinks from violence'.[109] But Lane's editorial continued:

but because we should endure to the utmost for the sake of the Humanity which shrinks from violence even against the violators of human rights and which realises all the horrors and misery of civil war, and which sees how our real enemies — the *absentee* capitalists — escape mostly while those who have wronged us ignorantly or by compulsion suffer, with ourselves, the most. Once let us win a fair franchise, once let the bushmen march up with us all to the ballot-box, once let

107. *A New Britannia*, p.83.
108. Ibid., p.193.
109. Ibid., p.193.

the plural vote and the revision-trick be abolished, and there
will be none to blame but ourselves if the Law is wrong . . .
And if they persistently refuse the ballot to us as they have
persistently refused it in the past: if Parliament refuses to do
us justice and scorns our demand to be made full citizens; then
we shall have full justification for any action we may adopt,
even if that action is revolution.[110]

And making the point quite clear, he stressed 'A Tyranny
has no claim upon us but that we should resist it'. The
editorial concludes, 'Those have rights who dare maintain
them — they alone, and none others'.

Lane at no point rejects the use of force. But force for him
is a last resort. Bloodshed is no proof of ideological
correctness. The real enemy — the absentee capitalists, for
instance, — are not the ones who suffer the most in any
violence. Peaceful means of change are always preferable to
violent means. And if violent means are used, they must be
successful; an unsuccessful revolution is counter-
revolutionary. In March 1891 'there were 29 officers and
509 men based at Barcaldine, with a nine-pounder and a
Nordenfeld gun in the middle of the Barcaldine en-
campment'.[111] For Lane to have recommended violence at
this point would have been suicidal. The shearers were not
adequately armed. They were not ideologically organized.
Lane was concerned to avoid provocation that could lead to
the excuse for a judicial massacre on the United States'
model. 'They'd like nothing better than a chance to shoot a
mob of us down like wild turkeys', Ned says (p.147).

The strike collapsed in June. In a *Worker* editorial in
October Lane brooded on the situation, repeating the

110. John Miller, 'The Editorial Mill', *The Worker* (Brisbane), II, 20, 21
    March 1891, p.2.
111. Kenway, *Prelude to Power*, p.116.

conclusion of his March editorial.

> Once or twice, in these columns, I have alluded to the inevitable necessity for violent reform where peaceful efforts to secure what is just and right are ignored and derided and suppressed by the brutal Force of class governments. I have said, as I say now and at all times, that a time always arrives, sooner or later, where tolerance of Wrong becomes itself a Wrong, and where those alone have rights who dare to maintain them. For this, it is alleged that the WORKER preaches sedition, as if one had to preach submission to oppression and injustice in order to be law-abiding.[112]

A time always arrives. He expected it within thirty years. The interim was to be used preparing for it.

His early beliefs in class collaboration had vanished by the time of the shearers' strike. He saw the class war in these confrontations. And it is not the class struggle, as many Marxists phrased it, but class war. Ned says to Strong ' "There is war between us, only I think it possible to be a little civilised and not to fight each other like savages as we are doing" ' (p.200). By the novel's end, the pretences of civilization are dropped in Ned's vision of Apocalypse.

> All the world over it was the same, two great ideas were crystallising, two great parties were forming, the lists were being cleared by combats such as this for the ultimate death-struggle between two great principles which could not always exist side by side. The robbed were beginning to understand the robbery; the workers were beginning to turn upon the drones; the dominance of the squatter, the mine-owner, the ship-owner, the land-owner, the shareholder, was being challenged; this was not the end, but surely it was the beginning of the end. (p.221)

On the last page he talks of 'these later days' and the new

Messiah of the Apocalypse (p.225).

His stress is on the achieved good society, not on the violence to be gone through to reach it. He accepts that a violent confrontation will occur but until the appropriate time any confrontation would be adventurism. In the interim there is the battle of ideas, the need to reveal the truth of communism to the world, to workers and bourgeoisie alike. In New Australia he would train the consciousness of a socialist army, and propaganda would be disseminated round the world. And perhaps a change of consciousness could avert the need for a violent confrontation; or at least make the inevitable socialist victory quick and overwhelming. When he took a strong, militarist anti-German line in World War I he was not in conflict with his earlier principles. Militarism, like racism, was never rejected in Lane's socialism.

How militant were the striking shearers? At the beginning of the novel Ned's unionism is naive, unpolitical. On his return to Sydney after the maritime strike he stresses to Nellie that the 'responsible' unionists who went round 'talking law and order to the chaps on strike and rounding on every man who even boo'd as though he were a blackleg' have realized the way they were co-opted and used by the 'authorities'.

> The man who told me vowed it would be a long time before he'd do policeman's work again. He said that for him Government might keep its own order and see how soon it got tired of it. (p.144)

The voices preaching moderation are introduced by Lane only to be discounted, to show how they had been used. 'Do you think there will be any trouble?', Nellie asks as the shearers' strike begins its slow start.

"Honestly, I don't, Nellie. At least nothing serious. Some of the fellows may start to buck if the Government does try to break up the camps and it might spread a little, but there are no guns and so I don't see how it could. There seems to be a lot of talk everywhere but that's hard fact. Ten thousand bushmen with rifles wouldn't have much trouble with the Government and the Government wouldn't have much trouble with ten thousand bushmen without rifles." (pp.146-7)

But it is a confrontation situation. Nellie, daughter of a selector, a subsistence farmer, reflects with anger 'the companions of her childhood were to be Gatling-gunned because of the squatters' (p.132).

The gunning down is all threatened from the squatters, the military and the 'special constables'. Lane had good reason for playing down any armed militancy of the shearers now that the strike had ended. Twelve leaders had been gaoled, but the Brisbane *Telegraph* complained 'it was worthless for the Government to arrest strike criminals when it was Lane who was the real criminal'. 'The Man Behind the Curtain' it called him.[113] The *Courier* alleged of the strike that

The details had all been considered and arranged not by the ignorant men now languishing in gaol, but by wiser men, of whom the chief plotter is a resident in Brisbane. His plans were at one time on paper, and possibly might have been secured; but it is certain that since the arrest of the first conspirators in Barcaldine they existed in black and white no longer. It was the rash precipitancy of these bush leaders which brought to confusion the carefully-planned scheme of the arch-conspirator in Brisbane.[114]

W. T. Stead called Lane 'The most dangerous man in

113. *A Peculiar People*, p.10.
114. Ibid., p.10.

Queensland'. 'In Australia', a Victorian Cabinet Minister corrected.[115]

Ned sets off for Queensland at the end of the novel and is clearly going to be one of those gaoled. But the movement of the book suggests that gaoling will only raise his militancy. What was the next stage?

The unions were desperately weakened by the loss of the strike. Kenway points out that 'the convictions for conspiracy removed from active life for over two years almost all the executive members of the Q.L.U. and the Q.S.U.' and that 'the cost to the unions of the 1891 strike was reckoned at £22,228, not including salaries'.[116] The Labour movement was preparing to move into parliamentary action. Lane correctly predicted that this would lead only to co-option and corruption. But the time was not yet ripe for revolution. He proposed to continue the strike by draining off the best bushmen to a communist settlement, New Australia, and land was acquired in Paraguay. Ernie Lane stresses

It was not merely an isolated Communist settlement in the depths of a Paraguayan forest that Will was visioning, but something far more ambitious and far-reaching. Talking to me of what the future might hold, he foresaw New Australia within 30 years from its establishment, a powerful Communist State, with a disciplined army of many thousands of Communists. "The world, then," he exclaimed, "will be ripe for Communism. The workers in all lands will be ready to revolt and only awaiting the match that will set ablaze the crumbling world of capitalism. What is there to prevent us — Communists who are living proof of our Communist faith —

---

115. Vance Palmer, *The Legend of the Nineties*, Melbourne University Press, 1963, p.83.
116. *Prelude to Power*, pp.118, 119. Q.L.U. — Queensland Labourers' Union; Q.S.U. — Queensland Shearers' Union.

coming forth and starting the world revolution that must inevitably come. We will write the future history of humanity on the rocks of the Andes![117]

The Association agreed with the Paraguayan government to settle 400 families within two years, 800 within four;[118] 'early in 1894 there should be fully a thousand people in the settlement.'[119] The first issue of *New Australia* considered the effect of 5-6,000 workers joining the movement,[120] arguing that since most of them did not have votes and they were spread over five or six colonies, the emigration would not seriously affect the electoral chances of the emerging parliamentary labour movement. The advertisement in the hardback edition of *The Workingman's Paradise* talked of acquiring land 'sufficient to carry 50,000 people' (p.78): 50,000 was the *Worker's* estimate of the unemployed in Australia.[121] As Lane predicted, within thirty years there was a revolutionary situation in 1917 in Russia. But New Australia had not survived.

It is important to stress that Lane's scheme was not a utopian retreat, but an attempt to produce a vanguard for the revolution.[122] Geisner outlines the scheme to Ned in *The Workingman's Paradise*. Socialism needs the 'right conditions' away from the corruptions and subversions of industrial capitalism.

Absolute isolation while the new conditions are being

117. *Dawn to Dusk*, p.49.
118. *New Australia*, I, 6, 8 April 1893, p.1.
119. *New Australia*, I, 8, 27 May 1893, p.1.
120. *New Australia*, I, 1, 19 November 1892, p.1.
121. Cited in *New Australia*, 5, 25 March 1893, p.2.
122. 'This expedition was to be the attack of the vanguard rather than a rearguard action', *William Lane and the Australian Labor Movement*, p.166.

established; colonists who are rough and ready and accustomed to such work and at the same time are thoroughly
saturated with Socialism; men accustomed to discuss and
argue and at the same time drilled to abide, where necessary,
by a majority decision. (p.118)

And expounding New Australia, Lane wrote

> Our argument must be that if Socialism is shown to be
> practicable and if an energetic state springs up on sound lines,
> it will set such an example and excite such determination in
> other states that a world revolution will be speedily brought
> about. We can get together men who are what the average men
> of hundreds of years hence will be, and, with the organisation
> and the discipline, will be able to render possible a genuinely
> democratic and co-operative community.[123]

'We must first show that Socialism is possible' were
Geisner's words to Mrs Stratton, she tells Ned at the end of
the novel (p.211). The military discipline, drill and
organization are unmistakable. Lane's vision of world
revolution springing from South America prefigures
Guevara's.

Geisner presents the idea of the New Australia movement
as a future strategy. New Australia is not named
specifically, but an advertisement in the bound edition of
The Workingman's Paradise announced a continuation of
the novel, *In New Australia: Being Nellie Lawton's Diary of
a Happier Life.* It was to follow through the story of Nellie
and Ned and 'deal with the scheme for complete co-
operation, on which the New Australia Co-operative
Settlement Association is based' (p.78).

George Reeve recalled

I have been told by a well-known writer who was at one time

123. *William Lane and the Australian Labor Movement*, p.172.

schoolmistress at Cosme, that the continuation of *The Workingman's Paradise* was actually written, but when it was submitted to her to pass opinion on, the abandonment of its publication was argued, as it was considered "washy", with no virile touch to the characters therein depicted, and lacking all the fire of the founder's old-time burning enthusiasm and glowing language.[124]

Mary Gilmore, the writer in question, replied:

In regard to the continuation of *The Workingman's Paradise* the chapters of the book begun in Paraguay did not relate to that at all [i.e. the expulsions and the split in the settlement]. The work did not strike me as "washy" (to use Mr Reeve's word), but thin and indicative of the low state of health in which Mr Lane then was. He was still weak and bloodless from an illness that all but killed him, and in no condition to write. As he grew stronger he took his share in the colony work, and there was no time to write, even if bodily fatigue allowed it.[125]

William Wood wrote to George Reeve from Cosme, 3 June 1926,

Two chapters of the book of *The Happier Life in New Australia* were read out at Sunday night meetings at Cosme at the end of the year 1895 . . . I heard nothing further about it . . .[126]

The New Australia pioneers planned to leave on 1 May 1893, May Day and the anniversary of the beginning of

124. George Reeve, 'New Australia, Cosme and Wm. Lane', *Ross's*, 16 August 1919, p.5.
125. Mary Gilmore, 'Colonia Cosme and New Australia', *Ross's*, 11 October 1919, p.4. Reeve replied to Mary Gilmore in *Ross's*, 15 November 1919, p.14.
126. William Wood, 'The Workingman's Paradise', *Windsor and Richmond Gazette*, undated clipping, New Australia papers, Mitchell Library.

the 1891 Rockhampton conspiracy trial. The N.S.W.
government harassed and obstructed them in order to
drain the Association's cash resources, the assembled
pioneers had to be housed in Balmain, and it was not until
16 July 1893 that the *Royal Tar* sailed with 220 colonists
and their children. One of the articles of the association was
that the settlement should be teetotal. As soon as South
America was reached, a group of 'rebels' persisted in
drinking and challenging Lane as chairman. One of them,
believed to have been a special constable during the
shearers' strike, was suspected of having joined the
movement in order to split it.[127] When Lane expelled him
and two others, 81 men, women and children left after
them. The pioneers were split before the second boatload
arrived; when they arrived, a further 200 of them, there
were further dissensions and in May 1894 Lane and fifty-
seven followers left New Australia to establish Colonia
Cosme on a separate site, some forty-five miles south.

> Cosme is a Commonhold of English speaking whites, who
> accept among their principles Life marriage, Teetotalism and
> the Color Line. And who believe that Communism is not
> merely expedient but is right.[128]

In 1896 Lane sailed to England to try and recruit new
members for Colonia Cosme. The March 1897 issue of
Cosme Monthly was printed in London to help with the

127. *New Australia*, I, 15, 27 February 1894, p.1; I, 16, 24 March 1894,
 p.2. *The Worker* (Brisbane), II, 25, 30 May 1891, p.2, carried an
 article on 'Private Capitalistic Police' detailing the use of Pinkerton
 detectives as undercover agents in anti-worker activities in the
 U.S.A., commenting 'the Griffith Government stands idly by and
 sees such a "damnable institution" established under its nose here
 in Queensland'.
128. *Cosme Monthly*, September 1896, p.4.

recruiting drive and, it announced

> Since February 1st, lectures on Cosme have been given in
> Scotland at Paisley, Glasgow, Bridge of Weir, Cambuslang,
> Clydebank, Galashiels, Edinburgh, Musselburgh, and
> Larbert; and in England at Bradford, Rochdale, Chorlton-
> cum-Hardy, Blackburn, Bolton, Halifax, Long Eaton,
> Gloucester, Cheltenham, Portsmouth, Reading, Birmingham,
> London, and St. Leonards. These have generally been under
> the auspices of the local I.L.P. or Labour Church branches,
> but occasionally by the arrangement of private friends.

Lane stayed in Britain until February 1898, but the
recruiting was not a success; few responded to the call, and
of those who did, few stayed in Cosme. In May 1899 Lane
announced he was not standing for further office and in
August he left Paraguay for Auckland. He worked on the
New Zealand Herald, returned to Australia as the first full-
time editor of the Sydney *Worker*, but after three months
resigned and was back with the *New Zealand Herald* by
June 1900. As leader writer and finally chief editor, he
continued to have a wide following. The popularity of his
articles

> is made manifest by the almost universal demand for their
> republication as soon as it was known that their author, the
> late William Lane, had laid down forever the pen which in life
> he had wielded so well.

So ran the introductory note to the posthumous *Selections
from the Writings of "Tohunga" (William Lane)*, published
in Auckland in 1917 by Wilson and Horton.

Lane was an activist, an organizer, but he was also a
thinker, a theoretician. He tested his ideas in practice. But
until the revolutionary moment came, it was the war of
ideas that engaged him. The major stress of *The*

Workingman's Paradise is on the power of ideas, the necessity for a consciousness change. Connie Stratton tells Ned at the end of the novel how Geisner 'is moulding the world as a potter moulds clay' (p.211). She sees evidence of his ideas taking effect everywhere. Like William Morris, Lane believed in the communist aim of reintegrating man to wholeness, resisting the separating and fragmenting forces of industrial capitalist specialization. He was a journalist who had also worked as copy-boy, printer's devil and compositor. In 1890 he dropped his salary from £12 a week to £3 when he became editor of the new *Worker*. 'An editor who wouldn't give up a lot to push the Cause can't think much of it', Ford says in *The Workingman's Paradise* (p.87). It was no narrow cause. Lane's radicalism was a broad humanizing force. Literature was a weapon in the struggle. At the same time, writing was something that demanded its own commitment from Lane. Whatever the vicissitudes of his career and the changes in his political commitments, he always wrote. He continued to write fiction in Paraguay; at least part of *The Happier Life* was written and according to William Wood he also 'started another work on Cosme to be called 'The King's Quest'.[129] Neither is known to have survived.

The New Australia movement had its journal from 19 November 1892. Colonia Cosme established *Cosme Monthly* in January 1895; initially handwritten and duplicated, from April 1897 it was printed on the colony's own press. A large part of the surplus went in printing and in mailing the journal to other communes and to communist and socialist journals and friends throughout the

---

129. *Windsor and Richmond Gazette.*

world.[130] The Paraguayan experiments were enacted socialism; their journals gave the necessary commentary, interpretation and theoretical component. The *Monthly* ceased to be issued regularly in 1904, declaring:

> had the money, time, thought and brains which have been expended on the paper during its ten years of life been put into the acquisition and care of a herd of cattle, we should now be in a very much better material position than we now occupy.[131]

But the thinking, the writing, the mail network were central to Lane's purpose. His essays appeared regularly in *Cosme Monthly*, and he had sent several 'John Miller' articles to *Seed Time*, the English journal of the American Fellowship of the New Life organization dedicated to 'the reconstruction of society'. When he announced he would not seek any re-election for any further office, 'W. Lane said that "apart from health reasons which alone were more than sufficient", he wished to become entirely free to propagandize'.[132] He returned to a public forum again — a large circulation paper, not the newsletter of a commune of a handful of people.

Always the writer, Lane spread his range of contacts into the literary-artistic world as well as the political. *The Boomerang* ran a regular column called 'Bohemia' which kept up with theatrical news and gossip. Bohemia was

---

130. 'The paper will, on application be mailed free to secretaries of trade unions, or other labor or democratic societies. Exchanges with labor, colony or progressive papers invited.' *Cosme Monthly*, August 1900, p.4. A list of forty-one 'papers and magazines regularly received on the colony' appeared in *Cosme Monthly*, December 1900, p.2.
131. *Cosme Monthly*, June 1904, p.1.
132. *Cosme Monthly*, June 1899.

always a part of Lane's world, and Australia had its well established Bohemian milieux. John Sibbald, who went to New Australia with Lane, recalled he was

> essentially a Bohemian, to whom a fixed residence and domesticity are distasteful, and who contemns on principle all those attentions to material amelioration which result in what we call comfort.[133]

Julian Ashton, the Sydney painter, recalled

> On many occasions [Lane] came to my studio and limped up and down talking about the wrongs under which mankind lived; for he was an idealist, but unlike most idealists he was reasonable and logical.[134]

In *The Workingman's Paradise* the Strattons are the focus of Lane's Bohemian world. According to Harry Taylor, who went with Lane to Paraguay, they were based on Agnes Rose-Soley and her husband and 'the scene of one of the principal chapters of the book is laid in her house'.[135] Agnes Rose-Soley was born in Scotland, educated at Newnham College, Cambridge, and wrote under the name 'Rose de Bohème'. A contributor to the *Bulletin Storybook* (1901), she wrote two volumes of poetry, *The Call of the Blood and Other War Verses* (1914) and *Stray Chords* (1923), and with her husband J. F. Rose-Soley, a newspaper editor,

---

133. John Sibbald, *A Short History of New Australia*, reprinted from *South Australian Register*, W. K. Thomas, printers, Adelaide, n.d., p.1.

134. Julian Ashton, *Now Came Still Evening On*, Angus and Robertson, Sydney 1941, p.126. Ashton's chapter on Lane includes an account of New Australia and Cosme by Mary Gilmore.

135. Harry Taylor, letter on the occasion of the death of Rose Scott, *The Register*, reprinted in *The Murray Pioneer*; undated clipping in A. G. Stephens' newspaper cuttings book, 'New Australia', p.128, Mitchell Library.

Manoupa, a South Sea novel. She founded the Sydney Lyceum Club in 1914. She wrote a marching song for New Australia,[136] and an account of the *Royal Tar*'s departure for *The Worker*.[137] With her husband she wrote under the joint pen-name 'A. J. Rose-Soley' a widely reprinted account of New Australia for the *Westminster Review*. As well as the movement they discuss Lane the writer.

> Speaking with a slight Yankee twang, he can write, when it pleases him, pure Yankee journalese. When it pleases him, also, he can pen eloquent, vibrating, absolutely pure Anglo-Saxon, with an old-fashioned simple grandeur which he himself attributes to the early influence of the Bible and John Bunyan. This power is nowhere more manifest than in the one book he has published, *The Workingman's Paradise,* a hastily thrown together, loosely constructed story, written for the benefit of the Union Prisoners' Defence Fund after the Queensland bush strike of 1891, and insufficiently revised. For some reasons Lane's friends wish the book had never been brought out, as many a line bears evidence of how much better he could have done had he given his work more leisure, for others they are glad that it saw the light with all its imperfections, as there are pages upon pages of grand, rhythmic, soul-stirring prose, such as seldom gets printed in these modern days — sonorous prose, fruitful in ideas, which the world cannot afford to lose and which leaves a lasting impression on the reader.[138]

The poem Arty delivers was written for the novel by Fred J. Broomfield, one of the Bohemians of the *Bulletin*. Lloyd

136. *New Australia,* I, 5, 25 March 1893, pp.1, 4.
137. *The Worker* (Brisbane), IV, 116, 22 July 1893, reprinted in *New Australia,* I, 10, 1 August 1893, p.2.
138. A. J. Rose-Soley, 'New Australia', *Westminster Review,* CXL (1893), pp.523-37; reprinted *Eclectic Magazine,* December 1893, pp.780-9; *New Australia,* I, 15, 27 February 1894, pp.2-4; summarized, *Review of Reviews* (Australian edition), VIII, p.514.

Ross suggests 'it is possible' that the character of Arty, 'the people's poet', was based on Henry Lawson,[139] an identification accepted by Denton Prout.[140] Lawson's poem 'My Literary Friend' (1891) is about Broomfield's unhelpful critical suggestions for Lawson's poems. On this occasion Broomfield 'supplied the book with a last minute verse which Lawson had forgotten to write'.[141]

Gresley Lukin, who took over *The Boomerang* after Lane resigned, brought Lawson to Brisbane for a job on the staff, which lasted March to September 1891. Lawson wrote regularly for both *The Boomerang* and Lane's *Worker* during this time. Hilton Barton stresses

> This Brisbane episode brought Lawson more directly under the personal influence of William Lane, with a corresponding strengthening of ideological bonds, including the philosophy of "Mateship" as a cementing principle in trade union and socialist endeavour . . . Henceforward Lane, the Propagandist of Mateship, and Lawson, the Poet of Mateship, moved along parallel paths in their devotion to the cause.[142]

At the height of the shearers' strike, Lane published Lawson's first contribution to *The Worker*, 'Freedom on the Wallaby':

> So we must fly a rebel flag
> As others did before us . . .

139. *William Lane and the Australian Labor Movement*, pp.6-7.
140. Denton Prout, *Henry Lawson: The Grey Dreamer*, Rigby, Adelaide 1963, p.61.
141. Colin Roderick (ed.), *Henry Lawson: Collected Verse*, Vol. I, Angus and Robertson, Sydney 1967, pp.152, 438. Ann-Mari Jordens, 'Fred J. Broomfield', *Australian Literary Studies*, IX, October 1980, p.468.
142. Hilton Barton, 'Lawson, Lane and "Mateship"', *Communist Review*, 244, April 1962, p.115.

> They needn't say the fault is ours
> If blood should stain the wattle.[143]

F. T. Brentnall quoted the poem in the Queensland
Legislative Council, in support of a motion thanking the
military and civil officers for 'the suppression of the late
organised attempt to subvert the reign of law and order'. To
Brentnall it was evidence of a political campaign for in-
surrection organized by the ALF and *The Worker*. The
poem was reprinted in *Hansard* to Lawson's delight, and
the inspiration of another poem, 'The Vote of Thanks
Debate' in *The Worker*, 25 July 1891.[144] Lawson returned
to Sydney, Jack Lang, his brother-in-law, recalled, 'with
glowing reports about Lane'.[145] Lawson kept in touch with
Lane; he wrote a couple of poems about the New Australia
venture, 'Otherside', which appeared in *The Bulletin*, 23
January 1892, and the first issue of *New Australia*, and
'Something Better', *New Australia*, 24 March 1894.[146]
Years later, around 1911-12, he recalled the period of his
association with Lane in Brisbane in 'The Old Unionist':

> The fighting, dying *Boomerang*
> Against the daily press,
> The infant *Worker* holding out;
> The families in distress;

143. Henry Lawson, 'Freedom on the Wallaby. (Written for the
     "Worker")', *The Worker* (Brisbane), II, 24, 16 May 1891, p.8.
144. Roderick (ed.), *Henry Lawson: Collected Verse*, Vol. I, pp.123-4,
     136-7, 435-6. Lawson's 'The Vote of Thanks Debate', *The Worker*
     (Brisbane), II, 30, 25 July 1891, p.3.
145. J. T. Lang, 'Australia's Experiment in Communism — Upheaval in
     Utopia,' *Truth*, 7 November 1954, p.36.
146. Roderick (ed.), *Henry Lawson: Collected Verse*, Vol. I, pp.171-2,
     256-7, 449. Henry Lawson, 'Otherside', *New Australia*, I, 1, 19
     November 1892, p.1; 'Something Better', *New Australia*, I, 16, 24
     March 1894, p.3.

> The sudden roars of beaten men—
>   O you remember that :—
> Are memories that make my pen
>   Not worth the while to rat.[147]

E. H. Lane describes another of Lane's contemporaries who appears in the novel.

> An outstanding figure in the Australian revolutionary movement at this time, J. A. Andrews, philosophical anarchist, poet and rebel, was a regular talker in Sydney Domain on Sundays. Clothed in an overcoat to cover his sometimes shirtless body and tattered clothes . . . a long pole with a small black flag attached to an overhead tree, he would deliver a two or three hours' exposition of the tenets of philosophic anarchy . . . a man of exceptional ability. He published a book of poems, *The Temple of Death*, and was a fair linguist. With true anarchic fervor, he issued irregularly a little paper, *Revolt*, printed by type he cut out of wood.[148]

Ernie Lane occasionally went round with him putting up anarchist slogans and posters in the early hours of the morning. In *The Workingman's Paradise* the anarchist Sim describes his fellow anarchist Jones, clearly based on Andrews.

> Jones hasn't got any type, and of course he can't afford to buy it, but he's got hold of a little second-hand toy printing press. To print from he takes a piece of wood, cut across the grain and rubbed smooth with sand, and cuts out of it the most revolutionary and blood-curdling leaflets, letter by letter . . . Every old scrap of paper he can collect or get sent him he prints his leaflets on and gets them distributed all over the country. (p.41)

---

147. Roderick (ed.), *Henry Lawson: Collected Verse*, Vol. III, Angus and Robertson, Sydney 1969, p.94.
148. *Dawn to Dusk*, p.31.

Joe Harris reproduces a page of Andrew's paper *Anarchy* 'printed in type he cut out of wood'.[149]

And then there was Mary Gilmore. Harry Taylor recalled 'William Lane once told me that the very striking character of the heroine in *The Workingman's Paradise* was derived from a composite of Miss Cameron and another'.[150] Nettie Palmer wrote in 1926, of 'Mary Gilmore, the woman Lane took for his heroine in his remarkable novel'.[151] But William Wood wrote from Cosme in reply to the article:

> I think it unlikely. I always understood that it (the heroine) was an imaginary character, and that "Ned Hawkins" was a composite of the strike leaders in Queensland, the bush strike in 1891, of the pastoral workers there. David R. Stevenson, who knew Mrs Gilmore (then Miss Cameron) in Sydney, says that William Lane and Miss Cameron had not met prior to the book's publication.[152]

But Mary Gilmore always claimed to be the original of Nellie. On 9 May 1947 she wrote to Mr Fadden, leader of the Country Party in the House of Representatives, enclosing a curriculum vitae: '14. I am "Nellie" in William Lane's book *The Workingman's Paradise*. Every incident, every person, every conversation in the book is real'.[153]

And according to Mary Gilmore, the model for Ned was David Russell Stevenson, a bushman who went with Lane

149. *The Bitter Fight*, p.106. *Anarchy* appeared in 1891 and *The Revolt* in 1893. See J. N. Rawling, 'Some Forerunners of our "Workers' Weekly"', *Communist Review*, II, vii, July 1935, pp.41-4.
150. Harry Taylor, letter to *The Register*, reprinted *The Murray Pioneer*, in A. G. Stephens' cutting book, 'New Australia', p.128, Mitchell Library.
151. *Australian Woman's Mirror*, 23 February 1926, p.8.
152. *Windsor and Richmond Gazette*.
153. Mary Gilmore, Letter to Fadden, 9 May 1947, Mary Gilmore papers, Mitchell Library.

to New Australia and Cosme, and who was related to the novelist Robert Louis Stevenson.[154] As for the revolutionary Geisner, Lane reputedly met at one of the Rose-Soley gatherings a San Domingo planter 'whose father had fought in the Paris Commune and had spent twelve years in prisoned exile', and this provided the model.[155]

'Mr Hawkins, this is Bohemia. You do as you like. You say what you like', Mrs Stratton announces in an unmistakable patrician, haut-bourgeois way (p.57). Class divisions permeate bourgeois Bohemia just as they permeate the rest of society.

> Ned's thoughts were in tumult, as he sat balancing his spoon on his cup after forcing himself to swallow the, to him, unpleasant drink that the others seemed to relish so. There were no conspirators here, that was certain. (p.59)

The emphasis is on bourgeois taste and bourgeois property and conspicuous consumption, in this beautiful waterfront house on the harbour.

> It was pleasant, of course, too pleasant. It seemed a sin to enjoy life like this on the very edge of the horrible pit in which the poor were festering like worms in an iron pot. Was it for this Nellie had brought him here? To idle away an evening among well-meaning people who were "interested in the Labour movement" . . .(p.59)

But the episode does more than contrast the middle-class

154. *William Lane and the Australian Labor Movement*, p.89; *A Peculiar People*, p.30.
155. *William Lane and the Australian Labor Movement*, p.110. Humphrey McQueen, 'Laborism and Socialism' in Richard Gordon (ed.), *The Australian New Left*, Heinemann, Melbourne 1970, p.49, incorrectly writes of 'the protagonist, Geisner (Lane himself)'.

comforts with the slums, doss-houses, and the homeless in
the Domain. It introduces the topic of the role of art. The
visitors discuss music and the *Zeitgeist*. 'What a waste of
words when the world outside needed deeds!' Ned fumes
inwardly (p.60) until he finally explodes:

> Is it by playing music in fine parlours that good is to be done?
> Is it by drinking wine, by smoking, by laughing, by talking of
> pictures and books and music, by going to theatres, by living
> in clover while the world starves? Why do you not play that
> music in the back streets or to our fellows? (p.66)

It is the culmination of his frustration at conversations
about environmental 'vandalism which the naval authorities
were perpetrating on Garden Island' (p.57), and at the ease,
comfort and irrelevance of the Strattons' 'culture'.

But in a sense Ned answers his own question. Geisner's
playing the *Marseillaise* has brought tears to Ned's eyes, to
everyone's eyes. Art has its radicalizing, inspirational role;
it is music that has prompted Ned's outburst. Ernie Lane
reminds us the *Marseillaise* was 'the then international
revolutionary song of the world's workers'.[156] The anarchist Larry Petrie, who tried to blow up a scab ship between
Sydney and Rockhampton, and later spent time at Cosme,
used to sing it to attract a crowd to his street-corner
speeches; he had had an arm amputated after a brawl with a
non-union scab, and when he sang 'To arms, my citizens',
waving his remaining arm in the air, the crowd was always
vastly amused.[157] Henry Lawson wrote 'The Australian
Marseillaise, or A Song for the Sydney Poor'.[158]

---

156. *Dawn to Dusk*, p.26.
157. *A Peculiar People*, p.64.
158. *Truth*, 23 November 1890; Roderick (ed.), *Henry Lawson: Collected Verse*, Vol. I, pp.87-8.

The discussion about whether 'Puritanism crushed the artistic sense out of the English' (p.63) relates directly to the book's politics. Geisner points out 'the Puritan period produced two of the masterpieces of English Art — Milton's *Paradise Lost* and Bunyan's *Pilgrim's Progress*' (p.64). The radical politics of the English revolution are here identified with the production of literary masterpieces. England may have 'no national music' (p.63) but there is a national literature that is also a radical, revolutionary literature.

The discussion about art is important to the novel; it validates Lane's own activity in writing the novel, it is his justification for taking time from direct organizing. The arts can be the transmitters of radical social messages; they work in alliance with the deeds of the activists. But Ned's specific question, 'Why do you not play that music in the backstreets?' is not answered by the bourgeois bohemians. They are shocked at Ned's ignorance in challenging a man who suffered so much for the cause. But Lane himself took up the challenge he has Ned deliver. Lane spread his ideas not through the rarified high arts and the private salons, but through the columns of *The Boomerang, The Worker, New Australia*, applying his art to this novel that was sold through the labour movement and reached into the backstreets. He didn't neglect the bourgeoisie — he spent considerable time haranguing Brisbane opinion leaders in attempts to radicalize them; but he reached beyond that to the bushmen and the urban workers, devoting his literary gifts to the specifics of propaganda.

Finally and ultimately there is Lane's religious sense which permeates *The Workingman's Paradise* as it did all his writings and activities. It was not a narrowly denominational religion; indeed, it was not narrowly

Christian. Geisner refers to 'Brahma and more than Brahma. What Prince Buddha thought out too. What Jesus the Carpenter dimly recognized. Not only Force, but Purpose . . .' (p.76). Lane wrote in 1898 of his

> absolute and unshakeable faith in what we commonly call "God". And when I say God I mean neither the idol built of wood or stone by the crude hands of savages nor the idol built of words and phrases by the equal heathenism of higher races. I mean by God the sense of the oneness, the livingness, the completeness, of that inconceivable power which working through matter called us and all the wondrous universe we see into being. That power I know and feel is supreme beyond all conceiving. Nothing is beyond its control.[159]

And it was this belief that was the basis of his communism:

> to me communism is part of God's law. He who tries to live for his fellow as for himself, he who strives unceasingly to be less selfish and more human, he who with all his heart and soul endeavours to be communist of himself, freely, and to mould upon communistic lines the social organization without which man cannot live on earth, he is, in so far, serving God and obeying God's law.[160]

THE PRESENT TEXT

The Worker (Brisbane), II, 33, 5 September 1891, p.4 announced as the first item in the regular 'Smoke-ho' column:

> "The Working Man's Paradise," written by the editor of the Worker in aid of the Prisoners' Defence Fund, will be

159. William Lane, 'Belief and Communism', *Cosme Monthly*, September 1898, p.2.
160. Ibid.

published in a few weeks: price 2s. 6d. Books containing a dozen order tickets will be issued shortly to all union secretaries and others willing to help in the sale. On receipt of 2s. 6d. the Worker will forward the books to any address in the colonies.

The notice was repeated in succeeding issues. On 31 October (II, 37, p.2) it was announced ' "The Workingman's Paradise" will be published as soon as advance subscriptions sufficient to cover costs are received'. A reminder that 'the book will not be sent to press until the cost of publication is guaranteed' appeared on 14 November (II, 38, p.2), and the following issue (28 November, II, 39, p.2) announced that the novel 'is going to press and will be out about New Year'. *The Worker* for 6 February 1892 (II, 44, p.2) announced it

is now in the press but will soon be out. Messrs. Warwick and Sapsford, of Brisbane, are doing the printing, and making an excellent job of it. Subscribers ... mustn't get impatient, because they're encouraging native industry in the printing line, and books of that class are not often printed in Queensland.

On 5 March (II, 46, p.2) it was announced

The last proofs of "The Workingman's Paradise" have been seen as the Worker goes to press. The delay, which has been as usual the printer's fault, has been uncontrollable by anybody else. The book will certainly be out this month.

Finally *The Worker* of 2 April 1892 (III, 48) announced 'The publication of "the Workingman's Paradise" is commenced this week' and the issue of 9 April (II, 49, p.3) declared ' "The Workingman's Paradise" after an irritating but unavoidable delay, has been published and forwarded to subscribers'. It was reviewed on the same page.

The Workingman's Paradise: An Australian Labour Novel
by John Miller was published by Edwards, Dunlop & Co.,
Sydney, Brisbane and London, and the Worker Board of
Trustees, Brisbane, 1892. The title page declared 'PRICE
2/6.' It was cloth bound.

A paperbound edition, with its title page declaring
'PRICE 1/3' appeared later. It was advertised for the first
time in *The Worker* (Brisbane) IV, 113, 1 July 1893, p.2:
'There is only a limited supply of the Cheap Edition.'

Both editions are dated 1892, and use the same
typesetting. The cloth bound edition advertises *The Worker*
and *In New Australia*, at the end of the text. The paperbound edition has a new, smaller advertisement for *The
Worker* and has replaced the announcement of the novel's
sequel with an advertisement for the New Australia
movement.

In 1948 the novel was reissued in cloth and paper bound
editions by Cosme Publishing Co., Box 675, GPO Sydney,
with a new seven page preface by E. H. Lane, and some
textual variation and excisions of unknown authority.

The text reproduced here is a facsimile of the cloth bound
first edition of 1892.

The epigraphs to parts I and II of the novel are from
Algernon Charles Swinburne's poem, 'Our Lady of Pain'.
Selected stanzas from the poem were published in *The
Worker* (Brisbane), II, 26, 13 June 1891, p.6, with a note by
Lane: 'I used to quote these verses to Chairman Bennett of
the C. D. Strike Committee, in Adelaide last February.
Anybody who doesn't see how they apply to him and his
mates had better read something else'.

Advertisement from the cloth bound first edition (1892) of *The Workingman's Paradise*

Advertisement from the paperbound first edition (1893) of *The Workingman's Paradise*

THE FACSIMILE TEXT

Price 2/6

THE

WORKINGMAN'S PARADISE:

AN AUSTRALIAN LABOUR NOVEL.

By JOHN MILLER.

———

IN TWO PARTS.

PART I.—THE WOMAN TEMPTED HIM.
PART II.—HE KNEW HIMSELF NAKED.

———

EDWARDS, DUNLOP & CO., SYDNEY, BRISBANE AND LONDON.

WORKER BOARD OF TRUSTEES, BRISBANE.

1892.

Brisbane:

WARWICK & SAPSFORD PRINTERS, &C., ADELAIDE STREET.

1892.

PREFACE.

THE naming and writing of THE WORKINGMAN'S PARADISE were both done hurriedly, although delay has since arisen in its publishing. The scene is laid in Sydney because it was not thought desirable, for various reasons, to aggravate by a local plot the soreness existing in Queensland.

While characters, incidents and speakings had necessarily to be adapted to the thread of plot upon which they are strung, and are not put forward as actual photographs or phonographs, yet many will recognise enough in this book to understand how, throughout, shreds and patches of reality have been pieced together. The first part is laid during the summer of 1888-89 and covers two days; the second at the commencement of the Queensland bush strike excitement in 1891, covering a somewhat shorter time. The intention of the plot, at first, was to adapt the old old legend of Paradise and the fall of man from innocence to the much-prated-of "workingman's paradise"—Australia. Ned was to be Adam, Nellie to be Eve, Geisner to be the eternal Rebel inciting world-wide agitation, the Stratton home to be presented in contrast with the slum-life as a reason for challenging the tyranny which makes Australia what it really is; and so on. This plot got very considerably mixed and there was no opportunity to properly re-arrange it. After reading the MSS. one friend wrote advising an additional chapter making Ned, immediately upon his being sentenced for "conspiracy" under George IV., 6, hear that Nellie has died of a broken heart. My wife, on the contrary, wants Ned and Nellie to come to an understanding and live happily ever after in the good old-fashioned style. This being left in abeyance, readers can take their choice until the matter is finally settled in another book.

Whatever the failings of this book are it may nevertheless serve the double purpose for which it was written:

(1) to assist the fund being raised for Ned's mates now in prison in Queensland, and (2) to explain unionism a little to those outside it and Socialism a little to all who care to read or hear, whether unionists or not. These friends of ours in prison will need all we can do for them when they are released, be that soon or late ; and there are too few, even in the ranks of unionism, who really understand Socialism.

To understand Socialism is to endeavour to lead a better life, to regret the vileness of our present ways, to seek ill for none, to desire truth and purity and honesty, to despise this selfish civilisation and to comprehend what living might be. Understanding Socialism will not make people at once what men and women should be but it will fill them with hatred for the unfitting surroundings that damn us all and with passionate love for the ideals that are lifting us upwards and with an earnest endeavour to be themselves somewhat as they feel Humanity is struggling to be.

All that any religion has been to the highest thoughts of any people Socialism is, and more, to those who conceive it aright. Without blinding us to our own weaknesses and wickednesses, without offering to us any sophistry or cajoling us with any fallacy, it enthrones Love above the universe, gives us Hope for all who are downtrodden and restores to us Faith in the eternal fitness of things. Socialism is indeed a religion—demanding deeds as well as words. Not until professing socialists understand this will the world at large see Socialism as it really is.

If this book assists the Union Prisoners Assistance Fund in any way or if it brings to a single man or woman a clearer conception of the Religion of Socialism it will have done its work. Should it fail to do either it will not be because the Cause is bad, for the Cause is great enough to rise above the weakness of those who serve it.

J.M.

CONTENTS.

PART I.

THE WOMAN TEMPTED HIM.

Ah thy people, thy children, thy chosen,
* Marked cross from the womb and perverse !*
They have found out the secret to cozen
* The gods that constrain us and curse ;*
They alone, they are wise, and none other ;
* Give me place, even me, in their train,*
O my sister, my spouse, and my mother,
* Our Lady of Pain.*

—SWINBURNE.

THE WORKINGMAN'S PARADISE.

CHAPTER I.

WHY NELLIE SHOWS NED ROUND.

NELLIE was waiting for Ned, not in the best of humours.

"I suppose he'll get drunk to celebrate it," she was saying, energetically drying the last cup with a corner of the damp cloth. "And I suppose she feels as though it's something to be very glad and proud about."

"Well, Nellie," answered the woman who had been rinsing the breakfast things, ignoring the first supposition. "One doesn't want them to come, but when they do come one can't help feeling glad."

"Glad!" said Nellie, scornfully.

"If Joe was in steady work, I wouldn't mind how often it was. It's when he loses his job and work so hard to get——" Here the speaker subsided in tears.

"It's no use worrying," comforted Nellie, kindly. "He'll get another job soon, I hope. He generally has pretty fair luck, you know."

"Yes, Joe has had pretty fair luck, so far. But nobody knows how long it'll last. There's my brother wasn't out of work for fifteen years, and now he hasn't done a stroke for twenty-three weeks come Tuesday. He's going out of his mind."

"He'll get used to it," answered Nellie, grimly.

"How you do talk, Nellie!" said the other. "To hear you sometimes one would think you hadn't any heart."

"I haven't any patience."

B

"That's true, my young gamecock!" exclaimed a somewhat discordant voice. Nellie looked round, brightening suddenly.

A large slatternly woman stood in the back doorway, a woman who might possibly have been a pretty girl once but whose passing charms had long been utterly sponged out. A perceptible growth of hair lent a somewhat repulsive appearance to a face which at best had a great deal of the virago in it. Yet there was, in spite of her furrowed skin and faded eyes and drab dress, an air of good-heartedness about her, made somewhat ferocious by the muscularity of the arms that fell akimbo upon her great hips, and by the strong teeth, white as those of a dog, that flashed suddenly from between her colourless lips when she laughed.

"That's true, my young gamecock!" she shouted, in a deep voice, strangely cracked. "And so you're at your old tricks again, are you? Talking sedition I'll be bound. I've half a mind to turn informer and have the law on you. The dear lamb!" she added, to the other woman.

"Good morning, Mrs. Macanany," said Nellie, laughing. "We haven't got yet so that we can't say what we like, here."

"I'm not so sure about that. Wait till you hear what I came to tell you, hearing from little Jimmy that you were at home and going to have a holiday with a young man from the country. We'll sherrivvery them if he takes her away from us, Mrs. Phillips, the only one that does sore eyes good to see in the whole blessed neighborhood! You needn't blush, my dear, for I had a young man myself once, though you wouldn't imagine it to look at me. And if I was a young man myself it's her "—pointing Nellie out to Mrs. Phillips—"that I'd go sweethearting with and not with the empty headed chits that—"

"Look here, Mrs. Macanany!" interrupted Nellie. "You didn't come in to make fun of me."

"Making fun! There, have your joke with the old woman! You didn't hear that my Tom got the run yesterday, did you?"

"Did he? What a pity! I'm very sorry," said Nellie.

"Everybody'll be out of work and then what'll we all do?" said Mrs. Phillips, evidently cheered, nevertheless, by companionship in misfortune.

"What'll we all do! There'd never be anybody at all out of work if everybody was like me and Nellie there," answered the amazon.

"What did he get the run for?" asked Nellie.

"What can we women do?" queried Mrs. Phillips, doleful still.

"Wait a minute till I can tell you! You don't give a body time to begin before you worry them with questions about things you'd hear all about it if you'd just hold your tongues a minute. You're like two blessed babies! It was this way, Mrs. Phillips, as sure as I'm standing here. Tom got trying to persuade the other men in the yard—poor sticks of men they are!—to have a union. I've been goading him to it, may the Lord forgive me, ever since Miss Nellie there came round one night and persuaded my Tessie to join. 'Tom,' says I to him that very night, 'I'll have to be lending you one of my old petticoats, the way the poor weak girls are beginning to stand up for their rights, and you not even daring to be a union man. I never thought I'd live to be ashamed of the father of my children!' says I. And yesterday noon Tom came home with a face on him as long as my arm, and told me that he'd been sacked for talking union to the men.

"'It's a man you are again, Tom,' says I. 'We've lived short before and we can live it again, please God, and it's myself would starve with you a hundred times over rather than be ashamed of you,' says I. 'Who was it that sacked you?' I asked him.

"'The foreman,' says Tom. 'He told me they didn't want any agitators about.'

"'May he live to suffer for it,' says I. 'I'll go down and see the boss himself.'

"So down I went, and as luck would have it the boy in the front office wasn't educated enough to say I was an old image, I suppose, for would you believe it I actually heard him say that there was a lady, if you please, wanting to see Mister Paritt very particularly on personal business, as I'd told him. So of course I was shown in directly, the very minute, and the door was closed on me before the old villain, who's a great man at church on Sundays, saw that he'd made a little mistake.

"'What do you want, my good woman?' says he, snappish like. 'Very sorry,' says he, when I'd told him that I'd eleven children and that Tom had worked for him for four years and worked well, too. 'Very sorry,' says he, 'my good woman, but your husband should have thought of that before. It's against my principles,' says he, 'to have any unionists about the place. I'm told he's been making the other men discontented. I can't take him back. You must blame him, not me,' says he.

"I could feel the temper in me, just as though he'd given me a couple of stiff nobblers of real old whisky. 'So you won't take Tom back,' says I, 'not for the sake of his eleven children when it's their poor heart-broken mother that asks you?'

"'No,' says he, short, getting up from his chair. 'I can't. You've bothered me long enough,' says he.

"So then I decided it was time to tell the old villain just what I thought of his grinding men down to the last penny and insulting every decent girl that ever worked for him. He got as black in the face as if he was smoking already on the fiery furnace that's waiting for him below, please God, and called the shrimp of an office boy to throw me out. 'Leave the place, you disgraceful creature, or I'll send for the police,' says he. But I left when I got ready to leave and just what I said to him, the dirty wretch, I'll tell to you, Mrs. Phillips, some time when she"—nodding at Nellie—"isn't about. She's getting so like a blessed saint that one feels as if one's in church when she s about, bless her heart!"

"You're getting very particular all at once, Mrs. Macanany," observed Nellie.

"It's a wonder he didn't send for a policeman," commented Mrs. Phillips.

"Send for a policeman! And pretty he'd look with the holy bible in his hand repeating what I said to him, wouldn't he now?" enquired Mrs. Macanany, once more placing her great arms on her hips and glaring with her watery eyes at her audience.

"Did you hear that Mrs. Hobbs had a son this morning?" questioned Mrs. Phillips, suddenly recollecting that she also might have an item of news.

"What! Mrs. Hobbs, so soon! How would I be hearing when I just came through the back, and Tom only just gone out to wear his feet off, looking for work? A boy again! The Lord preserve us all! It's the devil's own luck the dear creature has, isn't it now? Why didn't you tell me before, and me here gossiping when the dear woman will be expecting me round to see her and the dear baby and wondering what I've got against her for not coming? I must be off, now, and tidy myself a bit and go and cheer the poor creature up for I know very well how one wants cheering at such times. Was it a hard time she had with it? And who is it like the little angel that came straight from heaven this blessed day?

The dear woman! I must be off, so I'll say good-day to you, Mrs. Phillips, and may the sun shine on you and your sweetheart, Nellie, even if he does take you away from us all, and may you have a houseful of babies with faces as sweet as your own and never miss a neighbour to cheer you a bit when the trouble's on you. The Lord be with us all!"

Nellie laughed as the rough-voiced, kind-hearted woman took herself off, to cross the broken dividing wall to the row of houses that backed closely on the open kitchen door. Then she shrugged her shoulders.

"It's always the way," she remarked, as she turned away to the other door that led along a little, narrow passage to the street. "What's going to become of the innocent little baby? Nobody thinks of that."

Mrs. Phillips did not answer. She was tidying up in a wearied way. Besides, she was used to Nellie, and had a dim perception that what that young woman said was right, only one had to work, especially on Saturdays when the smallest children could be safely turned into the street to play with the elder ones, the baby nursed by pressed nurses, who by dint of scolding and coaxing and smacking and promising were persuaded to keep it out of the house, even though they did not keep it altogether quiet.

Mrs. Phillips "tidied up" in a wearied way, without energy, working stolidly all the time as if she were on a tread-mill. She had a weary look, the expression of one who is tired always, who gets up tired and goes to bed tired, and who never by any accident gets a good rest, who even when dead is not permitted to lie quietly like other people but gets buried the same day in a cheap coffin that hardly keeps the earth up and is doomed to be soon dug up to make room for some other tired body in that economical way instituted by the noble philanthropists who unite a keen appreciation of the sacredness of burial with a still keener appreciation of the value of grave-lots. She might have been a pretty girl once or she might not. Nobody would ever have thought of physical attractiveness as having anything to do with her. Mrs. Macanany was distinctly ugly. Mrs. Phillips was neither ugly nor pretty nor anything else. She was a poor thin draggled woman, who tried to be clean but who had long ago given up in despair any attempt at looking natty and had now no ambition for herself but to have something "decent" to go out in. Once it was her ambition also to have a "room." She had scraped and saved and pared in dull times for this "room" and when once Joe had a long run of steady work she had launched out into what those who know how workingmen's wives *should* live would have denounced as the wildest extravagance. A gilt framed mirror and a sofa, four spidery chairs and a round table, a wonderful display of wax apples under a glass shade, a sideboard and a pair of white lace curtains hanging from a pole, with various ornaments and pictures of noticeable appearance, also linoleum for the floor, had finally been gathered together and were treasured for a time as household gods indeed. In those days there was hardly a commandment in the decalogue that Mephistopheles might not have induced Mrs. Phillips to commit by judicious praise of her "room." Her occasional "visitors" were ushered into it with an air of pride that was alone enough to illuminate the dingy, musty little place. Between herself and those of her neighbours who had "rooms" there was a fierce rivalry, while those of inferior grade—and they were in the majority—regarded her with an envy not unmixed with dislike.

But those times were gone for poor Mrs. Phillips. We all know how they go, excepting those who do not want to know. Work gradually became more uncertain, wages fell and rents kept up. They had one room of the small five-roomed house let already. They let another—"they" being her and Joe. Finally, they had to let *the* room. The chairs, the round table and the sofa were bartered at a second-hand store for bedroom furniture. The mirror and the sideboard were brought out into the kitchen, and on the sideboard the wax fruit still stood like the lingering shrine of a departed faith.

The "room" was now the lodging of two single men, as the good old ship-phrase goes. Upstairs, in the room over the kitchen, the Phillips family slept, six in all. There would have been seven, only the eldest girl, a child of ten, slept with Nellie in the little front room over the door, an arrangement which was not in the bond but was volunteered by the single woman in one of her fits of indignation against pigging together. The other front room was also rented by a single man when they could get him. Just now it was tenantless, an additional cause of sorrow to Mrs. Phillips, whose stock card, "Furnished Lodgings for a Single Man," was now displayed at the front window, making the house in that respect very similar to half the houses in the street, or in this part of the town for that matter. Yet with all this crowding and renting of rooms Mrs. Phillips did not grow rich. She was always getting into debt or getting out of it, this depending in inverse ratio upon Joe being in work or out. When the rooms were all let they barely paid the rent and were always getting empty. The five children—they had one dead and another coming—ate so much and made so much work. There were boots and clothes and groceries to pay for, not to mention bread. And though Joe was not like many a woman's husband yet he did get on the spree occasionally, a little fact which in the opinion of the pious will account for all Mrs. Phillips' weariness and all the poverty of this crowded house. But however that may be she was a weary hopeless faded woman, who would not cause passers-by to turn, pity-stricken, and watch her when she hurried along on her semi-occasional escapes from her prison-house only because such women are so common that it is those who do not look hopeless and weary whom we turn to watch if by some strange chance one passes.

The Phillips' kitchen was a cheerless place, in spite of the mirror that was installed in state over the side-board and the wax flowers. Its one window looked upon a diminutive back yard, a low broken wall and another row of similar two-storied houses. On the plastered walls were some shelves bearing a limited supply of crockery. Over the grated fireplace was a long high shelf whereon stood various pots and bottles. There were some chairs and a table and a Chinese-made safe. On the boarded floor was a remnant of linoleum. Against one wall was a narrow staircase.

It was the breakfast things that Nellie had been helping to wash up. The little American clock on the sideboard indicated quarter past nine.

Nellie went to the front door, opened it, and stood looking out. The view was a limited one, a short narrow side street, blinded at one end by a high bare stone wall, bounded at the other by the almost as narrow by-thoroughfare this side street branched from. The houses in the thoroughfare were three-storied, and a number were used as shops of the huckstering variety, mainly by Chinese. The houses in the side street were two-storied, dingy, jammed tightly together, each one exactly like the next. The pavement was of stone, the roadway of some composite, hard as iron; roadway and pavement were overrun with children. At the corner by a dead wall was a lamp-post. Nearly opposite Nellie a group of excited women were standing in an open doorway. They talked loudly, two or three at a time, addressing each other indiscriminately. The children screamed and swore, quarrelled and played and fought, while a shrill-voiced mother occasionally took a hand in the diversion of the moment, usually to scold or cuff some luckless offender. The sunshine radiated that sickly heat which precedes rain.

Nellie stood there and waited for Ned. She was 20 or so, tall and slender but well-formed, every curve of her figure giving promise of more luxurious development. She was dressed in a severely plain dress of black stuff, above which a faint line of white collar could be seen clasping the round throat. Her ears had been bored, but she wore no earrings. Her brown hair was drawn away from her forehead and bound in a heavy braid on the back of her neck. But it was her face that attracted one, a pale sad face that was stamped on every feature with the impress of a determined will and of an intense womanliness. From the pronounced jaw that melted its squareness of profile in the oval of the full face to the dark brown eyes that rarely veiled themselves beneath their long-lashed lids, everything told that the girl possessed the indefinable something we call character. And if there was in the drooping corners of her red lips a sternness generally unassociated with conceptions of feminine loveliness one forgot it usually in con-templating the soft attractiveness of the shapely forehead, dashed beneath by straight eyebrows, and of the pronounced cheekbones that crossed the symmetry of a Saxon face. Mrs. Phillips was a drooping wearied woman but there was nothing drooping about Nellie and never could be. She might be torn down like one of the blue gums under which she had drawn in the fresh air of her girlhood, but she could no more bend than can the tree which must stand erect in the fiercest storm or must go down altogether. Pale she was, from the close air of the close street and close rooms, but proud she was as woman can be, standing erect in the door-way amid all this pandemonium of cries, waiting for Ned.

Ned was her old playmate, a Darling Downs boy, five years older to be sure, but her playmate in the old days, nevertheless, as lads who have no sisters are apt to be with admiring little girls who have no brothers. Selectors' children, both of them, from neighbouring farms, born above the frost line under the smelting Queensland sun, drifted hither and thither by the fitful gusts of

Fate as are the paper-sailed ships that boys launch on flood water pools, meeting here in Sydney after long years of separation. Now, Nellie was a dressmaker in a big city shop, and Ned a sunburnt shearer to whom the great trackless West was home. She thought of the old home sadly as she stood there waiting for him.

It had not been a happy home altogether and yet, and yet—it was better than this. There was pure air there, at least, and grass up to the door, and trees rustling over-head; and the little children were brown and sturdy and played with merry shouts, not with these vile words she heard jabbered in the wretched street. Her heart grew sick within her—a habit it had, that heart of Nellie's—and a passion of wild revolt against her surroundings made her bite her lips and press her nails against her palms. She looked across at the group opposite. More children being born! Week in and week out they seemed to come in spite of all the talk of not having any more. She could have cried over this holocaust of the innocents, and yet she shrank with an unreasoning shrinking from the barrenness that was coming to be regarded as the most comfortable state and being sought after, as she knew well, by the younger married women. What were they all coming to? Were they all to go on like this without a struggle until they vanished altogether as a people, perhaps to make room for the round-cheeked, bland-faced Chinaman who stood in the doorway of his shop in the crossing thoroughfare, gazing expressionlessly at her? She loathed that Chinaman. He always seemed to be watching her, to be waiting for something. She would dream of him sometimes as creeping upon her from behind, always with that bland round face. Yet he never spoke to her, never insulted her, only he seemed to be always watching her, always waiting. And it would come to her sometimes like a cold chill, that this yellow man and such men as he were watching them all slowly going down lower and lower, were waiting to leap upon them in their last helplessness and enslave them all as white girls were sometimes enslaved, even already, in those filthy opium joints whose stench nauseated the hurrying passers-by. Perhaps under all their meekness these Chinese were braver, more stubborn, more vigorous, and it was doomed that they should conquer at last and rule in the land where they had been treated as outcasts and intruders. She thought of this— and, just then, Ned turned the corner by the lamp.

Ned was a Downs native, every inch of him. He stood five feet eleven in his bare feet yet was so broad and strong that he hardly looked over the medium height. He had blue eyes and a heavy moustache just tinged with red. His hair was close-cut and dark; his forehead, nose and chin were large and strong; his lips were strangely like a woman's. He walked with short jerky steps, swinging himself awkwardly as men do who have been much in the saddle. He wore a white shirt, as being holiday-making, but had not managed a collar; his pants were dark-blue, slightly belled; his coat, dark-brown; his boots were highly polished; round his neck was a silk handkerchief; round his vestless waist, a discoloured leather belt; above all, a wide-brimmed cabbage tree hat, encircled by a narrow leather strap. He swung himself along rapidly, unabashed by the stares of the women or the impudent comment of the children. Nellie, suddenly, felt all her ill-humour turn against him.

He was so satisfied with himself. He had talked unionism to her when she met him two weeks before, on his way to visit a brother who had taken up a selection in the Hawkesbury district. He had laughed when she hinted at the possibilities of the unionism he championed so fanatically. "We only want what's fair," he said. "We're not going to do anything wild. As long as we get £1 a hundred and rations at a fair figure we're satisfied." And then he had inconsistently proceeded to describe how the squatters treated the men out West, and how the union would make them civil, and how the said squatters were mostly selfish brutes who preferred Chinese to their own colour and would stop at no trick to beat the men out of a few shillings. She had said nothing at the time, being so pleased to see him, though she determined to have it out with him sometime during this holiday they had planned. But somehow, as he stepped carelessly along, a dashing manliness in every motion, a breath of the great plains coming with his sunburnt face and belted waist, he and his self-conceit jarred to her against this sordid court and these children's desolate lives. How dared he talk as he did about only wanting what was fair, she thought! How had he the heart to care only for himself and his mates while in these city slums such misery brooded! And then it shot through her that he did not know. With a rapidity, characteristic of herself, she made up her mind to teach him.

"Well, Nellie," he cried, cheerily, coming up to her. "And how are you again?"

"Hello, Ned," she answered, cordially, shaking hands. "You look as though you were rounding-up."

"Do I?" he questioned, seriously, looking down at himself. "Shirt and all? Well, if I am it's only you I came to round up. Are you ready? Did you think I wasn't coming?"

"It won't take me a minute," she replied. "I was pretty sure you'd come. I took a holiday on the strength of it, anyway, and made an engagement for you to-night. Come in a minute, Ned. You must see Mrs. Phillips while I get my hat. You'll have to sleep here to-night. It'll be so late when we get back. Unless you'd sooner go to a hotel."

"I'm not particular," said Ned, looking round curiously, as he followed her in. "I'd never have found the place, Nellie, if it hadn't been for that pub. near the corner, where we saw that row on the other night."

The women opposite had suspended their debate upon Mrs. Hobbs' latest, a debate fortified by manifold reminiscences of the past and possibilities of the future. It was known in the little street that Nellie Lawton intended taking a holiday with an individual who was universally accepted as her "young man," and Ned's appearance upon the stage naturally made him a subject for discussion which temporarily over-shadowed even Mrs. Hobbs' baby.

"I'm told he's a sort of a farmer," said one.

"He's a shearer; I had it from Mrs. Phillips herself," said another.

"He's a strapping man, whatever he is," commented a third.

"Well, she's a big lump of a girl, too," contributed a fourth.

"Yes, and a vixen with her tongue when she gets started, for all her prim looks," added a fifth.

"She has tricky ways that get over the men-folks. Mine won't hear a word against her." This from the third speaker, eager to be with the tide, evidently setting towards unfavorable criticism.

"I don't know," objected the second, timidly. "She sat up all night with my Maggie once, when she had the fever, and Nellie had to work next day, too."

"Oh, she's got her good side," retorted the fifth, opening her dress to feed her nursing baby with absolute indifference for

all onlookers.   "But she knows a great deal too much for a girl
of her age.   When she gets married will be time enough to
talk as she does sometimes."   The chorus of approving murmurs
showed that Nellie had spoken plainly enough on some subjects
to displease some of these slatternly matrons.

"She stays out till all hours, I'm told," one slanderer said.

"She's a union girl, at any rate," hazarded Nellie's timid
defender.   There was an awkward pause at this.   It was an
apple of discord with the women, evidently.   A tall form turning
the corner afforded further reason for changing the subject.

"Here's Mrs. Macanany," announced one.   "You'd better not
say anything against Nellie Lawton when she's about."   So they
talked again of Mrs. Hobbs' baby, making it the excuse to leave
undone for a few minutes the endless work of the poor man's
wife.

And sad to tell when, a few minutes afterwards, Ned and Nellie
came out again and walked off together, the group of gossipers
unanimously endorsed Mrs. Macanany's extravagant praises, and
agreed entirely with her declaration that if all the women in
Sydney would only stand by Nellie, as Mrs. Macanany herself
would, there would be such a doing and such an upsetting and
such a righting of things that ever after every man would be his
own master and every woman would only work eight hours and
get well paid for it.   Yet it was something that of six women
there were two who wouldn't slander a girl like Nellie behind
her back.

CHAPTER II.

"WELL! Where shall we go, Nellie?" began Ned jauntily, as they walked away together. To tell the truth he was eager to get away from this poor neighborhood. It had saddened him, made him feel unhappy, caused in him a longing to be back again in the bush, on his horse, a hundred miles from everybody. "Shall we go to Manly or Bondi or Watson's Bay, or do you know of a better place?" He had been reading the newspaper advertisements and had made enquiries of the waitress, as he ate his breakfast, concerning the spot which the waitress would prefer were a young man going to take her out for the day. He felt pleased with himself now, for not only did he like Nellie very much but she was attractive to behold, and he felt very certain that every man they passed envied him. She had put on a little round straw hat, black, trimmed with dark purple velvet; in her hands, enclosed in black gloves, she carried a parasol of the same colour.

"Where would you like to go, Ned?" she answered, colouring a little as she heard her name in Mrs. Macanany's hoarse voice, being told thereby that she and Ned were the topic of conversation among the jury of matrons assembled opposite.

"Anywhere you like, Nellie."

"Don't you think, Ned, that you might see a little bit of real Sydney? Strangers come here for a few days and go on the steamers and through the gardens and along George-street and then go away with a notion of the place that isn't the true one. If I were you, Ned, right from the bush and knowing nothing of towns, I'd like to see a bit of the real side and not only the show side that everybody sees. We don't all go picnicking all the time and we don't all live by the harbour or alongside the Domain."

"Do just whatever you like, Nellie," cried Ned, hardly understanding but perfectly satisfied, "you know best where to take a fellow."

"But they're not pleasant places, Ned."

"I don't mind," answered Ned, lightly, though he had been looking forward, rather, to the quiet enjoyment of a trip on a harbour steamer, or at least to the delight of a long ramble along some beach where he thought he and Nellie might pick up shells. "Besides, I fancy it's going to rain before night," he added, looking up at the sky, of which a long narrow slice showed between the tall rows of houses.

There were no clouds visible. Only there was a deepening grey in the hard blueness above them, and the breathless heat, even at this time of day, was stifling.

"I don't know that you'd call this a pleasant place," he commented, adding with the frankness of an old friend : " Why do you live here, Nellie ?"

She shrugged her shoulders. The gesture meant anything and everything.

"You needn't have bothered sending me that money back," said Ned, in reply to the shrug.

"It isn't that," explained Nellie. "I've got a pretty good billet. A pound a week and not much lost time ! But I went to room there when I was pretty hard up. It's a small room and was cheap. Then, after, I took to boarding there as well. That was pretty cheap and suited me and helped them. I suppose I might get a better place but they're very kind, and I come and go as I like, and— " she hesitated. " After all," she went on, "there's not much left out of a pound."

"I shouldn't think so," remarked Ned, looking at her and thinking that she was very nicely dressed.

"Oh! You needn't look," laughed Nellie. " I make my own dresses and trim my own hats. A woman wouldn't think much of the stuff either."

"I want to tell you how obliged I was for that money, Ned," continued Nellie, an expression of pain on her face. "There was no one else I could ask, and I needed it so. It was very kind—"

"Ugh ! That's nothing," interrupted Ned, hiding his bashfulness under a burst of boisterousness. " Why, Nellie, I'd like you to be sending to me regular. It might just as well come to you as go any other way. If you ever do want a few pounds again, Nellie," he added, seriously, " I can generally manage it. I've got plenty just now—far more than I'll ever need." This with wild exaggeration. " You might as well have it as not. I've got nobody."

"Thanks, just the same, Ned! When I do want it I'll ask you.
I'm afraid I'll never have any money to lend you if you need it,
but if I ever do you know where to come."

"It's a bargain, Nellie," said Ned. Then, eager to change the
subject, feeling awkward at discussing money matters because
he would have been so willing to have given his last penny to
anybody he felt friends with, much less to the girl by his side:
"But where are we going?"

"To see Sydney!" said Nellie.

They had turned several times since they started but the
neighborhood remained much the same. The streets, some wider,
some narrower, all told of sordid struggling. The shops were
greasy, fusty, grimy. The groceries exposed in their windows
damaged specimens of bankrupt stocks, discolored tinned goods,
grey sugars, mouldy dried fruits; at their doors, flitches of fat
bacon, cut and dusty. The meat with which the butchers' shops
overflowed was not from show-beasts, as Ned could see, but the
cheaper flesh of over-travelled cattle, ancient oxen, ewes too aged
for bearing; all these lean scraggy flabby-fleshed carcasses surrounded and blackened by buzzing swarms of flies that invaded
the foot-path outside in clouds. The draperies had tickets, proclaiming unparalleled bargains, on every piece; the whole stock
seemed displayed outside and in the doorway. The fruiterers
seemed not to be succeeding in their rivalry with each other and
with the Chinese hawkers. The Chinese shops were dotted
everywhere, dingier than any other, surviving and succeeding,
evidently, by sheer force of cheapness. The roadways everywhere
were hard and bare, reflecting the rays of the ascending sun until
the streets seemed to be Turkish baths, conducted on a new and
gigantic method. There was no green anywhere, only unlovely
rows of houses, now gasping with open doors and windows for air.

Air! That was what everything clamoured for, the very stones,
the dogs, the shops, the dwellings, the people. If it was like this
soon after ten, what would it be at noon?

Already the smaller children were beginning to weary of play.
In narrow courts they lolled along on the flags, exhausted. In
wider streets, they sat quietly on door-steps or the kerb, or announced their discomfort in peevish wailings. The elder children
quarrelled still and swore from their playground, the gutter, but
they avoided now the sun and instinctively sought the shade—
and it is pretty hot when a child minds the sun. At shop doors,

shopmen, sometimes shopwomen, came to wipe their warm faces
and examine the sky with anxious eyes. The day grew hotter
and hotter. Ned could feel the rising heat, as though he were in
an oven with a fire on underneath. Only the Chinese looked
cool.

Nellie led the way, sauntering along, without hurrying.
Several times she turned down passages that Ned would hardly
have noticed, and brought him out in courts closed in on all sides,
from which every breath of air seemed purposely excluded.
Through open doors and windows he could see the inside of
wretched homes, could catch glimpses of stifling bedrooms and
close, crowded little kitchens. Often one of the denizens came to
door or window to stare at Nellie and him; sometimes they
were accosted with impudent chaff, once or twice with pitiful
obscenity.

The first thing that impressed him was the abandonment that
thrust itself upon him in the more crowded of these courts and
alley-ways and back-streets, the despairing abandonment there of
the decencies of living. The thin dwarfed children kicked and
tumbled with naked limbs on the ground; many women leaned
half-dressed and much unbuttoned from ground floor windows, or
came out into the passage-ways slatternly. In one court two
unkempt vile-tongued women of the town wrangled and abused
each other to the amusement of the neighborhood, where the
working poor were huddled together with those who live by
shame. The children played close by as heedlessly as if such
quarrels were common events, cursing themselves at each other
with nimble filthy tongues.

" There's a friend of mine lives here," said Nellie, turning into
one of these narrow alleys that led, as they could see, into a
busier and bustling street. '' If you don't mind we'll go up and
I can help her a bit, and you can see how one sort of sweating is
done. I worked at it for a spell once, when dressmaking was
slack. In the same house, too.''

She stopped at the doorway of one of a row of three-storied
houses. On the doorstep were a group of little children, all barefooted and more or less ragged in spite of evident attempts to
keep some of them patched into neatness. They looked familiarly
at Nellie and curiously at Ned.

"How's mother, Johnny?" asked Nellie of one of them, a
small pinched little fellow of six or seven, who nursed a baby of

a year or so old, an ill-nourished baby that seemed wilting in the heat.

"She's working," answered the little fellow, looking anxiously at Nellie as she felt in her pocket.

"There's a penny for you," said Nellie, "and here's a penny for Dicky," patting a little five-year-old on the head, "and here's one to buy some milk for the baby."

Johnny rose with glad eagerness, the baby in his arms and the pennies in his hand.

"I shall buy 'specks' with mine," he cried joyfully.

"What's 'specks?'" asked Ned, puzzled, as the children went off, the elder staggering under his burden.

"'Specks!' Damaged fruit, half rotten. The garbage of the rich sold as a feast to these poor little ones!" cried Nellie, a hot anger in her face and voice that made Ned dumb.

She entered the doorway. Ned followed her through a room where a man and a couple of boys were hammering away at some boots, reaching thereby a narrow, creaking stairway, hot as a chimney, almost pitch dark, being lighted only by an occasional half-opened door, up which he stumbled clumsily. Through one of these open doors he caught a glimpse of a couple of girls sewing; through another of a woman with a baby in arms tidying-up a bare floored room, which seemed to be bedroom, kitchen and dining room in one; from behind a closed door came the sound of voices, one shrilly laughing. Unused to stairways his knees ached before they reached the top. He was glad enough when Nellie knocked loudly at a door through which came the whirring of a sewing machine. The noise stopped for a moment while a sharp voice called them to "come in," then started again. Nellie opened the door.

At the open window of a small room, barely furnished with a broken iron bedstead, some case boards knocked together for a table and fixed against the wall, a couple of shaky chairs and a box, a sharp featured woman sat working a machine, as if for dear life. The heat of the room was made hotter by the little grate in which a fire had recently been burning and on which still stood the tea-pot. Some cups and a plate or two, with a cut loaf of bread and a jam tin of sugar, littered the table. The scanty bed was unmade. The woman wore a limp cotton dress of uncertain colour, rolled up at the sleeves and opened at the neck for greater coolness. She was thin and sharp; she was so busy you understood that

C

she had no time to be clean and tidy. She seemed pleased to see Nellie and totally indifferent at seeing Ned, but kept on working after nodding to them.

Nellie motioned Ned to sit down, which he did on the edge of the bed, not caring to trust the shaky chairs. She went to the side of the sharp-featured woman, and sitting down on the foot of the bed by the machine watched her working without a word. Ned could see on the ground, in a paper parcel, a heap of cloth of various colours, and on the bed some new coats folded and piled up. On the machine was another coat, being sewn.

It was ten minutes before the machine stopped, ten minutes for Ned to look about and think in. He knew without being told that this miserable room was the home of the three children to whom Nellie had given the pennies, and that here their mother worked to feed them. Their feeding he could see on the table. Their home he could see. The work that gave it to them he could see. For the first time in his life he felt ashamed of being an Australian.

Finally the machine stopped. The sharp-faced woman took the coat up, bit a thread with her teeth, and laying it on her knee began to unpick the tackings.

"Let me!" said Nellie, pulling off her gloves and taking off her hat. "We came to see you, Ned and I," she went on with honest truthfulness, "because he's just down from the bush, and I wanted him to see what Sydney was like. Ned, this is Mrs. Somerville."

Mrs. Somerville nodded at Ned. "You're right to come here," she remarked, grimly, getting up while Nellie took her place as if she often did it. "You know just what it is, Nellie, and I do, too, worse luck. Perhaps it's good for us. When we're better off we don't care for those who're down. We've got to get down ourselves to get properly disgusted with it."

She spoke with the accent of an educated woman, moving to the make-shift table and beginning to "tidy-up." As she passed between him and the light Ned could see that the cotton dress was her only covering.

"How are the children?" asked Nellie.

"How can you expect them to be?" retorted the other.

"You ought to wean the baby," insisted Nellie, as though it was one of their habitual topics.

"Wean the baby! That's all very well for those who can buy plenty of milk. It's a pity it's ever got to be weaned."

"Plenty of work this week?" asked Nellie, changing the subject.

"Yes; plenty of work this week. You know what that means. No work at all when they get a stock ahead, so as to prevent us feeling too independent I suppose." She paused, then added: "That girl downstairs says she isn't going to work any more. I talked to her a little but she says one might just as well die one way as another, and that she'll have some pleasure first. I couldn't blame her much. She's got a good heart. She's been very kind to the children."

Nellie did not answer; she did not even look up.

"They're going to reduce prices at the shop," went on Mrs. Somerville. "They told me last time I went that after this lot they shouldn't pay as much because they could easily get the things done for less. I asked what they'd pay, and they said they didn't know but they'd give me as good a show for work as ever if I cared to take the new prices, because they felt sorry for the children. I suppose I ought to feel thankful to them."

Nellie looked up now—her face flushed. "Reduce prices again!" she cried. "How can they?"

"I don't know how they can, but they can," answered Mrs. Somerville. "I suppose we can be thankful so long as they don't want to be paid for letting us work for them. Old Church's daughter got married to some officer of the fleet last week, I'm told, and I suppose we've got to help give her a send-off."

"It's shameful," exclaimed Nellie. "What they paid two years ago hardly kept one alive, and they've reduced twice since then. Oh! They'll all pay for it some day."

"Let's hope so," said Mrs. Somerville. "Only we'll have to pay them for it pretty soon, Nellie, or there won't be enough strength left in us to pay them with. I've got beyond minding anything much, but I would like to get even with old Church."

They had talked away, the two women, ignoring Ned. He listened. He understood that from the misery of this woman was drawn the pomp and pride, the silks and gold and glitter of the society belle, and he thought with a cruel satisfaction of what might happen to that society belle if this half-starved woman got hold of her. Measure for measure, pang for pang, what torture, what insults, what degradation, could atone for the life that was suffered in this miserable room? And for the life of "that girl downstairs" who had given up in despair?

"How about a union now?" asked Nellie, turning with the first pieces of another coat to the machine.

"Work's too dull," was the answer. "Wait for a few months till the busy season comes and then I wouldn't wonder if you could get one. The women were all feeling hurt about the reduction, and one girl did start talking strike, but what's the use now? I couldn't say anything, you know, but I'll find out where the others live and you can go round and talk to them after a while. If there was a paper that would show old Church up it might do good, but there isn't."

Then the rattle of the machine began again, Nellie working with an adeptness that showed her to be an old hand. Ned could see now that the coats were of cheap coarse stuff and that the sewing in them was not fine tailoring. The cut material in Nellie's hands fairly flew into shape as she rapidly moved it to and fro under the hurrying needle with her slim fingers. Her foot moved unceasingly on the treadle. Ned watching her, saw the great beads of perspiration slowly gather on her forehead and then trickle down her nose and cheeks to fall upon the work before her.

"My word! But it's hot!" exclaimed Nellie at last, as the noise stopped for a moment while she changed the position of her work. "Why don't you open the door?"

"I don't care to before the place is tidy," answered Mrs. Somerville, who had washed her cups and plates in a pan and had just put Ned on one of the shaky chairs while she shook and arranged the meagre coverings of the bed.

"Is he still carrying on?" enquired Nellie, nodding her head at the partition and evidently alluding to someone on the other side.

"Of course, drink, drink, drink, whenever he gets a chance, and that seems pretty well always. She helps him sometimes, and sometimes she keeps sober and abuses him. He kicked her down stairs the other night, and the children all screaming, and her shrieking, and him swearing. It was a nice time."

Once more the machining interrupted the conversation, which thus was renewed from time to time in the pauses of the noise. The room being "tidied," Mrs. Somerville sat down on the bed and taking up some pieces of cloth began to tack them together

with needle and thread, ready for the machine. It never seemed
to occur to her to rest even for a moment.

"Nellie's a quick one," she remarked to Ned. "At the shop
they always tell those who grumble what she earned one week.
Twenty-four and six, wasn't it, Nellie? But they don't say she
worked eighteen hours a day for it."

Nellie flushed uneasily and Ned felt uncomfortable. Both
thought of the repayment of the latter's friendly loan. The girl
made her machine rattle still more hurriedly to prevent any
further remarks trending in that direction. At last Mrs. Somerville, her tacking finished, got up and took the work from Nellie's
hands.

"I'm not going to take your whole morning," she said. "You
don't get many friends from the bush to see you, so just go away
and I'll get on. I'm much obliged to you as it is, Nellie."

Nellie did not object. After wiping her hands, face and neck
with her handkerchief she put on her gloves and hat. The
sharp-faced woman was already at the machine and amid the din,
which drowned their good-byes, they departed as they came.
Ned felt more at ease when his feet felt the first step of the
narrow creaking stairway. It is hardly a pleasant sensation for a
man to be in the room of a stranger who, without any unfriendli-
ness, does not seem particularly aware that he is there. They
left the door open. Far down the stifling stairs Ned could hear
the ceaseless whirring of the machine driven by the woman who
slaved ceaselessly for her children's bread in this Sydney sink.
He looked around for the children when they got to the alley
again but could not see them among the urchins who lolled about
half-suffocated now. The sun was almost overhead for they had
been upstairs for an hour. The heat in this mere canyon path
between cliffs of houses was terrible. Ned himself began to feel
queerly.

"Let's get out of this, Nellie," he said.

"How would you like never to be able to get out of it?" she
answered, as they turned towards the bustling street, opposite to
the way they had previously come.

"Who's that Mrs. Somerville?" he asked, not answering.

"I got to know her when I lived there," replied Nellie. "Her
husband used to be well off, I fancy, but had bad luck and got
down pretty low. There was a strike on at some building and he
went on as a laborer, blacklegging. The pickets followed him to

the house, abusing him, and made him stubborn, but I got her
alone that night and talked to her and explained things a bit and
she talked to him and next day he joined the union.   Then he
got working about as a labourer, and one day some rotten scaffold-
ing broke, and he came down with it.   The union got a few
pounds for her, but the boss was a regular swindler who was
always beating men out of their wages and doing anything to get
contracts and running everything cheap, so there was nothing to
be got out of him.''

" Did her husband die ?"

''Yes, next day.   She had three children and another came
seven months after.   One died last summer just before the baby
was born.   She's had a pretty hard time of it, but she works all
the time and she generally has work.''

" It seems quite a favour to get work here," observed Ned.

" If you were a girl you'd soon find out what a favour it is
sometimes," answered Nellie quietly, as they came out into the
street.

CHAPTER III.

SHORN LIKE SHEEP.

"How many hours do you work?" asked Nellie of the waitress.

"About thirteen," answered the girl, glancing round to see if the manager was watching her talking. "But it's not the hours so much. It's the standing."

"You're not doing any good standing now," put in Ned. "Why don't you sit down and have a rest?"

"They don't let us," answered the waitress, cautiously.

"What do they pay?" asked Nellie, sipping her tea and joining in the waitress' look-out for the manager.

"Fifteen! But they're taking girls on at twelve. Of course there's meals. But you've got to room yourself, and then there's washing, clean aprons and caps and cuffs and collars. You've got to dress, too. There's nothing left. We ought to get a pound."

"What——"

"S-s-s!" warned the waitress, straightening herself up as the manager appeared.

* * * *

They were in a fashionable Sydney restaurant, on George-street, a large, painted, gilded, veneered, electro-plated place, full of mirrors and gas-fittings and white-clothed tables. It was not busy, the hour being somewhat late and the day Saturday, and so against the walls, on either side the long halls, were ranged sentinel rows of white-aproned, white-capped, black-dressed waitresses.

They were dawdling over their tea—Ned and Nellie were, not the waitresses—having dined exceedingly well on soup and fish and flesh and pudding. For Ned, crushed by more sight-seeing and revived by a stroll to the Domain and a rest by a fountain under shady trees, further revived by a thunderstorm that suddenly rolled up and burst upon them almost before they could reach the shelter of an awning, had insisted on treating Nellie to "a good dinner," telling her that afterwards she could take him anywhere she liked but that meanwhile they would have something to cheer them up. And Nellie agreed, nothing loth, for she too longed for the momentary jollity of a mild dissipation, not to mention that this would be a favorable opportunity to see if the restaurant girls could not be organised. So they had "a good dinner."

"This reminds me," said Nellie, as she ate her fish, "of a friend of mine, a young fellow who is always getting hard up and always raising a cheque, as he calls it. He was very hard up a while ago, and met a friend whom he told about it. Then he invited his friend to go and have some lunch. They came here and he ordered chicken and that, and a bottle of good wine. It took his last half-sovereign. When he got the ticket the other man looked at him. 'Well,' he said, 'if you live like this when you're hard up, how on earth do you live when you've got money?'"

"What did he say?" asked Ned, laughing, wondering at the same time how Nellie came to know people who drank wine and spent half-sovereigns on chicken lunches.

"Oh! He didn't say anything much, he told me. He couldn't manage to explain, he thought, that when he was at work and easy in his mind he didn't care what he had to eat but that when he didn't know what he'd do by the end of the week he felt like having a good meal if he never had another. He thought that made the half-sovereign go furthest. He's funny in some things."

"I should think he was, a little. How did you know him?"

"I met him where we're going to night. He's working on some newspaper in Melbourne now. I haven't seen him or heard of him for months."

She chatted on, rather feverishly.

"Did you ever read 'David Copperfield?'"

Ned nodded, his mouth being full.

"Do you recollect how he used to stand outside the cookshops? It's quite natural. I used to. It's pretty bad to be hungry and it's just about as bad not to have enough. I know a woman who has a couple of children, a boy and a girl. They were starving once. She said she'd sooner starve than beg or ask anybody to help them, and the little girl said she would too. But the boy said he wasn't going to starve for anybody, and he wasn't going to beg either; he'd steal. And sure enough he slipped out and came back with two loaves that he'd taken from a shop. They lived on that for nearly a week." Nellie laughed forcedly.

"What did they do then?" asked Ned seriously.

"Oh! She had been doing work but couldn't get paid. She got paid."

"Where was her husband?"

"Don't husbands die like other people?" she answered, pointedly. "Not that all husbands are much good when they can't get work or will always work when they can get it," she added.

"Are many people as hard up as that in Sydney, Nellie?" enquired Ned, putting down his knife and fork.

"Some," she answered. "You don't suppose a lot of the people we saw this morning get over well fed, do you? Oh, you can go on eating, Ned! It's not being sentimental that will help them. They want fair play and a chance to work, and your going hungry won't get that for them. There's lots for them and for us if they only knew enough to stop people like that getting too much."

By lifting her eyebrows she drew his attention to a stout coarse loudly jewelled man, wearing a tall silk hat and white waistcoat, who had stopped near them on his way to the door. He was speaking in a loud dictatorial wheezy voice. His hands were thrust into his trouser pockets, wherein he jingled coins by taking them up and letting them fall again. The chink of sovereigns seemed sweet music to him. He stared contemptuously at Ned's clothes as that young man looked round; then stared with insolent admiration at Nellie. Ned became crimson with suppressed rage, but said nothing until the man had passed them.

"Who is that brute?" he asked then.

"That brute! Why, he's a famous man. He owns hundreds of houses, and has been mayor and goodness knows what. He'll be knighted and made a duke or something. He owns the whole block where Mrs. Somerville lives. You ought to speak respectfully of your betters, Ned. He's been my landlord, though he doesn't know it, I suppose. He gets four shillings a week from Mrs. Somerville. The place isn't worth a shilling, only it's handy for her taking her work in, and she's got to pay him for it being handy. That's her money he's got in his pocket, only if you knocked him down and took it out for her you'd be a thief. At least, they'd say you were and send you to prison."

"Who's the other, I wonder?" said Ned. "He looks more like a man."

The other was a shrewd-looking, keen-faced, sparely-built man, with somewhat aquiline nose and straight narrow forehead, not at all bad-looking or evil-looking and with an air of strong determination; in short, what one calls a masterful man. He was dressed well but quietly. A gold-bound hair watch guard that crossed his high-buttoned waistcoat was his only adornment; his slender hands, unlike the fat man's podgy fingers, were bare of rings. He was sitting alone, and after the fat man left him returned again to the reading of an afternoon paper while he lunched.

"His name's Strong," said Nellie, turning to Ned with a peculiar smile. "That fat man has robbed me and this lean man has robbed you, I suppose. As he looks more like a man it won't be as bad though, will it?"

"What are you getting at, Nellie?" asked Ned, not understanding but looking at the shrewd man intently, nevertheless.

"Don't you know the name? Of course you don't though. Well, he's managing director of the Great Southern Mortgage Agency, a big concern that owns hundreds and hundreds of stations. At least, the squatters own the stations and the Agency owns the squatters, and he as good as owns the Agency. You're pretty sure to have worked for him many a time without knowing it, Ned."

Ned's eyes flashed. Nellie had to kick his foot under the table for fear he would say or do something that would attract the attention of the unsuspecting lean man.

"Don't be foolish, Ned," urged Nellie, in a whisper. "What's the good of spluttering?"

"Why, it was one of their stations on the Wilkes Downs that started cutting wages two years ago. Whenever a manager is particularly mean he always puts it down to the Agency. The Victorian fellows say it was this same concern that first cut wages down their way. And the New Zealanders too. I'd just like to 'perform' on him for about five minutes."

Ned uttered his wish so seriously that Nellie laughed out loud, at which Ned laughed too.

"So he's the man who does all the mischief, is he?" remarked Ned, again glaring at his industrial enemy. "Who'd think it to look at him? He doesn't look a bad sort, does he?"

"He looks a determined man, I think," said Nellie. "Mr. Stratton says he's the shrewdest capitalist in Australia and that he'll give the unions a big fight for it one of these days. He says he has a terrible hatred of unionism and thinks that there's no half-way between smashing them up and letting them smash the employers up. His company pays 25 per cent. regularly every year on its shares and will pay 50 before he gets through with it."

"How?"

"How! Out of fellows like you, Ned, who think themselves so mighty independent and can't see that they're being shorn like sheep, in the same way, though not as much yet, as Mrs. Somerville is by old Church and the fat brute, as you call him. But then you rather like it I should think. Anyway, you told me you didn't want to do anything 'wild,' only to keep up wages. You'll have to do something 'wild' to keep up wages before he finishes."

"That's all right to talk, Nellie, but what can we do?" asked Ned, pulling his moustache.

"Hire him instead of letting him hire you," answered Nellie, oracularly. "Those fat men are only good to put in museums, but these lean men are all right so long as you keep them in their place. They are our worst enemies when they're against us but our best friends when they're for us. They say Mr. Strong isn't like most of the swell set. He is straight to his wife and good to his children and generous to his friends and when he says a thing he sticks to it. Only he sees everything from the other side and doesn't understand that all men have got the same coloured blood."

"How can we hire him?" said Ned, after a pause. "They own everything."

Nellie shrugged her shoulders.

"You think we might take it," said Ned.

Nellie shrugged her shoulders again.

"I don't see how it can be done," he concluded.

"That's just it. You can't see how it can be done, and so nothing's done. Some men get drunk, and some men get religious, and others get enthusiastic for a pound a hundred. You haven't got votes up in Queensland, and if you had you'd probably give them to a lot of ignorant politicians. Men don't know, and they don't seem to want to know much, and they've got to be squeezed by men like him"—she nodded at Strong—"before they take any interest in themselves or in those who belong to them. For those who have an ounce of heart, though, I should think there'd been squeezing enough already."

She looked at Ned angrily. The scenes of the morning rose before him and tied his tongue.

"How do you know all these jokers, Nellie?" he asked. He had been going to put the question a dozen times before but it had slipped him in the interest of conversation.

"I only know them by sight. Mrs. Stratton takes me to the theatre with her sometimes and tells me who people are and all about them."

"Who's Mrs. Stratton? You were talking of Mr. Stratton, too, just now, weren't you?"

"Yes. The Strattons are very nice people. They're interested in the Labour movement, and I said I'd bring you round when I go to-night. I generally go on Saturday nights. They're not early birds, and we don't want to get there till half-past ten or so."

"Half-past ten! That's queer time."

"Yes, isn't it? Only——"

At that moment a waitress who had been arranging the next table came and took her place against the wall close behind Nellie. Such an opportunity to talk unionism was not to be lost, so Nellie unceremoniously dropped her conversation with Ned and enquired, as before stated, into the becapped girl's hours. The waitress was tall and well-featured, but sallow of skin and growing haggard, though barely 20, if that. Below her eyes were bluish hollows. She suffered plainly from the disorders caused by constant standing and carrying, and at this end of her long week was in evident pain.

*　　　*　　　*　　　*

"You're not allowed to talk either?" she asked the waitress, when the manager had disappeared.

"No. They're very strict. You get fined if you're seen chatting to customers and if you're caught resting. And you get fined if you break anything, too. One girl was fined six shillings last week."

"Why do you stand it? If you were up in our part of the world we'd soon bring 'em down a notch or two." This from Ned.

"Out in the bush it may be different," said the girl, identifying his part of the world by his dress and sunburnt face. "But in towns you've got to stand it."

" Couldn't you girls form a union ?" asked Nellie.

" What's the use, there's plenty to take our places."

" But if you were all in a union there wouldn't be enough."

"Oh, we can't trust a lot of girls. Those who live at home and just work to dress themselves are the worst of the lot. They'd work for ten shillings or five."

" But they'd be ashamed to blackleg if once they were got into the union," persisted Nellie. " It's worth trying, to get a rise in wages and to stop fining and have shorter hours and seats while you're waiting."

" Yes, it's worth trying if there was any chance. But there are so many girls. You're lucky if you get work at all now and just have to put up with anything. If we all struck they could get others to-morrow."

" But not waitresses. How'd they look here, trying to serve dinner with a lot of green hands ?" argued Nellie. " Besides, if you had a union, you could get a lot without striking at all. They know now you can't strike, so they do just exactly as they like."

" They'd do what they——" began the waitress. Then she broke off with another "s-s-s" as the manager crossed the room again.

" They'd do what they like, anyway," she began once more. "One of our girls was in the union the Melbourne waitresses started. They had a strike at one of the big restaurants over the manager insulting one of the girls. They complained to the boss and wanted the manager to apologise, but the boss wouldn't listen and said they were getting very nice. So at dinner time, when the bell rang, they all marched off and put on their hats. The customers were all waiting for dinner and the girls were all on strike and the boss nearly went mad. He was going to have them all arrested, but when the gentlemen heard what it was about they said the girls were right and if the manager didn't apologise they'd go to some other restaurant always. So the manager went to the girl and apologised."

" By gum ! " interjected Ned. "Those girls were hummers."

"I suppose the boss victimised afterwards ?" asked Nellie, wiser in such matters.

"That's just it," said the girl, in a disheartened tone. "In two or three weeks every girl who'd had anything to do with stirring the others up was bounced for something or other. The manager did what he liked afterwards."

"Just talk to the other girls about a union, will you?" asked Nellie. "It's no use giving right in, you know."

"I'll see what some of them say, but there's a lot I wouldn't open my mouth to," answered the waitress.

"What time do you get away on Thursdays?"

"Next Thursday I'm on till half-past ten."

"Well, I'll meet you then, outside, to see what they say," said Nellie. "My name's Nellie Lawton and some of us are trying to start a women's union. You'll be sure to be there?"

"All right," answered the waitress, a little dubiously. Then she added more cordially, as she wrote out the pay ticket: "My name's Susan Finch. I'll see what I can do."

So Ned and Nellie got up and, the former having paid at the counter, walked out into the street together. It was nearly three. The rain had stopped, though the sky was still cloudy and threatening. The damp afternoon was chilly after the sultry broiling morning. Neither of them felt in the mood for walking so at Nellie's suggestion they put in the afternoon in riding, on trams and 'busses, hither and thither through the mazy wilderness of the streets that make up Sydney.

Intuitively, both avoided talking of the topics that before had engaged them and that still engrossed their thoughts. For a while they chatted on indifferent matters, but gradually relapsed into silence, rarely broken. The impression of the morning walk, of Mrs. Somerville's poor room, of Nellie's stuffy street, came with full force to Ned's mind. What he saw only stamped it deeper and deeper.

When, in a bus, they rode through the suburbs of the wealthy, past shrubberied mansions and showy villas, along roads where liveried carriages, drawn by high-stepping horses, dashed by them, he felt himself in the presence of the fat man who jingled sovereigns, of the lean man whose slender fingers reached north to the Peak Downs and south to the Murray, filching everywhere from the worker's hard-earned wage. When in the tram they were carried with clanging and jangling through endless rows of houses great and small, along main thoroughfares on either side of which crowded side-streets extended like fish-bones, over less crowded districts where the cottages were generally detached or semi-detached and where pleasant homely houses were thickly sprinkled, even here he wondered how near those who lived in happier state were to the life of the slum, wondered what struggling and pinching and scraping was going on behind the half-drawn blinds that made homes look so cosy.

What started him on this idea particularly was that, in one tram, a grey-bearded propertied-looking man who sat beside him was grumbling to a spruce little man opposite about the increasing number of empty houses.

"You can't wonder at it," answered the spruce little man. "When the working classes aren't prospering everybody feels it but the exporters. Wages are going down and people are living two families in a house where they used to live one in a house, or living in smaller houses."

"Oh! Wages are just as high. There's been too much building. You building society men have overdone the thing."

"My dear sir!" declared the spruce little man. "I'm talking from facts. My society and every other building society is finding it out. When men can't get as regular work it's the same thing to them as if wages were coming down. The number of surrenders we have now is something appalling. Working men have built expecting to be able to pay from 6s. to 10s and 12s. a week to the building societies, and every year more and more are finding out they can't do it. As many as can are renting rooms, letting part of their house and so struggling along. As many more are giving up and renting these rooms or smaller houses. And apparently well-to-do people are often in as bad a fix. It's against my interest to have things this way, but it's so, and there's no getting over it. If it keeps on, pretty well every workingman's house about Sydney will be a rented house soon. The building societies can't stop that unless men have regular work and fair wages."

"It's the unions that upset trade," asserted the propertied-looking man.

"It's the land law that's wrong," contended the spruce man. "If all taxes were put on unimproved land values it would be cheaper to live and there would be more work because it wouldn't pay to keep land out of use. With cheap living and plenty of work the workingman would have money and business would be brisk all round."

"Nonsense!" exclaimed the propertied man, brusquely.

"It's so," answered the spruce little man, getting down as the tram stopped. "There's no getting away from facts and that's fact."

So even out here, Ned thought, looking at the rows of cottages with little gardens in front which they were passing, the squeeze was coming. Then, watching the passengers, he thought how worried they all seemed, how rarely a pleasant face was to be met with in the dress of the people. And then, suddenly a shining, swaying, coachman-driven brougham whirled by. Ned, with his keen bushman's eyes, saw in it a stout heavy-jawed dame, large of arm and huge of bust, decked out in all the fashion, and insolent of face as one replete with that which others craved. And by her side, reclining at ease, was a later edition of the same volume, a girl of 17 or so, already fleshed and heavy-jawed, in her mimic pride looking for all the world like a well-fed human animal, careless and soulless.

Opposite Nellie a thin-faced woman, one of whose front teeth had gone, patiently dandled a peevish baby, while by her side another child clutched her dingy dust-cloak. This woman's nose was peaked and her chin receded. In her bonnet some gaudy imitation flowers nodded a vigorous accompaniment. She did not seem ever to have had pleasure or to have been young, and yet in the child by her side her patient joyless sordid life had produced its kind.

They had some tea and buttered scones in a cheaper café, where Nellie tried to "organise" another waitress. They lingered over the meal, both moody. They hardly spoke till Ned asked Nellie:

"I don't see what men can get to do but can't single women always get servants' places?"

"Some might who don't, though all women who want work couldn't be domestic servants, that's plain," answered Nellie. "But by the number of girls that are always looking for places and the way the registry offices are able to bleed them, I should imagine there were any amount of servant girls already. The thing is there are so many girls that mistresses can afford to be particular. They want a girl with all the virtues to be a sort of house-slave, and they're always grumbling because they can't get it. So they're always changing, and the girls are always changing, and that makes the girls appear independent."

"But they have good board and lodging, as well as wages, don't they?"

"In swell houses, where they keep two or three or more girls, they usually have good board and decent rooms, I think, but they don't in most places. Any hole or corner is considered good enough for a servant girl to sleep in, and any scraps are often considered good enough for a servant girl to eat. You look as though you don't believe it, Ned. I'm talking about what I know. The average domestic servant is treated like a trained dog."

"Did you ever try it?"

"I went to work in a hotel as chamber maid, once. I worked from about six in the morning till after ten at night. Then four of us girls slept in two beds in a kind of box under the verandah stairs in the back yard. We had to leave the window open to get air, and in the middle of the first night a light woke me up and a man was staring through the window at us with a match in his hand. I wanted the twelve shillings so I stood it for a week and then got another place."

"What sort was that?"

"Oh! A respectable place, you know. Kept up appearances and locked up the butter. The woman said to me, when I'd brought my box, 'I'm going to call you Mary, I always call my girls Mary.' I slept in a dark close den off the kitchen, full of cockroaches that frightened the wits out of me. I was afraid to eat as much as I wanted because she looked at me so. I couldn't rest a minute but she was hunting me up to see what I was doing. I hadn't anybody to talk with or eat with and my one night out I had to be in by ten. I was so miserable that I went back to slop-work. That's what Mrs. Somerville is doing."

"It isn't all honey, then. I thought town servant girls had a fair time of it."

"An occasional one does, though they all earn their money, but most have a hard time of it. I don't mean all places are like mine were, but there's no liberty. A working girl's liberty is scanty enough, goodness knows"—she spoke scornfully—"but at least she mixes with her own kind and is on an equality with most she meets. When her work is over, however long it is, she can do just exactly as she likes until it starts again. A servant girl hasn't society or that liberty. For my part I'd rather live on bread again than be at the orders of any woman who despised me and not be able to call a single minute of time my own. They're so ignorant, most of these women who have servants, they don't know how to treat a girl any more than most of their husbands know how to treat a horse."

D

The naïve bush simile pleased Ned a little and he laughed, but soon relapsed again into silence. Then Nellie spoke of " Paddy's Market," one of the sights of Sydney, which she would like him to see. Accordingly they strolled to his hotel, where he put on a clean shirt and a collar and a waistcoat, while she waited, looking into the shops near by; then they strolled slowly Haymarketwards, amid the thronging Saturday night crowds that overflowed the George-street pavement into the roadway.

CHAPTER IV.

PADDY'S Market was in its glory, the weekly glory of a Sydney Saturday night, of the one day in the week when the poor man's wife has a few shillings and when the poor caterer for the poor man's wants gleans in the profit field after the stray ears of corn that escape the machine-reaping of retail capitalism. It was filled by a crushing, hustling, pushing mass of humans, some buying, more bartering, most swept aimlessly along in the living currents that moved ceaselessly to and fro. In one of these currents Ned found himself caught, with Nellie. He struggled for a short time, with elbows and shoulders, to make for himself and her a path through the press; experience soon taught him to forego attempting the impossible and simply to drift, as everybody else did, on the stream setting the way they would go.

He found himself, looking around as he drifted, in a long low arcade, brilliant with great flaring lights. Above was the sparkle of glass roofing, on either hand a walling of rough stalls, back and forward a vista of roofing and stalls stretching through distant arches, which were gateways, into outer darkness, which was the streets. On the stalls, as he could see, were thousands of things, all cheap and most nasty.

What were there? What were not there? Boots and bootlaces, fish and china ornaments, fruit, old clothes and new clothes, flowers and plants and lollies, meat and tripe and cheese and butter and bacon! Cheap music-sheets and cheap jewellery! Stockings and pie-dishes and bottles of ink! Everything that the common people buy! Anything by which a penny could be turned by those of small capital and little credit in barter with those who had less.

One old man's face transfixed him for a moment, clung to his memory afterwards, the face of an old man, wan and white, grey-bearded and hollow-eyed, that was thrust through some hosiery hanging on a rod at the back of a stall. Nobody was buying there, nobody even looked to buy as Ned watched for a minute; the stream swept past and the grizzled face stared on. It had no body, no hands even, it was as if hung there, a trunkless head; it was the face of a generation grown old, useless and unloved, which lived by the crumbs that fall from Demos' table and waited wearily to be gone.   It expressed nothing, that was the pain in it.   It was haggard and grizzled and worn out, that was all.   It knew itself no good to anybody, knew that labouring was a pain and thinking a weariness, and hope the delusion of fools, and life a vain mockery.   It asked none to buy.   It did not move.   It only hung there amid the dark draping of its poor stock and waited.

Would he himself ever be like that, Ned wondered.   And yet! And yet!

All around were like this.   All! All! All!   Everyone in this swarming multitude of working Sydney.   On the faces of all was misery written.   Buyers and sellers and passers-by alike were hateful of life.   And if by chance he saw now and then a fat dame at a stall or a lusty huckster pushing his wares or a young couple, curious and loving, laughing and joking as they hustled along arm in arm, he seemed to see on their faces the dawning lines that in the future would stamp them also with the brand of despair.

The women, the poor women, they were most wretched of all; the poor housewives in their pathetic shabbiness, their faces drawn with child-bearing, their features shrunken with the struggling toil that never ceases nor stays ; the young girls in their sallow youth that was not youth, with their hollow mirth and their empty faces, and their sharp angles or their unnatural busts ; the wizened children that served at the stalls, precocious in infancy, with the wisdom of the Jew and the impudence of the witless babe ; the old crones that crawled along—the mothers of a nation haggling for pennies as if they had haggled all their lives long.   They bore baskets, most of the girls and housewives and crones ; with some were husbands, who sometimes carried the basket but not always; some even carried children in their arms, unable even for an hour to escape the poor housewife's old-man-of-the-seas.

The men were absorbed, hidden away, in the flood of wearied women.   There were men, of course, in the crowd, among the stallkeepers—hundreds.   And when one noticed them they were wearied also, or sharp like ferrets ; oppressed, overborne, or cunning, with the cunning of those who must be cunning to live ; imbruted often with the brutishness of apathy, consciousless of

the dignity of manhood, only dully patient or viciously keen as
the ox is or the hawk. Many sottish-looking, or if not sottish
with the beery texture of those whose only recreation is to be
bestially merry at the drink-shop. This was the impression in
which the few who strode with the free air of the ideal Australian
workman were lost, as the few comfortable-seeming women were
lost in the general weariness of their weary sex.

Jollity there was none to speak of. There was an eager
huckling for bargains, or a stolid calculation of values, or a loud
commendation of wares, or an oppressive indifference. Where
was the " fair " to which of old the people swarmed, glad-hearted ?
Where was even the relaxed caution of the shopping-day ?
Where was the gay chaffering, the boisterous bandying of wit ?
Gone, all gone, and nothing left but care and sadness and a
careful counting of hard-grudged silver and pence.

Ned turned his head once or twice to steal a glance at Nellie.
He could not tell what she thought. Her face gave no sign of
her feeling. Only it came home to him that there were none
like her there, at least none like her to him. She was sad with a
stern sadness, as she had been all day, and in that stern sadness
of hers was a dignity, a majesty, that he had not appreciated
until now, when she jostled without rudeness in this jostling
crowd. This dark background of submissive yielding, of hopeless
patience, threw into full light the unbending resolution carved in
every line of her passionate face and lithesome figure. Yet he
noticed now on her forehead two faint wrinkles showing, and in
the corners of her mouth an overhanging fold; and this he saw
as if reflected in a thousand ill-made mirrors around, distorted
and exaggerated and grotesqued indeed but nevertheless the
self-same marks of constant pain and struggle.

They reached the end of the first alley and passed out to the
pavement, slippery with trodden mud. There was a little knot
gathered there, a human eddy in the centre of the pressing throng.
Looking over the heads of the loiterers, he could see in the centre
of the eddy, on the kerb, by the light that came from the gateway, a girl whose eyes were closed. She was of an uncertain age
—she might be twelve or seventeen. Beside her was a younger
child. Just then she began to sing. He and Nellie waited. He
knew without being told that the singer was blind.

It was a hymn she sang, an old-fashioned hymn that has in its
music the glad rhythm of the " revival," the melodious echoing of

the Methodist day. He recollected hearing it long years before, when he went to the occasional services held in the old bush schoolhouse by some itinerant preacher. He recalled at once the gathering of the saints at the river; mechanically he softly hummed the tune. It was hardly the tune the blind girl sang though. She had little knowledge of tune, apparently. Her cracked discordant voice was unspeakably saddening.

This blind girl was the natural sequence to the sphinx-like head that he had seen amid the black stockings. Her face was large and flat, youthless, ageless, crowned with an ugly black hat, poorly ribboned; her hands were clasped clumsily on the skirt of her poor cotton dress, ill-fitting. There was no expression in her singing, no effort to express, no instinctive conception of the idea. The people only listened because she was blind and they were poor, and so they pitied her. The beautiful river of her hymn meant nothing, to her or to them. It might be; it might not be; it was not in question. She cried to them that she was blind and that the blind poor must eat if they would live and that they desire to live despite the city by-laws. She begged, this blind girl, standing with rent shoes in the sloppy mud. In Sydney, in 1889, in the workingman's paradise, she stood on the kerb, this blind girl, and begged—begged from her own people. And in their poverty, their weariness, their brutishness, they pitied her. None mocked, and many paused, and some gave.

They never thought of her being an impostor. They did not pass her on to the hateful charity that paid parasites dole out for the rich. They did not think that she made a fortune out of her pitifulness and hunt her with canting harshness as a nuisance and a cheat. Her harsh voice did not jar on them. Her discords did not shock their supersensitive ears. They only knew that they, blinded in her stead, must beg for bread and shelter while good Christians glut themselves and while fat law-makers white-wash the unpleasant from the sight of the well-to-do. In her helplessness they saw, unknowing it, their own helplessness, saw in her Humanity wronged and suffering and in need. Those who gave gave to themselves, gave as an impulsive offering to the divine impulse which drives the weak together and aids them to survive.

Ned wanted to give the blind girl something but he felt ashamed to give before Nellie. He fingered a half-crown in his pocket, with a bushman's careless generosity. By skilful manœuvring and convenient yielding to the pressure of the crowd he managed to get near the blind girl as she finished her hymn. Nellie turned round, looking away—he thought afterwards: was it intentionally?—and he slipped his offering into the singer's fingers like a culprit. Then he walked off hastily with his companion, as red and confused as though he had committed some dastardly act. Just as they reached the second arcade they heard another discordant hymn rise amid the shuffling din.

There were no street-walkers in Paddy's Market, Ned could see. He had caught his foot clumsily on the dress of one above the town-hall, a dashing demi-mondaine with rouged cheeks and unnaturally bright eyes and a huge velvet-covered hat of the Gainsborough shape and had been covered with confusion when she turned sharply round on him with a "Now, clumsy, I'm not a door-mat." Then he had noticed that the sad sisterhood were out in force where the bright gas-jets of the better-class shops illuminated the pavement, swaggering it mostly where the kerbs were lined with young fellows, fairly-well dressed as a rule, who talked of cricket and race horses and boating and made audible remarks concerning the women, grave and gay, who passed by in the throng. Nearing the poorer end of George-street, they seemed to disappear, both sisterhood and kerb loungers, until near the Haymarket itself they found the larrikin element gathered strongly under the flaring lights of hotel-bars and music hall entrances. But in Paddy's Market itself there were not even larrikins. Ned did not even notice anybody drunk.

He had seen drinking and drunkenness enough that day. Wherever there was poverty he had seen viciousness flourishing. Wherever there was despair there was a drowning of sorrow in drink. They had passed scores of public houses, that afternoon, through the doors of which workmen were thronging. Coming along George street, they had heard from more than one bar-room the howling of a drunken chorus. Men had staggered by them, and women too, frowsy and besotted. But there was none of this in Paddy's Market. It was a serious place, these long dingy arcades, to which people came to buy cheaply and carefully, people to whom every penny was of value and who had none to throw away, just then at least, either on a brain-turning carouse or on a painted courtesan. The people here were sad and sober and sorrowful. It seemed to Ned that here was collected, as in the centre of a great vortex, all the pained and tired and ill-fed and wretched faces that he had been seeing all day. The accumulation of misery pressed on him till it sickened him at the heart. It felt as though something clutched at his throat, as though by some mechanical means his skull was being tightened on his brain. His thoughts were interrupted by an exclamation from Nellie.

"There's a friend of mine," she explained, making her way through the crowd to a brown-bearded man who was seated on the edge of an empty stall, apparently guarding a large empty basket in which were some white cloths. The man's features were fine and his forehead massive, his face indicating a frail constitution and strong intellectuality. He wore an apron rolled up round his waist. He seemed very poor.

"How d'ye do, Miss Lawton?" said he getting off the stall and shaking hands warmly. "It's quite an age since I saw you. You're looking as well as ever." Ned saw that his thin face beamed as he spoke and that his dark brown eyes, though somewhat hectic, were singularly beautiful.

"I'm well, thanks," said Nellie, beaming in return. "And how are you? You seem browner than you did. What have you been doing to yourself?"

"Me! I've been up the country a piece trying my hand at farming. Jones is taking up a selection, you know, and I've been helping him a little now times aren't very brisk. I'm keeping fairly well, very fairly, I'm glad to say."

"This is Mr. Hawkins, Mr. Sim," introduced Nellie; the men shook hands.

"Come inside out of the rush," invited Sim, making room for them in the entrance-way of the stall. "We haven't got any armchairs, but it's not so bad up on the table here if you're tired."

"I'm not tired," said Nellie, leaning against the doorway. Ned sat up on the stall by her side; his feet were sore, unused to the hard paved city streets.

"I suppose Mr. Hawkins is one of us," said Sim, perching himself up again.

"I don't know what you call 'one of us,'" answered Nellie, with a smile. "He's a beginner. Some day he may get as far as you and Jones and the rest of the dynamiters."

Sim laughed genially. "Do you know, I really believe that Jones would use dynamite if he got an opportunity," he commented. "I'm not joking. I'm positively convinced of it."

"Has he got it as bad as that?" asked Nellie. Ned began to feel interested. He also noticed that Sim used book-words.

"Has he got it as bad as that! 'Bad' isn't any name for it. He's the stubbornest man I ever met, and he's full of the most furious hatred against the capitalists. He has it as a personal feeling. Then the life he's got is sufficient to drive a man mad."

"Selecting is pretty hard," agreed Nellie, sadly.

"Nellie and I know a little about that, Mr. Sim," said Ned.

"Well, Jones' selection is a hard one," went on Sim, good-humouredly. "I prefer to sell trotters, when I sell out like this, to attempting it. The soil is all stones, and there is not a drop of water when the least drought comes on. Poor Jones toils like a team of horses and hardly gets sufficient to keep him alive. I never saw a man work as he does. For a man who thinks and has ideas to be buried like that in the bush is terrible. He has no one to converse with. He goes mooning about sometimes and muttering to himself enough to frighten one into a fit."

"Does he still do any printing?" asked Nellie, archly.

"Oh, the printing," answered Sim, laughing again. "He initiated me into the art of wood-engraving. You see, Mr. Hawkins"—turning to Ned—"Jones hasn't got any type, and of course he can't afford to buy it, but he's got hold of a little second-hand toy printing press. To print from he takes a piece of wood, cut across the grain and rubbed smooth with sand, and cuts out of it the most revolutionary and blood-curdling leaflets, letter by letter. If you only have patience it's quite easy after a few weeks' practice."

"Does he print them?" asked Ned.

"Print them! I should say he did. Every old scrap of paper he can collect or get sent him he prints his leaflets on and gets them distributed all over the country. Many a night I've sat up assisting with the pottering little press. Talk about Nihilism! Jones vows that there is only one way to cure things and that is to destroy the rule of Force."

"He's a long while starting," remarked Nellie with a slight sneer. "Those people who talk so much never do anything."

"Oh, Jones isn't like that," answered Sim, with cheerful confidence. "He'll do anything that he thinks is worth while. But I suppose I'm horrifying you, Mr. Hawkins? Miss Lawton here knows what we are and is accustomed to our talk."

"It'll take considerable to horrify me," replied Ned, standing down as Nellie straightened herself out for a move-on. "You can blow the whole world to pieces for all I care. There's not much worth watching in it as far as I can see."

"You're pretty well an anarchist," said the brown-bearded trotter-seller, his kindly intellectual face lighted up. "It'll come some day, that's one satisfaction. Do you think that many here will regret it?" He waved his hand to include the crowd that moved to and fro before them, its voices covered with the din of its dragging feet.

"That'll do, Sim!" said Nellie. "Don't stuff Ned's head with those absurd anarchistical night-mares of yours. We're going; we've got somewhere to go. Good-bye! Tell Jones you saw me when you write, and remember me to him, will you? I like him —he's so good-hearted, though he does rave."

"He's as good-hearted a man as there is in New South Wales," corroborated Sim, shaking hands. "I'm expecting to meet a friend here or I'd stroll along. Good-bye! Glad to have met you, Mr. Hawkins."

He re-mounted the stall again as they moved off. In another minute he was lost to their sight as they were swallowed up once more in the living tide that ebbed and flowed through Paddy's Market.

After that Ned did not notice much, so absorbed was he. He vaguely knew that they drifted along another arcade and then crossed a street to an open cobble-paved space where there were shooting-tunnels and merry-go-rounds and try-your-weights and see-how-much-you-lifts. He looked dazedly at wizen-faced lads who gathered round ice-cream stalls, and at hungry folks who ate stewed peas. Everything seemed grimy and frayed and sordid; the flaring torches smelt of oil; those who shot, or ate, or rode, by spending a penny, were the envied of standers-by. Amid all this drumming and hawking and flaring of lights were swarms of boys and growing girls, precocious and vicious and foul-tongued.

Ten o'clock struck. "For God's sake, let us get out of this, Nellie!" cried Ned, as the ringing bell-notes roused him.

"Have you had enough of Sydney?" she asked, leading the way out.

"I've had enough of every place," he answered hotly. She did not say any more.

As they stood in George-street, waiting for their 'bus, a high-heeled, tightly-corsetted, gaily-hatted larrikiness flounced out of the side door of a hotel near by. A couple of larrikin acquaintances were standing there, shrivelled young men in high-heeled pointed-toed shoes, belled trousers, gaudy neckties and round soft hats tipped over the left ear.

"Hello, you blokes!" cried the larrikiness, slapping one on the shoulder. "Isn't this a blank of a time you're having?"

It was her ideal of pleasure, hers and theirs, to parade the street or stand in it, to gape or be gaped at.

CHAPTER V.

NEITHER Ned nor Nellie spoke as they journeyed down George-street in the rumbling 'bus. "I've got tickets," was all she said as they entered the ferry shed at the Circular Quay. They climbed to the upper deck of the ferry boat in silence. He got up when she did and went ashore by her side without a word. He did not notice the glittering lights that encircled the murky night. He did not even know if it were wet or fine, or whether the moon shone or not. He was in a daze. The horrors of living stunned him. The miseries of poor Humanity choked him. The foul air of these noisome streets sickened him. The wretched faces he had seen haunted him. The oaths of the gutter children and the wailing of the blind beggar-girl seemed to mingle in a shriek that shook his very soul.

If he could have persuaded himself that the bush had none of this, it would have been different. But he could not. The stench of the stifling shearing-sheds and of the crowded sleeping huts where men are packed in rows like trucked sheep came to him with the sickening smell of the slums. On the faces of men in the bush he had seen again and again that hopeless look as of goaded oxen straining through a mud-hole, that utter degrada-tion, that humble plea for charity. He had known them in Western Queensland often in spite of all that was said of the free, brave bush. It was not new to him, this dark side of life; that was the worst of it. It had been all along and he had known that it had been, but never before had he understood the significance of it, never before had he realised how utterly civilisation has failed. And this was what crushed him—the hopelessness of it all, the black despair that seemed to fill the universe, the brutal weariness of living, the ceaseless round of sorrow and sin and shame and unspeakable misery.

Often in the bush it had come to him, lying sleepless at night under the star-lit sky, all alone excepting for the tinkling of his horse-bell: "What is to be the end for me? What is there to look forward to?" And his heart had sunk within him at the prospect. For what was in front? What could be? Shearing and waiting for shearing—that was his life. Working over the sweating sheep under the hot iron shed in the sweltering summer time; growing sick and losing weight and bickering with the squatter till the few working months were over; then an occasional job, but mostly enforced idling till the season came round again; looking for work from shed to shed; struggling against conditions; agitating; organising; and in the future years, aged too soon, wifeless and childless, racked with rheumatism, shaken with fevers, to lie down to die on the open plain perchance or crawl, feebled and humbled, to the State-charity of Dunwich. He used to shut his eyes to force such thoughts from him, fearing lest he go mad, as were those travelling swagmen he met sometimes, who muttered always to themselves and made frantic gestures as they journeyed, solitary, through the monotonous wilderness. He had flung himself into unionism because there was nothing else that promised help or hope and because he hated the squatters, who took, as he looked at it, contemptible advantage of the bushmen. And he had felt that with unionism men grew better and heartier, gambling less and debating more, drinking less and planning what the union would do when it grew strong enough. He had worked for the union before it came, had been one of those who preached it from shed to shed and argued for it by smouldering camp fires before turning in. And he had seen the union feeling spread until the whole Western country throbbed with it and until the union itself started into life at the last attempt of the squatter to force down wages and was extending itself now as fast as even he could wish to see it. "We only want what is fair," he had told Nellie; "we're not going in for anything wild. So long as we get a pound a hundred and rations at a fair figure we're satisfied." And Nellie had shown him things which had struck him dumb and broken through the veneer of satisfaction that of late had covered over his old doubts and fears.

"What is to be the end for me?" he used to think, then force himself not to think in terror. Now, he himself seemed so insignificant, the union he loved so seemed so insignificant, he was only conscious for the time being of the agony of the world at large, which dulled him with the reflex of its pain. Oh, these puny foul-tongued children! Oh, these haggard weary women! Oh, these hopeless imbruted men! Oh, these young girls steeped

in viciousness, these awful streets, this hateful life, this hell of
Sydney And beyond it—hell, still hell. Ah, he knew it now,
unconsciously, as in a swoon one hears voices. The sorrow of it
all! The hatefulness of it all! The weariness of it all! Why
do we live? Wherefore? For what end, what aim? The
selector, the digger, the bushman, as the townman, what has life
for them? It is in Australia as all over the world. Wrong
triumphs. Life is a mockery. God is not. At least, so it came
gradually to Ned as he walked silently by Nellie's side.

They had turned down a tree-screened side road, descending
again towards the harbour. Nellie stopped short at an iron gate,
set in a hedge of some kind. A tree spanned the gateway with
its branches, making the gloomy night still darker. The click
of the latch roused her companion.

"Do you think it's any good living?" he asked her.

She did not answer for a moment or two, pausing in the gateway. A break in the western sky showed a grey cloud faintly
tinged with silver. She looked fixedly up at it and Ned, his eyes
becoming accustomed to the gloom, thought he saw her face
working convulsively. But before he could speak again, she
turned round sharply and answered, without a tremor in her
voice :

"I suppose that's a question everybody must answer for themselves."

"Well, do you?"

"For myself, yes."

"For others, too?"

"For most others, no." The intense bitterness of her tone
stamped her words into his brain.

"Then why for you any more than anybody else?"

"I'll tell you after. We must go in. Be careful! You'd
better give me your hand!"

She led the way along a short paved path, down three or four
stone steps, then turned sharply along a small narrow verandah.
At the end of the verandah was a door. Nellie felt in the darkness for the bell-button and gave two sharp rings.

"Where are you taking me, Nellie?" he asked. "This is too
swell a place for me. It looks as though everybody was gone to
bed."

In truth he was beginning to think of secret societies and
mysterious midnight meetings. Only Nellie had not mentioned

anything of the kind and he felt ashamed of acknowledging his suspicions by enquiring, in case it should turn out to be otherwise. Besides, what did it matter? There was no secret society which he was not ready to join if Nellie was in it, for Nellie knew more about such things than he did. It was exactly the place for meetings, he thought, looking round. Nobody would have dreamt that it was only half an hour ago that they two had left Paddy's Market. Here was the scent of damp earth and green trees and heavily perfumed flowers; the rustling of leaves; the fresh breath of the salt ocean. In the darkness, he could see only a semi-circling mass of foliage under the sombre sky, no other houses nor sign of such. He could not even hear the rumbling of the Sydney streets nor the hoarse whispering of the crowded city; not even a single footfall on the road they had come down. For the faint lap-lap-lapping of water filled the pauses, when the puffy breeze failed to play on its leafy pipes. Here a Mazzini might hide himself and here the malcontents of Sydney might gather in safety to plot and plan for the overthrow of a hateful and hated "law and order." So he thought.

"Oh, they're not gone to bed," replied Nellie, confidently. "They live at the back. It overlooks the harbour that side. And you'll soon see they're not as swell as they look. They're splendid people. Don't be afraid to say just what you think."

"I'm not afraid of that, if you're not."

"Ah, there's someone."

An inside door opened and closed again, then they heard a heavy footstep coming, which paused for a moment, whereat a flood of colour streamed through a stained glass fanlight over the door.

"That's Mr. Stratton," announced Nellie.

Next moment the door at which they stood was opened by a bearded man, wearing loose grey coat and slippers.

"Hello, Nellie!" exclaimed this possible conspirator, opening the door wide. "Connie said it was your ring. Come straight in, both of you. Good evening, sir. Nellie's friends are our friends and we've heard so much of Ned Hawkins that we seem to have known you a long while." He held out his hand and shook Ned's warmly, giving a strong, clinging, friendly grip, not waiting for any introduction. "Of course, this is Mr. Hawkins, Nellie?" he enquired, seriously, turning to that young woman, whose hands he took in both of his while looking quizzingly from Ned to her and back to Ned again.

" Yes, of course," she answered, laughing. Ned laughed. The possible conspirator laughed as he answered, dropping her hands and turning to shut the door :

" Well, it mightn't have been. By the way, Nellie, you must have sent an astral warning that you were coming along. We were just talking about you."

*   *   *   *

They had been discussing Nellie in the Stratton circle, as our best friends will when we are so fortunate as to interest them.

In the pretty sitting-room that overlooked the rippling water, Mrs. Stratton perched on the music stool, was giving, amid many interjections, an animated account of the opera : a dark-haired, grey-eyed, full-lipped woman of 30 or so, with decidedly large nose and broad rounded forehead, somewhat under the medium height apparently but pleasingly plump as her evening dress disclosed. She talked rapidly, in a sweet expressive voice that had a strange charm. Her audience consisted of an ugly little man, with greyish hair, who stood at a bookcase in the corner and made his remarks over his shoulder; a gloomy young man, who sat in a reclining chair, with his arm hanging listlessly by his side ; and a tall dark-moustached handsome man, broadly built, who sat on the edge of a table smoking a wooden pipe, and who, from his observations, had evidently accompanied her home from the theatre after the second act. There was also her husband, who leant over her, his back turned to the others, unhooking her fur-edged opera cloak, a tall fair brown bearded man, evidently the elder by some years, whose blue eyes were half hidden beneath a strongly projected forehead. He fumbled with the hooks of the cloak, passing his hands beneath it, smiling slyly at her the while. She, flushing like a girl at the touch, talked away while pressing her knee responsively against his. It was a little love scene being enacted of which the others were all unconscious unless for a general impression that this long-married couple were as foolishly in love as ever and indulged still in all the mild raptures of lovers.

"Ever so much obliged," she said, pausing in her talk and looking at him at last, as he drew the cloak from her shoulders.

" You should be," he responded, straightening himself out. " It's quite a labour unhooking one of you fine ladies."

"Don't call me names, Harry, or I'll get somebody else to take it off next time. I'm afraid it's love's labour lost. It's quite chilly, and I think I'll wrap it round me."

"Well, if you will go about half undressed," he commented, putting the cloak round her again.

"Half undressed! You are silly. The worst of this room is there's no fire in it. I think one needs a fire even in summer time, when it's damp, to take the chill off. Besides, as Nellie says, a blazing fire is the most beautiful picture you can put in a room."

"Isn't Nellie coming to-night?" asked the man who smoked the wooden pipe.

"Why, of course, Ford. Haven't I told you she said on Thursday that she would come and bring the wild untamed bushman with her? Nellie always keeps her word."

"She's a wonderful girl," remarked Ford.

"Wonderful? Why wonderful is no name for it," declared Stratton, lighting a cigar at one of the piano candles. "She is extraordinary."

"I tell Nellie, sometimes, that I shall get jealous of her. Harry gets quite excited over her virtues, and thinks she has no faults, while poor I am continually offending the consistencies."

"Who is Nellie?" enquired the ugly little man, turning round suddenly from the book case which he had been industriously ransacking.

"I like Geisner," observed Mrs. Stratton, pointing at the little man. "He sees everything, he hears everything, he makes himself at home, and when he wants to know anything he asks a straightforward question. I think you've met her, though, Geisner."

"Perhaps. What is her other name?"

"Lawton—Nellie Lawton. She came here once or twice when you were here before, I think, and for the last year or so she's been our—our—what do you call it, Harry? You know—the thing that South Sea Islanders think is the soul of a chief."

"You're ahead of me, Connie. But it doesn't matter; go on."

"There's nothing to go on about. You ought to recollect her, Geisner. I'm sure you met her here."

"I think I do. Wasn't she a tall, between-colours girl, quite young, with a sad face and queer stern mouth—a trifle cruel, the mouth, if I recollect. She used to sit across there by the piano, in a plain black dress, and no colour at all except one of your roses."

E

"Good gracious ! What a memory ! Have you got us all ticketed away like that ?"

"It's habit," pleaded Geisner. "She didn't say anything, and only that she had a strong face, I shouldn't have noticed her. Has she developed ?"

"Something extraordinary," struck in Stratton, puffing great clouds of smoke. "She speaks French, she reads music, she writes uncommonly good English, and in some incomprehensible way she has formed her own ideas of Art. Not bad for a dress-making girl, who lives in a Sydney back street and sometimes works sixteen hours a day, is it ?"

"Well, no. Only you must recollect, Stratton, that if she's been in your placé pretty often, most of the people she meets here must have given her a wrinkle or two."

"You're always in opposition, Geisner," declared Mrs. Stratton. "I never heard you agree with anybody else's statement yet. Nellie is wonderful. You can't shake our faith in that. There is but one Womanity and Nellie is its prophet."

"It's all right about her getting wrinkles here, Geisner," contributed Ford, "for of course she has. It was what made her, Mrs. Stratton getting hold of her. But at the same time she is extraordinary. When she's been stirred up I've heard her tackle the best of the men who come here and down them. On their own ground too. I don't see how on earth she has managed to do it in the time. She's only twenty now."

"I'll tell you, if you'll light the little gas stove for me, Ford, and put the kettle on," said Mrs. Stratton, drawing her cloak more tightly round her shoulders. "I know some of you men don't believe it, but it is the truth nevertheless that Feeling is higher than Reason. Isn't it chilly ? You see, after all, you can only reason as to why you feel. Well, Nellie feels. She is an artist. She has got a soul."

"What do you call an artist ?" queried Geisner, partly for the sake of the argument, partly to see the little woman flare up.

"An artist is one who feels—that's all. Some people can fashion an image in wood or stone, or clay, or paint, or ink, and then they imagine that they are the only artists, when in reality three-quarters of them aren't artists at all but the most miserable mimics and imitators — highly trained monkeys, you know. Nellie is an artist. She can understand dumb animals and hear music in the wind and the waves, and all sorts of things. And to her the world is one living thing, and she can enjoy its joys and worry over its sorrows, and she understands more than most why people act as they do because she feels enough to put herself in their place. She is such an artist that she not only feels herself but impels those she meets to feel. Besides, she has a freshness that is rare nowadays. I'm very fond of Nellie."

"Evidently," said Geisner; "I've got quite interested. Is she dressmaking still?"

"Yes; I wanted her to come and live with us but she wouldn't. Then Harry got her a better situation in one of the government departments. You know how those things are fixed. But she wouldn't have it. You see she is trying to get the girls into unions."

"Then she is in the movement?" asked Geisner, looking up quickly.

Mrs. Stratton lifted her eye-brows. "In the movement! Why, haven't you understood? My dear Geisner, here we've been talking for fifteen minutes and—there's Nellie's ring. Harry, go and open the door while I pour the coffee."

The opera cloak dropped from her bare shoulders as she rose from the stool. She had fine shoulders, and altogether was of fashionable appearance, excepting that there was about her the impalpable, but none the less pronounced, air of the woman who associates with men as a comrade. As she crossed the room to the verandah she stopped beside the gloomy young man, who had said nothing. He looked up at her affectionately.

"You are wrong to worry," she said, softly. "Besides, it makes you bad company. You haven't spoken to a soul since we came in. For a punishment come and cut the lemon."

They went out on to the verandah together, her hand resting on his arm. There, on a broad shelf, a kettle of water was already boiling over a gas stove.

"What are you thinking of," she chattered. "We shall have some more of your ferocious poetry, I suppose. I notice that about you, Arty. Whenever you get into your blue fits you always pour out blood and thunder verses. The bluer you are the more volcanic you get. When you have it really bad you simply breathe dynamite, barricades, brimstone, everything that is emphatic. What is it this time?"

He laughed. "Why won't you let a man stay blue when he feels like it?"

She did not seem to think an answer necessary, either to his question or her own. "Have you a match?" she went on. "Ah! There is one thing in which a man is superior to woman. He can generally get a light without running all over the house. That is so useful of him. It's his one good point. I can't imagine how any woman can tolerate a man who doesn't smoke. I suppose one get's used to it, though.

He laughed again, turning up the gas-jet he had lighted, which flickered in the puffs of wind that came off the water below. "I could tell you a good story about that."

"That is what I like, a good story. Gas is a nuisance. I wish we had electric lights. Sydney only wants two things to be perfect, never to rain and moonlight all the time. Why, I declare! If there aren't Hero and Leander! Well, of all the spooniest, unsociable, selfish people, you two are the worst. You haven't even had the kindness to let us know you were in all the time, and you actually see Arty and me toiling away at the coffee without offering to help. I've given you up long ago, Josie, but I did expect better things of you, George."

While she had been speaking, pouring the boiling water into the coffee-pot meanwhile, Arty cutting lemons into slices, the two lovers discovered by the flickering gaslight got out of a hammock slung across the end of the verandah and came forward.

"You seemed to be getting along so well we didn't like to disturb you, Mrs. Stratton," explained George, shaking hands. He was bronzed and bright-eyed, not handsome but strong and kindly-looking; he had a kindly voice, too; he wore a white flannel boating costume under a dark cloth coat. Josie also wore a sailor dress of dark blue with loose white collar and vest; a scarlet wrap covered her short curly hair; her skin was milk-white and her features small and irregular. Josie and Connie could never be mistaken for anything but sisters, in spite of the eleven years between them. Only Josie was pretty and plastic and passionless, and Connie was not pretty nor plastic nor passion-less. They were the contrast one sees so often in children kin-born of the summer and autumn of life.

"Don't tell me!" said Mrs. Stratton. "I know all about that."

"Connie knows," said Josie, putting her arms over her sister's shoulders—the younger was the taller—and drawing her face back. "Do you know, Arty, I daren't go into a room in a house I know without knocking. The lady has been married twelve

years and when her husband is away he writes to her every day,
and though they have quite big children they send them to bed
and sit for hours in the same chair, billing and cooing. I've
known them—"

"I wonder who they can be," interrupted Mrs. Stratton,
twisting herself free, her face as red as Josie's shawl. "There's
Nellie's voice. They'll be wondering what we're doing here. Do
come along!" And seizing a tray of cups and saucers, on which
she had placed the coffeepot and the saucer of sliced lemon, she
beat a dignified retreat amid uproarious laughter.

*   *   *   *

Ned found himself in a narrow hall that ran along the side of
the house at right angles to the verandah and the road. The
floor was covered with oil-cloth; the walls were hung with curios,
South Sea spears and masks, Japanese armour, boomerangs,
nullahs, a multitude of quaint workings in wood and grass and
beads. Against the wall facing the door was an umbrella stand
and hat rack of polished wood, with a mirror in the centre.
There were two pannelled doors to the left; a doorless stairway,
leading downwards, and a large window to the right; at the end
of the passage a glazed door, with coloured panes. A gas jet
burned in a frosted globe and seeing him look at this Stratton
explained the contrivance for turning the light down to a mere
dot which gave no gleam but could be turned up again in a
second.

"My wife is enthusiastic about household invention," he
concluded, smiling. "She thinks it assists in righting women's
wrongs. Eh, Nellie? The freed and victorious female will put
her foot on abject man some day? Eh?"

Nellie laughed again. She held the handle of the nearest
door in one hand. Mr. Stratton had turned to take Ned's hat,
apologising for neglecting to think of that before. Ned saw the
girl's other hand move quickly up to where the gas bracket met
the wall and then the light went out altogether. "That's for
poking fun," he heard her say. The door slammed, a key turned
in it and he heard her laughing on the other side.

"Larrikin!" shouted Stratton, boisterously. "Come out here
and see what we'll do to you. She's always up to her tricks," he
added, striking a match and turning the gas on again. "She is
a fine girl. We are as fond of her as though she were one of the
family. She is one of the family, for that matter."

Ned hardly believed his ears or his eyes, either. He had not seen Nellie like this before. She had been grave and rather stern. Only at the gate he had thought he detected in her voice a bitterness which answered well to his own bitter heartache; he had thought he saw on her face the convulsive suppression of intense emotion. Certainly this very day she had shown him the horrors of Sydney and taught him, as if by magic, the misery of living. Now, she laughed lightly and played a trick with the quickness of a thoughtless school girl. Besides, how did it happen that she was so at home in this house of well-to-do people, and so familiar with this man of a cultured class? Ned did not express his thoughts in such phrases of course, but that was the effect of them. He had laughed, but he was still sad and sick at heart and somehow these pleasantries jarred on him. It looked as if there were some secret understanding certainly, some bond that he could not distinguish, between the girl of the people and this courteous gentleman. Nellie had told him simply that the Strattons were "interested in the Labour movement" and were very nice, but Stratton spoke of her as "one of the family" and she turned out his gas and locked one of his own doors in his face. If it was a secret society, well and good, no matter how desperate its plan. But why did they laugh and joke and play tricks? He was not in the humour. For the time his soul abhorred what seemed to him frippery. He sought intuitively to find relief in action and he began impatiently to look for it here.

"Hurry, Nellie!" cried Stratton. "Coffee's nearly ready."

"You won't touch me?" answered her merry voice.

"No, we'll forgive you this once, but look out for the next time."

She opened the door forthwith and stepped out quickly. Ned caught a glimpse of a large bedroom through the doorway. She had taken off her hat and gloves and smoothed the hair that lay on her neck in a heavy plait. At the collar of the plain black dress that fell to her feet over the curving lines of her supple figure she had placed a red rose, half blown. She was tall and straight and graceful, more than beautiful in her strong fresh womanhood, as much at home in such a house as this as in the wretched room where he had watched her sewing slop-clothes that morning. His aching heart went out towards her in a burst of unspoken feeling which he did not know at the time to be Love.

"Mrs. Stratton always puts a flower for me. She loves roses."
So she said to Ned, seeing him looking astonishedly at her. Then
she slipped one hand inside the arm that Stratton bent towards
her, and took hold of Ned's arm with the other. Stratton turned
down the gas. Linked thus together the three went cautiously
down the dim passage hall-way, towards the glass door through
one side of which coloured light came.

"Anybody particular here?" asked Nellie.

"That's a nice question," retorted Stratton. "Geisner is here,
if you call him 'anybody particular.'"

"Geisner! Is he back again?" exclaimed the girl. Ned felt
her hand clutch him nervously. A sudden repulsion to this
Geisner shot through him. He pulled his arm from her grasp.

They had reached the end of the passage, however, and she did
not notice. Stratton turned the handle and opened the door, held
back the half-drawn curtain that hung on the further side and
they passed in. "Here we are," he cried. "Geisner says he
recollects you, Nellie."

Ned could have described the room to the details if he had been
struck blind that minute. It was a double room, long and low
and not very broad, running the whole width of the house, for
there were windows on two sides and French lights on another.
The glazed door opened in the corner of the windowless side.
Opposite were the French lights, the further one swung ajar and
showing a lighted verandah beyond from which came a flutter of
voices. Beyond still were dim points of light that he took at
first for stars. Folding doors, now swung right back, divided
the long linoleum-floored room into two apartments, a studio
and a sitting-room. The studio in which they stood was littered with things strange to him; an easel, bearing a half-
finished drawing; a black-polished cabinet; a table-desk
against the window, on it slips of paper thrown carelessly
about, the ink-well open, a file full of letters, a handful of
cigarettes, a tray of tobacco ash, a bespattered palette, pens,
coloured crayons, a medley of things; a revolving office chair,
with a worn crimson footrug before it; a many-shelved glass
case against the blank wall, crammed to overflowing with shells
and coral and strange grasses, with specimens of ore, with
Chinese carvings, with curious lacquer-work; a large brass-bound
portfolio stand; on the painted walls plaster-casts of hands
and arms and feet, boxing gloves, fencing foils, a glaring tiger's

head, a group of photographs; in the corner, a suit of antique armour stood sentinel over a heap of dumb-bells and Indian clubs.

In the sitting room beyond the folded doors, a soft coloured rug carpet lay loosely on the floor. There were easy chairs there and a red lounge that promised softness; a square cloth-covered table; a whatnot in the corner; fancy shelves; a pretty walnut-wood piano, gilt lined, the cover thrown back, laden with music; on the music-stool a woman's cloak was lying, on the piano a woman's cap. A great book-case reached from ceiling to floor, filled with books, its shelves fringed with some scalloped red stuff. Everywhere were nick-nacks in china, in glass, in terra-cotta, in carved woods, in ivory; photo frames; medallions. On the walls, bright with striped hangings, were some dainty pictures. Half concealed by the hangings was another door. Lying about on the table, here and there on low shelves, were more books. The ground-glass globes of the gaslights were covered with crimson shades. There was a subdued blaze of vivid colouring, of rich toned hues, of beautiful things loved and cherished, over all. Sitting on the edge of the table was the moustached man who smoked the wooden pipe. And turning round from the book-case, an open book in his hand, was the ugly little man. Ned felt that this was Geisner.

The ugly little man put down his book, and came forward holding out his hand. He smiled as he came. Ned was angered to see that when he smiled his face became wonderfully pleasant.

"Yes; I think we know one another, Miss Lawton," he said, meeting them on the uncarpeted floor.

"I am so glad you are here to-night," she replied, greeting him warmly, almost effusively. "I recollect you so well. And Ned will know you, too—Mr. Geisner, Mr. Hawkins." Ned felt his reluctantly extended hand enclosed in a strong friendly clasp.

"Hawkins is the Queenslander we were expecting," said Stratton cheerfully. "You will excuse my familiarity, won't you?" he added, laying his hand on Ned's shoulder. "We don't 'Mister' our friends much here. I think it sounds cold and distant; don't you?"

"We don't 'Mister' much where I come from," answered Ned. He felt at home already. The atmosphere of kindness in this place stole over him and prevented him thinking that it was too "swell" for him.

"I don't know Queensland much——," Geisner was beginning, when the further verandah door was swung wide and the dark-haired little woman swept in, tray in hand, the train of her dress trailing behind her.

"I heard you, Nellie dear," she cried. "That unfeeling Josie was saying the cruellest things to me. I feel as red as red." Putting the tray down on the table she hurried to them, threw her plump bare arms round Nellie's neck and kissed her warmly on both cheeks. Then she drew back quickly and raised her finger threateningly. "Worrying again, Nellie, I can tell. My word! What with you and what with Arty I'm made thoroughly wretched. You mayn't think so to look at me, Mr. Hawkins," she rattled on, holding out her hand to Ned ; "but it is so. You see I know you. I heard Nellie introducing you. That husband of mine must leave all conventionalism to his guests, it seems. You're incorrigible, Harry."

There was a welcome in her every word and look. She put him on a friendly footing at once.

"You have enough conventionalism to-night for us both, my fine lady," twitted Stratton, pinching her arm.

"Stop that! Stop, this minute! Nellie, hit him for me. Mr. Hawkins, this is Bohemia. You do as you like. You say what you like. You are welcome to-night for Nellie's sake. You will be welcome always because I like your looks. I do, Harry, so there. And I'm going to call you Ned because Nellie always does. Oh! I forgot—Mr. Hawkins, Mr. Ford. Mr. Ford thinks he can cartoon. I don't know what you think you can do. And now, everybody, come to coffee."

The others came in from the verandah, still laughing, whereat Mrs. Stratton flushed red again and denounced Josie and George for hiding away, then introduced them and Arty to Ned. There was a babel of conversation for awhile, Josie and George talking of their boating, Connie and Ford of the opera, Stratton and Arty of a picture they had seen that evening. Geisner sat by Ned and Nellie, the three chatting of the beauty of Sydney harbour, the little man waxing indignant at the vandalism which the naval authorities were perpetrating on Garden Island. Mrs. Stratton, all the time, attended energetically to her coffee-pot. Finally she served them all, in small green-patterned china cups, with strong black coffee guiltless of milk, in each cup a slice of lemon floating, in each saucer a biscuit.

"I hope you like your coffee, Ned," she exclaimed, a moment

after. "I forgot to ask you. I'm always forgetting to ask new-comers. You see all the 'regulars' like it this way."

"I've never tasted it this way before," answered Ned. "I suppose liking it's a habit, like smoking. I think I'll try it."

She nodded, being engaged in slowly sipping her own. Geisner looked at Ned keenly. There was silence for a little while, broken only by the clatter of cups and an occasional observation. From outside came the ceaseless lap-lap-lapping of the waves, as if rain water was gurgling down from the roof.

CHAPTER VI.

"WE HAVE SEEN THE DRY BONES BECOME MEN."

NED's thoughts were in tumult, as he sat balancing his spoon on his cup after forcing himself to swallow the, to him, unpleasant drink that the others seemed to relish so. There were no conspirators here, that was certain. Nellie he could understand being one, even with the red rose at her neck, but not this friendly chattering woman whose bare arms and shoulders shimmered in the tinted light and from whose silk dress a subtle perfume stole all over the room; and most certainly not this pretty, mild-looking girl in sailor-costume who appeared from the previous conversation to have passed the evening swinging in a hammock with her sweetheart. And the men! Why, they got excited over music and enraptured over the "tone" of somebody's painting, while Geisner had actually gone back to the book-case, coffee cup in hand, and stood there nibbling a biscuit and earnestly studying the titles of books. It was pleasant, of course, too pleasant. It seemed a sin to enjoy life like this on the very edge of the horrible pit in which the poor were festering like worms in an iron pot. Was it for this that Nellie had brought him here? To idle away an evening among well-meaning people who were "interested in the Labour movement" and in some strange way, some whim probably, had taken to this working girl who in her plain black dress queened them all. He looked round the room and hated it. To his sickened soul its beauty blasphemed the lot of the toilers, insulted the wretchedness, the foulness, the hideousness, that he had seen this very day, that he had known and struggled against, all unconsciously, throughout his wayward life. And Geisner, Geisner at whom Nellie was looking fondly, Geisner who he supposed had written a book or a bit of poetry or could play the flute, and who raved about the spoiling of a bit of an island when the happiness of millions upon millions was being spoiled—well, he would just like to tell Geisner what he thought of him in emphatic bush lingo. Nellie, herself, seemed peacefully happy. Yet Mrs. Stratton had accused her of "worrying."

When Ned thought of this he felt as he did when fording a strange creek, running a banker. He did not know what was underneath.

"Try a cigar, Hawkins?" asked Stratton, pushing a box towards him.

"Thank you, but I don't smoke."

"Don't you really! Do you know I thought all bushmen were great smokers."

"Some are and some aren't," said Ned. "We're not all built to one pattern any more than folks in town."

"That's right, Ned," put in Connie, suddenly recollecting that she was chilly. "Will you hand me my cloak, please? You see," she went on as he brought it, "Harry imagines every bushman as just six feet high, proportionally broad, with bristling black beard streaked with grey, longish hair, bushy eyebrows, bloodshot eyes, moleskins, jean shirt, leathern belt, a black pipe, a swag—you call it 'swag,' don't you?—over his shoulders, and a whisky bottle in his hand whenever he is 'blowing in his cheque,' which is what Nellie says you call 'going on the spree.' Complimentary, isn't it?"

"Connie's libelling both me and my typical bushman," said Stratton, lighting his cigar, having passed the box around. Ned was laughing against his will. Connie had mimicked her husband's imaginary bushman in a kindly humorous way that was very droll.

The musical debate had started up again behind them. Ford and George argued for the traditional rendering of music. Nellie and Arty battled for the musical *zeit-geist*, the national sense that sees through mere notation to the spirit that breathes behind. They waxed warm and threw authorities and quotations about, hardly waiting for each other to finish what they wished to say. Connie turned round to the disputants and threw herself impetuously into the quarrel, strengthening with her wit and trained criticism the cause of the *zeit-geist*. Stratton, to Ned's surprise, putting his arms over her shoulders, opposed her arguments and controverted her assertions with unsparing keenness. Josie leaned back on the lounge and smiled across at Ned. The smile said plainly: "It really doesn't matter, does it?" Ned, fuming inwardly, thought it certainly did not. What a waste of words when the world outside needed deeds! This verbiage was as empty as the tobacco smoke which began to hang about the room in bluish clouds.

Suddenly Mrs. Stratton stood up. "Geisner!" she cried. "I'm ashamed of you. You hear us getting overwhelmed by these English heresies, and you don't come to the rescue. We have talked ourselves dry and you haven't said a word. Who says wine?"

Geisner slowly put down his book and went to the piano. "This is the only argument worth the name," he said. He ran his fingers over the keys, struck two or three chords apparently at hap-hazard, then sat down to play. A volume of sound rose, of clashing notes in fierce, swinging movement, a thrilling clamour of soul-stirring melody, at once short and sharp and long-drawn, at once soft as a mother's lullaby and savage as a hungry tiger's roar. It was the song of the world, the Marseillaise, the song that rises in every land when the oppressed rise against the oppressor, the song that breathes of wrongs to be revenged and of liberty to be won, of flying foes in front and a free people marching, and of blood shed like water for the idea that makes all nations kin. The hand of a master struck the keys and brought the notes out, clear and rhythmic, full strong notes that made the blood boil and the senses swim.

As the glorious melody rose and fell, sinking to a murmur, swelling out in heroic strains that rang like trumpet pealings, a great lump rose in Ned's throat and a mist of unquenchable tears filled his eyes. Roget de Lisle, dead and dust for generations, rose from the silent grave and spoke to him, spoke as heart speaks to heart, spoke and called and lived and breathed and was there, spoke of tortured lives and enslaved millions and of the fetid streets of great towns and of the slower anguish of the plundered country side, spoke of an Old Order based on the robbery of those who labour and on their weakness and on their ignorant sloth, spoke of virtue trampled down and little children weeping and Humanity bleeding at every pore and womanhood shamed and motherhood made a curse, spoke of all he hated and all he loved, pilloried the Wrong in front of him and bade him—to arms, to arms. "To arms!" with the patriot army whose trampling was the background of the music. "To arms!" with those whose desperate hands feared nothing and at whose coming thrones melted and kingdoms vanished and tyranny fled. To arms! To certain victory! To crash forward like a flood and sweep before the armed people all those who had worked it wrong!

Down Ned's cheeks the great tears rolled. He did not heed them. Why did not some one beat this mighty music through the Sydney slums, through those hateful back streets, through those long endless rows of mortgaged cottages and crowded apartment-houses? Why was it not carried out to the great West, hymned from shed to shed, told of in the huts and by the waterholes, given to the diggers in the great claims, to the drovers travelling stock, borne wherever a man was to be found who had a wrong to right and a long account to square? Ah! How they would all leap to it! How they would swell its victorious chanting and gather in their thousands and their hundred thousands to march on, march on, tramping time to its majestic notes! If he could only take it to them! If he could only make them feel as he felt! If he could only give to them in their poverty and misery all this wondrous music sounding here in this luxurious room! He could not; he could not. This Geisner could and would not, and he who would could not. The tears rained down his cheeks because of his utter impotence.

The music stopped. With a start he came to himself, ashamed of his weakness, and hastily blew his nose, fussing pretentiously with his handkerchief. But only one had noticed him—Geisner, who seemed to see and hear everything. Connie was sobbing quietly with her arms round Harry's neck, holding his head closely to her as he bent over her chair; all the while her foot beat time. Arty had suddenly grown moody again and sat with bent head, his cigar gone out in his listless hand. Ford had got up and was perched again on a corner of the table, smoking critically, apparently wholly engaged in watching the smoke wreaths he blew. George and Josie had taken each other's hands and sat breathlessly side by side on the lounge. Nellie lay back in her chair, her face flushed, a twisted handkerchief stretched over her eyes by both hands.

"I think that's the official version," observed Geisner, running his fingers softly over the keys again.

"It's above disputation, whatever it is," remarked Ford.

"Why should it be, if all true music isn't? And why should not this be the best rendering?"

He struck the grand melody again and it sounded softened, spiritualised, purified. Its fierce clamour, its triumphant crashing, were gone. It told of defeat and overthrow, of martyrs walking painfully to death, of prison cells and dungeons that never see the sun, of life-work unrewarded, of those who give their lives to Liberty and die before its shackled limbs are struck free. But it told, too, of an ideal held more sacred than life, rising ever from defeat, filling men's hearts and brains and driving them still to raise again the flag of Freedom against hopeless odds. It was a death march rolling out, the death march of sad-souled patriots going sorrowfully to seal their faith with all their earthly hopes and human loves and to meet, calm and pale, all that Fate has in store. They said to Liberty: "In death we salute thee." Without seeing her or knowing her, while the world around still slept in ignorance of her, they gave all up for her and in darkness died. Only they knew that there was no other way, that unless each man of himself dared to raise the chant and march forward alone, if need be, Liberty could never be.

"Well," said Geisner, coming unconcernedly into the circle where they sat in dead silence. "Don't you think the last rendering is the best, and isn't it the best simply because it expresses the composer's idea in the particular phase that we feel most at this present time?"

"Gracious! Don't start the argument again!" entreated Connie, vivacious again, though her eyes were red. "You'll never convert Ford or George or Harry here. They'll always have some explanation. Puritanism crushed the artistic sense out of the English, and they are only getting it back slowly by a judicious crossing with other peoples who weren't Puritanised into Philistinism. England has no national music. She has no national painting. She has no national sculpture. She has to borrow and adapt everything from the Continent. I nearly said she has no art at all."

"Here, I say," protested Ford. "Aren't you coming it a little too strong? You've got the floor, Geisner. I've heard you stand up for English Art. Stand up now, won't you?"

"Does it need standing up for?" asked Geisner. "Why, Connie doesn't forget that Puritanism with all its faults was in its day a religious movement, that is an emotional fervour, a veritable poem. That the Puritan cut love-locks off, wore drab, smashed painted windows and suppressed instrumental music in churches, is no proof of their being utterly inartistic. Their art-sense would simply find vent and expression in other directions if it existed strongly enough. And what do we find? This, that the Puritan period produced two of the masterpieces of English Art—Milton's 'Paradise Lost' and Bunyan's 'Pilgrim's Progress.' As an absolute master of English, of sentences rolling magnificently in great waves of melodious sound, trenchant in every syllable, not to be equalled even by Shakespeare himself, Milton stands out like a giant. As for Bunyan, the Englishman who has never read 'Pilgrim's Progress' does not know his mother tongue."

"Oh! Of course, we all admit English letters," interjected Connie.

"Do we?" answered Geisner, warming with his theme. "I'm not so sure of that; else, why should English people themselves put forward claims to excellencies which their nation has not got, and why should others dub them inartistic because of certain things lacking in the national arts? As far as music goes what has France got if you take away the Marseillaise? It is Germany, the kin of the English, which has the modern music. France has painting, England has literature and poetry—in that she leads the whole world."

"Still, to-day! How about Russia? How about France even—Flaubert, Zola, Daudet, Ohnet, a dozen more?"

"Still! Ay, still and ever! Will these men live as the English writers live, think you? Look back a thousand years and see English growing, see how it comes to be the king of languages, destined, if civilisation lasts, to be the one language of the civilised world. There, in the Viking age, the English sweep the seas, great burly brutes, as Taine shows them to us, gorging on half-raw meat, swilling huge draughts of ale, lounging naked by the sedgy brooks under the mist-softened sun that cannot brown their fair pink bodies, until hunger drives them forth to foray; drinking and fighting and feasting and shouting and loving as Odin loved Frega. And the most honoured of all was the singer who sang in heroic verse of their battling and their love-making and their hunting. English was conceived then, and it was a worthy conceiving."

"Other nations have literature," maintained Connie.

"What other living nations?" demanded Geisner. "Look at English! An endless list, such as surely before the world never saw. You cannot even name them all. Spencer and Chaucer living still. Shakespeare, whoever he was, immortal for all time, dimming like a noontide sun a galaxy of stars that to other nations would be suns indeed ! Take Marlow, Beaumont and Fletcher, a dozen playwrights ! The Bible, an imperishable monument of the people's English ! Milton, Bunyan and Baxter, Wycherly and his fellows ! Pope, Ben Johnson, Swift, Goldsmith, Junius, Burke, Sheridan ! Scott and Byron, De Quincey, Shelley, Lamb, Chatterton ! Moore and Burns wrote in English too ! Look at Wordsworth, Dickens, George Eliott, Swinburne, Tennyson, the Brontés ! There are gems upon gems in the second class writers, books that in other countries would make the writer immortal. Over the sea, in America, Poe, Whittier, Bret Harte, Longfellow, Emerson, Whitman. Here in Australia, the seed springing up ! Even in South Africa, that Olive Schreiner writing like one inspired. By heavens ! There are moments when I feel it must be a proud thing to be an Englishman."

"Bravo, Geisner ! You actually make me for the minute," cried Ford.

" You should be ! Has any other people anything to compare ? There is not one other whose great writers could not almost be counted on the fingers of one hand. Spain has Cervantes and he is always being thrown at us. Germany has Goethe, Heine, Schiller. France so seldom sees literary genius that a man like Victor Hugo sends her into hysterics of self-admiration. But I'm afraid I'm lecturing."

"It's all right, Geisner," remarked Connie. " It's not only what you say but how you say it. But what are you driving at ?"

"Just this ! Nations seldom do all things with equal vigour and fervour and opportunity, so one excels another and is itself excelled. England excels in the simplest and strongest form of expression, literature. She is defective in other forms and borrows from us. But so we others borrow from her. Puritanism did not crush English art. English art, in the national way of expressing the national feeling, kept steadily on."

" Thanks ! I think I'll sit down," he added, as Stratton handed him a tumbler half-filled with wine and a water-bottle. He filled the tumbler from the bottle, put them on the table, took cigarettes in a case from his pocket and lighted one at a gas jet behind him.

" Do you take water with your wine ?" asked Stratton of Ned.

"I don't take wine at all, thank you," said Ned.

F

"What!" exclaimed Connie, sitting up. "You don't smoke and you don't drink wine. Why, you are a regular Arab. But you must have something. Arty! Rouse up and light the little stove again! You'll have some tea, Ned. Oh! It's no trouble. Arty will make it for me and it will do him good. What do you think of this oration of Geisner's?"

"I suppose it's all right," said Ned. "But I can't see what good it does myself."

"How's that?"

"Well, it's no use saying one thing and meaning another. This talk of 'art' seems to me selfish while the world to most people is a hell that it's pain to live in. I am sorry if I say what you don't like."

"Never mind that," said Connie, as cheerfully as ever. "You've been worrying, too. Have it out, so that we can all jump on you at once! I warn you, you won't have an ally."

"I suppose not," answered Ned, hotly. "You are all very kind and mean well, but do you know how people live, how they exist, what life outside is?"

Geisner had sat down in a low chair near by, his cigarette between his lips, his glass of wine and water on a shelf at his elbow. The others looked on in amazement at the sudden turn of the conversation. Connie smiled and nodded. Ned stared fiercely round at Geisner, who nodded also.

"Then listen to me," said Ned, bitterly. "Is it by playing music in fine parlours that good is to be done? Is it by drinking wine, by smoking, by laughing, by talking of pictures and books and music, by going to theatres, by living in clover while the world starves? Why do you not play that music in the back streets or to our fellows?" he asked, turning to Geisner again. "Are you afraid? Ah, if I could only play it!"

"Ned!" cried Nellie, sharply. But he went on, talking at Geisner:

"What do you do for the people outside? For the miserable, the wretched, those weary of life? I suppose you are all 'interested in the Labour movement.' Well, what does all this do for it? What do you do for it? Would you give up anything, one puff of smoke, one drink of wine——"

"Stop, Ned! For shame's sake! How dare you speak to him like that?" Nellie interrupted, jumping up and coming between the two men. Ned leaned eagerly forward, his hands on his knees, his eyes flaming, his face quivering, his teeth showing Geisner leaned back quietly, alternately sipping his wine and water and taking a whiff from his cigarette.

"Never mind," said Geisner. "Sit down, Nellie. It doesn't matter." Nellie sat down but she looked to Mrs. Stratton anxiously. The two women exchanged glances. Mrs. Stratton came quickly across to Geisner.

"It does matter," she said to him, laying her hands on his head and shoulder and facing Ned thus. "Not to you, of course, but to Ned there. He does not understand, and I don't think you understand everything either. It takes a woman to understand it all, Ned," and she laughed at the angry man. "Why do you say such things to Geisner? He does not deserve them."

Ned did not answer.

"I'm not defending the rest of us, only Geisner. If you only knew all he has done you would think of him as we do."

"Connie!" exclaimed Geisner, flushing. "Don't."

"Oh! I shall. If men will keep their lights under bushel baskets they must expect to get the covers knocked off sometimes. Ned! This man is a martyr. He has suffered so for the people, and he has borne it so bravely."

There was a hush in the room. Ned could see Connie's full underlip pouted tremulously and her eyes swimming; her hands moved caressingly to and fro. His face relaxed its passion. The tears came again into his eyes, also. Geisner smoked his cigarette, the most unmoved of any.

"If you had only known him years ago," went on Connie, her voice trembling. "He used to take me on his knee when I was a little girl, and keep me there for hours while great men talked great things and he was greatest of them all. He was young then and rich and handsome and fiery, and with a brain—oh, such a brain!—that put within his reach what other men care for most. And he gave it all up, everything—even Love," she added, softly. "When he played the Marseillaise just now, I thought of it. One day he came to our house and played it so, and outside the people in the streets were marching by singing it, and—and—". she set her teeth on a great sob. "My father never came back nor my brother, and Harry there came one night and took Josie and me away. We had no mother. And when we saw this man again he was what he is now. It was worse than death, ten thousand times worse. Oh! Geisner, Geisner!" The head her hand rested on had sunk down. What were the little man's thoughts? What were they?

"But his heart is still the same, Ned," she cried, triumphantly, her sweet voice ringing clear again. "Ah, yes! His heart is still the same, as brave and true and pure and strong. Oh, purer, better! If it came again, Ned, he would do it. Sometimes, I think, he doubts himself but I know. He would do it all again and suffer it all—that worse than death he suffered. For, you see, he only lives to serve the Cause, in a different way to the old way but still to serve it. And I serve the Cause also as best I can, even if I wear—" she shrugged her shoulders. "And Harry serves it still as loyally as when, a beardless lad, he risked his life to care for a slaughtered comrade's orphan children. And Ford, too, and Nellie here, and Arty and Josie and George. But Geisner serves it best of all if it be best to give most. He has given most all his life and he gives most still. And we love him for it. And that love, perhaps, is sweeter to him than all he might have been."

She knelt by his side as she ceased speaking, and put her arms round his neck as he crouched there. "Geisner!" Nellie who was nearest heard her whisper in her childhood's tongue. "Geisner! We have seen the dry bones become men. We have poured our blood and our brain into them and if only for a moment they have lived, they have lived. Ah, comrade, do you recollect how you breathed soul into them when they shrank back that day? They moved, Geisner. They moved. We felt them move. They will move again, some day, dear heart. They will move again." Then, choking with sobs, she laid her head on his knees. He put his arms tenderly round her and they saw that this immovable little man was weeping like a child. One by one the others went softly out to the verandah. Only Ned remained. He had buried his face in his hands and sat, overwhelmed with shame, wishing that the floor would open and swallow him. From outside came the ceaseless lap-lap-lapping of water, imperceptibly eating away the granite rock, caring not for time, blindly working, destroying the old and building up the new.

The touch of a hand roused Ned. He looked up. Mrs. Stratton had gone through the door concealed by the hangings. Geisner stood before him, calmly lighting another cigarette with a match. There was no trace of emotion on his face. He turned to drop the match into an ash tray, then held out both hands, on his face the kindly smile that transfigured him. Ned grasped them eagerly, wringing them in a grip that would have made most men wince. They stood thus silently for a minute or two, looking at one another, the young, hot-tempered bushman, the grey-haired, cool-tempered leader of men; between them sprang up, as they stood, the bond of that friendship which death itself only strengthens. The magnetism of the elder, his marvellous personality, the strength and majesty of the mighty soul that dwelt in his insignificant body, stole into Ned's heart and conquered it. And the spirit of the younger, his fierce indignation, his angry sorrow, his disregard for self, his truth, his strong manhood, appealed to the weary man as an echoing of his own passionate youth. Then they loosened hands and without a word Geisner commenced to walk slowly backwards and forwards, his hands behind him, his head bent down.

Ned watched him, studying him feature by feature. Yes, he had been handsome. He was ugly only because of great wrinkles that scored his cheeks and disfigured the fleshless face and discoloured skin. His eyebrows and eyelashes were very thin, too. His hair looked dried up and was strongly greyed; it had once been almost black. His lips were thin, his mouth shapeless, only because he had closed them in his fight against pain and anguish and despair and they had set thus by the habit of long years. His nose was still fine and straight, the nostrils swelling wide. His forehead was rugged and broad under its wrinkles. His chin was square. His frame still gave one the impression of tireless powers of endurance. His blue eyes still gleamed unsubdued in their dark, overhanging caverns. Yes! He had lived, this man. He had lived and suffered and kept his manhood still. To be like him! To follow him into the Valley of the Shadow! To live only for the Cause and by his side to save the world alive! Ned thought thus, as Connie came back, her face bathed and beaming again, her theatre dress replaced by a soft red dressing gown, belted loosely at the waist and trimmed with an abundance of coffee coloured lace. Her first words were a conundrum to Ned:

"Geisner! Haven't you dropped that unpleasant trick of yours after all these years? Two long steps and a short step! Turn! Two long steps and a short step! Turn! Now, just to please me, do three long steps."

He smiled. "Connie, you are becoming quite a termagant."

She looked at Ned questioningly : "Well ? "

"Oh, Ned and I are beginning to understand one another," said Geisner.

"Of course," she replied. "All good men and women are friends if they get to the bottom of each other. Let us go on the verandah with the rest. Do you know I feel quite warm now. I do believe it was only that ridiculous dress which made me feel so cold. Give me your arm, Ned. Bring me along a chair, Geisner."

CHAPTER VII.

A MEDLEY OF CONVERSATION.

NED dreaded that rejoining the others on the verandah, but he need not have. They had forced the conversation at first, but gradually it became natural. It had turned on the proper sphere of woman, and went on without being interrupted by the new-comers. Nobody took any notice of them. The girls were seated. Stratton lay smoking in the hammock. The other men perched smoking on the railing. The gaslight had been turned down and in the gloom the cigar ends gleamed with each respiration. In spite of the damp it was very cosy. From the open door behind a ray of light fell upon the darkness-covered water below. Beyond were circling the lights of Sydney. Dotting the black night here and there were the signal lamps of anchored ships.

"We want perfect equality for woman with man," asserted Ford, in a conclusive tone of voice.

"We want woman in her proper sphere," maintained Stratton, from the hammock.

"What do you call 'her proper sphere?'" asked Nellie.

"This: That she should fulfil the functions assigned to her by Nature. That she should rule the home and rear children. That she should be a wife and a mother. That she should be gentle as men are rough, and, to pirate the Americanism, as she rocked the cradle should rock the world."

"How about equality?" demanded Ford.

"Equality! What do you mean by equality? Is it equality to scramble with men in the search for knowledge, narrow hipped and flat-chested? Is it equality to grow coarse and rough and unsexed in the struggle for existence? Ah! Let our women once become brutalised, masculinised, and there will be no hope for anything but a Chinese existence."

"Who wants to brutalise them?" asked Ford.

"What would your women be like?" asked Nellie.

"Look out for Madame there, Stratton!" said George.

"What would my women be like? Full-lipped and broad-hearted, fit to love and be loved! Full-breasted and broad-hipped fit to have children! Full-brained and broad-browed, fit to teach them! My women should be the embodiment of the nation, and none of them should work except for those they loved and of their own free will."

"Sort of queen bees!" remarked Nellie. "Why have them work at all?"

"Why? Is it 'work' for a mother to nurse her little one, to wash it, to dress it, to feed it, to watch it at night, to nurse it when it sickens, to teach it as it grows? And if she does that does she not do all that we have a right to ask of her? Need we ask her to earn her own living and bear children as well? Shall we make her a toy and a slave, or harden her to battle with men? I wouldn't. My women should be such that their children would hold them sacred and esteem all women for their sakes. I don't want the shrieking sisterhood, hard-voiced and ugly and unlovable, perpetuated. And they will not be perpetuated. They can't make us marry them. Their breed must die out."

"In other words," observed Nellie; "you would leave the present relationship of woman to Society unchanged, except that you would serve her out free rations."

"No! She should be absolutely mistress of her own body, and sole legal guardian of her own children."

"Which means that you would institute free divorce, and make the family matriarchal instead of patriarchal; replace one lop-sided system by another."

"Give it him, Nellie," put in Connie. "I haven't heard those notions of his for years. I thought he had recanted long ago."

"Well, yes! But you needn't be so previous in calling it lop-sided," said Stratton.

"It is lop-sided, to my mind!" replied Nellie. "What women really want is to be left to find their own sphere, for whenever a man starts to find it for them he always manages to find something else. No man understands woman thoroughly. How can he when she doesn't even understand herself? Yet you propose to crush us all down to a certain pattern, without consulting us. That's not democratic. Why not consult us first I should like to know?"

"Probably because they wouldn't agree to it if you led the opposition, Nellie. We are all only democratic when we think Demos is going our way." This from Ford.

Arty slipped quietly off the railing and went into the sitting-room. Connie leaned back and watched him through the open door. "He's started to write," she announced. "He's been terribly down lately so it'll be pretty strong, poor fellow." She laughed good-naturedly; the others laughed with her. "Go on, Nellie dear. It's very interesting, and I didn't mean to interrupt."

"Oh! He won't answer me," declared Nellie, in a disgusted tone.

"I should think not," retorted Stratton. "I know your womanly habit of tying the best case into a tangled knot with a few Socratic questions. I leave the truth to prove itself."

"Just so! But you won't leave the truth about woman to prove itself. You want us to be good mothers, first and last. Why not let us be women, true women, first, and whatever it is fitting for us to be afterwards?"

"I want you to be true women."

"What is a true woman? A true woman to me is just what a true man is—one who is free to obey the instincts of her nature. Only give us freedom, opportunity, and we shall be at last all that we should be."

"Is it not freedom to be secure against want, to be free to——"

"To be mothers."

"Yes; to be mothers—the great function of women. To cradle the future. To mould the nation that is to be."

"That is so like a man. To be machines, you mean—well cared for, certainly, but machines just the same. Don't you know that we have been machines too long? Can't you see that it is because we have been degraded into machines that Society is what it is?"

"How?" questioned Stratton.

"He knows it well, Nellie," cried Connie, clapping her hands.

"Because you can't raise free men from slave women. We want to be free, only to be free, to be let alone a little, to be treated as human beings with souls, just as men do. We have hands to work with, and brains to think with, and hearts to feel with. Why not join hands with us in theory as you do in fact? Do you tell us now that you won't have our help in the movement? Will you refuse us the fruit of victory when the fight is won? If I thought you would, I for one would cease to care whether the Cause won or not."

"I, too, Nellie. We'd all go on strike," cried Connie.

"What is it to you whether women are good mothers or not? What objections can you have to our rivalling men in the friendly rivalry that would be under fair conditions? Are our virtues, our woman instincts, so weak and frail that you can't trust us to go straight if the whole of life is freely open to us? Why, when I think of what woman's life is now, what it has been for so long, I wonder how it is that we have any virtues left." She spoke with intense feeling.

"What are we now," she went on, "in most cases? Slaves, bought and sold for a home, for a position, for a ribbon, for a piece of bread. With all their degradation men are not degraded as we are. To be womanly is to be shamed and insulted every day. To love is to suffer. To be a mother is to drink the dregs of human misery. To be heartless, to be cold, to be vicious and a hypocrite, to smother all one's higher self, to be sold, to sell one's self, to pander to evil passions, to be the slave of the slave, that is the way to survive most easily for a woman. And see what we are in spite of everything! Geisner said he would sometimes be proud if he were an Englishman. Sometimes I'm foolish enough to be proud I'm a woman.

"Why should we be mothers, unless it pleases us to be mothers? Why should we not feel that life is ours as men may feel it, that we help hold up the world and owe nothing to others except that common debt of fraternity which they owe also to us? Don't you think that Love would come then as it could in no other way? Don't you think that women, who even now are good mothers generally, would be good mothers to children whose coming was unstained with tears? And would they be worse mothers if their brains were keen and their bodies strong and their hearts brave with the healthy work and intelligent life that everybody should have, men and women alike?"

"You seem to have an objection to mothers somehow, Nellie," observed Geisner.

"Oh, I have! It seems to me such a sin, such a shameful sin, to give life for the world that we have. I can understand it being a woman's highest joy to be a mother. I have seen poor miserable women looking down at their puny nursing babies with such unutterable bliss on their faces that I've nearly cried for pure joy and sympathy. But in my heart all the time I felt that this was weakness and folly; that what was bliss to the mother, stupefying her for a while to the hollowness and emptiness of her existence, was the beginning of a probable life of misery to the child that could end only with death. And I have vowed to myself that never should child of mine have cause to reproach me for selfishness that takes a guise which might well deceive those who have nothing but the animal instincts to give them joy in living."

"You will never have children?" asked Geisner.

"I will never marry," she answered. "There is little you can teach a girl who has worked in Sydney, and I know there are ideas growing all about which to me seem shameful and unwomanly, excepting that they spare the little ones. For me, I shall never marry. I will give my life to the movement, but I will give no other lives the pain of living."

"You will meet him some day, Nellie," said Connie.

"Then I will be strong if it breaks my heart." Ned often thought of this in after days. Just then he hardly realised how the girl's words affected him. He was so breathlessly interested. Never had he heard people talk like this before. He began to dimly understand how it touched the Labour movement.

"You will miss the best part of life, my dear," said Connie. "I say it even after what you have seen of that husband of mine."

"You are wrong, Nellie," said Geisner, slowly. "Above us all is a higher Law, forcing us on. To give up what is most precious for the sake of the world is good. To give up that which our instincts lead us to for fear of the world cannot but be bad. For my part, I hold that no door should be closed to woman, either by force of law or by force of conventionalism. But if she claims entrance to the Future, it seems to me that she should not close Life's gate against herself."

"I would close Life's gate altogether if I could," cried Nellie, passionately. "I would blot Life out. I would—oh, what would I not do? The things I see around me day after day almost drive me mad."

There was silence for a moment, broken then by Connie's soft laugh. "Nellie, my dear child," she observed, "you seem quite in earnest. I hope you won't start with us."

"Don't mind her, Nellie," said Josie, softly, speaking for the first time. "Connie laughs because if she didn't she would cry."

"I know that," said Nellie. "I don't mind her. Is there one of us who does not feel what a curse living is?"

Geisner's firm voice answered: "And is there one of us who does not know what a blessing living might be? Nellie, my girl, you are sad and sorrowful, as we all are at times, and do not feel yet God in all working itself out in unseen ways."

"God!" she answered, scornfully. "There is no God. How can there be?"

"I do not know. It is as one feels. I do not mean that petty god of creeds and religions, the feeble image that coarse hands have made from vague glimpses caught by those who were indeed inspired. I mean the total force, the imperishable breath, of the universe. And of that breath, my child, you and I and all things are part."

Stratton took his cigar from his mouth and quoted:

" ' I am the breath of the lute, I am the mind of man,
  Gold's glitter, the light of the diamond and the sea-pearl's
    lustre wan.
I am both good and evil, the deed and the deed's intent—
Temptation, victim, sinner, crime, pardon and punishment.' "

"Yes," said Geisner; "that and more. Brahma and more than Brahma. What Prince Buddha thought out too. What Jesus the Carpenter dimly recognised. Not only Force, but Purpose, or what for lack of better terms we call Purpose, in it all."

"And that Purpose; what is it?" Ned was surprised to hear his own voice uttering his thought.

"Who shall say? There are moments, a few moments, when one seems to feel what it is, moments when one stands face to face with the universal Life and realises wordlessly what it means." Geisner spoke with grave solemnity. The others, hardly breathing, understood how this man had thought these things out.

"When one is in anguish and sorrow unendurable. When one has seen one's soul stripped naked and laid bare, with all its black abysses and unnatural sins; the brutishness that is in each man's heart known and understood—the cowardice, the treachery, the villainy, the lust. When one knows oneself in others, and sinks into a mist of despair, hopeless and heart-wrung, then come the temptations, as the prophets call them, the miserable ambitions dressed as angels of light, the religions which have become mere drugged pain-lullers, the desire to suppress thought altogether, to end life, to stupefy one's soul with bodily pain, with mental activity. And if," he added slowly, "if one's pain is for others more than for oneself, if in one's heart Humanity has lodged itself, then it may be that one shall feel and know. And from that time you never doubt God. You may doubt yourself but never that all things work together for good."

"I do not see it," cried Nellie.

"Hush!" said Connie. "Go on, Geisner."

"To me," the little man went on, as if talking rather to himself than to the others. "To me the Purpose of Life is self-consciousness, the total Purpose I mean. God seeking to know God. Eternal Force one immeasurable Thought. Humanity the developing consciousness of the little fragment of the universe within our ken. Art, the expression of that consciousness, the outward manifestation of the effort to solve the problem of Life. Genius, the power of expressing in some way or other what many thought but could not articulate. I do not mean to be dogmatic. Words fail us to define our meaning when we speak of these things. Any quibbler can twist the meaning of words, while only those who think the thought can understand. That is why one does not speak much of them. Perhaps we should speak of them more."

"It is a barren faith to me," said Nellie.

"Then I do not express it well," said Geisner. "But is it more barren-sounding than utter Negation? Besides, where do we differ really? All of us who think at all agree more or less. We use different terms, pursue different lines of thought, that is all. It is only the dullard, who mistakes the symbol for the idea, the letter for the spirit, the metaphor for the thought within, who is a bigot. The true thinker is an artist, the true artist is a thinker, for Art is the expression of thought in thing. The highest thought, as Connie rightly told us before you came, is Emotion."

"I recollect the Venus in the Louvre," interjected Harry. "When I saw it first it seemed to me most beautiful, perfect, the loveliest thing that ever sculptor put chisel to. But as I saw it more I forgot that it was beautiful or perfect. It grew on me till it lived. I went day after day to see it, and when I was glad it laughed at me, and when I was downhearted it was sad with me, and when I was angry it scowled, and when I dreamed of Love it had a kiss on its lips. Every mood of mine it changed with; every thought of mine it knew. Was not that Art, Nellie?"

"The artist in you," she answered.

"No. More than that. The artist in the sculptor, breathing into the stone a perfect sympathy with the heart of men. His genius grasped this, that beauty, perfect beauty, is the typifying not of one passion, one phase of human nature, but of the aggregation of all the moods which sway the human mind. There is a great thought in that. It is 'the healthy mind in the healthy body,' as the sculptor feels it. And 'the healthy mind in the healthy body' is one of the great thoughts of the past. It is a thought which is the priceless gift of Greek philosophy to the world. I hold it higher than that of the Sphinx, which Ford admires so."

"What does the Sphinx mean?" asked Ned.

"Much the same, differently expressed," answered Ford. "That Life with us is an intellectual head based on a brutish body, fecund and powerful; that Human Nature crouches on the ground and reads the stars; that man has a body and a mind, and that both must be cared for."

"They had a strange way of caring for both, your Egyptians," remarked Nellie. "The people were all slaves and the rulers were all priests."

At this criticism, so naïve and pithy and so like Nellie, there was a general laugh.

"At least the priests were wise and the slaves were cared for," retorted Ford, nothing abashed. "I recollect when I was a little fellow in England. My people were farm labourers, west of England labourers. We lived in a little stone cottage that had little diamond-paned windows. The kitchen floor was below the ground, and on wet days my mother used to make a little dam of rags at the door to keep the trickling water back. We lived on bread and potatoes and broad beans, and not too much of that. We got a little pig for half-a-crown, and killed it when it was grown to pay the rent. Don't think such things are only done in Ireland! We herded together like pigs ourselves. The women of the place often worked in the fields. The girls, too, sometimes. You know what that means where the people are like beasts, the spirit worn out of them. The cottages were built two together, and our neighbour's daughter, a girl of 18 or so, had two children. It was not thought anything. The little things played at home with our neighbour's own small children, and their grandmother called them hard names when they bothered her.

"My father was a bent-shouldered hopeless man, when I recollect him. He got six shillings a week then, with a jug of cider every day. When he stopped from the wet, and there was no work in the barns, his wages were stopped. So he worked in the wet very often, for it generally rains in England, you know. The wet came through our roof. Gives the natives such pretty pink skins, eh, Geisner?" and he laughed shortly. "My father got rheumatism, and used to keep us awake groaning at nights. He had been a good-looking young fellow, my old granny used to say. I never saw him good-looking. In the winter we always had poor relief. We should have starved if we hadn't. My father got up at four and came home after dark. My mother used to go weeding and gleaning. I went to scare crows when I was five years old. All the same, we were a family of paupers. Proud to be an Englishman, Geisner! Be an English pauper, and then try!"

"You'll never get to the priests, Ford, if you start an argument," interposed Mrs. Stratton.

"I'll get to them all right. Our cottage was down a narrow, muddy lane. On one side of the lane was a row of miserable stone hovels, just like ours. On the other was a great stone wall that seemed to me, then, to be about a hundred feet high. I suppose it was about twenty feet. You could just see the tops of trees the other side. Some had branches lopped short to prevent them coming over the wall. At the corner of the highway our lane ran to was a great iron gate, all about it towering trees, directly inside a mound of shrub-covered rockery that prevented anybody getting a peep further. The carriage drive took a turn round this rockery and disappeared. Once, when the gate was open and nobody about, I got a peep by sneaking round this rockery like a little thief. There was a beautiful lawn and clumps of flowers, and a summer house and a conservatory, and a big grey-fronted mansion. I thought heaven must be something like that. It made me radical."

"How do you mean?" asked Mrs. Stratton.

"Well, it knocked respect for constituted authority out of me. I didn't know enough to understand the wrong of one lazy idler having this splendid place while the people he lived on kennelled in hovels. But it struck me as so villainously selfish to build that wall, to prevent us outside from even looking at the beautiful lawn and flowers. I was only a little chap but I recollect wondering if it would hurt the place to let me look, and when I couldn't see that it would I began to hate the wall like poison. There we were, poor, ragged, hungry wretches, without anything beautiful in our lives, so miserable and hopeless that I didn't even know it wasn't the right thing to be a pauper, and that animal ran up a great wall in our faces so that we couldn't see the grass— curse him!" Ford had gradually worked himself into a white rage.

"He didn't know any better," said Geisner. "Was he the priest?"

"Yes, the rector, getting £900 a-year and this great house, and paying a skinny curate £60 for doing the work. A fat impostor, who drove about in a carriage, and came to tell the girl next door as she lay a-bed that she would go to hell for her sin and burn there for ever. I hated his wall and him too. Out in the fields I used to draw him on bits of slate. In the winter when there weren't any crows or any weeding I went to school. You see, unless you sent your children to the church school a little, and went to church regularly, you didn't get any beef or blanket at Christmas. I tell you English charity is a sweet thing. Well, I used to draw the parson at school, a fat, pompous, double-chinned, pot-bellied animal, with thin side-whiskers, and a tall silk hat, and a big handful of a nose. I drew nothing else. I studied the question as it were and I got so that I could draw the brute in a hundred different ways. You can imagine they weren't complimentary, and one day the parson came to the school, and we stood up in class with slates to do sums, and on the back of my slate was one of the very strongest of my first attempts at cartooning. It was a hot one." And at the remembrance Ford laughed so contagiously that they all joined. "The parson happened to see it. By gum! It was worth everything to see him."

"What did he do?"

"What didn't he do? He delivered a lecture, how I was a worthy relative of an uncle of mine who'd been shipped out this way years before for snaring a rabbit, and so on. I got nearly skinned alive, and the Christmas beef and blanket were stopped from our folks. And there another joke comes in. An elder brother of mine, 14 years old, I was about 12, took to going to the Ranters' meetings instead of to church. My mother and father used to tie him up on Saturday nights and march him to church on Sunday like a young criminal going to gaol. They were afraid of losing the beef and blanket, you see. He sometimes ran out of church when they nodded or weren't looking, and the curate was always worrying them about him. It was the deadliest of all sins, you know, to go to the Ranters. Well, when the beef and blanket were stopped, without any chance of forgiveness, we all went to the Ranters."

"I've often wondered where you got your power from, Ford," remarked Connie. "I see now."

"Yes, that great wall made me hate the great wall that bars the people from all beautiful things; that fat hypocrite made me hate all frauds. I can never forget the way we all swallowed those things as sacred. When I get going with a pencil I feel towards whatever it is just as I felt to the parson, and I try to make everybody feel the same. Yet would you believe it, I don't care much for cartooning. I want to paint."

"Why don't you?" asked Nellie.

"Well, there's money you know. Then it was sheer luck that made me a cartoonist and I can't expect the same run of luck always."

"Don't believe him, Nellie," said Connie. "He feels that he has a chance now to give all frauds such a hammering that he hesitates to give it up. You've paid the parson, Ford, full measure, pressed down and running over!"

"Not enough!" answered Ford. "Not enough! Not till the wall is down flat all the world over! Do you think Egypt would have lasted 20,000 years if her priests had been like my parson, and her slaves like my people?"

"I'd forgotten all about Egypt," said Nellie. "But I suppose her rulers had sense enough to give men enough to eat and enough to drink, high wages and constant employment, as M'Ilwraith used to say. Yes; it was wiser than the rulers of to-day are. You can rob for a long while if you only rob moderately. But the end comes some time to all wrong. It's coming faster with us, but it came in Egypt, too."

"Here is Arty, finished!" interrupted Connie, who every little while had looked through the door at the young man. She jumped up. "Come along in and see what it is this time."

They all went in, jostling and joking one another. Arty was standing up in the middle of the room looking at some much

G

blotted slips of paper. He appeared to be very well satisfied, and broke into a broad smile as he looked up at them all. Geisner and Ned found themselves side by side near the piano, over the keys of which Geisner softly ran his fingers with loving touch. "You are in luck to-night," he remarked to Ned. "You know Arty's signature, of course. He writes as ——," mentioning a well-known name.

"Of course I know. Is that him?" answered Ned, astonished. Verses which bore that signature were as familiar to thousands of western bushmen as their own names. "Who is Ford?" he added.

"Ford! Oh, Ford signs himself ——." Geisner mentioned another signature.

"Is he the one who draws in the *Scrutineer*?" demanded Ned, more astonished than ever.

"Yes; you know his work?"

Know his work! Had not every man in Australia laughed with his pitiless cartoons at the dignified magnates of Society and the utter rottenness of the powers that be?

"And what is Mr. Stratton?"

"A designer for a livelihood. An artist for love of Art. His wife is connected with the press. You wouldn't know her signature, but some of her work is very fine. George there is a journalist."

"But I thought the newspapers were against unions."

"Naturally they are. They are simply business enterprises, conducted in the ordinary commercial way for a profit, and therefore opposed to everything which threatens to interfere with profit-making. But the men and women who work on the press are very different. They are really wage-workers to begin with. Besides, they are often intelligent enough to sympathise thoroughly with the Labour movement in spite of the surroundings which tend to separate them from it. Certainly, the most popular exponents of Socialism are nearly all press writers."

"We are only just beginning to hear about these things in the bush," said Ned. "What is Socialism?"

"That's a big question," answered Geisner. "Socialism is——"

He was interrupted. "Silence, everybody!" cried Mrs. Stratton. "Listen to Arty's latest!"

CHAPTER VIII.

"Silence, everybody!" commanded Mrs. Stratton. "Listen to Arty's latest!"

She had gone up to him as they all came in. "Is it good?" she asked, looking over his arm. For answer he held the slips down to her and changed them as she read rapidly, only pausing occasionally to ask him what a more than usually obscured word was. There was hardly a line as originally written. Some words had been altered three and four times. Whole lines had been struck out and fresh lines inserted. In some verses nothing was left of the original but the measure and the rhymes.

"No wonder you were worrying if you had all this on your mind," she remarked, as he finished, smiling at him. "Let me read it to them."

He nodded. So when the buzz of conversation had stopped she read his verses to the others, holding his arm in the middle of the room, her sweet voice conveying their spirit as well as their words. And Arty stood by her, jubilant, listening proudly and happily to the rhythm of his new-born lines, for all the world like a young mother showing her new-born babe.

THE VISION OF LABOUR.*

There's a sound of lamentation 'mid the murmuring nocturne noises,
And an undertone of sadness, as from myriad human voices,
  And the harmony of heaven and the music of the spheres,
  And the ceaseless throb of Nature, and the flux and flow of years,
  Are rudely punctuated with the drip of human tears—
                    As Time rolls on!

Yet high above the beat of surf, and Ocean's deep resounding,
And high above the tempest roar of wind on wave rebounding,
  There's a burst of choral chanting, as of victors in a fight,
  And a battle hymn of triumph wakes the echoes of the night,
  And the shouts of heroes mingle with the shriekings of affright—
                    As Time rolls on!

---

* Kindly written by Mr. F. J. Broomfield for insertion here.

There's a gleam amid the darkness, and there's sight amid the blindness,
And the glow of hope is kindled by the breath of human kindness,
　　And a phosphorescent glimmer gilds the spaces of the gloom,
　　Like the sea-lights in the midnight, or the ghost-lights of the tomb,
　　Or the livid lamps of madness in the charnel-house of doom—
　　　　　　　　　　　　　　　　　As Time rolls on!

And amidst the weary wand'rers on the mountain crags belated
There's a hush of expectation, and the sobbings are abated,
　　For a word of hope is spoken by a prophet versed in pain,
　　Who tells of rugged pathways down to fields of golden-grain,
　　Where the sun is ever shining, and the skies their blessings rain—
　　　　　　　　　　　　　　　　　As Time rolls on!

Where the leafy chimes of gladness in the tree-tops aye are ringing,
Answering to the joyous chorus which the birds are ever singing;
　　Where the seas of yellow plenty toss with music in the wind;
　　Where the purple vines are laden, and the groves with fruit are lined;
　　Where all grief is but a mem'ry, and all pain is left behind—
　　　　　　　　　　　　　　　　　As Time rolls on!

But it lies beyond a desert 'cross which hosts of Death are marching,
And a hot sirocco wanders under skies all red and parching,
　　Lined with skeletons of armies through the centuries fierce and sere—
　　Bones of heroes and of sages marking Time's lapse year by year,
　　Unmoistened by the night-dews 'mid the solitudes of fear—
　　　　　　　　　　　　　　　　　As Time rolls on!

"Well done, Arty!" cried Ford. "I'd like to do a few 'thumb-nails' for that."

"Let me see it, please! Why don't you say 'rushes' for 'wanders' in the last verse, Arty?" asked George, reaching out his hand for the slips.

"Go away!" exclaimed Mrs. Stratton, holding them out of reach. "Can't you wait two minutes before you begin your sub-editing tricks? Josie, keep him in order!"

"He's a disgrace," replied Josie. "Don't pay any heed to him, Arty! They'll cut up your verses soon enough, and they're just lovely."

The others laughed, all talking at once, commending, criti-cising, comparing. Arty laughed and joked and quizzed, the liveliest of them all. Ned stared at him in astonishment. He seemed like somebody else. He discussed his own verses with a strange absence of egotism. Evidently he was used to standing fire.

"The metaphor in that third verse seems to me rather forced," said Stratton finally. "And I think George is right. 'Rushes' does sound better than 'wanders.' I like that 'rudely punctuated' line, but I think I'd go right through it again if it was mine."

"I think I will, too," answered Arty. "There are half-a-dozen alterations I want to make now. I'll touch it up to-morrow. It'll keep till then."

"That sort of stuff would keep for years if it wasn't for the *Scrutineer*," said Stratton. "Very few papers care to publish it nowadays."

"The *Scrutineer* is getting just like all the rest of them," commented George. "It's being run for money, only they make their pile as yet by playing to the gallery while the other papers play to the stalls and dress circle."

"It has done splendid work for the movement, just the same," said Ford. "Admit it's a business concern and that everybody growls at it, it's the only paper that dares knock things."

"It's a pity there isn't a good straight daily here," said Geisner. "That's the want all over the world. It seems impossible to get them, though."

"Why is it?" demanded Nellie. "It's the working people who buy the evening papers at least. Why shouldn't they buy straight papers sooner than these sheets of lies that are published?"

"I've seen it tried," answered Geisner, "but I never saw it done. The London *Star* is going as crooked as the others I'm told."

"I don't see why the unions shouldn't start dailies," insisted Nellie. "I suppose it costs a great deal but they could find the money if they tried hard."

"They haven't been able to run weeklies yet," said George, authoritatively. "And they never will until they get a system, much less run dailies."

"Why?" asked Ned. "You see," he continued, "our fellows are always talking of getting a paper. They get so wild sometimes when they read what the papers say about the unions and know what lies most of it is that I've seen them tear the papers up and dance a war-dance on the pieces."

"It's a long story to explain properly," said George. "Roughly it amounts to this that papers live on advertisements as well as on circulation and that advertisers are sharp business men who generally put the boycott on papers that talk straight. Then the cable matter, the telegraph matter, the news matter, is all procured by syndicates and companies and mutual arrangement between papers which cover the big cities between them and run on much the same lines, the solid capitalistic lines, you know. Then newspaper stock, when it pays, is valuable enough to make the holder a capitalist; when it doesn't pay he's still more under the thumb of the advertisers. The whole complex organisation of the press is against the movement and only those who're in it know how complex it is."

"Then there'll never be a Labour press, you think?"

"There will be a Labour press, I think," said George, turning Josie's hair round his fingers. "When the unions get a sound system it'll come."

"What do you mean by your sound system, George?" asked Geisner.

"Just this! That the unions themselves will publish their own papers, own their own plant, elect their own editors, paying for it all by levies or subscriptions. Then they can snap their fingers at advertisers and as every union man will get the union paper there'll be a circulation established at once. They can begin with monthlies and come down to weeklies. When they have learnt thoroughly the system, and when every colony has its weekly or weeklies, then they'll have a chance for dailies, not before."

"How would you get your daily?" enquired Geisner.

"Expand the weeklies into dailies simultaneously in every Australian capital," said George, waxing enthusiastic. "That would be a syndicate at once to co-operate on cablegrams and exchange intercolonial telegrams. Start with good machinery, get a subsidy of 6d. a month for a year and 3d. a month afterwards, if necessary, from the unions for every member, and then bring out a small-sized, neat, first-rate daily for a ha'penny, three-pence a week, and knock the penny evenings off their feet."

"A grand idea!" said Geisner, his eyes sparkling. "It sounds practical. It would revolutionise politics."

"Who'd own the papers, though, after the unions had subsidised them?" asked Ned, a little suspiciously.

"Why, the unions, of course," said George. "Who else? The unions would find the machinery and subsidise the papers on to their feet, for you couldn't very well get every man to take a daily. And the unions would elect trustees to hold them and manage them and an editor to edit each one and would be able to dismiss editors or trustees either if it wasn't being run straight. There'd be no profits because every penny made would go to make the papers better, there being no advertising income or very little. And every day, all over the continent, there would be printing hundreds of thousands of copies, each one advancing and defending the Labour movement."

" It's a grand idea," said Geisner again, " but who'd man the papers, George. Could Labour papers afford to pay managers and editors what the big dailies do ? "

" I don't know much about managers, but an editor who wouldn't give up a lot to push the Cause can't think much of it. Why, we're nothing but literary prostitutes," said George, energetically. " We just write now what we're told, selling our brains as women on the streets do their bodies, and some of us don't like it, some of the best too, as you know well, Geisner. My idea would be to pay a living salary, the same all round, to every man on the literary staff. That would be fair enough as an all round wage if it was low pay for editing and leader writing and fancy work. Many a good man would jump at it, to be free to write as he felt, and as for the rest of the staff by paying such a wage we'd get the tip-top pick of the ordinary men who do the pick-up work that generally isn't considered important but in my opinion is one the main points of a newspaper."

" Would you take what you call a ' living salary ' on such a paper ? " asked Connie.

" I'd take half if Josie——." He looked at her with tender confidence. The love-light was in her answering eyes. She nodded, proud of him.

" And they'd all publish my poetry ? " asked Arty.

" Would they ? They'd jump at it."

" Then when they come along, I'll write for a year for nothing."

" How about me ? " asked Ford, " Where do I come in ? "

" And me ? " asked Connie.

" You can all come in," laughed George. " Geisner shall do the political and get his editor ten years for sedition. Stratton will supply the mild fatherly sociological leaders. Mrs. Stratton shall prove that there can't be any true Art so long as we don't put the police on to everything that is ugly and repulsive. Nellie, here, shall blossom out as the Joan of Arc of women's rights, with a pen for a sword. And Arty we'll keep chained up on the premises and feed him with peppercorns when we want something particularly hot. Ford can retire to painting and pour his whole supply of bile out in one cartoon a week that we'll publish as a Saturday's supplement. Hawkins shall be our own correspondent who'll give the gentle squatter completely away in weekly instalments. And Josie and I'll slash the stuffing out of your 'copy' if you go writing three columns when there's only room for one. We'll boil down on our papers. Every line will be essence of extract. Don't you see how it's done already?"

"We see it," said Nellie, stifling a yawn. "The next thing is to get the unions to see it."

"That's so," retorted George, "so I'll give you my idea to do what you can with."

"We must go," said Nellie, getting up from her chair. "It must be after one and I'm tired."

"It's ten minutes to two," said Ford, having pulled out his watch.

"Why don't you stay all night, Nellie," asked Connie. "We can put Ned up, if he doesn't mind a shake-down. Then we can make a night of it. Geisner is off again on Monday or Tuesday."

"Tuesday," said Geisner, who had gone to the book-shelf again.

"Then I'll come Monday evening," said Nellie, for his tone was an invitation. "I feel like a walk, and I don't feel like talking much."

"All right," said Connie, not pressing, with true tact. "Will you come on Monday too, Ned?" she asked, moving to the door under the hangings with Nellie. Josie slipped quickly out on to the verandah with George.

"I must be off on Monday," replied Ned, regretfully. "There's a shed starts the next week, and I said I'd be up there to see that it shore union. I'm very sorry, but I really can't wait."

"I'm so sorry, too. But it can't be helped. Some other time, Ned." And nodding to him Connie went out with Nellie.

"So we shan't see you again," said Stratton, lighting a cigar at the gas. Ford had resumed his puffing at his black pipe and his seat on the table.

"Not soon at any rate," answered Ned. "I shall be in Western Queensland this time next week.

"The men are organising fast up that way, aren't they?" asked Stratton.

"They had to," said Ned. "What with the Chinese and the squatters doing as they liked and hating the sight of a white man, we'd all have been cleared out if we hadn't organised."

"Coloured labour has been the curse of Queensland all through," remarked Ford.

"I think it has made Queensland as progressive as it is, too," remarked Geisner. "It was a common danger for all the working classes, and from what I hear has given them unity of feeling earlier than that has been acquired in the south.

"Some of the old-fashioned union ideas that they have in Sydney want knocking badly," remarked Arty, smoking cheerfully.

"They'll be knocked safely enough if they want knocking," said Geisner. "There are failings in all organisation methods everywhere as well as in Sydney. New Unionism is only the Old Unionism reformed up to date. It'll need reforming itself as soon as it has done its work."

"Is the New Unionism really making its way in England, Geisner?" asked Stratton.

"I think so. A very intelligent man is working with two or three others to organise the London dock laborers on the new lines. He told me he was confident of success but didn't seem to realise all it meant. If those men can be organised and held together for a rise in wages it'll be the greatest strike that the world has seen yet. It will make New Unionism."

"Do you think it possible?" asked Ford. "I know a little about the London dockers. They are the drift of the English labour world. When a man is hopeless he goes to look for work at the docks."

"There is a chance if the move is made big enough to attract attention and if everything is prepared beforehand. If money can be found to keep a hundred thousand penniless men out while public opinion is forming they can win, I think. Even British public opinion can't yet defend fourpence an hour for casual work."

"Men will never think much until they are organised in some form or other," said Stratton. "Such a big move in London would boom the organisation of unskilled men everywhere."

"More plots!" cried Connie, coming back, followed by Nellie, waterproofed and hatted.

"It's raining," she went on, to Ned, "so I'll give you Harry's umbrella and let Ford take his waterproof. You'll have a damp row, Nellie. I suppose you know you've got to go across in George's boat, Ned."

Ned didn't know, but just then George's "Ahoy!" sounded from outside.

"We mustn't keep him waiting in the wet," exclaimed Nellie. She shook hands with them all, kissing Mrs. Stratton affectionately. Ned felt as he shook hands all round that he was leaving old friends.

"Come again," said Stratton, warmly. "We shall always be glad to see you."

"Indeed we shall," urged Connie. "Don't wait to come with Nellie. Come and see us any time you're in Sydney. Day or night, come and see if we're in and wait here if we're not."

Geisner and Stratton put on their hats and went with them down the verandah steps to the little stone quay below. Josie was standing there, in the drizzle, wrapped in a cloak and holding a lantern. In a rowing skiff, alongside, was George; another lantern was set on one of the seats.

"Are you busy to-morrow afternoon?" asked Geisner of Ned, as Nellie was being handed in, after having kissed Josie.

"Not particularly," answered Ned.

"Then you might meet me in front of the picture gallery between one and two, and we can have a quiet chat."

"All aboard!" shouted George.

"I'll be there," answered Ned, shaking hands again with Geisner and Stratton and with Josie, noticing that that young lady had a very warm clinging hand.

"Good-bye! Good-bye! Good-bye!" From the three on shore.

"Good-bye! Good-bye! Good-bye!" From the three in the boat as George shoved off.

"Good-bye!" cried Connie's clear voice from the verandah. "Put up the umbrella, Ned!"

Ned obediently put up the umbrella she had lent him, overcoming his objections by pointing out that it would keep Nellie's hat from being spoiled. Then George's oars began to dip into the water, and they turned their backs to the pleasant home and faced out into the wind and wet.

The last sound that came to them was a long melodious cry that Josie sent across the water to George, a loving "Good-bye!" that plainly meant "Come back!"

CHAPTER IX.

"THIS IS SOCIALISM!"

THE working of George's oars and the rippling of water on the bow were all that broke the silence as the skiff moved across the harbour. Suddenly Ned lost sight of the swinging lantern that Josie had held at the little landing stairs and without it could not distinguish the house they had left. Here and there behind them were lights of various kinds and sizes, shining blurred through the faint drizzle. He saw similar lights in front and on either hand. Yet the darkness was so deep now that but for the lantern on the fore thwarts he could not have seen George at all. There were no sounds but those of their rowing.

Nellie sat erect, half hidden in the umbrella Ned held over her. George pulled a long sweeping stroke, bringing it up with a jerk that made the rowlocks sound sharply. When he bent back they could feel the light boat lift under them. He looked round now and then, steering himself by some means inscrutable to the others, who without him would have been lost on this watery waste.

All at once George stopped rowing. "Listen!" he exclaimed.

There was a swishing sound as of some great body rushing swiftly through the water near them. It ceased suddenly; then as suddenly sounded again.

"Sharks about," remarked George, in a matter-of-fact tone, rowing again with the same long sweeping stroke as before.

Nellie did not stir. She was used to such incidents, evidently. But Ned had never before been so close to the sea-tigers and felt a creepy sensation. He would much rather, he thought, be thirty-five miles from water with a lame horse than in the company of sharks on a dark wet night in the middle of Sydney harbour.

"Are they dangerous?" he asked, with an attempt at being indifferent.

"I suppose so," answered George, in a casual way. "If one of them happened to strike the boat it might be unpleasant. But they're terrible cowards."

"Are there many?"

"In the harbour? Oh, yes, it swarms with them. You see that light," and George pointed to the left, where one of the lights had detached itself from the rest and shone close at hand. "That's on a little island and in the convict days hard cases were put on it—I think it was on that island or one like it—and the sharks saw that none of them swam ashore."

"They seem to have used those convicts pretty rough," remarked Ned.

"Rough's no name," said George after a few minutes. "It was as vile and unholy a thing, that System, as anything they have in Russia. A friend of mine has been working the thing up for years, and is going to start writing it up soon. You must read it when it comes out. It'll make you hate everything that has a brass button on. I tell you, this precious Law of ours has something to answer for. It was awful, horrible, and it's not all gone yet, as I know."

He rowed on for a space in silence.

"There's one story I think of, sometimes, rowing across here and hearing the sharks splash. At one place they used to feed the dead convicts to the sharks so as to keep them swarming about, and once they flung one in before he was dead."

Nellie gave a stifled exclamation. Ned was too horror-struck to answer; above the clicking of the oars in the rowlocks he fancied he could hear the swish of the savage sharks rushing through the water at their living prey. He was not sorry when George again rested on his oars to say:

"Will you land at the point this time, Nellie?"

"Yes, I think so."

"Well, here you are! We've had a pretty fastish pull over, considering."

Two or three more strokes brought them to a flight of low stone steps. By the light of the lantern Ned and Nellie were disembarked.

"I won't keep you talking in the rain, Nellie," said George. "I'm sorry you are going away so soon, Hawkins. We could have given you some boating if you had time. You might come out to-morrow afternoon—that's this afternoon—if you haven't anything better to do."

"I'm very much obliged, but I was going to meet Mr. Geisner."

"That settles it then. Anybody would sooner have a yarn

with Geisner. We'll fix some boating when you're down again. You'll come again. Won't he, Nellie? Good-bye and a pleasant trip! Good-bye, Nellie." And having shaken hands by dint of much arm stretching, George pushed his boat away from the steps and pulled away.

Nellie stood for a minute watching the lantern till it turned the point, heading eastward. Then straightening the waterproof over her dress she took Ned's arm and they walked off.

"He's a nice sort of chap," remarked Ned, referring to George.

"Yes, he's a great oarsman. He rows over to see Josie. Mrs. Stratton calls them Hero and Leander."

"Why? Who were they?"

"Oh! Leander was Hero's sweetheart and used to swim across the water to her so that nobody should see him."

"They're to be married, I suppose?"

"Yes, next month."

"Those Strattons are immense—what's that noise, Nellie?" he interrupted himself. A strange groaning from close at hand had startled him.

"Somebody asleep, I suppose," she answered, more accustomed to the Sydney parks. But she stopped while, under the umbrella, he struck a match with a bushman's craft.

By the light of the match they saw a great hollow in the rocks that bordered on one side the gravelled footway. The rocks leaned out and took in part of the path, which widened underneath. Sheltered thus from the rain and wind a number of men were sleeping, outcast, some in blankets, some lying on the bare ground. The sound they had heard was a medley of deep breathing and snoring. It was but a glimpse they caught as the match flared up for a minute. It went out and they could see nothing, only the faint outline of path and rock. They could hear still the moaning sound that had attracted them.

They walked on without speaking for a time.

"How did you know the Strattons?" resumed Ned.

"At the picture gallery one Sunday. She was writing some article defending their being opened on the 'Sawbath' and I had gone in. I like pictures—some pictures, you know. We got talking and she showed me things in the pictures I'd never dreamed of before. We stayed there till closing time and she asked me to come to see her.

"She's immense!"

"I'm so glad you like her. Everybody does."

"Has she any children?"

"Four. Such pretty children. She and her husband are so fond of each other. I can't imagine people being happier."

"I suppose they're pretty well off, Nellie?"

"No, I don't think they're what you'd call well off. They're comfortable, you know. She has to put on a sort of style, she's told me, to take the edge off her ideas. If you wear low-necked dress you can talk the wildest things, she says, and I think it's so. That's business with her. She has to mix with low-necked people a little. It's her work."

"Does she have to work?"

"No. I suppose not. But I think she prefers to. She never writes what she doesn't think, which is pleasanter than most writers find it. Then I should think she'd feel more independent, however much she cares for her husband. And then she has a little girl who's wonderfully clever at colours, so she's saving up to send her to Paris when she's old enough. They think she'll become a great painter— the little girl, I mean."

"What does that Josie do?"

"She's a music-teacher."

"They're all clever, aren't they?"

"Yes. But, of course, they've all had a chance. Ford is the most remarkable. He never got any education to speak of until he was over 20. The Strattons have been born as they live now. They've had some hard times, I think, from what they say now and then, but they've always been what's called 'cultured.' Everybody ought to be as they are."

"I think so, too, Nellie, but can everybody be as well off as they are?"

"They're not well off, I told you, Ned. If they spend £5 a week it's as much as they do. Of course that sounds a lot, but since if things were divided fairly everybody who works ought to get far more, it's not extravagant riches. Wine and water doesn't cost more than beer, and the things they've got were picked up bit by bit. It's what they've got and the way it's put that looks so nice. There's nothing but what's pretty, and she is always adding something or other. She idolises Art and worships everything that's beautiful.

"Do you think it's really that sort of thing that makes people better?" said Ned.

"How can it help making them better if their hearts are good? When what is ugly and miserable in life jars on one at every turn because one loves so what is harmonious and beautiful, there seems to me to be only one of two things to be done, either to shut your eyes to others and become a selfish egotist or to try with all your strength to bring a beautiful life to others. I'm speaking, of course, particularly of people like the Strattons. But I think that hatred of what is repulsive is a big influence with all of us."

"You mean of dirty streets, stuffy houses and sloppy clothes?"

"Oh! More than that. Of ugly lives, of ugly thoughts, of others, and ourselves perhaps, just existing like working bullocks when we might be so happy, of living being generally such a hateful thing when it might be so sweet!"

"I suppose the Strattons are happy?"

"Not as happy as everybody might be if the world was right. They understand music and pictures and colouring and books. He reads science a lot and paints—funny mixture, isn't it?—and she teaches the children a great deal. They go boating together. They both work at what they like and are clever enough to be fairly sure of plenty to do. They have friends who take an interest in the things that interest them and their children are little angels. They aren't short of money for anything they need because they really live simply and so have plenty to spend. And, then, they are such kind people. She has a way with her that makes you feel better no matter how miserable you've been. That's happiness, I think, as far as it goes. But she feels much as I do about children. She is so afraid that they will not be happy and blames herself for being selfish because other people's children never have any happiness and would do anything to alter things so that it would be different. Still, of course, they have a happy life as far as the life itself goes. I think, the way they live, they must both feel as if they were each better and knew more and cared for each other more the older they get."

"It must be very pleasant," said Ned, after a pause. They had reached the higher ground and were passing under branches from which the rain-drops, collected, fell in great splashes on the umbrella.

"Yes," said Nellie, after another pause.

"Do they go to church?" Ned began again.

"I never heard them say they did."

"They're not religious then ?"

"What do you call religious ?"

"They don't believe anything, do they ?"

"I think they believe a very great deal. Far more than most people who pretend to believe and don't," answered Nellie. There was a longer pause. Then :

"What do they believe ?"

"In Socialism."

"Socialism ! Look here, Nellie ! What is Socialism ?"

They had passed the fig-tree avenue, turning off it by a cross path, where a stone fountain loomed up gigantic in the gloom and where they could hear a rushing torrent splashing. They were in the region of gas-lamps again. Nellie walked along with a swiftness that taxed Ned to keep abreast of her. She seemed to him to take pleasure in the wet night. In spite of their long walking of the day before and the lateness of the hour she had still the same springy step and upright carriage. As they passed under the lamps he saw her face, damp with the rain, but flushed with exercise, her eyes gleaming, her mouth open a little. He would have liked to have taken her hand as she steadied the umbrella, walking arm in arm with him, but he did not dare. She was not that sort of girl.

He had felt a proud sense of proprietorship in her at the Strattons'. It had pleased him to see how they all liked her, but pleased him most of all that she could talk as an equal with these people, to him so brilliant and clever. The faint thought of her which had been unconsciously with him for years began to take shape. How pleasant it would be to be like the Strattons, to live with Nellie always, and have friends to come and see them on a Saturday night ! How a man would work for a home like that, so full of music, so full of song, so full of beauty, so full of the thoughts which make men like unto gods and of the love which makes gods like unto men ! Why should not this be for him as well as for others when, as Nellie said, it really cost only what rich people thought poverty, and far less than the workingman's share if things were fairly divided ? And why should it not be for his mates as well as for himself ? And why, most of all, why not for the wretched dwellers in the slums of Sydney, the weary women, the puny children, the imbruted men ? For the first time in his life, he coveted such things with a righteous covetousness, without hating those who had them, recognising without words that to have and to appreciate such a life was to desire ceaselessly to bring it within the reach of every human being. He could not see how this was all to come about. He would have followed blindly anybody who played the Marseillaise as Geisner did. He was ready to echo any ringing thought that appealed to him as good and noble. But he did not know. He could see that in the idea called by Mrs. Stratton "the Cause" there was an understood meaning which fitted his aspirations and his desires. He had gathered, his narrow bigotry washed from him, that between each and all of those whom he had just left there was a bond of union, a common thought, an accepted way. He had met them strangers, and had left them warm friends. The cartoonist, white with rage at the memory of the high rectory wall that shut the beautiful from the English poor; the gloomy poet whose verses rang still in his ears and would live in his heart for ever ; the gray-eyed woman who idolised Art, as Nellie said, and fanned still the fire in which her nearest kin had perished; the pressman, with his dream of a free press that would not serve the money power; the painter to whom the chiselled stone spoke; the pretty girl who had been cradled amid barricades ; the quiet musician for whom the bitterness of death was past, born leader of men, commissioned by that which stamped him what he was ; the dressmaking girl, passionately pleading the cause of Woman ; even himself, drinking in this new life as the ground sucks up the rain after a drought; between them all there was a bond—"the Cause." What was this Cause ? To break down all walls, to overthrow all wrong, to destroy the ugliness of human life, to free thought, to elevate Art, to purify Love, to lift mankind higher, to give equality to women, to—to—he did not see exactly where he himself came in—all this was the Cause. Yet he did not quite understand it, just the same. Nor did he know how it was all to come about. But he intended to find out. So he asked Nellie what the Strattons believed, feeling instinctively that there must be belief in something.

" What do they believe ?" he had asked.

" In Socialism," Nellie had answered.

" Socialism ! Look here, Nellie ! What is Socialism ?" he had exclaimed.

They neared a lamp, shining mistily in the drizzle. Close at hand was a seat, facing the grass. In the dim light was what

H

looked like a bundle of rags thrown over the seat and trailing to the ground. Nellie stopped. It was a woman, sleeping.

There, under a leafy tree, whose flat branches shielded her somewhat from the rain, slept the outcast. She had dozed off into slumber, sitting there alone. She was not lying, only sitting there, her arm flung over the back of the seat, her head fallen on her shoulder, her face upturned to the pitying night. It was the face of a street-walker, bloated and purplish, the poor pretence of colour gone, the haggard lines showing, all the awful life of her stamped upon it; yet in the lamplight, upturned in its helplessness, sealed with the sleep that had come at last to her, sore-footed, as softly as it might have come to a little baby falling asleep amid its play, there enhaloed it the incarnation of triumphant suffering. On the swollen cheeks of the homeless woman the night had shed its tears of rain. There amid the wind and wet, in the darkness, alone and weary, shame-worn and sin-sodden, scorned by the Pharisee, despised by the vicious, the harlot slept and forgot. Calm as death itself was the face of her. Softly and gently she breathed, as does the heavy-eyed bride whose head the groom's arm pillows. Nature, our Mother Nature, had taken her child for a moment to her breast and the outcast rested there awhile, all sorrows forgotten, all desires stilled, all wrongs and sins and shame obscured and blotted out. She envied none. Equal was she with all. Great indeed is Sleep, which teaches us day by day that none is greater in God's sight than another, that as we all came equal and naked from the Unknown so naked and equal we shall all pass on to the Unknown again, that this life is but as a phantasy in which it is well to so play one's part that nightly one falls asleep without fear and meets at last the great sleep without regret!

But, oh, the suffering that had earned for this forsaken sister the sweet sleep she slept! Oh, the ceaseless offering of this sin-stained body, the contumelious jeers she met, the vain search, through streets and avenues this wild night, for the blind lust that would give her shelter and food! Oh, the efforts to beg, the saints who would not wait to listen to such a one, the sinners who were as penniless! Oh, the shivering fits that drove her to walk, walk, walk, when the midnight hours brought silence and solitude, the cramps that racked her poor limbs when she laid down, exhausted, in dripping garments, on the hard park seats, the aching feet that refused at last the ceaseless tramping in their soaked and broken shoes! Oh, the thoughts of her, the memories, the dreams of what had been and what might be, as she heard the long hours toll themselves away! Oh, the bitter tears she may have shed, and the bitter words she may have uttered, and the bitter hate that may have overflowed in her against that vague something we call Society! And, oh, the sweet sleep that fell upon her at last, unexpected—as the end of our waiting shall come, when we weary most—falling upon her as the dew falls, closing her weary eye-lids, giving her peace and rest and strength to meet another to-day!

Ned stopped when Nellie did, of course. Neither spoke. A sense of great shame crept upon him, he hardly knew why. He could not look at Nellie. He wished she would move on and leave him there. The silent pathos of that sleeping face cried to him. Lowest of the low, filthy, diseased probably, her face as though the womanliness had been stamped from her by a brutal heel of iron, she yet was a woman. This outcast and Nellie were of one sex; they all three were of one Humanity.

A few hours before and he would have passed her by with a glance of contemptuous pity. But now, he seemed to have another sense awakened in him, the sense that feels, that sympathises in the heart with the hearts of others. It was as though he himself slept there. It was as though he understood this poor sister, whom the merciful called erring, and the merciless wicked, but of whom the just could only say: she is what we in her place must have become. She was an atom of the world of suffering by which his heart was being wrung. She was one upon whom the Wrong fell crushingly, and she was helpless to resist it. He was strong, and he had given no thought to those who suffered as this poor outcast suffered. He had lived his own narrow life, and shared the sin, and assisted Wrong by with-holding his full strength from the side of Right. And upon him was the responsibility for this woman. He, individually, had kicked her into the streets, and dragged her footsore through the parks, and cast her there to bear testimony against him to every passer-by; he, because he had not fought, whole-souled, with those who seek to shatter the something which, without quite understanding, he knew had kicked and dragged and outcasted this woman sleeping here. Ned always took his lessons personally. It was, perhaps, a touch in him of the morbidity that seizes so often the wandering Arabs of the western plains.

Suddenly Nellie let go the umbrella, leaving it in his hand. She bent forward, stooped down. The strong young face, proud and sad, so pure in its maiden strength, glowing with passionate emotion, was laid softly against that bruised and battered figure-head of shipwrecked womanhood; Nellie had kissed the sleeping harlot on the cheek.

Then, standing erect, she turned to Ned, her lips parted, her face quivering, her eyes flashing, her hand resting gently on the unconscious woman.

"You want to know what Socialism is," she said, in a low, trembling voice. "This is Socialism." And bending down again she kissed the poor outcast harlot a second time. The woman never stirred. Seizing Ned's arm Nellie drew him away, breaking into a pace that made him respect her prowess as a walker ever after.

Until they reached home neither spoke. Nellie looked sterner than ever. Ned was in a whirl of mental excitement. Perhaps if he had been less natural himself the girl's passionate declaration of fellowship with all who are wronged and oppressed—for so he interpreted it by the light of his own thoughts—might have struck him as a little bit stagey. Being natural, he took it for what it was, an outburst of genuine feeling. But if Nellie had really designed it she could not have influenced him more deeply. Their instincts, much akin, had reached the same idea by different ways. Her spontaneous expression of feeling had fitted in her mind to the Cause which possessed her as a religious idea, and had capped in him the human yearnings which were leading him to the same goal. And so, what with his overflowing sympathy for the sleeping outcast, and his swelling love for Nellie, and the chaotic excitement roused in him by all he had seen and heard during the preceding hours, that kiss burnt itself into his imagination and became to him all his life through as a sacred symbol. From that moment his life was forecast—a woman tempted him and he ate.

For that kiss Ned gave himself into the hands of a fanaticism, eating of the fruit of the Tree of Knowledge, striving to become as a god knowing good from evil. For that kiss he became one of those who have the Desire which they know can never be satiated in them. For that kiss he surrendered himself wholly to the faith of her whose face was sad and stern-mouthed, content ever after if with his whole life he could fill one of the ruts that delay the coming of Liberty's triumphal car. To that turning-point in his life, other events led up, certainly, events which of themselves would likely have forced him to stretch out his hand and pluck and eat. It is always that way with life changes. Nothing depends altogether upon one isolated act. But looking back in after years, when the lesser influences had cleared away in the magic glass of Time, Ned could ever see, clear and distinct as though it were but a minute since, the stern red lips of that pale, proud, passionate face pressed in trembling sisterliness to the harlot's purple cheek.

As she put the key in the door Nellie turned to Ned, speaking for the first time:

" You'd better ask Geisner about Socialism when you see him to-morrow—I mean this afternoon."

Ned nodded without speaking. Silently he let her get his candle, and followed her up the stairs to the room concerning which the card was displayed in the window below. She turned down the bedclothes, then held out her hand.

"Good-night or good-morning, whichever it is!" she said, smiling at him. "You can sleep as long as you like Sunday morning, you know. If you want anything knock the wall there."

" Good-night, Nellie !" he answered, slowly, holding her fingers in his. Then, before she could stop him, he lifted her hand to his lips. She did not snatch it away but looked him straight in the eyes, without speaking; then went out, shutting the door softly behind her. She understood him partly; not altogether, then.

Left alone in the scantily-furnished room, Ned undressed, blew out the candle and went to bed. But until he fell asleep, and in his dreams afterwards, he still saw Nellie bending down over a purpled, sin-stained face, and heard her sweet voice whisper tremblingly:

"This is Socialism !"

CHAPTER X.

WHERE THE EVIL REALLY LIES.

GEISNER was betimes at his appointment in the Domain. It was still the dinner hour, and though it was Sunday there were few to be seen on the grass or along the paths. So Ned saw him afar off, pacing up and down before the Art Gallery like a sentinel, an ordinary looking man to a casual passer-by, one whom you might pass a hundred times on the street and not notice particularly, even though he was ugly. Perhaps because of it.

Neither of them cared to stroll about, they found. Accordingly they settled down at a shady patch on a grassy slope, the ground already dried from the night's rain by the fierce summer sunshine of the morning. Stretched out there, Geisner proceeded to roll a cigarette and Ned to chew a blade of grass.

Below them a family were picnicking quietly. Dinner was over; pieces of paper littered the ground by an open basket. The father lay on his side smoking, the mother was giving a nursing baby its dinner, one little child lay asleep under a tree and two or three more were playing near at hand.

"How do you mean?"

"Well, this way. The wealth production of thickly settled countries is proportionately greater than that of thinly settled countries. Of course, there would be a limit somewhere, but so far no country we know of has reached it."

"You don't mean that a man working in England or France earns more than a man working in Australia?" demanded Ned, sitting up. "I thought it was the other way."

"I don't mean he gets more but I certainly mean that he produces more. The appliances are so much better, and the sub-division of labour, that is each man doing one thing until he becomes an expert at it, is carried so much further by very virtue of the thicker population."

"That's to say they have things fixed so that they crush more to the ton of work."

"About that. Taking the people all round, and throwing in kings and queens and aristocrats and the parsons that Ford loves so, every average Englishman produced yesterday more wealth—more boots, more tools, more cloth, more anything of value—than every average Australian. And every average Belgian produced yesterday, or any day, more wealth than every average Englishman. These are facts you can see in any collection of statistics. The conservative political economists don't deny them; they only try to explain them away."

"But how does it come? Men produce more there than we do here and earn less. How's that?"

"Simply because they're robbed more.

"Look here, Mr. Geisner!" said Ned, gathering his knees into his arms. "That's what I want to know. I know we're robbed. Any fool can see that those who work the least or don't work at all get pretty much everything, but I don't quite see how they get it. We're only just beginning to think of these things in the bush, and we don't know much yet. We only know there's something wrong, but we don't know what to do except to get a union and keep up wages."

"That's the first step, to get a union," said Geisner. "But unless unionists understand what it's all about they'll only be able to keep up wages for a little while. You see, Ned, this is the difficulty: a man can't work when he likes."

"A man can't work when he likes!"

"No; not the average man and it's the average man who has to be considered always. Let's take a case—yourself. You want to live. Accordingly, you must work, that is you must produce what you need to live upon from the earth by your labour or you must produce something which other working men need and these other men will give you in exchange for it something they have produced which you need. Now, let's imagine you wanting to live and desiring to start to-morrow morning to work for your living. What would you do?"

"I suppose I'd ask somebody."

"Ask what?"

"Well, I'd have to ask somebody or other if there was any work."

"What work?"

"Well, if they had a job they wanted me to do, that I could do, you know."

"I don't 'you know' anything. I want you to explain. Now what would you say?"

"Oh! I'd kind of go down to the hut likely and see the boys if 'twas any use staying about and then, perhaps, or it might be before I went to the hut, that would be all according, I'd see the boss and sound him."

"How sound him?"

"Well, that would be all according, too. If I was pretty flush and didn't care a stiver whether I got a job or not I'd waltz right up to him just as I might to you to ask the time, and if he came any of his law-de-dah squatter funny business on me I'd give him the straight wire, I promise you. But it stands to reason—don't it?—that if I've been out of graft for months and haven't got any money and my horses are played out and there's no chance of another job, well, I'm going to humor him a bit more than I'd like to, ain't I?"

Geisner laughed "You see it all right, Ned. Suppose the first man you sounded said no?"

"I'd try another."

"And if the other said no?"

"Well, I'd have to keep on trying."

"And you'd get more inclined to humour the boss every time you had to try again."

"Naturally. That's how they get at us. No man's a crawler who's sure of a job."

"Then you might take lower wages, and work longer hours, after you'd been out of work till you'd got thoroughly disheartened than you would now."

"I wouldn't. Not while there was—I might have to, though I say I'd starve or steal first. There are lots who do, I suppose."

"Lots who wouldn't dream of doing it if there was plenty of work to be had?"

"Of course. Who'd work for less than another man if he needn't, easily? There isn't one man in a thousand who'd do another fellow out of a job for pure meanness. The chaps who do the mischief are those who're so afraid the boss'll sack them, and that another boss won't take them on, that they'd almost lick his boots if they thought it would please him."

"Now we're coming to it. It is work being hard to get that lowers wages and increases hours, and makes a workman, or work-woman either, put up with what nobody would dream of putting up with if they could help it?"

"Of course that's it."

"Now! Is the day's work done by a poorly-paid man less than that done by a highly-paid one?"

"No," answered Ned. "I've seen it more," he added.

"How's that?"

"Well, when a man's anxious to keep a job and afraid he won't get another he'll often nearly break his back bullocking at it. When he feels independent he'll do the fair thing, and sling the job up if the boss tries to bullock him. It's the same thing all along the line, it seems to me. When you can get work easily you get higher wages, shorter hours, some civility, and only do the fair thing. When you can't, wages come down, hours spin out, the boss puts on side, and you've got to work like a nigger."

"Then, roughly speaking, the amount of work you do hasn't got very much to do with the pay you get for it?"

"I suppose not. It's not likely a man ever gets more than his work is worth. The boss would soon knock him off and let the work slide. I suppose a man is only put on to a job when it's worth more than the boss has to pay for getting it done. And I reckon the less a man can be got to do it for the better it is for the fellow who gets the job done."

"That's it. Suppose you can't get work no matter how often you ask, what do you do?"

"Keep on looking. Live on rations that the squatters serve out to keep men travelling the country so they can get them if they want them or on mutton you manage to pick up or else your mates give you a bit of a lift. You must live. It's beg or steal or else starve."

"I think men and women are beginning to starve in Australia. Many are quite starving in the old countries and have been starving longer. That's why the workers are somewhat worse off there than here. The gold rushes gave things a lift here and raised the condition of the workers wonderfully. But the same causes that have been working in the old countries have been working here and are fast beating things down again."

"That reminds me of Paris," remarked Geisner, watching them.

"I suppose you are French?"

"No. I've been in France considerably."

"It's a beautiful country, isn't it?"

"All countries are beautiful in their way. Sydney Harbour is the most beautiful spot I know. I hardly know where I was born. In Germany I think."

"Things are pretty bad in those old countries, aren't they?"

"Things are pretty bad everywhere, aren't they?"

"Yes," answered Ned, meditatively. "They seem to be. They're bad enough here and this is called the workingman's paradise. But a good many seem glad enough to get here from other countries. It must be pretty bad where they come from."

"So it is. It is what it is here, only more so. It is what things will be in a very few years here if you let them go on. As a matter of fact the old countries ought to be more prosperous than the new ones, but our social system has become so ill-balanced that in the countries where there are most people at work those people are more wretched than where there are comparatively few working."

"A gold rush!" exclaimed Ned. "That's the thing to make wages rise, particularly if it's a poor man's digging."

"What's that?"

"Don't you know? An alluvial field is where you can dig out gold with a pick and shovel and wash it out with a pannikin. You don't want any machines, and everybody digs for himself, or mates with other fellows, and if you want a man to do a job you've got to pay him as much as he could dig for himself in the time."

"I see. 'Poor man's digging,' you call it, eh? You don't think much of a reefing field?"

"Of course not," answered Ned, smiling at this apparent ignorance. "Reefing fields employ men, and give a market, and a few strike it, but the average man, as you call him, hasn't got a chance. It takes so much capital for sinking and pumping and crushing, and things of that sort, that companies have to be formed outside, and the miners mostly work just for wages. And when a reefing field gets old it's as bad as a coal-field or a factory town. You're just working for other people, and the bigger the dividends the more anxious they seem to be to knock wages."

"Then this is what it all amounts to. If you aren't working for yourself you're working for somebody else who pays as little as he can for as much as he can get, and rubs the dirt in, often, into the bargain."

"A man may not earn wages working for himself," answered Ned.

"You mean he may not produce for himself as much value as men around him receive in wages for working for somebody else.

Of course! You might starve working on Mount Morgan or Broken Hill with a pick and pannikin, though on an alluvial your pick and pannikin would be all you needed. That's the kernel of the industrial question. Industry has passed out of the alluvial stage into the reefing. We must have machinery to work with or we may all starve in the midst of mountains of gold."

"I don't quite see how you mean."

"Just this. If every man could take his pick on his shoulders and work for himself with reasonable prospect of what he regarded as a sufficient return he wouldn't ask anybody else for work."

"Not often, anyway."

"But if he cannot so work for himself he must go round looking for the man who has a shaft or a pump or a stamping mill and must bargain for the owner of machinery to take the product of his labour for a certain price which of course isn't it's full value at all but the price at which, owing to his necessities, he is compelled to sell his labour.

"Things are getting so in all branches of industry, in squatting, in manufacturing, in trading, in ship-owning, in everything, that it takes more and more capital for a man to start for himself. This is a necessary result of increasing mechanical powers and of the economy of big businesses as compared to small ones. For example, if there is a great advantage in machine clipping, as a friend of mine who understands such things tells me there is, all wool will some day be clipped that way. Then, the market being full of superior machine-clipped wool, hand-clipped would have little sale and only at lower price. The result would be that all wool-growers must have machines as part of their capital, an additional expense, making it still harder for a man with a small capital to start wool-growing.

"All this means," continued Geisner, "that more and more go round asking for work as what we call civilisation progresses, that is as population increases and the industrial life becomes more complicated. I don't mean in Australia only. I'm speaking generally. They can only work when another man thinks he can make a profit out of them, and there are so many eager to be made a profit on that the owner of the machine has it pretty well his own way. This system operates for the extension of its own worst feature, the degradation of the working masses. You see, such a vast amount of industrial work can be held over that employers, sometimes unconsciously, sometimes deliberately, hold work over until times are what they call 'more suitable,' that is when they can make bigger profits by paying less in wages. This has a tendency to constantly keep wages down, besides affording a stock argument against unionist agitations for high wages. But, in any case, the fits of industrial briskness and idleness which occur in all countries are enough to account for the continual tendency of wages to a bare living amount for those working, as many of those not working stand hungrily by to jump into their places if they get rebellious or attempt to prevent wages going down."

"That's just how it is," said Ned. "But we're going to get all men into unions, and then we'll keep wages up."

"Yes; there is no doubt that unions help to keep wages up. But, you see, so long as industrial operations can be contracted, and men thrown out of work, practically at the pleasure of those who employ, complete unionism is almost impracticable if employers once begin to act in concert. Besides, the unemployed are a menace to unionism always. Workmen can never realise that too strongly."

"What are we to do then if we can't get what we want by unionism?"

"How can you get what you want by unionism? The evil is in having to ask another man for work at all—in not being able to work for yourself. Unionism, so far, only says that if this other man does employ you he shall not take advantage of your necessity by paying you less than the wage which you and your fellow workmen have agreed to hold out for. You must destroy the system which makes it necessary for you to work for the profit of another man, and keeps you idle when he can't get a profit out of you. The whole wage system must be utterly done away with." And Geisner rolled another cigarette as though it was the simplest idea in the world.

"How? What will you do instead?"

"How! By having men understand what it is, and how there can be no true happiness and no true manliness until they over-throw it! By preaching socialistic ideas wherever men will listen, and forcing them upon them where they do not want to listen! By appealing to all that is highest in men and to all that is lowest—to their humanity and to their selfishness! By the help of the education which is becoming general, by the help of art and of science, and even of this vile press that is the incar-

nation of all the villainies of the present system! By living for
the Cause, and by being ready to die for it! By having only one
idea: to destroy the Old Order and to bring in the New!" Geisner
spoke quietly, but in his voice was a ring that made Ned's blood
tingle in his veins.

"What do you call the Old Order?" asked Ned, lying back and
looking up at the sky through the leaves.

"Everything that is inhuman, everything that is brutal,
everything which relies upon the taking advantage of a
fellow-man, which leads to the degradation of a woman or
to the unhappiness of a child. Everything which is opposed
to the idea of human brotherhood. That which produces
scrofulous kings, and lying priests, and greasy millionaires,
and powdered prostitutes, and ferret-faced thieves. That
which makes the honest man a pauper and a beggar, and
sets the clever swindler in parliament. That which makes you
what you are at 24, a man without a home, with hardly a future.
That which tries to condemn those who protest to starvation, and
will yet condemn them to prison here in Australia as readily as
ever it did in Europe or Russia.

"You want to know what makes this," he went on. "Well, it
is what we have been talking of, that you should have to ask
another man for work so that you may live. It doesn't matter
what part of the world you are in or under what form of government, it is the same everywhere. So long as you can't work
without asking another man for permission you are exposed to
all the ills that attend poverty and all the tyranny that attends
inordinate power and luxury. When you grip that, you understand half the industrial problem."

"And the other half, what's that?" asked Ned.

"This, that we've got over the alluvial days, if they ever did
exist industrially, and are in the thick of reefing fields and
syndicates. So much machinery is necessary now that no
ordinary single man can own the machinery he needs to work
with as he could in the old pick and pannikin days. This makes
him the slave of those who do own it for he has to work to live.
Men must all join together to own the machinery they must have
to work with, so that they may use it to produce what they need
as they need it and will not have to starve unless some private
owner of machinery can make a profit out of their labour. They
must pull together as mates and work for what is best for all,

not each man be trying only for himself and caring little whether others live or die. We must own all machinery co-operatively and work it co-operatively."

"How about the land? Oughtn't that to be owned by the people too?"

"Why, of course. The land is a part of the machinery of production. Henry George separates it but in reality it is simply *one* of the means by which we live, nowadays, for no man but an absolute savage can support himself on the bare land. In the free land days which Henry George quotes, the free old German days when we were all barbarians and didn't know what a thief was, not only was the land held in common but the cattle also. Without its cattle a German tribe would have starved on the richest pastureland in Europe, and without our machinery we would starve were the land nationalised to-morrow. At least I think so. George's is a scheme by which it is proposed to make employers compete so fiercely among one another that the workman will have it all his own way. It works this way. You tax the landowner until it doesn't pay him to have unused land. He must either throw it up or get it used somehow and the demand for labour thus created is to lift wages and put the actual workers in what George evidently considers a satisfactory position. That's George's Single Tax scheme."

"You don't agree with it?" asked Ned.

"I am a Socialist. Between all Socialists and all who favour competition in industry, as the Single Tax scheme does, there is a great gulf fixed. Economically, I consider it fallacious, for the very simple reason that capitalism continues competition, not to selling at cost price but to monopoly, and I have never met an intelligent Single Taxer, and I have met many, who could logically deny the possibility of the Single Tax breaking down in an extension of this very monopoly power. Roughly, machinery is necessary to work land most profitably, profitably enough even to get a living off it. Suppose machine holders, that is capitalists, extend their organisation a little and 'pool' their interests as land users, that is refuse to compete against one another for the use of land! Nellie was telling me that at one land sale on the Darling Downs in Queensland the selectors ab ut arranged matters among themselves beforehand. The land sold, owing to its situation, was only valuable to those having other land near and so was all knocked down at the upset price though worth four times as much. It seems to me that in just the same way the capitalists, who alone can really use land remember, for the farmer, the squatter, the shopkeeper, the manufacturer, the merchant, are nowadays really only managers for banks and mortgage companies, will soon arrange a way of fixing the values of land to suit themselves. But apart from that, I object to the Single Tax idea from the social point of view. It is competitive. It means that we are still to go on buying in the cheapest market and selling in the dearest. It is tinged with that hideous Free Trade spirit of England, by which cotton kings became million-aires while cotton spinners were treated far worse than any chattel slaves. There are other things to be considered besides cheapness, though unfortunately, with things as they are we seem compelled to consider cheapness first."

They lay for some time without speaking.

CHAPTER XI.

"You think land and stock and machinery should be nationalised, then?" asked Ned, turning things over in his mind.

"I think land and machinery, the entire means and processes of the production and exchange of wealth, including stock, should be held in common by those who need them and worked co-operatively for the benefit of all. That is the socialistic idea of industry. The State Socialists seek to make the State the co-operative medium, the State to be the company and all citizens to be equal shareholders as it were. State Socialism is necessarily compulsory on all. The other great socialistic idea, that of Anarchical Communism, bases itself upon voluntaryism and opposes all organised Force, whether of governments or otherwise."

"Then Anarchists aren't wicked men?"

"The Anarchist ideal is the highest and noblest of all human ideals. I cannot conceive of a good man who does not recognise that when he once understands it. The Anarchical Communists simply seek that men should live in peace and concord, of their own better nature, without being forced, doing harm to none, and being harmed by none. Of course the blind revolt against oppressive and unjust laws and tyrannical governments has become associated with Anarchy, but those who abuse it simply don't know what they do. Anarchical Communism, that is men working as mates and sharing with one another of their own free will, is the highest conceivable form of Socialism in industry."

"Are you an Anarchist?"

"No. I recognise their ideal, understand that it is the only natural condition for a community of general intelligence and fair moral health, and look to the time when it will be instituted. I freely admit it is the only form of Socialism possible among true Socialists. But the world is full of mentally and morally and socially diseased people who, I believe, must go through the school of State Socialism before, as a great mass, they are true Socialists and fit for voluntary Socialism. Unionism is the drill for Socialism and Socialism is the drill for Anarchy and Anarchy is that free ground whereon true Socialists and true Individualists meet as friends and mates, all enmity between them absorbed by the development of an all-dominant Humanity."

"Mates! Do you know that's a word I like?" said Ned. "It makes you feel good, just the sound of it. I know a fellow, a shearer, who was witness for a man in a law case once, and the lawyer asked him if he wasn't mates with the chap he was giving evidence for.

"'No,' says Bill, 'we ain't mates.'

"'But you've worked together?' says the lawyer.

"'Oh, yes!' says Bill.

"'And travelled together?'

"'Oh, yes!'

"'And camped together?'

"'Oh, yes!'

"'Then if you're not mates what is mates?' says the lawyer in a bit of a tear.

"'Well, mister,' says Bill, 'mates is them wot's got one pus. If I go to a shed with Jack an' we're mates an' I earn forty quid and Jack gets sick an' only earns ten or five or mebbe nothin' at all we puts the whole lot in one pus, or if it's t'other way about an' Jack earns the forty it don't matter. There's one pus no matter how much each of us earns an' it b'longs just the same to both of us alike. If Jack's got the pus and I want half-a-crown, I says to Jack, says I, "Jack, gimme the pus." An' if Jack wants ten quid or twenty or the whole lot he just says to me, "Bill," says he "gimme the pus." I don't ask wot he's goin' to take and I don't care. He can take it all if he wants it, 'cos it stands to reason, don't it, mister?' says Bill to the lawyer, 'that a man wouldn't be so dirt mean as to play a low-down trick on his own mate. So you see, mister, him an' me warn't mates 'cos we had two pusses an' mates is them wot's got one pus.'"

Geisner laughed with Ned over the bush definition of "mates."

"Bill was about right," he said, "and Socialism would make men mates to the extent of all sharing up with one another. Each man might have a purse but he'd put no more into it than his mate who was sick and weak."

"We'd all work together and share together, I take it," said Ned. "But suppose a man wouldn't work fairly and didn't want to share?"

I

"I'd let him and all like him go out into the bush to see how they could get on alone. They'd soon get tired. Men must co-operate to live civilised."

"Then Socialism is co-operation?" remarked Ned.

"Co-operation as against competition is the main industrial idea of Socialism. But there are two Socialisms. There is a socialism with a little 's' which is simply an attempt to stave off the true Socialism. This small, narrow socialism means only the state regulation of the distribution of wealth. It has as its advocates politicians who seek to modify the robbery of the workers, to ameliorate the horrors of the competitive system, only in order to prevent the upheaval which such men recognise to be inevitable if things keep on unchanged."

"But true Socialism? I asked Nellie last night what Socialism was, but she didn't say just what."

"What did she say?"

"Well! We were coming through the Domain last night, this morning I mean. It was this morning, too. And on a seat in the rain, near a lamp, was a poor devil of a woman, a regular hard-timer, you know, sleeping with her head hung over the back of the seat like a fowl's. I'd just been asking Nellie what Socialism was when we came to the poor wretch and she stopped there. I felt a bit mean, you know, somehow, but all at once Nellie bent her head and kissed this street-walking woman on the cheek, softly, so she didn't wake her. 'That's Socialism,' says Nellie, and we didn't speak any more till we got to her place, and then she told me to ask you what Socialism was." Ned had shifted his position again and was sitting now on his heels. He had pulled out his knife and was digging a little hole among the grass roots.

Geisner, who hardly moved except to roll cigarettes and light them, lay watching him. "I think she's made you a Socialist," he answered, smiling.

"I suppose so," answered Ned, gravely. "If Socialism means that no matter what you are or what you've been we're all mates, and that Nellie's going to join hands with the street-walker, and that you're going to join hands with me, and that all of us are going to be kind to one another and have a good time like we did at Mrs. Stratton's last night, well, I'm a Socialist and there's heaps up in the bush will be Socialists too."

"You know what being a Socialist means, Ned?" asked Geisner, looking into the young man's eyes.

" I've got a notion," said Ned, looking straight back.

" There are socialists and Socialists, just as there is socialism and Socialism. The ones babble of what they do not feel because it's becoming the thing to babble. The others have a religion and that religion is Socialism."

" How does one know a religion ?"

" When one is ready to sacrifice everything for it. When one only desires that the Cause may triumph. When one has no care for self and does not fear anything that man can do and has a faith which nothing can shake, not even one's own weakness."

There was a pause. " I'll try to be a Socialist of the right sort," said Ned.

" You are young and hopeful and will think again and again that the day of redemption is dawning, and will see the night roll up again. You will see great movements set in and struggle to the front and go down when most was expected of them. You will see in the morning the crowd repent of its enthusiasm of the night before. You will find cowards where you expected heroes and see the best condemned to the suffering and penury that weaken the bravest. Your heart will ache and your stomach will hunger and your body will be bent and your head gray and then you may think that the world is not moving and that you have wasted your life and that none are grateful for it."

" I will try not," said Ned.

" You will see unionism grow, the New Unionism, which is simply the socialistic form of unionism. You will see, as I said before, penal laws invoked against unionism here in Australia, under the old pretence of ' law and order.' You will see the labour movement diverted into political action and strikes fought and lost and won at the polling booths."

" Will it not come then ?"

" How can it come then ? Socialism is not a thing which can be glued like a piece of veneering over this rotten social system of ours. It can only come by the utter sweeping away of competition, and that can only come by the development of the socialistic idea in men's hearts."

" Do you mean that unions and political action and agitations don't do any good ?"

" Of course they do good. A union may make an employer rob his men of a few shillings weekly less. An act of Parliament may prevent wage-slaves from being worked sixteen hours a

day. An act of Parliament, granted that Parliament represented the dominant thought of the people, could even enforce
a change of the entire social system. But before action
must come the dominant thought. Unions and Parliaments
are really valuable as spreading the socialistic idea. Every
unionist is somewhat socialist so far as he has agreed not
to compete any longer against his fellows. Every act of
Parliament is additional proof that the system is wrong and
must go before permanent good can come. And year after
year the number of men and women who hold Socialism as a
religion is growing. And when they are enough you will see this
Old Order melt away like a dream and the New Order replace it.
That which appears so impregnable will pass away in a moment.
So!" He blew a cloud of smoke and watched it disappear circling
upwards.

"Listen!" he went on. "It only needs enough Faith. This
accursed Competitivism of ours has no friends but those who fear
personal loss by a change of system. Not one. It has hirelings,
Pretorian guards, Varangians, but not a devoted people. Its
crimes are so great that he is a self-condemned villain who knowing them dreams of justifying them. There is not one man who
would mourn it for itself if it fell to-morrow. A dozen times this
century it has been on the verge of destruction, and what has
saved it every time is simply that those who assailed it had not
a supreme ideal common among them as to how they should
re-build. It is exactly the same with political action as with
revolutionary movements. It will fail till men have faith."

"How can they get it?" asked Ned, for Geisner had ceased
speaking and mused with a far-off expression on his face.

"If we ourselves have it, sooner or later we shall give it to
others. Hearts that this world has wounded are longing for the
ideal we bring ; artist-souls that suffering has purified and edged
are working for the Cause in every land ; weak though we are we
have a love for the Beautiful in us, a sense that revolts against
the unloveliness of life as we have it, a conception of what might
be if things were only right. In every class the ground is being
turned by the ploughshare of Discontent ; everywhere we can
sow the seed broadcast with both hands. And if only one seed in
a thousand springs up and bears, it is worth it."

"But how can one do it best?"

" By doing always the work that comes to one's hand. Just now, you can go back to your union and knowing what the real end is, can work for organisation as you never did before. You can help throw men together, tie the bushmen to the coastmen, break down narrow distinctions of calling and make them all understand that all who work are brothers whether they work by hand or brain. That is the New Unionism and it is a step forward. It is drill, organisation, drill, and we need it. Men must learn to move together, to discuss and to decide together. You can teach them what political action will do when they know enough. And all the time you can drive and hammer into them the socialistic ideas. Tell them always, without mincing matters, that they are robbed as they would probably rob others if they had a chance, and that there never can be happiness until men live like mates and pay nothing to any man for leave to work. Tell them what life might be if men would only love one another and teach them to hate the system and not individual men in it. Some day you will find other work opening out. Always do that which comes to your hand."

" You think things will last a long time?" asked Ned, reverting to one of Geisner's previous remarks.

" Who can tell? While Belshazzar feasted the Medes were inside the gate. Civilisation is destroying itself. The socialistic idea is the only thing that can save it. I look upon the future as a mere race between the spread of Socialism as a religion and the spread of that unconditional Discontent which will take revenge for all its wrongs by destroying civilisation utterly, and with it much, probably most, that we have won so slowly and painfully of Art and Science."

" That would be a pity," said Ned. He would have spoken differently had he not gone with Nellie last night, he thought while saying it.

" I think so. It means the whole work to be done over again. If Art and Science were based on the degradation of men I would say 'away with them.' But they are not. They elevate and ennoble men by bringing to them the fruition of elevated and noble minds. They are expressions of high thought and deep feeling; thought and feeling which can only do good, if it is good to become more human. The artist is simply one who has a little finer soul than others. Mrs. Stratton was saying last night before you came that Nellie is an artist because she has a soul. But it's only comparative. We've all got souls."

"Mrs. Stratton is a splendid woman," began Ned, after another pause.

"Very. Her father was a splendid man, too. He was a doctor , quite famed in his profession. The misery and degradation he saw among the poor made him a passionate Communist. Stratton's father was a Chartist, one of those who maintained that it was a bread-and-butter movement."

For some few minutes neither spoke.

"One of the most splendid men I ever knew," remarked Geisner, suddenly, " was a workman who organised a sort of co-operative housekeeping club among a number of single fellows. They took a good-sized 'flat' and gradually extended it till they had the whole of the large house. Then this good fellow organised others until there were, I think, some thirty of them scattered about the city. They had cards which admitted any member of one house into any other of an evening, so that wherever a man was at night he could find friends and conversation and various games. I used to talk to him a great deal, helping him keep the books of an evening when he came home from his work. He had some great plans. Those places were hotbeds of Socialism," he added.

" What became of him ?"

Geisner shrugged his shoulders without answering.

"Isn't it a pity that we can't co-operate right through in the same way ?" said Ned.

"It's the easiest way to bring Socialism about," answered Geisner. " Many have thought of it. Some have tried. But the great difficulty seems to be to get the right conditions. Absolute isolation while the new conditions are being established ; colonists who are rough and ready and accustomed to such work and at the same time are thoroughly saturated with Socialism ; men accustomed to discuss and argue and at the same time drilled to abide, when necessary, by a majority decision ; these are very hard to get. Besides, the attempts have been on small scales, and though some have been fairly successful as far as they went, have not pointed the great lesson. One great success would give men more Faith than a whole century of talking and preaching. And it will come when men are ready for it, when the times are ripe."

They were silent again.

" We would be free under Socialism ?" asked Ned.

" What could stop us, even under State Socialism. The basis of all slavery and all slavish thought is necessarily the monopoly of the means of working, that is of living. If the State monopolises them, not the State ruled by the propertied classes but the State ruled by the whole people, to work would become every man's right. Nineteen laws out of twenty could then be dropped, for they would become useless. We should be free as men have never been before, because the ideal of the State would be toleration and kindness."

"Let's go and hear the speaking," he added, jumping up. " I've talked quite enough for once."

"You couldn't talk too much for me," answered Ned. " You ought to come up to a shed and have a pitch with the chaps. They'd sit up all night listening. I've to meet Nellie between five and six at the top of the steps in the garden," he added, a little bashfully. " Have we time ?"

" Plenty of time," said Geisner, smiling. " You won't miss her."

CHAPTER XII.

LOVE AND LUST.

THE picnic party had moved on while they talked, but a multitude of sitters and walkers were now everywhere, particularly as they climbed the slope to the level. There the Sunday afternoon meetings were in full swing.

On platforms of varying construction, mostly humble, the champions of multitudinous creeds and opinions were holding forth to audiences which did not always greet their utterances approvingly. They stood for a while near a vigorous iconoclast, who from the top of a kitchen chair laid down the Law of the Universe as revealed by one Clifford, overwhelming with contumely a solitary opponent in the crowd who was foolish enough to attempt to raise an argument on the subject of "atoms." Near at hand, a wild-eyed religionary was trying to persuade a limited and drifting audience that a special dispensation had enabled him to foretell exactly the date of the Second Coming of Christ. Then came the Single Tax platform, a camp-stool with a board on it, wherefrom a slender lad, dark-eyed and good-looking, held forth, with a flow of language and a power of expression that was remarkable, upon the effectiveness of a land tax as a remedy for all social ills.

Ned had never seen such a mass of men with such variegated shades of thought assembled together before. There was a well-dressed bald-headed individual laying down the axioms of that very Socialism of which Geisner and he had been talking. There was an ascetic looking man just delivering a popular hymn, which he sang with the assistance of a few gathered round, as the conclusion of open-air church. There was the Anarchist he had seen at Paddy's Market, fervidly declaring that all government is wrong and that men are slaves and curs for enduring it and tyrants for taking part in it. There was the inevitable temperance orator, the rival touters for free trade and protection, and half-a-dozen others with an opinion to air. They harangued and shouted there amid the trees, on the grass, in the brilliant afternoon sunshine that already threw long shadows over the swaying, moving thousands.

It was a great crowd, a good many thousands altogether, men and women and children and lads. It was dressed in its Sunday best, in attire which fluctuated from bright tints of glaring newness to the dullness of well-brushed and obtrusive shabbiness. There were every-looking men you could think of and women and girls, young and old, pretty and plain and repulsive. But it was a working-people crowd. There was no room among it for the idlers. Probably it was not fashionable for them to be there.

And there was this about the crowd, which impressed Ned, everybody seemed dissatisfied, everybody was seeking for a new idea, for something fresh. There was no confidence in the Old, no content with what existed, no common faith in what was to come. There was on many a face the same misery that he had seen in Paddy's Market. There was no happiness, no face free from care, excepting where lovers passed arm-in-arm. There was the clash of ideas, the struggling of opinions, the blind leading the blind. He saw the socialistic orator contending with a dozen others. Who were the nostrum vendors? Which was the truth?

He turned round, agitated in thought, and his glance fell on Geisner, who was standing with bent head, his hands behind him, ugly, impassive. Geisner looked up quickly: "So you are doubting already," he remarked.

"I am not doubting," answered Ned. "I'm only thinking."

"Well?"

"It is a good thought, that Socialism," answered Ned slowly, as they walked on. "There's nothing in it that doesn't seem fit for men to do. It's a part with Nellie kissing that woman in the wet. What tries to make us care for each other and prevent harm being done to one another can't be very far wrong and what tries to break down the state of affairs that is must be a little right. I don't care, either, whether it's right or wrong. It feels right in my heart somehow and I'll stand by it if I'm the only man left in the world to talk up for it."

Geisner linked his arm in Ned's.

"Remember this when you are sorrowful," he said. "It is only through Pain that Good comes. It is only because the world suffers that Socialism is possible. It is only as we conquer our own weaknesses that we can serve the Cause."

They strolled on till they came to the terraced steps of the Gardens. Before them stretched in all its wondrous glory the matchless panorama of grove and garden, hill-closed sea and villa'd shore, the blue sky and the declining sun tipping with gold and silver the dark masses of an inland cloud.

"What is Life that we should covet it?" said Geisner, halting there. "What is Death that we should fear it so? What has the world to offer that we should swerve to the right hand or the left from the path our innermost soul approves? In the whole world there is no lovelier spot than this, no purer joy than to stand here and look. Yet, it seems to me, Paradise like this would be bought dearly by one single thought unworthy of oneself."

"We are here to-day," he went on, musingly. "To-morrow we are called dead. The next day men are here who never heard our names. The most famous will be forgotten even while Sydney Harbour seems unchanged. And Sydney Harbour is changing and passing, and the continent is changing and passing, and the world is changing and passing, and the whole universe is changing and passing.

"It is all change, universal change. Our religions, our civilisations, our ideas, our laws, change as do the nebulæ and the shifting continents we build on. Yet through all changes a thread of continuity runs. It is all changing and no ending. Always Law and always, so far as we can see, what we call progression. A man is a fool who cares for his life. He is the true madman who wastes his years in vain and selfish ambition.

"Listen, Ned," he pursued, turning round. "There, ages ago, millions and millions of years ago, in the warm waters yonder, what we call Life on this earth began. Minute specks of Life appeared, born of the sunshine and the waters some say, coming in the fitness of Time from the All-Life others. And those specks of Life have changed and passed, and come and gone, unending, reproducing after their kind in modes and ways that changed and passed and still are as all things change and pass and are. And from them you and I and all the forms of Life that breathe to-day have ascended. We struggled up, obedient to the Law around us and we still struggle. That is the Past, or part of it. What is the Future, as yet no man knows. We do more than know—we feel and dream, and struggle on to our dreaming. And Life itself to the dreamer is as nothing only the struggling on.

"And this has raised us, Ned, this has made us men and opened to us the Future, that we learned slowly and sadly to care for each other. From the mother instinct in us all good comes. This is the highest good as yet, that all men should live their life and lay down their life when need is for their fellows. With all our blindness we can see that. With all our weakness we can strive to reach nearer that ideal. It is but Just that we should live so for others since happiness is only possible where others live so for us."

He turned again and gazed intently across the sail-dotted harbour.

"There is one thing I would like to say." He spoke without turning. "Man without Woman is not complete. They two are but one being, complete and life-giving. Love when it comes is the keystone of this brief span of Life of ours. They who have loved have tasted truly of the best that Life can give to them. And this is the great wrong of civilisation to-day, that it takes Love from most and leaves in us only a feverish, degrading Lust. It is when we lust that Woman drags us down to the level of that Lust and blackens our souls with the blackness of hell. When we love Woman raises us to the level of Love and girds on us the armour that wards our own weakness from us.

"Love comes to few, I think. Society is all askew and, then, we have degraded women. So they are often well-nigh unfit for loving as men are often as unfit themselves. Physically unfit for motherhood, mentally unfit to cherish the monogamic idea that once was sacred with our people, sexually unfit to rouse true sex-passion—such women are being bred by the million in crowded cities and by degenerate country life. They match well with the slaves who 'move on' at the bidding of a policeman, or with the knaves who only see in Woman the toy of a feeble lust.

"There are two great reforms needed, Ned, two great reforms which must come if Humanity is to progress, and which must come, sooner or later, either to our race or to some other, because Humanity must progress. One reform is the Reorganisation of Industry. The other is the Recognition of Woman's Equality. These two are the practical steps by which we move up to the socialistic idea.

"If it ever comes to you to love and be loved by a true woman, Ned, let nothing stand between you and her. If you are weak and lose her you will have lost more than Life itself. If you are strong and win her you can never lose her again though the universe divided you and though Death itself came between you, and you will have lived indeed and found joy in living."

" Should one give up the Cause for a woman ?" asked Ned.

Geisner turned round at last and looked him full in the face.

" Lust only," he answered, " and there is no shame to which Woman cannot drag Man. Love and there is nothing possible but what is manly and true."

As he spoke, along the terraced path below them came Nellie, advancing towards them with her free swinging walk and tall lissom figure, noticeable even at a distance among the Sunday promenaders.

"See !" said Geisner, smiling, laying his hand on Ned's arm. " This is Paradise and there comes Eve."

[END OF FIRST PART.]

PART II.

HE KNEW HIMSELF NAKED.

In yesterday's reach and to-morrow's,
  Out of sight though they lie of to-day,
There have been and there yet shall be sorrows
  That smite not and bite not in play.
The life and the love thou despisest,
  These hurt us indeed and in vain,
O wise among women, and wisest,
      Our Lady of Pain.

—SWINBURNE.

THE WORKINGMAN'S PARADISE.

PART II.

━━━ ■▶◀■ ━━━

CHAPTER I.

THE SLAUGHTER OF AN INNOCENT.

Mrs. Hobbs' baby was dying.

"It had clung to its little life so long, in the close Sydney
"streets, in the stuffy, stifling rooms which were its home; it
"had battled so bravely; it was being vanquished at last.

"The flame of its life had flickered from its birth, had shrunk
"to a bluish wreathing many a time, had never once leapt
"upward in a strong red blaze. Again and again it had lain at
"its mother's breast, half-dead; again and again upon its baby
"face Death had laid the tips of its pinching fingers; again and
"again it had struggled moaning from the verge of the grave
"and beaten back the grim Destroyer by the patient filling of
"its tiny lungs. It wanted so to live, all unconsciously. The
"instinct to exist bore it up and with more than Spartan courage
"stood for it time and again in the well-nigh carried breach.
"Now, it was over, the battling, the struggling. Death loitered
"by the way but the fight was done.

"The poor little baby! Poor unknown soldier! Poor unaided
"heroic life that was spent at last! There were none to help it,
"not one. In all the world, in all the universe, there was none to
"give it the air it craved, the food it needed, the living that its
"baby-soul faded for not having. It had fought its fight alone.
"It lay dying now, unhelped and helpless, forsaken and betrayed.

*   *   *   *

So thought Nellie, sitting there beside it, her head thrown back, over her eyes her hands clasped, down her cheeks the tears of passionate pity streaming.

* * *

"What had its mother done for it? The best she could, "indeed, but what was that? The worst she could when she "gave it life, when she bore it to choke and struggle and drown "in the fetid stream that sweeps the children of the poor from "infancy to age; the life she gave it only a flickering, half-"lighted life; the blood she gave it thin with her own weariness "and vitiate from its drunken sire; the form she gave it soft-"boned and angle-headed, more like overgrown embryo than "child of the boasted Australian land. Even the milk it drew "from her unwieldy breasts was tainted with city smoke and "impure food and unhealthy housing. Its playground was the "cramped kitchen floor and the kerb and the gutter. Its food "for a year had been the food that feeds alike the old and the "young who are poor. All around conspired against it, yet for "two years and more it had clung to its life and lived, as if "defying Fate, as if the impulse that throbbed in it from the "Past laughed at conditions and would have it grow to manhood "in spite of all. In the strength of that impulse, do not millions "grow so? But millions, like this little one, are crushed and "overborne.

"It had no chance but the chance that the feeble spark in it "gave it. It had no chance, even with that, to do more than "just struggle through. None came to scatter wide the prison "walls of the slum it lived in and give it air. None came to lift "the burden of woe that pressed on all around it and open to it "laughter and joy. None came to stay the robbery of the poor "and to give to this brave little baby fresh milk and strengthening "food. In darkness and despair it was born; in darkness and "despair it lived; in darkness and despair it died. To it Death "was more merciful than Life. Yet it was a crime crying for "vengeance that we should have let it waste away and die so.

* * *

So thought Nellie, weeping there beside it, all the woman in her aching and yearning for this poor sickly little one.

* * *

"It was murdered, murdered as surely as if a rope had been "put round its neck and the gallows-trap opened under it; mur-"dered as certainly as though, dying of thirst, it had been denied

"a sup of water by one who had to spare; murdered, of sure
"truth, as though in the dark one who knew had not warned it
"of a precipice in the path.

"It had asked so little and had been denied all; only a little
"air, only a little milk and fruit, only a glimpse of the grass and
"the trees, even these would have saved it. And oh! If also in
"its languid veins the love-life had bubbled and boiled, if in its
"bone and flesh a healthy parentage had commingled, if the
"blood its mother gave it had been hot and red and the milk
"she suckled it to white and sweet and clean from the fount of
"vigorous womanhood! What then? Then, surely it had been
"sleeping now with chubby limbs flung wide, its breathing so
"soft that you had to bend your ear to its red lips to hear it,
"had been lying wearied with dancing and mischief-making and
"shouting and toddling and falling, resting the night from a
"happy to-day till the dawn woke it betime for a happy
"to-morrow. All this it should have had as a birthright, with
"the years stretching in front of it, on through fiery youth, past
"earnest manhood, to a loved and loving old age. This is the
"due, the rightful due, of every child to whom life goes from
"us. And that child who is born to sorrow and sordid care, pot-
"bound from its mother's womb by encircling conditions that
"none single-handed can break, is wronged and sinned against
"by us all most foully. If it dies we murder it. If it lives to
"suffer we crucify it. If it steals we instigate, despite our
"canting hypocrisy. And if it murders we who hang it have
"beforehand hypnotised its will and armed its hand to slay.

*   *   *   *

So Nellie thought, the tears drying on her cheeks, leaning forward to watch the twitching, purpled face of the hard-breathing
child.

*   *   *   *

"Is there not a curse upon us and our people, upon our
"children and our children's children, for every little one we
"murder by our social sins?

"Can it be that Nemesis sleeps for us, he who never slept yet
"for any, he who never yet saw wrong go unavenged or heard
"the innocent blood cry unanswered from the ground? Can it be
"that he has closed his ears to the dragging footfalls of the harlot
"host and to the sobs of strong men hopeless and anguished
"because work is wanting and to the sighing of wearied women

K

"and to the death-rattle of slaughtered babes? Surely though
"God is not and Humanity is weak yet Nemesis is strong and
"sleepless and lingers not! Surely he will tear down the slum
"and whelm the robbers in their iniquity and visit upon us all
"punishment for the crime which all alike have shared! Into
"the pit which we have left digged for the children of others
"shall not our own children fall? Is happiness safe for any
"while to any happiness is denied?

"It is a crime that a baby should live so and die so. It is a
"villainy and we all are villains who let it be. No matter how
"many are guilty, each one who lives with hands unbound is as
"guilty as any. It were better to die alone, fighting the whole
"world single-handed, refusing to share the sin or to tolerate it
"or to live while it was, than with halting speech to protest and
"with supple conscience to compromise. He is a coward who
"lets a baby die or a woman sink to shame or a fellow-man be
"humbled, alone and unassisted and unrighted. She is false to
"the divinity of womanhood who does not feel the tigress in her
"when a little one who might be her little one is tossed, stifled
"by unholy conditions, into its grave. But where are the men,
"now, who will strike a blow for the babies? Where are the
"women who will put their white teeth into the murderous
"hands of the Society that throttles the little ones and robs the
"weak and simple and cloaks itself with a " law and order"
"which outrages the Supreme Law of that Humanity evolving
"in us?

"Surely we are all tainted and corrupted, even the best of
"us, by the scrofulous cowardice, the fearsome selfishness, of a
"decaying civilisation! Surely we are only fit to be less than
"human, to be slave to conditions that we ourselves might
"govern if we would, to be criminal accomplices in the sins of
"social castes, to be sad victims of inhuman laws or still sadder
"defenders of inhumanity! Oh, for the days when our race was
"young, when its women slew themselves rather than be shamed
"and when its men, trampling a rotten empire down, feared
"neither God nor man and held each other brothers and hated,
"each one, the tyrant as the common foe of all! Better the days
"when from the forests and the steppes our forefathers burst,
"half-naked and free, communists and conquerors, a fierce ava-
"lanche of daring men and lusty women who beat and battered
"Rome down like Odin's hammer that they were! Alas, for the

"heathen virtues and the wild pagan fury for freedom and for
"the passion and purity that Frega taught to the daughters of
"the barbarian! And alas, for the sword that swung then,
"unscabbarded, by each man's side and for the knee that never
"bent to any and for the fearless eyes that watched unblenched
"while the gods lamed each other with their lightnings in the
"thunder-shaken storm! Gone forever seemed the days when
"the land was for all, and the cattle and the fruits of the field,
"and when, unruled by kings, untrammelled by priests, untyran-
"nised by pretence of " law," our fathers drank in from Nature's
"breast the strength and vigour that gave it even to this little
"babe to fight its hopeless fight for life so bravely and so long.
"Odin was dead whose sons dared go to hell with their own
"people and Frega was no more whose magic filled with molten
"fire the veins of all true lovers and nerved with desperate
"courage the hand of her who guarded the purity of her body
"and the happiness of her child. The White Christ had come
"when wealth and riches and conquests had upheaped wrongs
"upon the heads of the wrongers; the cross had triumphed over
"the hammer when the fierce freedom of the North had worn
"itself out in selfish foray; the shaven-pated priest had come to
"teach patience as God-given when a robber-caste grew up to
"whom it seemed wise to uproot the old ideas from the mind of
"the people whose spent courage it robbed. Alas, for the days
"when it was not righteous to submit to wrong nor wicked
"to strike tyranny to the ground, when one met it, no matter
"where! Alas, for the men of the Past and the women, their
"faith and their courage and their virtue and their gods, the
"hearts large to feel and the brains prompt to think and the
"arms strong to do, the bare feet that followed the plough and
"trod in the winepress of God and the brown hands that milked
"cows and tore kings from their thrones by their beard! They
"were gone and a feebler people spoke their tongue and bore
"their name, a people that bent its back to the rod and bared its
"head to the cunning and did not rise as one man when in its
"midst a baby was murdered while all around a helpless kins-
"folk were being robbed and wronged.

" For the past, who would not choose it? Who would not, if
"they could, drop civilisation from them as one shakes off a
"horrid nightmare at the dawning of the day? Who would not
"be again a drover of cattle, a follower of the plough, a milker

"of cows, a spinner of wool-yarn by the fireside, to be, as well,
"strong and fierce and daring, slave to none and fearing none,
"ignorant alike of all the wisdom and all the woes of this hateful
"life that is ?

"For only one moment of the past if the whole past could not
"be ! Only to be free for a moment if the rest were impossible !
"Only to lose one's hair and bare one's feet and girdle again the
"single garment round one's waist and to be filled with the
"frenzy that may madden still as it maddened our mothers when
"the Roman legions conquered ! Only to stand for a moment, free,
"on the barricade, outlawed and joyous, with Death, Freedom's
"impregnable citadel, opening its gates behind—and to pass
"through, the red flag uplifted in the sight of all men, with
"flaming slums and smoking wrongs for one's funereal pyre!"

*　　*　　*　　*

So Nellie thought in her indignation and sorrow, changing the
wet cloth on the baby's head, powerless to help it, uncomforted
by creeds that moulder in the crimson-cushioned pews. She
knew that she was unjust, carried away by her tumultuous emotions, knew also, in her heart, that there was something more to
be desired than mere wild outbreaks of the despairing. Only she
thought, as we all think, in phases, and as she would certainly
have talked had opportunity offered while she was in the mood,
and as she would most undoubtedly have written had she just
then been writing. The more so as there was a wave of indignation and anger sweeping over Australia, sympathetic with the
indignation and anger of the voteless workers in the Queensland
bush. The companions of her childhood were to be Gatling-
gunned because of the squatters, whose selfish greed and
heartless indifference to all others had made them hateful to
this selector's daughter. Because the bushmen would not take
the squatters' wage and yield his liberty as a workman to the
squatter's bidding and agree to this and to that without consulta-
tion or discussion, the scum of southern towns and the sifted
blacklegs of southern "estates" were to be drafted in hordes to
Queensland to break down the unionism that alone protected the
bushman and made him more of a man than he had been when
the squatter could do as he would and did. From the first days
she could remember she had heard how the squatters filched
from the bushmen in their stores and herded the bushmen in vile
huts and preferred every colour to white when there were workers

wanted; and how the magistrates were all squatters or squatters' friends and how Government was for the squatters and for nobody else on the great Western plains; and she knew from Ned of the homeless, wandering life the bushmen led and how new thoughts were stirring among them and rousing them from their aimless, hopeless living. She knew more, too, knew what the bushman was: frank as a child, keeping no passing thought unspoken, as tender as a woman to those he cared for, responsive always to kindly, earnest words, boiling over with anger one moment and shouting with good humour the next, open-handed with sovereigns after months and years of lonely toiling or sharing his last plug of tobacco with a stranger met on the road. His faults she knew as well: his drunkenness often, his looseness of living, his excitability, all born of unnatural surroundings; but his virtues she knew as well, none better, and all her craving for the scent of the gums and to feel again the swaying saddle and to hear again the fathomless noon-day silence and to see again the stock rushing in jumbling haste for the water-hole, went out in a tempestuous sympathy for those who struggled for the union in the bush. And Ned! She hardly knew what she thought about Ned.

She was unjust in her thoughts, she knew, not altogether unjust but somewhat. There had been heroism in the passive struggle of six months before, when the seamen left the boats at the wharves for the sake of others and when the "lumpers" threw their coats over their shoulders and stood by the seamen and when the miners came up from the mines so that no coal should go to help fight comrades they had never seen. Her heart had thrilled with joy to see so many grip hands and stand together, officers and stewards and gasmen and lightermen and engine-drivers and cooks and draymen, from Adelaide to far-off Cooktown, in every port, great and small, all round the eastern coast. As the strike dragged on she lived herself as she had lived in the starving hand-to-mouth days of her bitter poverty, to help find bread for the hungry families she knew. For Phillips and Macanany were on strike, while Hobbs, who had moved round the corner, had been sacked for refusing to work on the wharves; and many another in the narrow street and the other narrow streets about it were idling and hungering and waiting doggedly to see what might happen, with strike pay falling steadily till there was hardly any strike pay at all. And Nellie's heart, that had thrilled with joy when New Unionism uprose in its strength and drew the line hard and fast between the Labour that toiled and the Capitalism that reaped Labour's gains, ached with mingled pride and pain to see how hunger itself could not shake the stolid unionism about her. She saw, too, the seed that for years had been sown by unseen, unknown sowers springing up on every hand and heard at every street corner and from every unionist mouth that everything belonged of right to those who worked and that the idle rich were thieves and robbers. She smiled grimly to watch Mrs. Macanany and viragoes like her pouring oil on the flames and drumming the weak-kneed up and screaming against "blacklegging" as a thing accurst. And when she understood that the fight was over, while apparently it was waxing thicker, she had waited to see what the end would be, longing for something she knew not what. She used to go down town, sometimes of an evening, to watch the military patrols, riding up and down with jingling bits and clanking carbines and sabres as if in a conquered city. She heard, in her workroom, the dull roar of the angry thousands through whose midst the insolent squatters drove in triumphal procession, as if inciting to lawlessness, with dragoon-guarded, police-protected drays of blackleg wool. Then the end came and the strike was over, leaving the misery it had caused and the bitter hatreds it had fostered and the stern lesson which all did not read as the daily papers would have had them. And now the same Organised Capitalism which had fought and beaten the maritime men and the miners, refusing to discuss or to confer or to arbitrate or to conciliate, but using its unjust possession of the means of living to starve into utter submission those whose labour made it rich, was at the same work in the Queensland bush, backing the squatters, dominating government, served by obsequious magistrates and a slavish military and aided by all who thought they had to gain by the degradation of their fellows or who had been ground so low that they would cut each other's throats for a crust or who, in their blind ignorance, misunderstood what it all meant. And there were wild reports afloat of resistance brooding in Queensland and of excited meetings in the bush and of troops being sent to disperse the bushmen's camps. Why did they endure these things, Nellie thought, watching and waiting, as impotent to aid them as she was to save the baby dying now beside her. Day by day she expected Ned.

She knew Ned was in the South, somewhere, though she had not seen him. He had come down on some business, in blissful ignorance of the nearness of the coming storm, but would be called back, she knew, now this new trouble had begun. And then he would be arrested, she was sure, because he was outspoken and fearless and would urge the men to stand out till the last, and would be sent to prison by legal trickery under this new law the papers said had been discovered; all so that the unions might break down and the squatters do as they liked. Which, perhaps, was why her thoughts for the time being were particularly tinged with pessimism. If the vague something called "law and order" was determined to be broken so that the bush could be dragooned for the squatter it seemed to her as well to make a substantial breakage while men were about it—and she did not believe they would.

She placed a cool damp cloth on the baby's head, wishing that its mother would come up, Mrs. Hobbs having been persuaded to go downstairs for some tea and a rest while Nellie watched by the sick child and having been entangled in household affairs the moment she appeared in the dingy kitchen where Mrs. Macanany, to the neglect of her own home, was "seeing to things." The hard breathing was becoming easier. Nellie brought the candle burning in a broken cup. The flushed face was growing paler and more natural. The twitching muscles were stilling. There was a change.

One unused to seeing Death approach would have thought the baby settling down at last to a refreshing, health-reviving sleep. Nellie had lived for years where the children die like rabbits, and knew.

"Mrs. Hobbs!" she called, softly but urgently, running to the stairs.

The poor woman came hastily to the foot. "Quick, Mrs. Hobbs!" said Nellie, beckoning.

"Oh, Mrs. Macanany! The baby's dying!" cried poor Mrs. Hobbs, tripping on her dragging skirts in her frantic haste to get upstairs. Mrs. Macanany followed. The children set up a boohoo that brought Mr. Hobbs from the front doorstep where he had been sitting smoking. He rushed up the stairs also. When he reached the top he saw, by the light of the candle in Nellie's hand, a little form lying still and white; its mother crouched on the floor, wailing over it.

It was a small room, almost bare, the bedstead of blistered iron, the mattress thin, the bedding tattered and worn. A soapbox was the chair on which Nellie had been sitting; there was no other. Against the wall, above a rough shelf, was a piece of mirror-glass without a frame. The window in the sloping roof was uncurtained. On the poor bed, under the tattered sheet, was the dead baby. And on the floor, writhing, was its mother, Mrs. Macanany trying to comfort her between the pauses of her own vehement neighbourly grief.

Nellie closed the dead baby's eyes, set the candle on the shelf and moved to the door where Mr. Hobbs stood bewildered and dumbfoundered, his pipe still in his hand. "Speak to her!" she whispered to him. "It's very hard for her."

Mr. Hobbs looked hopelessly at his pipe. He did not recollect where to put it. Nellie, understanding, took it from his fingers and pushed him gently by the arm towards his wife. He knelt down by the weeping woman's side and put his hands on the head that was bent to the ground. "Sue," he said, huskily, not knowing what to say. "Don't take on so! It's better for 'im."

"It's not better," she cried in answer, kneeling up and frantically throwing her arms across the bed. "How can it be better? Oh, God! I wish I was dead. Oh, my God! Oh, my God!"

"Don't, Sue!" begged Mr. Hobbs, weeping in a clumsy way, as men usually do.

"It's not right," cried the mother, rolling her head, half-crazed. "It's not right, Jack. It's not right. It didn't ought to have died. It didn't ought to have died, Jack. It wouldn't if it had a chance, but it hadn't a chance. It didn't have a chance, Jack. It didn't have a chance."

"Don't, Sue!" begged Mr. Hobbs again. "You did what you could."

"I didn't," she moaned. "I didn't. I didn't do what I could. There were lots of things I might have done that I didn't. I wasn't as kind as I might have been. I was cross to it and hasty. Oh, my God, my God! Why couldn't I have died instead? Why couldn't I? Why don't we all die? It's not right. It's not right. Oh, my God, my God!"

And she thought God, whatever that is, did not hear and would not answer, she not knowing that in her own pain and anguish were the seeds of progression and in her cries the whetting of the sickle wherewith all wrongs are cut down when they are ripe for the reaper.   So she wept and lamented, bewailing her dead, rebellious and self-reproachful.

"Take the baby, dear!" quoth Mrs. Macanany, reappearing from a descent to the kitchen with a six months' infant squalling in her arms.   "Give it a drink now!   It'll make you feel better."

Poor Mrs. Hobbs clutched the baby-in-arms convulsively and sobbed over it, finding some comfort in the exertion.   To Mrs. Macanany's muttered wrath Nellie intervened, however, with warnings of "fits" as likely to follow the nursing of the child while its mother was so excited and feverish.   Mr. Hobbs loyally seconded Nellie's amendment and with unexpected shrewdness urged the mother to control her grief for the dead for the sake of the living.   Which succeeding, to some extent, they got the poor woman downstairs and comforted her with a cup of tea, Nellie undressing and soothing the crying children, who sobbed because of this vague happening which the eldest child of 11 explained as meaning that "Teddy's going to be put in the deep hole."

It was after 10 when Nellie went.   Mrs. Hobbs cried again as Nellie kissed her "good-night."   Mr. Hobbs shook hands with genuine friendship.   "I don't know whatever we'd have done without you, Miss Lawton," he said, bashfully, following her to the door.

"I don't know what they'll do without you, Mr. Hobbs," retorted Nellie, whose quick tongue was noted in the neighbourhood.

He did not answer, only fumbled with the door-knob as she stood on the step in the brilliant moonlight.

"Give it up!" urged Nellie.   "It makes things worse and they're bad enough at the best.   It's not right to your wife and the children."

"I don't go on the spree often," pleaded Mr. Hobbs.

"Not as often as some," admitted Nellie, "but if it's only once in a life-time it's too often.   A man who has drink in him isn't a man.   He makes himself lower than the beasts and we're low enough as it is without going lower ourselves.   He hurts himself and he hurts his family and he hurts his mates.   He's worse than a blackleg."

"I don't see as it's so bad as that," protested Mr. Hobbs.

"Yes, it is," insisted Nellie, quickly.   "Every bit as bad.   It's drink that makes most of the blacklegs, anyway.   Most of them are men whose manhood has been drowned out of them with liquor and the weak men in the unions are the drunkards who have no heart when the whisky's out of them. Everybody knows that. And when men who aren't as bad feel down-hearted and despairing instead of bracing up and finding out what makes it they cheer up at a pub and imagine they're jolly good fellows when they're just cowards dodging their duty. They get so they can't take any pleasure except in going on the spree and if they only go on once in a month or two"—this was a hit at Hobbs— "they're the worse for it. Why, look here, Mr. Hobbs, if I hadn't been here you'd have gone to-night and brought home beer and comforted yourselves getting fuddled. That's so, you know, and it wouldn't be right. It's just that sort of thing"—she added softly—" that stops us seeing how it is the little ones die when they shouldn't. If everybody would knock off drinking for ten years, everybody, we'd have everything straightened out by then and nobody would ever want to go on the spree again."

She stood with her back to the moonlight, fingering the post of the door. Mr. Hobbs fumbled still with the door-knob and looked every way but at her. She waited for an answer, but he did not speak.

"Come," she continued, after a pause. "Can't you give it up? I know it's a lot to do when one's used to it. But you'll feel better in the end and your wife will be better right away and the children, and it won't be blacklegging on those who're trying to make things better. No matter how poor he is if a man's sober he's a man, while if he drinks, no matter if he's got millions, he's a brute.

" You never drink anything, Miss Lawton, do you?" asked Mr. Hobbs, swinging the door.

" I never touched it in my life," said Nellie.

" Do you really think you're better for it?"

" I think it has kept me straight," said Nellie, earnestly. " I wouldn't touch a drop to save my life. Some people call us who don't drink 'fools' just because a few humbugs make temperance a piece of cant. I think those who get drunk are fools or who drink when there's a prospect of themselves or those they drink with getting drunk. Drink makes a man an empty braggart or a contented fool. It makes him heartless not only to others but to himself."

There was another pause.

"If you won't for the sake of your wife and your children and yourself and everybody, will you do it to please me?" asked Nellie, who knew that Mr. Hobbs regarded her as the one perfect woman in Australia and, woman-like, was prepared to take advantage thereof.

"You know, Miss Lawton, I'm not one of the fellows who swear off Monday mornings and get on the spree the next Saturday night. If I say I'll turn temperance I'll turn." So quoth the sturdy Hobbs.

"I know that. If you were the other sort do you think I'd be bothering you?" retorted Nellie.

"Well, I'll do it," said Mr. Hobbs. "So help me ——"

"Never mind that," interrupted the girl. "If a man's a man his word's his word, and if he's not all the swearing in the world won't make any difference. Let's shake on it!" She held out her hand.

Mr. Hobbs dropped the door-knob and covered her long, slender hand with his great, broad, horny-palmed one.

"Good night, Mr. Hobbs!" she said, the "shake" being over. "Get her to sleep and don't let her fret!"

"Good night, Miss Nellie!" he answered, using her name for the first time. He wanted to say something more but his voice got choked up and he shut the door in her face, so confused was he.

*　　　*　　　*　　　*

"Hello, Nellie!" said a voice that made her heart stand still, as she crossed the road, walking sadly homewards. At the same time two hands stretched out of the dense shadow into the lane of moonlight that shone down an alley way she was passing and that cut a dazzling swath in the blackness made still blacker by the surrounding brilliancy. "I've been wondering if you ever would finish that pitch of yours."

It was Ned.

CHAPTER II.

WHILE NELLIE had been talking temperance to Mr. Hobbs, Ned had been watching her impatiently from the other side of the street. For an hour and more he had been prowling up and down, up and down, between the Phillipses and the Hobbses, having learned from Mrs. Phillips, who looked wearier than ever, where the Hobbses lived now and why Nellie had gone there after hardly stopping to swallow her dinner. At seven he had acquired this information and returned soon after nine to find Nellie still at the house of sickness, now, alas, the house of death. So he had paced up and down, up and down, waiting for her. He had seen the Hobbs' door open at last and had watched impatiently, from the shadow opposite, the conversation on the door step. His heart gave a great leap as she stepped across the road full in the moonlight. He saw again the sad stern face that had lived as an ideal in his memory for two long eventful years. There was none like her in the whole world to him, not one.

The years had come to her in this stifling city, amid her struggling and wrestling of spirit, but the strong soul in her had borne her up through all; she had aged without wearying, grown older and sadder without withering from her intense womanhood. Broader of hip a little, as Ned could see with the keen eyes of love, not quite so slender in the waist, fuller in the uncorsetted bust, more sloping of shoulder as though the pillared neck had fleshed somewhat at the base; the face, too, had gathered form and force, in the freer curve of her will-full jaw, in the sterner compression of fuller lips that told their tale of latent passions strangely bordering on the cruel, in the sweeter blending of Celt and Saxon shown in straight nose, strong cheek-bones and well-marked brows. She trod still with the swinging spring of the hill-people, erect and careless. Only the white gleam of her collar and a dash of colour in her hat broke the sombre hue that clothed her, as before, from head to foot.

Ned devoured her with his eyes as she came rapidly towards him, unconscious of his presence. She was full grown at last, in woman's virgin prime, her mind, her soul, her body, all full and strong with pure thoughts, natural instincts and human passions. Her very sadness gave her depths of feeling that never come to those who titter and fritter youth away. Her very ignoring of the love-instincts in her, absorbed as her thoughts were in other things, only gave those instincts the untrammelled freedom that alone gives vigorous growth. She was barbarian, as her thoughts had been beside the dying baby: the barbarian cultured, as Shakespeare was, the barbarian wronged, as was Spartacus, the barbarian hating and loving and yearning and throbbing, the creature of her instincts, a rebel against restrictions, her mind subject only to her own strong will. She was a woman of women, in Ned's eyes at least. One kiss from her would be more than all other women could give, be their self-abandonment what it might. To be her lover, her husband, a man might yield up his life with a laugh, might surrender all other happiness and be happy ever after. There was none like her in the whole world to Ned, not one—and he came to say good-bye to her, perhaps for ever.

In the black shadows thrown by the high-rising moon, the crossing alley-way cut a slice of brilliancy as if with a knife. From the shadow into the moonshine two hands stretched towards her as Ned's voice greeted her. She saw his tall form looming before her.

"Ned!" she cried, in answer, grasping both his hands and drawing him forward into the light. "I was expecting you. I've been thinking of you every minute for the last week. How tired you look! You're not ill?"

"No! I'm all right," he answered, laughing. "It's those confounded trains. I can't sleep on them, and they always give me a headache. But you're looking well, Nellie. I can't make out how you do it in this stuffed-up town."

"I'm all right," she replied, noticing a red rose in his coat but saying nothing of it. "Nothing seems to touch me. Did you come straight through?"

"Straight through. We rushed things all we could but I couldn't get away before. Besides, as long as I get Saturday's boat in Brisbane it'll be as soon as it's possible to get on. That gives me time to stay over to-night here. I didn't see you going down and I began to wonder if I'd see you going back. You can do a pitch, Nellie. When a fellow's waiting for you, too."

Nellie laughed, then sobered down. "The baby's dead," she said, sadly. "You recollect it was born when you were here before, the day we went to the Strattons."

"I don't wonder," he answered, looking round at the closed-in street, with its dull, hopeless, dreary rows of narrow houses and hard roadway between. "But I suppose you're tired, Nellie. Let's go and get some oysters!"

"I don't care to, thanks. I feel like a good long walk," she went on, taking his arm and turning him round to walk on with her. "I'm thirsting for a breath of fresh air and to stretch myself. I'm a terrible one for walks, you know."

"Not much riding here, Nellie;" walking on.

"That's why I walk so. I can go from here right down to Lady Macquarie's Chair in under half-an-hour. Over two miles! Not bad, eh, Ned?"

"That's a good enough record. Suppose we go down there now, Nellie, only none of your racing time for me. It's not too late for you?"

"Too late for me! My word! I'm still at the Phillipses and they don't bother. I wouldn't stay anywhere where I couldn't come and go as I liked. I'd like to go if you're not too tired."

"It'll do me good," said Ned, gleefully. So they set off, arm in arm. After they had walked a dozen yards he stopped suddenly.

"I've brought you a rose, Nellie," he exclaimed, handing it to her. "I'm so pleased to see you I forgot it."

"I knew it was for me," she said, fondly, pinning it at her throat. "How ever did you recollect my colour?"

"Do you think I forget anything about you, Nellie?" he asked. She did not answer and they walked on silently.

"Where is Geisner?" he enquired, after a pause.

"I don't know. Why?"

"Oh, nothing. Only he'd advise us a little."

After a pause: "What do you think of things, Ned?"

"What do I think? We couldn't get any wires through that explained anything. There was nothing on but the ordinary strike business when I came down. I suppose some of the chaps have been talking wild and the Government has snapped at the chance to down the union. You know what our fellows are."

"Yes. But I don't quite see what the Government's got to gain. Proclamations and military only make men worse, I think."

"Sometimes they do and sometimes they don't," answered Ned. "A crowd that's doing no harm, only kicking up a bit of a row, will scatter like lambs sometimes if a single policeman collars one of them. Another time the same crowd will jump on a dozen policemen. The Government thinks the crowd'll scatter and I'm afraid the crowd'll jump."

"Why afraid?" enquired Nellie, biting her lips.

"Because it has no chance," answered Ned. "These are all newspaper lies about them having arms and such nonsense. There aren't 500 guns in the whole Western country and half of them are old muzzle-loading shot guns. The kangarooers have got good rifles but nineteen men out of twenty no more carry one than they carry a house."

"But the papers say they're getting them!"

"Where are they to get them from, supposing they want them and naturally the chaps want them when they hear of military coming to 'shoot 'em down'? You can reckon that the Government isn't letting any be carried on the railways and even if they did I don't believe you could buy 500 rifles in all Queensland at any one time."

"Then it's all make-up that's in the papers? It certainly seemed to me that there was something in it."

"That's just it, there is something in it. Just enough, I'm convinced, to give the Government an excuse for doing what they did during the maritime strike without any excuse and what the squatters have been planning for them to do all along."

"One of the Queensland men who was here a week or two ago was telling me about the maritime strike business. It was the first I'd heard of that. Griffith didn't seem to be that way years ago," said Nellie.

"Griffith is a fraud," declared Ned, hotly. "I'd sooner have one of the Pure Merinoes than Griffith. They do fight us out straight and fair, anyway, and don't cant much about knowing that things aren't right, with Elementary Property Bills and 'Wealth and Want' and that sort of wordy tommy-rot. I like to know where to find a man and that trick of Griffith at the maritime strike in Brisbane showed where to find him right enough."

"Was it Griffith?" asked Nellie.

"Of course it was Griffith. Who else would it be? The fellows in Brisbane feel sore over it, I tell you. When they'd been staying up nights and getting sick and preaching themselves hoarse, talking law and order to the chaps on strike and rounding on every man who even boo'd as though he were a blackleg, and when the streets were quieter with thousands of rough fellows about than they were ordinary times, those shop-keepers and wool-dealers and commission agents went off their heads and got the Government to swear in 'specials' and order out mounted troopers and serve out ball cartridges. And all the time the police said it wasn't necessary, that the men on strike were perfectly orderly. Who'd ever do that but Griffith? And what can we expect from a government that did such a thing?"

"The Brisbane men do seem sore over that," agreed Nellie. "The man who told me vowed it would be a long time before he'd do policeman's work again. He said that for him Government might keep its own order and see how soon it got tired of it."

"Well, it's the same thing going on now. I mean the Government and the squatters fixing up this military business between them just to dishearten our fellows. Besides, they've got it into their heads, somehow, that most men are only unionists through fear and that if they're sure of 'protection' they'll blackleg in thousands."

"That's a funny notion," said Nellie. "But all employers have it or pretend to have it. I fancy it comes through men, afraid of being victimised if they display independence, shifting the responsibility of their sticking up for rules upon the union and letting the boss think they don't approve of the rules but are afraid to break them, when they're really afraid to let him know they approve them."

"That's about it, Nellie, but most people find it easy to believe what they want to believe. Anyway, I've got it straight from headquarters that the squatters expect to get blacklegs working under enough military protection to make blacklegging feel safe, as they look at it, and then they think our unions will break right down. And, of course, what maddens our crowd is that blacklegs are collected in another part of the world and shipped in under agreements which they can be sent to prison if they break, or think they can, which amounts to the same, and are kept guarded away from us, like convicts, so that we can't get to them to talk to them and win them over as is done in ordinary strikes in towns."

"That's shameful!" said Nellie. "The squatter governments have a lot to answer for."

"And what can we do?" continued Ned. "They won't let us have votes. There are 20,000 men in the back country altogether and I don't believe 5000 of them have votes and they're mostly squatters and their managers and 'lifers' and the storekeepers and people who own land. I've no vote and can't get one. None of the fellows in my lot can get votes. We can't alter things in Parliament and the law and the government and the military and the police and the magistrates and everything that's got authority are trying to down us and we can't help ourselves. Do you wonder that our chaps get hot and talk wild and act a little wild now and then?"

Nellie pressed his arm answeringly.

"I feel myself a coward sometimes," went on Ned. "Last drought-time some of us were camped 'way back at a water-hole on a reserve where there was the only grass and water we could get for hundreds of miles. We had our horses and the squatter about wanted the grass for his horses and tried to starve us away by refusing to sell us stores. He wouldn't even sell us meat. He was a fool, for we took his mutton as we wanted it, night-times, and packed our stores from the nearest township, a hundred and eighty miles off. I used to think that the right thing to do was to take what we wanted off his run and from his store, in broad daylight, and pay him fair prices and blow the heads off anybody who went to stop us. For we'd a better right to the grass than he had. Only, you see, Nellie, it was easier to get even with him underhand and we seem to do always what's easiest."

"They've always acted like that, those squatters, Ned," said Nellie. "Don't you recollect when they closed the road across Arranvale one drought 'cause the selectors were cutting it up a bit, drawing water from the reserve, and how everybody had to go seven miles further round for every drop of water? I've often wondered why the gates weren't lifted and the road used in spite of them."

"They'd have sent for the police," remarked Ned. "Next year Arranvale shed was burned," he added.

"It's always that way," declared Nellie, angrily. "For my part I'd sooner see the wildest, most hopeless outbreak, than that sort of thing."

"So would the squatters, Nellie," retorted Ned, grimly. "I feel all you do," he went on. "But human nature is human

L

nature and the squatters did their level best, ignorantly, I admit, to make the men mere brutes, and the life alone has made hundreds mad, so we can't wonder if the result isn't altogether pleasant. They've made us hut in with Chinese and Malays. They've stuck up prices till flour that cost them tuppence a pound I've seen selling us for a shilling. They've cut wages down whenever they got a chance and are cutting them now, and they want to break up our unions with their miserable 'freedom of contract' agreement. Before there were unions in the bush the only way to get even with a squatter was by some underhand trick and now we've got our unions and are ready to stand up manly and fight him fair he's coming the same dodge on us that the shipowners came on the seamen, only worse. Going to use contract labour from the South that we can't get near to talk to and that can't legally knock off if we did talk it over, and going to break up the camps and shoot down unarmed men just to stop the strike. How can you wonder if a few fires start or expect the chaps to be indignant if they do? Besides, half the fires that happen at times like this are old shanties of sheds that are insured above their value. It's convenient to be able to put everything down to unionists."

" It worries me," said Nellie, after a few minutes' silence.

" Me too," said Ned. " We've got such a good case if both sides could only be shown up. We've been willing to talk the whole thing over all along and we're willing yet or to arbitrate it either. We're right and lots of these fellows know it who abuse us. And if our chaps do talk a bit rough and get excited and even if they do occasionally carry on a bit, it's not a circumstance to the way the other side talk and get excited and carry on. Only all the law is against us and none against them. Our chaps are so hot that they don't go at it like lawyers but like a bull at a gate, when they talk or write. And so the Government gets a hold on us and can raise a dust and prevent people from seeing how things really are."

" Ned," she said, after a pause. " Tell me honestly! Do you think there will be any trouble?"

" Honestly, I don't, Nellie. At least nothing serious. Some of the fellows may start to buck if the Government does try to break up the camps and it might spread a little, but there are no guns and so I don't see how it could. There seems to be a lot of talk everywhere but that's hard fact. Ten thousand bushmen with rifles wouldn't have much trouble with the Government and the Government wouldn't have much trouble with ten thousand bushmen without rifles. Besides, we're trying to do things peacefully and I don't see why we shouldn't win this round as things stand and get votes soon into the bargain."

" But if there is trouble, Ned?" she persisted. " Supposing it does start ?"

"I shall go with the chaps, of course, if that's what you mean."

" Knowing it's useless, just to throw your life away ?" she asked, quietly, not protestingly, but as one seeking information.

" I've eaten their bread," answered Ned. " Whatever mad thing is done, however it's done, I'm with them. I should be a coward if I stood out of it because I didn't agree with it. Besides——"

" Besides what ?"

" I believe in Fate somehow. Not as anything outside bossing us, you know, but as the whole heap of causes and conditions, of which we're a part ourselves. But I don't feel that there'll be any real trouble though some of us'll get into trouble just the same."

" The Government will pick the big thistles, you mean."

" Those they think the big thistles, I suppose. Of course the Government is only the squatters and the companies in another shape and they only want to break down the strike and are glad of any excuse that'll give them a slant at us. They have a silly idiotic notion that only a few men keep the unions going and that if they can get hold of a dozen or two the others will all go to work like lambs just as the squatter wants. The fellows here have heard that the Government's getting ready to make a lot of arrests up there. I'm one."

Nellie squeezed his arm again ; " I've heard that. I suppose they can do anything they like, Ned, but surely they won't dare to really enforce that old George the Fourth law they've resurrected ?"

" Why not ? They'll do anything, Nellie. They're frantic and think they must or the movement will flood them out. They'd like nothing better than a chance to shoot a mob of us down like wild turkeys. They have squatter magistrates and squatter judges—you know we've got some daisies up in Queensland—and they'll snap up all the best lawyers and pack the jury with a lot of shopkeepers who're just in a panic at the newspaper yarns.

The worst interpretation 'll be put on everything and every foolish word be magnified a thousand times. I know the gentry too well. They'll have us sure as fate and all I hope is that the boys won't be foolish enough to give them an excuse to massacre a few hundred. It'll be two or three years apiece, the Trades Hall people have heard. However, I suppose we can stand it. I don't care so long as the chaps stick to the union."

"Do you think they will?" asked Nellie, after another pause.

"I'm sure they will. They can rake a hundred of us in for life and knock the union endways and in a year there'll be as much fight in the boys as there is now, and more bitter, too. Why they're raising money in Sydney for us already and I'm told that it was squeezed as dry as a bone over the maritime strike. The New South Wales fellows are all true blue and so they are down Adelaide way, as good as gold yet. The bosses don't know what a job they tackled when they started in to down unionism. They fancy that if they can only smash our fellows they'll have unionism smashed all over Australia. The fun will only just have started then."

"What makes you so sure the men will stick, Ned?" enquired Nellie.

"Because they all know what the squatter was before the union and what he'll be the minute he gets another chance. The squatters will keep the unions going right enough. Besides everybody's on for a vote now in the bush and, of course, the Government is going to keep it from them as long as possible. Without unionism they'll never get votes and they know it."

They had reached the path by Wooloomooloo Bay. Ned took off his hat and walked bareheaded. "This is lovely!" he remarked, refreshed.

"What a fool Griffith is!" cried Nellie, suddenly.

"He's not as cunning as he ought to be," assented Ned. "But why?"

"Do you know what I'd do if I were him?" answered Nellie. "I'd send all the military and all the police home and go up into the bush by myself and have a chat with the committee and the men at the camps and find out just how they looked at the thing and ask them to assist in keeping order and I'd see that they got justice if Parliament had to be called together specially to do it."

"He's not smart enough to do that," answered Ned. "Besides, the squatters and the capitalistic set are the Parliament and wouldn't let him. I suppose he believes every lie they stuff him with and never gives a minute's thought to our having a side."

"He didn't use to be a bad man, once," persisted Nellie.

"I suppose he's not a bad man now," cried Ned, boiling over. "He's not on the make like most of them and he fancies he's very patriotic, I imagine, but what does he know of us or of the squatter? He sees us at our worst and the squatter at his best and we've got different ways of talking and when we get drunk on poisoned rum that the Government lets be sold we aren't as gentlemanly as those who get drunk on Hennessy and champagne. We don't curse in the same gentlemanly way and we splash out what we think and don't wear two faces like his set. And so he thinks we're ruffians and outlaws and he can't feel why the bushmen care for the unions. The squatter has taken up all the land and the squatter law has tied up what hasn't been taken and most of us are a lot of outcasts, without homes or wives or children or anything that a man should have barring our horses. We've got no votes and every law is set against us and we've no rights and the squatter 'd like to throw us all out to make room for Chinese. There's nothing in front of the bushman now unless the union gets it for him and they're trying to break up our union, Griffith and his push, and, by God, they shan't do it. They haven't gaols enough to hold every good unionist, not if they hang a thousand of us to start with."

"What does it matter, after all, Ned?" said Nellie, gently. "The Cause itself gains by everything that makes men think. There'll never be peace until the squatter goes altogether and the banks and the whole system. And the squatter can't help it. I abuse him myself but I know he only does what most of our own class in his place would do."

"Of course he can't help it, Nellie," agreed Ned. "They're mostly mortgaged up to the neck like the shopkeepers and squeeze us partly to keep afloat themselves. It's the system, not the squatters personally. A lot of them are decent enough, taking them off their runs and some are decent even on their runs. Even the squatters aren't all bad. I don't wish them any harm individually but just the same we're fighting them and they're fighting us and what I feel sorest about is that it's just because the New Unionism is teaching our chaps to think and to be better and to have ideas that they are trying so hard to down it."

" They don't know any better," repeated Nellie.

" That's what Geisner says, I recollect. I mind how he said they'd try sending us to prison here in Australia. They're beginning soon."

They were right at the point now.

" There's only one thing I'd like to know first, Nellie."

" What is it, Ned ? " she asked, unconsciously, absorbed in her fear for him.

CHAPTER III.

"NELLIE!"

It was a husky whisper. His throat was parched, his lips dry, his mouth also. His heart thumped, thumped, thumped, so that it sickened him. He shook nervously. His face twitched. He felt burning hot; then deadly cold. He turned his hat slowly round and round in his trembling fingers.

It was as though he had turned woman. He did not even feel passion. He dared not look at her. He could feel her there. He did not desire as he had desired so often to snatch her to him, to crush her in his arms, to smother her with kisses, to master her. All his strength fled from him in an indescribable longing.

He had dreamed of this moment, often and often. He had rehearsed it in his mind a thousand times, when the reins dropped on his horse's neck, when he lay sleepless on the ground, even as he chatted to his mates. He had planned what to say, how to say it, purposing to break down her stubborn will with the passionate strength of his love for her, with mad strong words, with subtle arguments. He had seen her hesitating in his dreaming, had seen the flush come and go on her cheeks, her bosom heaving beneath the black dress he knew so well. He had made good his wooing with the tender violence that women forgive for love's sake, had caught her and kissed her till her kisses answered and till she yielded him her troth and pledged herself his wife. So he had dreamed in his folly. And now he stood there like a whipped child, pleading huskily:

"Nellie!"

He had not known himself. He had not known her. Even now he hardly understood that her glorious womanliness appealed to all that was highest in him, that in her presence he desired to be a Man and so seemed to himself weak and wicked. It was not her body only, it was her soul also that he craved, that pure, clear soul of hers which shone in every tone and every word and every look and every gesture. Beautiful she was, strong and lithe and bearing her head up always as if in stern defiance;

beautiful in her cold virginity; beautiful in the latent passion that slumbered lightly underneath the pale, proud face. But most beautiful of all to him, most priceless, most longed for, was the personality in her, the individuality which would have brought him to her were she the opposite, physically, of all she was. He had wondered in reading sometimes of the Buddhist thoughts if it were indeed that she was his mate, that in re-incarnation after re-incarnation they had come together and found in each other the completed self. And then he had wondered if there were indeed in him such power and forcefulness as were in her and if he were to her anything more than a rough, simple, ignorant bush fellow, in whom she was interested a little for old acquaintance sake and because of the common Cause they served. For to himself, he had been still the same as before he ate from her hands the fruit of the Tree of Knowledge. Absorbed in his work, a zealot, a fanatic, conscious of all she had and of all he lacked, he had not noticed how his own mind had expanded, how broader ideas had come to him, how the confidence born of persistent thought gave force to his words and how the sincerity and passion that rang in his voice reached if but for a moment the hearts of men. When he thought of her mentality he doubted that she would be his, she seemed so high above him. It was when he thought of her solely as a Woman, when he remembered the smile of her parting, the hand-clinging that was almost a caress, the tender "Come back to me again, Ned!" that he felt himself her equal in his Manhood and dreamed his dream of how he would woo and win her.

And now! Ah, now, he knew himself and knew her. He realised all that he was, all that he might have been. He would have wooed her and Nemesis struck him on the mouth, struck him dumb.

There come moments in our lives when we see ourselves. For years, for a generation, till dying often, we live our lives and do not know except by name the Ego that dwells within. We face death unflinchingly, as most men do, and it never speaks. We love and we hate, with a lightness that is held civilised, and it never stirs. We suffer and mourn and laugh and sneer and it lies hidden. Then something stirs us to the very base of our being and self-consciousness comes. And happy, thrice happy, in spite of all sorrow and pain, no matter what has been or what awaits him, is he to whom self-consciousness does not bring the self-reproach that dieth not, the remorse that never is quite quenched.

He would have wooed and he was dumb. For with a flash his life uprose before him. He saw himself naked and he was ashamed.

Tremblingly, shaken with anguish, he saw himself—unfit to look into the eyes of a woman such as this. Like loathsome images of a drunkard's nightmare scenes that were past came to him. Upon his lips were kisses that stung and festered, around his neck were the impress of arms that dragged him down, into his eyes stared other eyes taunting him with the evil glances that once seemed so dear. What had he of manhood to offer to this pure woman. It seemed to him a blasphemy even to stand there by her. His passion fled. He only felt a pitiful, gnawing, hopeless, indescribable longing.

What he had been! How he had drunk and drunk and drunk again of the filthy pools wherewith we civilised peoples still our yearnings for the crystal spring of Love, that the dragon of Social Injustice guards from us so well! His sins rose in front of him. They were sins now as they had never been before. The monogamy of his race triumphed in him. For men and for women alike he knew there was the same right and the same wrong.

His soul abhorred itself because of his unfitness to match with this ideal woman of his people. He could feel her purity, as he stood there by her. He could feel that her lips still waited for the lover of her life, that round her waist the virgin zone still lay untied, that she could still give herself with all the strength of unsullied purity and unweakened passion. And he, who had thought in his miserable folly that at least he was as much Man as she was Woman? He could only give her the fragments of a life, the battered fragments of what once had been well worth the having.

He knew that now. He saw himself naked and he knew what he was and what he had been. He had feared comparison with her intellectually and he towered above her, even now; he knew it. He knew now that to him it had been given to sway the thoughts of men, to feel the pulse of the great world beat, to weld discontent into action, to have an idea and to dare and to give to others faith and hope. That came to him also, without conceit, without egotism—with a rush of still more bitter infinitely more unbearable, pain. For this, too, he had wasted, flung away, so it seemed to him in his agony of degradation, because he had not been true to his higher self, because he had not done as a true Man would. And so, he had been blind. He saw it plainly, now, the path he should have trod, trampling his weaknesses down, bending his whole life in one strong effort, living only for the work at hand. And to him it came that, perchance, on him was this great punishment that because of his unworthiness the Cause must wait longer and struggle more; that because he had not been strong little children would sob who might have laughed and men would long for death who might have joyed in living. And he knew, too, that had he but been what he might have been he would have stood fearlessly by her side at last and won her to cast in her lot with his. For there was a way out, indeed, a way out from the house of bondage, and none had been so near to it in all time as he had all his life, none had had their feet pointed so towards it, none had failed so strangely to pick up the track and follow it to the end. Years ago, as he thought, sleepless, under the stars, he had touched on it. Geisner had brought him near to it. And still he had not seen it, had not seen as he saw now that those who seek to change the world must first of all show the world that change is possible, must gather themselves together and go out into the desert to live their life in their own way as an example to all men. Who could do this as the bushmen could, as he and his houseless, homeless, wandering mates could? If he only could lead them to it, Geisner helping him! If another chance might be his as the chance had been! Now, life seemed over. He had a prescience of misfortune. A Queensland gaol would swallow him up. That would be the end of it all.

He did not think that he was much the same as others, more forceful perhaps for evil as for good but still much the same. He did not think that social conditions had been against him, that Society had refused him the natural life which gives morality and forced upon him the unnatural life which fosters sin. What did that matter? The Puritan blood that flowed in his veins made him stern jury and harsh judge. He tried himself by his own ideal and he condemned himself. He was unworthy. He had condemned those who drank; he had condemned those who cursed and swore meaninglessly; he had looked upon smoking as a weakness, almost a fault. Now, he condemned himself, without reservation. He had sinned and his punishment had begun. He had lived in vain and he had lost his love. It never occurred to him that he might play a part before her—he was too manly. Yet his great longing grew greater as he realised everything. All the loneliness of his longing spoke in that hoarse whisper :

" Nellie !"

And Nellie ? Nellie loved him.

She had held him as a brother for so long that this love for him had crept upon her, little by little, inch by inch, insidiously, unperceived. She remembered always with pleasure their school days together and their meetings since, that meeting here in Sydney two years before most of all. She had felt proud of him, of his strength and his fiery temper, of his determined will, of the strong mind which she could feel growing and broadening in the letters he had sent her of late. She could not but know that to him she was very much, that to her he owed largely the bent of his thinking, that to her he still looked as a monitress. But she lulled herself with the delusion that all this was brotherliness and that all her feelings were sisterless. His coming that night, his gift of the rose, had filled her with a happiness that mingled strangely with the pain of her fears.

Coming along, arm in arm with him, she had been thinking of him, even while she spoke earnestly of other things. Would she ever see him again, she wondered with a sinking of the heart, would she ever see him again. Never had he thought or care for himself, never would he shrink from fear of consequences if it seemed to him that a certain course was "straight." She would not have him shrink, of course. He was dear to her because he was what he was, and yet, and yet, it pained her so to think that she nevermore might see him. Seldom she saw him it was true, only now and then, years between, but she always hoped to see him. What if the hope left her ! What should she do if she should see him again nevermore ?

The kaleidoscope of her memories showed to her one scene , one of the episodes that had gone to make up her character, to strengthen her devotion : the whirring of a sewing machine in a lamp-lit room and a life-romance told to the whirring, the fate of a woman as Geisner's was the fate of a man. A romance of magnificent fidelity, of heroic sacrifice illumined by a passionate love, of a husband followed to the land of his doom from that sad isle of the Atlantic seas, of prison bars worn away by the ceaseless

labour of a devoted woman and of the cruel storm that beat the
breath from her loved one as freed and unfettered he fled to
liberty and her ! She heard again the whirr of the machine, saw
again the lamplight shine on the whitening head majestic still.
For Ned, while he lived, no matter where, she would toil so.
Though all the world should forget him she would not. But
supposing, after all, she never saw him more. What should she
do ? What should she do ? And yet, she did not know yet that
she loved him.

They walked along, side by side, close together, through the
dull weary streets, by barrack-rows of houses wrapped in slumber
or showing an occasional light ; through thoroughfares which
the windows of the shops that thrive, owl-like, at night still made
brilliant ; down the long avenue of trim-clipped trees whereunder
time-defying lovers still sat whispering ; past the long garden
wall, startling as they crossed the road a troop of horses
browsing for fallen figs ; along the path that winds, water-lapped,
under the hollowed rocks that shelter nightly forlorn outcasts of
Sydney. She saw it all as they passed along and she did not see it.
Afterwards she could recall every step they took, every figure they
passed, every tree and seat and window and lamp-post on the way.

At one corner a group of men wrangled drunkenly outside a
public-house. Down one deserted street another drunkard
staggered, cursing with awful curses a slipshod woman who kept
pace with him on the pavement and answered him with nerveless
jeers. Just beyond a man overtook them, walking swiftly, his
tread echoing as he went ; he turned and looked at her as he
passed ; he had a short beard and wore a "hard hitter." Then
there was a girl plying her sorry trade, talking in the shadow with
a young man, spruce and white-shirted. They had to wait at one
street for a tram to rush past screeching and rattling. At
one crossing Ned had seized her arm because a cab was coming
carelessly. One of the lovers in the avenue was tracing lines on
the ground with a stick, while her sweetheart leaned over her.
Down under the rocks she saw the forms of sleepers here and
there ; from one clump of bushes came a sound of heavy snoring.
She saw all this, everything, a thousand incidents, but she did
not heed them. She was as one in a daze ; or as one who moves and
thinks and sees, sleep-walking.

So they reached the point by Lady Macquarie's Chair, paused
for a moment at the turn, hesitated, then together, as of one

accord, went down the grassy slope by the landing stairs and out upon the rough wave-eaten fringe of rock to the water's edge. They were alone together, alone in Paradise. There were none others in the whole world.

Above them, almost overhead, in the starry sky, the full round moon was sailing, her white glare falling upon a matchless scene of mingling land and water, sea and shore and sky. Like a lake the glorious harbour stretched before them and on either hand. In its bosom the moon sailed as in a mirror; on it great ships floated at anchor and islets nestled down; all round the sheltering hills verily clapped their hands. In the great dome of the universe there was not a cloud. Through the starless windows of that glorious dome they could see into the fathomless depths of Eternity. Under the magic of the moon not even the sordid work of man struck a discordant note. At their feet the faint ripplings of this crystal lake whispered their ceaseless lullaby and close behind them the trees rustled softly in the languid breathings of the sleeping sea. Of a truth it was Paradise, fit above all fitness to gladden the hearts of men, worthy to fill the soul to overflowing with the ecstasy of living, deserving to be enshrined as a temple of the Beautiful wherein all might worship together, each his own God.

The keen sense of its loveliness, its perfect beauty, its sublime simplicity, stole over Nellie as she stood silently by Ned's side in the full moonlight and gazed. Over her angry soul, tortured by the love she hardly knew, its pure languor crept, soothing, softening. She looked up at the silvery disc and involuntarily held out her hands to it, its radiance overpowering her. She wrenched her eyes away from it suddenly, a strange fearfulness leaping in her who knew no fear; the light at the South Heads flashed before her, the convent stood out in the far distance, a ferry-house shone white, the towers and roofs of Sydney showed against the sky, the lights on the shipping and on the further shore were as reflections of the stars above. And there in the water, as in a mirror, was that glowing moon. Startled, she found herself thinking that it would be heavenly to take Ned's hand and plunge underneath this crystal sheet that alone separated them from peace and happiness. She looked up again. There was the moon itself, swimming amid the twinkling stars, full and round and white and radiant. As its rays enwrapped her eyes, she heard the leaves rustling in melody and the wavelets rippling in tune.

All Nature lived to her then. There was life in the very rocks under her feet, language in the very shimmer of the waters, a music, as the ancients dreamed, in the glittering spheres that circled there in space. The moon had something to say to her, something to tell her, something she longed to hear and shrank from hearing. She knew she was not herself somehow, not her old self, that it was as though she were being bewitched, mesmerised, drawn out of herself by some strange influence, sweet though fearful. Suddenly a distant clock struck and recalled her wandering thoughts.

"Half-past! Half-past eleven I suppose! I thought it was later, ever so much later. It has seemed like hours, it is so beautiful here, but we haven't been here many minutes," she said. Adding incongruously : "Let's go. It's getting very late." She spoke decidedly. She felt that she dare not stay ; why, she had not the least idea.

Then she heard Ned, who was standing there, rigid, except that he was twirling his soft straw hat round and round in his fingers, say in a low tremulous husky whisper :

"Nellie ! "

Then she knew.

She was loved and she loved. That was what the stars sang and the little ripples and the leaves. That was what the hard rock knew and what the shimmer of the water laughed to think of and what the glowing moon had to tell her as it swam high in heaven, looking down into her heart and swelling its tumultuous tide. The moon knew, the full moon that ever made her pulse beat strong and her young life throb till its throbbing was a pain, the full white moon that, dethroned on earth, still governs from the skies the lives of women. She was loved. She was loved. And she, who had vowed herself to die unmarried, she loved, loved, loved.

She knew that those only laugh at Love to whom the fullness of living has been denied, in whose cold veins, adulterate with inherited disease, a stagnant liquid mocks the purpose of the rich red blood of a healthy race ; that in that laugh of theirs is the knell of them and of their people ; that the nation which has ceased to love has almost ceased to live.

She knew that every breath she had ever drawn had been drawn that she might live for this moment ; that every inch of her stature and every ounce of her muscle and every thought of her brain had built up slowly, surely, ultimately, this all-absorbing passion; that upon her was the hand of the Infinite driving her of her own nature to form a link in the great Life-chain that stretches from the Whence into the Whither, to lose herself in the appointed lot as the coral insect does whose tiny body makes a continent possible.

She knew that Love is from the beginning and to all time, knew that it comes to each as each is, to the strong in strength and to the weak in weakness. She knew that to her it had come with all the force of her grand physique and vigorous brain and dominant emotionality, that in her heart one man, one hero, one lover, was enshrined and that to him she would be loyal and true for ever and ever, choosing death rather than to fail him.

She knew that they do rightly and for themselves well who in Love's strength brush aside all worldly barriers and insensate prejudice. She knew that it is the one great Democrat strong as Death—when it comes, though sad to say in decaying states it comes too seldom; that its imperious mandate makes the king no higher than the beggar-girl and binds in sweet equality the child of fortune and the man of toil. She knew that the mysterious Power which orders all things has not trusted to a frail support in resting the conservation of the race upon the strength of loving.

All this she knew and more, knew as by instinct as her love flamed conscious in her.

She knew that there was one thing to which love like hers could not link itself and that was to dishonour, not the false dishonour of conventionalism but the real dishonour of proving untrue to herself. She knew that when she ceased to respect herself, when she shrank from herself, then she would shrink before him whom she loved and who loved her. She knew that she could better bear to lose him, to go lonely and solitary along the future years, than shame that self-consciousness which ever she had held sacred but which was doubly sacred now he loved her.

How she loved him! For his soul, for his body, for his brain, for his rough tenderness, for his fiery tongue! She loved his broad shoulders and his broad mind. She loved his hearty laugh and his hearty hand-grip and his homely speech and his red-hot enthusiasm. She loved him because she felt that he dared and because she felt that he loved her. She loved him because she had learned to see in him her ideal. She loved him because he was in danger for the Cause and because he was going from her and because she had loved him for years had she but known. She loved him for a thousand things. And yet! Something held her back. It only needed a word but the word did not come. It was on her lips a dozen times, that one word " Ned!" which meant all words, and she did not say it.

They stood there side by side, motionless, silent, waiting, Ned suffering anguish unspeakable, Nellie plunged in that great joy which comes so seldom that some say it only comes to herald deeper sadness. To him the glorious scene around spoke nothing, he hardly saw it; to her it was enchanted with a strange enchantment, never had it seemed so, all the times she had seen it. How beautiful life was! How sweet to exist! How glad the world!

"Nellie!" said Ned, at last, humbly, penitently, hopelessly. " I'm not a good man. I haven't been just what you think I've been." He stopped, then added, slowly and desperately as if on an afterthought: "If—your own heart—won't plead—for—me— it's not a bit of use my saying anything."

When one speaks as one feels one generally speaks to the point and this sudden despairing cry of Ned's was a better plea than any he could by long thinking have constructed. Wonderful are the intricacies of a man's mind, but still more intricate the mind of woman. Nellie at the moment did not care whether he had been saint or sinner. She felt that her love was vast enough to wash him clean of all offending and make amend in him for all shortcoming. She could not bear to see him in pain thus when she was so happy; in uncertainty, in despair, when the measure of her love was not to be taken, so huge was it and all for him. If he had sinned, and how men sin there is little hid from the working girl, it was not from evil heart. If he had not been good he would be good. He would promise her.

" But you will be good now, will you not, Ned?" she asked, softly, not looking at him, dropping her hand against his, stealing her slender fingers into the fingers that nervously twirled the hat.

From bitter despondency Ned's thoughts changed to ecstatic hope. He swung round, his hand in Nellie's, his brain in a whirl. Was it a dream or was she really standing there in the strong moonshine, her lovelit eyes looking into his for a moment before the downcast lids veiled them, her face flushed, her bosom heaving, her hand tenderly pressing his? He dropped his hat, careless of the watery risk, and seizing her by both arms above the elbows, held her for a moment in front of him, striving to collect himself, vainly trying to subdue the excitement that made him think he was going to faint.

"Nellie!" he whispered, passionately, his craving finding utterance. "Kiss me!" She lifted up the flushed face, with the veiled downcast eyes and soft quivering lips. He passed his hands under her arms and bent down. Then a white mist came over his eyes as he crushed her to him and felt on his parched lips the burning kiss of the woman he loved. For a moment she rested there, in his arms, her mouth pressed to his. The rose, shattered, threw its petals as an offering upon the altar of their joy.

The Future, what did it matter to him? The scaffold or the gaol might come or go, what did it matter to him? It flashed through his mind that Nellie could be his wife before he went and then all the governments in the world and all the military and all the gatling guns might do their worst. They could not take from him a happiness he had not deserved, but which had come to him as a free gift in despite of his unworthiness. And as he thought this, Nellie shook herself out of his arms, pushing him so violently that he staggered and almost fell on the uneven rocks.

"I cannot," she cried, holding up her arms as if to ward him off. "I cannot, Ned. You mustn't touch me. I cannot."

"Nellie!" he replied, bewildered. "What on earth is the matter?"

"I cannot," she cried again. "Ned, you know I can't."

"Can't what?" he asked, gradually understanding.

"I can't marry. I shall never marry. It's cruel to you, contemptible of me, to be here. I forgot myself, Ned. Come along! It's madness to stay here."

She turned on her heel and walked off sharply, taking the upper path. He picked up his hat and hastily followed. There was nothing else to be done. Overtaking her, he strode along by her side in a fury of mingled rage, sorrow, anger and disappointment.

She paused at the corner of her street. As she did so bells far and near began to strike midnight, the clock at the City Hall leading off with its quarters. They had been gone an hour and a quarter. To both of them it seemed like a year.

M

CHAPTER IV.

THE WHY OF THE WHIM.

NELLIE stopped at the corner of her street, under the lamp-post. Ned stopped by her side, fuming by now, biting his moustache, hardly able to hold his tongue. Nellie looked at him a moment, sadly and sorrowfully. The look of determination that made her mouth appear somewhat cruel was on her whole face; but with it all she looked heart-broken.

"Ned," she begged. "Don't be angry with me. I can't. Indeed, I can't."

"Why not?" he demanded, boiling over. "If you wouldn't have had me at first I wouldn't have blamed you. But you say you love me, or as good as say, and then you fly off. Nellie! Nellie, darling! If you only knew how for years I've dreamed of you. When I rode the horse's hoofs kept saying 'Nellie.' I used to watch the stars and think them like your eyes, and the tall blue gum and think it wasn't as full of grace as you. Down by the water just now I thought you wouldn't have me because I wasn't fit, and I'm not, Nellie, I'm not, but when I thought it I felt like a lost soul. And then, when I thought you loved me in spite of all, everything seemed changed. I seemed to feel that I was a man again, a good man, fit to live, and all that squatter government of ours could do, the worst they could do, seemed a bit of a joke while you loved me. And——"

"Ned! Ned!" begged Nellie, who had put her hands over her face while he was speaking. "Have pity on me! Can't you see? I'm not iron and I'm not ice but I can't do as others do. I cannot. I will not."

"Why not?" he answered. "I will speak, Nellie. Do you——"

"Ned!" she interrupted, evidently forcing herself to speak. "It's no use. I'll tell you why it's not."

"There can be no reason."

"There is a reason. Nobody knows but me. When I have said I would never marry people think it is a whim. Perhaps it is, but I have a reason that I thought never to tell anyone. I only tell you so that you may understand and we may still be friends, true friends."

"Go on! I'll convince you that it doesn't mean what you think it does, this reason, whatever it is."

"Ned! Be reasonable!" She hesitated. She looked up and down the street. Nothing moved. The moon was directly overhead. There were no shadows. It was like day. An engine whistle sounded like a long wail in the distance. In the silence that followed they could hear the rushing of a train. Ned waited, watching her pain-drawn face. A passionate fear assailed him, blotting out his wrath.

"You recollect my sister?" she asked, looking away from him. He nodded.

"You heard she died? You spoke of her two years ago." He nodded again.

"I did not tell you the whole truth then. . . . . . I did not tell anybody. . . . . . I came down here so as not to tell. . . . . . I could not bear to go home, to chance any of them coming down to Brisbane and seeing me. . . . . . You know." She stopped. He could see her hands wringing, a hunted look in the eyes that would not meet his.

"Never mind telling me, Nellie," he said, a great pity moving him. "I'm a brute. I didn't mean to be selfish but I love you so. It shall be as you say. I don't want to know anything that pains you to tell."

"That is your own self again, Ned," she answered, looking at him, smiling sadly, a love in her face that struck him with a bitter joy. "But you have a right. I must tell you for my own sake. Only, I can't begin." Her mouth trembled. Great tears gathered in her eyes and rolled down her cheeks. A lump rose in his throat. He seized her hands and lifted them reverently to his lips. He could not think of a word to say to comfort her.

"Ned!" she said, in a tone almost inaudible, looking at him through her tears. "She died in the hospital but I didn't tell you how. . . . . . She died, oh, a terrible death. . . . . . She had gone . . . . . down, Ned. Right down. Down to the streets, Ned."

He pressed her hands, speechless. They stood thus facing one another, till down his face, too, the sad tears rained in sympathy, sad tears that mourned without reproach the poor dead sister whom the hard world had crushed and scorned, sad tears that fell on his passion like rain on fire and left in him only a yearning desire to be a comforter. Nellie, snatching her hands away, pressed them to her mouth to stifle the frantic sobs that began to shake her, long awful sobs that drew breath whistling through clenched fingers. And Ned, drawing her to him, laid her head on his shoulder, stroking her hair as a mother does, kissing her temple with loving, passionless kisses, striving to comfort her with tender brotherly words, to still her wild cries and frantic sobs in all unselfishness. There were none to see them in all this moonlit city. The wearied toilers, packed around them, slumbered or tossed unconsciously. Above them, serene and radiant, the full moon swam on amid the stars.

"She was so good, Ned," cried Nellie, choking, with sobs, almost inarticulate, pouring out to him the pent-up thinking of long years. "She was so good. And so kind. Don't you remember her, Ned? Such a sweet girl, she was. It killed her, Ned. This cruel, cruel life killed her. But before it killed her—oh!—oh!—oh!—oh! Why are we ever born? Why are we ever born?"

It was heart-rending, her terrible grief, her abandonment of anguish which she vainly endeavoured to thrust back into her throat. With all her capacity for passionate love she bewailed her sister's fate. Ned, striving to soothe her, all the while mingled his tears with hers. A profound sadness overshadowed him. He felt all his hopes numbed and palsied in the face of this omnipotent despair. This girl who was dead seemed for the time the symbol of what Life is. He had hated Society, hated it, but as its blackest abyss opened at his very feet his hate passed from him. He only felt an utter pity for all things, a desire to weep over the helpless hopelessness of the world.

Nellie quieted at last. Her sobs ceased to shake her, her tears dried on her pale face, but still she rested her head on Ned as if finding strength and comfort in him. Her eyelids were closed Except for an occasional belated lingering sob she might have been asleep. Her grief had exhausted her. At last a coming footfall roused her. She raised her head, putting her hands instinctively to her hat and hair, pulling herself together with a strong breath.

"You are very kind to me, Ned," she said, softly. "I've been so silly but I'm better now. I don't often carry on like that." She smiled faintly. "Let's walk a bit! I shall feel better and I have such a lot to tell you. Don't interrupt! I want you to

know all about it, Ned." And so, walking backwards and forwards in the moonlit streets, deserted and empty, passing an
occasional night prowler, watched with suspicious eyes by ener-
getic members of the "foorce" whose beats they invaded, stopping
at corners or by dead-walls, then moving slowly on again, she
told him.

*   *   *   *

"You know how things were at home on the Darling Downs,
Ned. Father a ' cocky,' going shearing to make both ends meet,
and things always going wrong, what with the drought and the
wet and having no money to do things right and the mortgage
never being cleared off. It wasn't particularly good land, either,
you know. The squatters had taken all that and left only stony
ridges for folks like ours. And we were all girls, six of us.
Your father was sold up, and he had you boys to help him. Well,
my father wasn't sold up but he might as well have been. He
worked like a horse and so did mother, what with the cows and
the fowls and looking after things when father was away, and we
girls did what we could from the time we were little chits.
Father used to get up at daybreak and work away after dark
always when he was at home. On Sunday mornings after he'd
seen to the things he used to lie on his back under that tree in
front if it was fine or about the house if it was wet, just dead
beat. He used to put a handkerchief over his face but he didn't
sleep much. He just rested. In the afternoon he used to have a
smoke and a read. Poor father! He was always thought queer,
you recollect, because he didn't care for newspapers except to see
about farming in and took his reading out of books of poetry
that nobody else cared about. On Monday he'd start to work
again, with only a few hours for sleep and meals, till Saturday
night. Yet we had only just a living. Everything else went in
interest on the mortgage. Twelve per cent. Mother used to
cry about it sometimes but it had to be paid somehow.

"When Mary was fifteen and I was thirteen, you remember,
she went to Toowoomba, to an uncle of ours, mother's brother,
who had four boys and no girls and didn't know what to put the
boys to. Father and mother thought this a splendid chance for
Mary to learn a trade, there were so many of us at home, you
know, and so they took one of my cousins and uncle took Mary
and she started to learn dressmaking. Uncle was a small con-
tractor, who had a hard time of it, and his wife was a woman

who'd got frozen about the heart, although she was as good as gold when it melted a little. She was always preaching about the need for working and saving and the folly of wasting money in drink and ribbons and everything but what was ugly. She said that there was little pleasure in the world for those who had to work, so the sooner we made up our minds to do without pleasure the better we'd get on. Mary lived with them a couple of years, coming home once in a while. Then she got the chance of a place where she'd get her board and half-a-crown a week. She couldn't bear aunt and so she took it and I went to live at uncle's and to learn dressmaking, too. That was six months after you went off, Ned. I wasn't quite fifteen and you were eighteen, past. Seven years ago. I was so sorry when you went away, Ned.

"Aunt wasn't pleasant to live with. I used to try to get on with her and I think she liked me in her way but she made me miserable with her perpetual lecturing about the sin of liking to look nice and the wickedness of laughing and the virtue of scraping every ha'penny. I used to help in the house, of course, when I came from work and I was always getting into trouble for reading books, that I borrowed, at odd minutes when aunt thought I ought to be knitting or darning or slaving away somehow at keeping uncomfortable. I used to tell Mary and Mary used to wish that I could come to work where she did. We used to see each other every dinner hour and in the evening she'd come round and on Sundays we used to go to church together. She was so kind to me, and loving, looking after me like a little mother. She used to buy little things for me out of her half-crown and say that when she was older aunt shouldn't make me miserable. Besides aunt, I didn't like working in a close shop, shut up. I didn't seem to be able to take a good breath. I used to think as I sat, tacking stuff together or unpicking threads that seemed to be endless, how it was out in the bush and who was riding old Bluey to get the cows in now I was gone and whether the hens laid in the same places and if it was as still and fresh as it used to be when we washed our faces and hands under the old lean-to before breakfast. And Toowoomba is fresher than Sydney. I don't know what I'd have thought of Sydney then. I used to tell Mary everything and she used to cheer me up. Poor Mary!

"For a long while she had the idea of going to Brisbane to work. She said there were chances to make big wages there, because forewomen and draping hands were wanted more and girls who had anything in them had a better show than in a little place. I used to remind her that it was said there were lots too many girls in Brisbane and that unless you had friends there you couldn't earn your bread. But she used to say that one must live everywhere and that things couldn't be worse than they were in Toowoomba. You see she was anxious to be able to earn enough to help with the mortgage. Father had been taken sick shearing and had to knock off and so didn't earn what he expected and that year they'd got deeper into debt and things looked worse than ever. One day he came into Toowoomba with his cart, looking ten years older. Next day, Mary told me she didn't care what happened, she was going to Brisbane to see if she couldn't earn some money or else they'd lose the selection and that she'd spoken for her place for me and I was to have it. She'd been saving up for a good while what she could by shillings and sixpences and pennies, doing sewing work for anybody who'd pay her anything in her own time. She said that when she'd got a five-pound-a-week place she'd come back for a visit and bring me a new dress, and mother and father and the others all sorts of things and pay the interest all herself and that I should have the next best place in the shop and come to live with her. We talked about going into business together and whether it wouldn't be better for father to throw up the selection after a while and live with us in Brisbane. Ah! What simple fools we were! If we had but known!

"So Mary went to Brisbane, with just a few shillings beside her ticket and hardly knowing a soul in the big town. I went to the station with her in the middle of the night. She was going by the night train because then she'd get to Brisbane in the morning and have the day in front of her and she had nowhere to go if she got in at night. I recollect thinking how sweetly pretty she looked as she sat in the carriage all alone.

"You remember her, Ned? Well, she got prettier and prettier as she grew older, not tall and big and strong-looking like me but smaller than I was even then and with a fresh round face that always smiled at you. She had small feet and hands and hair that curled naturally and her skin was dark, not fair like mine. People in Toowoomba used to turn and look at her when she went out and everybody liked her. She was so kind to everybody. And she was full of courage though she did cry a little when she kissed me good-bye, because I cried so. I could never have stopped crying had I but known how I should see her again.

"She wrote in two or three days to say that she had got a place, just enough to pay her board, and expected to get a better one soon. She was always expecting something better when she wrote and my aunt when I saw her wagged her head and said that rolling stones gathered no moss. The interest-day came round and father just managed to scrape the money together. They'd got so poor and downhearted that I used to cry at night thinking of them and I used to tell Mary when I wrote. I used to blame myself for it once but I don't now. We all get to believe at last in what must be will be, Ned. And then I had a letter from Mary telling me she had a much better place and in two or three weeks mother wrote such a proud pleased letter to say that Mary had sent them a five-pound note. And for about a year Mary sent them two or three pounds every month and at Christmas five pounds again. Then her letters stopped altogether, both to them and to me. To me she had kept writing always the same, kind and chatty and about herself. She told me she had to save and scrape a little but that she had hope some day to be able to get me down. I never dreamed it was not so, not even when the letters stopped, though afterwards, when I went through them, I saw that the handwriting, in the later ones, was shaky a little.

"We waited and waited to hear from her but no letter came to anybody. There was a girl I knew whose father had been working in Toowoomba and who was in the same shop for a little while and her father was going to Brisbane to a job and they were all going. He was a carpenter. She and I had got to be friendly after Mary went away and she promised to find her but couldn't. You see we were bush folks still and didn't think anything of streets and addresses and thought the post office enough. And when two months passed and no letter came mother wrote half crazy, and I didn't know what to do, and I wrote to the girl I knew to ask her to get me work so that I could go to look for Mary. It just happened that they wanted a body hand in her shop and they promised me the place and I went the next day I heard. They wanted a week's notice where I was working and didn't want to give up my things without but aunt went and got them and gave me the money for my fare and told me if I wanted to come back to write to her and she'd find the money again. Poor old aunt! I shall never forget her. Her heart was all right if she had got hard and unhappy. That's how I got to Brisbane to look for Mary.

"I went to board with the girl I knew. I was earning ten shillings a week and paid that for my board and helped with the ironing for my washing. Her father had got out of work again for times were bad and they were glad to get my money. Lizzie got ten shillings a week and she had a brother about fourteen who earned five shillings. That was about all they had to live on often, nine in the family with me and the rent seven shillings for a shell of a place that was standing close up against other humpies in a sort of yard. There were four little rooms unceiled and Lizzie and I slept together in a sort of shelf bedstead, with two little sisters sleeping on the floor beside us. When it was cold we used to take them in with us and heap their bedclothes on top of us. The wind came through the walls everywhere. Out in the bush one doesn't mind that but in town, where you're cooped up all day, it doesn't seem the same thing. We had plenty of bread and meat and tea generally but the children didn't seem to thrive and got so thin and pale-looking that I thought they were going to be ill. Lizzie's father used to come home, after tramping about for work, looking as tired as my father did after his long day in the fields and her mother fretted and worried and you could see things getting shabbier and shabbier every week. I don't know what I should have done only Lizzie and I now and then got a dress to make for a neighbour or some sewing to do, night-times. Lizzie's mother had a machine and we used that and they always made me keep my half of what we got that way, no matter how hard up they were. They never thought of asking for interest for the use of the machine. And all the while I was looking for Mary.

"I used to stand watching as the troops of girls went by to work and from work, morning and evening, going to a new place every day so that I shouldn't miss her and in the dinner hours I used to go round the work rooms to see if she worked in one of them or if anybody knew her. At first, when I had a shilling to spare, I put an advertisement that she would understand in the paper, but I gave that up soon. I never dreamed of going to the police station, any more than we had dreamed of it in Toowoomba. I just looked and looked but I couldn't find her.

"I shall never forget the first time I got out of work. One Saturday, without a minute's warning, a lot of us were told that we wouldn't be wanted for a week or two. Lizzie and I were both told. She could hardly keep herself from crying but I couldn't cry. I was too wretched. I thought of everything and there seemed nothing to do anywhere. At home they couldn't help me. I shrank from asking aunt, for she'd only offered to help me to come back and what could I do in Toowoomba if I got there? And how could I find Mary? I had only ten shillings in the world and I owed it all for my board. I got to imagining where I should sleep and how long I could go without dying of hunger and I hated so to go into the house with Lizzie to tell them. Lizzie's mother cried when she heard it and Lizzie cried, but I went into the bedroom when I'd put my money on the table and began to put my things in my box. They called me to dinner and when I didn't come and they found out that I meant to go because I couldn't pay any more they were so angry. Lizzie's mother wanted to know if they looked altogether like heathens and then we three cried like babies and I felt better. I used to cry a good deal in those days, I think.

"Lizzie's father got a job next week a few miles out of Brisbane and went away to it and on the Monday I answered an advertisement for a woman to do sewing in the house and was the first and got it. She was quite young, the woman I worked for, and very nice. She got talking to me and I told her how I'd got out of work and about Mary. I suppose she was Socialist for she talked of what I didn't understand much then, of how we ought to have a union to get wages enough to keep us when work fell off and of the absurdity of men and women having to depend for work upon a few employers who only worked them when they could get profit. She thought I should go to the police-station about Mary but I said Mary wouldn't like that. What was more to me at the time, she paid me four shillings a day and found me work for two weeks, though I don't think she wanted it. There are kind people in the world, Ned.

"I got back to regular work again, not in the same shop but in another, and then Lizzie's folks moved out to where her father was working. I and another girl got a room that we paid five shillings a week for, furnished, with the use of the kitchen. It cost us about ten shillings a week between us for food, and I got raised to twelve-and-six a week because they wanted me back where I'd worked before. So we weren't so badly off, and we kept a week ahead. Of course we lived anyhow, on dry bread and tea very often, with cakes now and then as a treat, boiled eggs sometimes and a chop. There was this about it, we felt free. Sometimes we got sewing to do at night from people we got to hear of. So we managed to get stuff for our dresses and we kept altering our hats and we used to fix our boots up with waxed threads. And all the time I kept looking for Mary and couldn't see her or hear of her.

"I had got to understand how Mary might live for years in a place like Brisbane without being known by more than a very few, but I puzzled more and more as to how she'd got the money she'd sent home. The places where she might have earned enough seemed so few that everybody knew of them. In all dressmaking places the general run of girls didn't earn enough to keep themselves decently unless they lived at home as most did. Even then they had a struggle to dress neatly and looked ill-fed, for, you see, it isn't only not getting enough it's not getting enough of the right food and getting it regularly. Most of the girls brought their lunch with them in a little paper parcel, bread and butter, and in some places they made tea. Some had lots of things to eat and lots to wear and plenty of pocket money and didn't seem to have to work but they weren't my sort or Mary's.

"What made me think first how things might be was seeing a girl in the second place I worked at. She looked so like Mary, young and fresh and pretty and lively, always joking and laughing. She was very shabby and made-over when I saw her first, with darned gloves and stitched-up boots down at heel and bits of ribbon that she kept changing to bring the best side up. Then she got a new dress all at once and new boots and gloves and hat and seemed to have money to spend and the girls began to pass remarks about her when she wasn't hearing and sometimes to her face when they had words with her. I didn't believe anything bad at first but I knew she wasn't getting any more pay and then, all at once, I recollected being behind her one night when we came out of the shop and seeing a young fellow waiting in a doorway near. He was a good-looking young fellow, well-dressed and well to do, and as she passed with some other girls he dropped his stick out in front of her and spoke to her. She laughed and ran back to the shop when we'd gone on a little further and spoke to him for a second or two as she passed him. It was after that she was well dressed and I saw her out with him once or twice and—and—I began to think of Mary. You see, I knew how hard the life was and how wearying it is to have to slave and half-starve all the time, and then Mary wanted money so to send home to help them. And when the girls talked at work they spoke of lots of things we never heard of in the bush and gradually I got to know what made me sick at heart.

"I was nearly mad when I thought of that about Mary, my sister Mary who was so good and so kind. I hated myself for dreaming of such a thing but it grew and grew on me and at last I couldn't rest till I found out. I didn't think it was so but it began to seem just possible, a wild possibility that I must satisfy to myself, the more I couldn't find her. I somehow felt she was n Brisbane somewhere and I learnt how easily one slips down to the bottom when one starts slipping and has no friends. So I used to go on Queen Street at night and look for her there. But I never saw her. I wanted to ask about her but I couldn't bear to. I thought of asking the Salvation Army people but when I went one night I couldn't.

"At last one night when we'd been working late at the shop, till eleven, as we did very often in busy times without getting any overtime pay though they turned us off as they pleased when work got slack, I saw a girl coming that I thought I'd ask. She was painted up and powdered and had flaring clothes but she looked kind. It was a quiet street where I met her and before I had time to change my mind she got to me and I stopped and asked her. I told her I'd lost my sister and did she know anything of her. She didn't laugh at me or say anything rude but talked nice and said she didn't think so and I mustn't think about that but if I liked she'd find out. I told her the name but she said that wasn't any good because girls always changed their name and she looked like crying when she said this. I had a photograph of Mary's that I always carried with me to show anybody who might have seen her without knowing her and the girl said if I'd trust her with it for a week she'd find Mary if she was in Brisbane and meet me. So I lent it to her. And we were just talking a bit and she was telling me that she was from London and that when she was a little girl a great book-writer used to pat her on the head and call her a pretty little thing and give her pennies and how she'd run away from home with a young officer, who got into trouble afterwards and came out to Australia without her and how she came out to find him and would some day, when a policeman came along and asked us what we were doing. She said we weren't doing anything and that he'd better mind his business and he said he knew her and she'd better keep a civil tongue in her head. Then he wanted to know what my name was and where I lived and the girl told me not to tell him or he'd play a trick on me and I didn't. But I told him I worked at dressmaking and roomed with another girl and he gave a kind of laugh and said he thought so and that if I didn't give him my name and address I'd have to come along with him. I began to cry and the girl told him he ought to be ashamed of himself ruining a poor hard-working girl who was looking for her sister and he only laughed again and said he knew all about that. I don't know what would have happened only just then an oldish man came along, wearing spectacles and with a kind sharp face, who stopped and asked what was the matter. The policeman was very civil to him and seemed to know him and told him that I wouldn't give him my address and that I was no good and that he was only doing his duty. The girl called the policeman names and told how it really was, only not my name, and the man looked at me and told the policeman I was shabby enough to be honest and that he'd answer for me and the policeman touched his hat and said 'good-night, sir,' and went on. Then the man told me I'd had a narrow escape and that it should be a lesson to me to keep out of bad company and I told him the girl had told the truth and he laughed, but not like the policeman, and said that was all the more reason to be careful because policemen could do what they liked with dressmakers who had no friends. Then he pulled out some money and told me to be a good girl and offered it to me, so kindly, but of course I didn't take it. Then he shook hands and walked off. There are kind people in the world, Ned, but we don't always meet them when we need them. I didn't know then how much he did for me or what cruel, wicked laws there are.

"Next week I met the girl again. I wanted so to find Mary I didn't care for all the policemen. I knew when I saw her coming that she'd found her. I didn't seem to care much, only as though something had snapped. It was only afterwards, when Mary was dead, that I used to get nearly crazy. I never told anybody, not even my room-mate, that I'd found her.

"She was in the hospital, dying, Mary was. I've heard since how that awful life kills the tender-hearted ones soon and Mary wasn't 21. She was in a bleak, bare ward, with a screen round her, and near by you could hear other girls laughing and shouting. You wouldn't have known her. Only her eyes were the same, such loving, tender eyes, when she opened them and saw me.

She looked up and saw me standing there by the bedside and before she could shrink away I put my arms round her neck and kissed her forehead, where I used to kiss her, because I was the tallest, just where the hair grew. And I told her that she mustn't mind me and that she was my dear, dear sister and that she should have let me known because it had taken me so long to find her. And she didn't say anything but clung tight to me as though she would never let me go and then all at once her arms dropped and when I lifted my head she had fainted and her eyelids were wet.

" She died three days after. I made some excuse to get away and saw her every day. She hardly spoke she was so weak but she liked to lie with my hand in hers and me fanning her. She said that first day, when she came to, that she thought I would come. But she wouldn't have written or spoken a word, Mary wouldn't. She didn't even ask after the folks at home or how I was getting on. She said once she was so tired waiting and I knew she meant waiting to die. She didn't want to live. The last day she lay with her eyes half-closed, looking at me, and all at once her lips moved. I bent down to her and heard her murmur : 'I did try, Nellie, I did try,' and I saw she was crying. I put my arms round her and kissed her on the forehead and told her that I knew she had, and then she smiled at me, such a sweet pitiful smile, and then she stopped breathing. That was the only change.

"I couldn't stay in Brisbane. I was afraid every minute of meeting somebody who'd known Mary and who might ask me about her, or of father or uncle or somebody coming down. I wrote home and said I'd found out that Mary had died in the hospital of fever and they never thought of wanting to know any more, they were so full of grief. And then I got wondering how I should get away, somewhere, where nobody would be likely to come to ask me about her, and I couldn't go because I had no money and I was just wishing one day that I could see you when who should I meet but that Long Jack. He gave me your address and I wrote to ask you to lend me thirty shillings, the fare to Sydney, and you sent me five pounds, Ned. That's how I came here. Mary wouldn't have anybody know if she could help it and I couldn't have stayed there to meet people who knew her and would have talked of her.''

CHAPTER V.

AS THE MOON WANED.

THE shadows were beginning to throw again as Nellie finished telling her story. The quarters had sounded as they walked backwards and forwards. It was past one when they stopped again under the lamp-post at the corner.

"You see, Ned," she went on. "Mary couldn't help it. It's easy enough to talk when one has everything one wants or pretty well everything but when one has nothing or pretty well nothing, it's different. I've been through it and know. The insults, the temptations, the constant steady pressure all the time. If you are poor you are thought by swagger people fair game. And even workingmen, the young ones, who don't think themselves able to marry generally, help hunt down their working sisters. Women can't always earn enough to live decently and men can't always earn enough to marry on ; and when well-to-do men get married they seem to get worse instead of better, generally. So upon the hungry, the weary, the hopeless, girls who have to patch their own boots and go threadbare and shabby while others have pretty things, and who are despised for their shabbiness by the very hypocrites who cant about love of dress, and who have folks at home whom they love, and who are penniless as well and in that abject misery which comes when there isn't any money to buy the little things, upon these is forced the opportunity to change all this if only for a little while. Besides, you know, women have the same instincts as men—why do we disguise these things and pretend they haven't and shouldn't when we know that it is right and healthy that they should ?—and though it is natural for a woman to hate what is called vice, because she is better than man—she is the mother-sex, you know—yet the very instincts which if things were right would be for good and happiness seem to make things worse when everything is wrong. Women who work, growing girls as many are, have little pleasure in their lives, less even than men. And wiseacres say we are light and frivolous and chattering, because most women can only find relief in that and know of nothing else, though all the time in the bottom of their hearts there are deep wells of human passion and human love. If you heard sewing-room talk you would call us parrots or worse. If you knew the sewing-room lives you would feel as I do."

He did not know what to say.

"For myself," straightening herself with unconscious pride, "it has not been so much. I have been hungry and almost ragged, here in Sydney, wearing another girl's dress when I went to get slop-work, so as to lcok decent, living on rye bread for days at a time, working for thirty-eight hours at a stretch once so as to get the work done in time to get the money. That's sweating, isn't it? Of course I'm all right now. I get thirty shillings a week for draping and the wife of the boss wants to keep on friendly terms with Mrs. Stratton and I'm a good hand, so I can organise without being victimised for it. But even when I was hardest up it wasn't the same to me as to most girls. As a last resort I used to think always of killing myself. That would have been ever so much easier to me than the other thing. But I am hard and strong. I've heard my mother say that her father was the first of his people to wear boots. They went barefooted before then and I'm barefooted in some things yet. Mary wasn't like me, but better, not so hard or so selfish. And so, she couldn't help it, any more than I can."

"Nellie," he said, speaking the thought he had been thinking for an hour. "What difference does all this make between you and me?"

"Don't you understand?" she cried. "When people marry they have children. And when my sister Mary ended so, who is safe? Nothing we can do, no care we can take, can secure a child against misery while the world is what it is. I try to alter things for that. I would do anything, everything, no matter what, to make things so that little children would have a chance to be good and happy. Because the unions go that way I am unionist and because Socialism means that I am Socialist and I love whatever strikes at things that are and I hate everything that helps maintain them. And that is how we all really feel who feel at all, it is the mother in us, the source of everything that is good, and mothers do not mind much how their children are bettered so long as they are bettered. No matter what the bushmen do up there in Queensland, my heart is with them, so long as they shake this hateful state of things. I can't remember when everybody round weren't slaving away and no good coming of it. My father has only a mortgaged farm to show for a life of toil. My sister, my own sister, who grew up like a flower in the Queensland bush and worked her fingers to the bone and should have been to-day a happy woman with happy children on her knee, they picked her up when she lay dying in the gutter like a dog and in their charity gave her a bed to die on when they wouldn't give her decent wages to live on. Everywhere I've been it's the same story, men out of work, women out of work, children who should be at school the only ones who can always get work. Everywhere men crawling for a job, sinking their manhood for the chance of work, cringing and sneaking and throat-cutting, even in their unionism. In every town an army of women like my Mary, women like ourselves, going down, down, down. Honesty and virtue and courage getting uncommon. We're all getting to steal and plunder when we get a chance, the work people do it, the employers do it, the politicians do it. I know. We all do it. Women actually don't understand that they're selling themselves often even when a priest does patter a few clap-trap phrases over them. Oppression on every hand and we dare not destroy it. We haven't courage enough. And things will never be any better while Society is as it is. So I hate what Society is. Oh! I hate it so. If word or will of mind could sweep it away to leave us free to do what our inner hearts, crushed by this industrialism that we have, tell us to do it should go. For we've good in our hearts, most of us. We like to do what's kind, when we've a chance. I've found it so, anyway. Only we're caught in this whirl that crushes us all, the poor in body and the rich in soul. But till it goes, if it ever goes, I'll not be guilty of bringing a child into such a hell as this is now. That to me would be a cruelty that no weakness of mine, no human longing, could excuse ever. For no fault of her own Mary's life was a curse to her in the end. And so it may be with any of us. I'll not have the sin of giving life on me."

They stood face to face looking into each other's eyes. Unflinchingly she offered up her own heart and his on the altar of her ideal.

He read on her set lips the unalterability of her determination. It was on his tongue to suggest that it was easy to compromise, but there was that about her which checked him. Above all

N

things there was a naturalness about her, an absence of artificiality, the emanation of a strong and vigorous womanliness. The very freedom of her speech was purity itself. The dark places of life had been bared to her and she did not conceal the fact or minimise it but she spoke of it as something outside of herself, as not affecting her excepting that it roused in her an intense sympathy. She was indeed the barefooted woman in her conception of morality, in her frankness and in her strong emotions untainted by the gangrene of a rotting civilisation. To suggest to her that fruitless love, that barren marriage, which destroys the soul of France and is spreading through Australia, would be to speak a strange language to her. He could say nothing. He was seized with a desire to get away from her.

"Good-bye!" he said, holding out his hand. She took it in both her own.

"Ned!" she cried. "We part friends, don't we? If there is a man in the world who could make me change my mind, it's you. Wherever you go I shall be thinking of you and all life through I shall be the same. You have only to let me know and there's nothing possible I wouldn't do for you gladly. We are friends, are we not? Mates? Brother and sister?"

Brother and sister! The spirit moved in Ned's hot heart at the words. Geisner's words came to him, nerving him.

"No!" he answered. "Friends? Yes. Mates? Yes. Brother and sister? No, never. I don't feel able to talk now. You're like a thorn bush in front of me that it's no use rushing at. But I'm not satisfied. You're wrong somewhere and I'm right and the right thing is to love when Love comes even if we're to die next minute. I'm going away and I may come back and I mayn't but if I do you'll see my way. I shall think it out and show you. Why, Nellie, I'm a different man already since you kissed me. You and I together, why, we'd straighten things out if they were a thousand times as crooked. What couldn't we do, you and me? And we'll do it yet, Nellie. When I come back you'll have me and we two will give things such a shaking that they'll never be the same again after we've got through with them. Now, goodbye! I'll come back if it's years and years, and you'll wait for me, I know. Good-bye, till then."

She felt her feet leave the ground as he lifted her to him in a hug that made her ribs ache for a week, felt his willing lips on her passive ones, felt his long moustache, his warm breath, his reviving passion. Then she found herself standing alone, quivering and pulsating, watching him as he walked away with the waddling walk of the horseman.

In her heart, madly beating, two intense feelings fought and struggled. The dominant thought of years, to end with herself the life that seems a curse and not a blessing, to be always maid, to die in the forlorn hope and to leave none to sorrow through having lived by her, was shaken to its base by a new-born furious desire to yield herself utterly. It came to her to run after Ned, to go with him, to Queensland, to the bush, to prison, to the gallows if need be. An insane craving for him raged within her as her memory renewed his kisses on her lips, his crushing arm-clasp, the strength that wooed with delicious bruisings, the strong personality that smote against her own until she longed to stay the smiting. It flashed through her mind that crowning joy of all joys would be to have his child in her arms, to rear a little agitator to carry on his father's fight when Ned himself was gone for ever.

Then—she stamped her foot in self-contempt and walked resolutely to her door. When she got up to her room she went to the open window and, kneeling down there, watched with tearless eyes the full white moon that began to descend towards the roofs amid the gleaming stars of the cloudless sky.

The hours passed and she still knelt watching, tearless and sleepless, mind and body numbed and enwrapped by dull gnawing pain.

*   *   *   *

Pain is to fight one's self and to subdue one's self. Nellie fought with herself and conquered.

A paradox this seems but is not, for in truth each individual is more than one, far more. Every living human is a bundle of faggot faculties, in which bundle every faculty is not an inert faggot but a living, breathing, conscious serpent. The weakling is he in whose forceless nature one serpent after another writhes its head up, dominant for a moment only, doomed to be thrust down by another fancy as fickle. The strong man is he whose forceful nature casts itself to subdue its own shifting desires by raising one supreme above the others and holding it there by identifying the dearest aspirations with its supremacy. And we call that man god-like whose heart yearns towards one little ideal, struggling for existence amid the tumultuous passions that clash in him around it, threatening to stifle it, and whose personality drives him to pick this ideal out and to lift it up and to hold it supreme lifelong.   He himself is its bitterest enemy, its most hateful foe, its would-be murderer.   He himself shrinks from and cowers at and abhors the choking for its sake of faculties that draw titanic strength from the innermost fibres of his own being. Yet he himself shelters and defends and battles for this intruder on his peace, this source of endless pain and brain-rending sorrow. A strength arises within him that tramples the other strength underfoot ; he celebrates his victory with sighs and tears.   So the New rises and rules until the Old is shattered and broken and fights the New no more ; so Brutality goes and so Humanity comes.

Nellie fought with herself kneeling there at her window, watching the declining moon, staring at it with set eyes, grimly willing herself not to think because to think was to surrender.   Into heart and ear and brain the serpents hissed words of love and thoughts of unspeakable joy.   Upon her lips they pressed again Ned's hot kisses.   Around her waist they threw again the clasping of his straining arms.   "Why not ? Why not ?" they asked her.   "Why not ? Why not ?" they cried and shouted.   "Why not ? Oh, why not ?" they moaned to her.   And she stared at the radiant moon and clenched her fingers on the window sill and would not answer. Only to her lips rose a prayer for death that she disowned unuttered.   Had she fallen so low as to seek refuge in superstition, she thought, and from that moment she bore her agony in her own way.

It did pass through her mind that the ideal she had installed in her passionate heart did not aid her, that it had shrunk back out of sight and left her alone to fight for it against herself, left her alone to keep her life for it free from the dominance of these mad passions that had lifted their heads within her and that every nerve in her fought and bled for.   She crushed this back also.   She would not think.   Only she would be loyal to her conception of Right even though the agony of her loyalty drove her mad.

She knew what Pain meant, now.   She drank to the very dregs the cup of human misery.   To have one's desires within one's reach, to have one's whole being driving one to stretch out one's hand and satisfy the eternal instincts within, and to force one's self to an abnegation that one's heart revolts from, that indeed was Pain to her. She learnt the weakness of all the philosophies as in a flash of lightning one sees clearly. She could have laughed at the sophism that one chooses always that which pleases one most. She knew that there are unfathomed depths in being which open beneath us in great crises and swallow up the foundations on which we builded and thought sure. She paralysed her passion intuitively, waiting, as one holds breath in the water when a broken wave surges over.

Gradually she forgot, an aching pain in her body lulling the aching pain of her mind. Gradually the white disc of the moon expanded before her and blotted out all active consciousness. Slowly the fierce serpents withdrew their hissing heads again. Slowly the ideal she had fought for lifted itself again within her. She began to feel more like her old self, only strangely exhausted and sorrowful. She was old, so old; weary, so weary. Hours went by. She passed into abstraction.

The falling of the moon behind the roofs roused her. She gazed at its disappearing rim in bewilderment, for the moment not realising. Then the sense of bodily pain dawned on her and assured her of the Reality.

She stood up, feeling stiff and bruised, her back aching, her head swimming, all her desiring ebbing as the moon waned. Already the glimmer of dawn paled the moonshine. She could hear the crowing of the cocks, the occasional rumble of a cart, the indescribable murmur that betokens an awakening city. The night had gone at last and the daylight had come and she had worn herself out and conquered. She thought this without joy; it was her fate not her heart. Nature itself had come to her rescue, the very Nature she had resisted and denied.

She struck a light and looked into the glass, curious to know if she were the same still. Dark circles surrounded her eyes, her nose was pinched, her cheeks wan, on her forehead between the brows were distinct wrinkles, from the corners of the mouth were chiselled deeply the lines of pain. She was years older. Could it be possible that only five hours ago she had flung herself into a lover's arm by the moonlit water, a passionate girl, in womanhood's first bloom? She had cast those days behind her for ever, she thought; she would serve the Cause alone, henceforth, while she lived. Rest, eternal rest, must come at last; she could only hope that it would come soon. At least, if she lived without joy, she would die without self-reproach.

Exhausted, she sank to sleep almost as her head touched the pillow. And in her sleep she lived again that night at the Strattons with Ned and heard Geisner profess God and condemn her hatred of maternity. "You close the gates of Life," he said. Taking her hand he led her to where a great gate stood, of iron, brass bound, and there behind it a great flood of little children pressed and struggled, dashing and crashing till the great gates shook and tottered.

"They will break the gates open," she cried to him in anguish.

"Did you deem to alter the unalterable?" he asked. And his voice was Ned's voice and turning round she saw it was Ned who held her hand. They stood by the harbour side again and she loved him. Again her whole being melted into his as he kissed her. Again they were alone in the Universe, conscious only of an ineffable joy.

      *   *   *   *

"Time to get up, Nellie!" called Mrs. Phillips, who was knocking at the door. Nellie's working day began again.

CHAPTER VI.

AFTER ten minutes' walking Ned reached a broad thoroughfare. Hesitating for a moment, to get his bearings, he saw across the way one of the cheap restaurants of which "all meals sixpence" is the symbol and which one sees open until all sorts of hours. The window was still lighted, so Ned, parched with thirst, entered to get a cup of coffee. It was a clean-looking place, enough. He saw on the wall the legend "Clean beds" as he gulped down his coffee thirstily from the saucer.

"Can you put me up to-night?" he asked, overpowered with a drowsiness that dulled even his thoughts about Nellie and unwilling to walk on to his hotel.

"Yes, sir," answered the waiter, a young man who was making preparations to close for the night. "In half a minute."

Soon a cabman had finished his late midnight meal and departed. But another passer-by dropped in, who was left over a plate of stew while the waiter led Ned to a narrow stair at the end of the room, passing round a screen behind which a stout, gray-haired man slumbered in an arm chair with all the appearance of being the proprietor. The waiter showed Ned the way with a lighted match, renewed when burnt out. Ned noticed that the papered walls and partitions of the stairway and upper floor were dirty, torn and giving way in patches. From the first landing a dark narrow passage led towards the front street while three or four ricketty, cracked doors were crowded at the stair-head. Snoring sounds came from all quarters. The waiter turned up a still narrower twisting stairway. As they neared the top Ned could see a dim light coming through an open doorway.

The room to which he was thus introduced was some fifteen feet long and as many broad, on the floor. Two gabled windows, back and front, made with the centre line of the low-sloping ceiling a Greek cross effect. A single candle, burning on a backless chair by one of the windows, threw its flickering light on the choked room-full of old-fashioned iron bedsteads, bedded in make-shift manner, six in all, four packed against the wall opposite the door at which the stairs ended and one on each side of the window whereby was the light. On one of these latter beds a bearded man lay stretched, only partly undressed; on its edge sat a youth in his shirt. Although it was so late they were talking.

" Not gone to bed yet ?" asked the waiter.

" Hullo, Jack !" replied the youth. " Aren't you coming to bed yet ?"

"A gentleman of Jack's profession," said the bearded man, whose liquorous voice proclaimed how he had put in his evening, " doesn't require to go to bed at all. 'Gad, that's very good. You understand me ?" He referred his wit to the youth. He spoke with the drawling hesitation of the English " swell."

" I understand you," replied the youth, in a respectful voice that had acquired its tone in the English shires.

" I don't get much chance whether I require it or not," remarked Jack, with an American accentuation, proceeding to make up the other bed by the light. There was nothing on the grimy mattress but a grimy blanket, so he brought a couple of fairly clean sheets from a bed in the opposite corner and spread them dexterously.

" Have we the pleasure of more company, Jack ? " enquired the broken-down swell. " You understand me ? "

" I understand you," said the English lad.

"This gentleman's going to stay," replied Jack, putting the sheet over the caseless pillow.

" Glad to make your acquaintance, sir," said the swell to Ned, upon this introduction. " We can't offer you a chair but you're welcome to a seat on the bed. If you can't offer a man wine give him whisky, and if you haven't got whisky offer him the best you've got." This last to the youth. " You understand me ? "

" I understand you," said the youth. " I understand you perfectly."

" Thanks," replied Ned. " But it won't hurt to stand for a minute. There ain't much room to stand though, is there ?"

His head nearly touched the ceiling in the highest part ; on either side it sloped sharply, the slope only broken by the window gables, the stair casement being carried into the very centre of the room to get height for the door. The plaster on the ceiling had come off in patches, as if cannon-balled by unwary heads, showing the lath, and was also splashed by the smoke-wreaths of carelessly held candles; the papering was half torn from the shaky plastering of the wall; the flooring was time-eaten. A general impression of uncleanness was everywhere. On a ricketty little table behind the candle was a tin basin and a cracked earthenware pitcher. Excepting a limited supply of bedroom ware, which was very strongly in evidence, there was no other furniture. Looking round, Ned saw that on the bed opposite the door, hidden in the shadows, a man lay groaning and moaning. Through the windows could be seen the glorious moonlight.

"No. A man wants to be careful here," said the waiter, throwing the blanket over the sheets and straightening it in a whisk. "There," he went on, "will that suit you?"

"Anything 'll suit me," said Ned, pulling off his coat and hanging it over the head of the postless bed. "I'm much obliged."

"That's all right," replied Jack, cheerfully. "I'll be up to bed soon," he informed the others and ran down stairs again.

"Will you have a cigarette?" asked the English lad, holding out a box.

"Thanks, but I don't smoke," answered Ned, who had pulled off his boots and was wrestling with his shirt. Finally it came over his head. He lay down in his underclothing, having first gingerly turned back the blanket to the foot.

"I don't desire to be personal," said the broken-down swell. "You'll excuse me, but I must say you're a finely built man. You understand me? No offence!"

"He is big," chipped in the youth.

"You don't offend a man much by telling him he's well built," retorted Ned, with an attempt at mirth.

"Certainly. You understand me. It's not the size, my boy"— to the youth. "Size is nothing. It's the proportion, the capacity for putting out strength. I've been an athlete myself and I'm no chicken yet. But our friend here ought to be a Hercules. Will you take a drink? You'll excuse the glass." He offered Ned a flask half full of whisky.

"Thanks just the same but I never drink," answered Ned, stretching himself carelessly. The lad refused also.

"You're wise, both of you," commented the other, swallowing down a couple of mouthfuls of the undiluted liquor. "If I'd never touched it I should have been a wealthy man to-day. But I shall be a wealthy man yet. You understand me?"

"Yes," answered Ned, mechanically. He was looking at the frank, open, intelligent face and well-made limbs of the half-naked lad opposite and wondering what he was doing here with this grizzled drunkard. The said grizzled drunkard being the broken-down swell, whose highly-coloured face, swollen nose and slobbery eyes told a tale that his slop-made clothes would have concealed. "How old are you?" he asked the lad, the drunkard having fallen asleep in the middle of a discourse concerning a great invention which would bring him millions.

"I'm nineteen."

"You look older," remarked Ned.

"Most people think I'm older," replied the lad proudly.

"You're not a native."

"No. I'm from the west of England."

"Which county?"

"Devon."

"My father's Devon," said Ned, at which the poor lad looked up eagerly, as though in Ned he recognised an old friend.

"That's strange, isn't it? How you meet people!" he remarked.

"I've never been there, you know," explained Ned. "Fact is, I don't think it would be well for me to go. If all my old dad used to say is true I'd soon get shipped out."

"How's that?"

"Why, they transport a man for shooting a rabbit or a hare, don't they? My dad told me a friend of his was sent out for catching salmon and that his mother was frightened nearly to death when she knew he'd been off fishing one night. Of course, they don't transport to here any more. We wouldn't have it. But they do it to somewhere still, I suppose."

"I don't know, I'm sure," answered the lad. "I never heard much about that. I came out when I was fourteen."

"How was that?"

"Well, there was nothing to do in England that had anything in it and everybody was saying what a grand country Australia was and how everybody could get on and so I came out."

"Your folks come?"

"My father was dead. I only had a stepfather."

"And he wanted to get rid of you, eh?" enquired Ned, getting interested.

"I suppose he did, a little," said the lad, colouring.

"You came out to Sydney?"

" No. To Brisbane. That didn't cost anything."

" You hadn't any friends ?"

" No. I got into a billet near Stanthorpe, but when I wanted a raise they sacked me and got another boy. Then I came across to New South Wales. It wasn't any use staying in Queensland. I wish I'd stayed in England," he added.

" How's that ?"

" I can't get work. I wouldn't mind if I could get a job but it's pretty hard when you can't."

"Can't you get work ?"

" I haven't done a stroke for ten weeks."

" Well, are you hard up ?" enquired Ned, to whose bush experience ten weeks out-of-work meant nothing.

" Look here," returned the lad, touching the front of his white shirt and the cuffs. Ned saw that what he had taken for white flannel in the dim candle-light was white linen, guileless of starch, evidently washed in a hand-basin at night and left to dry over a chair till morning. "A man's pretty hard up—ain't he ?—when he can't get his shirt laundried."

"That's bad," said Ned, sympathetically, determining to sympathise a pound-note. Starched shirts did not count to him personally but he understood that the town and the bush were very different.

" I've offered three times to-day to work for my board," said the lad, not tremulously but in the matter-of-fact voice of one who had looked after himself for years.

"Where was that ?" asked Ned, wide-awake at last, alarmed for the bushmen, rapidly turning over in his mind the effect of strong young men being ready to work for their board.

" One place was down near the foot of Market Street, a produce merchant. He told me he couldn't, that it was as much as he could do to provide for his own family. Another place was at a wood and coal yard and the boss said I'd leave in a week at that price so it wasn't any good talking. The other was a drayman who has a couple of drays and he said he'd never pay under the going wage to anybody and gave me sixpence. He said it was all he could afford because times were so bad."

" Are you stumped then ?" asked Ned.

" I haven't a copper."

Just then the broken-down swell woke up from his doze and demanded his flask. After some search it was found underneath him. Then, heedless of his interruptions, Ned continued the conversation.

" Do they take you here on tick ?" he enquired.

" Tick ! There's no tick here. That old man downstairs is as hard as nails. Why, if it hadn't been for this gentleman I'd have had to walk about all night or sleep in the Domain."

" Fair dues, my boy, fair dues !" put in the broken-down swell. " Never refer to private matters like that. You make me feel ashamed, my boy. I should never have mentioned that little accommodation. You understand me ?"

" I understand you," replied the lad. " I understand you perfectly."

" That's all right," said Ned, suddenly feeling a respect for this grizzled drunkard. " We must all help one another. How was it ?"

" Well," said the lad. " I met a friend of mine and he gave me sixpence and this box of cigarettes. It was all he had. I've often slept here and so I came and asked the old man to trust me the other half. He wouldn't listen to it. I was going away when this gentleman came along. He only had threepence more than his own bed-money but he persuaded the old man to knock off threepence and he'd pay threepence. I thought I'd have had to go to the Domain."

" But that's nothing," said Ned. " I'd just as soon sleep out as sleep in."

" I've never come down to sleeping out yet," returned the lad, simply. " Perhaps your being a native makes a difference." Ned was confronted again with the fact that the bushman and the townsman view the same thing from opposite sides. To this lad, struggling to keep his head up, to lie down nightly in the Domain meant the surrender of all self-respecting decency.

" I shouldn't have brought up the subject. You understand me ?" said the drunkard. " But now it's mentioned I'll ask if you noticed how I talked over that old scoundrel downstairs. You understand me ? Where's that flask ? My God ! I am feeling bad," he continued, sitting up on the bed.

" You're drinking too much," remarked Ned.

The man did not reply, but, with a groan, pushed the lad aside, sprang from the bed, and began to retch prodigiously into the wash basin, after which he announced himself better, lay down and took another drink. Meanwhile the man in the far corner tossed and groaned as if he were dying.

" You're friend's still worse," said the lad.

" He's just out of the hospital. I told him he shouldn't mix his drinks so soon but he would have his own way. He'll be all right when he's slept it off. A man's a fool who gets drunk. You understand me ?"

" I understand you," said the lad. " I never want to get drunk. All I want is work."

" Why don't you go up to Queensland ?" asked the man, to Ned's hardly suppressed indignation. " The pastoralists would be glad to get a smart-looking lad like you. Good pay, all expenses paid, and a six months' agreement ! I believe that's the terms. You understand me ?"

" I understand you," said the English lad. " I understand you perfectly. But that's blacklegging and I'd sooner starve than blackleg. I ain't so hard up yet that I'll do either."

" Put it there, mate," cried Ned, stretching his hand out. " You're a square little chap." His heart rose again at this proof that the union spirit was spreading."

" You're a good boy," said the drunkard, slapping his shoulder. " I'm not a unionist and I'm against the unions. You understand me ? I am a gentleman "—poor drunken broken-down swell— " and a gentleman must stick to his own Order just as you should stick to your Order. I'd like to see the working classes kept in their places, but I despise a traitor, my boy. You understand me ?"

" I understand you perfectly," said the lad.

" Yet you'd work for your board ?" said Ned, enquiringly.

" I suppose I shouldn't," said the lad. " But one must live. I wouldn't cut a man out of a job by going under him when he was sticking up for what's right but where nobody's sticking up what's the use of one kicking. That's how I look at it. Of course, a lot don't."

" They'll get a lot to go then ? "

" I think they'll get a lot. Some fellows are so low down they'll do anything and a lot more don't understand. I didn't use to understand."

" Would you go up with them for the union ? " asked Ned, after a pause.

" You mean to come out again ? "

" Yes, and to get as many to come out as you can by explaining things. It may mean three months' gaol so you want to make up your mind well."

"I wouldn't mind going to gaol for a thing like that. It's not being in gaol but what you're in for that counts, isn't it?"

So they talked while the two drunkards groaned and tossed, the stench of this travellers' bedroom growing every moment more unbearable. Finally the waiter returned.

"Not gone to bed yet," he exclaimed. "Phew! This is a beauty to-night, a pair of beauties. Ain't it a wonder their insides don't poison 'em?"

"I thought I'd never get to bed," he went on, coming to light his pipe at the candle and then returning to the bed he had taken Ned's sheets from. "First one joker in, then another, and the old man 'ud stay open all night for a tanner. Past two! Jolly nice hour for a chap that's to be up at six, ain't it?"

He pulled off his boots and vest and threw himself down on the bare mattress in his trousers. "Ain't you fellows going to bed to-night?" he enquired.

"It's about a fair thing," said Ned, feeling nervous and exhausted with lack of sleep. So the young fellow blew the candle out and went over to the bed adjoining Jack's. As he lay down Jack picked up a boot and tapped the wall alongside him gently. "I think I hear her," he remarked. In a few moments there was an answering tap.

"Who's that?" asked Ned.

"The slavey next door," answered Jack, upon which an interchange of experience took place between Jack and the young fellow in which gable windows and park seats and various other stage-settings had prominent parts.

At last they all slept but Ned. Drowsy as he was he could not sleep. It was not that he thought much of Nellie, at least he did not feel that he was thinking of her. He only wanted to sleep and forget and he could not sleep. The moonshine came through the curtainless window and lit up the room with a strange mysterious light. The snoring breathing that filled the room mingled with other snoring sounds that seemed to come up the stairway and through the walls. The stench of the room stifled him. The drunkards who tossed there, groaning; this unemployed lad who lay with his white limbs kicked free and bathed in the moonlight; the tired waiter who lay motionless, still dressed; were there with him. The clock-bells struck the quarters, then the hour.

Three o'clock.

He had never felt so uncomfortable, he thought, so uneasy. He twisted and squirmed and rubbed himself. Suddenly a thought struck him. He leaned up on his elbow for a moment, peering with his eyes in the scanty light, feeling about with his hand, then leaped clean out of the bed. It swarmed with vermin.

Like most bushmen, Ned, who was sublimely tolerant of ants, lizards and the pests of the wilds generally, shivered at the very thought of the parasites of the towns. To strip himself was the work of an instant, to carefully re-dress by the candle-end he lighted took longer; then he stepped to the English lad's side and woke him.

"Hello !" said the lad, rubbing his eyes in sleepy astonishment. "What's the matter ?"

"I can't sleep with bugs crawling over me," said Ned. "I'm going to camp out in the park. Here's a 'note' to help you along and here's the address to go to if you conclude to go up to Queensland for the union. I'll see about it first thing in the morning so he'll expect you. The 'note's' yours whether you go or not."

"I'm ever so much obliged," said the lad, taking the money and the slip of paper. "I'll go and I'll be square. You needn't be afraid of me and I'll pay it back, too, some day. Do you know the way out ?"

"I'll find it all right," replied Ned.

"Oh! I'll go down with you or you'd never find it. It's through the back at night." So the good-hearted young fellow pulled on his trousers and conducted Ned down the creaking stairway, through the kitchen and the narrow back yard to the bolted door that led to the alley behind.

"Shall I see you again ?" asked the lad. Somehow everybody who met Ned wanted to see more of him.

"My name's Hawkins," replied Ned. "Ned Hawkins. Ask anybody in the Queensland bush about me, if you get there."

"I suppose you're one of the bushmen," remarked the lad, pausing. "If they're all as big as you it ought to be bad for the blacklegs."

"Why, I'm a small man up on the Diamantina," said Ned, laughing. "Which is the way to the park ?"

"Turn to your right at the end of the alley, then turn to the left. It's only five minutes' walk."

"Thanks. Good-bye !" said Ned.

"It's thank you. Good-bye !" said the lad.

They shook hands and parted. In a few minutes Ned was in the park. He stepped over a low railing, found a branching tree and decided to camp under it. He pulled his boots off and his coat, loosened his belt, put boots and coat under his head for a pillow, stretched out full length on the earth and in ten seconds was in a deep slumber.

He was roused—a moment after, it seemed to him; in reality it was nearly six hours after—by kicks on the ribs. He turned over and opened his eyes. As he did so another kick made him stagger to his feet gasping with pain. A gorilla-faced constable greeted him with a savage grin.

"Phwat d'ye mane, ye blayguard, indaycently exposing yersilf in this parrt av th' doomane? Oi've as good a moind as iver a man had in the wurrld to run yez in. Can't ye find anither place to unthdress yersilf in, ye low vaygrant?"

Ned did not answer. He buttoned up the neck of his shirt, which had opened in the night, tightened his belt again, drew on his boots and thrust his arms into his coat. While he did so the constable continued his abuse, proud to show his authority in the presence of the crowd that passed in a continuous stream along the pathway that cut through the carefully tended flower-bedded lawn-like park. It was one of Ned's strong points that he could control his passionate temper. Much as he longed to thrash this insolent brute he restrained himself. He desired most of all to get back to Queensland and knew that as no magistrate would take his word against a "constable's" as to provocation received, to retaliate now would keep him in Sydney for a month at least, perhaps six. But his patience almost gave way when the constable followed as he walked away, still abusing him.

"You'd better not go too far," warned Ned, turning round.

It suddenly dawned upon the constable that this was not the ordinary "drunk" and that it was as well to be satisfied with the exhibition of authority already made. Ned walked off unmolested, chewing the cud of his thoughts.

This sentence of Geisner's rang in his ears:

"The slaves who 'move on' at the bidding of a policeman."

CHAPTER VII.

"IT can't do any good. We have made up our minds that the matter might just as well be fought out now, no matter what it costs. We've made all our arrangements. There is nothing to discuss. We are simply going to do business in our own way."

"It can't do any harm. There is always something to be said on the other side and I always find workingmen fairly reasonable if they're met fairly. At any rate, you might as well see how they look at it. The labour agitation itself can't be stifled. The great point, as I regard it, is to make the immediate relations of Capital and Labour as peaceable as possible. The two parties don't see enough of each other."

"I think we see a great deal too much of them. It's a pretty condition of things when we can't go on with our businesses without being interfered with by mobs of ignorant fools incited by loud-tongued agitators. The fools have got to be taught a lesson some day and we might as well teach it to them now."

"You know I'm no advocate of Communism or Socialism or any such nonsense. I look at the matter solely from a business standpoint. I am a loser by disturbances in trade, so I try to prevent disturbances. I've always been able to prevent them in my own business and I think they can always be prevented."

"Well, Melsom, you may be right when it's a question of wages, but this is a question of principle. We're willing to confer if they'll admit 'freedom of contract.' That's all there is to say about it."

"But what is 'freedom of contract?' Besides, if it is questioned, there can't be much harm in understanding why. For my part, I find it an interminable point of discussion when it is raised and one of the questions that settles itself easily when it isn't."

"It is the key of the whole position. If we haven't a right to employ whoever we like at any terms we may make with any individual we employ what rights have we?"

O

"Hear what they think of it, Strong! It can surely do no harm to find out what makes them fight so."

And so on for half an hour.

"Well, I don't mind having a chat with one of them," conceded Strong at last. "It's only because you persist so, Melsom. I suppose this man you've been told is in town is an oily, ignorant fellow, who'll split words and wrangle up a cloud of dust until nobody can tell what we're talking about. I've heard these fellows."

*　　　*　　　*　　　*

Thus it was that Ned, calling at the Trades-Hall, after having washed and breakfasted at his hotel and seen to various items of union business about town, was greeted with the information that Mr. Melsom was looking for him.

"Who's Melsom?"

"Oh! A sort of four-leaved clover, a reasonable employer," answered his genial informant. "He's in a large way of business, interested in a good many concerns, and whenever he's got a finger in anything we can always get on with it. He's a great man for arbitration and conciliation and has managed to settle two or three disputes that I never thought would be arranged peaceably. He's a thoroughly decent fellow, I can assure you."

"What does he want with me, I wonder?"

"He wants you to see Strong, just to talk matters over and let Strong know how you Queenslanders look at things."

"Who's Strong?"

"Don't you know? He's managing director of the Great Southern Mortgage Agency. He's the man who's running the whole show on the other side and a clever man, too, don't you forget it."

Ned recollected the man he had seen at the restaurant and what Nellie had said of him, two years ago.

"But I can't see him without instructions. I must wire up to know what they say about it," said Ned.

"That's just what you mustn't do, old man. Strong won't consent to any formal interview, but told Melsom that he'd be glad to see anybody who knew how the other side saw things, to chat the matter over as between one man and another. I told Melsom yesterday that you were in town till to-night and he came this morning to get you to see Strong at eleven. He'll be back before then. I told him I thought it would be all right."

"I don't see how I can do that without instructions," repeated Ned.

"If it were formal there could be only one possible instruction, surely," urged the other. "As it is absolutely informal and as all that Melsom hopes is that it may lead to a formal conference, I think you should go. You'd talk to anybody, wouldn't you? Besides, Melsom has his heart set on this. I don't believe it will lead to anything, mind you, but it will oblige him and he often does a good turn for us."

"That settles it," said Ned. "Only I'll have to say I'm only giving my own opinion and I'll have to talk straight whether he likes it or not."

"Of course. By the way, here are some wires that'll interest you, and I want to arrange about sending money up in case they proclaim the unions illegal. Heaven knows what they can't do now-a-days! Have you heard what they did here during the maritime strike?"

* * * *

Shortly before eleven, Strong was closeted in his private office with a burly man of unmistakably bush appearance, modified both in voice and dress by considerable contact with the towns. Of sandy complexion, broad features and light-coloured eyes that did not look one full in the face, the man was of the type that attracts upon casual acquaintance but about which there is an indefinable something which, without actually repelling, effectually prevents any implicit confidence.

"You have been an officer of the shearers' union, you say?" enquired Strong, coldly.

"I've been an honorary officer, never a paid one," answered the man, who held his hat on his knee.

"There's a man in Sydney now, named Hawkins. Do you know him?"

"Yes. I've shorn with him out at the — "

"What sort of a man is he?" interrupted Strong.

"He's a young fellow. There's not much in him. He talks wild."

"Has he got much influence?"

"Only with his own set. Most of the men only want a start to break away from fellows like Hawkins. I'm confident the new union I was talking of, admitting 'freedom of contract,' would break the other up and that Hawkins and the rest of them couldn't stop it."

"It seems feasible," said Strong, sharply. "At any rate, there's nothing lost by trying it. This is what we will do. We will pay you all expenses and six pounds a week from to-day to go up to Queensland, publicly denounce the union, support 'freedom of contract' and try to start another union against the present one; generally to act as an agent of ours. Payment will be made after you come out. Until then you must pay your own expenses."

"I think I should have expenses advanced," said the man.

"We know nothing of you. You represent yourself as so-and-so and if you are genuine there is no injustice done by our offer. You must take or leave it."

"I'll take it," said the man, after a slight hesitation.

"There's another matter. Do you know the union officials in Brisbane?"

"I know all of them, intimately."

"Then you may be able to do something with them. We are informed that they are implicated in all that's going on, the instigators of it. Bring us evidence criminally implicating them and we will pay well."

"This is business," said the man, a little shamefacedly. "What will you pay?"

Strong jotted some figures on a slip of paper. "If you are a friend of these men," he said, passing the slip over, "you will know their value apiece to you." A sneer he could not quite conceal peeped from under his business tone.

"That concludes our business, I think," he continued, tearing the slip up, having received it back. "I will instruct our secretary and you can call on him this afternoon."

He touched an electric bell-button on his desk. A clerk appeared at the door instantly.

"Show this man out by the back way," ordered Strong, glancing at the clock. "Good-day!"

The summarily dismissed visitor had hardly gone when another clerk announced Mr. Melsom.

"Anybody with him?"

"Yes, sir. A tall, bush-looking man."

"Show them both in."

"What sneaking brutes what these fellows are!" Strong thought, contemptuously, jotting instructions on some letters he was glancing through, working away as one accustomed to making the most of spare minutes.

* * * *

Mr. Melsom had left Ned and Strong together, having to attend to his own business which had already been sufficiently interfered with by his exertions on behalf of his pet theory of " getting things talked over." Ned had felt inwardly agitated as he walked under the great archway and up the broad iron stairway that led to the inner offices of this great fortress-like building, the centre of the southern money-power. He had noted the massive walls of hewn stone, the massive gates and the enormous bolts, chains and bars. In the outer office he had glanced a little nervously around the lofty, stuccoed, hall-like room, of which the wood-work was as massive in its way as were the stone walls without and of which the very glass of the partitions looked put in to stay, while the counters and desks, with their polished brass-work and great leathern-bound ledgers, seemed as solid as the floor itself ; he wondered curiously what all these clerks did who leaned engrossed over their desks or flitted noiselessly here and there on the matting-covered flagstones of the flooring. Why he should be nervous he could not have explained. But he was cool enough when, after a minute's delay, a clerk led Melsom and himself through a smaller archway opening from this great office hall and up a carpetted stone stairway leading between two great bare walls and along a long lofty passage, wherein footfalls echoed softly on the carpetted stone floor. Finally they reached a polished, pannelled door which being opened showed Strong writing busily at a cabinet desk placed in the centre of the handsomely furnished office-room. The great financier greeted Melsom cordially, nodded civilly enough to Ned and agreed with the latter's immediate statement that he came, as a private individual solely, to see a private individual, at the request of Mr. Melsom.

" Now, where do we differ ?" Strong asked, when Melsom had gone.

" We are you and me, of course," said Ned, putting his hat on the floor.

Strong nodded.

" Well, you have sat down at your desk here and drawn up a statement as to how I shall work without asking me. I object. I say that, as I'm concerned, you and I together should sit down and arrange how I shall work for you since I must work for you."

"In our agreement, that you refer to, we have tried to do what is fair," replied Strong, looking sharply at Ned.

"Do you want me to talk straight?" asked Ned. "Because, if you object to that, it's better for me to go now than waste words talking round the subject."

"Certainly," answered Strong. "Straight talk never offends me."

"Then how do I know you have tried to do fairly?" enquired Ned. "Our experience with the pastoralists leads us to think the opposite."

"There have been rabid pastoralists," admitted Strong, after a moment's thought, "just as there have been rabid men on the other side. I'll tell you this, that we have had great difficulty in getting some of the pastoralists to accept this agreement. We had to put considerable pressure on them before they would moderate their position to what we consider fair."

Ned did not reply. He stowed Strong's statement away for future use.

"Besides," remarked Strong, after a pause, during which he arranged the letters before him, "There is no compulsion to accept the agreement. If you don't like it don't work under it, but let those who want to accept it."

"I fancy that's more how it stands than by being fair," commented Ned, bitterly.

"Well! Isn't that fair?" asked Strong, leaning back in his office chair.

"Is it fair?" returned Ned.

"Well! Why not?"

"How can it be fair? We have nothing and you have everything. All the leases and all the sheep and all the cattle and all the improvements belong to you. We've got to work to live and we can't work except for you. What's the sense of your saying that if we don't like the agreement we needn't take it? We must either break the agreement or take it. That's how we stand."

"Well, what do you object to in it?"

"I don't know what the others object to in it. I know what I object to."

"That's what I want to know."

"Well, for one thing, when I've earned money it's mine. The minute I've shorn a sheep the price of shearing it belongs to me and not to the squatter. It's convenient to agree only to draw pay at certain times, but it's barefaced to deliberately withhold my money weeks after I've earned it, and it's thieving to forfeit wages in case a squatter and I differ as to whether the agreement's been broken or not."

"There ought to be some security that a pastoralist won't be put to loss by his men leaving him at a moment's notice," asserted Strong.

"You've got the law on your side," answered Ned. "You can send a man to prison, like a thief, if he has a row with a squatter after signing an agreement, but we can't send the squatter to prison if he's in fault. The Masters and Servants Act is all wrong and we'll alter it when we get a chance, I can assure you, but you're not content with the Masters and Servants Act. You want a private law all in your own hand."

"We've had a very serious difficulty to meet," said the other. "Men go on strike on frivolous pretext and we must protect our interests. We've not cut down wages and we don't intend to."

"You have cut down wages, labourers' wages," retorted Ned.

"That has been charged," replied Strong, lifting his eyebrows. "But I can show you the list of wages paid on our stations during the last five years and you will see that the wages we now offer are fully up to the average."

"That may be," said Ned. "But they are less than they were last year. I'm speaking now of what I know."

"Oh! There may be a few instances in which the unions forced up wages unduly which have been rectified,". said Mr. Strong. "But the general rate has not been touched."

"The pastoralists wouldn't dare arbitrate on that," answered Ned. "In January, 1890, they tried to force down wages and we levelled them up. Now, they are forcing them down again. At least it seems that way to me."

"That matter might be settled, I think," said Strong, dismissing it. "What other objections have you to the agreement?"

"As an agreement I object to the whole thing, the way it's being worked. If it were a proposal I should want to know how about the Eight Hours and the Chinese."

"We don't wish to alter existing hours," answered Strong.

"Then why not put it down?"

"And we don't wish to encourage aliens."

" A good many pastoralists do and we are determined to try to stop them. It looks queer to us that nothing is said about it."

" Some certainly did urge that Chinese should be allowed in tropical Queensland but our influence is against that and we hope to restrain the more impetuous and thus prevent friction."

Ned shrugged his shoulders without answering.

" We hope—" began Strong. Then he broke off, saying instead : " I do not see why the men should regard the pastoralists as necessarily inimical and as not desirous of doing what is fair."

" Look here, Mr. Strong," said Ned leaning forward, as was his habit when in earnest. " We are beginning to understand things. We know that you people are after profits and nothing else, that to you we are like so many horses or sheep, only not so valuable because we're harder to break in and our carcasses aren't worth anything. We know that you don't care a curse whether we live or die and that you'd fill the bush with Chinese to-morrow if you could see your way to making an extra one per cent. by it."

" *You* haven't much confidence in us, at any rate," returned Strong, coolly. " But if we look carefully after profits you must recollect that a great deal of capital is trust funds. The widow and the orphan invest their little fortunes in our hands. Surely you wouldn't injure them ?"

" I thought we were talking straight to one another," said Ned. " You will excuse me, Mr. Strong, for thinking that to talk ' widow and orphan ' isn't worthy of a man like you unless you've got a very small opinion of me. When you think about our widows and orphans we'll think about your widows and orphans. That's only clap-trap. It doesn't alter the hard fact that you're only after profit and don't care what happens to us so long as you get it."

The financier bit his lips, flushing. He took up a letter and glanced over it before replying.

" Do you care what happens to us ?"

" As things are, no. How can we ? The worst that could happen to one of you would leave you as well off as the most fortunate of us. There is war between us, only I think it possible to be a little civilised and not to fight each other like savages as we are doing."

" I am glad you admit that some of your methods are savage."

" Of course I admit it," answered Ned. " That is my opinion of the way both sides fight now. Instead of conferring and arbitrating on immediate questions and leaving future questions to be talked over and understood and thoroughly threshed out in free discussion, we strike, you lockout, you victimise wholesale and, naturally, we retaliate in our own ways."

"You prefer to be left uninterrupted to preach this new socialistic nonsense?"

"Why not, if it is sound? And if it isn't sound, why not? Surely your side isn't afraid of discussion if it knows it's right."

"Do you really think that we should leave our individual rights to be decided upon by an ignorant mob?"

"My individual rights are at the mercy of ignorant individuals at present," said Ned. "I am not allowed to work if I happen to have given offence to a handful of squatters."

"I think you exaggerate," answered Strong. "I know that some pastoralists are very vindictive but I regard most of them as honorable men incapable of a contemptible action."

"Of course they are," said Ned. "The only thing is what do they call contemptible? You and I are very friendly, just now, Mr. Strong. You're not small enough to feel any hatred just because I talk a bit straight but you know very well that you'd regard it as quite square to freeze me out because I do talk straight."

The two men looked into each other's eyes. Strong began to respect this outspoken bushman.

"I think that one of the most fundamental of all rights in any civilised society is the right of a man to employ whom he likes at any terms and under any conditions that he can get men to enter his employment. It seems to me that without this right the very right to private property itself is disputed for in civilisation private property does not mean only a hoard, stored up for future use, but savings accumulated to carry on the industrial operations of civilisation. These savings have been prompted by the assurance that society will protect the man who saves in making, with the man who has not saved, the contracts necessary to carry on industry, unhampered by the interference of outsiders. That seems to me, I repeat, a fundamental right essential to the very existence of society. The man who disputes it seems to me an enemy of society. Whether he is right or wrong, or whether society itself is right or wrong, is another question with which, as it is a mere theory, practical men have nothing to do." Strong had only been fencing in his talk before. Now that he was ready he stated his position, quite coolly, with a quiet emphasis that made his line of argument clear as day.

"Then why confer at all, under any conditions, even if unionists admitted all this?" asked Ned.

"Simply for convenience. Some of our members object to any conference but the general opinion is that it does not involve a sacrifice of principle to discuss details provided principles are admitted. In the same way, some favoured the employment of men at any wage arranged between the individual man and his employer, but the general opinion was that it is advisable and convenient for pastoralists in the same district to pay the same wages."

"Then the pastoralists may combine but the bushmen mayn't."

"We don't object to the bushmen forming unions. We claim the right to employ men without asking whether they are unionist or non-unionist."

"Which means," said Ned, "the right to victimise unionists."

"How is that?" asked Strong.

"We know how. Do you suppose for a moment, Mr. Strong, that ideas spring up with nothing behind them? All those who are acquainted with the history of unionism know that 'close unionism,' the refusal to work with non-unionists, arose from the persistent preference given by employers to non-unionists, which was a victimising of unionists."

"That may have been once, but things are different now," answered Strong.

"They are not different now. Wherever employers have an opportunity they have a tendency to weed out unionists. I could give you scores of instances of it being done. The black list is bad enough now. It would be a regular terrorism if there was nothing to restrain the employer. Then down would come wages, up would go hours and in would come the Chinese. If it is a principle with you, it is existence itself with us."

"I think the pastoralists would agree not to victimise, as you call it," said Strong, after thinking a minute.

"Who is to say? How are we to know?" answered Ned. "Supposing, Mr. Strong, you and I had a dispute in which we both believed ourselves right would you regard it as a fair settlement to submit the whole thing, without any exception, to an arbiter whom we both chose and both believed to be fair?"

"Certainly I should," said Strong.

"The whole dispute, no matter what it was? You'd think it fair to leave it all to the arbiter?"

"Certainly."

"Then why not leave 'freedom of contract' to arbitration?" demanded Ned. "You say you are right. We say we are right. We have offered to go to arbitration on the whole dispute, keeping nothing back. We have pledged ourselves to stand by the arbitration. Isn't that honest and fair? What could be fairer? It may be that we have taken a wrong method against victimising in close unionism. But it cannot be that we should not have some defence against victimising, and close unionism is the only defence we have as yet, that any union has had, anywhere, except in Sheffield and I don't suppose you want rattening to start here. Why not arbitrate?"

"It is a question of principle," answered Strong, looking Ned in the face.

"That means you'll fight it out," commented Ned, rising and picking up his hat. Then he put his foot on his chair and, leaning on his knee, thus expressed his inward thoughts : "You can fight if you like but when it's all over you'll remember what I say and know it's the straight wire. You've been swallowing the fairy tales about ours being a union of pressed men but you will see your mistake, believe me. You may whip us; you've got the Government and the police and the P.M.'s and the money and the military but how much nearer the end will you be when you have whipped us? You'll know by then that the chaps up North, like men everywhere else, will go down fighting and will come up smiling to fight again when you begin to take it out of them because they're down. And in the end you'll arbitrate. You'll have no way out of it. It's fair and because it's fair and because we all know it's fair we'll win that or—" Ned paused.

"I'm sorry you look at the matter so," said Strong, arranging his papers.

"How else should we look at it? If we pretend to give in as you want us to do, it'll only be as a trick to gain time, as a ruse to put you off until we're readier. We won't do that. For my part, and for the part of the men I know, the union is a thing which mustn't get a bad name. We may lie individually but the union's word must be as good as gold no matter what it says. If the union says the sheep are wet, they're wet, and if it says they're dry, they are dry—if the water's dripping off 'em," added Ned, with a twinkle in his eye. " I mean, Mr. Strong, that we're trying to be better men in our rough way and the union is what's making us better and some of us would die for it. But we'd sooner see it die than see it do what's cowardly."

" I am sorry that men like you are so deceived as to what is right," said Strong.

"Perhaps we're all deceived. Perhaps you're deceived. Perhaps the whole of life is a humbug." So Ned said, with careless fatalism. " Only, if your mates were in trouble you'd be a cur if you didn't stand by them, wouldn't you? That's the difference between you and me, Mr. Strong. You don't believe that we're all mates or that the crowd has any particular troubles and I do. And as long as one believes it, well, it doesn't matter to him whether he's deceived or not, I think. I won't detain you any longer. It's no use our talking, I can see."

Strong got up and walked towards the door.

" I think not," he said. " But I am glad to have met you, Mr. Hawkins, and I can't help feeling that you're throwing great abilities away. You'll get no thanks and do no good and you'll live to regret it. It's all very well to talk lightly of the outlook in Queensland but when you have become implicated in lawlessness and are suffering for it the whole affair will look different. Don't misunderstand me! You are a young man, capable, earnest. There is no position you might not aspire to. Be warned in time. Let me help you. I shall be only too glad. You will never repent it for I ask nothing dishonourable."

" I don't quite understand," said Ned, sternly, his brow knitting.

" I'm not offering a bribe," continued Strong, meeting Ned's gaze unflinchingly. "That's not necessary. You know very well that you will hang yourself with very little more rope. I am talking as between one man and another. I meet only too few manly men to let one go to destruction without trying to save him. The world doesn't need saviours; it needs masters. You can be one of them. Think well of it! Not one in a million has the chance."

"You mean that you'll help me to get rich?"

" Rich!" sneered Strong. "What is rich? It is Power that is worth having and to have power one must control capital. In your wildest ranting of the power of the capitalist you have hardly touched the fringe of the power he has. Only there are very few who are able to use it. I offer you the opportunity to become one of the few. I never make a mistake in men. If you try you can be. There is the offer, take it or leave it."

For an instant Ned dreamed of accepting it, of throwing over everything to become a great capitalist, as Strong said so confidently he could be, and then, after long years, to pour his wealth into the treasuries of the movement, now often checked for lack of funds. Then he thought of Nellie and of Geisner, what they would say, still hesitating. Then he thought of his mates expecting him, waiting for him, and he decided.

" I was thinking," he said, straightforwardly, " whether I wouldn't like to make a pile so as to give it to the movement. But, you see, Mr. Strong, the chaps are expecting me and that settles it. I am much obliged but it would be dishonourable in me."

" You know what is in front ?" asked Strong, calmly, making a last effort.

" I think so. I'm told I'm one of those to be locked up. What does that matter ? That won't lose me any friends."

" A stubborn man will have his way," remarked Strong. Adding, at a venture : " Particularly when there is a woman in it."

" There is a woman in it," answered Ned, flushing a little ; " a woman who won't have me."

Strong opened the door. " I've done my best for you," he said. " Don't blame me whatever happens. You, at least, had your choice of peace or war, of more than peace."

" I understand. Personally, I shan't blame you," said Ned. " I choose war, more than war," and he set his mouth doggedly.

" War, at any rate," answered Strong, holding out his hand, his face as grave as Ned's. The two men gripped hands tightly, like duellists crossing swords. Without another word they shook hands heartily and separated.

Strong closed the door and walked up and down his room, hurriedly, deep in thought, pulling his lip. He sat down at his desk, took up his pen, got up and paced the room again. He went to the window and looked out into the well that admitted light to the centre of the great fortress-building. Then walked back to his desk and wrote.

" He is a dangerous man," he murmured, as if excusing himself. " He is a most dangerous man."

A youth answered a touch of the button. Strong sent for his confidential clerk.

"Send this at once to Queensland in cipher," he instructed, in a business tone, when the man appeared; "this" being:

> *Prominent bush unionist named Hawkins leaves Sydney to-night by train for Central Queensland via Brisbane. Have him arrested immediately. Most important.*

CHAPTER VIII.

THE REPUBLICAN KISS.

"I've never felt so before," said Ned. "For about ten minutes I wanted to go back and kill him."

"Why?"

"Because he is like a wall of iron in front of one. If he were a fat hulking brute, as some of them are, I wouldn't have minded. I could have pitied him and felt that he wasn't a fair specimen of Humanity. But this man is a fair specimen in a way. He looks like a man and he talks like a man and you feel him a man, only he's absolutely unable to understand that the crowd are the same flesh and blood as he is and you know that he'd wipe us down like ninepins if he could see he'd gain by it. He's all brains and any heart he's got is only for his own friends. He is Capitalism personified. He made me feel sick at heart at the hopelessness of fighting such men in the old ways. I felt for a little while that the only thing to do was to clear them out of the way as they'd clear us if they were in our shoes."

"You've got over it soon."

"Of course," admitted Ned, with a laugh. "He can live for ever, for me, now. It was a fool's thought. It's the system we're fighting, not the products of it, and he's only a product just like the fat beasts we abuse and the ignorant drunken bushmen he despises. I was worrying, as you call it, or I shouldn't have even thought of it."

Ned was talking to Connie. After having had dinner at a restaurant with his Trades Hall friend, to whom he related part of his morning's interview, he had found himself with two or three hours on his hands. So he had turned his steps towards the Strattons, longing for sympathy and comfort, being strangely depressed and miserable without being able to think out just how he felt.

He found Mrs. Stratton writing in her snug parlour. The rooms had the same general appearance that they had two years before. The house, seen by daylight for the first time, was embowered in trees and fringed back and front with pretty flower beds and miniature lawns. Connie herself was fair and fresh as ever and wore a loose robe of daintily flowered stuff; the years had passed lightly over her, adding to rather than detracting from the charms of her presence. She welcomed him warmly and with her inimitable tact, seeing his trouble, told him how they all were, including that Josie had married and had a beautiful baby, adding with a flush that she herself had set Josie a bad example and bringing in the example for Ned to admire. The other children were boating with George and Josie, she explained, George not having yet escaped from that horrible night-work. Harry was well and would be home after a while. He was painting a series of scenes from city life, the sketches of which she showed him. Arty was married to a very nice girl, who knew all his poetry, every line, by heart. Ford was well, only more bitter than ever. When Ned asked after Geisner, she said he had not been back since and she had only heard once, indirectly, that he was well. Thus she led him to talk and he told her partly what took place between Strong and himself. Strong's offer he could not tell to anyone.

"You didn't get on with Nellie last night?" she asked, alluding to his "worrying." Having taken the baby out she had sat down on the stool by the open piano.

Ned looked up. "How do you know? Has she been here?"

"No. She hasn't been here, but I can tell. You men always carry your hearts on your sleeve, when you think you aren't. You asked her to marry you, I suppose, and she said 'No.' Isn't that it?"

"I can't tell you all about it, Mrs. Stratton," answered Ned, frankly. "That's about it. But she did quite right. She thought she shouldn't and when Nellie thinks anything she tries to do it. That's what should be."

Mrs. Stratton strummed a few notes. "I'll show you something," she said, finally, getting up. "It passes the time to show old curiosities."

She left the room, returning in a few minutes with a quaint box of dark wood, bound with chased iron work and inlaid with some semi-transparent substance in the pattern of a coat-of-arms. She opened it with a little key that hung on her watch chain. Inside were a number of compartments, covered with little lids.

She lifted them all, together, exposing under the tray a deeper recess. From this she took a miniature case.

"Look at it!" she said, smiling. "I ought to charge you sixpence but I won't."

Ned pressed the spring, the lid of the case flew up, and there, in water-colour, was the head and bust of a girl. The face was a delicate oval, the mouth soft and sweet, the eyes bright with youth and health, the whole appearance telling of winning grace and cultured beauty. The fullness of the brows betrayed the artist instinct. The hair was drawn to the top of the head in a strange foreign fashion. The softly curving lines of face and figure showed womanhood begun.

"She is very beautiful," commented Ned. Then, looking at it more closely : "Do you know that somehow, although it's not like her, this reminds me of Nellie ? "

"I knew you'd say that," remarked Connie, swinging round on the music stool so as to reach the keys again and striking a note or two softly. "It has got Nellie's presentment, whatever you call it. I noticed it the first time I saw Nellie. That was how we happened to speak first. Harry noticed it, too, without my having said a word to him. They might be sisters, only Nellie's naturally more self-reliant and determined and has had a hard life of it, while she"—nodding at the miniature—"had been nursed in rose-leaves up to the time it was taken."

"I don't see just where the likeness comes in," said Ned, trying to analyse the portrait.

"It's about the eyes and the mouth particularly, as well as a general similitude," explained Connie.

"As I tell Nellie, she's got a vicious way of setting her lips, so," and Mrs. Stratton, mimicking, drew the corners of her mouth down in Nellie's style. "Then she draws her brows down till altogether she looks as though the burden of the whole world was on her. But underneath she has the same gentle mouth and open eyes and artist forehead as the picture and one feels it. It's very strange, don't you know, that Geisner never seemed to notice it and yet he generally notices everything. After all, I don't know that it is so strange. It's human nature."

"Geisner !" said Ned, clumsily, having nothing particular to say. "Has he seen it ?"

"Once or twice," observed Connie. "It belongs to him. He leaves it with me. That's how Harry's seen it and you. It's the

P

only thing he values so he takes care of it by never having it about him, you know," she added, in the flippant way that hid her feelings.

"I suppose it is—that it's—it's the girl he——" stumbled Ned, beginning to understand suddenly.

"That's her," said Connie, strumming some louder notes. "She died. They had been married a few days. She was taken ill, very ill. He left her, when her life was despaired of. She would have him go, too. She got better a little but losing him killed her."

Ned gazed at the portrait, speechless. What were his troubles, his grief, his sorrows, beside those of the man who had loved and lost so! Nellie at least lived. At least he had still the hope that in the years to come he and she might mate together. His thoughts flew back to Geisner's talk on Love on the garden terrace, in the bright afternoon sunshine. Truly Geisner's had been the Love that elevated not the Lust that pulled down. The example nerved him like fresh air. The pain that had dumbed his thoughts of Nellie passed from him.

"He is a man!" cried Ned.

"That wasn't all," went on Connie, taking the case from his hands and officiously dusting it with her handkerchief. "When she was pining for him, dying of grief, because she had lost her strength in her illness, they offered him his liberty if he would deny the Cause, if he would recant, if he would say he had been fooled and misled and desired to redeem his position. They let him hear all about her and then they tempted him. They wanted to disgust the people with their leaders. But it wasn't right to do that. It was shameful. It makes me wild to think of it yet. The way it was done! To torture a man so through his love! Oh, the wretches! The miserable dogs! I'd——" Connie broke off suddenly to put the handkerchief to her indignant eyes. The thunderstorm of her anger burst in rain. She was a thorough woman. "I suppose they didn't know any better, as he always says of everybody that's mean. It's some consolation to think that they overshot the mark, though," she concluded, tearfully.

"How?"

"How! Why if they had let Geisner go and everybody else, there'd be no martyrs to keep the Cause going. Even Geisner, if his wife had lived, poor girl, and if children had grown up, could hardly be quite the same, don't you know. As it is he only lives for the Cause. He has nothing else to live for. They crushed his weakness out of him and fitted him to turn round and crush them."

"It's time he began," remarked Ned, thoughtfully.

"He has begun."

"Where?"

"Everywhere. In you, in me, in Nellie, in men like Ford and George and Harry, in places you never dream of. in ways nobody knows but himself. He is moulding the world as a potter moulds clay. It frightens me, sometimes. I open a new book and there are Geisner's very ideas. I see a picture, an illustrated paper, and there is Geisner's hand passed to another. I was at a new opera the other night and I could hardly believe my ears; it seemed as though Geisner was playing. From some out of the way corner of the earth comes news of a great strike; then, on top of it, from another corner, the bubbling of a gathering rising; and I can feel that Geisner is guiding countless millions to some unseen goal, safe in his work because none know him. He is a man! He seeks no reward, despises fame, instils no evil, claims no leadership. Only he burns his thoughts into men's hearts, the god-like thoughts that in his misery have come to him, and every true man who hears him from that moment has no way but Geisner's way. A word from him and the whole world would rock with Revolution. Only he does not say it. He thinks of the to-morrow. We all suffer, and he has passed through such suffering that he is branded with it, body and soul. But he has faced it and conquered it and he understands that we all must face it and conquer it before those who follow after us can be freed from it. 'We must first show that Socialism is possible,' he said to me two years ago. And I think he hoped, Ned, that some day you would show it."

"You talk like Geisner," said Ned, watching her animated face. He had come to her for comfort and upon his sad heart her words were like balm. Afterwards, they strengthened the life-purpose that came to him.

"Of course. So do you when you think of him. So does everybody. His wonderful power all lies in his impressing his ideas on everybody he meets. Strong is a baby beside him when you consider the difference in their means."

"I wish Strong was on our side, just the same."

"Why? The Strongs find the flint on which the Geisners strike the steel. Do you think for a single moment that the average rich man has courage enough or brains enough to drive the people to despair as this Strong will do?"

"Yes, monopoly will either kill or cure."

"It will cure. This Strong is annihilating the squatters as fast as he's trying to annihilate the unions. I hear them talking sometimes, or their wives, which is the same thing. They fairly hate him. He's doing more than any man to kill the old employer and to turn the owners of capital into mere idle butterflies, or, if you like it better, into swine wallowing in luxury, living on dividends. Not that they hate that," went on Connie, contemptuously. "They're an idle, vicious set, taken all round, at the best. But he's ruining a lot of the old landocrats and naturally they don't like it. Of course, very few of them like his style or his wife's."

"Too quiet? Nellie was telling me something of him once."

"Yes. He's very quiet at home. So is his wife. He reads considerably. She is musical. They have their own set, quite a pleasant one. And fashionable society can rave and splutter but is kept carefully outside their door. They don't razzle-dazzle, at any rate."

"Don't what?" asked Ned, puzzled.

"Don't razzle-dazzle!" repeated Connie, laughing. "Don't dance on champagne, like many of the society gems?"

"The men, you mean."

"The men! My dear Ned, you ought to know a little more about high life and then you'd appreciate the Strongs. I've seen a dozen fashionable women, young and old, perfectly intoxicated at a single fashionable ball. As for the men, most of them haven't any higher idea of happiness than a drunken debauch. While as for fashionable morality the less you say about it the better. And the worst of the lot are among the canting ones. The Strongs and their set at least are decent people. Wealth and poverty both seem to degrade most of us."

"Ah, well, it can't last so very much longer," remarked Ned.

"It could if it weren't for the way both sides are being driven," answered Connie. "These fat wine-soaked capitalists would give in whenever the workmen showed a bold front if cast-iron capitalists like Strong didn't force them into the fight and keep them fighting. And you know yourself that while workmen get a little what they want they never dream of objecting to greater injustices. And if it weren't for the new ideas workmen would go on soaking themselves with drink and vice and become as unable to make a change as the depraved wealthy are to resist a change. Everything helps to make up the movement."

"I know I'm inconsistent," she went on. "I talk angrily myself often but it's not right to feel hard against anybody. These other people can't help it, any more than a thief can help it or a poor girl on the streets. They're not happy as they might be, either. And if they were, I think it's better to suffer for the Cause than to have an easy time by opposing it. I'd sooner be Geisner than Strong."

"What a comparison!" cried Ned.

"Of one thing I'm sure," continued Connie, "that it is noble to go to prison in resisting injustice, that suffering itself becomes a glory if one bears it bravely for others. For I have heard Geisner say, often, that when penalties cease to intimidate and when men generally rise superior to unjust laws those special injustices are as good as overthrown. We must all do our best to prevent anything being done which is unmanly in itself. If we try to do that prison is no disgrace and death itself isn't very terrible."

"I know you mean this for me," said Ned, smiling. "I didn't mind much, you know, before. I was ready for the medicine. But, somehow, since I've been here, I've got to feel quite eager to be locked up. I shall be disappointed if it doesn't come off." He laughed cheerfully.

"Well, you might as well take it that way," laughed Connie. "I can't bear people who take everything seriously."

"There was one thing I wanted you to do," said Ned, after a while. "Nellie promised me years ago to tell me if ever she was hard up. I've got a few pounds ahead and what my horses are worth. If anything happens can I have it sent down to you so that you can give it to her if she needs it?"

Connie thought for a moment, "You'd better not," she answered. "We'll see that Nellie's all right. I think she'd starve rather than touch what you'll need afterwards."

"Perhaps so," said Ned. "You know best about that. I must go now," rising.

"Can't you wait for dinner?" asked Connie. "Harry will be here then and you'd have time to catch the train."

" I've a little business to do before," said Ned. " I promised one of our fellows to see his brother, who lives near the station."

" Oh! You must have something to eat first," insisted Connie. " You'll miss your dinner probably. That won't do." So he waited.

They had finished the hurriedly prepared meal, which she ate with him so that he might feel at home, when Stratton came in.

" He's always just in time," explained Connie, when the greetings were over. " He gives me the cold shivers whenever we're going to catch a train. Say 'good-bye' to Ned now, and don't delay him! I'll tell you all he said, all but the secrets. He's going to Queensland to-night and hasn't a minute to spare."

" I'm sorry you can't stay overnight," said Harry, heartily. " I'd like to have a long talk but I suppose my fine society lady here hasn't wasted time."

"I've talked enough for two, you may depend upon it," announced Connie, as they went to the front door together, chatting.

" Well, good-bye, if you must go," said Harry, holding Ned by both hands. " And remember, whatever happens, you've got good friends here, not fair-weather friends either."

"He must go, Harry," cried Connie. " I've kept him just to see you. You'll make him miss the next boat. Come, Ned! Good-bye!"

Ned turned to her, holding out his hand.

" Bend down!" she said, suddenly, her lips smiling, her eyes filling. " You're so tall."

He bent to her mechanically, not understanding. She took his head between her hands and kissed him on both cheeks.

" The republican kiss!" she cried, trying to laugh, offering her own cheek to him as he stood flushed and confused. Something choked him as he stooped to her again, touching the fair face with his lips, reverentially.

" Good-bye!" she exclaimed, her mouth working, grasping his hands. " Our hearts are with you all up there, but, oh, don't let your good heart destroy you for no use!" Then she burst into tears and, turning to her husband, flung herself into the loving arms that opened for her. "It's beginning again, Harry. It's beginning again. Will it never end, I wonder? And it's always the best it takes from us, Harry, the bravest and the best." And she sobbed in his arms, quietly, resignedly, as she had sobbed, Ned recollected, when Geisner thundered forth that triumphant Marseillaise.

Her vivid imagination showed her friends and husband and sons going to prison and to death as friends and father and brother had gone to prison and to death in the days gone by. She knew the Cause so well—had it not suckled her and reared her?—with all the depth of the nature that her lightness of manner only veiled as the frothy spray of the flooded Barron veils the swell of the cataract beneath, with all the capacity for understanding that made her easily the equal of brilliant men. It was a Moloch, a Juggernaut, a Kronos that devoured its own children, a madness driving men to fill with their hopes and lives the chasm that lies between what is and what should be. It had lulled a little around her of late years, the fight that can only end one way because generation after generation carries it on, civilisation after civilisation, age after age. Now its bugle notes were swelling again and those she cared for would be called, sooner or later, one by one. Husband and children and friends, all must go as this bushman was going, going with his noble thoughts and pure instincts and generous manhood and eager brain. At least, it seemed to her that they must. And so she bewailed them, as women will even when their hearts are brave and when their devotion is untarnished and undimmed. She yearned for the dawning of the Day of Peace, of the Reign of Love, but her courage did not falter. Still amid her tears she clung to the idea that those whom the Cause calls must obey.

"Ned'll be late, Harry," she whispered. "He must go." So Ned went, having grasped Harry's hand again, silently, a great lump in his throat and a dimness in his eyes but, nevertheless, strangely comforted.

He was just stepping on board the ferry steamer when Harry raced down, a little roll of paper in his hand. "Connie forgot to give you this," was all he had time to say. "It's the only one she has."

Ned opened the little roll to find it a pot-shot photograph of Nellie, taken in profile as she stood, with her hands clasped, gazing intently before her, her face sad and stern and beautiful, her figure full of womanly strength and grace. He lovered it, overjoyed, until the boat reached the Circular Quay. He kept taking it out and stealing sly peeps at it as the bus rolled up George-street, Redfern way.

CHAPTER IX.

NED GOES TO HIS FATE.

At the station some of the Sydney unionists were waiting to see Ned off. As they loaded him with friendly counsel and encouraged him with fraternal promises of assistance and compared the threats made in Sydney during the maritime strike with the expected action of the Government in Queensland, a newspaper boy came up to them, crowded at the carriage door.

"Hello, sonny! Whose rose is that?" asked one of the group, for the little lad carried a rose, red and blowing.

"It's Mr. Hawkinses rose," answered the boy.

"For me!" exclaimed Ned, holding out his hand. "Who is it from?"

"I'm not to say," answered the urchin, slipping away.

The other men laughed. "There must be a young lady interested in you, Hawkins," said one jocularly; "our Sydney girls always have good eyes for the right sort of a man." "I wondered why you stayed over last night, Hawkins," remarked another. "Trust a Queenslander to make himself at home everywhere," contributed a third. Ned did not answer. He did not hear them. He knew who sent it.

Then the guard's whistle blew; another moment and the train started, slowly at first, gradually faster, amid a pattering of good-byes.

"Give him a cheer, lads!" cried one of his friends. "Hip-hip-hurrah!"

"And one for his red rose!" shouted another. "Hip-hip-hurrah!"

"And another for the Queensland bushmen! Hip-hip-hurrah!"

Ned leaned over the door as the train drew away, laughing genially at the cheering and waving his hand to his friends. His eyes, meanwhile, eagerly searched the platform for a tall, black-clad figure.

He saw her as he was about to abandon hope; she was half concealed by a pillar, watching him intently. As his eyes drank her in, with a last fond look that absorbed every line of her face and figure, every shade of her, even to the flush that told she had heard the cheer for " his red rose," she waved her handkerchief to him. With eager hands he tore the fastening of a fantastically-shaped little nugget that hung on his watch-chain and flung it towards her. He saw her stoop to pick it up. Then the train swept on past a switch-house and he saw her no more, save in the picture gallery of his memory stored with priceless paintings of the face he loved; and in the little photo that he conned till his fellow-passengers nudged each other.

* * * *

At Newcastle he left the train to stretch himself and get a cup of tea. As he stepped from the carriage a man came along who peered inquisitively at the travellers. He was a medium-sized man, with a trimmed beard, wearing a peaked cap pulled over his forehead. This inquisitive man looked at Ned closely, then followed him past the throng to the end of the platform. There, finding the bushman alone, he stepped up and, clapping his hand on Ned's shoulder, said quietly in his ear :

" In the Queen's name ! "

Ned swung round on his heel, his heart palpitating, his nerves shaken, but his face as serene as ever. It had come, then. After all, what did it matter ? He would have preferred to have reached his comrades but at least they would know he had tried. And no man should have reason to say that he had not taken whatever happened like a man. At the time he did not think it strange that he was not allowed to reach the border. The squatters could do what they liked he thought. If they wanted to hang men what was to stop them? So he swung round on his heel, convinced of the worst, calm outwardly, feverish inwardly, to enquire in a voice that did not shake :

" What little game are you up to, mister ? "

The inquisitive man looked at him keenly.

" Is your name Hawkins ? " he asked.

" Suppose it is ! What does that matter to you ? " demanded Ned, mechanically guarding his speech for future contingencies.

" It's all right, my friend," replied the other, with a chuckle. " I'm no policeman. If you're Hawkins, I've a message for you. Show me your credentials and I'll give it."

" Who're you, anyway ? " asked Ned. " How do I know who you are ? "

The inquisitive man stopped a uniformed porter who was passing. "Here, Tom," he said, "this gentleman wants to know if I'm a union man. Am I?"

"Go along with your larks!" retorted the man in uniform. "Why don't you ask me if you're alive?" and he passed on with a laugh as though he had heard an excellent joke.

"Hang it!" said the inquisitive man. "That's what it is to be too well known. Let's see the engine-driver. He'll answer for me."

"The other's good enough," answered Ned, making up his mind, as was his habit, from the little things. "Here's my credentials!" He pulled out his pocket-book and taking out a paper unfolded it for the inquisitive man to read.

"That's good enough, too," was the stranger's comment. "You answer the description but it's best to be sure. Now"—lowering his voice and moving still further from the peopled part of the platform—"here's the message. 'Dangerous to try going through Brisbane. Police expecting him that way. Must go overland from Downs.' Do you understand it?"

"I understand," said Ned, arranging his plans quickly. "It means they're after me and I'm to dodge them. I suppose I can leave my portmanteau with you?"

"I'm here to help you," answered the man.

"Well, I'll take my blankets and leave everything else. I'm a Darling Downs boy and can easily get a horse there. And when I'm across a horse in the bush they'll find it tough work to stop me going through."

"You'd better take some money," remarked the man, after Ned had handed out his portmanteau. "You may have to buy horses."

"Not when I'm once among the camps," said Ned. "I can get relays there every few miles. I've got plenty to do me till then. How do you fellows here feel about things?"

"Our fellows are as sound as a bell. If everybody does as much as the miners will you'll have plenty of help. We don't believe everything the papers say. You seem a cool one and if the others will only keep cool you'll give the squatters a big wrestle yet."

So they talked on till the train was about to start again.

"Take my advice," said the man, drawing back further out of hearing and putting the portmanteau down between them, "and get a cipher for messages. We had to arrange one with Sydney during the end of the maritime strike and that's what they've used to-night to get the tip to you. If it wasn't for that the other side would know what was said just as well as we do. Now, good-bye! Take care of yourself! And good luck to you!"

"Good-bye, and thanks!" said Ned, shaking hands as he jumped into his carriage. "You've done us a good turn. We won't forget the South up in Queensland. You didn't tell me your name," he added, as the train moved.

The man answered something that was lost in the jarring. Ned saw him wave his hand and walk away with the portmanteau. The train sped on, past sheds and side-tracked carriages, past steaming engines and switch-houses and great banked stacks of coal, out over the bridge into the open country beyond, speeding ever Queenslandwards.

Ned, leaning over the window, watched the sheen of the electric lights on the wharves, watched the shimmering of the river, watched the glower that hung over the city as if over a great bush fire, watched the glorious cloudless star-strewn sky and the splendid moon that lit the opening country as it had lit the water front of Sydney last night, as it would light for him the back-tracks of the mazy bush when he forced his horses on, from camp to camp, six score miles and more a day. It was a traveller's moon, he thought with joy; let him once get into the saddle with relays ahead and let the rain hold off for four or five days more, then they could arrest him if they liked; at least he would have got back to his mates.

Newcastle faded away. He took his precious photo out again and held it in his hand after studying its, outlines for the hundredth time; unobserved he pressed the red rose to his lips.

His heart filled with joy as he listened to the rumbling of the wheels, to the puffing of the engine, to the rubble-double-double of the train. Every mile it covered was a mile northward; every hour was a good day's journeying; every post it flew by was a post the less to pass of the hundred-thousand that lay between him and his goal. He would get back somehow. Where "the chaps" were he would be, whatever happened. And when he got back he could tell them, at least, that the South would pour its willing levies to help them fight in Queensland the common enemy of all. It never struck him that he was getting further and further from Nellie. In his innermost soul he knew that he was travelling to her.

What good fellows they were down South here, he thought, with a gush of feeling. Wherever he went there were friends, cheering him, watching over him, caring for him, their purses open to him, because he was a Queensland bushman and because his union was in sore trouble and because they would not see brother unionists fall into a trap and perish there unaided. From the Barrier to Newcastle the brave miners, veterans of the Labour war, were standing by. In Adelaide and Sydney alike the town unions were voting aid and sympathy. The southern bushmen, threatened themselves, were sending to Queensland the hard cash that turns doubtful battles. If Melbourne was cool yet, it was only because she did not understand; she would swing in before it was over, he knew it. The consciousness of a continent throbbing in sympathy, despite the frowns and lies and evil speakings of governments and press and capitalistic organisations and of those whom these influence, dawned upon him. All the world over it was the same, two great ideas were crystallising, two great parties were forming, the lists were being cleared by combats such as this for the ultimate death-struggle between two great principles which could not always exist side by side. The robbed were beginning to understand the robbery ; the workers were beginning to turn upon the drones; the dominance of the squatter, the mine-owner, the ship-owner, the land-owner, the shareholder, was being challenged ; this was not the end, but surely it was the beginning of the end.

" Curse them ! " muttered Ned, grinding his teeth, as he gazed out upon the moonlit country-side. " What's the good of that ? " he thought. " As Geisner says, they don't know any better. A man ought to pity them, for they're no worse than the rest of us. They're no better and no worse than we'd be in their places. They can't help it any more than we can."

A great love for all mankind stole over him, a yearning to be at fellowship with all. What fools men are to waste Life in making each other miserable, he thought ! Why should not men like Strong and Geisner join hands ? Why should not the republican kiss pass from one to another till loving kindness reigned all the world round ? Men were rough and hasty and rash of tongue and apt to think ill too readily. But they were good at heart, the men he knew, and surely the men he did not know were the same. Perhaps some day—— He built divine castles in the air as he twisted Nellie's rose between his fingers. Suddenly a great wonder seized him—he realised that he felt happy.

Happy! When he should be most miserable. Nellie would not be his wife and his union was in danger and prison gates yawned in front and already he was being hunted like an outlaw. Yet he was happy. He had never been so happy before. He was so happy that he desired no change for himself. He would not have changed of his free will one step of his allotted path. He hated nobody. He loved everybody. He understood Life somewhat as he had never understood before. A great calm was upon him, a lulling between the tempest that had passed and the tempests that were coming, a forecast of the serenity to which Humanity is reaching by Pain.

"What does it matter, after all?" he murmured to himself. "There is nothing worth worrying over so long as one does one's best. Things are coming along all right. We may be only stumbling towards the light but we're getting there just the same. So long as we know that what does the rest matter?"

"What am I?" he thought, looking up at the stars, which shone the brighter because the moon was now hidden behind the train. "I am what I am, as the old Jew God was, as we all are. We think we can change everything and we can change nothing. Our very thoughts and motives and ideals are only bits of the Eternal Force that holds the stars balanced in the skies and keeps the earth for a moment solid to our feet. I cannot move it. I cannot affect it. I cannot shake it. It alone is."

"No more," he thought on, "can Eternal Force outside of me move me, affect me, shake me. The force in me is as eternal, as indestructible, as infinite, as the whole universal force. What it is I am too. The unknown Law that gives trend to Force is manifest in me as much as it is in the whole universe beside, yet no more than it is in the smallest atom that floats in the air, in the smallest living thing that swims in a drop of water. I am a part of that which is infinite and eternal and which working through Man has made him conscious and given him a sense of things and filled him with grand ideals sublime as the universe itself. None of us can escape the Law even if we would because we are part of the Law and because every act and every thought and every desire follows along in us to that which has gone before and to the influences around, just as the flight of a bullet is according to the weight of the bullet, and its shape, and the pressure, and the direction it was fired, and the wind."

"It is as easy," he dreamed on, "for the stars to rebel and start playing nine-pins with one another, as it is for any man to swerve one hair's breadth from that which is natural for him to do, he being what he is and influences at any given time being what they are. None of us can help anything. We are all poor devils, within whom the human desire to love one another struggles with the brute desire to survive one another. And the brute desire is being beaten down by the very Pain we cry out against and the human desire is being fostered in us all by the very hatreds that seem to oppose it. And some day we shall all love one another and till then, I suppose, we must suffer for the Cause a little so that men may see by our suffering that, however unworthy we are, the Cause can give us courage to endure."

"I must think that out when I have time," he concluded, as the train slowed down at a stopping-place where his last fellow-passenger got out. "I'll probably have plenty of time soon," he added, mentally, chuckling good-humouredly at his grim joke. "It's a pity, though, one doesn't feel good always. When a fellow gets into the thick of it, he gets hot and says things that he shouldn't and does things, too, I reckon."

He had not heeded the other passengers but now that he found himself alone in the carriage he got down his blankets and made his bed. He took off his boots and coat as he had done in the park, stretched himself out on the seat, and slept at once the sleep of contentment. For the first time in his life the jarring of the train did not make his head ache nor its perpetual rubble-double irritate and unnerve him. He slept like a child as the train bore him onward, passing into sleep like a child, full of tenderness and love, slept dreamlessly and heavily, undisturbed, with the photo against his heart and the rose in his fingers and about his hands the hand-clasp of friends and on his cheeks the republican kiss as though his long-dead mother had pressed her lips there.

* * * *

In Queensland the chain was prepared already whereto he was to be fastened like a dog, wherewith he was to be driven in gang like a bullock because his comrades trusted him. Yet he smiled in his sleep as the train sped on and as the moon stole round and shone in on him.

Over the wide continent the moon shone, the ever-renewing moon that had seen Life dawn in the distant Past and had seen Humanity falter up and had witnessed strange things and would witness stranger. It shone on towns restless in their slumbering; and on the countryside that dreamed of what was in the womb of Time; and on the gathering camps of the North; and on the Old Order bracing itself to stamp out the new thoughts; and on the New Order uplifting men and women to suffer and be strong. Did it laugh to think that in Australia men had forgotten how social injustice breeds social wrongs and how social wrongs breed social conflicts, here as in all other lands? Did it weep to think that in Australia men are being crushed and women made weary and little children born to sorrow and shame because the lesson of the ages is not yet learned, because Humanity has not yet suffered enough, because we dare not yet to trust each other and be free? Or did it joy to know that there is no peace and no contentment so long as the fetters of tyranny and injustice gall our limbs, that whether we will or not the lash of ill-conditions drives us ever to struggle up to better things? Or did it simply not know and not care, but move ever to its unknown destiny as All does, shedding its glorious light, attracting and repelling, ceaseless obeying the Law that needs no policeman to maintain it?

The moon shone down, knowing nothing, and the moon sank down and the sun rose and still Ned slept. But over him and over the world, in moonlight and in darkness and in sunlight, sleeping or waking, in town and country, by land and sea, wherever men suffer and hope, wherever women weep, wherever little children wonder in dumb anguish, a great Thought stretched its sheltering folds, brooding godlike, pregnant, inspiring, a Thought mightier than the Universe, a Thought so sublime that we can trust like children in the Purpose of the forces that give it birth.

To you and to me this Thought speaks and pleads, wherever we are, whoever we are, weakening our will when we do wrong, strengthening our weakness when we would do right. And while we hear it and listen to it we are indeed as gods are, knowing good from evil.

It is ours, this Thought, because sinful men as we all are have shed their blood for it in their sinfulness, have lived for it in their earnest weakness, have felt their hearts grow tender despite themselves and have done unwittingly deeds that have met them in the path, deeds that shine as brightly to our mental eyes as do the seen and unseen stars that strew the firmament of heaven.

The brute-mother who would not be comforted because her young was taken gave birth in the end to the Christs who have surrendered all because the world sorrows. And we, in our yearnings and our aspirations, in our longings and our strugglings and our miseries, may engender even in these later days a Christ whom the world will not crucify, a Hero Leader whose genius will humanise the grown strength of this supreme and sublime Thought.

Let us not be deceived! It is in ourselves that the weakness is. It is in ourselves that the real fight must take place between the Old and the New. It is because we ourselves value our miserable lives, because we ourselves cling to the old fears and kneel still before the old idols, that the Thought still remains a thought only, that it does not create the New Order which will make of this weary world a Paradise indeed.

Neither ballots nor bullets will avail us unless we strive of ourselves to be men, to be worthier to be the dwelling houses of this Thought of which even the dream is filling the world with madness divine. To curb our own tongues, to soften our own hearts, to be sober ourselves, to be virtuous ourselves, to trust each other—at least to try—this we must do before we can justly expect of others that they should do it. Without hypocrisy, knowing how we all fall far short of the ideal, we must ourselves first cease to be utterly slaves of our own weaknesses.

JOHN MILLER.

Warwick & Sapsford, Printers, &c., Brisbane.

Q

BETTY BURTON

Josephine and Harriet

HarperCollins*Publishers*

HarperCollins*Publishers*
77–85 Fulham Palace Road,
Hammersmith, London W6 8JB

www.harpercollins.co.uk

First published in Great Britain by
HarperCollins*Publishers* 2004

ISBN 0 00 775519 8

Set in Sabon by Palimpsest Book Production Limited,
Polmont, Stirlingshire

Printed and bound in Great Britain by
Clays Ltd, St Ives plc

This book is for Sheila Burton.

Acknowledgements

Much of the truth that lies at the heart of *Josephine and Harriet* was unearthed by ace researcher Elizabeth Murray. Thanks to her.

Thanks also to my editor, Susan Opie, and copy editor, Penelope Isaac. They took my script by its shoulders and shook it until it made sense.

Harriet ran home as fast as her young legs could carry her.

Alarmed – but without reason.

Embarrassed – but not knowing why.

Fearful of the vicar, because what she had done might have been sinful.

Scoldings from Mam were always over before the sun went down. 'Sleep not on thy wrath.'

Punishments from Pa could be worked off in extra chores, or, 'Sing to me my little throstle and we'll call it quits.'

But sinning?

God dealt out punishments for that, and not until you were dead.

She didn't believe that she had sinned too much, not yet, but by the time she was dead, she might be weighed down with sins.

She might end up at the left hand of Jesus, with the goats.

The coin that was clutched in her hand became hot and sweaty. Perhaps if she threw it away then the sin would go with it. No. It was money, and money was fair short at home. For the life of her, the seven-year-old couldn't decide. 'Tell the truth and shame the Devil.'

So, when she reached home, she opened her palm to her mam.

'Oh, and where'd y' get that, me girl?'

'Gaffer gid it me.'

Her mother turned. She was making flour and water 'floaters' to put into knuckle-bone broth, flour hanging like rags from her fingers. 'Is that so then?'

Mam's look was enough. She was trying to be like always, but by Mam's straight face Harriet knew that something serious had happened. Money was always trouble with Mam and Jesus. He didn't like rich men, He turned over the money-lenders' tables in the temple, and He was sold out by Judas for pieces of silver. There hadn't seemed to be anything wrong about standing on a stool in Gaffer's workshop and taking a ha'penny for singing a song.

But, clearly, even if she wasn't sure what, she had committed a sin, and she did not want to confess it to her mam. She fed a few coals into the fire under the stewpot as a good deed.

'And why'd he give ya a whole ha'penny then? Has he give you money before?'

'Naw, Mam.'

2

Mam turned her back on her child and plunged her hands into the flour and water, gathering it into a ball. 'Well then?'

'I sang to him.'

'Oh.' Her mam chopped the ball of dough into little 'floaters' and put them aside to dry out a bit. 'Is that all?'

'Yes, Mam, I sang him the Easter song, just that one, no more.'

'Oh. Well, my pet. It's true that you have a sweet voice, but it's as well not to get paid for a gift of God. And don't go inside Gaffer's door if y're on y'r own self. You understand that?'

'Yes, Mam.'

'No harm done. Put the ha'penny in the jar and it'll add to fair money when time comes round.'

The coin was dealt with, but Harriet Burton knew that she had sinned. The greater sin was not in letting Gaffer touch her, but telling her mam a barefaced lie, and the day would come when she would pay for it.

Harriet placated people; that was how she made her way in the world.

Like me, please.

Like me, I'm not really a bad girl.

Nor was she.

Josephine Thomson, the other young woman involved in this story, also, as a child, had an experience that would follow her into womanhood.

Only she of her entire family had survived the ravages of a contagious fever that spread like wildfire.

She was saved by a visit to Hani's remote home village – Hani being the Thomsons' living-in help and friend, and teacher to the children. But saved for what? To succeed? To live up to the belief her father had had that women were as capable as men of making 'something of themselves'? But what was this Something? She was almost twenty before a talent was revealed; unfortunately it was not a talent that English provincial society expected women to possess.

Josephine Thomson's early years living far from England, with parents who hardly differentiated in the upbringing of herself and her twin brother, had given her a liberal view of what women should expect for themselves. This view was confirmed when tragedy forced her to come to live in England under the care of an intelligent and powerful uncle and his wealthy high-society wife; she also held quite advanced views on the capability of her own gender. Even so, Josephine's aunt believed that women's lives were improved by marriage to a loving man, as her own had been.

Josephine grew into blooming, ambitious womanhood with cobwebs of guilt clinging to her subconscious.

Christmas Eve 1872

Harriet Burton. Pretty, dainty, probably a few years older than she appeared. Not much of her native Norfolk dialect left since she had become a Londoner.

As her first-floor tenant tripped lightly downstairs, Mrs Wright waylaid her in a friendly manner, and asked cheerfully, 'Off then, Miss Burton? You look very nice.'

'Thank you, Mrs Wright.'

'Did Mr Wright remind you about the rent?'

'He did, but he didn't have need to. I realize I'm a bit behind, but, like I told him, I'll have it tonight when I get back from the theatre.'

'You got a booking then?'

'I think so. I'll know when I get there.'

'Good luck, then. Christmas Eve don't hardly seem the time when your sort of songs is best appreciated. No choruses, is there?'

5

No choruses . . . absolutely no choruses. Harriet Burton's act was simple: a pretty woman who sang sweet, sentimental ballads. No choruses. Her name was never high on the list of acts at the Alhambra Palace.

'True, but it's a time when a deal of drink is taken, and the audience does incline to get sentimental. They don't necessarily care about choruses.'

'Hard, though, working the Palace. I know what it's like.' Mrs Wright nodded at herself, having been on the halls before she got lucky and became a landlady.

'Ah well . . . when needs must . . .'

'I hope you got your boots on, it's snowing like anything.'

'Is it?' Harriet looked down at her pretty embroidered shoes. 'I'd better go back and change.'

On her second appearance outside the Wrights' apartment the singer was wearing her old boots, the embroidered shoes tucked into a dolly-bag, along with her little pots of eyes and lips. Through the hall-door window she saw that big snowflakes were beginning to lie. 'I'm off then. I'll say hello when I come in. I might be late.'

'That don't matter – you know Mr Wright likes to see who's coming into my house.'

Mrs Wright held that if any blame for vice on the streets of London be laid at anyone's door, it should be at the doors of men who used the girls – but men got off scot-free. Having narrowly escaped life on the streets, she did what she could to redress the balance by letting rooms to girls who were decent but down on their luck. So, 12 Great Coram Street was not a brothel, nor even

6

a house of ill-repute – nowhere near that, because Mrs Wright took nothing extra from her girls if they brought a man-friend to visit. Just the rent when it was due. Her girls looked after her in other ways: a bit of fruit here, a tot or two there, a few hot pies . . . Little treats, free tickets to the shows – but no money except the rent.

Number 12 Great Coram Street then was a lodging house for young women. Like the rest of the long, brick-built terrace of iron-railed, large houses, it comprised a large basement kitchen and scullery, ground floor accommodation for the Wrights, and three other floors of rooms rented out to young women. Mrs Wright would never take men as boarders. Although there was a turnover of young women, they remained her girls.

Josephine Thomson. In her twenties, a journalist on the staff of The News, *one of the new-style and outrageous 'rags', as they were known. In her professional life, Josephine Thomson became Jemima Ferguson.*

When a church clock struck twelve, Josephine collected together the piece she had ready for her editor, Mr George Hood. Her career in journalism had started with contributions to the *English Woman's Domestic Magazine.* She chose her name because she had read an article concerning women's rights by an American woman whose name was Ferguson. To have used the name Thomson could prove awkward for her family, in particular her uncle James, who had brought her up as a daughter. Uncle James was Detective Superintendent

James Thomson – Thomson of the Met., well known far beyond his Bow Street manor for his modern ideas of policing, and his determination to transform the police from a body of men who were shown little respect by the public into a well-trained, well-equipped force. A man with such revolutionary ideas made enemies, so Josephine did not intend making matters worse by having the name Thomson tagged to any piece of mud she might throw in her columns.

Being ambitious and sure of herself, she had made this decision long before her name ever appeared attached to a column. A good decision on her part, now that she had joined *The News*. This had transformed itself by quadrupling a two-page Sunday rag into a daily paper that 'tickled', in Fleet Street terms.

> Tickle the public, make 'em grin,
> The more you tickle, the more you'll win,
> Teach the public, you'll never get rich,
> You'll live like a beggar and die in a ditch.

The News lived and expanded following this philosophy. Women columnists tickled the public, as did murder and scandal. Josephine liked to be given assignments where she could stir consciences and create indignation. Mostly it was here-today, gone-tomorrow journalism, but Josephine believed that constant irritation made people want to scratch – eventually. Once she began working in Fleet Street, she learned how to give an edge

8

to her 'women's articles', and tried to give something more insightful than a paragraph or two of fact. Of course, the real plums were given to the men, but she had an ally in the editor, Mr Hood. It had been he who had 'stolen' her from *The Echo* a couple of years ago. That was when *The News* had transformed itself by bringing in Oxbridge men to try to give it some gravitas, but degrees in literature hardly ever gave those men a taste for the kind of 'tickle' that sold the paper: this came from the editorial talents of George Hood.

Josephine had 'tickle' in bags-full. Although that endeared her to her editor, it never brought her the plums she was ambitious for. However, she had faith that the future belonged to her and women like her. Her time would come.

Today, instead of handing the pages she had finished to the youth whose job it was to get them to the editor, she decided to take them herself to Mr Hood. Quickest way to get his approval – or not.

She would have given much not to have come into *The News* office today. She felt as though she might have caught a cold, the weather was worsening under a snow-laden sky, and the stove in her office had sulked.

But, when she had been offered a post as a 'filler' columnist – as opposed to the reviewer and fashion writer she had been with *The Echo* – she determined to prove herself equal to the Oxbridge men with their decent offices and time for lunch. This, of course, meant that, like other women in the profession, she had to be better than they were. Which was why she turned up regardless of colds, chills and freezing offices.

Josephine Thomson had determined to report on the lives of women, to be an investigator and reporter. And heaven alone knew there was much material here in London. The piece she had just completed was good. Mr Hood would like it. Death by starvation of an educated woman who had been unable to find work of any kind. Josephine – having picked her way through the apathy of other lodgers in the rooming-house, who themselves had come and gone as unrecognized and worthless as the woman known only as Jane – had pieced together the last weeks of Jane's life. Josephine's passion was evident in every seven-word sentence and five-line paragraph – the preferred style of *The News*.

As she made her way through the buzz of reporters at work and the familiar smell of cigar and tobacco smoke – and this morning wine, too, she was aware of the looks she got. They were not friendly. The male reporters who resented her most were those 'men of letters', 'Oxbridge men', men who had been persuaded to join *The News* for much the same reason as Josephine: to change the formula and appearance of the 'old rag', to give it a bit of dignity and gravitas and, in Josephine's case, to broaden its outlook. George Hood had warned her that in entering the world of male professional writers and male opinions, she had a hard furrow to plough. This, of course, did not daunt Josephine one jot. Her parents – missionaries of unorthodox views – had taught her and brought her up no differently from her twin brother.

The Thomson twins had a great sense of their own self-worth, while also valuing other people.

As always the door to the editor's office stood open. The name 'George Hood', and his title painted on the glass panel, was therefore not revealed until one was inside the room. 'Miss Ferguson, come in.'

'My piece about that woman Jane.'

'How many words?'

'Seven fifty. I know you wanted five hundred, but . . .'

He held out a hand for the copy, read swiftly, then nodded. 'But?'

'That's as spare as I can make it without it becoming . . . well, trivial.'

He read it over again quickly. 'I agree. We'll run it in the next edition.'

Josephine warmed with gratification. 'Anything else for me?'

'Not today. Going to your family?'

'Yes, I can't foresee a Christmas when I won't.'

'Was that a sigh?'

'No . . . well, yes . . . probably.'

'Families, eh? Can't do with 'em, can't do without 'em.'

'That about sums it up for me – not that I don't love them dearly.'

'What do they think of you? I mean, working here, it's not the most usual job for a young woman of your education. They must have very advanced views.'

Avoiding his eyes she answered reluctantly. 'They, um . . . they have no idea what I do.'

11

'I'm sorry, bad thing intruding on private life. I had assumed . . . sorry.'

'I left home some time ago. I have rooms, I share with another young professional woman. I have no parents.'

'Oh.'

'It's all right, I was orphaned when I was quite young, my uncle and his wife took me in and educated me. I am like a daughter to them – an only child, in fact. I owe them everything. I love them, too. They would never understand this world – well, my aunt wouldn't. My uncle knows it but wouldn't approve.'

George Hood pondered for a few moments on this uncle, but no ideas came immediately, nor could he think of a Ferguson who might fit the bill. 'What do they suppose you do with your time?'

'Write,' she smiled. 'I show them the pamphlets I have written up for one or two historical societies, and I have contributed to a London guide. My aunt is quite proud of me. Her friends ask me to produce little collections of kitchen receipts.'

A faint flicker of amusement crossed his face, and he arched his brows. 'Do they pay you?'

'They do. My aunt insists upon it, she tells them that they would not expect to get their hats trimmed free. Actually, they pay me quite well. Some of them have their collections printed up in little booklets of ten pages or so.'

'Do you get signed copies?'

'Actually, I do, I have quite a collection. It's a very good disguise for the work I do here.'

Now they both laughed outright. 'Miss Ferguson, you are a wonder.'

'I know, Mr Hood. I just need to prove that to the male reporters. They think I'm a joke.'

'I don't, and I am the only one who matters here. I brought you in because I had noticed your pieces for *The Echo*.'

'And you offered me a good arrangement to come to work on *The News*.'

'Just be patient, Miss Ferguson. Of course there is prejudice against women in professions.'

'Why "of course"? There doesn't have to be.'

'There doesn't have to be prejudice against producing newspapers every day of the year, but there is, and we can only chip away at rusty minds.'

Five years ago, the only females working on newspapers were in America, and mostly were daughters of owners and editors. Josephine might be a 'filler' writer, but at least she'd had no preferential treatment because she knew the right people. She had come to *The News* on merit. George Hood had noticed her work with *The Echo* and asked to meet her. The deal he offered was better than she could ever have expected. She had been bold in asking for more important assignments than 'Just for Women' pieces.

'Get you off, then.'

'Can I ask you something, Mr Hood?'

'Ask away.' He made a point of editing her piece as he talked to indicate that he was a busy man.

'When am I going to be given a chance to do

13

something that will get me on the front page? I can judge my own work, and I know that it's good. I like doing social conditions, but—'

'But nothing, Miss Ferguson. You are everybody's favourite She-Radical.'

'Everybody's what!'

'*The News*'s She-Radical.'

Josephine stiffened and drew back.

'From me, that is a compliment, Miss Ferguson.'

'I had no idea . . . I'd prefer to be thought of as a journalist, not a "she" anything. A journalist . . . a reporter like the rest. Do you have any He-Reporters, He-Overseas-Correspondents? Or . . . or He-Editors for that matter?'

'I like what you are . . . you wear your allegiance on your sleeve. Everything you write shouts Injustice, Unfairness, Favouritism. Readers warm to your indignation.'

Josephine stood there, speechless after her outburst. She took her work seriously, and put a lot of effort into her research.

Dropping his blue editing pencil, he got out of his seat and came out from behind his large desk.

If he patted her shoulder, or said one sweet word to placate her, she would walk right out.

He went to the window and looked down. 'When you come in tomorrow, I'd advise you to carry a shovel and get in some dry wood for that stove of yours.'

Josephine shook her head and wondered where her outburst had got her.

14

'Now don't get huffy at what I am about to say. You didn't apply to work on *The News*, we enticed you away. You were wasted on *The Echo*, filling their ladies' corners. *The News* is just finding its feet. One or two of the American dailies have got splendid women on their staff writing and reporting, the best ones being good writers. This business needs all the good writers it can get; if the Man in the Moon lands on Earth, what good is it if the reporter who sees it can't paint the word-picture for the rest of us?'

Josephine could only shrug her shoulders. He was stating the obvious.

'This piece,' he leaned over and picked up her Jane story, 'is a beautifully-written obit. to this woman. On this one page you have distilled the tragedy of a woman's life. You can *write*, Miss Ferguson . . . Jemima. You have an instinct that any of our BA and DLit word machines would give a lot to have. I'd swear none of them could whip up a storm and prick consciences in the same way as you have in Jane's story.

'I'll tell you something,' he continued, grinning and tapping the side of his nose, 'confidential. Now, the word "blood". Do you think there is any better description of . . . well, *blood*?'

'I don't. In any context it is the word I would use – life-blood, bloodstained, bloodshed . . . It is an evocative word.'

'Not the "crimson stream of life"?'

Smiling, she said, 'No, never the "crimson stream of life".'

15

'A dog's tail – a "cordial appendage"? An oyster a "succulent bivalve"? And coffee . . . oh yes, let coffee be "the fragrant berry of Mocha". You may well laugh, Miss Ferguson, but my blue pencil has often been needed to make our Oxbridge men into journalists. You, Miss, never use two words where one will do – and that one word will be choice.'

'So why am I not being given the chance to report on parliamentary debates, or something like that?'

Folding his arms across his chest, he looked her directly in the eyes, 'Is that what you *really* want? To sit in the House listening to men ("the male of our species") who, you will quickly learn, you are worth two of, day in, day out, writing up their boring speeches so that they sound profound for their constituents.'

'But those reports are prominent, and the correspondent's name is prominent too.'

'So?'

'So, people in power, MPs, members of the House of Lords, people who can change things . . . they read those articles and editorials.'

'Sorry,' he grinned, 'editor's job is taken.'

'My "Jane" will be read with breakfast and be gone by dinner.'

'And what do you suppose happens to the great chunks of editorials? Do you suppose that when the master throws down his newspaper, that his wife and subsequently his servants rush to read a report on a speech made in the House of Lords by Lord Tom Noddy on the price of pig iron?'

16

Josephine grinned in spite of herself.

'No, no, the great newspaper readers of this nation are those who turn to the tickle and titbit pieces – and that is not to say that tickle can't have serious content. *News* readers will remember "Jane's" life and death. There will be people, maybe just a few, who the next time they are about to turn a woman away because of some prejudice, will be a bit more understanding.'

'So, what are you saying, Mr Hood? That I must not aspire to the front page?'

'I am saying no such thing. You must aspire to the front page. To your own by-line. I am confident that you will have front page—'

'Even though I wear skirts?'

'The day will come when skirts will no longer excite comment in our world. Don't worry, it will come for you. It is a matter of finding something that will launch you. Something current, something we get before the opposition . . . and something that shocks the socks off our readers. And it will be something that the "Young Lions" won't have the passion or experience to handle. You will know when it comes, and so will I. Now, ' "Starved to Death in a Garret". Good, honest-to-God writing, but I shall alter that title, and make it a paragraph heading.' Josephine frowned. 'Don't worry, your words are safe. What I propose is placing it on the Obit. page, black-border it.' He squared his thumbs and fingers. "Jane" and her dates, by Jemima Ferguson.'

Taking a deep breath, Josephine let it out expressively.

'That's marvellous, Mr Hood. You're the best editor in London.'

'I know, that's why I get paid such a large salary and work such long hours. Now be off – and take this with you,' and handing her an envelope said, 'A bonus, a Christmas box . . . recognition that *The News* is pleased that you are with *us* and no longer with the opposition.' Returning to his desk he started marking up her work again. 'And don't forget what I said about a shovel and some dry sticks tomorrow.'

'Christmas Day tomorrow, Mr Hood.'

'Ah, yes, but I shall be here – at least for as long as I can to escape a house full of aunts and cousins and grannies.' He grinned. 'News editors have similar privileges to doctors and cabbies – a reason to be at work when families get too much.'

'You really love your work, don't you, Mr Hood?'

Spreading his hands, indicating the untidy office, he said, 'What is there not to love? Ambition fulfilled.'

'Merry Christmas, Mr Hood.'

'Thank you, Miss Ferguson.'

Back in her office, she opened the envelope. Twenty pounds! More than some could earn in a year.

She walked through the bustling streets where an icy wind whipped skirts and coat-tails, and flakes of snow were blown into corners of buildings where they settled in little pyramids. Christmas. She had always loved those few days of magic, ever since she had lived in England. Several family traditions had emerged from a single event – like Hani and Cooper, her aunt's general factotum, going out in the early hours to visit the flower market, and coming back with Cooper pushing a handcart laden with a tree and great bunches of chrysanthemums, holly, mistletoe and ivy. As a child 23 December had been the accepted beginning of the Christmas holiday. Uncle James kept well out of the way, coming home only when it was time to trim the tree – at least, coming home when his duties allowed. There had been times when he had sent a police messenger to say that he would be late but to wait for the tree. Aunt Ann would say, 'Wait for the tree, wait for the tree, does he think we can go many more hours with a naked tree?' But usually he came. Now Josephine was the one not to be there on the 23rd. It was still, in her mind, the start of Christmas, but she was creating her own traditions.

Yesterday evening had been the most enjoyable since she had left her uncle's Thames-side house at Chiswick to set up a home of her own. Boot Street was a world away in style from the sylvan area of Chiswick. Josephine's rooms – a few steps away from the very old timbered and jettied 'Boot Inn' – overlooked a busy street of shops, inns and dining rooms. She leased an apartment in a substantial building that had been built in the time of King George; since its heyday as a town house, like most of the houses in the street, it had had its ground floor made over into shops. Josephine's independence consisted of four large first-floor rooms fronting the street. The lease was cheap and the entertainment constant: London life passed back and forth all day and much of the night. Two of the large, high-ceilinged rooms she sublet to

Liliana Wilde, a painter; they shared a kitchen and other facilities at the dark back of the house. Liliana also had rooms on the Left Bank of the Seine in Paris, and divided her life between the two.

Yesterday evening Josephine and Liliana and ten of their friends had gathered in the public dining rooms that were next door and up a few steps. There they had shared a long table and a feast of roast beef and rich pudding. Later they had retired to Josephine's big first-floor room, where, due to the lack of many comfortable chairs, they had sat on cushions on the floor, eating fruit and sugared plums and drinking coffee made in the French manner by Liliana. The aroma of ground coffee beans drifted along the hallway, mingling with cigar smoke – some of the women smoked small cigars, not because they particularly liked the experience, but because it was outrageous. Josephine's friends enjoyed rejecting conventions, not for the sake of it, but so that they would not let prejudice or snobbery preclude experience. Josephine didn't particularly enjoy the cigars, but she did like Scotch whisky – not often the chosen drink of women brought up in high society as she had been. Most of all she liked the freedom to do as she chose within her own rooms.

The first time they had organized this pre-Christmas gathering, there had been only Jo, Lili, her brother David and Christine. David Wilde was a 'notorious' preacher, and Christine Derry an art-lover, who held shows of paintings and sculptures in her Bloomsbury home. Liliana, David and Christine were all dissidents of a kind – not revolutionary, but unwilling to accept everything that society deemed acceptable. One of the men had met the reformer Edwin Chadwick and persuaded them to read his treatise, 'London Labour and the London Poor'.

Josephine had been very influenced by this, for although – like all of her 'comfortably off' friends – she saw poverty at almost every corner as she went about London, she had not understood its nature: that destitute people were part of the same society in which she lived, and that quite minor events, such as a girl not being given a 'character' from her mistress, could push her over the line and onto the streets. Any children she might have would never know anything else. But, although Josephine and her friends were often very serious in their talk, they also knew how to enjoy life.

She was able to make most of her purchases in Boot Street, where she was greeted as a valued customer and friendly neighbour. When she went into the interior of 'Zammit – Silversmith', the owner opened his palms and greeted her like a relation. 'Miss Josephine!' He grinned, showing teeth ground down from years of gritting them in concentration while practising his craft. 'You were right, look, my first modern piece, you remember I said that the colours . . . oh, the oddness . . . Egyptian, you said, soon all London will be asking for copies of the jewels of the ancients . . .' On and on he went, relating his protests and her insistences, until he unwrapped a piece of suede revealing a row of large squares of colours, silver-set and linked.

21

'Mr Zammit! That's absolutely beautiful, more than I imagined.' She ran a finger over the smooth surface of the small tiles of stone. 'Jasper?' He nodded. 'Hardstone? Obsidian?'

Nodding, he gently polished where her finger had touched the vivid stone. 'And not one piece of jet. A few people have seen me working upon it and agree with me that exotic pieces like these will become popular. I have got the boy to go to the museum and make drawings. I will show you when I have finished the drop-earrings in the style of miniature oil jars – amphorae, so he says.'

Josephine paid him, much less than his beautiful work warranted, but he insisted that he would gain when other women saw the bracelet and coveted one like it, so she purchased pairs of filigree earrings in more conventional style for her aunt and Hani.

Liliana as usual was engrossed in her work, the room fuggy with the smell of oil paints, turpentine, and wood smoke from a small log that had fallen from the fire and lay smouldering on the tiled hearth. Josephine was about to admonish her friend when she was shocked into speechlessness at seeing the portrait that Lili was in the act of signing in tiny letters. Liliana turned and beamed, 'Christmas present, Jo. Merry Christmas.'

Josephine stepped forward to look at the small portrait – of herself. Not a formal pose – Josephine had never sat for Liliana, and Liliana hardly ever painted portraits – but a half profile, head slightly tilted, captured as though Josephine had turned, leaned back and was about to ask a question as she sat at her desk.

'Say something. Do you like it?'

'Of course I like it, Lili. I love it . . . you have made me look quite beautiful.'

'Good Lord, woman, you *are* beautiful. I *have* got you, don't you think?'

'Definitely me, I wonder what I was asking you? How did you manage it without me sitting for you?'

'Josephine, when you are working away at that desk, you don't know what is going on around you. In effect you have been sitting for me from the day you took me in. I don't suppose you even realize how many times you look over your shoulder like that to call out to me.'

'Liliana Wilde, you are so talented. Is Christine going to put it in her show?'

'If you agree, it's yours now.'

'Of course I agree. It's the kind of thing that will get you commissions. Thank you, Lili.' She handed Liliana the jeweller's box. 'Merry Christmas. I wish I could say this is my work. But it *is* my design . . . Mr Zammit took a lot of persuading.'

When Liliana saw the variety and colour of the linked tiles, she drew a breath of surprise. 'Jo! *Your* design?'

'With a little help from some ancient Egyptians.'

'You should give up scribbling for a living and set up with Mr Zammit.'

Josephine glowed with pleasure. It was always difficult to choose gifts for an artist. She had, some months ago, dealt with her feelings of guilt at spending her money so frivolously.

David Wilde had helped her with that. 'Josephine, if

you continue to rub your conscience sore every time you spend for pleasure, then there is nothing for it but to disown what your parents left you, wear a blanket and sandshoes and carry your begging-bowl as some Eastern priests do. Of course, you might then add to society's problems. I believe that your friends would prefer it if you go on being the generous, considerate person that you are and enjoy the life God has given to you.'

When Liliana had said that her brother David was a preacher, Josephine's prejudice created in her mind a sober, opinionated man, but that was before she met him, before she had heard him say anything. Then, like the scores who went to listen to him speak in the open air of London's Hyde Park, and the hundreds who attended his meetings at St Giles (meetings, not orthodox Christian services, talks not sermons), she became charmed by his voice and manner. He certainly held strong opinions, and saw it as his duty to express them. For the most part his views turned out to be quite in line with Josephine's own. He was amiable, funny, the tone of his voice as easy to listen to as a professional singer, and the sincerity of his beliefs simple and honest. This ideal man might have become self-satisfied, except that he had Liliana for a sister, and Liliana had been keeping him in his place since she was four and he eight.

Also, he had enemies. Churchgoers who did not necessarily live very Christian lives, factory-owners who did not like what he had to say about the way they acquired their wealth, and most newspaper-owners.

The 'Rabble Rouser' or the 'Ranting Priest' was always good for several column inches. Fleet Street saw him as fair game to hold up to ridicule. Water off a duck's back.

David's words had been nice to hear, but Jo guessed that she would never be easy living comfortably whilst London teemed with hardship.

Detective Superintendent James Thomson of Bow Street 'E' Division. Well-known in the Metropolitan Police area for his advanced views on police methods. He firmly believed that the force would not be efficient and strong until the public respected the men they wished to protect them. This meant training – both police and public. He also believed that the future of detection must be in applying scientific methods at all scenes of crime, and ordered that there be no big boots until he himself or Sergeant Kerley had been called. Such attention to detail was almost unknown in a high-ranking officer.

Josephine's famous uncle, James Thomson, festooned with little parcels, put the key in the lock of his own front door and went to step inside, only to be greeted by his wife's firm voice, 'Boots, boots, James.' Handing her his parcels, he hooked off his elastic-sided overboots, only to be stopped again by Hani's soft voice, 'S'ippers, s'ippers, Mister James.'

Ann Martha Thomson, shutting the inner hall door against the icy blast that had accompanied James's entrance, then offering her pretty pink cheek for a kiss, asked, 'What's all this, James? Home so early . . . have Londoners stopped knifing one another?'

'What then, shall I go out and find a felon to keep me busy for an hour or two?' James Thomson at home was a genial and comfortable man to be with. James Thomson, Detective Superintendent Thomson of the Metropolitan Police, working out of Bow Street, was something else. There were times when he carried shreds of his profession home with him. Then he would shut himself away in a small room that was his own only because Ann Martha could see no use for it as part of her well-kept home. An iron stove, an old, large wooden table, an armchair and an old rocker.

'No, James, I am pleased that you will be here to welcome Josephine. I have one or two purchases still to make, and in any case I like to be out when it's snowing.'

'And nothing to do with the new fur-trimmed cloak and hood?'

Ann tripped lightly up the thickly carpeted stairs. 'Oh James, how well you know me!' Almost immediately she returned, now wearing the said cloak. James, seated on a bench inlaid in the new style, watched as she swooped around the hallway trying to produce the effect she hoped gusts of wind would have on the fur. 'Doesn't it just ripple beautifully, James?'

'Beautifully, Ann. It is amazing how rippling a few dead animals can be.'

'James!'

'Don't take on – I'm teasing. The cloak is beautiful,

26

much better on you than on the nasty little foxes. You have saved the lives of many chickens. Now go and enjoy the snowstorm.'

'You heard what I said about Josephine, you haven't forgotten?'

'Is it likely?'

'It's not unknown for you to doze.'

'I keep him 'wake, Miss Ann.'

Mrs Thomson smiled warmly at Hani. 'I'm sure you will,' and brushed a kiss on her husband's cheek, wafting a cloud of perfume around him. He had never discovered what it was, something discreet and elegant, probably very expensive – like Ann herself – lingering on the senses.

The warm tone of this little scene was unforced and quite usual. Detective Superintendent Thomson, Ann Martha and Hani. Harmonious under one roof where there was respect and a mutual caring. There used to be a fourth – Josephine. The light of all their lives.

It was Christmas Eve and they were each busy in their different ways, keen to shower her with affection as they had years ago when Hani had brought the orphaned child to London.

The interior of the Alhambra Palace was in direct contrast to the afternoon darkness and windy blasts of snow outside. Inside it was close and fuggy, lights burned around the walls, and spots lit up the stage. From time to time, the audience, some seated at tables, laughed and applauded. It didn't matter at what, the noise and music were at one with the atmosphere. Gaiety and Christmas cheer enveloped everyone as they entered, whether by the front of house or the stage door . . .

Young Man, age unknown. By the cut of his clothes, and the style of his hat, not English. Dark-haired. Not tall, but not short. Occupation unknown, but he appears excessively interested in the women who, between acts at the Alhambra Palace, often kept company with any man who appeared not to have a partner. He could make a single glass of beer last, taking sips of that as he took sips of the women.

Watching the parade of women – 'actresses', as some called themselves and some were – the young man was enjoying himself, a dark beer in one hand, a cigar in the other.

Back at the hotel on the far side of London, his wife would still be enjoying her fury but having to swallow it in the company of their fellow countrymen.

Until this morning, it had been weeks since he'd had satisfactory marital relations with her. Marital relations was her phrase, his own was coarser, something else to add fuel to her fire of resentment. Well, she was the one who had suggested the venture. If she regretted it, it was now far too late. No going back. Even though there had been a hiatus and they found themselves unexpectedly in England, there was still no going back.

Soon after their arrival at Kroll's German Hotel and their bags were taken up, she had slipped the latch against him. The latch had been as easily overcome as she had herself. He had thrust his strength, first against the fastened room and then against her body, and gained easy entrance to both. He had pushed her onto the bed, lifted her skirts and opened his trousers. Straddling her face, he had forced her to look at his erection. 'No more excuses. We can enjoy ourselves for as long as we like. The bed is sprung, the walls are thick and the room next to this is mine.'

For many days now she had pleaded menstruation as the reason. Before that it had been fear of an untimely pregnancy, and always the claim that, aboard ship, the walls to the cabins were paper thin and that she would never be able to face other passengers who might overhear the crudity of his love-making.

Not here, she said. When we get to our new country.

No, no, not now, she said.

Not tonight. Wait a little.

Others will hear us.

Be patient, she said.

Wait until we have a room to ourselves.

At the last moment he withdrew, spilling semen over her, and saw that this time she was actually telling the truth about her long-lasting menstrual condition.

It was then she had spat at him. 'Brute!' Literally spat. 'Lecher!' He had slapped her very hard on her buttocks, had felt neither brutish, debauched nor lecherous – only extraordinary. Standing where she was forced to look at him, he used her petticoats to wipe away her blood. Its intensity of colour on the white petticoat had excited him into erection again, making him feel doubly powerful.

This time he expelled himself inside her, confident that there could be no pregnancy whilst she bled.

He would never again accept that as an excuse. Wallowing in her blood was more exciting than he could ever have imagined.

Thoughts of how it would be when they were once again en route for Brazil, and yet again when they arrived and he was leader and responsible for the future of an entire colony of souls and bodies, including *hers*. All of them relying upon him to create a future. *She* of all of them was entirely reliant upon him. If she did not like the life he intended for them, to whom could she complain? She could write all the letters home she liked; he could let them go, or not, as he pleased. It was her extravagance and love of position and high-life that had brought them to the very edge. Only his own wits and shrewd planning had brought them back from the brink. She used to be outrageous and funny, daring him, drawing him into her fantasies of love. Love! He realized too late that she wasn't capable of love. Only of sexual excess – but on her terms. All those, 'No, no, not now. Not tonight. Wait a little. People will hear what we are doing. Wait until we have a room to ourselves.'

Well, that morning they had had a room to themselves, and in a moment of revelation he realized that he had been master all along. He could do as he pleased. She could not leave him; she was attached to him now. She had burnt her boats along with his. She could go nowhere, except with him.

His hand warmed and his heart swelled at the memory

of that subduing slap. All that he wanted from her was passivity. He would give her pleasure, he liked to do that, but only when she was passive. In their early days together, there had been such fever in her. He had loved to take her almost to ecstasy, but then withhold until she had performed some novelty on him, and then, if she would only lie quietly, he would give her satisfaction.

He felt the beginnings of arousal as he remembered how submissive she had become this morning, how explosively he had ejaculated.

A new actress came in.

At the side of the bar, the young man watched as she took off her boots, gave them to the barmaid, who stowed them behind the bar and slipped on some pretty embroidered shoes, after which she bought a tot of something and stood for a while, chatting to the barmaid in a low voice. He could not hear what she said, but was pleased to see from their glances that he was their topic.

Harriet said, 'Haven't seen him before, Tryphena, have you?'

Tryphena Douglas gave a section of the bar counter a hard polish. 'No, and I can't say as I mind if I don't see him again. He's been hanging on to that drink for an hour. I don't mind them hanging around, except if they don't shell out for a drink or two. Anybody'd think I was a charity.'

'He doesn't look too bad to me.'

'Full of himself.'

'Aren't they all?'

'Harriet, love. Don't get yourself all upset. Have you heard from him?'

'Oh yes, he writes regular, describes all the goings-on aboard ship, and the ports where they have to stop off. Last letter, he said the temperature was over one hundred.'

'And do you reckon you'd like that?'

'Of course I will, and it's not as hot as that where we shall be. He says the temperature is lovely, like summer all the year round. Can you imagine that? Not having to huddle around half the year trying to keep out the chill; always wearing lawns and silks.'

'When do you think he'll send for you?'

'As soon as he gets settled in a bigger house – the one he had before was just a bachelor place.'

Tryphena, worldly-wise, thought, Oh yes, he's sure to do that, just like he's sure to marry you. Harriet Burton wasn't silly, just too trusting of any man who was kind to her. And here she was, calling herself 'Clara' once again, 'Clara' because the man who arranged bookings for her said that was a better name for a performer. Here she was, back on the halls, doing her singing act because another man left her. Here she was, 'Clara Burton', bottom of the bill, Christmas Eve, looking for a man who would buy her a meal and a few drinks. 'See you later, Harriet. If you ask me there's something queer about a chap who wears a hat like that.'

True, it was a strange style. Harriet caught his eye, still

smiling at Tryphena's comment about the hat. Young, not bad looking, decently dressed. Tryphena said that he was careful, but he looked as though he could afford a bit of supper, and the rent she owed Mrs Wright. She had made her pick. He would do.

As he made his way to the bar, Harriet smiled briefly, shyly.

Like me, please like me. I'm not a bad girl.

The young man indicated to the barmaid that he would buy Harriet a drink. He had made his pick. She was the one. She would do. A pretty head held erect on a delicate neck. A submissive type, he could see that. And, by the look of the boots hidden behind the bar, she would not be the sort of London woman he had been told about, who would fleece a man of his last coin. He had never had an Englishwoman before. The idea appealed to him very much, although he couldn't explain why that was. Perhaps it was merely that she wasn't the one to whom he had somehow found himself married. Well, not actually *found* himself married. He needed a wife. There was no way that he would have been appointed to start a colony had he been an unmarried man.

The Thomsons' servants had been told not to pull curtains across the windows yet. 'It looks so welcoming and seasonal to see lamps glowing in every house.' As well, Ann Martha Thomson did not mind too much if passers-by caught glimpses of her art, which was the creation of beautiful interiors.

Josephine, who had come across London in an omnibus, alighted at the end of the square, not that there was much chance of Aunt Ann seeing her niece using that form of transport. Jo was very much her own woman now that she had her own accommodation, but it did no good going against Aunt Ann's wishes that Jo should always travel by cab. She did a deal with a street urchin to carry her bags from the bus to the house.

'Ha'penny *and* a bag of hot ches'nuts.'

'Lord save us, you drive a hard bargain.'

'I wouldn't have the strength to lift yer bags, miss, 'less I have a bit of something warm in me belly.' He could read her like a book. He knew she was soft.

Jo carried the chestnuts inside her muff to make sure that he kept his part of the bargain.

One day . . . one . . . day I'm going to write about these little lads. 'Here, give me one of the bags.'

'Not likely, you said a whole penny.'

'You'll get it. Come on, your arms will snap off.' As he still appeared reluctant, she bent down and said quietly, 'I can easily carry them myself, but I don't want my auntie to know I came here on a 'bus, because I shall get a good ticking off if she finds out.'

The boy found that reasonable.

Just before they reached the house, she gave him the penny, put chestnuts in both side-pockets of his man-sized jacket then, slipping her black fur muff from its cord, she placed it on his head. The boy jumped back, 'Here, what d'you want to go and do that for?'

'Keep your head warm.'

34

'You're right, it is that, but it must look pretty daft. Never heard of a chap wearing a muff on 'is head.'

'Do you know what a Cossack is?' He shook his head, wondering what this queer woman would come up with next.

'They are soldiers who live in Russia, where the snow gets as deep as houses. If they don't keep their heads warm, it freezes their brains, so they wear fur hats. In fact if they saw you wearing that, they would think you were one of them.'

He didn't know whether to believe her or not. But the hat felt a treat, the smell and warmth of the chestnuts seemed like it was pouring down his neck. 'Somebody will think I pinched it.'

'If any person says it's not yours, tell them Miss Josephine Thomson gave it to you – and if they need proof, then you just bring them to this house, and I will soon tell them to recognize the truth when they hear it.'

He grinned at her, showing a few half-grown second teeth.

Dear Lord forgive us! Working on the streets and still with baby teeth in his head.

'What's your name?'

'Who wants to know?'

'Me, because I am a polite person and I like to give people a name when I am speaking with them.'

'What's yours?'

'I've just told you.'

'Oh yes, Josafeen. I never knew nobody called that.'

'Well you do now. Now, come on, tell.'

'Micky Smiff . . . *th*.'

'Is it Michael, really?'

'How d' you know that?'

'Because I'm quite old, and I've picked things up over the years. My head's full of bits of information like that. Can I call you Michael?'

'You can, but I don't expect you'm be likely to see me again. Well, not unless you gets off the bus at Coram's Fields or round there. That's my patch.'

'If I give you another penny, will you promise not to spend it today?'

He didn't reply at once. 'If you *gives* us a 'nother penny, then it's mine.'

Jo nodded.

'Then you can't tell me what to do with it – because it's mine.'

It was too serious a statement for Jo to smile at. 'You're right, Michael. I have absolutely no right to interfere in your life or the way you spend your well-earned money.'

She handed him his penny and moved towards the glass porch of her aunt and uncle's house. The lamps within sparkled the glass panels, making her wish that he would go so that she could pull the bell. She didn't want him to watch her welcomed and disappear into the orange glow. Consciences were not salved by pennies and chestnuts.

'Miss, why do you think I ought to hold on to one penny?'

'I suppose I thought you might go throwing it around and somebody might wonder how you came by it and make trouble for you.'

'It's all right, some days I can make as much as thruppence. It's the hat that I'll have to be careful about.'

As he disappeared into the falling snow she watched as he cracked open a chestnut, threw it in the air and caught it expertly in his open mouth.

Frank Kerley. Detective Sergeant, Metropolitan Police Force, 'E' Division, Bow Street, London. An exact 5 feet 11 inches, fair skinned, light haired, broad and healthy at thirty-eight years old.

The Kerleys' house was up three steps. One of a long terrace of well-kept homes of lower middle-class families. Door brasses polished daily, lace curtains regularly washed and starched, and windows cleaned of London grime every Friday.

Today, Frank Kerley noticed that, instead of the healthy aspidistra which was usually placed centrally in the front window, Elizabeth had stood a small fir tree bedecked with baubles and tinsel and small gifts wrapped in red paper. She had done the same every year since Christmas Trees became popular. In the hallway she would have hung a large bunch of mistletoe, and behind every picture and mirror would be sprigs of holly. As he entered, he was not disappointed. Home for Christmas. He wished himself a bit of a good time for himself, Elizabeth and Frances this year. A plain-clothes detective sergeant in Superintendent Thomson's hand-picked company of men, Sergeant Kerley was well aware that wishing had nothing to do with being home for Christmas. But still, delegation being the super's philosophy, unless some particularly heinous crime was committed during the next couple of days . . .

Elizabeth Kerley's heart lifted when she heard the jangle of Frank's keys, the creak of the front door followed by a resolute cleaning of snow from his boots on the coconut mat. 'Are you there, Elizabeth Kerley?'

'You know I am, Francis.'

'Well, come here and let's see if this mistletoe works.'

She appeared from the kitchen, her face alive with pleasure, her apron showing signs of baking. 'It works all right, I tested it on the milkman.'

They kissed one another as they had always kissed, with passion and deep affection and good humour.

Harriet Burton. Josephine Thomson. Detective Superintendent Thomson. Detective Sergeant Frank Kerley, and a young man who thus far has no name – all with plans for the Christmas holiday.

Harriet Burton appeared twice on stage that evening. She decided that, instead of something from her usual repertoire, she would sing a Christmas carol. It went down well and the stage manager said that she could have a second spot later. When she went back to the bar, Tryphena, the barmaid said, 'Your bloke must be

38

keen, he's passed over two or three of the girls who gave him the eye.'

'Well, he's going to have to wait, I've got a second turn to do.'

'You'll be in the money, then.' She nodded in the direction of the young man who was now seated at a table. 'You could tell him to sling his hook.'

'I thought about having a day in the country tomorrow . . . visiting. And I still owe this week's rent.' Harriet smiled cheerfully at Tryphena. 'Anyway, if he really wants me, I reckon I'll get supper out of him.'

'I told you, he don't seem that free with his money.'

'We'll see.'

The Thomsons' house was pretty, in a pretty part of London, beside the River Thames. Built in modern times, it had the advantage of stylish detail that could be ordered from a catalogue, and a terrazzo laid by Italian specialist gangs who were working their way through England, creating – in halls and glass orangeries – elegant stone floors inlaid with classical patterns.

Everything had been new when Josephine landed up here as a child. It still looked as fresh today, but many things within had been changed. Ann Martha Thomson was a great lover of the latest innovation and of style. It was a wonderful home to enter, and although Josephine now had a modest place of her own, she still enjoyed returning to the home in which she had grown up.

Surprisingly it was Uncle James who opened the door to Josephine.

'Uncle James! What are you doing at home so early in the day? Has London gone all honest, or have you got all the villains locked up?'

'Josie! I am beset by women who talk as though I am never at home. Not too grown-up for a kiss?'

'I shall never be that, Uncle James.'

'Good. You certainly look grown-up. Your hat is white with snow. You should be using a muff over those thin gloves.'

'Muffs are for old ladies. Who cares about snowy hats? It's Christmas and I'm happy and absolutely ravenous for some crumpets and tea.'

The familiar clip-clop of heeled slippers and Hani's gentle voice. 'Almond cake too, 'osie.'

'Hani, Hani, my darling Hani.' Jo clasped the exotic little woman and started to hug the life out of her.

'Stop it, silly gir'.' Hani's normally impassive features creased with joy.

Of course . . . and almond cake.

All the traditional English foods.

Josephine, shedding her outdoor clothes, looked at herself in one of the many mirrors that Ann Martha used to bring lightness into every room, and approved of herself. The skirt of her new street costume was a great success: tiered pleating, along with the hemline which was well clear of the ground, allowed Josephine to walk quickly and with longer strides than Aunt Ann's springy paces.

40

James Thomson put a fond arm about his niece's shoulder and guided her up a few steps towards the orange glow from red coals and peach-shaded lamps that radiated from the front room and shone out onto the street. Hani started to pull the curtains across, but James halted her. 'A little longer, Hani, you know how Mrs Ann likes to look in upon her handiwork.'

'Also street-feefs see what you have.'

'Street feefs also know that "Thomson of the Yard" lives here, so stop worrying.'

Hani's position in the household had always been ambiguous. She was neither servant nor family, yet the household would not function as perfectly as it did, nor the family be as united as it was without Hani. Between leaving Malacca and arriving in England, Hani had been all the family that Josephine had. London had been a shock for both of them. Hani, not much more than a girl herself in those days, was the means by which the girl Josephine had come to accept that a dirty city in a cold country would be her home.

'Where is Aunt Ann?'

'Gone out in the snow to fly her new foxes.'

'Miss Ann Mar'a has new cloat. Is very fine, suit her very much.'

'Uncle James – has he been teasing her again, Hani?'

Hani wagged her head and smiled, 'I think she don't mind.'

'She loves it. It shows her I notice, and I should soon be told of it if I tried outright flattery.'

'Go wash hands, 'osie.'

41

Jo went, as she had always done, at Hani's firm command, answering back childishly, 'I'm not a child any more, Hani.'

'I say you wash hand. I bring tea. Quick now.'

'It's not tea-time yet.'

'Tea-time when I say, 'osie. You have more tea-time when MisAnn come home.'

Jo was glad to get rid of the smell of roasted chestnuts. *Maybe, though, I should keep wearing the smell to remind me that there are children who don't have crumpets and almond cake.* Jo's conscience often tried to guide her to the high moral ground, but her resolve was weak.

This troublesome conscience was a legacy from her father. From an early age she and her twin brother Joseph had had to learn how to deal with being privileged in a land where poverty lay outside the gate, along the dusty track, becoming denser as it infested the city streets. He had not lived to complete the job he had started, teaching his daughter how to cope with the world. But in many ways he lived on in his brother, James, alike physically and with a well-developed sense of duty. But Father could never have done the same work as Uncle James. Josephine was proud of Uncle James.

Maybe she should tell him that. Yes. And tell Aunt Ann that she loved her for having taken on such an angry child, and the stubborn young woman who would not leave the child in a strange country. The child soon settled, but Hani stayed on, each year saying that she must soon return to her home. It was pretty certain that

42

Hani would go home once Josephine was settled in a good marriage. Josephine had told her often enough that the love of her life was her work. Big joke, Josie, silly gir' must not wait long time, man not want old women for marriage.

As she washed her hands in the warm water that flowed from a tap, she looked into her own eyes, facing her in the mirror – a very modish mirror she noticed, new since she was last here. What else was new? She and Aunt Ann would take a tour later, looking at the changes made. There would be changes. There always would be whilst Ann was mistress of a London house.

Hani was here now, living in Uncle James's household. Under five foot tall, smooth skinned, delicately boned, beautiful as a moonflower, moving about as she had done in her parents' medical missionary compound in Malacca. Softly, unobtrusively taking care of the details of the household. Hani was as near to a mother as Jo had now, and Uncle James as near to a father. Ann Martha? Younger than her husband, perhaps more like an older sister to Josephine. An older sister with firm views on society and how one lives in it, and the proprieties to be observed to keep the wheels of social intercourse running smoothly. An older sister who was sensible enough to see that, as she and her husband's niece had dissimilar views on women's roles, their relationship would be all the stronger if Josephine were allowed to set up in rooms of her own.

During the time when Josephine had for the first time shown how serious she was about having rooms of her own, life in the Thomson household had been difficult. Josephine had reverted to speaking only Malay, until came a day when Hani had packed the small bag with which she had arrived, and walked into the room where the three Thomsons were sitting at breakfast.

'I go back where children know their place in family, and fathers are wise to let grown daughters go from home. This daughter is good. She not bring shame on us. Josie – you now speak English, I am not your language servant.'

This was probably the longest speech in English that Hani had ever made. It worked. Josephine took rooms, but on the condition that she let one room to another woman. Hani stayed on with the Thomsons.

On Jo's way to the sitting room, Aunt Ann swept in, a swirl of red fox and snow. 'Josephine! My dear girl, there you are. Now the celebrations can truly begin.' Aunt Ann pressed her cheek to Jo's with warm affection.

'Aunt Ann! That cloak! It is exactly your style.'

'You think so? I knew that you would think so. Your undiscerning uncle referred to dead animals . . . well, of course they *were*, but not any more.'

'Absolutely, they have gone to heaven and come back as beautiful trimmings to suit your hair and complexion.'

Aunt Ann kissed her again, and, as the soft fur brushed her face, Josephine understood its appeal, as little Micky Smiff had with the muff on his head. Perhaps there would come a time when Jo would be ready to step out in furs, but not yet, not for a hundred years or more. Until then she would stick to her high necks and plain and practical skirts and a wonderful cashmere shawl that she used daily.

'Where's Hani?'

'Where do you think, Aunt, in the sitting room, hovering over the chafing dish.'

'Oh, she has been so excited, click-clacking all over the house. She has emptied Covent Garden of chrysanthemums.'

Jo laughed, having already seen some of Hani's exotic arrangements of flowers and bamboo sticks.

'I will just take my things into the airing room and then I shall be with you. Josephine, dearest, I can't tell you how much we shall love having you with us again.' She spoiled it slightly by adding, 'If only for a short while.'

'I am looking forward to my visit.'

'Josephine, I should quite like it if you would use my name without the "aunt".'

'All right, Ann, so I shall. Maybe you could call me Josie.'

'I don't think so, dear, Josephine is such a beautiful name. Your parents chose it, so I think we should keep to it.'

Josephine went through into the glowing sitting room where the small woman, who still had only sufficient English on which to get by, said everything that was necessary with her eyes: *My dearest child, you are here, my life is complete, my heart is full and I shall not give one thought to the time when you leave again.*

'Crumpets, 'osie, eat.'

'I suppose you won't sit with us, Hani?'

Hani smiled. 'Is plenty butter, 'osie.'

As always, right from when Jo and Joseph were little, Hani had made the rules. Hani in the room attending to food and comfort, organizing every meal down to the smallest detail. With the family, but not of it. Nothing to do with status, as Father had once explained when the twins had said he must tell Hani that she should eat with them. 'Hani chooses to be with our family in her own way. Don't embarrass her by expecting her to change to our ways. Has it ever occurred to you that she might find our ways at the table strange, even unpleasant?' No, it never had. Hani was a law unto herself.

The Thomsons knew that Hani would not stay with them for ever. Josephine too wondered about that, now that she herself was in rooms of her own, but she didn't like to think about it. Recently, she had been turning over in her mind the idea of having Hani to live with her. There was a spare bedroom, but what on earth would she do when Jo was off and about, as she was most days, often working long into the evening in her office? Josephine had no idea of Hani's age: say she was seventeen when she accompanied Josephine to England, she could be approaching thirty now. Hani was probably still young enough to have a husband and children. In her own country, but not here. England, and London in particular with its grey pavements and solid brick buildings, seemed to be too heavy and dark for her.

Overcome with love for Hani, Jo jumped up and twirled Hani round.

'Oh Hani, Hani, Hani.'

'You tell 'osie stand in wall-corner till she know manner, Mister James, Miss Ann Martha?'

Four people woven together by tragedy and love. Jo leaving to set up on her own had pulled a thread, but it had held, and the three older members had not demurred when she left, but still waited for her to return. Hani kept Josie's room always ready for when she would want to come back and live in the circle again.

It would not happen.

'What y' got there, kid?'

A scabby hand reached out for Micky Smith's bit of fur.

'Get off, it's mine.'

'Let's have a look then.'

'No! You'll only take it.'

'I won't, honest.'

'Get out of my way. This is my patch.'

'I don't want yer bleedin' patch, I wants to have a see of that ear-warmer.'

'It's a sojer's hat.'

'Queer sort of sojer.'

A wide figure stepped in front of Micky's assailant. 'And you're a queer sort of feef. Get off and leave the kid to hisself.'

The aggressor sloped off.

'You all right, Micky?'

'Yeah, I'm all right. Here, Chink, want a couple of ches'nuts?'

Chink crushed the shells easily and picked out the

cooked centre. 'I tell ya', if he gets after you again, fake as if you're going to run off, then get your heel up under his bollocks, hard.'

The yellow-skinned youth and the skinny white boy laughed at the thought. 'OK, Chinky.'

'Anyway, what is that thing – did you feeve it?'

'Truth, it was give to me by a customer. Best thing I had in my whole life. You can try it if you like.'

'Nah, don't want to breed your fleas along of mine.' Chinky's eyes disappeared into thin lines when he laughed. 'Tell you what, though. If you was to turn it inside out, you'd have the fur against your ears which'd be warmer, and feefs like that one won't be so interested.'

Micky turned the hat. Yeah. It felt good. Chinky was all right. He was quite old, probably a man, but Micky couldn't tell with Chinks. Anyway, Micky knew that Chinky was all right.

A warm, wonderful smell of grilled chops and cigar smoke rushed to surround Harriet Burton as the waiter opened the door for her, reawakening her hunger pangs, which had been kept dormant for hours by a tot of Irish and a glass of stout. The stout had been only temporarily filling, and, although her hunger was for meat, she did not hurry as she followed William, the assistant head waiter, to a table close to the side, halfway down the room. She was a regular client here and, although he guided her to her usual table, he went through the motions of asking whether this position pleased her without reference to her young male companion, who followed in sullen silence.

She smiled directly at the waiter, as though he had done her a favour by offering this table. 'William, thank you, this is splendid.' He held the chair and she arranged her full skirts, then the waiter moved a chair under the surly-looking man.

Harriet liked William. Whenever she went to the Cavour restaurant he saw to it that she was served a man-sized dish. It was he who had recommended stout because of its nourishing qualities, and Harriet had very much taken to the taste of it. He also always referred to her as a professional soprano.

'What's on the board tonight, William?'

It was the usual fare, but he presented the food as something exceptional and to the occasion. 'Ah, madam, tonight we have some splendid grilled chops. Or, if you prefer it, steaks? Finest tenderloin. Then there is fowl also. Yes, the fowl is excellent. Succulent, roast or boiled, both hot or cold.'

She enquired of the young man, 'Boiled fowl would be nice, don't you think?' to which he acquiesced with just a curt, 'Cold for me.'

'The cold boiled fowl is particularly good, sir.'

'Thank you, William, and for me. Plenty of chutney and potatoes mashed with cream.' William smiled, nodding approvingly at her nutritious choice. 'And William, ask Oscar to fetch me a bottle of stout and serve it now.'

Oscar, the head waiter, always dealt with the drinks.

He considered the pretty singer an adornment to the establishment, particularly when she came into the dining room still wearing the fine feathers in which she performed on stage at the Alhambra. Not that she was ever in other than good gowns and accessories of quality. He flourished the bottle, making much of the pouring of the stout. This was the first time he had seen her without at least one piece of nice jewellery. He hoped that this didn't mean that she had been forced to pawn them.

Harriet liked it when there were men around her. She knew that she possessed an aura of fragility and femininity. She had a magnetism that drew them to her. Until recently, since she had come to live in London, she had seldom wanted for a protector. Not casual protectors, but men who were bachelors or widowers who set her up in comfortable apartments and bought her pretty clothes, jewellery and adornments, and who stayed for months, even a year or more.

But how they did all want to '*improve*' her. All of them, in one way or another, told her how they loved her. She was graceful and lovely, she was carefree, generous and good-hearted – all this and more. And then, to a man, they set about trying to change her, improve her. Her most recent protector had gone back abroad where he was to make ready a home for the two of them. He would be almost there by now, and it would only be a matter of a few weeks until she would be able to collect her own ticket from his agent.

Just at this moment, Christmas Eve, she was a bit down on her luck, owning more pawn tickets than pieces of jewellery, and she was hungry. The man who would pay for supper was perhaps terse and less generous than she was used to, but if she went to bed satisfied with meat and brandy, she could easily stand his silence.

'Isn't this good? The Cavour always has very good fowls. Are you enjoying it?'

'I like it. You eat it all, you do not waste what has to be paid for.' This was about the longest sentence he had put together. She could tell that he was a foreigner, but he spoke in a low tone, as if he didn't want to be overheard. She had wondered if he couldn't speak English, but so far he had managed to buy her a tot at the Alhambra, and then negotiate a half-sovereign to go to her room. But she had insisted, 'First, a decent supper, and you pay for the omnibus tickets.' He couldn't have pondered longer had it been a deal between nations.

She always included food in her negotiations with men. Why else would she go with a casual if it wasn't to keep body and soul together? Money they might try to get back, but they couldn't do that with a decent meal and a couple of drinks.

'Don't you worry about me wasting food. Look, I can't keep on chatting to you if you won't tell me your name. Go on, call yourself anything you like. Who's going to know?'

In a low voice, he said, 'You call me Karl.'

'Ah, ha.' Harriet playfully waved her fork at him. 'That's what I've been trying to place. First off I thought you were Dutch – Dutch sailors always like the Alhambra.' She leaned forward and laughed lightly, the mixture of rum and stout relaxing her and making it easier for her to flirt. 'They like the Alhambra because it doesn't matter if you don't know a word of English. A lot of the acts are dancers and conjurors and trapeze artists. But Karl's a German name. You're a German, right?'

'Is not necessary to speak so aloud.'

'I'm not, this is just normal conversation. Sorry, Karl, I . . .' She noticed he looked at all the tables near enough to overhear, but nobody was interested.

She hoped that when he had eaten a good supper and had a couple more drinks he would join in the party-like atmosphere that was gathering in the restaurant.

'Do you celebrate Christmas much at home?'

'We do.'

'Of course you do, it was our queen's husband who thought of Christmas trees.' She smiled at him. 'A good idea, it's really become the fashion.' Harriet lowered her voice and shielded her words by her glass. 'You know our queen married a German?'

'Of course.'

'Germans are very popular since he became her husband – prince consort, not king.'

'Oh yes. But he is now dead.'

'Terrible. Just over ten years now. But the queen still favours anything German, you know.'

'Does she? Are you not eating this?'

'Um . . . all right, you can have it if you like.'

He scooped up the large portion of forcemeat, transferred it to his own plate and served himself some pickles and more potato yellow with butter and cream.

At the end of the meal not a scrap of food was left. She hoped that he was satisfied that they had eaten everything he was going to pay for. William came to remove the dishes, and Oscar to ask how they would like their coffee.

Karl shook his head. Harriet ignored him. 'A large pot, if you please, Oscar. French roast . . . heavy cream, and brandies.'

Oscar didn't consult Miss Burton's friend, but went off quickly to give orders to the kitchen. The man had not been pleased. Oscar didn't want him as a regular, and hoped that the young lady's luck would soon turn.

Harriet waited whilst the young man carefully counted out the coins to pay Oscar's wife who was seated at the little desk beside the door. Oscar handed her the bag containing her evening shoes. 'Have you got another booking soon, Ma'am?'

'Yes, two in fact.'

'Good, so I hope you'll pay us a visit. Are you doing anything special tomorrow?'

'I thought I would have a day in the country. I have a sister who begs me to visit, so I think that I shall, provided the snow doesn't lie too deep.'

'I think the gentleman is ready to leave.'

'Let him wait. Did any man ever find it so difficult to buy two liqueur brandies?'

Oscar held open the exit door. 'Goodnight, Ma'am, and a Merry Christmas. Good night, sir.' He did not add his usual hope that sir would pay the Cavour another visit.

* * *

On the omnibus travelling to the whore's room, the young man was irritated with himself for having let her have a name: that had been stupid. He withdrew into himself, ignoring the chatter that went on between her and some other women she knew.

There was ice in the air when they alighted. Although they had travelled a fair distance, he had made mental notes so that he could find his way back to his hotel. She pulled at his arm. Apples this time. She was certainly proving more expensive than he had anticipated. Women were alike when it came to getting them to open their drawers. They always wanted something. Marriage was the biggest payment. This one had said a half-sovereign and supper, and he had agreed before he had calculated how much this was in English money. And now apples. He let her carry them.

'Here we are then.'

He looked up at the house. It appeared to be very respectable. As they entered, a woman looked out into the hallway, checking to see who was coming in.

'Hello, Mrs Wright, this is a friend, just coming in to have a night-cap. Haven't got a couple of bottles of stout have you?' Mrs Wright had. Harriet twiddled her fingertips at the friend, indicating that he should pay.

Mrs Wright craned her neck to follow the man's progress up the stairs to where he waited on the landing. With a sardonic look, 'Isn't he just the eager type?'

'I only hope he's just as eager to go home. If you just hold on a minute please, Mrs Wright, I'll be back down with the rent arrears. Meantime, here are some apples for being so patient. I'll just take a couple, one for myself for the morning.'

When Harriet Burton returned with the half-sovereign, she was quite gleeful. 'I thought I might have had to squeeze it out of him.'

'Tight?'

Harriet Burton grinned. 'As my pa would have said, "tight as a bull's bum in August".'

Mrs Wright laughed, 'Well, I can't say as I ever heard that, but you got something out of him. Just tell him he's got to be out before morning. No breakfasts, tell him. I don't run a hotel.'

'Don't want him gone more than I do. I'd like to have a good sleep-in tomorrow.'

'Breakfast won't be till late, we're just having a few drinks round the fire tonight. We'll give you a knock when breakfast is ready.'

'You're a gem, Mrs Wright, I never had such a good landlady before. You won't get trouble from me.'

Christmas Morning 1872

In the two hours he had been with her, the man had twice gratified his lust. The second time – after she had gone downstairs for more bottles of beer – he suspected that, although she had gone through the motions of response and made the sounds of pleasure, she had actually been half asleep and half intoxicated. He didn't mind at all, he was able to enjoy her without being called 'brute!' She even snored a little as he turned her face down and sat astride and entered her as he had never tried with his wife. There was blood on him as he withdrew. He mopped it with his handkerchief, recalling the earlier episode with his wife's petticoats.

When he turned her over again, she was as pliable as a rag doll. As he was bending close to see whether she was breathing, her eyes snapped open close to his own. 'Got your money's worth?' Her speech was slurred. 'Reg'lar ol' Jew-boy you are.' Briefly tugging at his member she opened her eyes for a moment and made horns of her fingers. Her head fell back onto the pillow and she closed her eyes, a faint smile on her lips.

In the glow of the small nightlight he looked at his pocket watch. He had spent more time here than he had anticipated, but it was worth it. The last mauling of her would stay with him. Once the Christmas holiday was over, he knew only too well that it would be a return to his own fists and fantasies, but he was going to take with him a fantasy that he had never expected to have any chance of living.

Through the fringe of her lashes, she watched as, with his back to her, he sat on the bed and checked his money and numerous things he carried in his pockets. He was going. Thank God for that.

She closed her eyes and let herself drift into a deep, warm sleep. She did not hear him take a bite from the apple, nor feel him pull the counterpane up to her chin, did not hear him pour water from the jug into the hand-basin and wash his hands, did not see him pull on his trousers and jacket. Nor was she aware that he took his overcoat from the back of a chair, or that he picked up his boots and locked the door from the outside and took away her key. Neither did she hear him go stealthily down the back stairs and let himself out of Number 12 Great Coram Street by the back door.

He did not try to leave by the front door, but easily found the kitchen where it was as dark as the back of an oven, except for the lighter black square of window. He knew from observing it last night that the door was next to the window, and steps led up to the street from there.

Dark as the back of an oven, and wonderfully warm.

The warmest spot was beside the iron cooking range, where the girl, Daisy, lay curled up, making the most of the last few minutes before she must do the front steps and start the fires. It was Christmas morning, so nobody would be about early. Some of the girls had brought a chap home and the missis and mister had been drinking late with some friends. The girls would have got their chaps to bring a bit of something for the missis. The girls knew how to keep the missis sweet, particularly if they was behind with their rent. Some of them remembered Daisy and left little presents for her, some wrapped sweets, a side-comb with a flower, even a pair of fancy knee-socks, two sixpences and a pretty bottle still half-full of scent – not that she could use it in the house in case it contaminated the cooking.

When Daisy heard the pump in next-door's yard going, she knew that their girl, Minn, would soon be starting on their steps. Poor little beggar, her missis was heavy-handed. Daisy was fourteen, which she knew was true because her pa had once took her to look at the Parish Register at All Souls.

The oven warmth and thinking of her pa acted on her like a sleeping draught, causing her to drift away again into that pleasant state of half-sleep. She had been really proud that day.

Pa had said, 'I brought you here, Daisy, so as you will

58

always know who you are and be proud of yourself. Your name is put down in this big book which anybody can see if they asks the verger.' Daisy had never learned to read very well, but the letters that made up her name she could always see as clear as day . . . if anybody would have asked, she could write it herself. Sometimes she did that on steamed-up windows.

Stretching her toes she felt the side of the iron stove. Still enough fire left from yesterday, no need for paraffin rag and sticks. That gives me another ten minutes, not having to fire the stove from scratch. As she was about to move from her little cubby-hole and start the day, she heard the back stairs creak. Oh, Lord, one of the chaps had stopped longer than the missis liked.

He crept quickly through the kitchen, found the door-bolt, slid it along carefully, left the door open a few moments as he put on his hat and coat, then closed it very quietly and walked off in the direction of the main road.

Daisy tied her sack apron round her waist and started her day.

The lamplighter had not yet started along this street, but the sky was already lightening and the reflection from the snow enhanced the appearance of daylight.

The young man remembered, it was the morning of Christmas. He looked forward to a fine breakfast at Kroll's Hotel.

Having pulled on his boots, he walked away, thinking that if he should take a cab, it would be best to find one well away from this area. He enjoyed taking chances, but not foolish ones.

Frank Kerley – on duty. His were the only big boots to enter the crime scene. Waiting for the arrival of his super, he examined the bedroom, making detailed notes as he went, using the formula that he and the super had worked out between them. It was unfortunate that the room had been entered, but there was likely to be no tampering of evidence – the witness had not stayed long enough. He had, however, vomited copiously on the landing and, as Kerley had forbidden anyone to come up to this floor until the chief arrived, the combined odour of last night's boozing and that emanating from the area of the bed was a thing to be stoic about.

Frank Kerley waited beside the body of 'E' Division's first reported murder victim of the day. Christmas Day. Harriet Burton: that much he knew. A singer.

She had come home last night in the company of a man who had left silently without leaving any sign that he had ever been here. Any sign, that is, if you discounted the bloody water, the bloody petticoat used to wipe a weapon, the bloody handprint on the mantelpiece. That is if you discounted the corpse lying like a sleeping woman. Having replaced the counterpane as he had found it, he looked down at the peaceful face of the young woman and felt unprofessional sadness for her.

A country girl, he guessed. A village lad himself until he was twenty, he was pretty sure that she had not been a product of London's mean streets, where so many limbs never recover from a childhood spent in choking air and being fed poor and adulterated food. She had the look of a girl who had not been many years away from fresh air, barley broth, the smell of gillyflowers, and haymaking and harvesting. Frank had been away for more years than he liked to think of, but those early years were the stanchions of his own childhood. The longer he lived away from it, the more he forgot that haymaking and harvesting were sunny and healthy only in his memory.

Perhaps in twenty years or so, he would return to Dorset and retire to back there in Gunville, the village he had left in order to better himself. He withdrew his gaze. Francis Kerley, you're soft as butter. He and the super knew better. DS Kerley could be as hard as nails.

And in his innermost heart, he knew that, having lived as many years breathing London's air as he had that of Gunville, he had become a Londoner. A star of the Met. A faint smile crossed his face. He had once allowed an aspiring young journalist to question him about his work. Not something he would normally think of doing, but she had just started out, and Elizabeth had told him straight that he should do it, he'd been glad enough of a bit of a leg-up himself when he was young. 'She's a woman in a man's world, it's not asking much to answer a few questions. And in any case, if it gets printed at all, it won't be anywhere prominent.' That proved to be so. *A Day in the Life of* was short and sweet and appeared on the inside back page of a London magazine next to a receipt for a summer pudding, but it had helped her get a regular piece in *The Echo*. There had followed a whole series of *A Day in the Life of. A Star of the Metropolitan Police* . . . She had written a note apologizing for that. 'Sergeant Kerley, I have no say in the titles of my pieces. I hope that you were not embarrassed by the title (and, as agreed, the article gives no clue as to the identity of my "star"). But you should not be, because in my mind that is what I believe you are. I have always been a great admirer of London policemen. Jemima Ferguson.'

He continued examining the room. Lifting small items with his pencil and allowing them to drop again as they had been. He made lists and diagrams, knowing that to miss an item might be to miss a piece of evidence that could later prove crucial. But the murderer appeared to have left nothing behind him, except, maybe, his teethmarks on the apple and a bloody handprint. The super might have something to say about that.

Harriet Burton appeared to have few possessions, unless they were elsewhere. Most were scattered on the one or two bits of furniture, or hanging behind the door. On and in the chest of drawers were much the same oddments that he might have found on Elizabeth's dressing table, plus a few that he might not. Elizabeth did not use rouge or eye-black – nor, as far as he knew, did she use contraceptive sponges, a small porcelain jarful of which were beside the hand-basin, soaking in vinegar. That was the one smell that always pointed to the possibility of a woman involved in prostitution.

He opened the drawers one by one, from each of which escaped the smell of faded lavender. Then the various decorated boxes in which she kept her haberdashery and frippery: some good lace collars, a set of ornamental buttons, bits of well-chosen, cheap jewellery, nice-looking beads and ear-drops. But few of these things were worth more than a shilling or two, although her gloves, millinery and gowns were of good quality. A couple of pairs of light shoes, very pretty, nicely made and to Frank's taste – he liked a woman to have a shapely foot. Both pairs, as well as some newish embroidered eastern-looking slippers, were in good repair. The clue to her fortune was in the snow-damaged, badly worn, high-buttoned boots – the ones she must have worn last night, which were in need of repair; he had noticed them propped up against the skirting board on the landing. It was quite likely that the embroidered slippers had been gifts from a man, or men. The young woman might well have preferred the gift of a stout pair of boots, but men liked to give impractical chilly silk and beads. Poor young thing, such cold feet. Permanently cold now.

Although the room was stuffy with the smells of bedding and clothes, soap, scent, cosmetic powder, lavender and vinegar mingling with the vomit and blood, it had that chill about it which only comes with dampness and a habitual lack of heating, and is a hallmark of poverty. Without having uncovered the victim more than a few inches, Frank Kerley knew that her life's blood had drained away. Looking under the bed he had seen the shine of a small pool that had gathered there. The rest would have been absorbed by the feather mattress. Thank God for a cold night. In summer the room would already have been stinking and buzzing with blowflies. Frank had a great hatred for the creatures. Even so, he was forced to admit, many a corpse might have lain undiscovered had it not been for those grisly investigators.

Not wanting to proceed without the super, and having seen as much as he could without making too much disturbance, Frank Kerley lowered his large frame to sit on the edge of the bed, almost as if he were a visitor with a sick person. Holding the counterpane by his fingertips he, for a second time, pulled it away from the young woman, and for a second time observed the gaping wounds that transformed a peaceful sleeper into a gruesome cadaver. She lay on her back, hands on her breasts, legs apart, the skirt of her nightdress raised to the waist, revealing above an unremarkable black triangle the marked and crumpled belly of a woman who has carried a child full-term. Frank Kerley could not remember having seen a more macabre sight than this: a bloody corpse, knees bent, legs spread wide, laid out ready for sex.

Covering her again, he said, 'How much did he pay you to do this?' He laid a large warm hand on her icy wax brow. 'Here's a promise, Harriet, we'll get him if we have to go to the ends of the earth to find him.'

This was not his usual way with murdered prostitutes. He had seen any number. Such cases were usually easily solved: a blow on the head in the street, or a knife in the ribs in a back alley; clients intent on getting their money back, or lost in rage because they couldn't get hard and blamed the woman; sometimes pimps who had fallen for a girl and then went mad with jealousy. Many times it was pimps cutting a girl for holding money back, and as a lesson to the others of his string not even to think of it.

This was no sudden frenzy. This looked thought-out, maybe planned. Here was a violent death, yet no sign of it in her expression. She was asleep, but with gaping wounds slashed deeply from ear to ear, fine cuts done in one swipe in each direction. This had been carried out with a thin and very sharp blade.

A young uniformed constable lurked discreetly across the square that fronted a church whose bells were ringing out proclaiming Christmas. Mass was over, and communicants streamed out into the clear, cold London air.

Ann Martha Thomson, one arm linked with her husband whose other arm was linked with Josephine's, stiffened as she drew breath to speak.

'It's all right, my dear, I see him too.'

'Oh James! Even on Christmas morning. People are too bad.'

'And if they were not, my ever-forbearing wife –' he raised her finely gloved knuckles to his lips and engaged her with twinkling eyes – 'I should be unemployed and you would complain because I was always under your feet.'

Making their way to where the constable was standing with a cab at the ready, Ann Martha said, 'I know that you told me what the life of a detective's wife might be before we married, but James . . . Christmas morning?'

'Well, Constable?'

The man said in a low voice, 'It's murder, sir. Sergeant Kerley's at the scene, Great Coram Street, number 12.'

'Would you like me to call you a cab, Ann?'

'No, you go, James, we do know how to call a cab . . . and James, do try to get something to eat.' The ritual of Holy Communion was always performed before food was consumed.

As soon as the cab with the policemen pulled away, Ann Martha and Josephine walked to a cab rank close by. 'Do you mind if I don't go with you, Ann? I think I would like to drop in on the service at St Giles's and then walk back. I can do with some exercise if I'm to be fed for two days like a *foie-gras* goose.' Ann Martha stepped into the open-sided cab and, taking both of Josephine's hands, she squeezed them as she pressed her cheek to Josephine's, wafting her delicate perfume. She said, 'That man is becoming quite famous . . . or notorious. I do read newspapers, Josephine.'

'He speaks up for poor people, Aunt. He's bound to tread on toes doing that.'

Ann Martha noticed the flush rise and fall on Josephine's cheeks. They said the new preacher at St Giles was young and handsome. 'I doubt if James will be back for lunch, but I do hope that you will be: we have guests.'

'Of course, Aunt. I just want to—'

'It's quite all right, darling, you can tell me what the preacher has to say about Christmas feasting.'

Josephine felt herself flushing again. Clearly Ann Martha was aware of the attraction at St Giles, although not that he had been part of the Boot Street group enjoying her niece's hospitality.

'I'll be in time for the meal. Promise.'

As the cab drew away, Josephine was stepping into the next in line. 'Coram's Fields. I will tell you where to stop when we get there.'

As the cab door closed, so had Superintendent James Thomson's mind closed on domestic affairs.

'Well, Constable?'

'Murder, sir. A young woman. Sometime during the night. In her own bed. Sergeant Kerley's waiting. We was called in not more than an hour since. Mr Kerley sent me straight over to find you. The lady at your house said where you'd be.'

Something tried to click into place in James Thomson's fact-filled memory. 'Coram Street, rings a bell. Do you know anything?'

'*Great* Coram Street to be right, sir. It's on my beat. To my knowledge it's a respectable street, not every house occupied by a single family.'

'What then? Sub-lettings, that kind of thing?'

'I believe so, sir. I don't recollect any trouble in the area.'

'Ah, sub-letting . . . doesn't make our job any easier . . . that's the first step on the downward path. You'll see, in ten years, every house will be let by the room or by the floor. The shared services will break down. Inhabitants will stop taking a pride, railings will not be painted, and no one will care except the beat bobby who will want to carry a night-stick in daylight hours.'

'I hope not to be a beat bobby in ten years, sir.'

'Ambitious are you, Constable?'

'The detection squad, sir. I believe that to be the bright future of police work.'

'Good. Start on the beat, that's where a good detective gains experience. Now, when we reach Great Coram Street, I shall get out a little distance from the scene. In answer to the question you would like to ask, it's easier for one to slip through the gawping crowd if one doesn't arrive in a cab with a constable up front. You will be the distraction. Whilst you make a good show of opening the cab door, I will be inside in two ticks.'

James got out at the end of the street, and walked on. Dressed in his church clothes, he was able to make his way unobtrusively along Great Coram Street. As he did so, memories of walking this particular area came tumbling into his mind. There had been a time as a uniformed officer when he could have written a very detailed report on this street.

He could see where number 12 must be.

The houses were large, quite impressive, but not grand, having no rising entrance to the front doors, but just areas enclosed in black-painted iron railings. The generous-sized front doors were set in shallow archways, beside a pair of windows with fancy iron window-boxes. First floors: three full-length windows, some dressed with blinds and drapes, linked by wrought-iron balconies. Second floors: three four-paned sashed windows and, symmetrically above these, three smaller sashed windows with the six panes typical of nurseries and servants' quarters. Then flat, slate roofs and large blocks of chimney stacks with numerous pots, most of them sending coal smoke straight up into the windless air. The architecture of the houses composing the terrace held no secrets or surprises as to the layout of the interior. Any secrets were what went on within.

Quietly insinuating his way between the sensation-mongers who were being kept at bay by some of his big-boots Bow Street men – 'Keep back there. Keep back, nothing to see—' he reached the iron railings of number 12. At the exact moment when the cab drew up and his constable opened the cab door with a flourish, the superintendent slipped into the house, making a mental note to tell the ambitious young policeman that he did well. Praise booted a man forward much more successfully than criticism.

Josephine alighted at the opposite end of Great Coram Street, closer to number 12 than the police vehicle had ended up, her sensible cabbie knowing how the numbers ran. Having told the driver well done and giving him a generous fare, she was able to mingle with the crowd just as her uncle went into the house. Her disguise was simple. Her fashionable beaded velvet tam-o'-shanter was turned inside out and pulled well down over her ears, her jacket was clutched around her and her hands tucked under her arms so that she appeared huddled and dragged down by the cold, much like many of the women who had come here with just a shawl hastily thrown around their shoulders.

'What's goin' on then?' A lowered, husky voice, words running together, she used the language of the city which she knew from experience usually got a response. Nobody interesting ever responded to a 'toff's' voice.

Without taking their eyes off the door of number 12, several of the crowd offered certain knowledge.

'Murder.'

'Whatappened?'

'Woman done in last night. One of her lodgers, her "girls", she likes to call them.'

'Who?'

'Hatty Wright, she lets out rooms to actresses and that.'

'D'you think it's one of them who's been—'

'Done in?' somebody offered. 'Bound to be, innit? *She's* been at the door, and it's him what found the body, and as the son was sent to fetch the police, must of been one of the girls.'

Josephine huddled closer to her informants. 'They all actresses, then?' That question got quite a bit of response, but still nobody bothered to turn round to see who was asking, just in case something might happen should they take their eyes off the door for a moment.

'Yeah. She used to be on the stage herself one time . . .'

'Quite a bit ago by the looks of her.'

'Yeah, well, you got to hand it to her for havin' a bit of sense. Once girls starts losing their looks they got two choices, an 'usband, or the other thing.'

'Or do what Hatty Wright done and start a lodging house.'

''atty still looks good . . .'

'But fat, she run to fat and couldn't get in the box no longer.'

Josephine stayed quiet for a while, not wanting to appear more-than-averagely nosy. She wanted to know *what box*? She needn't have worried, people who have seen something – a bag-snatch, a horse dropping dead – love to prove they know everything about everybody and will tell anyone whatever they wish to hear.

''atty Wright used to be a saw-in-half woman and a knife-thrower's gal.'

Josephine said, 'Is that the truth? Never met one of them before.'

''Ang around and you're bound to see her come out.'

'A knife-throwing act? I shouldn't like that,' Josephine said, warming to the gossip.

'Fancy trusting a fella like that!'

The fact of murder didn't prevent a bit of harmless chat.

'She'll be loving all this, 'specially if she thinks she'll get her name in papers.'

And not only the landlady. Enjoying the notoriety that comes with crime as long as it is once removed, the entire street was loving it. Christmas morning and a murder

71

right in their midst. Her own activity? Josephine didn't question it. She was at work. This could be what was needed to get Jemima Ferguson's name on page one of *The News*.

Mrs Wright waylaid the superintendent in her hallway. 'He's up in her room, sir, your sergeant. He said to look out for you because he wouldn't leave the dear girl unattended.'

'Good, that is the correct thing to do. As few people as possible should move about this house until the sergeant gives permission.'

'Oh yes, sir, Mister Kerley said that.'

'And if you could keep to your quarters until then, it would be a great help.'

'I've already given instructions to everybody. Mr Kerley said that once everybody was up and decent, that they come down here,' she gestured, 'into my apartments, which of course I gladly agreed to.'

'Good.'

'Anyway, sir, I assure you, sir, having seen the state of my husband when he came down, I don't think anybody's likely to want to go up there. I reckon it's not going to be easy letting that room again.'

James Thomson wanted no opinions of any sort, so just looked at her until she became embarrassed.

'I won't show you right up, sir, if that's all right. It's this way.'

Thomson followed Mrs Wright up the first flight of stairs, mentally taking notes as they progressed.

'I let rooms on a monthly rent but most of them pay weekly when they settle for any meals they have had, but I don't do a lot of that.'

Her full-skirted gown swayed as she led him. She was quite young, probably in her thirties, but with a full matronly bosom and the swell and roundness of a woman who had borne children, and would no doubt bear more yet.

She halted on the first landing, getting her breath. 'I hope nobody's going to ask me to look at her, sir. Seeing my husband's face was enough for me.'

'No, no, Mrs Wright. Possibly later, when she has been taken to the . . . hospital, my men will accompany Mr Wright for formal identification.'

'Wouldn't one of her own family do that?'

'If we can find one.'

'I know she's got a sister. She has mentioned her, though I never have seen her.'

A door opened and closed, and Frank Kerley came down the few stairs to greet his superior officer, nodding at the patch Mr Wright had deposited on the lower landing. 'Watch where you step, sir.' Stepping round it, Thomson thanked Mrs Wright, and allowed his sergeant to lead the way. 'Door's busted, sir. Wright, the landlady's husband, said he did it.'

'The door was locked.'

'Yes, sir, but it's queer. Locked on the outside, no sign of a key, and they don't have a spare.'

Thomson casually inspected the damaged lock. 'No other in the house to fit?'

'Most doors haven't got keys anyhow; some have got bolts.'

'So?'

'Looks like our man thought he might gain himself a bit of time by locking the room and taking the key?'

'And did it?'

'Save him time? Probably not necessary, by the looks of the victim, always supposing he left quite soon after the deed was done. I'd estimate that he left in the early hours, and nobody in the house stirred until breakfast, which was later than usual because of Christmas.'

James Thomson looked at his pocket-watch, and, not believing that it was only fifteen minutes since he had left the church, shook it. 'The victim's name is?'

'Harriet Burton. Miss or Mrs I'm not certain.'

'And she was found at what time?'

'There's still a bit of confusion about that, but breakfast was ready by about eight thirty. Mrs Wright had said that she would give the victim a call. She was planning to have a day in the country apparently – the victim, that is. Mr Wright knocked,' the sergeant indicated the broken door, 'and, not receiving any answer, went down to ask his wife what to do. I believe he must have tried the door-handle, but he doesn't like to say.'

'Why?'

'Don't want to be thought of as a landlord who'd go into a girl's room uninvited. Well, that's my theory . . . Anyway, Mrs Wright then came up and knocked and it was she who tried the handle; they looked for a key, but couldn't find one. They were both a bit concerned, so decided to use force on the door.'

'Didn't it occur to them that she might have gone out and locked the door behind her?'

'I asked that, but nobody gets in or out of this house without the Wrights knowing about it. You've seen the layout. Front door, there's a kind of warning buzzer beneath the mat.'

'But anyone who knew about the buzzer could let themselves out quietly, which means surely that they might have reasonably supposed that the victim had risen early and gone out.'

'It was a possibility, but she wasn't very well off for sensible footwear, as you will see, and Mr Wright noticed that her only decent boots were on the landing drying out.' He indicated the pathetic boots. 'Quite the detective, sir. It's my belief that the murderer must have gone out through the basement.'

James Thomson fell silent, looking around, up the next flight of stairs, down the ones he had just climbed. 'Hardly call them decent boots. What's in there?'

'Just a kind of ablutions cupboard: water tap, buckets, chamber-pots.' Kerley opened the door and held it. 'Not the most savoury of places. I haven't taken a close look, but I mean to when you've looked over the room.' Shutting the closet door and pushing open the busted one, he continued, 'By the time Wright broke in, I reckon she'd already been dead a fair few hours by then. She's covered by a lot of bedding, but the room's cold. After you, sir.'

* * *

Josephine didn't wait for the appearance of the landlady, but backed her way through the crowd and slipped unseen down the steps of the house opposite number 12. She knocked softly on the basement door, which was opened a crack by a pale-faced girl who blocked entry with her thin body.

'Can you let me in? I just want to talk to you for five minutes.' Josephine Thomson's 'toff's' speech was gone again; she was missing the odd 't' and running words together as she had previously.

'I can't do that.' The girl spoke in a whisper, her eyes darting upwards to the front entrance, half fearful, but still curious. 'Who are you, miss? I don't know who you are. What do you want?'

Josephine took the hint, speaking in a whisper too. 'Five minutes. I can pay you.' Josephine dipped into her jacket pocket and took out a florin, pressing against the door as she did so. The coin, which happened to be a bright and shining, newly minted one, caught the girl's attention. 'My name's Jemima, what's yours?'

Watching the florin as it threatened to return to Josephine's pocket, 'Why would you want to pay me all that money for five minutes?'

'Because you live opposite where all that is going on, and I want to know about it.'

'I don't know nothink.'

'I'm sure you do . . . what's your name?'

'Edith, miss.'

'Well, Edith, you must see more than most about what goes on in the houses opposite.'

76

'D'you think I got time to stand around peeping through the shutters like . . . ?' She jerked a thumb upwards, took Josephine's proffered florin and opened the door wide enough for Josephine to slip in. The girl gently closed the door behind her, then went to the bottom of a flight of stairs and listened. 'The master will give me a right beltin' if he finds you here.'

'Is he likely to?'

'Well, I suppose not. They're all upstairs watchin' out the front winda, but I'm on my own here till teatime. Cook had to go and see her badly mother . . . *they* didn't like it, but they know Cook will up and go if they don't be easy with her – they don't keep staff – the maids have been sent to morning service with the children. When they gets back, we has to send up something cold.'

'It's nowhere near dinner-time, I expect they won't want serving yet.'

'That's true, specially with everything that's been going on over there.'

'Do you know somebody was murdered in number 12?'

The girl's hand flew to her mouth and she stared at Josephine. 'I hoped she wasn't killed, I hoped she was just beat up. I guessed it might be bad because of the police and that, but I never thought murder.' Shaken, Edith lowered herself onto a wooden kitchen chair. Josephine dipped a beaker into a bowl collecting water from a filter. Edith drank without realizing it. 'Oh, miss, I never thought . . . He could easy come after me, I could be found dead.'

'Edith', Josephine touched the girl on the shoulder, 'whoever did this is probably far away by now. He's not likely to come back to this road again.'

'He could. He's a bold one, he is. When he gets to thinking about it, he might realize that anybody could have seen him: the streetlights was on, and he stopped to pull his boots on.'

Chilled and thrilled at the same time, Josephine said casually, 'You saw a man leaving number 12 then?'

Edith nodded uncertainly. 'Could ov, but he never acted like he was a murderer.'

'Were there people about?'

'Oh no, only me, and he wouldn't know I was looking. I never makes any noise in the morning, I'd get a right belting for that.'

'What did you see?'

'I see him come up the area steps. Then he bends down and does something to his boots, like straightening his socks, and off he goes.'

'You didn't notice which way he went when he left Great Coram Street?'

Edith shook her head. 'No, I only know he didn't go towards Marchmont Street.'

'So, once he reached the corner he might have gone towards Euston Road, or Southampton Row?'

'Could ov gone anywhere.'

How true. This was an area of crescents, squares, interlocking streets and roads. Euston Station, St Pancras, King's Cross, and the underground train stations and main bus routes were all within easy walking distance.

Once he turned the corner of Great Coram Street, he could disappear.

Edith's eyes kept flicking at the row of bells, any of which, Josephine knew, could jangle and bounce around at any moment, summoning Edith to above stairs. 'Look, they'll want me before long. If I don't eat my dinner now, I don't know when—'

'Edith, I am so sorry. Just tell me how he looked and I'll be gone and the florin is yours.'

'He was youngish, not that tall, he had on a short sort of coat – not a jacket, a real top-coat, but short. And he had on a round sort of hat, a bit like a billy-cock, only not the same. His boots, his coat and his hat . . . all queer sort of clothes, I'd say.'

'Foreign?'

Edith gazed off for a moment. 'Yes, I suppose that could be it. Yes, kind of foreign, I'd say. But, it wasn't that light.'

'Do you know anyone who lives there?'

'Only Daisy, who's the skivvy, like me. I know the missis is called Wright. Far as the lodgers go, they're just women lodgers. Though Daisy did say that one of the new ones was on the stage at the 'lhambra Palace – Clara Burton. I hope it wasn't her, because Daisy and me was hoping to go and see her next time we got an hour or two off at the same time. Clara said she could get us in cheap.'

'Thank you, Edith, thank you very much. I would be very grateful if you didn't mention to anyone what you have told me.'

79

Edith dipped thick bread into thick broth and snorted. 'I an't likely to do that. He'd have the skin off my back if he knew I even let you into the house. They wouldn't want to get mixed up in anything like that, especially if, like you say, it wasn't a bashin' but somebody was done in. Waa, miss, I just thought: I seen a murderer. Don't tell nobody, please, miss. I'd just as soon give you back your money.'

'I swear I won't tell a soul that you've spoken to me . . . In any case, I wouldn't want anyone to know how I got to know what you told me. I'll tell you something, Edith, I'd be in hot water myself if you told anybody I was here asking questions. If I were you, I would keep quiet about what you saw.'

'You don't think the police is going to start asking questions from everybody?'

'Ah well, the police is another matter. It's your mistress they will talk to if they talk to anybody . . . and even if they do ask you questions, you can just tell them the truth, like you told me, but you don't have to tell them that I was here.' Edith looked a bit doubtful, but she thought of a whole florin to herself, to spend it on anything she liked . . . 'All right, Edith?'

'Yes, miss. But you'd better get out before she rings that bell.'

Josephine had the great good fortune to be sneaking up the area steps just as the mortuary wagon arrived, compressing the audience, making it even denser.

Ann Martha Thomson stood in the bow window of her

'Divertimento Gallery', a room she had invented to delight herself and any of her friends who liked to gather there. The divertissements provided by Ann Martha were as many and varied as she could provide to indulge simple and innocent whims: arts and games, books, magazines, craft objects and small gardening experiments, such as growing little trees from pips, musical instruments and music boxes, pens, water-colour boxes, crystallized fruits and boxed chocolates.

It could not be truly said to be a gallery, but it was the wide, high window that bowed far out into the back garden that gave it the appearance of such. What gave the room its delightful ambience was the clear view beyond the walled garden across the River Thames as it flowed towards Chiswick. There was a public footpath at the bottom of the garden, hidden from their view of it and the public's view of the Thomsons'. From the gallery it was almost possible to believe that the house stood on its own beside river and fields. It was an illusion, of course, one had only to open the glazed doors and step onto the balcony to see the truth of that.

Ann Martha stayed inside the window this morning, drinking mid-morning café au lait. Hani had been in and out several times. She used the room to make her stylized flower arrangements, often of a single flower, a stone and a reed, which must surely be mathematically placed, because when Ann and her friends tried their own versions they could never get the proportions quite right.

Although Ann Martha gazed out, she was not taking

in how golden the undulations of the snowy fields were, lit by the far-off clear sun. Snow had frozen where it had fallen onto bare branches, and had finished the garden wall with a coping stone of white. She had intended to go down and look to see if the first of the chionodoxas had pushed through, but had been waylaid by her thoughts, not made less troubled by Hani.

'Why you let her go, MisAnn?'

'Do you think you could have stopped her? Our Josie has become very independent.'

'She come just for two short day, and first day she runs away. MistaJame, he does not know. Eh? When she come here, I tell her she had no bad manner when she live in this house. We both tell her we are cross. Eh?'

Ann Martha had given Hani the brief, sedate, one-armed hug that each understood to be as strong as any pressing of cheeks and clutching of shoulders. 'Hani, she is no longer our little girl. She has become independent. You would not like her to be a silly little miss gazing at herself in a mirror and making ribbon bows all day.'

'She think she can be like young man.'

'The world is changing, Hani. Many young women no longer look for an engagement ring. If they are intelligent and educated, they look around and see what domesticity can do to women.'

'It can do very well for MisAnn.'

'Perhaps she has taken you as a pattern to follow.'

Hani dismissed this notion with a puff of air. 'Because I not go home and find man?'

'Maybe because when she was an orphan child, you

82

were free to bring her here; there was no man to tell you what to do.'

Hani smiled wryly. 'Almost I was not free. This time when I take 'osie to my village, my father gave me to a man. If big fever did not happen, I should now be wife and mother to babies so.'

'Don't you want that?'

'Not first thing I choose now. First thing I choose is to live in London . . . live with you and MastaJame.' She sat neatly, her cup of jasmine-flower tea neatly placed on the saucer. 'You think I can live in London, MisAnn? I mean for all time? Not go back to my village?'

'Don't you want to go back?'

'To father to tell what I must do? To man who will not want old woman for wife?'

'Hani, you can't be thirty yet, that's not old.'

'I was, I think, thirteen year when 'osie came to my village, and my father gave me to village boy. I am *old*.' Looking over her cup at Ann Martha, she smiled, wrinkling her small flat nose, 'Also, I like red stone house like this, I like shop with windows, I like gaslamp, so. Snow, him I like, jus' for looking. En'lish man, some I like, big men like MistaJame men.'

Ann Martha laughed. 'Hani, you sly thing. So you are not totally opposed to domestic life – I mean, life with a man . . . a husband?'

'Not village man . . . too old for my village man now.'

Ann Martha had tried to keep the exchange light, but had come to realize that Hani was going as far as she was able to discuss her future. Hani had brought James's niece across thousands of miles when little more than a girl herself. Josephine had clung to her as to a life buoy during the first months; Hani had become an essential part of the household, almost part of the family. Ann Martha suddenly realized what a hole in all their lives there would be if Hani left them.

Her mind now off her earlier musings about Josephine, and what she was doing going to St Giles, Ann Martha took a seat opposite Hani, where they were at eye-level with one another, a feat not always achievable with the inches difference in their height. 'Are you saying that you want to make your future life here, in London?'

'Yes, it is what I mean. But I think, now 'osie is gone from here, you think I also must go?'

'Go? No, no, Hani. I have never given a thought to that . . . how self-centred we are. We don't want you to go. I can't remember how it felt before you brought Josephine here, but this is much more a home since you did.'

Hani, peering into her tea, sat still and quiet for some moments, 'Thank you, Miss Ann, I feel very good now. I still tell that girl she is doing bad manner not coming from church with you. Where she go? What she do with herself all time now she live in rooms. Rooms! What is rooms?'

'Rooms is where young people like to live in these strange times. Where they can make mistakes out of sight of fussy dragons like me and you.'

'Boot Street! I should like to see this Boot Street.'

'That is not a very good idea, Hani. If she thought that we were spying on her independent life, we might lose her altogether. We should go down and look to the cold collation, and I must prepare myself to tell our luncheon guests that their host will probably not be joining us, and his niece . . . ? Only the Lord knows what I shall tell them if she isn't here.'

'Maybe she will not be long away.'

'We can only hope, Hani.'

Having established from the ever-increasing crowd that the victim was Clara Burton, one of Hatty Wright's actresses, Josephine hurried away. In Tavistock Square, Josephine hailed a cab. '*The News* offices, please, cabby.' No directions needed: the offices of all the dailies were well known to cab drivers. She had bet on Mr Hood being in this morning, if only to check incoming stories and post. She told the cabby to wait for her. The nightwatchman said that Mr Hood had come in about half an hour ago and hadn't left. Her heels sounded, clacking up stairwells and through deserted corridors.

In the empty reporters' room she put down the outline of her report. George Hood appeared in the doorway. 'Miss Ferguson?'

'Yes, it's me, sir.'

'Where are the dry sticks?'

'I am quite warm enough without a stove. Look sir, I want you to read this. I know that it is going to become a big, big story. It's a big story which *The News* can publish first. Young actress, singer in the halls, meets

85

a man, takes him to her room . . .' She looked up from her notes to see his expression.

'And?'

'He killed her, then leaves in the early hours of *this* morning. He was seen leaving the house, bold as brass, with the streetlights still burning. Just a few hours ago. Murdered on Christmas morning.' She paused. 'It's all there, isn't it, sir? And I know that I'm the first home with the story. When I left the scene, I saw none of the opposition in the crowd. But they won't be long.'

Hood looked over her shoulder at what she had written, hands clasped, thumbnails pressed against his lips. Hardly daring to breathe aloud, she waited, then jumped out of her skin when he spun round and clapped his hands loudly. 'Yes, Jemima Ferguson, it is all there.'

'If we could get it out today . . .'

'Even if our customers and advertisers are not particularly God-fearing people, they will cry stinking fish if we don't observe Christmas Day, more so than Sundays and Good Friday.'

'They expect cabbies and gasometer workers to work.'

'You should try debating that with a Tory MP from the Shires and see where it gets you.'

'I shouldn't mind doing that.'

Hood smiled and held up a placating hand. 'Let's hope that you will one day get that opportunity, but for now—'

'Would there be any objection to starting the presses at midnight? Boxing Day?'

'They would never believe that we did not desecrate this Holy Day, but . . .'

She could almost hear the cogs of his mind turning.

'A Special Edition. A single fold. There are any number of pieces already set that I held back from the last edition, and some ready for the post-Christmas edition. Pictures, too, as fillers. Did you say she worked at the Alhambra Palace?'

'No, I said that she was an actress, and my source said that she *thought* so.'

'Library picture of the Alhambra will do. Where did the murder take place?'

'Number 12 Great Coram Street. Everything I have so far is in my notes.'

Hood shook his head. 'What's her name?'

'That I don't know for certain.'

'Who is on the case?'

'Superintendent Thomson.'

'Very, very well done, Miss Ferguson. We have a busy few hours before us. You go back and find out as much as you can whilst I start calling in a few of our typesetters.'

'Christmas Day, sir?'

'Boxing Day – stretched a bit. Sworn to secrecy and big bonuses. They will come.'

'Thank you, sir.'

Again that loud clap of hands. 'Have you heard of Miss Barbara Baker?'

'The American columnist? I have. Certainly. Yes. She's my model.'

'Did you know that her father owns the paper she works on?'

'I didn't.'

'I'm not saying that he bought it *for* her, but the relationship cannot be to her detriment.'

'Even so, she is a very good reporter. And she is opening a door for women into a very male profession.'

He put a friendly hand lightly on her shoulder. 'As *you* are Ferguson. You have the instincts.' Narrowing his eyes and giving her a tight smile, '*And*, I suspect, you have the ambition of a young man.'

'It is true, sir, I am ambitious. Many young women are.'

'But not for a diamond ring followed by a quiet life in Kensington, eh?'

'That is a disease known as *terminal ennui*.'

'No boredom in this establishment, Ferguson.'

As the hooves of the cab-horse clopped its way through the sparsely peopled streets towards the Haymarket, Josephine laid her fingers on the place where her chief, Hood, had touched her shoulder. She smiled to herself. Jemima Ferguson, MP. Here was another bastion of masculine power to be breached. There must come a day when women would sit in the House of Commons; that was where changes to society could be made.

Josephine Thomson often had such daydreams.

It was not the bed with its covered human form that first caught James Thomson's attention, but a polished apple placed on the mantelpiece, its bright red skin glowing except for where a single bite had been taken. Close to the apple was a hand-print of blood where

the killer must have grasped the mantelpiece for support.

'Get this over to that new department.'

'To make a cast, sir?'

'Long odds, Kerley, and I cannot detect any sign in
the toothmarks of any missing.'

Kerley peered closely at the apple. 'Nothing lost in
trying, sir.'

At New Scotland Yard, an embryonic department
was working towards establishing scientific methods of
detection. Plaster casts of footprints were not generally
accepted as firm evidence, but might be used to prompt
a confession.

His eye was now drawn to more blood. On the
washstand a bloodstained hand-towel, the marks on
which seemed consistent with someone wiping a dagger,
stiletto or knife on it, and a china hand-basin containing
bloodied water.

The superintendent now leaned forward to look at
the victim, the head of whom was the only part visible,
and was poleaxed to see the features of a woman he
recognized. Quickly recovering, he said, 'Such a peaceful
expression.'

Kerley didn't miss the super's sudden pallor. 'Yes,
well . . . Are you all right, sir?'

'Thank you, yes, Sergeant. I took Holy Communion
this morning and came straight here.'

'Ah, so you won't have eaten yet.' Frank Kerley hadn't
much time for a religion that forbade its followers to eat
a decent breakfast before pretending to eat the flesh and

drink the blood of a god like heathens. He had brought with him to London his simple Wesleyan religion, but had lost it in a life amid a welter of violence and sordid acts. The super, he knew, was Roman Catholic and observed the rituals. How could a man of such superior intelligence believe in all that? A hearty debate on the subject would have been good, but their ranks were too distant for that.

Kerley waited quietly as Thomson turned full circle and methodically checked the room, his eyes flickering up and down, noting mentally not only the layout and furnishing but quite likely the small detail that Frank himself needed to write up in his notebook. His super had the ability to look at a scene and set it firmly in his memory. Frank preferred to have things down in black and white; things might get lost if you kept them in your mind.

'Who is she?'

'Harriet Burton according to the landlady. There's a letter – it's written and addressed but not sent – to a "Mrs E. Horwood, Grove Hill, Hurst Green", her sister.'

Thomson lifted a page of notepaper from the envelope, read it, then handed it to Kerley. 'Make a note of the address and go yourself to break the bad news. I will take the letter with me. Notice, she signs herself "C" Burton, not Harriet.'

'Might not be the same woman?'

'Doubtful . . . ask Mrs Wright, and about the sister before you go there. See what she knows.'

Frank Kerley observed his superior officer. He appeared

90

reluctant to inspect the body. Frank watched and waited until at last the super appeared to force his gaze to rest on the bed.

Kerley took a step forward.

'No! Not yet, Kerley. Did you find her tucked up like that?'

'I did, sir. Wright swears he didn't touch a thing, he saw the blood-print on her forehead, and the bloody towel and the water . . .' Frank flipped back pages of his notebook. 'Exact words, "I took one look, and she was that white I knew straight off she was a goner".'

'He didn't see the injuries?'

'He says not, sir. I believe him. I think if he had he would have dropped the coverlet and ran.'

'So this is how you found her? You looked, made your notes and replaced the covers exactly so.'

'Yes, Superintendent, the scene is exactly as I found it.'

'Right.' Now, Thomson stepped closer to the bed. 'Is that blood mark on her forehead a fingerprint?'

'I reckon a thumbprint, sir. I can't make sense of it, unless he cut his own hand. Maybe we shall be able to work out what happened at the post-mortem.'

'Perhaps. But we must do our best to work out the events from what we see here. What else have you observed so far?'

'Her night-clothing is disturbed and stained, and there's a fair pool of blood under the bed; she's lying on her back and her legs are spread out, sir. It looks as though he could have misused her after death, sir . . .

not normal sexual contact, sir, an act of debasement, an abuse of her womanhood, perhaps. There is semen evident on the pubic hair. Perhaps the killing didn't satisfy him, or he may have wanted to abuse her more than he already had. An evil man, Superintendent, an evil, evil killer who wallowed in his debauchery.'

Ann Martha Thomson was seated in her own dining room with Lord and Lady Granville and Colonel and Mrs Henderson, invited as 'James's guests' because of their connection to the Home Office and the Metropolitan Police. The three other couples were Ann Martha's guests, invited for their lively knowledge of the London scene. All were eating an excellent cold luncheon and drinking wonderful French wines, of good vintage and more expensive than police pay – even that of a superintendent – would provide.

Lady Granville had been influential in recommending James Thomson to the police commissioner, the Granville-Thomson link going back to the Smyrna days, when James's mother held her celebrated gatherings in her salon, where any and every passing traveller of any note was certain of a welcome. There, the Granvilles had met more exotic foreigners in one visit than in an entire season in London. Ann Martha had never known whether to be pleased or cross when James was absent on important occasions. Without him, the ambience was more relaxing. James was not good with guests; one always had the feeling that he would not be sorry when they left. But Ann Martha very much liked to entertain;

guests and friends were part of the *raison d'être* for the attention she paid to her lovely home. Without people moving around in it, the house was an empty stage set.

Lady Granville took it as a compliment that her protégé was absent. 'You don't have to apologize to me for James's absence, Ann. I am pleased to know that he is so indispensable to the detection service.' Colonel Henderson, Chief Commissioner, nodded agreement. The Granvilles and Hendersons, if asked, would have to agree that their presence at the table of a detective superintendent, was unexpected – unique, even. But then, James Thomson's origins were exotic and unique, and his marriage to a lady with royal connections – albeit distant – set social distinctions on their head. It allowed them to pride themselves on their open minds and living at the hub of the universe. London, this could only happen in London.

Mrs Henderson asked whether Ann's niece would be joining them. 'Is she with you for Christmas?'

'Until tomorrow. She likes to walk in the snow – I expect she has lost all sense of time. Now, I do recommend this walnut pickle . . .' Her friends, all being fond of excellent food, were easily distracted from the subject of Josephine's absence.

The young men staying in Kroll's Hotel some distance from the St Pancras area of Great Coram Street, and from the house beside the Thames, enjoyed a meal of good German food and Rhenish wine. Not to all tastes, but this group of young people were all Germans.

Some of them had been out and about on Christmas Eve, and one complained of having caught a cold. His wife, whilst enjoying her food, cast dark looks at her husband.

Yesterday he had treated her despicably.

He had gone off with his friends into the city; at what time he had returned to his room she had no idea. All that she knew was that he appeared to be making amends by suggesting that all of them might go together to an entertainment. She knew how short of money they were, and hoped that there would not be another embarrassment about buying the tickets. At least the hotel bill would be paid for by the ship's agent. It would be sensible to stay in the hotel, where they did not have to find money. But . . . She became persuaded that the men were right. They would be many weeks at sea, and who knew whether there would be any civilized entertainment when they arrived at their destination in Brazil. And the ship might easily be blown off course again. Enjoy a civilized city whilst they could. Next week they might be back in their cramped quarters being tossed around by heavy seas. Enjoyment whilst it lasted. He'd had his pleasure last night; she would take her own whilst she could.

Watching the super's perusal of the room, picking up things here and there, moving objects, opening pots and bags, Sergeant Kerley noticed that he did not replace a rosary where it had lain, in a tiny porcelain dish, but kept it in his hand, fingering the beads absent-mindedly, rolling them between fingers and thumb. Eventually, he clenched his fist about the rosary and transferred it to his pocket.

What was he to make of his superior officer? They had viewed many bodies together, some bruised and battered, some knifed, some decomposing or bloated by Thames water, but the super was having difficulty viewing this one.

'Peel back the covers carefully, Sergeant.' James Thomson lowered his gaze to the dead woman.

Yes, he did know her. *Had* known her, before those gaping wounds had all but severed her head.

How had she come to end her life with her body set thus, so suggestive of abandonment and lust? He recollected how small and sweet her voice had been, so much at odds with the surroundings in which he had heard her sing. Each of her blood-drained hands cradled one of her own breasts beneath her bodice; her legs, bent at the knees, spread apart, gave the appearance of disgusting lewdness.

'He's a madman, sir.'

'No, Sergeant, he doesn't get away with that. Decadent and debauched, yes. Insane, no. Capable of planning – men don't just happen to have a surgical instrument in their pocket. This man came here with every intention of killing. I don't know about positioning her like this – maybe it was an afterthought; maybe he thought he didn't get value for money . . .'

'Semen is running from her, sir.'

'Even so, she may have demurred at further attempts.'

'But her face, sir, as peaceful and composed as if she was asleep.'

'I have no doubt that she was asleep, Sergeant, maybe a little gone in drink, dozing. Those wounds are so clean-cut that she may not have known she had been cut. You must have cut yourself a dozen times with a razor and not known until you saw blood.'

Frank Kerley nodded. 'It couldn't have happened any other way, sir. Had she felt even the slightest nick, her reaction would still have been there on her face.'

Thomson nodded. 'How did he deflect the blood from himself? Arterial blood gushes.'

'Naked, I would guess. Kept his hands under the bedclothes whilst he did it?'

'Which might show that he knew what he was doing blindfold, as you might say.'

Frank Kerley nodded. 'A surgeon perhaps?'

'Certainly somebody who would know that arterial blood gushes, and how to steer clear of it until it subsides . . . it doesn't take long.'

'A veterinary surgeon . . . It won't be a butcher; those cuts are done with a razor or scalpel. You notice that she had had a child, or children.' Frank Kerley gently touched the woman's wrinkled belly, with white stretch scars here and there.

In life her breasts, within boning, had appeared bouncy and high, but unsupported were the looser breasts of a mother who has suckled a child. Although she had, before death, the appearance of a young and lovely woman, the evidence of her motherhood was in the belly stretched and wrinkled from carrying.

'Motive, sir?'

'Motive, Sergeant? Will he have a motive that we would understand? Perhaps she said something that reminded him of an unpleasant experience and wished to punish her. Or he may not have liked to have other men touch her after him – a kind of desecration. Perhaps he liked knives, carried them, and the idea suddenly came upon him that he must have the experience of using them. He may not even remember what twisted motive he had by the time we reach him. Instead of motive, we'll have to make do with knowing of his cunning, his dissipation, arrogance, disdain for a woman sunk so low.'

'Yes, it occurred to me that he must be disdainful. Mrs Wright says she saw him, so he must have felt cock-sure of himself.'

'Not a man from her past, but a complete stranger.'

'Passing through, knows he won't return.'

'Even so, put a discreet watch on this place. A decadent, perverted and corrupt mind. When we find him I believe we shall discover a debauchee, someone who enjoys whoring, gambling, violence the lot. I'll wager he has been through our hands before today . . . Possibly he pulls the legs from spiders and the wings from butterflies. But he won't have the appearance of Caliban. He shall not get away with pleading insanity, Sergeant, we shall make sure of that.'

'He'll be as plausible as you and me, sir. I mean that

he has two eyes and speaks the Queen's English, and we shall need all our senses to find him. And if I follow your breakdown of his character correctly, then I fancy he's got about as much conscience as Iago.'

The superintendent now withdrew his gaze from the body, and found it captured by the knowing grey eyes of his large, fair detective sergeant. Handsome face, manly frame, and the broad honest features of a man who, one might imagine, would be better riding a shire horse over the ribbles of a ploughed field than riding a London Underground train.

Iago? Never underestimate Frank Kerley. Despite the rural accent, he was self-educated and as intelligent as they come.

The detective sergeant now moved to look out of the window. 'The mortuary cart's arrived, sir.'

'Is she going to have to be carried out through that gawping crowd?'

'The only other exit is through the basement, and that still comes up in the street.'

'I will go back to the station and send out some more men. Christmas Day ... I know, Frank, they won't like it.'

'I'll remind them that they'll get dinner tomorrow whereas she won't.'

'When they arrive, shut the Wrights in their room, remind the mortuary men that there are ghouls out there. Just keep them off her whilst she makes her last curtain call.'

'Right, sir, I shall threaten them with a charge for

obstructing police in the course of their duty if I have to.'

Frank was certain that the super had recognized the victim. 'We'll get the beggar, sir.'

'We have to, Sergeant. He has a taste for blood.'

Josephine decided that it would be better to make a late appearance at lunch than to leave Ann Martha to find an excuse for her absence. Mr Hood had sufficient material to get his special edition out. If Uncle James came home, she might do better to pick up some bit of information from him; even so, on her way back to the house she had the cabby stop off at the police mortuary. She came away with a prize. The victim's name was Burton. Once she had this, she ordered the cabby to take her to the Alhambra Palace where, on a billboard, she found 'Clara Burton – Songs and Ballads' listed almost at the bottom of the bill.

'I hope you know where you're goin', miss. We been over half London.'

'If you are worried about your fare, tell me what it is so far.' He did, and she paid him, then he drove her to West Central, where she arrived in time to join the gathering round the cold collation and make her apologies. Ann Martha was mollified at having at least one other member of the Thomson family there and, as Colonel Henderson commented, such a bright and sparkling young conversationalist at that.

By the time Kerley got round to taking statements from the inhabitants of number 12, Mrs Wright had changed into a dark red gown, very suited to her colouring. In the living room she placed on the table a tray with best china and a rich fruit cake for the delectation of the good-looking police sergeant. She had taken a few nips of best London gin to stop the shakes.

The thought that she had set eyes upon the killer was terrifying.

Having given the lodgers permission to return to their rooms to dress and hold themselves in readiness for giving statements. Sergeant Kerley questioned Mrs Wright first. He accepted tea and cake and spoke gently. 'I understand that this will be a great ordeal for you, Mrs Wright.'

'I don't care about that, Mr Kerley, you just get him. She was a nice quiet sort, not at all the sort you might think'd get herself murdered.'

Costermonger Flack. He wasn't on his stand, so Kerley went back to Bow Street looking for one of the uniformed men who walked the Great Coram Street beat and who would likely know where Flack lived.

'You come with me, Constable. He'll know you, so he won't take fright at a detective come knocking at his door late on Christmas Day.'

George Flack had the gravelly voice of a costermonger, and his accent was true Bow Bells. 'I would 'a come dahn to the nick in the mornin'. When I heard that one of Mrs Wright's lodging girls had been murdered. I thought maybe it was the one who stopped and bought stuff from me off the late 'bus. Mind, most of the girls was taking fruit home for to eat on Christmas afternoon. But this one, the cove with 'er, he never seemed kosher. Summit about him, if you know what I mean.'

'No . . . what?'

'First off, you tell me if the girl who was killed was the singer.'

'Why?'

'Because, if it was, then you can be sure it was the bloke who was with her. He was shifty – you don't do a job like mine with 'arf London coming and going and not be able to pick out a bad'n. He really didn't want to buy her no fruit. A real miser. He was counting out his pence as though they was pieces of gold. She really wanted a pineapple. I mean, a pineapple at Christmas, what a treat.'

'But he didn't buy her one?'

'Did he hell-as-like. "Enough!" he said. "Too much cost." So, there's a clue for you, Mr Kerley. He never spoke proper English. Any ordinary sort of cove would'a said "It's too dear, you have the apples." Something like that, you know what I mean. He could speak English, but not proper.'

'Can you describe him? What he was wearing?'

'Oh yes, that's another thing that makes me think you've got to look for a foreigner. He had queer sort of clothes . . . and boots.'

Flack gave an even better description than Mrs Wright. The two of them together would give the artist as good a picture of the man as was possible.

'Sometime tomorrow, Mr Flack. I will send a message for you to attend at Bow Street and look at some sketches an artist will be making. Other people have seen a man of similar description to the man you saw, so together we should get it right.'

Boxing Day 1872

In the first hours of Boxing Day, James Thomson was seated in his little study, hardly tasting the single malt whisky, a gift from Josie who always had the good sense not to give the trumpery that young women often thought men would enjoy. Deep in thought, the wood stove burning hot, he had the letter that the victim had not posted, and the one from her sister, pleading with her to spend Christmas, spread out before him.

The letter that 'C. Burton' had written but not posted read:

My dear sister, Your letter came safely to hand. I have not answered before I have been in a great deal of trouble. I have left Mrs Hillerton and am living at the above address. I am sorry I cannot accept your kind invite for Christmas. I have so much to attend to or I would accept it with pleasure. With kindest love to all wishing you a Happy Christmas & Happy New Year to you all, from your ever affectionate sister C. Burton.

But where was the letter that had come safely to hand? Mrs Hillerton? He hoped that Kerley would have been able to get to her before she heard the news of her sister's death from the daily papers.

His conscience was troubling him. The rosary. He and Frank Kerley had worked together for a long time. They were like a long-married couple, opposites who complemented one another.

He couldn't remember any other occasion when he had not been entirely honest with Kerley. It distressed him. He should have said something the moment he recognized the woman, but he had been confused seeing the death-mask features that he had once known as animated. The moment passed and he was now faced with how to tell his sergeant. Kerley was as sensitive and cerebral as any of Thomson's own exalted circle who thought that their own class had a monopoly on such gifts. Kerley wouldn't have missed the pocketing of the rosary. It lay now on his desk; delicate pink beads linked with a chain and hung with a small plain cross.

Never underestimate Frank Kerley.

It couldn't be left. He must see Kerley first thing. If I become emotional, then so be it. There is no shame in tears. But there was indignity. Not at the station. Kerley must know before they met to organize the investigation.

There was a soft knock on the door. 'Who is it?'

'Me, Josie. Uncle James, may I come in?'

James opened the door for her; dressed in a cashmere shawl over a flannel nightgown and sensible slippers, she came in and he kissed her cheek. 'What are you doing roaming around at this ungodly hour?'

'I am going home in the morning, and I guessed that you would be away early. I wanted to give you this before I left.'

'But you have given me an excellent Christmas present,' he indicated the whisky. 'Truly to my taste, as you know.'

'This one is supplemental, and I am delivering it at midnight away from the curious eyes of my guardian angels.' She handed him a flat parcel that held no mysteries.

'A book? Thank you, Jo, my dear. Something to look forward to reading when the first rush of this new case slows down.'

'No, I should like you to look at it tonight. It contains something that I want you to know.' She felt nervous. 'I chose the binding and endpapers myself.' She paused. 'Could I have a nip of whisky?'

Quite taken aback, as she had expected, he exclaimed, 'Whisky?' Shaking his head ruefully, and reaching for a flat-bottomed glass, he said, 'Since when have you taken to strong drink?'

'Since I stopped having the guardian angels around. A little water please.'

James wondered if this was more of a gesture of proof

of independence than a taste for spirits. However, when she took a sip and held it in her mouth, savouring its flavour, he changed his mind.

Since she and Hani had arrived on their doorstep, each with few belongings, he and Ann had had many firm exchanges of view as to how Josephine was to be brought up, to say nothing of Hani's input. Often it was the two women against his decision, but when he thought it right, he overruled, because he thought he knew what Jo's father would have wanted for his daughter. There could be no argument about that.

As he looked at her now, confident, balanced, well-educated, and apparently happy, he thought that the four of them had done pretty well. She had come into his and Ann's life at a time when the prospects of a family of their own had been pretty bleak.

'Was the cold collation a success?'

'Yes, it was.'

'I am sorry that I could not be there. Thank the Lord for a wife like Ann who understands my duties.'

'Uncle James! You aren't at all sorry, you hate cold collations.'

'It is not the cold food, it is the artificiality of such occasions.'

'You like Lady Granville.'

He smiled over his spectacles as he picked at the red string knotted around the parcel. 'I do.'

'But not the Hendersons.'

'Josephine, do not put words into my mouth. Chief Commissioner Henderson is my superior by far, and it is not usual that a police commissioner will eat under the roof of a lowly super. It is an honour not extended to others of my rank.'

'He likes to hobnob with blue blood, and he knows there will always be some around Aunt Ann's table. I like Lady Granville. I shouldn't mind it if I grow old like her.'

James Thomson laughed. 'I am certain that you can become imperious if you set your mind to it.'

She held her glass out. 'A tiny nip, please. I need a bit of Dutch courage.' When he didn't respond she started, 'There is something that I've wanted to admit to for months now.'

'A young man?' He tipped a generous tot into her glass.

'Open your parcel.' He did so and looked at her, puzzled that it was a scrapbook of newspaper cuttings. Flicking through them he said, 'What is this?'

'This is everything written by Jemima Ferguson. She used to write for *The Echo* and now she writes for *The News*.'

'Ah, the gossip sheet that likes to "tickle" its readers.'

'There is no need to look down your nose at the gossip sheets, Uncle James. They have readers like Ann, and thousands of other sensible people – Lady Granville too, I wouldn't be surprised. There's nothing wrong with a bit of light-heartedness mixed in with the serious and heavy stuff. I know that you don't take *The News*, but have you ever sat down to read it from front page to back?'

He smiled, 'Ah, so this is your method of enlightening me. A woman newspaper writer? Well, I must say you have captured my interest. If you think this lady has something to say of interest, then I am sure that she has.'

'Don't be so patronizing, Uncle James.'

He raised his eyebrows. This was the first time that the child who had brought joy into their marriage had spoken to him as an adult, as an equal. It was very late. He was very weary. He wasn't sure he knew how to respond or handle her.

'Jemima Ferguson is a good journalist. Though she writes about minor events, she tries to draw attention to all kinds of injustices. I know that they are short pieces, but if you read them you will see how concerned and serious-minded she is.'

'Josie, my dear, I am sorry if I'm not responding as you hoped, but I am at a loss to know what you want me to say, or why you have gone to such trouble as to make a collection of cuttings.'

She finished off the dregs of the whisky, placed the glass firmly on the desk and looked directly at him. 'Because, Uncle James, I am Jemima Ferguson.'

James Thomson looked closely at the pasted cuttings as though he had never encountered newsprint before, and then at Josephine.

'What made you think of doing this? Journalism is not exactly a world for women.'

'Which is *such* a good reason to enter it. You're behind the times, Uncle James. In America . . .'

108

'Ah *America*.'

She heaved an exasperated sigh. 'Oh what a put-down. They are centuries ahead of this country where women are concerned. Women can be *anything* they choose.'

'A slight exaggeration, Josephine. One or two women, *maybe*, have broken into one or two professions—'

'One or two women are enough to break open the gates and let in other women. Well, I intend to break open the gates to the newspaper empire here. If you read the next edition of *The News* you will see my name – Jemima's name – on the front page, and again in the Obituaries.'

'You should have told me . . . us.'

'I wanted to make something of myself in the newspaper world first.'

'Did you think that I wouldn't approve? Well, I tell you this, Josephine, I don't.'

Josephine was dashed. 'Not approve? There is nothing not to approve of. I do good work. If you will read those pieces, you will see that.'

'I see reporters every day of my life. I don't have great regard for them.'

'Why?'

'They can be like vultures over a kill, each of them scrabbling for the best bits before the rest. I don't want you to be part of that, Josephine.'

'I am already part of it. Except that my methods are not to scrabble. Don't underestimate me, Uncle James.'

'Since you came to us, I have always been guided by what I thought your father would have wanted for you. I hardly think that he would have wanted his only daughter to work for a newspaper.'

'What my father would have wanted has nothing to do with it. And, I have to say this, Uncle James, what you want for me has nothing to do with it. You and Ann have given me everything, I love you for it, and shall always be grateful. But I am on my own now. I can now pay my own way. I have an income and received a twenty pounds bonus from my editor. *He* thinks I am good at what I do.'

'Because of this?' Indicating the cuttings.

'Because of that and the fact that *The News* wanted to employ women on their staff. I am the first. It was important that I do well. And I have done that. As you will see when tomorrow's edition arrives on the streets.'

Pausing for moments before he did so, he moved aside a pile of documents, and pulled out a fold of newsprint. 'You mean this?'

When she saw the distinctive head, she snatched the paper from him. Mr Hood had done it. Following the Duke of Wellington's attitude of 'Publish and be damned', he had got the special edition onto the streets ahead of the rest.

MURDER
ACTRESS KILLED ON
CHRISTMAS MORNING

Josephine quickly scanned the brief account. Most of her words had survived the blue pencil. But George Hood had not kept his promise: there was no byline giving Jemima's name, just the anonymous, 'by a *News* crime reporter'. Disgusted, she flung the paper down. 'He promised me . . . he actually said that I had broken the news ahead of everybody and deserved my name on the front page. And I do. Have you read this, Uncle James? Every word about the murder was written by me.'

James Thomson seized the paper and scanned the report. 'By you?'

'As Jemima Ferguson, yes.'

He read aloud, '". . . the man seen leaving the house in the early hours of Christmas morning was described to our crime reporter as young, of average height, wearing a short topcoat, pull-on boots and a billy-cock type of hat. He walked away in the direction of Great Coram Street."' James lowered the paper and put his head in his hands.

'How did you come by this information, and that he went in the direction of Great Coram Street?'

'In the way good reporters do – I went to the obvious place, and asked.'

Holding his head in his hands, he was silent for long moments. 'Josephine, I would be well within my rights to take you to Bow Street for questioning.'

'I might not mind that, Uncle James. Experience.'

'It is not amusing to me, Josephine. You have plastered across the front page evidence that the police might not like to have the general public know. He may well not be the murderer, and as a consequence the police will be inundated with sightings of a young man wearing a short coat and a billy-cock hat.'

'And one of them may well be the man who killed the singer.'

James was confused. Outside 12 Great Coram Street, only Kerley and himself knew that the victim was a singer. 'Josie, the police can only make two and two facts make four pieces of evidence – never three, or five or seven. *That* way we get to the truth.'

'Are you saying that *Harriet* Burton is not the victim, or that *Clara* Burton is not a singer?'

'I am saying nothing about anything, Josie. I am on dangerous ground here. As you must realize, our relationship could be damaging to the investigation. If it becomes known that *The News* crime reporter is the niece of the senior officer investigating this case, I should be compromised.' Long moments of silence fell between them. 'I have to be up and about early, and as you are several hours of rest ahead of me, I am going to bed. I'm sorry, but I can't leave you here as I have evidence that I must lock away. Sadly, I cannot trust you.'

'I would never look at evidence like that. I might keep my ears open to get a clue as to where you shot off to when we came from church. but I would never—'

'Who told you about the man in the billy-cock hat?'

'Uncle James!'

'Urgently, Josie. I must verify this sighting.'

'Who have you interviewed so far?'

'The inhabitants of number 12.'

'Including the skivvies, Mrs Wright's girl and Edith who works on the opposite side of the road?'

James stiffened. When Mrs Wright had assembled all the inhabitants, there had been no scullery maid, just a maid-of-all-work who he and Kerley had assumed was the bottom of the Wright's household pile.

'Her name is Daisy, and she is quite friendly with Edith, who lives opposite. I interviewed Edith.' She turned as she was leaving his stuffy study. 'Now you won't need to take me down to Bow Street for questioning. Goodnight, Uncle James, I expect our paths will cross tomorrow – well, actually it will be today.'

'Josie—'

'Oh, don't worry, Uncle James, I would never embarrass you by letting it be known that we are in any way connected.'

'Nothing to do with embarrassment, Josephine; it can never be known that I have the slightest connection with news reporters. Already I am compromised.'

'How? I made sure that I kept well away from where you and Sergeant Kerley were.'

'How did you know where to go?' His voice was not gentle.

Neither was hers when she said, 'I have good hearing. You mentioned "Coram" to your cabby, so I went to Coram's Fields, and saw the spectators in Great Coram Street.' If it was not the exact truth, it was only to save the young constable from a dressing-down.

*   *   *

113

James Thomson left the house very early, leaving a note of apology to Ann and a little box containing a necklace of jet that she had admired.

Having made a decision regarding Harriet Burton's rosary, which he had taken from the scene of crime, he now strode out with purpose to Bow. The air was still frosty and snow had rutted in the gutters. It was perfect weather for clearing the head. Should he tell Kerley about Josephine?

'Francis.' Elizabeth Kerley called from the back kitchen door. 'You said you wanted to be about early. It's nigh on six forty-five.'

'I'm not so deaf I can't hear the bells, and there'll be no pies if I don't give the rabbits their turnip-tops.'

His wife was the only person who had never dropped his given name. He liked that; it was something close and personal between Elizabeth and himself. He could still recollect the thrill of the first time she said, 'Oh, Francis,' as they broke away from their first passionate embrace. They had married soon after that, each knowing that, when they were in the presence of one another, they could easily snap together like magnets. They had laughed loudly when Elizabeth had said, 'I think we should go for consummation as quick as possible, Francis.'

'You mean consummation as in you and me getting wed?'

Elizabeth, with her arms around his neck, and smiling up at him, said, 'I was thinking that, or something.'

'We could have the first banns called on Sunday.'

'And get wed after three weeks.' She had kissed him hard. 'Because I tell you, Francis Kerley, consummation with you don't hardly leave my mind since you walked me home – for my safety's sake, wasn't it?'

Having found the bare small of her back, he had slid his hands down until he had one firm cheek in each hand. He had laughed into her neck, making her squirm. 'Three weeks is a long time, my lover?'

Without coyness she felt his erection.

'What say to the banns on Sunday?'

She had kissed him close to his ear and whispered, 'Marriage end of August, and prenuptial consummation here and now.'

It had been August, warm, the smell of straw and corn on the air, and the brook chattering, bats flying, nightingales and owls calling, full cows lowing for the milkmaids' tugging fingers. As they lay side-by-side, astonished at what they had discovered, Elizabeth had said, 'Oh Francis, do you realize that we have just consummated?'

Frank Kerley knew a score of other words, but for a reason not understood by them, the word, and the act, were destined to become an important part of their married life together.

The following May, their daughter Frances had been born.

And to an extent their marriage had continued like that. Their physical enjoyment, cementing their growing respect for – and liking of – one another. It would be

115

hard to find a better marriage than that of the Kerleys. It was seldom now that they needed to say the word they had once found so amusing: a look was enough. Their physical attraction for one another had never waned, but had grown full and satisfying.

Frank came into the kitchen, washed his hands, and sat at the table, where Elizabeth put a proper breakfast before him. Plenty of meat and eggs, and bread. Plenty of tea in a large covered pot.

'I'll go up and wash and dress. I'll be down by the time you've finished.' She kissed him lightly as he began to eat.

'Elizabeth.' She looked back at him from the doorway. 'I'm sorry I was sarcastic about . . . when you reminded me about the time.'

'Francis Kerley, you went out and didn't come back till late yesterday, and I reckon it won't be any different today. You're weary and will be even wearier before you sort out this terrible case.'

'They will write her up as a prostitute. She was just a poor young woman, trying to keep her head above water.'

'Isn't that what all of them are?'

Frank looked at her. She was a woman's woman, always turning things on their head, siding with women, defending their actions. 'She picked a bad'n, and he did for her.'

'More likely that he picked her, wouldn't you say, Francis. Oh Lord! There's the front door. You answer it, I'm not respectable.'

* * *

116

Josephine's two guardian angels hovered around Josephine as she made ready to return to her other home. ''osie, I have fetch your overshoes from shoe cupboard. These are warm for you.'

It was no good protesting, and it was sensible because snow had fallen on snow overnight. Josephine stepped into the waterproofs whilst Ann wound a silk scarf about her throat. 'There is nothing like silk to hold the body's warmth.'

Josephine smiled and allowed the scarf to be knotted artfully. 'You taught me that, the first winter after we came to England. In the East silk is for airiness, in England for warmth.'

Hani ran to answer a sharp rap on the front door. 'Cab is here.'

Josephine said her warm thanks and goodbyes.

'You know that you can stay longer, Josephine.'

'I know that, Ann, and I appreciate it, but I believe that Liliana will have returned by now, and we promised ourselves a visit to the shops to try for bargains.'

Ann Martha waved that thought aside. 'There are no such things as bargains, Josephine, only out-of-date fashions and soiled goods. If you want a new hat, buy one, not a thing that has been on a hundred heads before yours.'

The cab driver collected her bags and waited with the cab door open ready. 'I promise that I won't buy a single hat.'

'Good, and I am certain that your friend who spends

117

time in Paris would never dream of such a waste of good money.'

The three women hugged and kissed goodbye, and the cabby was away before Josephine could wave at her guardian angels.

James Thomson sat with Kerley whilst he finished his breakfast. The cup of tea was very different from the China he usually took in the morning, but this was good, Indian; it had a lot of body and taste.

On his way to Bow, his mind had dwelt upon his meeting with the girl he had always remembered with warmth and gratitude. She had been a kind person, and he had gained the opinion that – given different circumstances – she would have made a fine wife. Perhaps she had done; so far, all that they knew of her as a resident of the Wrights was that her life as a singer did not bring in enough to keep a roof over her head so she had been forced to take men home. Men? Perhaps not men, perhaps just this one man. Perhaps because it was Christmas and she was being the good-natured and sympathetic woman he had known briefly. He tried to conjure up an image of her last night. Perhaps she had been singing. A man had complimented her on her sweet voice, as he himself had once done. She would have glowed with gratitude. The man, a stranger, a foreigner, and she had been kindly to him.

He was greatly troubled by Josephine. He and Ann Martha and Hani had given her more freedom to make decisions than most children would have been given.

118

He and Ann Martha had discussed such matters of her upbringing on many occasions. His brother had had many unusual ideas regarding the disciplining of young children, and encouraged them when they were old enough to make their own decisions and their own mistakes. But he himself was not her father. Quite possibly, because he was endeavouring to—

Frank Kerley's voice broke into this preoccupation. 'Is the tea to your liking, sir? Not too strong?'

'Oh dear, I am sorry, I was miles away.'

Frank Kerley could see that, all right, and the expression of pain and trouble that flickered across his brow.

'Would it trouble you if I were to use your first name when we are not on duty?'

'I should be glad, sir.'

'The tea is excellent. What is it?'

'The tea? It's just ordinary breakfast tea. We don't ever drink any other, except when Elizabeth has some of her delicate artist friends to visit her.'

James at once wanted to ask about the artist friends, but this was neither the time nor the place. And it was possible that there would never be a good opportunity. Their lives were set well apart. How sad that the rules and proprieties of their profession prevented a close friendship. He had no friends to speak of. Some acquaintances, people whose company he and Ann Martha invited, but most of them were Ann's friends. No one close, except Gwendoline Granville, who had known him in Smyrna when he was a youthful palace-aide in a fanciful uniform. Frank Kerley would be

119

a good man to count as a friend. This visit was likely to be as close as they would ever get.

'This would not have been so difficult for me had I spoken yesterday.'

To help his super, Frank cut himself a generous slice of cheese and indicated that the super should help himself.

Absent-mindedly, James cut a small crumbly corner but did not eat it. 'Unless I have underestimated you, I suspect that you already know why I have come before we both start work today.'

'The victim was not a stranger to you.'

James nodded. 'Though I did not know her, except as a singer.' James handed Frank the large envelope containing the letter and the rosary. 'It's all there.'

'I am sure it is, sir.'

'But you will check against your list.'

Frank grinned. 'You wouldn't keep me on as your DS if you thought I wouldn't. Trust is one thing, evidence is another.'

'The woman, Burton, was once very kind to me. Perhaps at a more appropriate time and place, I shall tell you more, but I swear – on oath if you like – that my meeting with the victim has nothing to do with this investigation.'

'Very well, sir. Let's leave it at that, shall we?'

Frank got up from the table and took his plate to the sink, where he scraped the leavings into a dish. 'I'll just take these to the chickens, if you don't mind. Should you care to take a look, I'm proud of them.'

Frank Kerley led the way to the bottom of the long, narrow garden. Brussels sprouts grew in straight rows. Spinach, too, and other brassicas that James didn't recognize in their growing state. 'What's that with the leaves?'

'Curly kale. We like it, but mostly it goes to the chickens and rabbits.'

'Rabbits too?'

Frank snapped off some leaves and held them to the cages. Several fat rabbits came to feed. 'And the chickens are through the gate.'

'You brought a bit of the countryside to London to remind you of it?'

'No, Mr Thomson, this isn't remotely like rural England. Nobody keeps animals boxed up like this. They roam free and take their chances with predators. In London, all of us is in boxes.'

'So why . . . ?'

'Food, fresh food. We know where they come from and what they've been fed on. If we could keep fish, too, then we would.'

'How do you find time?'

'Elizabeth. I like to feed the animals when I can, but she's the one who grows our food.'

'What good use she makes of her time.'

'Time, sir. We should be leaving.'

James nodded.

'About the rosary, sir?'

'It had been mine, I gave it to her, I don't know why, in the nature of a token of . . . I am a Roman Catholic,

Frank, and she acted as a confessor would. I told her something that I could never tell Ann. Nothing bad, Frank, just sad . . . very sad.'

A short silence ensued, after which James again took up his rank. 'Did we get a statement from Daisy, the scullery maid at number 12?' It was obvious from the sergeant's expression that they had not. '*The News* has brought out a kind of penny sheet. It's all on the front page. It's my guess that the sighting must have been from the house opposite, and the only person likely to be about at dawn must be the scullery maid.'

'Mrs Wright didn't say that she had a scullery maid . . .'

'You didn't interview one?'

'No, sir, Mrs Wright said she had assembled the entire household. Dammit, she didn't consider a scullery maid worthy of attention, I'll be bound. And I am as bad not asking.'

'Well, see to it, Sergeant.'

They were well on their way to the police station when Frank Kerley said, 'You say *The News* published details of a sighting? We should have them for withholding evidence.'

'Nothing was withheld, Sergeant: I told you, it's spread across the front of *The News*.'

At Bow Street Police Station, Frank Kerley gathered his squad of trained detectives and a few from the uniformed branch who would be working on the case.

'Notebooks, men. On the cover write "Harriet Burton, sometimes known as Clara Burton and Mrs Brown.

Murdered Christmas Day Eighteen Seventy-two. Page one you head with the name "Miss Burton". Write it in large letters. Whenever you refer to this victim you will use her *name* – not "dolly-mop" or "prossie" or "doxie," or any of the names you are inclined to use when referring to women who have nothing to sell but the parts of their body that they would much prefer to keep to themselves. Understand?' There was some embarrassed mumbling. 'I said "Understand?" That loud enough for you?'

There was a sibilant reply, 'Yess, Ssargeant.'

'You, DC Morrisy,' he indicated a detective standing at the back of the room. 'I want you to be present when the first three of our witnesses arrive to describe a suspect to the artist. I know that some of you think that sketches are a waste of time, but we have nothing better. This time we have two witnesses who saw the suspect clearly, so what I want is for you to oversee each of the attempts of the artist to catch an image, and then to see how each witness responds to the other sketches. By this means, we should get a good likeness. As we gather more information, we may amend the likeness. See that our witnesses are well taken care of, don't leave them hanging around in cold rooms, and remember they have work to do, same as you, and they won't be earning whilst they are here. I know I've said it before, but I'm saying it again – witnesses are our best evidence. Make them feel comfortable. We should all look pretty stupid questioning an empty witness box.' As usual this got a bit of a smile.

His longest-serving men were well used to Kerley's thinking: witnesses aren't keen to come forward, so make them glad that they have, make them feel important, which they usually are.

'The rest will be detailed off to make enquiries about the victim's movements from when she arrived at the Alhambra Palace on Christmas Eve to the point where she alighted from the late omnibus passing through Coram Fields and bought fruit from one of the witnesses coming in today. One last thing, put your hearts into this one. Superintendent Thomson says our murderer has a taste for blood . . . yes! He will do it again if we don't get him soon. He killed yesterday in the early hours, his trail must still be warm. You find him. As soon as we have a likeness, you shall have it.'

DC Morrisy paid close attention as he listened to the Wrights and Flack the costermonger, and watched the artist.

'He wasn't no more than average tall. Early twenties. Darkish. Rough complexion like he needed a shave . . .'

'I think he was a bit spotty . . .'

'He didn't have a beard but he wasn't clean-shaven.'

'He might have been a bit feverish, blotchy like . . .'

'He wore a queer sort of hat.'

'He had on a round billy-cock hat, but with a narrow brim.'

'He wore a round hat dented on the crown.'

'His topcoat was short.'

'He wore a short topcoat . . .'

'He had on a warm coat, but it only came to his knees.'

'His boots was like seamen's boots, or maybe elastic sided . . .'

'I can't really say about his boots except that they was pull-ons.'

'Sea boots, I remember definitely sea boots.'

'He looked a surly cove.'

'He wasn't English . . .'

'He had a distinct foreign accent.'

'He was a foreigner.'

As the detectives spread out across the area of Clara Burton's known activity on Christmas Eve, more and clearer descriptions came in. A sketch was printed, which all of the witnesses agreed was a fair likeness.

It was very early, but as on any other day in Fleet Street, reporters and editors, sub-editors and copy-writers were already working, providing the copy that would begin rolling off the presses that night, so that people could devour news and their breakfasts at the same table.

Although it was so early, George Hood was already seated at his desk. 'Ah-ha, the young woman of the moment. Come in, come in, Miss Ferguson. Sit down, sit down. I am very pleased with your piece. Very enterprising. You have the makings of an excellent reporter.'

'The makings? Excuse *me*, Mr Hood, I *am* an excellent reporter. You all but promised me that I should get my byline on the Great Coram Street Murder, and what is there? "*The News*'s Crime Reporter." All of our crime reporters are men: they will take the credit. I feel really let down. Really! Really! If any of the men had come in with this, the credit would have been given, front-page name.'

'I don't remember actually promising that your name would be on the piece.'

'Oh don't you, Mr Hood? Well I remember exactly. I may be a woman, and I may be one of the first to get a foot in the door as a serious reporter, but I will not let you or anyone try to put me down. I *earned* my name on that story.'

He held up his hands, palms out. 'Miss Ferguson, just sit down and let us talk about this.'

'No, Mr Hood. There is nothing to talk about. I got this story before anyone. What happened between my story and its publication?'

'Nothing. But we did discuss the problem of crossing the church.'

'Oh, so?'

'On reflection, I thought that *The News* should not try for too much notoriety at one go.'

'Do you mean that having a woman scoop up a story before anybody, and giving her credit for it, would be construed as *notorious*? I cannot believe it! I have always thought you to be more advanced in your thinking than the rest.'

'*The News* has plans to take on more and more women. On reflection I thought it might be too much of a poke in the eye having a woman reporter scoop the rest. That could well disrupt our plans to feminize our staff.'

'To have a successful woman reporter? That could push your plans ahead five years.'

'I'm sorry, Miss Ferguson, I daren't risk what we are achieving here.'

'Oh, and just what are you achieving – the double-crossing of a really good reporter because she wears skirts? I had a better opinion of you than that. I shall resign.'

'If you do that it will be *you* who will be putting the clock back.'

'You are turning this on its head.' She flung her hands in the air in despair.

'You *are* a good reporter, you have the instinct, the flair and such a way with words,' George Hood insisted.

'Not a lot of good if nobody reads them. Not even the police knew that the killer walked in the direction of Great Coram Street.'

'How do you know that?'

'You don't really expect me to tell you that, Mr Hood.'

Hood looked puzzled, possibly trying to fathom how she obtained police information. Maybe conjecture. She was bright enough. 'I don't want to lose you, Miss Ferguson. Quite possibly I made a slight miscalculation in not giving you the byline.'

'Not slight, Mr Hood. I have more information, a lot

more, but there's no way that I will give it to *The News* unless I have a guarantee that my name will head every word of mine that appears in print.'

Sudden inspiration. A book! Make Harriet Burton the heroine. The plot is there, I have only to research the detail of her life. No, a biography. A good, readable biography.

She knew that she could do it.

After Mrs Wright had approved the artist's sketch, she told the uniform keeping control of the front of house at Bow Street Police Station that she wished to see Sergeant Kerley. 'What's it in connection to?'

'With – in connection with. It is in connection with the murder of Miss Burton.'

'You're a witness, then.' He recalled DS Kerley's warning about witnesses.

'Of course I am, haven't I just come from the artist?'

'Please wait, ma'am. You can sit down if you care to, come round here, we have a little stove going. Your name?' He poised his pen to make an entry in the log.

'Wright, Mrs Frank Wright of 12 Great Coram Street. Near Russell Square, London.'

Tomorrow she would be in the London papers.

Sergeant Kerley came into the little public office. The constable hadn't been able to say what she wanted. 'You always say we should look after witnesses, and by God, sir, she's a top one. I reckon she must be the landlady.' Kerley was cautious because there were always people who, having had a taste of celebrity, wanted to hold on to it. There was no doubt that Mrs Wright liked to be up front; it occurred to him that she might have been on stage herself: she did tend to strut rather than walk.

'Mrs Wright, thank you for coming to the artist's session. I believe that we have come up with a very fair sketch of him. Were you satisfied?'

'All of us agreed that it was a good likeness, but disagreed a little as to detail.'

'Oh, please, tell me.'

'I thought that he was a little rough about the chin, and maybe a little shabby, but George Flack – I've known him for years, honest as they come, but maybe, being a man and a little rough himself, he might not have judged the murderer as a woman would.'

'Suspect, Mrs Wright, we mustn't make assumptions.'

'I'm a very good judge of character, Mr Kerley, and I would put money on him being the one. He was very shifty, that we did agree on. Mr Wright never had such a clear a view as I had, but he wasn't in no doubt that the man in the sketch was a very good likeness.'

'That's good, that's good. The constable said that you wanted—'

'Oh I do, Mr Kerley. I have discovered you a witness who can vouch to the time he left – give or take, you know. My Daisy . . . Saw him creep downstairs and let himself out of the basement door, and then up the area steps.'

'Mrs Wright, I requested yesterday that you assemble your entire household.'

'I know, but I never thought at the time . . . Well, you know how it is with scullery maids, you don't think of them as a member of the household, do you?'

One of his super's new-fangled methods of training his men was to put on a little scene – such as the one Frank was now involved in – and learn how to control the situation to the advantage of the interrogator. There were times when a fist banged on a table, combined with a threatening voice, could work wonders with, say, a law-abiding clerk. Mrs Wright, however, needed to believe that, as a main witness, she was held in high esteem by the police. 'I don't have a scullery maid, but I should have been more specific. So, tell me about Daisy.'

'Not a lot to tell really. I would say she might be about twelve, but she is bright, and I have never had any trouble with her. She's a useful little thing, and I've taught her to be honest and truthful, so you can believe what she tells you.'

'Mrs Wright, what I should like is for me to get a cab and for you to come with me to your house. I don't want her prompted at all, but I should like you to assure her that she has no need to be afraid.'

'Little scullery maid' is often the term describing the lowest of the lowly below-stairs domestics, but Mrs Wright's Daisy was just that. Not reaching five foot in height, she was dwarfed by the detective's mass. He smiled, a smile he knew how to use and varied according to whom he was questioning. Charming and friendly, 'Well, miss, I near forgot to come and talk to you.'

Her eyebrows shot up and she blushed.

'Is it all right with you, ma'am, if I question Miss Daisy on her home territory so to speak?' and he indicated to Daisy that she lead the way below stairs. In many houses, the below-stairs arrangements could be most comfortable. This was usually the case in an affluent household with a good mistress, but here the only sign of comfort was an old-fashioned day bed that had seen better days, and the glow from between the bars of the kitchen range, the surface of which had that sheen which only daily black-leading can achieve.

Frank Kerley took one of the four wooden chairs arranged around a bare wooden table upon which various utensils were obviously being used for the making of something very floury. 'Sorry if I interrupted your work, I shan't keep you long.' The little thing was scared half to death; he'd never get more than a word if he couldn't get her over that. 'That's a beautiful bit of black-leading. Mrs Kerley'd be quite jealous if she could see that.' She quickly looked up at him and then returned her gaze to somewhere about his elbow. 'Mrs Wright said you saw somebody.'

Daisy nodded apprehensively, not certain whether she should have seen him, or told her mistress that she had done so.

'When did you see him?' With the blunt end of his pencil he drew a funny smiling snowman face in the film of flour.

131

A little smile came upon her lips, enough to relax her throat and permit her voice to come whispering out. 'Morning.'

'Where?'

She flicked a forefinger quickly in the direction of a door that appeared to lead outside. Frank went to it and lifted the latch, which made the familiar sound of an iron latch being lifted. 'Were the bolts shot home?' She nodded. He slid both bolts back and forth – they were oiled but grated a bit when moved, then returned to his chair. 'I'd feel a lot easier if you'd sit down, miss. Men aren't supposed to be seated whilst ladies are standing.' He indicated the chair nearest the range, and she slid into it. There were times when he quite despised himself for the acts he put on. Until now, he had overlooked her possible presence in the house, and now he was behaving like a blooming dancing master. But she was hardly more than a child, and he knew no other way of persuading her that he was not about to cuff her, which was likely to be her more usual experience of authority. 'That's better.'

'So where were you when this man came through and let himself out?'

'I'd a just woke up, but I wasn't out of bed and I watched him come down the stairs.' A very long sentence for Daisy.

'Was there any light?'

She shook her head. 'On'y through the window.'

'From a streetlight?'

She nodded.

Frank walked where anyone coming from upstairs

132

would walk to reach the back door, looked at what he might see of the room, then went to sit on the edge of the worn and seedy day bed. 'I'm surprised he didn't see you from there. Doesn't the light get as far as this?'

'I wasn't there. I was abed.'

Making assumptions again, Frank Kerley. 'Perhaps you wouldn't mind showing me.'

She indicated a walled space about a couple of feet wide, between the kitchen range and the kitchen wall; a space usually used for the drying out of damp fuel or for sweeping brushes and the like. 'It's the warmest part of the house. The walls gets nice and hot.'

Frank saw that, from Daisy's point of view, this lobby-hole might well be preferable to the old day bed. 'Ah,' he said, 'I can see it must be.' He grinned, 'Bit of a tight squeeze for me I reckon.'

She lowered her lids as she grinned back. Had she been a little braver she might have said, 'Oh, go on with you.'

Frank saw that he had won her over. 'So, then, tell me the whole thing.'

'Well, I hadn't been awake more than a minute or two. I was hoping the clock would strike so I wouldn't have to get out of bed to see the time, an' I heard the landing creak. And then the bottom stairs, they creak and all. I never took no notice, really, because quite often there's gentlemen as goes out in the early hours.'

'Out of the front door?'

She nodded. 'That's why I was surprised when I heard somebody come on down the back stairs. Nobody don't

133

usually, not unless they got like gripes or something and they have to go out there in the night-time. So I just holded on because I never had on . . . I never had on my skirt and that.'

Frank added a top hat and collar to the face in the flour as he waited until she continued. 'I thought he was going to the pantry because he got a-hold of the latch. Then he must of realized it was the wrong door. Then he looked at the basement door and went on to that. He tried the latch first, then found the bolts. Only the bottom one works, the top one don't meet proper. He put down his coat and that and worked it open, then he picked up his things and lifted the latch and opened the door.' She looked at him apparently for approval or permission to continue.

Frank nodded encouragingly, 'And . . . ?'

'He put on his hat, then his coat. I tell you it was cold, the air don't half whip round that area, but it never took him more than a minute, then he shut the door, quiet.' She stopped. Frank hesitated before speaking in case there was more, but apparently not.

'You heard him go up the steps?'

She searched around in her memory. 'No, I never. I'll tell you why, I think he was in his socks and carrying his boots.'

'Did you see?'

'No, but he stopped and it sounded like he was pulling on his boots, grunting like, not loud.'

'Daisy, you are a very good observer. I have a very clear picture of what you saw.'

She blushed. 'It's not really very clever just to watch people.'

'Oh, you'd be surprised. So many people watch people but they never really see what's before their eyes. Not many would think to say about the putting on of his boots.' He grinned. 'Too much to hope for that you know what kind of hat?'

Had she known how, she might have preened with pleasure. 'Nearly like a billy-cock, only it wasn't just the same. And his coat wasn't a proper topcoat . . . well, it was, I mean it was a *top* coat, only it didn't come right down long.'

He went back upstairs to tell Mrs Wright that he had finished.

'Sergeant. I remembered something. She come from a place called "Wizzbeach". Queer sort of name, I remember thinking that when she told me.'

Well, my girl, you are on your own now. Although Josephine did not utter those exact words, this was her sentiment. When she had expected to cover the Great Coram Street murder, she had concocted a plan. This, now that she had no one to tell her otherwise, she could develop in more concrete terms. She would seek out the women amongst whom Harriet had lived and worked. David Wilde would know who to ask. If the poor and desperate prayed anywhere, it was where David Wilde was minister.

First, though, she must go to Harriet herself.

* * *

135

This was the second time in a few weeks that she had requested entry to the mortuary, the last being to look at Jane who had died of hunger. Although that had been the first time that she had seen a dead person – at least the first time that she had seen a dead white person. When she was a girl there had been several occasions when a native beggar had curled up waiting for her father, but had left it too late for any kind of medicine to help. That had not seemed so very bad: those people always wore clothes, were curled up and appeared to be asleep; but Jane and other corpses, awaiting a coroner's verdict, or to be claimed by a relative, were stiff and pale and unmistakably dead.

'You a relation?' The man guarding the entry shoved a piece of paper across the counter and, knowing from her last experience that relations were waved through on a signature, she said, 'Yes, distant.'

'She hasn't been here very long, you're the first, but I dare say there'll be plenty more once it gets around what happened. Are you going to do the identity?'

'No, I've just come to pay my respects before she is taken to be put in her coffin.'

'She was cut real bad . . . well, good in a way, quick for her. Don't remember seeing anything as clean and neat as that. Must have been a lot of blood.'

Josephine felt her cheeks burn with indignation, but bit back a scathing comment about her being a person not a curiosity. She had wanted to ask whether the wounds would be covered, but could not bear to be with the keeper any longer.

Harriet Burton was one of several corpses displayed for identification and the ministrations of a coroner. A raised walkway with a painted iron barrier surrounded the viewing area. Covered by a sheet, with only her head showing, she lay on her back in an odd position; her knees appearing to be bent outwards. Josephine frowned at what she feared might lie beneath the sheet. All the other corpses were as one would expect: toes turned up, tenting the covering sheet. A shiver ran through her – not the stark chill of the mortuary, but someone 'walking over her grave'. This could be Liliana or herself, a young woman who might have had another forty years of her life left.

Panic whirled in her chest, then anger. This was the second time in only weeks that she had stood and looked down at a young woman dead. 'Jane' and Harriet, dead because they were women. Dead because they were poor. Dead because nobody really cared enough to make changes. Better-off people would lose their servants and skivvies. Quite unexpectedly she found herself in tears. Sadness and frustration. Waste, loss, of women . . . children like little Micky 'Smiff'. She and her friends might talk the hind leg off a donkey about the conditions of the London poor, but what good did that do? They were talking to the converted.

A conversation that had happened only recently came back to her. Some of them had gathered round her kitchen table, drinking soup and airing their views and agreeing that 'The problem of "The London Poor" is holding back progress.'

'Of course something must be done.'

'But the very fact that even *we* can refer to "the London poor" is part of the problem. They are not "the" anything. They are individuals.'

David Wilde had said that. And he was right. Harriet was a pretty woman who could sing. She had talent, but not enough to give her a living. And so, being a woman, she had taken a man to her room.

That man had been so depraved and arrogant that he had not thought of her as a human being at all, but as a thing, a device to use to gratify his lust. Suddenly she understood what the strange angle of Harriet's legs indicated, and felt hot with guilt and shame.

How was it that a rather serious-looking young woman was able to contemplate depravity, or to consider lust? How could she understand the significance of the position of Harriet Burton's knees? The answer lay in the part that Hani had played in Jo's life long before they came to live in England, where girls and women were unenlightened about their own nature; where ignorance was considered to be innocence, and it was felt that unmarried girls should be kept that way.

But, perhaps in the whole of London, Josephine was unique: a young woman, raised in high society and not in the stews, who knew that men and women copulated, and did not think that a cab-horse with its organ engorged was losing its entrails. When the girl Hani had been taken in as nursery help by Josephine's mother (who had expected to give birth to one baby and got twins), Hani was well prepared for her future as a married woman, which, although at the time she had not reached puberty and thus bride age, was not distant. But, poor Ann Martha when she discovered the uncomfortable truth, who can imagine the problems she faced at the time? There was such a wide gulf between what was expected to be known by girls and women and what – in their case – must be forgotten. But as happened when Pandora opened her box, once knowledge is out, it cannot be put away, though years passed before Ann Martha could assure herself that Hani and Josephine were not damaged in any way by the extent of their knowledge.

Just a short time ago Jo had been shouting at her editor because he had omitted to give her credit for reporting this woman's murder. Like all the other news vultures, she had wanted her pound of Harriet's flesh with her own name upon it.

She said silently what she would have wished to say aloud. I am so sorry, Harriet. Truly, sorry to have used you. But I promise, no matter what comes to light during the police investigation, I will discover the rest of you. Not Harriet the singer who was killed on Christmas Eve, but Harriet the young woman who had family, friends, had a childhood, had dreams. When they are picking over the unclean parts of your life, I shall look for the rest.

Superintendent Thomson went into his study and closed the door. Ann, he knew, had been disappointed at his absence at both Christmas Day lunch and dinner, and her forbearance was, as he so often found it to be, unbearable. Had she discharged her feelings in some normal display of feminine emotion, the domestic atmosphere would have soon cleared; as it was, her reasonableness pushed him further into withdrawal. The truth was, as he knew only too well, he withdrew because he felt culpable. It was true that one Bow Street detective had been on duty but had been taken home with a high fever, so had been unable to undertake the enquiries at Great Coram Street, but it would have been no great difficulty for James to have handed over to another inspector. The truth was, though, that James liked being at the centre of an investigation. It was what he was trained to do, it was what he was very good at doing, and what he liked to do. A good murder enquiry depended upon efficient organization. He was an organizer. Recently he had successfully organized the amalgamation of the 'F' and 'E' divisions at a saving of £1,000 per annum. But the satisfaction of having achieved this did not compare with the stimulation he experienced in organizing a murder investigation.

He finished the writing he had come to do and crossed to the window. A winter garden. Spare elegant skeletons and white trunks of silver birches, a small border of the newest shades of species azalea, beneath which bloomed the snow-white heads of the Christmas hellebore, and the yellow jasmine, which he liked so much for its colour and perfume that reminded him of the sun. He loved the sun. He had been born and raised with sun overhead for months on end. In six months, if there was a favourable late spring, he and Ann would be sitting on the stone terrace taking tea on Sunday afternoons, or cold lemonade of a morning. And later, in July and August, there would be small gatherings of friends listening to piano-playing and enjoying the last of the sun before a light supper. In no way approaching his mother's salons, but pleasurable. Very pleasurable.

But not today. Today, he saw neither bird-bath nor brilliant firethorn berries. That scene was obliterated by another. A cluttered bedroom, discarded clothing scattered around, scent bottles and powder boxes, bits and pieces of cheap jewellery. He saw the counterpane and the hair jumbled upon the pillow, the closed eyes, the peaceful expression. He felt in his jacket pocket for his rosary, but was hardly conscious of the thanks he gave for that look of peace. What if it had been horror? Or terror? He had seen that often enough on the face of a murder victim.

A flight of sparrows busily pecking crumbs caught his attention for a moment, but they soon dissolved into the image of a rosary in a small porcelain bowl. Did its separateness indicate that it was special? Perhaps above all he wanted to know this. Did the rosary merely happen to find a home in the bowl, or had the girl placed it there?

Turning away from the window, he made a decision that he would continue to act as senior officer in this case. He had done good work since he had been in 'E' division, but had been too long involved in matters of administration. Having straightened his desk, he went to find Ann to tell her not to wait any meals for him, that he would be perfectly content with a plate of something cold.

The doors of the Alhambra Palace were ajar, although the bars were not yet open. On the list of attractions the name 'Clara Burton' still appeared. Here was a place that Josephine had often wanted to see, but for an unaccompanied woman to enter was to be misconstrued. A youth pushing a broom stepped in front of her. ''ello, sweetheart. Can I do anythink for you?'

In her London street-voice she said, 'I want to talk to somebody who works in the bar here.'

'Depends on which side of the bar you mean. The girls who works this side won't be here till the first show starts.' He grinned. 'If you're looking for that sort of work, you're a bit early in the day.'

'Are there any barmaids here yet?'

'Alice and Tryphena, but I haven't seen Alice yet.'

She followed him through the dimly lit interior of the famous music hall. The stage with its curtains drawn aside was a dark cavern. It must be wonderful to step onto it, into the limelight, and to have the ability to entertain an audience. She paused, trying to visualize Harriet doing that and to see her walking amongst the tables until a man stopped her. Was that how it was done?

'Are you coming, miss? I ain't got all day. You there, Tryphena?'

Just one lamp was burning behind the bar. A young woman appeared from behind a display of exotic drinks. 'What do you want, Billy?'

'A girl here wants you.'

Josephine engaged Tryphena's eyes. She was a striking-looking young woman who held her back straight so that her bosom was high in a close-bodiced frock of dark green. Over that she wore a waiter's long white apron tied snugly around her neat waist. Josephine held out her hand, which Tryphena shook firmly. 'I won't keep you long, Miss . . . ?'

'Douglas. All right, Billy, I'm quite able to talk to somebody without your ears flapping.' Billy went off, whistling shrilly. 'I haven't got a lot of time.'

Harriet or Clara? Clara or Harriet? If she chose wrongly she wouldn't engage the trust of this woman. 'I've just come from seeing Harriet.'

The barmaid clenched her fists and tightened her lips. 'Are you trying to have me on?'

She had chosen the right name. Tryphena obviously knew Harriet under her own name, and not just as one of the acts. 'No, no, I mean that I've just come from the mortuary. She looks very peaceful, and I wanted to talk to somebody who probably knew her.'

'My God! How could you do that? I shouldn't want to look at a cadaver.'

'I wasn't looking at a cadaver. I was looking at Harriet Burton and feeling angry at what had been done to her. If you saw her, wouldn't you feel like that?'

Tryphena Douglas's intelligent eyes engaged Josephine's,

143

and she nodded thoughtfully. 'I can feel like that without the need to look at her corpse. I could do with a drink. Do you want one?'

This reception was better than Josephine could have hoped for. 'Thanks, but nothing that's going to make me too tipsy. I've got a lot of work to do.'

'Gin and pep?'

'Thanks.' Whatever that might be. Experiences were tumbling over her. Even as she waited for Tryphena to mix the watery-looking drinks, Josephine was filled with certainty that her plan to write a book about Harriet's life could be done. The ease with which she was able to gain entrance to Harriet's place of work, and probably much of her life, and now her acceptance by the barmaid, gave her confidence. Tryphena took the drinks to a small table, whilst Josephine uprighted the two chairs cleaners had placed on it. 'Take the weight off of your feet for five minutes – it's all I can spare.'

'Busy day?'

'Every day's a busy day here.' She lifted the drink to her lips and took a small sip.

Josephine, not knowing how gin and pep might taste, did the same. It was a surprisingly pleasant drink, probably easy to get to like for the sweet peppermint stinging its way over the tongue. 'Look, Miss Douglas – may I call you Tryphena? My name's Josephine, but I get called Josie.' Tryphena nodded, and Josephine continued with what she hoped would appear open and honest, which it was. 'As I told you, I went to see Harriet this morning, not because I knew her, I didn't, but because I was so

144

shaken up by what happened to her I wanted to write a book about her life.'

'A book? What d'you mean? A book that would go into libraries and shops and that?' Josephine nodded. 'Who'd want to read a book about poor girls. You might just as well write about my life – fat lot of interest to anybody there.'

'It would interest me.'

'Of course it would.'

'Do you reckon, then, that if you were My Lady Tryphena that your life-story would be more interesting than this?'

'It's got to be.'

'My Lady Tryphena gets up, chooses what to wear, dresses, goes out, comes back, changes her dress, goes out again to another house just like her own, talks about the same things over and over again, comes back, changes her dress, eats her dinner, goes to bed. End of story. Don't tell me that Lady Tryphena's life is more interesting than yours. Ladies like that get so bored.'

'Easy life, though.'

'You think boring is easy. I tell you, I've seen quite a bit of it. I wouldn't have that life for anything. Behind your bar, you see hundreds of people every day, some of them very strange, I'll be bound. Things change every day, you . . . well, you do things like this. My Lady could never go home at the end of the day and say, "D'you know what? I had this mad woman come to see me today, and she thinks my life would be more interesting to people who read books than the lives of the gentry".'

Josephine had her hooked. Had she wanted, she could have taken Mr Hood two thousand words that would be perfect for a Jemima Ferguson piece. But, no, this project was infinitely more serious than a couple of column inches.

'What do you want to know?'

'About Harriet, about you, how she lived, what goes on here. I know that she was Clara Burton the singer, but I also know that she took a man home with her that night, and he killed her. Now, I can do nothing about that, but I can string words together so that people want to read what I write, and I want people to read it who know nothing of how a young woman like Harriet manages to keep going. She took a madman to her room, and he killed her. All those "My Ladies" who you think have stories worth telling, are kept women, but not in the kind of danger that the women who are picked up here must be.'

'Well, that's different.'

'What's different about it?'

'Husbands. If I had one, I'd be out of here like a shot from a gun.'

'Of course you would, but you'd still be a kept woman.'

'I'd earn my keep by cooking and cleaning.'

'And taking him to bed?'

'Of course.'

'But at the moment you are independent, like me.'

146

'How do you earn your keep then?'

That was the trouble with half-truths, one half could catch you out. 'I work in an office.'

'I often think I would have liked to do that. Another gin and pep?'

'Not now, but I would like to come back again, if you don't mind.'

'Why don't you come when we're open? It's always nice to have somebody to talk to when things are a bit slow.'

Coming here when the place was open was exactly what Josephine needed to start her research into Harriet's life.

'Come back early evening, you can stand at the end of the bar, and I'll talk to you when I can.'

'That's really nice. Why? I mean, why are you willing to help me?'

'I don't know, really. Probably what you said about toffs not knowing about what goes on. The men do, of course. A lot of the men who come here to pick up girls are toffs, lawyers, doctors, all that sort.' She grinned and downed the last of her drink. 'I shouldn't mind people knowing about that. They'd pay a girl to open her drawers, but give her a proper job in an office? Not in a million years.'

'Would Harriet's man have been a toff, do you think?'

'No, average. Mean with his money.'

Josephine chilled and, trying to keep the shock out of her voice because Tryphena appeared to be so nonchalant, asked, 'So you saw him, the man she took home?'

'Oh yes, he was in here some time. Had a drink, smoked a cigar, taking his time about who would get the privilege of him. That's what I thought, anyhow; thought a lot of himself.'

'What happened, do you think, to make him settle on Harriet?'

'Don't rightly know. I did see him watching her change from her old street boots to the little slippers she wears when she goes on stage.'

'Did she go on stage on Christmas Eve?'

'I can't say as I remember. I've seen her perform so many times . . . but I think she did a turn.'

'But you remember that he was watching her change into her slippers?'

'I have to say, the thought passed through my mind that he might have thought she would be cheap, her boots being so down-at-heel. Probably thought she was really down on her luck, which she was. He was a real mean sort. You quite often get them. Come in here, buy one drink, watch the girls parading, never buying them nor anybody a drop of anything, and then clear off back home to give their wives what for. Anyway, I was wrong about him.'

'Did he buy her a drink?'

'I think he did, but it was so busy, it being Christmas.'

'But you saw him throughout the evening.'

'Pretty much . . . you know, off and on.'

'What about when he left?'

'She, Harriet, asked for her boots which was under my bar, and put them on, just about here where we're sitting now. She was taking her time, I reckon he was anxious to get going. I said as much to her, and she just winked at me. "Oh, let him wait." She was like that with men. She was really nice, though. Never moaned, and if she was flush she'd always say, "And one for yourself, Tryphena." A really nice sort.'

'And then they left?'

'They did. She often takes a glass of something before she leaves.'

'And did she?'

'No. "Sorry, Tryphena," she said, "but I'm going to get handsome there to buy me a few at the Cavour."'

'The Cavour?'

'Restaurant. Just here in the Haymarket. It was Harriet's favourite place when she got somebody to foot the bill.'

'And was he handsome?'

'Depends on what you fancy.'

'And you didn't.'

'I don't like foreigners, and I don't like mean men, and he was both.'

'Suppose he comes back? He must know that you would recognize him.'

'Me and half a dozen more. He won't come back. One thing I'm sure of. The police will be round here soon, so he won't risk coming here once they get his description.'

Josephine was again astonished at her nonchalant attitude. 'I'd better not keep you any longer. You've been really helpful.' She put a florin down on the table. 'Will that be enough?'

149

'More than enough. Thanks, Josephine. And you'll come back?'

'Oh yes, I want to be here about the time Harriet would have come.'

'See you this evening then. And thanks for the drink.'

Billy came clomping in. 'Police is here. I told you they would.'

'Well, it's obvious that they would.'

'Oh, Lord. Is there another way out of here?'

Tryphena grinned. 'Not keen on the blue-bottles then? This way. Lets you out onto the unloading yard.'

'Don't say anything about me.'

'Why would I do that? Now get going.'

As Josephine went through a door behind the bar, she heard the clomping of feet and a voice she recognized well.

There wasn't much information that Sergeant Kerley obtained from Tryphena Douglas which Josephine did not have.

Tryphena and her sister Alice had travelled home on the same omnibus as Harriet Burton and the foreigner. He had looked very sour-faced. He had objected to having to pay for her ticket as well as his own. It was very late. The last bus to Coram Fields that day.

'Would you recognize him again?'

'No trouble, Sergeant. I'd pick him out of a hundred men if you asked me.'

She gave him a signed statement.

Frank Kerley left feeling immensely satisfied that he

had found such a witness. Miss Douglas would be excellent giving evidence.

All they had to do now was to find a foreigner and put him in an identification parade.

How many foreigners were there in London? Whittle it down to young men. Whittle again to men with the spots on their face that several witnesses had mentioned. But at least they now had several positive descriptions of the man seen with the victim late on Christmas Eve. Here at the Alhambra Palace, on the omnibus, buying fruit from a coster-barrow, and going upstairs in number 12 Great Coram Street.

Even for an officer with a rank as high as Superintendent Thomson's, there were few comforts in Bow Street Police Station, but the room in which he worked did have a blazing fire, and a constable did bring in tea and biscuits. Frank Kerley appreciated both as he sat with his superior and informally reported his findings.

He had come to the end of what he had to say and waited respectfully for the super to comment. Thomson supped tea and gazed inwardly, his eyes no longer moving as they had when taking in the surprising amount of Kerley's findings. At last he said, 'The victim went to the West End, performed on stage at the Alhambra Palace. She was seen leaving from there with a man fitting a similar description to that given by the costermonger . . . ?'

'Flack.'

'Yes, Flack, and very similar to the man seen by the Wrights.'

'We have three good witnesses there, especially Douglas, who had him in her sight for a great part of the evening, and then again on the late omnibus.'

'Has the driver been questioned?'

'Even as we speak, sir.'

'Now that we have a good description and his movements on that evening, I have secured permission to offer a reward.'

'That spells a great number of extra working hours. Rewards always do – brings every trickster and hopeful claiming to have seen something.'

The super smiled wryly. 'Especially if one hundred pounds is offered.'

'A hundred!'

'The man was brazen, Sergeant. If he is not apprehended very soon, he will come to believe that he is invulnerable.'

Frank Kerley nodded. 'And then who knows who his next victim might be. Perhaps a woman more respectable than Harriet Burton.'

As she opened the door to her rooms, the evocative smell of oil paint and turpentine drifted up her nose.

'Jo? Is that you?'

'It had better be or someone else has a key.'

Liliana Wilde, in a large white cook's apron, offered her cheek. 'I thought I'd try some little cakes. Madeleines. They are very French. I learned how to concoct them from a real patisserie-maker.' Liliana appeared as frail as Josephine did robust. This apparent frailty was brought about because her complexion, pale and smooth as alabaster, was framed by a wildness of flaxen curls that neither she nor any nursery maid had ever been able to control. In any gathering of women, Liliana Wilde was outstandingly beautiful. She cared very little for her appearance but, as Josephine had said, she had no need to. Her appearance cared for itself; there was little that could be done to make her an unattractive woman.

In looks they were in some ways similar, although Josephine's hair was a darker shade of blonde and not so spectacularly out of control as Liliana's. They were also similar in being above-average in height for women.

Josephine threw down her bags, unlaced her boots and followed Liliana into the tiny kitchen. 'And what were you doing that a cake-maker would give you lessons?'

'Making a drawing of him. Such a head! He must have a hundred jowls down to his shoulders, an enormous drooping moustache, and the wickedest eyes you ever saw. I have plans to make him the centre of an exhibition I have arranged with the Soho Gallery for this summer.'

'My, you have been busy.'

'Café?' Assuming that Josephine would always drink coffee made in the French way, in an enamelled pot, Liliana poured two breakfast-cupsful. 'There! They aren't a perfect shape, but they are good.'

Josephine ate one cake in two bites. 'Very good. I hope you have made dozens.'

'They are supposed to be a dainty delicacy.'

'But I am so hungry. I haven't found time to eat

anything except a pie from a pieman, and I had to eat that in a church doorway.'

'How did your piece on "Jane" go? I thought it exceptional. Did the great Mr Hood like it?'

'Don't mention his name to me.'

Liliana opened her very large, very long-lashed eyes wide, 'Oh?'

'I have resigned from *The News*.'

'For heaven's sake, Jo, did the man take liberties?'

'Had it been that, I could have slapped his face. Worse than that, Lili, I got the best story ever, before any of the opposition – I'm sorry, I absolutely must have another cake. Christmas Eve, a man picks up a girl from the Alhambra, wines and dines her. She takes him back to her room, he slits her throat and walks off early Christmas morning. I scooped up the story first.'

'Why, Jo, that's splendid. Not a resigning matter – go on take another, they are pretty scrumptious, and I can easily make more – yet you resigned.'

'Hood went back on his word to put my name on the piece. It was front page, but no byline, just by "A *News* Crime Reporter".' Eating with 'mmm's of appreciation, she related the duplicity of her editor and the unfairness heaped upon women who were in general more talented than men. 'I was so furious, I just walked out. After he had promised.'

'Oh, Jo, I am so sorry. Well, they are the losers.'

'He says that he is a forward-thinking man. Oh yes! Going to take more women on the staff . . . that kind of thing, big innovator, going to turn Fleet Street upside down.'

'Why do you think he reneged?'

'The shire MPs and bishops and police commissioners? I don't know ... I only know that, between when I handed in my story and its publication, he had taken my name out.'

'And we do like fame, don't we, me and you?'

'Nothing wrong with that. Power can go with fame. *That's* what I want most of all. I want to dictate terms. I want to show everyone that women are every bit as good as men, in *everything*. It is true, Lili, throughout history there is not a single profession in which at some time a woman hasn't excelled or surpassed males, and yet look at us!'

'We have been over this so many times, haven't we?'

'I know, I know – our problem is our wombs.'

'Of course. Wombs tell us to have babies. And we do. We create an amazing painting, and a child comes along and takes over any talent we might have.'

'Not you, I hope.'

'No, not me. I don't take notice of my womb. If it tries to make me notice it, and I have a lovely young man to hand, I send him away, and paint until it all settles down again. I expect it will get me in the end. I took to a kitten in Paris, but that didn't work, it just grew into a disgusting tom-cat and went off. I don't know where, and I don't care.'

Josephine just smiled. Liliana could always be relied upon to be entertaining on the subject of herself and her work. She was a very good artist; Josephine hoped one day to have one of her paintings on her bedroom wall, but Lili needed to get the highest price possible, so an L. Wilde painting was beyond her means at present. And possibly for some time to come.

'What will you do?'

'I have decided to write a book based on the life of Harriet Burton.'

'And what is she famous for?'

'For being young and pretty and dead. The murdered girl.'

'Can you do this? You have always said that you couldn't do it.'

'Because I never felt that I had a story to tell. But this, Lili . . . Harriet has got beneath my skin, and I shall not be able to leave it alone until I have discovered the story of her life.'

'It sounds to me as though you are becoming as absorbed with this person as you were with "Jane". Why these two? You have written about any number of incidents.'

'I looked at Harriet and "Jane" when they had been killed.'

'"Jane" wasn't killed.'

'Of course she was killed. She had no means to help her survive, and *we* were not willing to give it.'

'There are charities; I wonder why she didn't ask for help instead of starving to death?'

'Charities for women and children expect appeals to come from people without pride – ha! – and in my

156

"Jane's" case not to sound like an educated woman. That is wrong. No one should be without food and shelter.' She crammed a whole cake into her mouth and spoke through it with a lack of eating manners that Ann Martha would have despaired of. 'Oh, Lili, it makes me so angry!' She bit another dainty cone in half. 'This is the wealthiest city, in the richest country in the world, and women are dying needlessly.'

'And men and boys?'

'Yes, little boys too.' Josephine's face lightened as she remembered. 'On Christmas Eve, I met a little street urchin, trying to be a real passenger-help at my omnibus stop. He was tiny. Micky "Smiff", as he called himself. I gave him my muff to wear as a hat.'

'He's probably sold it by now . . . but you did a good thing there, Jo.'

'You are such a cynic.'

'Some of us have to be if they happen to be close to people like you and my brother. Have you been to any of his "rantings" since I have been away?'

'Yes. He doesn't rant, he speaks in a language ordinary mortals like me can understand. I let him see my piece about "Jane" before I handed it in.'

'And?'

'He complimented me on its sincerity.'

'He's very keen on sincerity, is David.'

'Isn't it about time that you stopped taking pot shots at him? Maybe you and your family had plans to see another Wilde as a great barrister. But David's who he is, and you should be proud of him.'

157

'You can do that, and I'll keep taking pot shots. Tell me more about the woman whose life you intend making into a book? Why this particular woman?'

'Like "Jane", you could say that she presented herself to me. On Christmas morning, I overheard my Uncle James's constable giving an address to the cabby taking him to the scene of a murder. So I went there. And I discovered that a young woman had been murdered. Later I discovered that she was Harriet Burton, a singer, known at the Alhambra as Clara, and that Clara was a heroine to some scullery maids who were saving up money to go to watch her perform.'

'That's so sad.'

'After that, I went to see her. At the mortuary. She was just a woman about our age, like you and me, except that she could neither write nor paint. But she could sing. All that she had was her voice and her body. Can you imagine how that must feel? Instead of getting recompense for doing something interesting, to have to wait until some man chooses you, and to have to take him home and let him do whatever he wishes.'

Liliana ruffled Josephine's hair. 'I do like being your lodger. Life here is never dull.'

'Tell me that when we get home tonight.'

'Where are we going?'

'I'm meeting someone at the Alhambra Palace, and it would be better if you came with me.'

James Thomson's team of investigating officers spread out through the heart of London, from Piccadilly and the Haymarket, and along the omnibus route from there to the Coram Fields area. The superintendent's tried-and-tested method was well-conducted police routine. Frank Kerley presented a report early enough in the day for James Thomson to order reward notices to be placed in newspapers.

'Sit down for a moment, Sergeant. I'll read your report later,' Thomson said, placing a hand on the sergeant's page of fine and clear handwriting, which was very different from his own heavy and, he had to admit, florid hand. 'Tell me.' Most of the investigating officers would have to face the super like this. On the page of a report, there were no inflections in speech, no hand movements, no facial expressions. 'Tell me.'

'Well, sir, if we ever get to putting witnesses on the stand, the barmaid at the Alhambra will be superb. She speaks well, is very clear in what she says she saw, and is a likeable personality.'

As ever, when he entered the gaudy portals of the Alhambra Palace, Frank Kerley felt the mixed emotions of guilt and elation. It was scarcely fair that the pleasant emotion that lifted his spirits and over which he had no control was spoiled by the other, which was equally out of his hands. A married policeman had no business feeling enjoyment at being in a place of low life and tastelessness. Yet, on the occasion when he had taken the trouble to analyse the nature of his relish for this particular theatre, he saw that it was perfectly reasonable to be reminded of days when he was a youth and had first ventured into a music hall. Gilding, plaster mouldings and heavy textiles, gold leaf and the smell of smoke and beer and brass polish, and, over it all, stale perfume. If it wasn't pleasant, it was certainly evocative. Not that he ever yearned for those days after he had met Elizabeth.

In some ways Miss Tryphena Douglas was typical of the kind of young women often found serving behind the bar of a music hall, in that she had an easy manner and was pretty and curled and smiling. She was, however, he soon discovered, well spoken and intelligent.

She was also, and this pleased him, elegant in her figure and restrained in her dress. So many of the girls in this line of work sought to catch the eye with necklines so low that one expected at any moment to discover a bare bosom escaping, which of course was their purpose, for no gentleman will count his change when this prospect presents itself. Tryphena, though, drew the eye more by a line of many neat buttons running from abdomen to neck of a bodice that covered her finely shaped bosom like a skin. A bosom such as Elizabeth had possessed – still did possess. She did not, as did so many fashionable women, ape the queen by wearing unnecessary black and jet. Women were best suited to colour. Well, that was Frank Kerley's opinion, which he omitted in the telling of his interview with the barmaid.

'Who is next on the list of possible witnesses?'

'Flack, the costermonger.'

'I can do that, Sergeant. By the bye, now that we have so many witnesses testifying to his possibly being German, I have ordered handbills to be printed giving notice of the reward, and showing the artist's impression of the suspect. There is always a chance that he may try to slip out of the country, so a printed letter from me, together with the handbill, will be sent out by tomorrow to police in Germany, France, Belgium, and to all the Channel ports.'

Frank Kerley knew the super would have translated the notice into the relevant languages, and was certain that the grammar in each of the letters would be impeccable. Anyone who could speak another tongue got Kerley's admiration, and the super spoke many.

After much discussion about what would be appropriate to wear, Josephine and Liliana set off by omnibus to the Haymarket. They had piled up one another's fair, curly hair into fetching topknots, attached long earrings to their lobes, and chose the only pretty hats they had that matched their bustly skirts.

'What shall we do if we get picked up, Jo?'

'Say that we are meeting someone. Though, of course, I wouldn't impose that on you, Lili, should you find some nice young man who takes your fancy! But I suppose we shouldn't make jokes. Harriet got herself all dolled up like this, and it wasn't for fun.'

'Oh, I know that, Jo. Just because we have a bit of banter doesn't mean that we are insensitive. I think that you are more apprehensive than I am.'

The two young women alighted from the 'bus and joined people who were pouring into the music hall. Since Josephine's earlier visit, the Alhambra had been transformed by light and colour. A band was playing lively music, accompanying the display of a group of contortionists dressed in glittering spangles, each spectacular climax being accompanied by a drum roll, a clash of cymbals and cheers from the noisy audience.

'I say, Jo, this beats baking cakes. I've been to halls in Paris, but never in London.'

Tryphena Douglas beckoned them to the end of the bar. 'Ladies, what can I get you?'

'This is my friend, Liliana. I think she should try your recommendation, gin and pep.'

Liliana spoke up, 'Have you absinthe?'

Tryphena raised her eyebrows. 'I have, but not many asks for it. Rots your socks, I'm told.'

Liliana laughed. 'I know, and I drink it with due respect.'

'Liliana spends quite a lot of time in Paris.'

Tryphena leaned across the counter, full of interest. 'Is it as bad a city as they say?'

'Worse. But not as bad as London.'

Josephine refused absolutely to take absinthe, but paid for Liliana's and her own gin and pep and one for Tryphena. Whenever she was offered a drink, the barmaid always chose something clear that would take peppermint, so that she could drink with customers but not actually become affected by alcohol. This showed a nice little profit for herself.

The two friends placed themselves at the far end of the bar where they could watch the passing scene, and to where the barmaid could return to sip her drink in between serving.

'You two look like sisters.'

'People have said that. Liliana's an artist.'

'Do you sing or recite or what?'

'She paints pictures.'

'And people buy them?'

'Some people, but others wouldn't have them to line a garden shed.'

'She paints light.'

'How do you do that? Could you paint the lights in here?'

Although the barmaid was not familiar with the term 'painting light', Liliana looked around at the gilding, and at the etched glass and mirrors reflecting numerous gaslamps: light as Tryphena saw it. Liliana's eyes sharpened with interest.

'I'd like to try. That huge mirror behind you, and the sparkling glass of the bottles and glasses; there are so many different kinds of light in just this one area.'

'I expect they wouldn't mind if you came when the place was empty.'

'But the light wouldn't be here then.'

Tryphena nodded in sombre agreement. 'I might be able to get you in.'

'Oh could you? Will you try?'

'Lili, just think, if you could do some pictures to complement my book.'

'Oh, Jo, it's not really my style, too figurative.'

'But think what you'd be doing: a picture is always worth a thousand words, isn't it? People would see your paintings and read my book.'

'That is David's territory – ranting, reform.'

The place was filling up now, and Josephine was concerned that she wouldn't get as much time from Tryphena as she would like.

'So, you and your sister went home on the same omnibus as Harriet?'

'We left here about a quarter-past midnight. It takes less than five minutes to get to Regent Circus, and we caught the last 'bus.'

'Is this where Harriet was waiting too?'

'That's right, we had to wait about five minutes for the omnibus. She was walking up and down, arm in arm with the man I told you about this morning. Well, the 'bus came and I got on with Alice, and Harriet and him followed right behind us and sat down.'

'Could you see them from where you were seated?'

'Oh yes, they took seats right opposite me and Alice . . . well, not exactly opposite me, Alice was opposite Harriet, I was in the first seat. Listen, let me go and get Alice, she can tell you.'

Alice Douglas was a slighter version of her sister. She too took a gin and pep.

'And the man?'

'He sat next to Harriet.'

'Which gave you a good view of him?'

'Oh yes, I could see him clear as I see you now.'

'Did you recognize any of the other passengers?'

Again she shook her head. 'Strangers to me, all of them.'

She broke off to serve a man porter, calling him Mr Pragnell and asking him if he was better of his cold. Having indicated that he might be once he had his porter, he took his drink away with the air of one who was familiar with the place and expected to take his usual seat.

'Please continue, tell me anything else about that journey. Anything at all.'

'Well, Tryphena was wide awake as she always is, but I was dog tired, and was leaning forward, drowsing. Harriet tapped me on the knee and asked if she could hold my parcel, as it seemed I was likely to let it fall. I said no. Then she asked if it was a turkey. I said no, but it was a goose, and we talked about a properly cooked goose being better any day than turkey.'

'Did the man take part in the conversation?'

'No. He never said a word. I asked her if she was doing anything for Christmas, and she said she thought she might go to the country next day with some friends. Then we talked about some occasions when we'd given the conductor the wrong money. I said I had once handed up a sovereign in mistake for a shilling, and Harriet said she once paid a Strand conductor ten shillings in gold for a sixpenny fare and the conductor was a bit off with her. It was only chit-chat, like you do on the 'bus.'

Alice went off for a few minutes serving quickly, bantering with girls and men, some of whom hung around close to the bar, others who took their drinks to the small tables. She came back and addressed Josephine. 'Tryphena said you was going to write a book. Does that mean that we might be in it?'

'Would you mind?'

'Depends.'

'If I get the book written, I will come back and talk to you to check that you agree with what I've had to say.'

'All right then. I'll have to go back to my own bar soon, but I'll tell you up to when I got off. I began to nod off again, and I dropped the goose. I looked across at Harriet, and she looked at the man, but he wasn't acting the gentleman, leaving it to Harriet to hand it to me. I think it was somewhere about the Tottenham Court Road area when Harriet nudges the man and said something. I didn't hear what he said, but I heard her say "sixpence". He gave her a black look, but dug into his trousers pocket and found a coin.'

'What was it the man said?'

'I never heard, leastways, I never took notice. I can't say I was very interested.' She smiled, 'He couldn't have been the sort I find attractive, else I might have.'

Tryphena came back. 'Maggie's just come on duty, so you're all right for a couple of minutes.'

'Thanks, 'Phe. So, there was people getting off at the different stops, everybody saying "Merry Christmas" and all that. Next day, it was all over everywhere that one of the Haymarket girls had got herself murdered. I couldn't hardly believe that it was Harriet. We'd only been with her a few hours before. It was a real shock to us, wasn't it, 'Phe?'

Tryphena Douglas acknowledged that it was. 'It makes you see how easy it is to get yourself killed. I can't say that I've ever thought of it happening to us, but there's plenty you hear of getting robbed and even worse. It's why Alice and me always try to work the same shifts.'

'Aren't there always policemen about at that time of night?'

'Oh yes, plenty,' Alice said, 'but no chap's going to try to rape you with the beat copper looking on. It's in the dark and lonely places, alleyways and such, that they'll get you. A lot of places like that between here and Islington. I'm not complaining about the police, they can't be everywhere at once, so girls who work late have to take their own precautions.'

'Except,' said Tryphena, 'a girl who makes a living picking up men don't have that choice. They have to keep away from the regular coppers' beats. No sort of precautions you could take against a monster with a knife in his pocket.' She wagged her head and frowned, sincerely disturbed at the dreadfulness of it all. 'I still can't hardly credit it. She wasn't the type to play up, in all the time she's been coming in here, I never knew her to have so much as a bruise or a black eye.'

'Is there much of that: women being hit?'

Alice gave her sister a wry smile. Josephine said crossly, 'You'll have to forgive my innocence, Miss Douglas. I can't help it that I don't know what goes on in a world that is strange to me, but I must learn as much as I can if I am to get truth into what I write about it. So tell me, then I shall not ask questions that make you smile.'

Tryphena answered. 'There's some that practically asks to get knocked about, they lead a man on so just to get maybe a glass of spirit. But Harriet? Never! She was the sort of girl people took to. A nice, friendly sort.'

'You liked her.'

'Well, I didn't really *know* her, it's too busy in here to do more than pass the time of day, but I reckon if I had a got to know her better, I could say "yes", she was the sort of girl I would like.'

Liliana asked, 'When you saw her that night, was she alone?'

'Yes, she came but joined three other girls.'

'Do girls often go about together?'

'Some do, but you got to realize, it being Christmas Eve, people were cheered up with each other, going about arm in arm. Usually she wasn't one to drink much: just a stout, which she didn't drink quick.'

'And is that what she drank then?'

'No, she took an Irish whiskey, which one of the others paid for.'

'You have an excellent memory.'

'Well, you know how it is, you remember some things, others just pass you by, but I do remember her taking a whiskey. She was in here just about as it was beginning to fill up, but there was not so many as I was rushed, else I probably wouldn't remember what she nor anybody

168

else had. It was quite lively, as you'd imagine, being Christmas Eve.'

'What time would that be?'

She frowned. 'Hard to say. The only time I ever really notice is when it's close to closing time. But I do remember her asking me if I wouldn't be glad when I could put my feet up. This job's very hard on the feet. And I said that my toes was hurting after being on them for so many hours, so it was probably about tennish, I'd say.'

Once Josephine and Liliana had overcome any awkwardness about posing as bar-butterflies, they began to enjoy the experience, and when Tryphena and Alice Douglas became used to being close-questioned, they tried to anticipate what Josephine wanted to know, pointing out or calling over women who had been particular friends of Harriet.

'This is Madame Margaret.' Tryphena introduced a woman, probably in her thirties, notable for her red hair and ample bosom. She accepted a port and lemon.

'I've known Harriet since she first come to town. She was in the family way, by the coachman where she had been in service. I seem to remember it was in Finchley, or somewhere like that, I don't rightly recall, but I do recall that his name was Burton. That's why she took it, probably thinking he might do something about the baby. Ha! Wasn't she the innocent country girl? He soon cleared off.'

'What year would that be?' Liliana too was being drawn into wanting to know, not just about Harriet, but about these other women who were part of the daily life of the hall and its bar. Jo might be right . . . women of light and dark . . . something to think about.

'February Eighteen Sixty-four.'

'That's very precise.'

'It would be, because I was living in the same lodgings as her at the time. Pleasant Row, Islington. Not only that, it was me and Mrs Atkins – she was the landlady – and Harriet's sister who delivered the baby.'

'Harriet was a mother?'

'Has been for eight year now.'

'What was it, the baby?'

'A girl. Kathryn. I was hoping she might of named her after me, but she never. Nobody ever called her Kathryn, always Katy.'

'So Katy would be eight years old now.'

'Nearly nine.'

'She didn't live with her mother, though.'

'Not of recent time, but back then Harriet had a real bit of luck. There was this Major Brown who took to Harriet, and he set her up in lodgings in Blackfriars Road.'

'Did she have Katy with her?'

'Far as I know. Oh yes, thanks, I will have another. Kind of you, I'm sure.'

She got the second port and lemon under false pretences, because she really didn't have anything more to tell Josephine. 'The thing is we sort of drifted apart after she left Mrs Atkins's. We'd see each other from time to time, and we'd gossip for a bit – you know how it is, nothing much, only vague bits about where we was both living, how things were going and that.'

'Was she still at Blackfriars Road when you last met her?'

'Don't think so. The time when she was living with Major Brown, she didn't have to work, but I know she still kept pally with Patty Lydney and Eliza Cavendish. They might be able to tell you.'

Josephine thought that she was now getting somewhere. Names were tumbling out; real people were attached to those names. Katy, Major Brown, Patty, Eliza. 'Do they come here?'

'No, don't need to now. Patty always had her head screwed on the right way. She and Eliza got some decent rooms together, and they're very choosy who they let in.'

Liliana wrote down Patty's address as Madame Margaret gave it to her. Madame Margaret tapped the side of her nose. 'Don't ever get in no trouble with the police – very respectable is Patty and Eliza now. I don't envy them . . . well, I sort of do . . . what I mean is, good luck to them. They had the sense to put a bit aside while they were young.'

'Do they take in lodgers or run a brothel?' Liliana asked.

Madame Margaret looked offended and, picking up her port and lemon, stood up. 'I can't tell you nothing else.'

Liliana turned to Tryphena, 'What did I say to offend her?'

'You used the word that the police use. It's a bad word to the likes of Madame Margaret.'

'I'm sorry, I didn't realize. There are plenty of brothels close by where I live.'

Josephine said, 'London's not Paris, Lili.'

Tryphena said, 'I don't think you'll get any of the other girls to talk to you now. Best you leave. You could always try Patty. She would have had Harriet in her house, but for the little girl.'

As they made ready to leave, Josephine said, 'I hope that I can write this account.'

'You have to, Miss Ferguson, not one of us knows if it won't happen to us.'

Josephine felt slightly uncomfortable. She and Liliana were not 'us', not part of the world of the girls of the Alhambra.

'These girls – Harriet, and the ones you've been with this evening, like Madame Margaret . . . they didn't start out dreaming of a life picking up men and letting them do it for money. There's some that probably was born to girls who did, knowing better than any what was the score, but they wouldn't have said to themselves, "That's what I want to do, pay my way in some side street with any man who has the price of it." I'm sorry if you think I'm being coarse, but that's what goes on here, night in, night out, year in, year out. In the end they nearly all end up the same: drunk, babes, disease, beatings. Alice and me, we're all right, this is hard work and long hours, but it's a good position. Another one of our sisters is in service, and I wouldn't want her life, but worst of all is when a girl gets so desperate that she has to get on the old game . . .'.

Josephine nodded.

Tryphena drew her eyebrows together, 'You don't believe that, do you? You don't think you could find yourself so down on your luck that you didn't have anything left except your own self.'

'That's true, and I count myself lucky enough to have family.'

'You might not always have; they might chuck you out . . . I'm not saying they would, but things happen.'

'I am also fortunate enough to be good at stringing words together, interviewing people. I can write things down very fast . . . reporting, you know.'

'As long as you hadn't got your fingers broke or something like that. I'm not saying that you might be one to go down, what I'm saying is that a woman is always at risk of finding herself having nowhere to turn to, and, high or low, town or country, women has the mucky end of the stick.'

Jo and Lili were transfixed by Tryphena's earnestness. A feeling of inadequacy overcame Josephine. She was embarking on the writing of a book about the lives of women about whom she knew nothing.

'Look, Miss Ferguson, this is all new to you, and I have to say that I admire you for wanting to tell people who talk about "fallen women" what their life is like. If you tell Harriet's life, then you'll be telling the life of all of them.'

'I shall do my best. The last time you saw Harriet, where was she, what was she doing?'

'Getting fruit from George Flack's stall. She picked up a pineapple and put it back.'

'Where is this stall?'

'Coram's Fields. He'll be there now till after midnight, but if you want to ask him about Harriet, you'd best go daytime, to his shop in Brunswick Square.'

Ann Martha had to learn from a daily newspaper that the detective in charge of investigating the case of the woman found so horribly murdered on Christmas morning was her own husband. Skilled herself at making deductions from her observations where James was concerned, she had already suspected this from two days of early risings, late returnings from duty and the alacrity with which he dressed in the morning.

Something was exercising his mind and body, and from past experience she knew that nothing did this half so well as tracking a murderer. When Hani said, 'Mister Jame, must be catching killer again,' Ann Martha could only smile wryly. 'Mr James is not easy to live with when he has a murder case.'

'I know. I speak to him, ask him if I tell Cook to make salt biff for supper, he look up, and I am not there.'

'Oh, Hani, you know him well enough by now to know that he means no disrespect to you.'

'Of course I know. But how shall Cook know to make salt biff for supper?'

'If he makes any complaints, we can always tell him

174

that he chose it. He never knows differently when he's absorbed in his work. I know that this is a very puzzling crime. Mrs Henderson told me that James has requested the commissioner to allow a big reward to be offered, and that hundreds of handbills are being printed and distributed, and to foreign cities as well.'

'Is good that wife of commissioner is friend to you.'

'Absolutely. Mr Henderson must tell his wife everything that he does. Lord, Hani, can you imagine how dull their conversation must be?'

'I hear him now, MisAnn,' and she clip-clopped away to welcome James home, handing him his slippers.

Ann Martha followed. 'You spoil him, Hani. He should receive a reprimand for neglecting us so shamefully. You are looking pleased with yourself, James.'

'Apples! I got them from an excellent witness.'

Hani took the bag. 'These pretty apple, make nice arrangement. Not so nice for eating.'

A meal was quickly assembled for him, and the two of them sat together for the first time since Christmas.

'The daily papers are referring to "The Great Coram Street Murder".'

He didn't respond, but helped himself to plain boiled potatoes with butter, a dish he would eat with almost anything, hot or cold.

'You might as well say something about it. I have to hear from friends that you are sending out handbills all over the world.'

'A slight exaggeration.'

'James! You are so infuriating. Perhaps we could do

it this way. An actress (so called) was murdered on the night of Christmas Eve. On Christmas morning, very early, you are collected from outside the church by a constable with a waiting cab. You jump in and rush off. I perform my duties as hostess *alone* – about which I am not complaining because I knew about policemen long before we married. You realize that you missed seeing Josephine off.'

'I know. But I did see her in the early hours of Boxing Day morning. Did you know she likes to drink whisky?'

'I try to gain your attention by expensive perfume, Josephine by drinking whisky in your presence.'

'Annie, my dearest . . .'

'Be sensible, James.'

'I will try. Yes, I am in charge of the investigation into the murder of Harriet Burton. She is . . . was, not an actress "so-called", she was a young woman who went on stage and sang. She got very little in payment. She had pawned everything decent she had owned. She owed rent. So that she would not get turned out of her room – one room – she took a man home and made him pay a sovereign. Woman of the world as you are, you have no need of me to explain further.'

Ann Martha pushed her winter salad around with a fork, looking very contrite. James was a good man, a truly good man. 'I do give generously to several of the charities for fallen women, James.'

'I know, Ann, but you should realize that such women

are not fallen, they are usually pushed by poor circumstances and by men. I am not suggesting that you should not give, but to make a difference an Act of Parliament and a change of heart in the British people as a whole is necessary.'

He rose from the table, wiped his mouth on immaculate linen and went to fetch his coat. Hani, working in the inner hall on an arrangement on a dish of the red apples, holly and spotted laurel, said, 'You find this man, MisaJame.'

'I will, Hani, yes, I certainly will.'

Similarly, Elizabeth Kerley waited for her husband to tell her something. Unlike Ann Martha, however, Elizabeth knew better than to question Francis when he was obsessed by an investigation. This was not the first of its kind he had been involved in. Each killing of a girl cut him to the quick. It became almost personal because of his love for their daughter, Frances. Knowing his girl was living at home, healthy and well, Francis found it necessary to double his efforts to find the killer of another man's daughter and see him on his way to the gallows.

He ate quickly, picked up the bowl of scraps and went down to the chickens. After he had been gone for ten minutes, Elizabeth took a bag and followed the path down to the chicken coop.

'These oats have gone weevily, Francis, the birds will like them.'

He nodded and flung some handfuls into the run. 'Where's Frances?'

'In her room, looking through a new piece.'

'I didn't hear her.'

'She's just reading through the music at the moment.' Their daughter was a talented musician who, having done well with the violin, had decided to take up the flute, too. Until this investigation was over, both Elizabeth and Frances knew that he would have less to worry about if he knew that his wife and his daughter were safely together. It was something unspoken between the three of them.

'We are on to him.' He flung oats at the scrabbling hens.

'Good.'

'We know what he looks like, how he dresses, how he speaks – he's a German.'

'All that so soon.'

'Right. All we've got to do now is to find him and it's all plain sailing.'

'Have you got some good witnesses?'

'The very best. Articulate and firm about what they saw.' He threw oats, bag and all, which sent the hens squawking and fluttering. 'They are firm about his description because he was a cocky bugger, an arrogant bugger. Every time I take a statement, I see him. Young bloody German, strutting around London in his bloody felt hat, his velvet collar, his jacket, his short coat, and, for God's sake, even his short boots. I see him. He came prepared for what he did, I'm pretty sure of that. Her throat was cut with something as sharp as a razor or a surgeon's scalpel. This was no spur of the moment act of madness. Nobody just happens to have a scalpel in their pocket.'

Elizabeth held back on her usual, 'Language, language, Francis,' knowing from years of experience of her husband's passionate nature that, where some men possessing such dominating presence and strength become physically violent, in anger and in love-making Francis Kerley was vocal but gentle. He had investigated many violent murders, but occasionally one would touch him in a way that was personal. Usually because of violence done to a woman; why one in particular rather than another she never knew, only that he became obsessive and withdrawn until the perpetrator was arrested.

'Why was he so brazen?'

'He just didn't care. It's as though he's cocking a snook at us . . . not just us, at everybody who saw him with his victim that night.'

Elizabeth put one hand over his large one. He turned hers palm up and kissed it tenderly, both still watching the chickens peck the brown bag and eat it. Suddenly he laughed, and squeezed her shoulder. 'What daft creatures they are.'

Elizabeth stood close, enjoying the warmth of his large body, then said quietly, 'Francis . . . I don't think you are going to find him in London.'

After a few silent moments, Frank Kerley said, 'No, nor do I.'

To the ever-increasing collection of files in which were contained information pertaining to the death of 'Harriet

Burton, sometimes known as Clara Burton', was added a daily shower of claims to the £100 reward. Each piece of information had to be recorded and evaluated.

Frank Kerley knocked and entered. 'I could go through some of these with you, sir. Maybe weed out the absolute cranks.'

'Excellent, Sergeant. So far in the cranks pile I have foreigners of all kinds, from a Swiss travelling band to Chinese and black Africans.'

'And the problem is, as always, that being a crank doesn't necessarily rule out possible evidence.'

'Which is why I wouldn't trust anyone but you to help sort the good from the dross.'

'And there'll be an abundance of dross, sir.'

Frank Kerley seated himself on an upright wooden chair that looked as though it might not uphold his bulk for long. Even in the most senior police offices, the furniture was nothing more than rough and functional. Not much at all to do with the police was of quality.

Ever since he had achieved his senior position three years previously, James Thomson had fought for better uniforms and conditions for his men. Possibly to keep him quiet, he was asked to write a report, which he did with his usual straightforward honesty and fearlessness. 'The stations are prison-like: cheerless and akin to military barracks.' It was the lack of care for the men that most concerned him. 'The men are clothed and shod and clean, but wanting in "finish" – but perhaps I am fastidious. If our men are to be respected by the public they serve, then they must be elevated above the common labourer. If they are to have authority, then respect and care for their well-being must come first.'

'You were correct in your prediction, Sergeant. Some of these claims are obviously a chance to point a finger at a neighbour, or enemies settling old scores.'

However, one or two pieces of information looked as though they might lead somewhere.

There was a firm knock and a uniformed policeman entered. 'Inspector Cruse, sir, it's about the veterinary surgeon.'

'Come in, come in. My sergeant and I were trying to make some order here.' By way of explanation to Frank, James Thomson said, 'A man came into the station reporting a veterinary surgeon who lived at the same address as himself had disappeared overnight. Carry on, Inspector.'

'To paraphrase, sir. The man reporting was Mr Nurse, of Wrotham Road, Camden Town. There had been a veterinary surgeon, Mr Studdert, living at the same address, and on Christmas Eve he disappeared. Nurse also said that Studdert consorted with prostitutes, one of whom he believed was Harriet Burton. He referred to her as Clara Burton, the singer. I visited Nurse today and asked for a statement. He said that maybe he was mistaken, and that it might be another veterinary surgeon who knew the victim, and that Studdert might have gone to Ireland. I pressed him as to why he had reported Studdert's disappearance. He said that he had seen Studdert come home with blood on him, and that he, Studdert, had said that he had been to the Alhambra music hall and had got into a fight.'

Frank Kerley said, 'Sounds to me as though he realized that one hundred pounds wasn't so easily had, and he changed his tune a little.'

'More than a little, Sergeant. When I asked him if he was certain that this had been on Christmas Eve, he said that it might have been, but he couldn't be certain.'

'Did you get a statement, Inspector?' the superintendent asked.

Cruse replied, 'He declined to give a statement, or to give Studdert's address in Ireland, although I am certain that he knew it.'

James said, 'You should have charged him with wasting police time.'

'I still might, sir. However, I did think that a veterinary surgeon who disappears on the very day of the murder was a good prospect. After all, we are looking for a man who knows how to use a scalpel. So I went to the Veterinary College. They have no address in Ireland, but said that he would no doubt be in London at the end of the week as he has to attend college on Monday next.'

'Good work, Inspector, keep with it. Get in touch with Ireland. I wouldn't confuse an Irish accent for German, but who knows?'

And so the investigation went on and on, hour after hour, day after day, chasing sightings, following leads that went nowhere. It all had to be done, but it all ate into the men's time. They all worked extra hours, but there were times when a conclusion appeared hopeless.

182

James and his senior officers spent time keeping the men's morale high in spite of the pages and pages of reports they had to make.

Josephine's early attempts at making her way into the newspaper business had taken her to many parts of London that her life as an educated young lady would not. To Ann Martha and her close friends, the merchant and trading areas were another country, whose inhabitants spoke an idiosyncratic version of English that Josephine understood perfectly well.

She enjoyed buying from street vendors – flowers, fruit, pies, boiled sweets, muffins – and enjoyed going back to her rooms with purchases in paper bags or wrapped in newspaper. Once she had told Hani about some of her favourite foods, and how it reminded her of the street-vendors of her childhood, but Hani had been scornful. 'You are lady now; my mistress your mother never buys eating food in market. She teach me, "Many bad things on food, girl: flies, dirty fingers, disease. Wash hands, boil water, Hani, make food in own house."'

Her sharp retort had shocked Hani. 'A lot of good it did her! Perhaps if she had allowed market food into our house we might have got used to the bad things, and they wouldn't have died.'

'That fever came on winds.'

Josephine continued buying delectable cooked eels, hand-raised pies, and spicy bread-pudding slices. Liliana liked to experiment with cooking, mostly French dishes, but Josephine loved to collect an assortment of street foods and assemble them into a meal. As a consequence, she knew several street-vendors. She certainly knew George Flack, but not that he owned a shop.

She discovered George Flack's small, open-fronted Brunswick Square shop was only a little better than the covered stall in the Strand where he stood on Saturday mornings.

Flack was typical of his kind, quick witted and apparently good-humoured, though Josephine wondered whether a costermonger's constant good humour was a skill acquired to be a successful salesman. The cry, 'Apples a pound, pears', and double-meaning jokes about peach fuzz and feeling melons, never failed to raise a smile.

He recognized her at once. 'Hello, luv, what you doing down here? Bit out of your manor.'

'Hello, George, I've come down here specially to see you.'

Continuing to serve other customers, asking, weighing, bantering, he said, 'Nah, nah, I'm a respectable married man.'

'Oh dear, and I hoped that you'd give me a few minutes of your private time.'

Leaving the shop to his apprentices, he bowed exaggeratedly to his customers, 'Sorry, ladies, duty calls,' and conducted Josephine to a cubby-hole at the back of the shop.

They were obliged to stand to drink the sugar-loaded strong tea that Flack pressed upon Josephine. 'Nice cup of tea, George, just as I like it. I won't take up much of your time. It's about the singer who was murdered.' She related briefly her interest in Harriet.

'Mrs Brown. That's who she was when I first knew her, some years back now.'

Flack looked pleased at the interest he had aroused. 'Ah, so you didn't know she was sometimes known by that name. I've known her years: Harriet Buswell, Clara Burton, Harriet Burton and Mrs Brown. Same girl, told people she was an actress. She did turns in the halls.'

'When was the last time you saw her?'

'Early hours of Christmas morning, same time as she often comes to my Coram Fields stand.'

'To buy fruit?'

Flack winked, 'Not for nothink else. I ain't got that sort of luck.' The little man became serious, 'Now don't get me wrong, no disrespect, that's just me . . . sort of just comes out without thinking. She might of been an actress, but she was a proper lady, like yourself, miss, decent and friendly, always had a smile and passed the time of day. She knew about my veins – never was a stall-holder that didn't have veins. She'd say, "How's your legs today, Mr Flack?" She knew I only had one foot, but I got a lot of pain in the one that has gone, and I'd have a bit of a joke about being fast enough to catch a hare in Hyde Park . . . you know? Sometimes we'd have a word about us coming from the same neck of the woods, and she'd put on that funny accent of hers.' Momentarily he stared off with a sad expression. 'She was just a nice, pretty kind of young woman. Not one to make you think you could take liberties.'

'What neck of the woods are you from then, Mr Flack?'

'Oh not me, I'm a proper Cockney, born within the sound of Bow Bells. No, it was my grandfather came from close to where she was from. Norfolk. Recognized it as soon as she opened her mouth, even though she had learned to speak more city-like.'

Josephine perched herself on a bench piled high with crates of fruit. 'What do you remember about the last time you saw her?'

'Like I said, it was about her usual time when she comes in at night. She comes off the last 'bus, as a rule. I was quite busy, it being Christmas Eve . . . well, Christmas morning by then. She was waiting, looking over everything, deciding what to have. She says she'll have a bag of Christmas apples – that's the big red ones. "Ain't the best ones for taste," I said to her. "That don't matter," she says, "I like their looks, real Christmassy." (I did have them all polished up nice.) So I weighed her out the ones she wanted, then she turns to this cove that was standing there—'

'You could see him?'

'A course, like I told the detective, I had two lamps burning, real bright, and they was standing full in the light. He wasn't very old, probably younger than Mrs Brown. He was clean-shaven, but a bit rough, as though he hadn't shaved since morning, or his whiskers grew quick, you know how a dark beard comes through late in the day. And he had spots, like he was getting over some kind of rash. Maybe he had been drinking, I myself

186

get a bit rashy if I take spirits – and my nose too. His coat was pretty short, I do remember that, and I think he had on some kind of boots. I seem to remember thinking they wasn't town boots, but he was walking off before I could see proper.'

'Did he take her arm?'

'I never realized he was with her till he spoke, because he never said nothing when she was choosing. When it come to paying, she sort of nudges him to cough up and he baulks at that, but she jokes him into it – well, shames him really – and he makes a to-do about not understanding what coins she wants. But that was all my eye – he knew all right how much they cost, though he made out he didn't. Probably testing her to see if she'd take more than she should.'

Suddenly, Flack slapped his forehead. 'Blimey, I nearly forgot the funny hat. I never seen one like it before. It was a soft felt, round, with a kind of fold down the centre of the crown. Not a hat I'd like myself, but there, him being German, I suppose that's why.'

'German? Are you certain?'

'Oh yes, miss, I can give you any accent you want. I know German when I hear it. I used to work down the docks until I lost my foot.' He stamped his wooden foot.

'What about your boys, did they see him?'

'They told the detective they did, but after he was gone, the young one says he wasn't so sure. I told him, "You got to be sure, because when they capture him we shall have to stand up and say so." I think he just wanted to boast a bit.'

'George, you're a wonder, thank you.'

'No thanks needed, miss. When they catch him and you write this book of yours, it's going to open people's eyes to how the other half lives. I never read a book, but I would have a go with that one.'

The Boot Street rooms were a hive of industrious activity, Josephine bent over her desk, writing furiously, whilst Liliana, whistling like a baker-boy, applied oil paint. When Josephine had written up her interview with George Flack, she went to find Lili to ask a favour.

'Please come with me, Liliana.'

'No Josie, *no*, absolutely *no*. I hate funerals. And a funeral in midwinter of someone I have no interest in? No, thank you very much.'

'You do have an interest in her.'

'A slight one, but not an obsession as you have.'

'Lili, it will be a workhouse funeral. Isn't that bad enough, without the fact that there will be no one concerned enough to be there.'

'She had friends who knew her when she was alive. How about Patty Lydney and—'

'All right, Lili. I will go without you.'

So Josephine went by omnibus alone to Brompton Cemetery.

Josephine had attended few enough funerals, and had expected, because of Harriet's poor circumstances, that, as she had told Liliana, this would be a 'parish funeral'.

Surprisingly there was an undertaker in attendance. A hearse arrived carrying a fine elm coffin, followed by a mourning coach from which stepped four people: a young man, and a woman – older, but not by much – leaning on the arm of a man who must be her husband. There was also another man who, Josephine estimated, was perhaps another relative. The younger man and the woman were much alike, and, even though she had seen Harriet only in death, there was a family likeness. Brother, sister and sister's husband, and a well-dressed man.

Superintendent Thomson and Sergeant Kerley were present at the premises of the undertaker in Drury Lane when the hearse and coach left. Although it was not late in the day, December gloom was descending into darkness. A small crowd of a poor class of people watched. These were mostly women, some of whom Frank Kerley recognized as women who had been brought in for questioning as to their whereabouts on Christmas Eve.

The brother. Appearing no more than a youth, although James knew him to be a young man, he looked pale and lost; beside him, an obviously well-to-do older gentleman made up the foursome of the chief mourners. Frank Kerley did not go into the chapel, but waited in the area of the open grave, standing well back and at a discreet distance from where the graveside service would take place, to observe who was there. He agreed with the super: such a murderer as they were looking for might well get satisfaction from watching the outcome of his handiwork.

And for James Thomson there was the added draw to Brompton Cemetery, because of the small part that Harriet Burton had played in his life some time ago. Arriving late for the chapel service, he was glad now that he had come alone. He spotted Kerley almost hidden by headstones and crosses.

When the mourners emerged from the chapel, he was glad to see that they had not brought the little girl with them. Although by now he was aware of the identity of the mourners, he had not yet spoken to any of them. This had been Kerley's role. From the sister, her husband and her brother, he transferred his attention to the third man of the party of mourners. A gentleman, tall and fair, and with an open, honest face. His bespoke apparel had been created for him by a tailor, a hatter and a boot-maker working in establishments the like of which a sergeant in the Met. would never see, except perhaps in the line of duty.

James Thomson was glad that in Harriet Burton's last appearance centre-stage, so to speak, she was attended with dignity by people of some refinement, even of quality. He was glad that he had come himself, too, and that he had troubled to dress appropriately to the occasion.

When Josephine had arrived, she had gone unobtrusively into the chapel and sat at the back. A surprising number of people were already gathered. Who were they? Why had they come to mourn Harriet? Having come this far, Josephine determined to follow the other mourners to the graveside. Still standing well back, she observed real grief in the brother and sister, the sister having to be supported by her husband and the youth unable to stop his streaming tears. Suddenly she saw herself as an interloper, a voyeur – yet she could not make herself leave. Within only a week, Harriet Burton had become important to her; every new piece of information was insight into her life. Who was the tall fair-haired gentleman? Could he be one of her gentlemen? She longed to know. Was Liliana right? Was she becoming obsessed?

No. She argued her own cause. Harriet Burton had been used and killed by some man who thought that her life was worthless compared with gratifying his own lust. It was not obsession to wish to open up to the public such a life as hers. And if she could do it, she would open his life as well. No matter what, she would write the account of Harriet.

A voice at her shoulder made her jump. 'Hello, Miss Ferguson?' She recognized the voice, but could not place it until she turned slightly. 'Oh. Yes, hello. Sergeant Kerley, isn't it?'

'It is. Are you here for one of your journals?'

Confused at having been discovered by one of her uncle's close Bow Street men, she blurted out, 'Oo, no, I am here on my own account, Sergeant. I have been writing for . . . other newspapers since you so kindly allowed me to interview you.'

'I thought it turned out rather well. My wife has made

a cutting and my daughter insists on showing it to all and sundry.'

'Thank you.'

'Well, it's not that often that the Force gets much recognition. So, what is your interest in this unfortunate woman?'

Any answer she gave would sound lame. 'General interest; a writer always needs to observe unusual occasions.'

The graveside service having ended, mourners were beginning to disperse. She and the sergeant stood respectfully, heads bowed.

'Josephine?' For a second time she jumped at a voice emanating from behind her. 'Sergeant Kerley. What is going on here?'

Josephine closed her eyes and prayed that this was not true. Her uncle had appeared as if from nowhere.

Speechless, she knew that embarrassment was flushing her cheeks, and hoped that the late afternoon gloom hid it.

Frank Kerley looked mystified. 'Sir?'

'Is this young lady persuading you to give her an interview, Mr Kerley?'

'No, sir. No.' Sensing that something was amiss, and not wanting to add anything to the situation, Frank Kerley thought on his feet. 'We just happened to find ourselves together.'

Josephine answered quickly, 'I was saying how surprised I was that there were so many well-dressed people present.'

'What did you expect, miss, a rabble?' And, turning on his heel, her uncle tipped his hat at her and left.

The sergeant, not knowing what was going on, said, 'Excuse me, Miss Ferguson. Nice to see you again,' and hastened to follow the superintendent.

Streetlights shone across the sleety pavements as Josephine rode the crowded omnibus. She really had intended to go and visit him and say that she was sorry for having said hot-headed things. But she had been too caught up in Harriet's life and too many days had gone by.

Uncle James could not stand finding himself caught on the back foot.

Nor for that matter could Josephine. She felt that she had come out of that meeting very badly. What on earth must Sergeant Kerley have thought?

Frank Kerley was puzzled. The super knew that the young woman he had made jump at the sound of his voice was a newspaper journalist, yet he had called her Josephine, and she had responded. It took hardly any time at all for an experienced detective to come up with a solution. He had a vague recollection of the name Josephine. Josephine Thomson – Jemima Ferguson? It fitted. He kept his counsel. If the super wanted him to know, then he would tell him.

That evening, when he was eating supper with Elizabeth and Frances, he asked, 'You remember me once telling you about Mr Thomson and his wife taking in his brother's child?'

Elizabeth nodded. 'That was years ago, but I do remember, it being so unusual for him to confide in you. A terrible tragedy, if memory serves.'

Frances, home from music college for one last meal before she returned to her studies, perked up. 'What, Ma? Tell us what happened.'

'I don't know. Anything I do know is what your father said at the time.'

'Mr Thomson had a brother who worked abroad – some kind of missionary.'

'Oh, Pa, how could he be *some kind* of a missionary. He was or he wasn't.'

'Don't always be so pedantic, Franny, let your father have his say.'

Frank continued. 'The brother and all the family was wiped out in some sort of plague, but the little girl had gone up-country in the care of a servant. Only the two of them survived.'

'That's tragic, Pa. What happened?'

'It's what I am trying to say. The child in the care of the servant was sent to England – the super being next-of-kin – and he and Mrs Thomson took them in and brought the girl up as their own.'

'What happened to the servant, Pa?'

'How would I know that? We work together, we aren't social equals.'

'Doesn't he talk about her, Francis?'

'He is my superior officer, Elizabeth. It's not my

194

place to ask about his family matters. Too personal.'

'But he came here only last week. Isn't that personal?'

Frank Kerley heaved a great sigh. 'A simple question, Elizabeth. I wondered if you remembered the girl's name.'

Elizabeth Kerley gave her husband what he would have described as a self-satisfied, cocky kind of look. 'As a matter of fact I *do*, but only because it was the same as my mother's.'

Franny said, 'Josephine.'

Frank Kerley said, 'I do believe you are right, Elizabeth. Not that it matters,' and said no more.

The morning following the funeral, when Frank Kerley reported, his super. handed him a sheaf of letters. Frank read.

'To the Coroner:
   Dear Sir,
   Could you not dispense with my servant's attendance at the inquest of his poor sister today and future days? An account of what goes on in a brothel does not tend to edification and brings him into a class of people he has not been used to. He is a very well-disposed lad and I want to keep him so.
   This is the third time I have troubled to write a letter. But you will, I am sure, understand and

excuse my anxiety. If you can spare him, please send him back here.

Faithfully yours, C. Knight Watson'

Frank raised his eyes and eyebrows questioningly.

'That was to the Coroner. Now read this.' This letter was anonymous, and sent to Bow Street Station. It drew the attention of the police to the fact that, with the connivance of Mr C. Knight Watson, Harriet Burton's brother was sleeping on the premises of the Society of Antiquities against the rules of membership.'

'Who is this Mr Knight Watson, sir?'

'Savile Row tailoring, Malacca palm cane with silver at both ends. Ring any bells at the funeral yesterday?'

'The gentleman of means.'

'Christopher Knight Watson, one of the mourners at the Burton funeral.'

'And do we suspect Mr Watson?'

'Not unless the man for whom we have put out a description changed his appearance at midnight. Mr Watson is, as you saw, as fair and tall as yourself. But we should call upon the gentleman. Discover what you can about his link with the Burtons.'

Frank Kerley held up the anonymous letter. 'I think I recognize this one's style. One of our regulars, sir. I'll have a word with the desk, but I think we shall find that this is not the first time he has tried to stir up trouble within the Society of Antiquities. He has some kind of axe to grind.'

* * *

Christopher Knight Watson might be as fair as Frank, and he was tall, but not quite equal to the sergeant's height. Nor was he the product of a village school, but most likely of one of the most ancient public schools followed by a favoured university. But not the services, Frank decided; there was nothing of the military or naval in him – more clerical, if anything. One thing was certain, he had wealth.

His greeting was gracious. 'It is not necessary to apologize, Sergeant Kerley. We all have our tasks, and where should we be without the police?'

'Nice of you to take it like that, sir.'

His manner changed subtly, soberly. 'This devil must be found, Sergeant. How can I assist?'

'It's only a matter of routine, we have to contact anyone who might be able to shed light on this dreadful crime. I believe you know the family?'

Watson smiled, 'And you have, no doubt, received a letter suggesting that you investigate my movements because I am a patron of young Buswell – you realize that his sister took the name Burton, of course.'

'My superintendent thought that I might speak with you about the concern at young Mr Buswell's presence in the coroner's court, as you expressed in your letter. I'm sorry, sir, but I'm not at liberty to say anything about such matters, or any other letter.'

The other man held up his hand, 'Of course not. All I meant was that my action in a small act of charity towards the Buswell boy has upset a certain member of the Society, who has done nothing but raise the matter

197

with other members. And, as for the coroner's court, he is a young man who is suffering greatly at the death of his sister, and to be forced to sit in court and listen to details of the kind of life she . . .' The idea of the hurt to the young man was obviously painful. 'I have sons of my own. I should not like it if they had such grief and ignominy to bear, Sergeant.'

'Right, sir. I don't have sons, but I have a grown daughter.'

'Good, Sergeant, good. Pity the man who does not see descendants.'

Whoever had written the cranky anonymous letter suggesting that this man had anything to do with the murder of Harriet Burton was as mad as a hatter. Frank Kerley was convinced that Mr Christopher Knight Watson had not a violent bone in his body.

A gentle man. The kind of man Frank often wished himself to be, occasionally believed himself to be. His grandfather would have said that it is no hardship to be gentle if you have wealth; it's poverty that makes men harsh. There had been a time when Frank accepted his grandfather's beliefs without question, but not so much now. Now he believed that gentleness is something of the spirit. 'I'd agree with that most heartily, sir.'

Christopher Watson started. 'I doubt that what I know will be of any assistance, except, of course, that it was only Harriet who was known as Burton. The family name is Buswell. Certain members of the Buswell family are known to me through the young man.'

'How came you to know him, sir?'

'He came to the Society as an employee, which he is still. Having nowhere to lodge, and little money, I permitted him to sleep in the building. It harms no one; indeed, if our offended member who takes such exception to the boy's presence did not search him out, then no one would be aware that this is where he lays his head.'

'He lives on the premises of the Society of Antiquities then?'

Watson nodded. 'He's a good lad, and the Buswells are a respectable family. Three of them left home to come to live in London . . .' He trailed off, and a pained expression crossed his face. 'The elder sister, as I am sure you must know, now lives in Sussex and the younger, Harriet . . . well, she is why you are here. This business has been devastating to them, Sergeant. They had been close and caring siblings.'

'Did you know Harriet Burton?'

'No, I did not know that poor unfortunate.'

'You knew her to be called Harriet and not Clara, sir?'

Watson nodded. 'She was never referred to by any other name as far as I know.'

'Clara was her professional name, I mean the name under which she appeared on the list of music-hall performers.'

'You know, of course, about the child?'

'Yes, sir.'

'Kate. Poor child. I don't know what will become of her. I believe her aunt hopes to take her, but for the present she is in a boarding school.'

'A rather expensive one, by all accounts.'

'I pay the fees, but perhaps you know that already also?'

'You pay the school fees, even though you have never met the mother? That is very generous of you, very charitable.'

'Do you ever give to the African mission charities?'

'When I can.'

'Yet you have never met the recipients? Very generous of you, Mr Kerley, very charitable. Read nothing into my wife and me helping the Buswell child. We are not poor people, our own sons are grown and want for nothing, and, if one is honest, the satisfaction one gets from any act of charity is something a Christian should admit to. Our consciences are salved by such acts, are they not? When we say, "There but for the grace of God go I", in our inner hearts we are relieved that God had the grace to stay his hand.'

'I'd agree with that in essence, sir, but even so I would say it is generous of you and your wife. I am sure that for the present, a good boarding school is the best place for the little girl. Away from everything. It will never be easy for her, a thing like this, for the rest of her life . . .'

'You are a most unusual policeman, Mr Kerley.' Frank raised his eyebrows, at which Mr Knight Watson hastily added, 'Impertinent fellow, that Knight Watson! I meant only that, when one relies on the daily press for one's acquaintance with other professions, I am afraid that one is apt to pick up the prejudices of the journalists. Perhaps you are not at all unusual, Mr Kerley. Perhaps all policemen are intelligent and compassionate?' It was a rhetorical question, and he went straight on. 'Well, what else can I tell you?'

'To eliminate you from our investigations, sir, your movements.'

'My movements. I was in the company of my family and friends on Christmas Eve. We played at cards till the early hours. We could vouch for young Buswell, too, if you wish. I shall be glad to give you details of those present.' He smiled, 'I could no doubt also give you the name of the member of the Society who objects to poor young Buswell sleeping on the premises.'

On the streets again, a short piece of poetry, straight from his youth, sprang into Frank's mind. Mr Knight Watson had been reading the poet, Frank had noticed. 'Ellen Brine'. Had Mr Knight Watson been reading it because he saw a similarity between the 'childern all in black' and the plight of the child Kate.

September come, wi' Shroton faer
But Ellen Brine were never there!
A heavy heart were on the maer
Their father rawd his homeward road
'Tis true he brought zome fearin's back
Ver them two childern all in black;
But they had now, wi' playthings new,
No muther ver to shew um to,
Ver Ellen Brine of Allenburn
Would never more return.

* * *

Liliana had been baking again, this time light but extremely oddly shaped croissants, made deliciously crispy by layered butter. By the time Josephine came warm from having a hot, soapy wash all over, Liliana had a dozen pieces of pastry cooling on a tray.

'Oh, Lili, I have died and gone to pastry-lovers' heaven. Will you marry me and bake croissants every day?' Josephine yanked her fair frizz to the top of her head and skewered it with a length of tortoiseshell.

'Peace-offering, Jo. As soon as you had left, I felt myself to be no end of a pig. I would have run after you except that ... well, it was so cold and gloomy, and the omnibuses appeared all steamed up, and I hate cemeteries and ...' She laughed and gave her friend a quick peck on the cheek, 'and it was so much nicer toasting in front of the fire.'

'Pass the butter, and I'll think about forgiving you.'

Having eaten, Josephine sat before the kitchen fire and pulled on thick stockings. 'You *are* coming with me to David's midnight meeting aren't you, Liliana?'

It was clear that Liliana had forgotten the promise to her brother to listen to his New Year message at the church where he was a preacher.

'Of course I'm coming. I've only to put on my boots and I'm ready.'

They set off walking to St Giles, where Liliana's brother was gaining a reputation for himself as a free-thinking preacher. The first time Josephine had heard him speak to his congregation, she discovered a human being in the guise of a preacher. If the *Telegraph* had a vendetta with him, this was more than compensated for by *The News*'s favouritism. The Reverend Wilde was a people's preacher. It was from hearing Mr Hood's good opinion that Josephine had gone to hear him. And from then to David Wilde mentioning that his sister was visiting and looking for accommodation. After which, finally, Liliana had become Josephine's sub-tenant and close friend.

David Wilde had eliminated from his ministrations anything that could be construed as confusing to the people of the area. No tolling bells, no high-flown ideals or language, no threats or warnings that his God was one who turned against the poor and favoured the rich. His God knew that it wasn't difficult for the wealthy not to steal. Over the period that he had been minister in London, those who had been offended by his speeches – which could not be called sermons – had dwindled away, but were replaced threefold by the poor and hungry. The better-off who did stay were stalwart and sincere, and doubly generous with donations.

So that by the last day of the year 1872, the people streaming into St Giles would hear him bring in a new year with a prayer and words of hope and advice, as well as a simple explanation about how the material world could be changed. When he was accused of preaching politics, he would ask where in all holy writ was there a single word that said that he was wrong. So ridicule and denigration were tried, but this was water off a duck's back.

Inside the atmosphere was more partylike than Christian service. Along the side-aisles trestle-tables had been erected, on which were piles of fresh loaves, large dishes

203

of brawn, and dozens of meat pies. It was obvious that the parishioners knew that there would be tea to drink, because each had brought along some kind of mug or cup. Those who might have expected anything stronger were disappointed, because David was much against alcohol.

Josephine and Lilian heard him before they saw him in the throng. Leaning over the pulpit in a very uncleric-like manner, he was trying to make himself heard. Gradually the hubbub died down.

'Good friends, I had hoped that you would come tonight and thank God for having let us live through another year – hard and bitter for many though it has been – but nevertheless we have come through. In about five minutes' time, we shall hear all the bells of Bow ring in another year – of pain and pleasure, of sadness and happiness, of want and very infrequently, of plenty. But, for a few minutes now, let us think of those whom we knew and loved, and those we hardly knew at all, but who will not be of this world in Eighteen Seventy-three. None of us can be certain of what lies ahead, or even whether there is another world waiting, but we can be certain of the here and now, and thank God for it. Our good neighbours – the grocery merchants, and butchers and bakers, oh, yes, and candle-makers – have contributed food and tea and light enough for us to celebrate the beginning of another year. Bless you all, and I hope that you will bless me.' Loud amens and hundreds of sibilant blessings filled the body of the church.

Josephine drew in her breath. Had he really said that?

That none of us could be certain that another world is waiting? That was agnosticism. If that was repeated, he would lose his living. The *Daily Telegraph* would blare out 'Blasphemy.'

Suddenly the distant and distinct sound of the bells of St Clement Danes, Whitechapel and Bow rang out, soon to be joined by others from all the bell-towers in London. Not all could be heard in Bow Street, but the sound of ringing was in the clear frosty air.

It was some time before Liliana could get to her brother. Josephine followed, wanting to speak with him again. Even if she could not speak with him, to be in his presence. The Reverend Wilde excited her, even more tonight when he had seemed to speak as an agnostic.

All the while they were talking, people were coming up to him and wishing him a Happy New Year, and thanking him for the 'eats'.

'Come on, Jo.' Liliana tried to lead her towards the generous tables. 'Let's try for some food.'

'All right, I'll be with you in a minute.' But Lili waited. 'David,' Josephine said, 'I realize that now is not the time, but I wanted some information from you.'

'She is obsessed by that singer who was killed. She is going to write a book about her life.'

'Lili! I wish you wouldn't interfere. I am quite capable of talking for myself.'

David said, 'Lili, go and get food like a good girl,' and to Josephine, 'Did you know Clara?'

Josephine shook her head. 'Only since her death, and

I find that I now know quite a lot about her – as Harriet, not Clara.'

'What is it you want from me?'

'To meet people she knew.'

'She knew me.'

That night, James Thomson too attended the night-watch service, not at his own church, but at St Giles, where he knew from past, secretive visits, he would come out refreshed and exhilarated. His visits to St Giles to listen to young Reverend Wilde were part of a life he kept separate from Ann. Ann was conventional and afraid to think otherwise than in the manner of her upbringing. It was not that he set out to have secrets from her, it was rather as a means of protecting her from his own upbringing in Turkey, which was, to say the least, cosmopolitan. 'Foreign,' Ann said of it.

He sat with his hat between his feet and watched as the church filled, not with the bonneted and well turned-out congregation he was used to – although there was a fair sprinkling of such – but with working men and, in greater numbers, working women and their children; people who, until Rev. Wilde came to St Giles, did not believe that such places as churches were for them. But they trusted this young clergyman; he did not frighten them with incense, and ritual, and robes and words that had no meaning. They came in crowds from London's infamous Baldwin's Gardens and its environs, London's poorest, to listen to the young clergyman who said things that had relevance to their mean lives.

Enemies called him the 'Ranting Priest', thinking it to be insulting, but James guessed that the young man himself would take it as a compliment, for he meant to raise these people up. This might be the only service in the year that they attended, but then what the clergyman said in his simple language was such rich fare that perhaps they were sustained for much longer than they would be by the thin stuff James and Ann were served weekly.

Certainly it had relevance to James's life at Bow Street.

He wondered where, and how frequently, Frank Kerley attended. Certainly he was Low Church – hadn't his father or grandfather been a preacher? Certainly radical. James wondered what his junior officer would think if he knew his superintendent supported such 'ranting' preachers as young Rev. Wilde. For that matter, he wondered what Ann would say, what Colonel Henderson would say, what Lady Granville would say. Earlier that day he had placed fifty sovereigns in the St Giles collection box.

It was inappropriate to finger a rosary at this unaffected watch-night service, so he sat as he had done on other occasions in this church, with his hands linked across his lap, allowing the easy atmosphere to deal with his anxieties.

He thought about Frank Kerley and what he might have made of Christopher Knight Watson, and admitted to himself that he had sent his sergeant out angling, but, even though he felt that there was nothing to be caught in those waters, James never made assumptions.

Never? He had assumed that Josephine would develop into a woman whose character would be much like Ann's; instead she had developed a character too much like his own to sit comfortably in a woman. How pleased he had always been when he had told her of his plans and hopes for a literate and modern police force trained in sciences and she had asked intelligent questions.

He had assumed that a girl as pretty as Josephine, with Ann Martha to guide her, would not develop ambitions that could never be fulfilled in a world as it now existed. Women were now pushing for places in universities; even Gwendoline Granville had been outspoken in her belief that Ann was as capable of voting as any man. Perhaps so, but not in their lifetime would it come about, and not until she understood that 'Fallen Women' needed more than charitable institutions to keep them off the streets.

With head bowed, he offered a silent prayer for Harriet Burton.

He stood and joined in the singing of a hymn.

He must find time to visit Josephine. He had been full of consternation at the thought of the kind of low life she would encounter if she continued to follow her mistaken dream that she could be a reporter. He realized he had allowed this anxiety to prejudice him. He had read her Jemima Ferguson cuttings and been moved by her sincerity and facility with words. He was optimistic that he might persuade her to make use of her talents by writing biography, perhaps, or even fiction.

Had Harriet Burton ever attended this service, so simple and cleansed of ritual? The rosary he had given her appeared to have religious meaning for her. What did it all amount to? She had been around the Bow Street district for something like six years; she had been a casual singer and a casual streetwalker; she had accepted a rosary from a stranger and a half-sovereign from another. She had died in a welter of blood with a peaceful expression. His instinct was to thank God for that peaceful expression, yet the fact of it somehow made the killing worse.

She had been no threat to her killer, and yet he had taken some razor-sharp instrument and drawn it twice across her throat.

James Thomson was aroused from meditation by the pealing first of Bow bells, then of St Clement Danes, then Whitechapel. He fixed his eyes upon the altar, crossed himself, and vowed that he would not rest until he had her murderer in a cell.

Josephine, standing in the crowd listening to David Wilde, let her gaze wander over the many, many faces looking towards him, and started when, to her great astonishment, she saw her uncle. She drew back, even though the oil-lamps did not, she thought, illuminate the gathering sufficiently for him to be able to see her in an aisle lit only by candles. But, from where she stood, she could watch him. On Christmas morning, when she attended church with him and Ann, she had thought his eyes were glazed with boredom by the long mass in Latin. But not here in St Giles; he sang the one hymn with gusto. Here, he reminded her of what she could remember of the full-hearted singing that had gone on in her father's mission. Uncle James, she thought, why aren't you more easy with yourself?

It was not until she had watched him leave that she had gone to speak to some women who Liliana's brother had said might be glad to talk to her. He was known to them as Young Father David. He had said, 'This is my sister's friend, I hope you will tell her what she wants to know about Clara.'

'What's to know, Father David? She did some singing, and picked up a wrong 'n.'

'People who don't know you as I do have no idea how difficult life on the streets is.' He smiled, 'You are "Bad Lots", and you have only yourselves to blame, isn't that the general opinion?'

'You are a sweet man, Father David, but I don't see what writing up Clara's life is going to do.'

Josephine interrupted, 'Listen, I'll be honest with you, a biography of Clara might not do much, but isn't that better than doing nothing? She had a daughter, didn't she?'

'Yeah, little Katy. Remember her from when Clara lived in Nelson Street. Katy wasn't very old then.'

David Wilde said, 'Josephine, these girls need to get back to the Haymarket. Maybe you could meet tomorrow.'

'Yeah, do that, about four o'clock. I always go to O'Sullivan's for me breakfast then.'

Josephine made an appointment to meet Violet on the following day.

January 1873

O'Sullivan's was a new experience for Josephine, and she liked it. A small eating place, made more accommodating by having long tables and benches. At the long serving hatch it seemed possible to request anything one fancied. Breakfast in name only. Everything from cold cuts to thick soup was written up in chalk on a large board. Items were deleted, others added. It being four in the afternoon, Josephine chose Welsh rarebit. It being Violet's breakfast time, she ordered ham and eggs and fried bread. When Josephine was about to ask for tea, Violet said, 'Have some stout, it's the best drink in the world.' And, once having got used to its bitterness, Josephine agreed.

Violet ate quickly, then sat back and sipped her stout. 'Look, I don't know what you want to know about Clara, but I'll tell you what I can remember from when I knew her. Her best times, I should think, was when she lived with Major Brown. Now, I don't know whether he rightly was a major or not, but he wasn't short of cash and he treated her really nice. Used to call herself Mrs Brown then, didn't have to go out to work. Twice she got in the family way by him, but both times they was stillbirths. If you ask me, that's a bad thing for a woman to suffer. Abortions and miscarriages are everyday things, but to carry a child full-term and then it be dead makes you think that, if there's someone up *there*, they a'nt very fond of women.'

'Did she have any live children with Major Brown?'

'Nah, he went off abroad. I think he died, but I can't remember who told me that. Anyway, the next one she takes up with was a different kettle of fish. He was lovely, good fun, had been living abroad. Falls head over heels in love with Clara, used to come and listen to her sing every time she was on. He had a nice place in Regent Square, and he set her up there.'

'Living with him?'

'Yes, but not taking his name as she did with the major. She knew all along that there'd come a time when he would have to go back to China, but he told her that he would send for her and they would live together out there.'

Josephine ordered Violet another glass of stout. 'I expect that you're going to tell me it was the old, old story – out of sight, out of mind, and she never heard from him again.'

'Well, that's where you'd be wrong. She heard from him regular.' Violet handed over a packet, a large, used

212

envelope bulging with papers. 'I did wonder if I ought to hand these over to the police, but . . . well, what would they do with love-letters except have a bit of a laugh? So you have them.'

Josephine was stunned at being presented with such an insight into Harriet's life. 'How did you come by them?'

'She asked me to keep them a few weeks back because she was on the move such a lot and she'd had stuff go missing in the past, and Willie's letters were more precious to her than her bits of jewellery. She knew with me they'd be safe from prying eyes because I can't read – never could.'

With the new year came a flurry of activity. The reward notices brought forth scores of people who, for the sake of a visit to Bow Street or the price of a penny letter, thought they would try their luck, no matter how little their statements fitted the details. Every type of foreigner was offered, from Japanese to a German travelling band, all members of which wore moustaches and all of whom had to be sought and interviewed. Neighbours seemed intent on settling old scores, and reported their suspicions. The working days of the detectives of 'E' Division were stretched at both ends. DCs and inspectors were sent out in all directions to check on every reported sighting. Each day, when the reports were assembled on James Thomson's desk, Frank usually found himself in the senior man's office, where he was often handed a report with the Met. heading. But they were getting nowhere. James's greatest hope was that the 'Wanted' notices spread throughout the country would produce a lead. But days slipped by, and, although there was a great deal of activity generated by the '£100 Reward' posters, there was little real progress.

New witnesses came into Bow Street who had sight of Harriet Burton and a man on Christmas Eve. Their reports added weight to the description they already had. He was young, surly and German.

Frank Kerley, and the DCs assigned to the case, went on wild-goose chases all around London, and for his own satisfaction Frank went over and over the ground between the Alhambra and Regent Circus. At last he came up with something that seemed to be part of the story and went gladly back to report to the superintendent, who for the first time bade him take a chair and warm his legs.

'She calls herself Madame Margaret, and she says that on the Friday before Christmas she and her friend met a foreigner in Leicester Square. It was the man who started the conversation.'

James Thomson raised his eyebrows.

Frank Kerley smiled, 'I know, that's what she would say, but it doesn't matter really . . . The three of them went for a drink at The Falcon in Princes Street. Then, according to Madame Margaret, he asked if she and her friend would go to a coffee house with him and spend the night. He offered to pay them ten shillings.'

'Did they take it?'

'Apparently they didn't like his appearance. I reckon

it was more that they were huffed at five shillings a head for depravity of that kind.'

'What sort of price do you suppose she puts on herself then?'

Josephine was beginning to have insight into the kind of woman Harriet was, and she liked her. Tryphena had obtained a billboard picture of 'Sweet Clara Burton'. She could not possibly have been as demure as depicted, but her features were dainty and pretty. Josephine could see how she must have captivated men, especially if her voice was as appealing as her looks.

At Somerset House in London, every birth in Britain was on record. Josephine spent a productive few hours there, and returned home to find Liliana stretching a new canvas with her brother David helping. He was in his shirtsleeves and looking very un-clergyman-like. And certainly not as 'brotherly' as she had considered him heretofore. Her feeling of elation surprised her. Even so, she knew that she could never be romantically interested in a clergyman. Since having heard an outdoor speaker on Humanism at Hyde Park's Speakers' Corner, she felt more at home with those views than any religion that offered rewards in Heaven for behaving well.

Liliana asked eagerly, 'Did you find Harriet?'

'I have Lili, I have. My coster friend was correct she was born in Norfolk, at Wisbech. I found two other siblings: one a sister three years older, and a brother, much younger.'

'What next then?' David asked.

'She plans to go to Wisbech,' Liliana said. 'Right, Jo?'

'Of course, what else? I found the last address of their mother and father on death certificates. I shall start there – there are bound to be other Buswells. If not, Wisbech is a small town; I shall find someone who knows the Buswell family.'

David said, 'That's a tall order, it could take a while.'

'I hope not, but I have to do it. Birthplace and early conditions are what makes us who we become as adults.'

'Would you like some company?'

'You want to come with me to Norfolk?'

'If you'll have me, and you would be doing me a kindness.' He smiled wryly, 'I need someone to be kind to me.'

'Listen to the man, he has only himself to blame,' Lili scoffed.

'What is this about?' Josephine asked.

'My church seniors have come down on me like a ton of bricks, and I'm in limbo until they decide whether I am fit to continue to be a clergyman.'

'I'm not surprised,' Liliana said. 'You practically announced yourself an agnostic.'

'I didn't mean it like that. I said that we should live as well as we can in the present.'

'And the *Daily Telegraph* quoted you. "The Ranting Priest".'

'Ignoramuses! I am not a priest. Just a clergyman . . . a preacher if anything.'

'It's strange, I can never think of you as a clergyman.'

He responded with a burst of laughter. 'I can never think of myself as a clergyman either.'

'Perhaps you are a politician.'

After a long pause, he gave a wry, lopsided smile. 'I am, Josephine, I am, but that doesn't preclude me holding Christian views.'

'Perhaps we might discuss those views and my own on our long train journey to Wisbech. Go and put some things in an overnight bag, David. I should really like to have your company.'

They arrived in Wisbech the next day.

Wisbech turned out to be not as small as Josephine had supposed, and they wasted an hour wandering around wondering where to start. David's idea that they should go to a vicarage gave them what they wanted.

Mrs Burnett was the best sort of woman for a vicar to have as a wife: welcoming, interested and helpful. David, being a churchman himself, established Josephine's bona fides as a serious and concerned person. 'My husband is away from home, but I might be more helpful to you – I am born and bred local. Known the Buswells all my life. A nice, hard-working, respectable family. In a way, with all this scandal about Harriet, it is a blessing that her parents have gone on to a better place. There is only one Buswell left now, on either side of the family – Harriet and Mary's uncle. He's a poor soul, and has taken it hard – the Buswells have always been a respectable family.'

Mrs Burnett insisted that they leave their bags and stay

217

the night, and that it was no trouble for her to take them to Albion Place and introduce them as people sincerely concerned in the Buswell tragedy.

Josephine was grateful to have found such a mediator, but Mrs Burnett's naiveté was concerning. Josephine might easily have been going to write a column for a London newspaper.

Harriet's uncle might be a poor soul, but he was articulate and educated, and by no means as naive as Mrs Burnett. It took some direct questions about motive and an assurance that he would see what she proposed writing before he agreed to talk.

'Would you ah wrote about our Harriet if she hadn't got herself dead in the manner she did?' Both his accent and phrasing were intriguing.

She answered him honestly and told him that she had been a newspaper reporter. 'I might have written something, but not a history of her life.'

'That seems a mighty undertaking for a bit of a girl like Harriet.'

'Mr Buswell, your niece had a child . . .'

'Ah, Katy, so I'm told.'

'When she is older, she is bound to want to know about her mother. I think what I will write is going to be better for her than newspaper articles. When was the last time you saw Harriet – when she left home?'

'No, since then. Five years. She and Mary came and stayed a week. I was surprised to know that she had had a little one. What has happened to it?'

'She's well cared for. In a boarding school at present.'

218

'That's for the best. I don't see our Harriet making much of a mother. She wasn't the type. I don't say she was the black sheep, but Harriet's mother was a trained machinist, and my brother had a very respectable living. He was a seaman.'

'How came your nieces to leave home?'

'Well they both died, didn't they? First my brother and then my sister-in-law. That was when the girls decided they'd try their hand in service in London.'

'Was Harriet in service before that?'

'Ah, she went as a servant to a man who lived near here.'

'Can you give me the address?'

'I could, but you won't get no change from him. He's been up the graveyard this four years.

'I was hoping Mary might come. I wrote to her, but I haven't heard back yet. You haven't seen her, I suppose?'

'At a distance. I attended Harriet's funeral.'

Tears welled but did not spill over. 'I should ha' like to be there, but I can't make distances these days. What sort of affair was it?'

'Very dignified. Your other niece and nephew, several well-to-do people, I don't know who they were, but they were comforting your nephew.'

'That would be the Knight Watsons. Mary once wrote to tell me that there was a philanthropic gentleman who had provided for the boy, and had offered to pay for Harriet's child to be schooled.'

'Is there a connection between your family and these people?'

'Mary's husband, I believe. Good, charitable people Mary believed them to be. Have you spoken to Mary?'

'No. She will not want any more questioning, what with the police and the newspapers. Now that you have been kind enough to speak to me, I shall probably not try.'

'Lately, I've been wondering if there was something I could have done for the two girls, but I don't know what. It seemed at the time to be the best thing for them to get away from here with the deaths of their mother and father hanging over their lives.'

'Mary has stood by her sister, even though it couldn't have been easy.'

'Oh yes, I think there were times when Harriet pushed Mary to distraction, but being the older, she felt responsible. When they came here I asked them straight, how Harriet managed to get herself into trouble and Mary didn't. I wasn't finding fault, what was done was done, and it weren't no business of mine.

'Harriet said, so innocent, "I believed him, uncle. He was a coachman." When he found that he had got her in trouble, he said it would be all right, that they should go down to London where coachmen were always wanted. Once they got to London, he disappeared.'

There being no other person Mrs Burnett could think of who could help Josephine, they caught an early train next morning.

Josephine thought to herself how pleasant it was to have a male companion. Independent as she liked to be, she enjoyed having her bag taken from her and handed to a porter, having a daily paper and a box of jelly sweets purchased for her, having a window seat found for her. When she was settled, he sat beside her.

'Shall we go over your notes together?'

'You mean the Wisbech or the London ones?'

'All of it.'

It wasn't easy to talk about the life of a murder victim with other passengers within earshot, but by reading together and each making pencil notes for the other to consider, they managed very well. When at last Josephine returned her sheaf of notes to a document case, he placed his hand over hers. 'I have to say that I am very impressed, very, very impressed.'

'Really? What impresses you?'

'Your tenacity for one thing – perhaps dedication is the better word. Your passion for your subject. I read the "Jane" obituary: that must have touched many people who read it.'

'But for how long? Until the newspaper is used to light a fire?'

'Mr Gladstone's words must end up like that, too.'

'Maybe that is no bad thing . . . but Jemima Ferguson's words, now that's another matter entirely.'

He now took full charge of her hand in both of his briefly, 'You are incorrigible, Miss Ferguson.'

'I don't know whether to take offence at that,' she grinned, 'mostly because I don't know exactly what incorrigible means. Incurable?'

He smiled, 'Unrepentant?'

She shrugged, still not taking her hand from his. 'That

will do. I repent of nothing. My work, my beliefs, my views.'

'Good. I am glad that you and Liliana found one another.'

Slowly he released her hand, which remembered his for the rest of the journey.

Liliana, very taken with her new-found creative interest, had prepared coq au vin, the aroma of which pervaded the entire floor as her brother, David, in company with Josephine, went through into Josephine's apartment. David deposited two small travelling bags in the hall.

'Ah, the wanderers return. Was it worth the journey?'

'Josephine is the judge of that.'

'Well worth it.'

Liliana served the melting pieces of chicken floating in its flavoursome sauce in wide earthenware bowls. As they ate with the appetites of the young, healthy people they were, Josephine related what they had discovered. 'We seemed to get at some true picture of Harriet.'

Liliana looked up from dipping bread into the remains of the crock of sauce. '*We*, David? *We* get at the truth? Have you appointed him, Jo?'

'No I have not. But whilst David is wallowing in free time until his fate is sealed . . .'

'My fate will not be sealed. I intend to carry on my crusade to improve conditions . . .'

'Yes, yes, David,' Liliana interjected, 'I know all about that.'

'Lili, listen,' Jo said. 'At the moment, David is being very useful to me. He knows who to ask what. It could take me hours of questioning and researching to discover something that David has at his fingertips. He's such a help . . . knows most of the prostitutes in the Haymarket . . .'

Tapping the table with a spoon to make himself heard over Liliana's unladylike whoops and laughs, he said, 'Josephine, I don't think that you will help my quest to be given back my living if you praise me like that.'

Frank Kerley had also visited Mr Buswell. His report on his visit to Wisbech was thin, as James Thomson had expected but, just as he had sent his sergeant to Christopher Knight Watson to 'fish' so Thomson had sent him to discover the only remaining member of Harriet Burton's family not to have been questioned.

'She came from a nice family who lived in a nice town. I visited the graveyard, sir, she would have been better buried there. Used to work for a man with almost the same name as yourself. Spelled with a P. He's dead. I went to look at the headstone.'

That was what James himself would have done. Dotted the i's and crossed the t's. Turnstone. The closer he worked with Kerley, the more he had come to admire him and acknowledge his character and intelligence. Kerley was open in his opinions, yet understood protocol and recognized the proprieties that adhere to rank. In other circumstances, James would have been delighted to have Ann invite the Kerleys socially. But then, why not? He and Ann Martha had often been received at the Hendersons'. Until recently he had imagined Mrs Kerley to be the daughter of an apple-cheeked farmer's wife. Now that he had met her, if only briefly, he felt that she and Ann would get on splendidly. One day he hoped to find a suitable opportunity to ask the sergeant how a Dorsetshire farmboy came to have an artist wife and a musical daughter. Or was he perhaps no less prejudiced than many of his own class, who thought that to be from the working classes was to be lacking in taste and sophistication.

'Have you considered applying for higher rank, Sergeant? You know that I have always been impressed by the way you work, and I like the way you think. I should be pleased to give you a recommendation.'

Kerley smiled. 'Thank you, sir, thank you very much. I will give it some thought, but I reckoned time enough when my feet give up. I like to be out and about.'

'Don't leave it too late. You're a good man to have on a murder investigation – *any* investigation at all.'

'Thank you, sir. I might not have got a trip to Wisbech if I was an inspector. I'd have been a sight too expensive.' Then, seriously, 'I'm a happy man, sir. My philosophy is, "Don't change something that don't need it".'

'You might find that you were happier, or at least more fulfilled, with more authority.'

'"Might" is the important word there, sir. To my

mind, happiness and fulfilment aren't always inter-changeable. Mrs Kerley might be fulfilled if she'd stayed single and been a full-time painter, but she'd tell you herself, she wouldn't have been happier.'

Frank Kerley was beginning to feel that they were losing their quarry. Time was running out. No German answering the description had been seen in the dockland area, or Soho, or any of the other places foreigners tended to gather. He found himself checking and rechecking, realized that often he was reading a report hurriedly, as though that would speed up the discovery of a vital piece of information that would allow them to pounce on him.

Every dark-haired, sallow-skinned, clean-shaven man of twenty-five years he passed in the street was a possible suspect, yet it was impossible to stop every man who fitted the description to discover whether they spoke with a German accent. He read every report from every investigating officer and, as did his super-intendent, made notes and chased up every line of enquiry.

He read and re-read the antecedents. And the reports that were still not cleared. He noted in several of these that the investigating officer had been told of the victim's reported indifference to the men she brought home. 'Let him wait' was mentioned more than once.

This was not something helpful to the victim's char-acter. The newspapers would soon hint – or worse – that she had brought it on herself.

*　　*　　*

Josephine gave a lot of thought about how to persuade Harriet's landlady to talk to her.

Liliana had the answer. 'Money, Jo. Don't be subtle. Offer her a decent sum and she will tell.'

'How mercenary, Lili,' she smiled, raising her eyebrows. 'How much is a decent sum?'

They decided that five pounds sounded mercenary, but five guineas was a more respectable fee.

Josephine used a little flattery, and the suggestion that a place in history in a book was a much better thing than the Wright name in newspapers, particularly as she would get a fee for her time. In this way she achieved her interview with Mrs Wright, who, given the option, chose to meet Josephine at one of London's most expensive tearooms.

There was no doubt about it, Mrs Wright had presence. With an erect posture, full, swaying skirts and a high, complicated hat, she allowed herself to be conducted to where Josephine was waiting, at a table that was beautifully laid up for tea, with dainty sandwiches and little cakes highly decorated with sugar and cream. Josephine was not insincere when she said, 'If you don't mind me saying so, you have a wonderful way of making an entrance.'

'Thank you, Miss Ferguson, it's on account of my theatre training. It's something that comes natural once you're trained.' She was obviously not intimidated by her surroundings, but unbuttoned her gloves and turned them back on the wrist, and adjusted the folds of her skirt. 'This is nice, very nice. It's quite a while since I was entertained to tea. I must try to come up West more often, I'm glad of you suggesting Claridges, Miss Ferguson.'

'It occurred to me that you might like to talk away from . . .' Tailing off, not wanting to mention Great Coram Street directly.

Accepting milk for her tea and some small triangular sandwiches, Mrs Wright said, 'Did you know that my name's Harriet too? She called herself Clara for her act because it's a modern name. Which always seemed queer to me because her act was real old-fashioned.'

'In what way?'

'Well, she never tried to put any spice into her act. She had a pretty enough voice, but no . . . ?' Mrs Wright raised her chin and pouted provocatively, 'She never tried to be fetching.'

'So she wasn't the sort of girl to . . . act provocatively on the stage.'

'Not any time I saw her. I don't think she had it in her. No, what men liked in her was that sweet kind of girlishness. It wasn't false, she was a kind person, would give away her last sixpence. Which wasn't a good idea when she had to find her rent.'

'Did she get behind with that?'

'She may have done before she came to me, but I never let my girls get behind. It's no good to anybody to have debts dragging them down. No, when she went out on Christmas Eve, she owed me rent and I reminded her.'

'When she went out to go to the Alhambra Palace?'

'Yes. She was the only one of my girls who had an

act there last Christmas . . . you understand that many of my girls are on the stage.'

'No, I didn't know that.'

'I like having them around. Most of them haven't got people of their own. You see, when a girl gets stars in her eyes about treading the boards, a lot of them just ups tracks and comes to London. What they don't realize is that, even if they're good, it don't last. I was lucky, I didn't need talent, only this.' She ran her hands down her curvaceous figure. 'I was always the sweetmeat in the magician's box, the distraction whilst he moved mirrors and panels. Of course, I was only a little bit of a thing, and a real contortionist inside those boxes.'

'You say that you didn't need talent, but that is what you had. I would say to do those things you must have had amazing talent.'

'Well, thank you, there's not many who's ever seen it like that.' She smiled, showing that she had all her front teeth and that they were very good. 'What I did have a talent for was money. I saw the writing on the wall when I was very young, so I lived quite simple – not meagre – and always put money aside, bought good stones that would keep their value. Diamonds and gold always keep their value. It's what I try to tell my girls. It's why I don't like them getting into debt.'

'And Harriet?'

'She'd known good times; she had decent protectors she lived with for long stretches at a time. She'd had several good pieces given to her – modern stuff, but stuff to hold their value. One in particular, Major Brown, she was with him for quite some time. Trouble with that set-up is that, although Harriet still did her turns on the halls, she never looked at that as her income. To my mind, if he wanted her to be Mrs Brown, then she ought to have lived off of him and put her own earnings to one side.'

'And didn't she?'

Mrs Wright shook her head. 'I dare say she expected to be the major's lady for ever.'

'What happened?'

'She never told me that. But I know people who knew her then, and they say he went abroad. Twice that happened to her. The second one, I don't know his name, he was young, never gave her anything to salt away.'

'I hope you don't mind me asking, but was she in debt to you?'

'She had been behind ... not much, but when she come home that night, first thing she did was to pay the rent she owed, and she give us a bag of apples for Christmas, just took a couple for herself.'

'Does that mean she made the man she brought home with her pay ... I don't know how to put this ...'

'Pay up front of what he was expecting?' Josephine nodded. 'Wisest thing, and to hand it over for safe-keeping if it's possible. In Harriet's case, she got the money off of him and paid her rent arrears with it. My girls a'nt whores, Miss Ferguson, not at all; there's thousands of girls out there having to do what they can to keep body and soul together.'

'I know, but before I decided to take an interest in Harriet's life – well, and death really, I didn't know how many girls have to go with men on the streets. It's a terrible thing.'

'Miss Ferguson, you won't know the half of it, I'll be bound. Girls by the hundred, come in from country places into service, like Harriet. Gets in the fam'ly way by some man who tells her a tale about better'n herself because he's got a position in the household, like Harriet, or it could be by the master, or the son of the house. It's often the innocent country girls who come off worst.'

'So, I suppose they are turned out.'

'To fend for theirselves and the young one. Nobody cares a tuppenny toss.'

Mrs Wright sounded so resentful that Josephine wondered whether Mrs Wright's own story had been similar. 'But you care, I can tell.' Josephine called for fresh tea to be made and another selection of cakes.

'I can't do much. But at least a dozen girls out of hundreds who would have been going up dark alleyways with any Tom, Dick and Harry, could have a place with a family.' Tears welled in her eyes and she blotted them before they fell. 'I always thought they wouldn't be in any danger living under my roof. Yet she was; she wasn't no safer there than if she had gone with him like . . .'

Josephine tentatively rested her hand upon Mrs Wright's. 'I hope that you are not feeling guilty or anything like that. You have no reason to, none at all.'

'Not guilty, but useless. What men do to women don't bear thinking about.'

'There are good men.'

Mrs Wright nodded. 'Oh yes, but sometimes you can't tell which ones is which until it's too late.'

Josephine decided that she must hand over to the police Harriet's letters that Violet had given her. Before doing so, though, she began recording them as part of her research, and as she did so read them aloud to Liliana.

'Point do Galle (Ceylon)
Sunday 13 November 1870

My Dearest Harriet,

I have travelled as far as Ceylon in safety, and next Sunday hope to be in *Singapore*, and *there* to receive your *first* letter before going on to my Hong Kong home. Not a day passes that I do not think about you many times, regretting that I do not possess the *original* instead of the photograph you gave me, not at all a flattering one – and I often wonder if you have had resolution enough to fly from London associations to the shelter of your sister's roof. My anxiety about you, dear Harriet, is very great, and *if* there is no letter from you at Singapore when we arrive there next Sunday, I shall not know what to think, and I shall fear all sorts of mishap have befallen you.

My chief dread is that the quiet, perhaps monotonous life of Hurst Green with your

sister may soon weary you, and that then the
temptations of your old friends – female as well
as male – with the attractions of London to your
excitable self, may have led you back to a life
from which I would gladly preserve you. Though
a month has passed since I left you. I am not a bit
more reconciled to my solitary banishment than I
was before leaving London, and increasingly regret
that time did not permit me to have arranged for
you to have accompanied me, as you sometimes
said you would like to do. I should then have felt
that my best days were not spent *alone* in acquiring
wealth without myself to expend it upon selfishly.
Indeed, after living so pleasantly in London, I *do*
feel that I want a companion to love and be loved
by. I do so *much* fear your being left in London.'

Josephine lowered the long, finely-written letter she had
been reading aloud to Liliana. 'I've just thought, how
would Willie ever get to know that the woman he loved
is murdered? It's not as though he's kin or family or
betrothed or anything? Imagine what it would be like
for him receiving a newspaper from England and reading
that his sweetheart is the victim of the Great Coram
Street murderer?'

'If he had not abandoned her, then she would not have
been the victim. Are you going to hand over the letters
to the police?'

'I have to, Lili, it would be withholding evidence or
something if I didn't, and I don't want to get on the

wrong side of Uncle James any more than I already am.' She continued reading and writing as they huddled around the kitchen range, which was almost red hot against the chill of the bitter January fog that seemed to be able to creep into any house.

'Now, before telling you more about my voyage, let me remind you of your promise to write to me everything about all your arrangements and plans for the future. Do, my dear girl, tell me everything about what you have been doing and thinking. Tell me, too, what arrangements you can make with your sister about keeping you, I mean remuneration for your board and lodging. I think you should not pay more than a pound a week, if so much. *I must know all your circumstances* before I can decide what to do when I reach Hong Kong. So, Harriet *mia*, pray keep nothing back from me. You may really confide in me.

'Men! Even when they say they are in love, they cannot leave women alone to be themselves. Listen to this . . .

'Another thing, my dear, I must remind you about. You promised to make some attempt at improvement in your writing and reading. You are so quick, intelligent, yet so young, that you need not despair of overcoming any defects.

'Defects Lili, defects! Such a man, to have no defects of his own.

'I know you would be a very good docile pupil, if I could only be near you to assist or direct your studies.

'After writing to you from Alexandria we crossed the desert by daylight on Saturday the twenty-ninth of October in very good railway carriages – can you fancy a railway laid in the midst of miles of sand? We reached Suez in time for dinner at seven. We got on board the rail steamer on Saturday morning and started down the Red Sea (you know it is the place you read of in the Bible whence the Egyptian Host were overwhelmed when pursuing the Israelites) . . .'

'Jo, the man's a monster,' Liliana chipped in. 'Who does he think he is, commenting on her defects, telling her how to live, and now geography and Bible lessons? I hate him, Jo. And so should you, writing in such a tone to Harriet. She was obviously sweet and nice to him. He was never going to bring her to China.'

'Just let me finish before you pass judgement. There's a lot more yet, and several other letters.'

'Mercy.'

'Aden is in Arabia, a dusty village without a tree, nothing to be seen but long strings of camels laden with dates, and half-naked Africans and Arabs. I went as hire to see the English soldiers' barracks and you would have laughed to see the black Natives with very little more clothing than father Adam's primitive fig leaf diving in the deep seas to pick up the money we threw in for them, quite fearless of the sharks abounding there.

'Another evening we had some "Christy's Minstrels", who gave us much fun. All this goes on, on the fire deck, with such a glorious *Moon* over us. (By the way, my dear, the *Moon* will, I suppose, be full with you again.)'

Josephine lowered the letter again. 'You realize what he means by this?'

'Of course. He hopes that he has not left her with child. Full moon!'

'And he mentions it so casually. How could he have gone off to China not knowing? He couldn't have loved her. "By the way," he says after he's related all that about entertainment. And that, "I suppose". Can you believe, Jo, that a man who is physically implicated with a woman can ever *suppose* that he had not left her carrying a child? Go on, let's hear it to the bitter end.'

'I try to banish thoughts of my pleasant evenings with you by chess-playing and reading, but I am now a believer in the saying, "*'tis not good for man to be alone.*"

'Now, my dearest, goodbye, write me in return. May God bless you, and keep you out of harm. I shall expect your answer to my Alexandria letter after we reach China.

'Again, Harriet *mia*, Good-bye. Yours as ever, Willie

'There is such a glorious Moon just rising on the sea – it reminds me of my *disappointment* in number thirty-four when the Moon (I mean *your Moon* came to the *Full* a couple of days sooner than was agreeable. W.K.'

'And how very inconvenient of her,' Lili said crossly, 'to have a full moon when it did not agree with her lover.'

'He wasn't all bad; he was sending her money.'

'Josephine, I dislike being coarse, but she probably cost him a lot less putting her up in his rooms than if he had to go out and pay . . . whatever it is women ask.'

'It's a half-sovereign, Lili, for a nice lady such as Harriet.'

'Jo!'

'What?'

'How on earth can you know such a thing?'

'I asked the girls.'

Josephine was now very busy looking into every corner of Harriet's existence. She went to see George Hood, who greeted her warmly. 'Miss Ferguson, I hope that this is to tell me that you are ready to return to us.'

'No, but I have come to say that I should have been a bit more mature about . . .'

'If I am honest, I should have done better. Come and sit down, tell me whether your project is proceeding well.'

'Better than I ever supposed it would.'

'Excellent. In what way better?'

'Well, although my story is the biography of Harriet Burton, I find myself being drawn to writing about her world and other girls in it. Thousands find themselves in Harriet's predicament, and nobody, except a few limp charities, is interested. Charity is worse than useless.'

'Why do you think that?'

'Those people who *do* have some concern are misled into believing that if they give money that is enough, but that if the girls don't *reform* then they only have themselves to blame. A prayer meeting and a dormitory doesn't come near helping. It is the other end of the problem that must be tackled. The reasons *why* they have to take to the streets.'

'Come back to us, Miss Ferguson. If you will, then I will promise you a regular place and you can write on any subject you choose.'

'Really?'

'One proviso: that your pieces will be short, but not very sweet. I would want you to prick consciences, stir up trouble, but always based on irrefutable facts.'

'My Harriet work keeps me very busy. I doubt if I should have time, even if I did want to come back to *The News*.'

'It might be easier working from here. You could have your old desk back, and an assistant – a female.'

'A woman assistant?'

George Hood nodded. 'She is very good, sensible, well-read, intelligent. Mrs Fisher. You probably wouldn't be able to have her all to yourself, but . . .'

'All right, I will give it a try, but you must understand that my Harriet work comes first.'

'Understood.'

'Also, I have had to do quite a bit of travelling and will have to do more.'

George Hood grinned. 'Are you bargaining with me, Miss Ferguson?'

'I am asking to be able to claim expenses. I wouldn't be unreasonable, or unfair.'

'Anything else?'

'The archives. I might want help in researching back numbers.'

'Mrs Fisher can do all that.'

'Now?'

'If you wish.'

When George Hood took Josephine into the general office to speak to Mrs Fisher, the lady was reading copy through wire-framed eyeglasses. She looked up and nodded. 'Yes, Mr Hood?'

Mrs Fisher was a slim, straight-backed woman of perhaps forty years. It was not until she removed the pince-nez that it was possible to see her striking features to advantage.

Large eyes with laughter wrinkles, long nose – noble or Roman or just big, but well suited to her bony face and high cheekbones. Most amazing of all was her hair. Many men wore their hair longer; it was dark and shiny as coal but had grown white at the temples where there were two badger-like streaks. Her facial bone-structure, short hair and white temples might have given her a masculine appearance, but it was not so, for everything was softened by her long-lashed eyes and plump, pink mouth that had a natural smile curve.

'Mrs Fisher, this is Miss Ferguson, she will be using *The News* offices for a scheme she is working on.'

When Mrs Fisher stood up with alacrity and held out her hand, she proved to be a very tall lady indeed. 'You are Jemima Ferguson?'

'She is, Emmeline, the very same.'

'George knows what I think of you. We're old friends –' she smiled at him – 'good friends. He knows how downcast I was when he said that you were no longer with *The News*.'

'Well, now she is. Not reporting, not yet, but having use of all the facilities that *The News* can give her. This includes some of your time and research expertise.'

Taking Josephine's hand again, Mrs Fisher pressed it. 'Better and better. George knows how much I am in favour of women being represented in all the professions, and he has given me the title of "research assistant".'

'I'll leave you to get acquainted, and for Miss Ferguson to tell you Emmeline how you can best help with her current scheme.'

Josephine drew a chair close to Mrs Fisher's desk. 'I wasn't expecting help, merely a desk, and access to *The News* archive. I have one friend who helps me when he can, but not in the way I need it.'

'You must have found it difficult being the only skirted reporter.'

'I was never a reporter, but it was always my ambition to be.'

Indicating over her shoulder in the direction of the room where *The News* reporters worked, Emmeline Fisher said, 'They must know that their monopoly of this profession will end soon.'

'Did you hear that they refer to me as the "She-Radical"?'

'I hope that you took that as a compliment.'

Josephine smiled. 'It rather got my hackles up, but now that you mention it . . .'

'My dear Miss Ferguson, I am *so* pleased that George persuaded you back.'

'Not exactly back.'

'Ah, but working here, that's the important thing. Can I tell you something in confidence?'

'It's not necessary to ask that.'

'Of course, but it concerns George, and he's a long-time and loyal friend.'

'I understand that. I owe him loyalty, too.'

'George knows that he made a big mistake over that story you wrote enabling *The News* to be first on the streets with the Great Coram Street tragedy.'

'I think so too. He lost his nerve.'

'He did; he had said as much to me, but with the best of motives . . . Well, perhaps not the best, but sincere motives. He took fright at the last moment. He knows that you should have had your name on the front page.'

'I should have, but I understand what he is up against – proprietors of other papers are envious of our growing popularity . . . and he *did* produce a newsheet to beat our competitors.'

'Miss Ferguson, I should very much like to work with you, if you agree.'

Josephine found herself smiling broadly. 'Deal done, Mrs Fisher.'

'Shall we start right away?'

Josephine claimed a desk by the window and placed her notebooks on it. Mrs Fisher took a box of new pencils, notebooks and some packets of paper, and arranged them neatly before Josephine. 'If those fellows call me the "She-Radical", they must have a name for you,' Josephine observed.

'"Brock". Oh, how original and clever.' Mrs Fisher strained her hair away from her face, emphasizing her white streaks. 'Water off a duck's back – my husband has been calling me "Brock" for twenty years. Now, tell me what you would like me to do.'

'It may be clutching at straws . . . on the other hand . . . I thought, the personal advertisements . . . I don't know what I expect to find, but a morning spent reading back over the month or so before the murder. Perhaps she met this man through the small advertisements.'

'Ah, yes. What a good idea.'

'I don't hold out much hope, but skip through all the likely newspapers leading up to Christmas. One never knows . . .'

Mrs Fisher smiled widely, 'One never does.'

At the end of her first morning, Mrs Fisher laid some notes on Josephine's desk.

'These all refer to "Clara" in some way but are no use to us. However,' she pointed to a copy of *The Echo* – 'this jumped out at me. German Gentleman . . .'

Josephine read the small advertisement. 'GERMAN GENTLEMAN. The lady who met German Gentleman near St Pancras Church last week regrets failing in her evening appointment and would arrange another interview – 172 Caledonian Street.'

Josephine smiled as she scribbled down the address. 'Mrs Fisher, would you care for a walk?'

The door at 172 Caledonian Street was opened by 'Madame Margaret', the woman who had left the Alhambra Palace bar in a huff.

'It's you again.'

'Yes, it's me, and this lady is Mrs Fisher. I'm sorry if what I said at the Alhambra—'

'What d'you want?'

'Firstly to say that I'm sorry.'

'How did you find me?'

'That's the other reason why I've come. It's this.' Mrs Fisher showed her the newspaper clipping. Madame Margaret became uneasy. 'Can I talk to you?' Josephine asked.

'Not in here you can't, there're too many nosey parkers.'

'How would it be if I were to buy you breakfast at O'Sullivan's? Would you talk to me there?'

'You know O'Sullivan's?'

'Of course, Welsh rarebit and stout is my favourite.' She said this with such assurance that Madame Margaret began to feel that, although this was a strange woman who talked posh, she might be all right.

This was a test of whether Mrs Fisher would be of use in Josephine's investigations; in the event she proved to be entirely at ease, as if she was used to breakfasting with a prostitute and a young woman who did not stand on ceremony.

Over a seven-item breakfast for Madame Margaret, and for Mrs Fisher and Josephine a repetition of the meal she had had with Violet, Josephine waited for Madame Margaret to talk. Eventually, when she was enjoying a second serving of fried bread, she spoke. 'About the German. Well, it was like this. My friend and I was picked up by this man, and he asks us to have a drink with him. So we took him to The Falcon, the pub. We thought we'd have a bit of a day off. Well, what happened, this German says would we go with him to a coffee house and spend the night with him – the both of us for a half-sovereign. At least, that's the coins he showed us.'

'A coffee house?'

'We reckoned he meant a hotel, but didn't know the right words. Anyway, we wasn't too keen. So he said, "I will give you each two gold pieces."'

'Well, to us that's a decent bit of money, so we said

we would meet him where we met him before, outside St Pancras Church.'

'But you got cold feet.'

'Sort of. We said maybe he wanted ropes tied and that kind of thing.'

Josephine didn't, but she was fast learning about the Haymarket women.

'I've never had nothing to do with that kind of thing, I leave that to them who don't mind. I don't like being hurt any more than is normal, so we didn't turn up.'

'What made you change your mind?'

'Debts. I said to my friend, as there's two of us, we're not likely to come to harm. So we decided to put that in the paper.'

'Did he fit the description the police have put out?'

'Oh, yes, he fits.'

'And you think that your German was the one that came back and picked up Harriet?'

Madame Margaret's hard face began to crease, and she gripped her lips together to hold back tears. 'Of course I bloody think that. It was my fault that Clara got done in, wasn't it?'

Mrs Fisher handed the other woman a handkerchief. Josephine said, 'No, it was *not* your fault. It was the fault of the man. He killed her, not you. Now you just stop thinking like that.'

'If I hadn't put that advert in the paper, he would of stayed away.'

'You do not know that. He . . .' Josephine had been

about to say that he had come prepared to kill and would have done so anyway.

'Yes, miss . . . he was going to kill one of us, wasn't he?'

David Wilde gathered his cloak about him and held it close to his chest. Fog and smoke created a thick air, yellow as tallow and hard to breathe. St Giles was but a few hundred yards from his home, not a traditional vicarage or manse, but a two-storey house in a row of similar houses. Although he was not permitted to preach, he could go into St Giles and talk to anyone who needed him. He liked his life and had no complaints. Today's dinner-time broth would have a ham-bone as its base. On other days there were pigs' feet, marrowbone, onions or leeks as the stock. Bread, pearl-barley or dumplings were additions in rotation. Mrs Chapman, the woman who cleaned and cooked for any minister living in the church's tied house, might not be an imaginative cook, but she was an excellent one.

He was so hungry he could scarcely wait to get home. 'David.' He at once recognized the voice calling him as Josephine's. He looked around eagerly and saw her hurrying towards him out of the fog's yellow gloom. 'Jo. What a treat. Are you in a rush?'

'No, but if you are I'm sorry to hold you up. I wanted to ask your advice. Could I walk with you?'

'Better than that, you could join me in a bowl of Mrs Chapman's soup. I can assure you that it will be wonderful, it always is.'

245

So, unexpectedly, Josephine found herself seated with David and his housekeeper in a comfortable below-stairs kitchen, eating thick broth and chunks of bread. She had never imagined him living like this; in fact, she had never envisioned his home life at all; until now he had always been part of the public supper rooms' group of would-be reformers, or a visitor to hers and Liliana's kitchen.

'Good, isn't it?' he grinned. 'Ham-bone and chicken broth with cider. Not Liliana's *coq au vin*; Mrs Chapman is a country cook ... the very best, aren't you, Mrs Chapman?'

'Giving out prizes, then, are you, Young Father? You don't get round me so easy. Going out like that when I told you there was a hole in your sock.' She wagged her head in mock exasperation, but it was obvious that she enjoyed caring for David. Jo knew that he disliked the popular name he had been given – Young Father David – but he let it go.

If Mrs Chapman was a country cook, then the country must be situated within the sound of Bow bells. 'I would give you a prize, Mrs Chapman ... in fact I would like to ask if you would give me the receipt for the women's page of a journal I write for.'

'I'm glad you like it, miss, but my soups don't never have a receipt. I wouldn't want it always turning out the same. My soups grow out of what gets give by people in a small way of business who can't always give money to the church.'

Josephine was glad that David was looked after so

well, and by such a nice friendly woman who didn't stand on ceremony.

Mrs Chapman cleared the table and took the dishes through to the scullery.

'You remember that you introduced me to Violet?' He nodded. 'We met, and she gave me these.' Josephine produced the packet and placed it on the table. 'Love letters written to Harriet. Violet had been keeping them for Harriet whilst she, Harriet, was moving to new lodgings. Violet was trusted because she could not read. She says that no one else has seen them, and I believe her. However, I *have* read them. They are from a man with whom Harriet obviously lived for a while: Willie Kirby.'

'I remember Willie.'

'You do? Ah, that is just what I wanted to know.'

'He was yet another of Clara's – Harriet's – ships that passed in the night. Each of them, I'm certain, she believed to be her knight in shining armour, who was going to take her away from her life here. I think he was on leave from somewhere in the Far East.'

'Hong Kong. The letters were written whilst he was on board ship returning there.'

'Liaisons such as these are not so uncommon. Young men come home on leave, set up with a pretty young woman for six months or so, even a year. The young women can scarcely believe their good luck and see a bright future for themselves. I never know whether to be pleased that young women have had a period in their lives when they are off the streets, or angry that they have their hopes dashed.'

'He did write her very many letters. Do you think that a good sign? That he did intend to send for her? He says so . . . but promises are easy to put in a love-letter aren't they?'

'Unfortunately I've never had occasion to write one.'

'Never? Poor David, you must be at least twenty-eight . . . you'd better hurry or you'll be left on the shelf.'

Giving her a mock pathetic smile, 'Twenty-nine. I couldn't even hazard a guess about his intentions. Harriet did bring him along to our meetings on occasion, but he didn't impress me as being the kind of man who would saddle himself with a wife.'

'I think one doesn't have to read between the lines to come to that conclusion.'

He left the table, took down a brown earthenware teapot from a shelf and proceeded to make tea. 'I'm sorry, we don't run to coffee here.'

'I prefer tea.' That wasn't quite true, but she was fascinated to watch him move about the kitchen, able, without searching, to lay his hands on any utensil necessary. A man who could fend for himself in a kitchen was rare. She doubted that Uncle James would have been able to find a spoon. The more she got to know David Wilde, the more he grew in her estimation. 'So, tell me, what must I do with his letters? I wondered if you would take them. If he ever returns . . .'

'No, no, even if he did return, they are not *his* letters. They are part of Harriet's estate, and they might even be evidence. I think you must take them to the police.'

'I did think about doing that, but what good are they to the police? Willie Kirby isn't a suspect. From the dates on the letters, he is still in China.'

'The police will be trying to discover as much about Harriet as you are, and who knows what information or evidence they may have that you do not.' He fingered the package. 'And there must be a great deal of information in here.'

'There is, but nothing that would help discover who killed Harriet. They do reveal a lot about Willie Kirby, though, and about the way that men in general think of girls like Harriet.'

'And what do "men in general" think of girls like Harriet?'

'I'm sorry, I didn't mean to imply *all* men.' She felt flustered. 'I meant . . .'

Smiling at her discomfort, he said, 'No, no, maybe you are right, but I cannot agree or disagree with you if you don't explain.'

'It is obvious from the start of our lives that boys are led to believe that their lives are more worthwhile than their sisters'; mothers favour sons over daughters, daughters learn to defer to brothers, sons model themselves on their father. Little boys learn, by osmosis if not by explicit lessons, that the world is fashioned to suit the male of our species, and that they are entitled to any advantage given to them.'

'I can't deny that.'

Wrong-footed by his acceptance, she said, 'Oh.'

'What, specifically, does Willie Kirby write that makes

him an object lesson on men's attitude to the Harriets of this world?'

'I don't know how they met, but we can make a good guess at that. He takes to her – more than that, I believe that he is fascinated by her, he certainly liked mixing with her friends: "the sisterhood", he calls them. He enjoyed that world, and yet he picks at her constantly to change. He wants her to dress differently, to be more sober and sensible in her ways, to stop being flighty, to read seriously, to practise her spelling and writing. He begs her to leave London and go to live a more proper life in the country when, for goodness' sake, it was her very impropriety and carefree life that he found so engaging.'

'She did leave London for a short while after Willie left.'

'Did she? I would guess that it *was* for a short while.'

'She went to her sister. I believe that her sister was as intent on improving Harriet as was Willie.'

'That doesn't surprise me; in fact it upholds my belief that women must be moulded to what men believe they should be. I have seen Harriet's sister; she appeared the epitome of properness. Willie Kirby found a light-hearted woman like Harriet, and liked her enough to have her live with him, then proceeded to try to make her serious and ladylike; to force her to work at her grammar and spelling.'

'In many ways, Harriet already *was* a thoughtful and serious woman. She might have lived an unstable life, but she always cared for her child and tried to keep her away from the Haymarket scene. Whilst the child's father was off and away, Harriet did what she could for the child in the only way she knew how – to entertain.'

'I hadn't realized that you knew her so well.'

'I didn't, but like so many of the people who live and work in my part of London, I know *about* them. I get to know their circumstances and usually their problems. Harriet Burton's greatest problem was trying to bring up and educate a child. And you are right about Willie Kirby. He was willing to keep Harriet, but not her daughter . . . She was sent to the country, perhaps to Harriet's sister, I really don't know.'

'I suppose you are right about these letters.'

'I am. As part of Harriet's estate they belong to her child, or her sister.'

'I didn't think of that.'

'You would have.'

She rose from the table and put the packet of letters into the document case she always carried. 'Thank you for the soup and advice. Come soon and visit Liliana and me. I will persuade Liliana to continue with her French cuisine.'

He grinned. 'I'm not sure whether that is a threat or a promise, but I will take a gamble.'

She had met many young men at Ann Martha's soirees, luncheons and dinner parties, but not one with whom she had felt as comfortable as she did with David Wilde. Best not tell Ann Martha, or she would start making guest lists and choosing wedding clothes.

* * *

251

James Thomson was seated in his office when the front desk sent in to say that a *Miss* Thomson wished to see him. James was up and out of his chair at once. They had not met since Harriet's funeral, and he was wondering what to do about it.

'Josephine, my dear, come in, come in.'

His expression was so kindly and welcoming that she felt assured that they were back in one another's good books again.

'Uncle James.' She kissed him on the cheek. 'Lovely fire. It is so cold out there. More snow on its way, I shouldn't wonder.'

'I will get some fresh tea made.'

'Don't trouble on my account.'

'No trouble,' he smiled widely. 'What is rank for if it is not to have the privilege of having tea and biscuits brought to one's desk?'

The tea having been brought and poured into heavy institutional cups, Josephine pushed the envelope containing Willie's letters across his desk. 'These were given to me.'

'Letters?'

'Love-letters, from a Willie Kirby. You may have heard of him in your investigations.' His expression was closed. 'She was kept by him for a while, and I believe that he sent her money until very recently. That is only gossip, but I've been told that it stopped, which was why she was forced on the streets again. I brought them to you because I don't want to be charged with withholding evidence.'

'Josie—'

'Uncle James, you may not like what I do, but I am determined to do it. I am back working as a correspondent for *The News* and I am writing a biography of Harriet Burton. I have interviewed very many of her friends. I think they trust me more than they might a policeman.'

'It is not surprising that they respond to another woman.'

'Then you should have women in the police force, shouldn't you?'

'Josie, let's not get into a discussion again about the place of women in the world. I agree, women could have a greater role to play than they have at present, but I don't make the rules.' He emphasized the last four words.

'I know. I know. I am just sounding off to someone who I know will not call me a madwoman.' She paused for a few seconds. 'And, Uncle James, as well as handing over the letters, it did occur to me that you might like to read what I have written of Harriet's biography so far.'

'That is very generous of you.'

'Ah, but the offer has strings.'

'Dearest girl, you know that you cannot make bargains with me regarding this investigation.'

'How close are you to catching him?'

He didn't reply.

'Not close at all?'

'I cannot answer that.'

'Do you know "Madame Margaret"?'

'Madame Margaret's name has been mentioned as one of many of the girls who frequented the bar at the Alhambra Palace, that I can tell you.'

'And The Falcon public house?'

'I don't recall that place in connection . . .'

'Madame Margaret and a friend took a German there before Christmas. The description of the man tallies with that of your suspect.'

James Thomson was all attention now. Nothing of this had come out in Kerley's report on his interview with the prostitute. 'Do you intend telling me, or do you intend dragging out your story?'

'All right, Uncle James, I was going to make a bargain with you. All the information contained in my manuscript for a promise to let me meet him – all right, at least see him – as soon as you have made an arrest.'

With the lack of success they had had so far in apprehending the suspect, he thought he was pretty safe in telling her, 'No promises, but I will try to let you know somehow.'

'That is all I ask. And I promise that nothing I will do will compromise you or give any clue that you have any connection with "Jemima". Give Ann my love, but don't you dare tell her what I have been doing.'

'You may be sure of that.'

'And you will send me a telegraph as soon as you find him?'

'Josie, I said that I would do my best to at least give you a hint, but certainly not telegraph you. That is the best I can offer, and maybe that is not exactly within the rules of the Met.'

She hugged his shoulders and placed a kiss on his thin, plastered-down hair. 'I am the last person in the world to jeopardize your career, Uncle James. I expect you to be commissioner one day.'

He held on to her hand. 'Don't you dare wish that upon me! I'm a Scotland Yard detective, and that is all that I want to be.'

Only days after Josephine had extracted a half-hearted deal with her uncle, there was a dramatic breakthrough in the investigation that slowed down every other line of enquiry.

It came from Ramsgate in Essex, a seaport on the eastern coast of southern England, not a hundred miles from London.

A sergeant in the Ramsgate force was so eager for promotion that he perused every piece of paper that passed over his desk. As he was contemplating what to keep and what to discard, several things came together: the £100 Reward notice that had been pinned to the station notice board for weeks, the artist's impression of the wanted man, the description mentioning that he might have a German accent, and a report of yet another incident connected with a German vessel named *Wangerland*.

The *Wangerland* was an emigrant ship en route from Danzig to Brazil, blown off course by a violent storm and onto the treacherous Goodwin Sands. The vessel had been tied up for repairs for weeks now, and from time to time trouble had broken out – not from the poor devils kept on board, but from the officials and agents who were living ashore in Ramsgate. Only minor incidents, except for the letting off of a firearm from a hotel window, but collectively a nuisance that the Ramsgate police could do without.

He took his suspicions to Superintendent Buss, who at once saw that there might well be a connection – it was a relatively short train journey between Ramsgate and London.

'Well spotted, Sergeant. Make a telegraph connection with Bow Street.'

Josephine was about to leave after making a short duty visit with Ann, Hani and Uncle James, when there arrived the same eager young constable who had been waiting for James Thomson with a cab on Christmas morning. He stood respectfully in the outer hall, awaiting an answer to the note he had carried here.

'Right then, Constable, I shall be no longer than two minutes.'

A maid was sent to fetch the small overnight bag he kept ready for such quick departures. 'I am sorry, Ann, and you too, Josie, but I must go to the station at once.'

'Is it him, the German?' Ann asked.

James Thomson flicked a glance at Josie.

'You know that I cannot tell you that, Ann. I am sorry that I could not enjoy an entire morning with you both but—'

'I know, I know, duty calls.'

Josephine saw the eagerness on her uncle's face and knew at once that the note contained dramatic information.

'I was about to send for a cab, so perhaps I could ride part of the way with you.' She hastened to take her kapok-lined jacket and hat from the hall stand, gave Ann Martha and Hani a quick hug and joined her dismayed uncle in leave-taking.

With the constable on top with the driver, James at once set about admonishing Josephine in a low voice. 'What do you think that you are doing, Josie? You simply cannot impose yourself like this.'

'All I want is a ride in your cab. You haven't forgotten your promise that you would let me see him?'

'For heaven's sake, Josie, I have no idea whether I am going to be seeing *him*. I cannot emphasize enough that if it gets known that I am closely related to a member of the newspaper fraternity then I could be compromised.'

'We have been over this. You know that I would never do that . . . Don't you trust me, Uncle James?'

'That's not the point, Josie.'

'Do you or don't you have faith in my promise not to compromise you in any way? You have to do what you must, and so must I. If there is one thing that I absolutely must do, it is to see the monster who ended Harriet's life.'

He withdrew into his thoughts, looking out at the busy London streets as the cab forced its way through the congestion of the centre. Josie knew that she had said enough to prick his conscience a little. And he *had* said that he would do his best. Eventually he said, 'I did say that I might find some way . . . but I tell you this most seriously, Josephine. You must never, ever, try to extract promises of that nature from me, ever again.'

'I do understand, Uncle James. And really, honestly, I shall never ask such a favour again.'

'The best that I can do is to say that I shall be catching the afternoon train to Ramsgate. You are *not* to try to do the same. If at any time you do arrive in that town, you will keep well away from us.'

'Uncle James, I have said that you can trust me, haven't I?' He continued to look out at the traffic. 'Look at me, Uncle James. I am serious. And thank you, thank you. You understand that I *have* to do this.'

The cab stopped and he got out. 'Bow Street, Josie. Do you wish to take the cab on?'

'I think I shall, Uncle James.'

Touching her hand, he said, 'I do understand, Josie. I was very touched by what you have so far written.'

Good as her word, Josephine did not try to travel to Ramsgate on the same train as her uncle, the sergeant and some of the most reliable eyewitnesses. Instead, she went straight to the railway station and caught a much earlier train to Ramsgate.

The spirits of the two detectives and the entire 'E' Division lifted, as would the spirits of any team of detectives whose suspect is a German who killed with a 'scalpel or similar thin-bladed instrument' and is offered a German surgeon.

The constables had been very successful in speedily rounding up the witnesses, and awaiting the two detectives were Oscar Philippe and William Stalker of the Cavour Restaraunt, Tryphena Douglas, George Flack and his two assistants.

'I didn't call Mrs Wright; she is still overwrought at the thought of confronting the suspect, nor the two scullery maids.'

'Those six will do us well enough.'

They were now on their way to Ramsgate in a first-class 'reserved' compartment. In another, but third class, accompanied by two constables, were the witnesses.

Superintendent Buss of Ramsgate was waiting at the station with three cabs, and greeted the two detectives warmly. 'It is fortunate that the repairs to the ship have taken longer than expected. It was thought to have sailed directly after Christmas.'

'So, if this surgeon you suspect is the one, then we have our only bit of good luck in weeks.'

They were now travelling in a cab from the railway station. Thomson asked, 'What is the story behind these people who came to London, Mr Buss?'

'I have to admit that it is one of mishaps and coincidences.' He related how an emigrant ship, the *Wangerland*, came to be tied up in a Ramsgate ship-repair yard.

'How long has she been there?' Frank Kerley asked.

259

Superintendent Buss was much more concerned with protocol than his Bow Street equal. 'My sergeant and I have worked together for many years. I encourage him to ask questions,' James Thomson explained.

Unused to such a relationship, Buss's answer was still directed at the senior officer. 'November. The damage proved greater than first expected.'

'So, what have they been doing, these people who suddenly found themselves in Ramsgate instead of en route for Brazil?'

'They *are* still en route, merely delayed some two months. You can hear all this yourself via an excellent translator I have engaged, but, to paraphrase, this ship has just one cargo – emigrants. I tell you, Mr Thomson, a more sorry lot you never saw in your life. They have invested everything they possessed to sail away to a new land. There is to be a German colony in this place, Bahai.'

Kerley asked, 'How do they think they are going to set up there?'

'There is an agent, Mr Hermes. Herr Hermes, whose job – as far as I can ascertain – is to arrange the practicalities of the settlement.'

'Ah. And they are taking along their own surgeon, sir?'

'Right. Our suspect, ship's surgeon Karl Wolebe. There is also a doctor, Franzen, and a pastor, the Reverend Hessel and his wife. I don't know what would possess anyone to take on such a venture. The emigrants are mostly families, but the others – the professionals, so to speak – are all young people. None of them thirty, I would say.'

'Idealists?' James Thomson asked. 'See themselves as present-day Founding Fathers, like those who sailed to America?'

'I speak frankly, and I have no evidence to support this: I believe that this is nothing more than a money-making venture, using the poor wretches below-decks for the purpose.'

'Poor wretches?'

'They have not been on dry land since they sailed. We have no jurisdiction over the arrangements on board, and it appears that they have no papers which give them the right to be in England – so there they stay, in the most degrading of situations.'

'And the others?'

'They all have passports, which is how Wolebe and his friends were able to travel to London.'

'Do they live aboard?' Frank asked.

'Oh no, they all have rooms at Hiscock's Royal Hotel, along with the ship's captain, Captain Wilken, and others. They come and go as they please. Others come to visit them – agents, vice-consuls, officials from Danzig – which is where this venture all began.'

Superintendent Buss and the entire entourage of police, witnesses and the prisoner were conducted to where the chairman of the bench of magistrates and twenty other justices were assembled, plus a formally dressed group of three august gentlemen. Superintendent Buss

261

introduced the second group who were (as Frank Kerley would later describe them to Elizabeth) most definitely important as well as being self-important. But for the present Frank's mood was in no way frivolous, but entirely correct and mostly unnoticed by the important gentlemen.

The magistrates arranged themselves to flank the chairman and the august gentlemen, whilst James's witnesses were put into a room to one side of the court. Then a number of dark-haired, clean-shaven young men of medium build were lined up facing the bench.

'You have done well to find so many likenesses to the suspect,' James commented.

'All German emigrants – not difficult to find around the port.'

The line-up was ready. Thomson and Kerley stood with the Ramsgate men. The chairman ordered the surgeon to be brought in and the manacles taken off. 'You may choose your place in the line, Herr Wolebe.' Frank Kerley noticed the respect afforded the murder suspect. A surgeon, well turned-out, of the class of person that commands respect. Wolebe chose a central position. He was thinner and paler than Kerley had expected, but men kept in custody, even though only for a day or so, often appeared altered. Nevertheless, the likeness to the charcoal portrait was easy to see.

'If you are ready then, Mr Buss, bring in the first witness.' However, before this could be done, there was a disturbance. A young man burst in, and said, 'I must stand by my friend. I insist. I am his pastor and must give him my support.'

'Who are you, sir?'

The German consul spoke up. 'This is a countryman of mine, Reverend Godfried Hessel. A clerical gentleman and colleague of Herr Wolebe.'

'He wishes to stand with the suspect?'

Hessel spoke up. 'It is my duty to support my dear friend Karl Wolebe.'

'Very well.'

'Thank you, I will stand beside my friend.'

Frank Kerley felt a terrible, inexplicable apprehension. Something untoward was taking place, but he could not understand what it was.

An usher opened the door to the room in which the witnesses were penned. He allowed Tryphena Douglas into the court.

James was proud of her: she would make the ideal witness with her quiet manner and her bearing. Never mind that her accent was that of a London barmaid, the girl had a refined air about her and she spoke up. Tryphena walked steadily and looked carefully at each man in the line, but stopped only when she reached the suspect. Then, speaking clearly and pointing, she said, 'To the best of my belief, this is the man who met Harriet in the bar and was with her on the omnibus.'

'Please touch on the shoulder the man you believe you saw.'

Tryphena Douglas reached out and touched a shoulder to the sound of gasps being drawn. James and Kerley looked at one another, then at Buss. Frank Kerley felt his spirits plummet.

The wrong man.

She had picked out the friend, the clergyman.

The rest of the London witnesses were brought in one by one. Without exception, they each touched the clergyman and said, as Tryphena had done, 'To the best of my belief, this is the man.'

On arriving at Ramsgate, Josephine, not having any plan, decided to sit in the station tearoom and watch the trains from London arrive. Her stomach turned with excitement when she saw her uncle and his entourage being greeted and taken off in cabs. She had no need to follow on their heels, but waited to give them a head start, then engaged a cab to take her to the vicinity of the town hall. If there was to be an identification parade, that is where it would take place.

Although she had not seen her uncle arrive at the town hall, she did see other comings and goings that led her to believe that she had chosen the right place. A number of uniformed policemen arrived on foot, accompanied by men who were obviously chosen for their likeness to the man on the Wanted poster.

The air carried the smell of the sea, from where came sharp, gusting winds. Josephine was glad to have a woollen scarf and hat on her perambulation around the vicinity of the town hall. Her attention was attracted by two young people carrying on a fierce argument as they hurried along. The woman clutched a shawl about her, apparently oblivious to the fact that she was without a hat and her hair was being torn from its pins by the gusts.

Josephine could hear nothing, but their actions spoke for them. The woman was angrily trying to stop the man from doing whatever it was he intended. From time to time she pulled his arm, making him stop and face her, still arguing. He shook her off. She hurried after him, again pulling at him. He pushed her away. She clenched her fists at him in frustration. As they reached the entrance to the town hall, he twisted away from her and rushed inside, leaving her standing.

Now what was all that about?

It was as much as she could do to hold herself back from entering the building herself. But good sense prevailed: if this was an identification parade to put the finger on Harriet's killer, then she would need to prove to Uncle James that she was responsible, and serious. If she put so much as a foot wrong, she would never achieve what she planned, which was to come face-to-face with the killer.

Had she known that this was the clergyman who was to put the cat amongst the pigeons, she might not have waited so patiently eating a pie and drinking tea to pay for her observation place in a pie shop facing the town hall.

She was lingering over yet another cup of tea when she saw several cabs drive up to a side entrance. The only person she could identify was Sergeant Kerley, his fair head visible as he doffed his hat to climb into a cab.

What to do now? Go back to London and hope that her uncle would do another favour? No. If they had apprehended the man, he would not be happy to see her. Stay in Ramsgate? Try to discover what had gone on?

Having decided to stay, she went to the offices of the Ramsgate evening paper, where she presented herself as Jemima Ferguson, assistant to George Hood of *The News*. Her honesty, charm, and the mention of the well-respected George Hood gave her access to the information she sought. The crime reporters were eagerly writing copy for the next edition.

From their office she gleaned nuggets of gold.

There had been a startling outcome to a parade where a Great Corham Street murder-suspect was to be viewed by some London witnesses. A man – a clergyman, no less – had at the last moment thrust his way in and insisted that he stand beside his friend – the suspect – to support him in his hour of need. As he was a clergyman, the magistrate allowed it.

Then, what happened? The London witnesses had identified him, the clergyman, as the murderer, and *not* the surgeon. There had been two London detectives in attendance, but the arrest had been made by a Ramsgate detective. The suspect would be taken to London.

The scene of the arguing couple came back vividly to Josephine. The incident appeared to fit the facts. Better far than returning to London, having ascertained where the Germans involved were staying, she found a modest emporium, purchased a small leather bag and a few items that would make her a bona fide visitor and took a cab to the hotel where the Germans were putting up.

The arrested man had been taken by cab to Bow Street, but James Thomson chose to travel back by train.

For the first while he and his sergeant travelled in silence, each within their own thoughts about the startling outcome. 'He fits, Frank.'

'He does, sir. A gambler, even with his own life.'

'A gambler, certainly, but an arrogant one who believes that he can outwit the rest of us. You may be sure, Frank, that he knows what he is doing.'

'It could have been collusion on both their parts: his and the surgeon's. How did he keep quiet so long and not make a statement about the visit to London?'

'I believe that we shall find that this party of young people have been living in a hotbed of intrigue.'

'But to be accused and not say what he must have known about the clergyman?'

'It is possible that the surgeon has his own secret.'

'Each has a hold over the other?'

'It would make sense. Which has the better chance of escaping a charge of murder: a bachelor surgeon or a married clergyman?'

'No, sir, he's not going to escape. He did it, clergyman or not, and he will get the rope. No magistrate is going to ignore the evidence of six witnesses – plus Mrs Wright and the two scullery maids if necessary . . . and who is to say what will be found out in Ramsgate?'

'I hope that you are right, Frank. Buss agrees that you

should go back there tomorrow when his men examine Hessel's possessions, and they question the rest of the London party and the hotel servants.'

They fell into a thoughtful silence.

Frank's thoughts went back to what had troubled him since it had been mentioned in the early days of the investigation. His senior's connection with the dead girl. Although it appeared that the investigation was drawing to a close, he wished that the super would come clean about his relationship with Harriet Burton.

Suddenly, the super leaned across and tapped Frank on the knee. 'You have something on your mind, Kerley?'

'Have I, sir? Mrs Kerley tells me she can read me like a book.' He smiled.

'No doubt she is more astute than I, but although I have yet to see you reveal your mind during an interrogation of a witness or a suspect, I think I know you well enough.'

'I have no reason to hide my thoughts from Elizabeth.'

'But from your superior officer? A colleague of long standing?'

'Sorry, sir, I never intended to imply that.' Frank could not avoid the shrewd scrutiny of the dark brown eyes. 'You would not thank me for revealing the nit-picking nature of my concern.'

'I won't ever be patronized, Kerley. Particularly not by a man under my command, and most particularly not by an officer for whom I have high regard and whose character and intelligence I esteem.'

'I'm sorry if my reticence smacks of condescension,

sir. It springs from an equal regard for an officer under whose command I hope to remain.'

'Thank you, Kerley.' The two men did not unlock eyes. 'And will you now kindly tell me what this is all about?'

Frank paused only long enough to try to assemble the right words, then, grasping the bull by the horns, said, 'It's been at the back of my mind what you once said about having at some time spoken to Harriet Burton. You said at the time that you once saw her perform. Then there was the matter of the beads. I am sorry, sir, but you won't be satisfied with less than honesty.' James gave a nod in acknowledgement. 'Had you been any man other than my superior officer, I might have questioned you further on the occasion when you first saw the body and revealed that she was known to you.'

Don't ever underestimate Frank Kerley.

James Thomson pulled from his pocket an expensive leather case containing two cigars and proffered it to Frank.

'I can't get on with them, thank you, sir. I use a pipe.'

The superintendent indicated that he should go ahead if he wanted, and Frank made a long job of filling a pipe and tamping the tobacco.

'You can be assured that, had my meeting with her had the slightest bearing on the case, then I should have added that to the evidence, but you are right to ask. It has no bearing, but I am glad to have the opportunity of telling you.'

269

This was an extraordinary turn of events. Hitherto James Thomson could never have conceived of an occasion when an officer of lower rank would speak with such candour to his superior officer, and that officer himself had so trampled down the barrier of class and rank as to put himself at a disadvantage.

'In the antecedents, as you no doubt recall, there is a list of lodgings and people with whom she lived, which includes a Major Brown?'

'Of course, sir, they lived at One hundred and seventeen Stamford Street, and before that in Blackfriars Road – Forty-eight Nelson Square. Not likely to forget, sir, I must have read them a dozen times lately. That's when she started calling herself Mrs Brown – she had a stillborn child by him.'

'She had two.' James Thomson leaned forward to unstrap the window a little to expel the accumulating tobacco smoke. 'Has Mrs Kerley had such an experience, Frank?'

'Thank God, no, sir.'

'Then you and she are fortunate. It is the most grievous experience one can imagine. Not only for the woman, but for the man also – a thing few people think much of. It is fearful to see one's wife experiencing anguish and misery and be quite unable to do anything to assuage it. He must be strong and give her hope, make her believe that she will bear another child. Yet his own heart is broken. Whilst the woman is surrounded by her comforting relatives and friends, the man's grief is not seen. People do not expect a man who has had his hopes

270

of fatherhood dashed to be anything but supportive, strong and brave, yet he feels none of those things, he feels weak and greatly in need of comfort.'

Frank Kerley took in the expression he saw in the superintendent's eyes, and saw that the man had experienced an inexpressible pain.

James Thomson continued. 'It is a little while since this unfortunate occurrence. She had been passing herself off as the wife of Major Brown. I hardly know now how I came to find myself seated in a music hall. My wife was still lying-in and the house was filled with women bent on drawing her out of her despair. If I am to tell you the whole story, then I must say that I most likely went in the direction of the Haymarket, bent on trying to deal with my own despair in whatever manner took hold of me. Nothing seemed to be worth a thing without the little children I had seen laid in the ground. Unconsecrated ground, Frank! Unconsecrated because they were twins who never drew breath. Yet these were my children. My wife has never realized that they did not receive a Christian burial. I have always persuaded her not to visit their resting place – if resting place it is.'

He stood up and, pulling at the leather strap sharply, shut the window again against the cold air and soots from the engine.

Frank, with the happiest of memories of his own daughter's birth, would have done anything not to have been the recipient of this sad tale, but he had been the reason for its telling, and must suffer whatever consequences came from it.

'Where I found myself eventually was seated in the bar of the Alhambra Palace, a bottle of brandy before me, staring without knowing what was passing before my gaze until eventually this sweet, unusual voice penetrated my dull brain. I had never heard quite that kind of voice before.

'The ballad was poignant and sentimental. Not the kind of song I am very partial to, and I hardly think it was the sentimentality that affected me, but that sweet voice spoke of vulnerability. She may have felt unconfident in that place where voices are most often strident and coarse, I doubt hers always reached the back of the theatre, but perhaps it did not matter, she was a most feminine and pretty young woman. She looked no more than nineteen, although she was of course older than this. If you were to question me as a suspect, then you would be right to suppose that what I say is not true, but I was not attracted to her . . . to her physically. During the entire encounter I never once wanted to experience a sexual relationship with her.'

To spare his senior officer embarrassment, Frank knocked the ash from his pipe into the little brass cup attached to the side of the door for the purpose. It was notoriously unsuited unless one was most careful, so the operation provided a distraction.

'I don't know where my thoughts had been – they may have been in a stupor from the brandy I had been drinking – but suddenly I looked up and there she was, seated beside me, the curtains on the stage pulled and the lights gone up for an interval. She said, "If you want me to go away, you have only to say so." I think I probably indicated that she should stay, and offered her some of the brandy. "A lemonade, if you please, and I'll take a dash with it.'

'She was with you for the evening?'

James Thomson nodded. 'Until quite late. After the first drink of brandy and lemonade, she drank only lemonade, and I joined her in drinking that too. The waiter seemed not to mind, I paid him for the bottle of brandy which he would be able to sell a second time. Once she began to draw out of me the reason for the melancholy she had observed when she came from the stage, a table in the Alhambra stalls was hardly the place. So we walked. Nowhere in particular. Her discretion was touching; she did not enquire a thing about me except to ask when we looked for a place to take refreshment whether it was a place where I would be recognized, as she was sure I would not wish to be seen in her company. (I shall never know, but I do believe that she may have recognized me.) But I tell you sincerely, Frank, I don't think I should have minded much at that moment, for I had discovered a fellow human being who recognized my suffering and my absolute need to talk of it.'

'And you talked of stillborn children.'

'We did, for the entire time. She said that she had experienced that grief not just once, but a second time. I asked her what it was like for the woman, and she told me of the sense of having failed her husband (she called him that) and the longing, at first, the woman has to

273

replace the lost child. "But you see," she said to me, "I soon found out that a baby isn't replaceable. It is itself and is unique, and its parents must mourn it and then get over it." She said, "People will tell your wife to have another child quickly and she will forget the first, but that is not true. Each child is remembered for itself, no matter how long it lived or whether it lived at all."

'You have no idea how wise that girl seemed to be. What a comfort it was to be told something by one who was an authority on the subject which no one else would talk about with me. She was open and honest. I have to confess I admired her strength of character and despised my own weakness, but she assured me that it was no weaker for a father to grieve for a dead child than for its mother. She said that I would find it a painful experience, but that she was certain that I would survive it, as she had herself. She told me about her daughter and the circumstances in which she herself had been at the time she put the child out to foster. "I have even survived that," she said.'

Again he met Frank Kerley's eyes full on. 'That really constitutes the entire story. It was late when I walked with her to Russell Square, where she had been living since Brown left her to fend for herself. I did not go to her room, nor had any desire to do so. She had done more for me that evening than any relative or friend had done. She gave me hope that I would arise from my state of despair and soon see that the future would lose its bleakness. It could not have been easy for her to spend an evening with such a grim companion, to say nothing of having resurrected her own experience. I felt that I must pay her but felt clumsy when it came offering money for something that money really cannot buy. However, her straightforward manner when I broached the subject swept away any awkwardness. "I have no income at present, and my voice is not exactly my fortune. I have to eat and clothe myself, and landladies do not give free lodging." She refused the five guineas I offered, saying that she would take a sovereign, though when she left, I slipped the rest into her pocket. She kissed me on the cheek.

'She was right. From that day I began to return to the real world, where the twin children who should have been did not exist. I might have sought her out and told her this, but I did not. Wounds heal, and more often than not one forgets to bless the means by which they are healed.'

'That's a common human trait, sir.'

'Thank you, Frank. You cannot imagine how much I wished myself a better person on that morning.'

'Sir, may I ask you something?' Thomson nodded. 'Were you and I working together during that period, for I can think of no time when you appeared anything but professional.'

'Yes. That too was my salvation, I could leave home and immerse myself in "E" Division. That was the time when I worked on the orphanage.'

Frank hardly knew what to say. Superintendent Thomson had received great commendation for the months of work and donations he had contributed to the setting-up of a police orphanage. 'And the Police Reward Fund. You were the first person to understand the lives of ordinary policemen.'

James Thomson gave a wry smile. 'Commissioners and ministers are rewarded – titles and the like. It was difficult to get anyone to see that ordinary people too need to have their exceptional deeds recognized . . . and their orphaned children cared for.'

'It made you enemies, Mr Thomson.'

'Small-minded people are not worthy of being recognized as enemies. The enemy in "E" Division is still the awful poverty and degradation under which the greater portion of the people live.'

'I often think, sir, that if we could house and feed children as is only right, our job would be to catch the real villains, grotesques like the one we nabbed today.'

They were now racing towards London through the flat and featureless countryside of Kent. The composure of both men regained, the matter that Frank had raised was done with, but it would be a thing that would link them to the end of their careers.

After two nights away from home, all the pleasures of coming back to her own rooms returned to Josephine. A clutter of animated voices came from within, making her return doubly pleasurable. She dropped her bag and put hat and jacket on a hall peg.

Without so much as a greeting, Liliana said, 'Here's Jo, she will agree with *me*.'

The door that linked the two parts of the accommodation was propped open, as it often was when Liliana wanted to keep at work but not miss anything going on in the kitchen. Christine Derry, the promoter of new art, was stirring something on the newly installed gas stove; David Wilde was placing spoons and dishes on the table.

Briefly she took in the scene. This was the kind of homecoming she had envisioned whilst she was still trying to break out of the cocoon spun by her guardian angels.

Smiling broadly, she said, 'Jo will agree with nothing nor no one until she is given a cup of chocolate.' Chocolate, always warm and ready to drink, was served dark and thick, in the European style that Liliana had introduced.

David Wilde stepped forward and offered to shake her hand. 'I hope you don't mind us rabble invading your territory like this. My sister said that you would not.'

'I already said that I hoped you would come. I'm pleased. And Christina, making your amazing hotpot?'

Christina, who had stopped stirring to pour chocolate, said, 'You have arrived at the exact moment of readiness. I must say this new stove is a marvel, from a flame to a glimmer in an instant.'

Liliana, who had been intent on entering whilst still cleaning her hands with turpentine, was shooed back to wash with soap. In five minutes the four young people were seated around the wooden table, ladling meat and vegetables from the central crock and breaking bread from a large loaf. Not at all in the style of Ann Martha and Hani. They would be dismayed at their casual manners, but that was the point: they would never see Josephine's new way of living.

What it was that Jo would have agreed with Liliana about was forgotten in their eagerness to hear – and her own need to share with somebody – the extraordinary happenings at Ramsgate. She began by telling them how she had rushed to the railway station and arrived ahead of the Bow Street detectives and the witnesses.

'How did you know to go to Ramsgate?' Christina asked.

'Professional secret, and anyway it doesn't matter. Only that I did the right thing. It was a strange feeling stalking the police. When I saw them arrive with the witnesses in tow, I knew that something important had happened.'

'You didn't go prepared to stay,' said Liliana.

'No, but as soon as I knew that the suspect had been released and another arrested, I had to. I bought a few things and took a room at Hiscock's Royal Hotel, where this party of Germans had been staying for the two months since they arrived in Ramsgate.'

'What were they doing there?'

'Shipwrecked, apparently, and waiting for their ship to put to sea again. Don't interrupt me, Lili, and I will tell you the whole thing, most of which I got from the staff at the Royal. Particularly Somers, a girl on the hotel staff who I engaged as a personal maid.

'As you can imagine, the staff were agog as the news

leaked into their life below stairs. They see everything. Know all the gossip. And I am not an amateur at engaging in gossip.'

'Is that an inherent trait in you, or can it be learned?'

'You don't need me to tell you that, David. I see you doing it every time I come in to hear you talk to your audience.'

Christine said, 'I think it is being at ease with oneself and with the other person. I confess, I haven't that skill.'

'And so . . . ?' Liliana prompted.

'And so, from what Somers said, there were several of these young shipwrecked Germans travelling together. They were quite rackety, always falling in and falling out. One of them, the man who has been charged with Harriet's murder, always carried a revolver, and had already received a warning from the police for firing a shotgun from his bedroom window.

'However, all of this was minor compared to what happened a few days ago, when the young surgeon was arrested on suspicion and taken into custody. Jane Somers said that it was as if the public rooms had been turned into a disturbed beehive. The German consul and the ship's agent were back and forth, talking and arguing with the captain, the ship's doctor and some of the other passengers.'

'"Never act up before the servants" was my mother's advice,' Christine said.

'And never act up before your mistress if you are a servant,' Liliana retorted. 'That way you are out and no reference.'

'As far as I am concerned,' Josephine continued, 'I should have been lost without Jane, my fount of all knowledge where these young Germans were concerned. So, she told me that they had acted up from the very beginning. However, what happened on the day that I arrived was beyond anything that had gone before.

'The surgeon, whose name is Karl Wolebe, had been arrested on suspicion of murdering Harriet, and was to be put up for identification by the London witnesses. The consul was going to the town hall as his representative. Before he left, he, plus the ship's captain, the agent, the ship's doctor and two others – the ship's pastor and his wife – had foregathered in one of the Royal's public rooms. And, as my informant Jane put it, "there was a right ding-dong", a lot of it in German, but that didn't stop the servants getting the gist of it as one of the porters had been with a family who lived for years in Germany.'

'So what was the "ding-dong" about?' asked David.

'It was about the consul insisting that the ship's pastor – one Reverend Hessel – should support the surgeon at the identification parade, to which the Reverend Hessel apparently replied, "Very well then, if you insist." Then the wife was supposed to have said in jest, "If you are accused, a wife will not be allowed to vouch for evidence." I assume she meant that she wouldn't be able to give evidence against him.'

'Why would she even think that she might be called to do so?' David asked.

'Unless she knew that he was in danger of being identified,' Liliana said.

'Or,' said Christina, 'that the surgeon *was* likely to be identified, and she *could* give evidence against him.'

David said, 'That's a tortuous kind of conspiracy . . . all three of them would have had to be colluding.'

'Who is to say that there was not something more?'

Josephine looked sceptical. 'What, Lili, that the wife was an adulteress?'

'Have you thought that both men might be implicated in Harriet's murder?' David suggested.

'I have thought of that. And it may still be a possibility. You remember, David, that you introduced me to Violet and some of her friends? Well, there was one, "Madame Margaret", who had met a German prior to Christmas and had been offered money to—'

Liliana looked quite gleeful. 'Both of them? Lord help us! London gets more like Paris every year.'

'Lili,' David chided, 'let Josephine continue with her story. Facts not conjecture. And did he go to the identity parade?'

Josephine gave a gleeful grin. 'He most certainly did. What happened in the town hall is almost unbelieveable, but true. Just as the line-up was formed and the witnesses ready to come in, Mr Hessel came bursting in and demanded loudly to stand by his friend. Of course, there were no members of the public at the identification parade, except for those brought in to stand in line. It was from these that my friends in the local newspaper office paid for the inside story. Anyway, in short, dear friends, the clergyman has been arrested and brought to London, and the surgeon released.'

281

'Heavens!' The other three were hanging on Josephine's words.

'How extraordinary,' David said, 'how came this turnaround?'

'Simple. After being allowed to get in the line – by now his attitude was one of magnanimity rather than his earlier reluctance, "I shall stand by my friend!" – he was identified by the six witnesses as the man who had been seen in any number of places in the company of Harriet on Christmas Eve. I know some of these witnesses, and if they say it was the clergyman, then I believe them one hundred per cent. You remember, Tryphena and Alice, Lili? You'd trust their word wouldn't you?'

'I would, especially Tryphena. I was greatly impressed by her, I even have plans to ask her to let me paint her – all that dignity and posture set before the array of bottles of spirits and liqueurs.'

'Well, once this news got back to the hotel, all sorts of gossip came my way.'

'Such as?' Liliana asked.

'Such as the vicar having a separate bedroom from his wife and sometimes getting up in the middle of the night to sleep on board – there was some nose-tapping about that. Such as the two of them strutting about arm in arm. Mrs Hessel flirted with every young man.

'It was generally agreed, according to Somers, that *something* had happened in London. Because when the party returned, there was odd behaviour. First, Karl Wolebe (the surgeon, you remember) gave up his room at the Royal and sent his bags on board, saying he was going back there to stay until the ship sailed. Then he changed his mind and said that he was going to sleep in the hotel. Then, to cap it all, after everybody's in bed and asleep, he starts kicking up a fuss and getting servants out of bed to let him out. He went off only half dressed, rushing out in the middle of the night and demanding to be let on board to sleep there.'

Christina intervened, 'Did you see the wife?'

'Only outside the town hall when she was making a spectacle of herself trying to stop her husband going in.'

'What about when she returned to the hotel?'

'She didn't actually return there before I left, but had gone on board the ship.'

'Go on,' David urged.

'Well, on the return from London of this rackety group, Somers recalled that Reverend Hessel sent down for a large bottle of turpentine to clean his trousers of some blood from a nosebleed. He used an entire quart bottle.'

Liliana said, 'Turps is no good for removing blood.'

'Which is as Somers said. And the laundress – this will make spectacular evidence if she is ever called as a witness – in the Hessel's bundle of washing on return from London were a great number of blood-soaked handkerchiefs, and some petticoats. Again he explained the amount of blood away as a nosebleed.' Josephine smiled. 'You realize of course that no comment was made by Jane Somers or the laundress at the time, except that it must have been a mighty nosebleed.'

'With hindsight then,' Christine said, 'the saturated handkerchiefs suddenly became evidence that the man could be a murderer.'

'I believe that is what he is – Harriet Burton's killer.'

The prisoner Godfried Hessel was once again brought to stand in an identification line, this time at Bow Street police station.

James Thomson, tense with his wish to get it over, watched as the two overawed scullery maids, Mrs Wright, Madame Philippe from the Cavour Restaurant, and Alice Douglas walked the line of men. Again a positive identification was made, but Hessel appeared to rise above the proceedings – cocksure, disdainful and self-important.

It would not be professional for James to feel triumphant, but it was hard not to.

'We've got you!'

When earlier Mr Buss ordered the prisoner to empty his pockets, James had shared with Frank Kerley that most satisfactory moment. One gold coin, some silver and copper, a gold watch, a corkscrew, a penknife with sharpened blade, a fine, slim, steel fisherman's gutting blade, and a long, spring-loaded knife.

Hessel had not expected to be arrested, so had joined the line-up carrying what was normal for him. One could only surmise that he never went out without them. What kind of clergyman is it who carries a sharpened fisherman's blade and a spring-loaded knife?

All that he had to do now was to select from the many witnesses who had identified Godfried Hessel, those best suited to face the questioning of the likes of the Mr Polands and Magistrate Vaughans of the world of the London courts.

Before David had left, he asked whether she would be interested in meeting a friend of his. 'You won't have heard of her yet, but you will. Her name is Isabella Varley and she has written a book. I thought that she might be of use to you in telling you how she managed to get her own book published.'

'Really? Do you believe that someone might be interested in publishing "Harriet"? That will be my title: "Harriet – The Biography of a Country Girl in London". Is Miss Varley's a novel? I should think that fiction is much more likely to find a publisher than the biography of an unknown woman.'

'You could ask her.'

'Thank you, David, you really are a nice, thoughtful man.'

'Oh dear. How dull that makes me sound.'

'I don't think you dull at all. Quite the opposite. You are all fireworks when you speak in St Giles. What you say is not only true, it is inspiring. When I have been listening to you, I want to go out and make the world better. I expect that is how the Knights of St George went off to the Crusades.'

He laughed, 'Do you see yourself on a charger?'

'Not me. I am scared to death of horses.' Shaking his

hand to take leave of him, she said, 'Thank you for offering me your friend Miss Isabella Varley. When I am ready, I may ask you to let me meet her.'

Still holding her hand, absent-mindedly it might seem, as he had done on the train, 'Very well, but it leaves me disappointed. I had hoped that I had found a reason to ask you to go somewhere with me.'

'Lord above, David, you don't have to stand on ceremony with a woman who has your eccentric sister as a sub-tenant. I should very much like to go somewhere with you.'

'Really?'

'Better still, would you come out with me tomorrow morning?'

'I would.'

'You have church duties to perform, don't you?'

'No longer. I have parish duties – there I am my own master. I will go with you.'

'But you don't know where it is.'

'Then it shall be a surprise.'

She grinned, handing him his thick scarf to wind twice around his neck. 'I would rather not surprise you. Tomorrow morning, Harriet's killer will appear in Bow Street magistrate's court to answer the charge of murder.'

'And you would rather not go alone?'

'Oh no, not in the sense that I am apprehensive – no, I should like to have another person there to give an independent view of the man. I think I have been too involved with Harriet to be impartial. Also, I would like

286

Madame Margaret to be there, and I wondered if you would ask her.'

He laughed, 'Margaret going voluntarily to Bow Street court?'

'Which is why I hoped that you might persuade her. She was propositioned by a German, and I want to know if she recognizes the man who's been arrested.'

The court was crowded, as was usual if a murder case was to be heard. Josephine, David and Madame Margaret sat squashed together, high up at the back in the public seats. Madame Margaret had been reluctant to get out of bed so early, but Young Father David was a favourite of hers, so she was in court, almost unrecognizable without her extravagant dress and cosmetics. Only her red, red hair, partly covered with a shawl, distinguished her.

'I don't like this, Father David. I don't like this at all, miss. What if it's *my* German bloke? I don't know why you would want to know, miss.'

Josephine decided not to try to explain, but to rely on a promised payment for Madame Margaret's trouble in getting up so early. After three short cases she became quite absorbed in watching the court in action from a different perspective, away from her usual place in the dock on charges of soliciting or disturbing the peace.

There was a short recess and a great deal of bowing and scraping as the chief magistrate retired. 'Pee and tea,' Madame Margaret explained. 'I've often wondered

287

what's behind that door. I always imagine there's probably a really nice comfy room.'

The chatter subsided as a door opened and two uniformed policemen, not wearing helmets, appeared one each side of a manacled prisoner.

Instantly, Madame Margaret hunched down, pulling her shawl well down over her sweat-beaded brow and covering her mouth and nose with her cupped hands. She had no need to whisper, 'That's him.' David was seated between the two of them so that Josephine could not give the other woman's hand an assuring squeeze, but she was moved to see David take one of the prostitute's hands between his own and try to calm its trembling.

They were so wedged in by others in the crowded public gallery that it was impossible to leave, so they sat on and heard Josephine's Uncle James give evidence as to the circumstances of arrest, the victim's brother-in-law as to the identification of Harriet, and listened to the prosecution and defence cases in outline.

It was only at this point that Josephine discovered that Reverend Hessel's defence would be that, although he had been in London at the time of the murder, he had been taken ill on 22 December and been confined to his room at Kroll's Hotel in the Minories, well away from the site of the murder, and that Herr Kroll and his servants would give evidence to that effect.

It was well past noon when Josephine and her companions stepped out into snow that had fallen in the streets during their absence.

'I can't stop shaking and feel right sick,' Madame Margaret complained.

'O'Sullivan's,' Josephine commanded. 'Take her other arm, David.'

Once in the humid warmth of the breakfast rooms, and having taken a double shot of rum, Madame Margaret's cheeks regained some colour. 'Do you mind fetching us some food?' she asked David. Pulling a wry face he said, 'I'm sorry, Jo, but I don't have any money with me.' Which raised a laugh from the prostitute. 'You and me both, Father David.'

Josephine felt wretched at her assumption that all people carried money when they went out and, pulling a half-crown from her pocket, she passed it to him. He was not at all embarrassed, as many men would be, but picked it up and went to the serving hatch. 'Are you feeling better, Margaret . . . may I call you by your name?'

'It's as good as most things I've been called in my time, though my true name isn't that, it's Bella, but I don't use it except only when I'm not on the street. Call me Bella if you like.'

Bella, with a face clean of cosmetics, and seated hunched instead of displaying her usual projection of chin and bosom, was a different woman. So vulnerable that Josephine felt some guilt at having subjected her to the confrontation with the German. But she had really wanted to know whether the clergyman had been in London prior to his Christmas jaunt.

*   *   *

289

Following Hessel's remand, Herr Kroll called at Bow Street and handed in a written statement for the attention of Detective Superintendent Thomson. A voluntary written statement was unusual, and so promptly delivered. James read, 'I voluntarily tender, as suggested by my legal representative, a written statement of what was asked by your detectives as to what could be proved at the hotel.' There followed a detailed account of the comings and goings of the party from Ramsgate. It was a precise list of rooms, occupants, times, registrations, and everything else the owner of a first-class hotel might keep account of. Solid alibis. Irrefutable evidence by Herr Kroll and his servants.

This was to be Hessel's entire defence. He was not there. He could not have been there. He was confined to his rooms. He was heard to cough. His boots were put out for cleaning on Christmas Eve – he had no other boots than those.

James's earlier spirits dropped. His witnesses against Hessel's. Low-class witnesses against wealth and respectability.

There must be more to be uncovered in Ramsgate.

Frank Kerley returned to Ramsgate at once and went to Hiscock's Royal Hotel.

Although Superintendent Buss was nominally in charge of the questioning here, he was quite willing to give way to Frank Kerley in the questioning of Hessel's wife.

In all their weeks of speculation about Harriet Buswell's killer, neither of them had seriously considered a wife for him. But here she was, a young woman, who in other circumstances must have been lively but was now bewildered and strained at the turn of events at the town hall. And, Frank observed, she was angry.

Although she spoke reasonable English, Frank was correct and to the letter, and insisted that someone from the German consulate be present at all times.

'I regret, madam, that I must ask you to accompany me on board to examine your husband's chests and boxes.'

Through the consul, she said that these contained nothing but wearing apparel and dirty linen and that she would not wish this to be examined.

'I assure you, madam, that in any other circumstances but these I would avoid having to do so, and the consul will, I am certain, advise you that you do not have the right to prevent this happening.'

In sympathetic, gentle words the consul confirmed that this was the case – in English, after Frank had requested that he do so.

'You cannot make me go there,' she said. 'There is smallpox aboard the *Wangerland*.'

The consul retreated from her as though she might be a carrier of the dread disease. 'I had not heard of this.'

'Ask Captain Wilken, ask Karl Wolebe, ask Doctor Franzen . . . They know it.'

And so it proved true. The agents and captain were trying to prevent the discovery of the disease, hoping, Frank assumed, that they could make their escape before it was discovered. He was under no illusion as to what would happen to any of the emigrants found carrying smallpox.

Karl Wolebe, the original suspect, was not to be found, but Captain Wilken and the doctor agreed to accompany Frank Kerley aboard the vessel in order that he carry out his search, the kind of demeaning task he loathed. As it turned out, what she said about dirty linen was the truth. Crammed into sea-chests without laundering or care, silverfish and insects were nesting. The smell was repugnant.

'I noticed that Dr Hessel was wearing what appeared to be a new suit of clothes. Where are those he wore to London?' The search continued. More trunks were opened. Sergeant Buss came aboard as a cabin chest stowed in the Hessels' accommodation was opened.

It was obvious that the Germans were ill at ease, whether from the close proximity of smallpox below decks, or from discovering the contents of the cabin chest. 'If you are willing that the superintendent and myself list and take away some of the contents of this chest, we need not detain you any longer.'

With the captain and doctor gone, Kerley and Buss listed the items. 'One black dress coat, one black cloth vest. A quantity of clean and dirty linen consisting of men's shirts, collars and cuffs, two woollen shirts, some papers and books written in a foreign language, one worn suit, a six-barrel revolver, three packets of cartridges, two cases containing scalpels and other surgical instruments, a minister's black gown and cap, one black mackintosh, one pair of patent-leather side-opening boots.' All of which were later carried ashore by some of Buss's men.

'Mr Buss, sir,' Kerley said as they made their way along the dockside, 'I believe that someone should make a report on the conditions aboard this ship.'

'I am not sure that I should be the one to make the report.' The superintendent looked ill-at-ease. 'I understand your concern, but at least aboard the ship any disease is contained. A report might mean that the infection could escape and ravage the whole of Ramsgate. Do you understand my concern?'

'Sir, I also understand the plight of those poor wretches huddled in such poor conditions as I saw on my last visit.'

'It has not so far been confirmed as the smallpox. It might not be that.'

'What are those two doctors doing?'

'I really don't know.'

'Well, sir, if I might suggest—'

'Sergeant Kerley, you may have a less formal relationship with your own superior than my men have with me, but I am not open to suggestions from lower ranks.'

Frank felt his blood rage through his body. However, he knew better than to oppose a man of superior rank, and one who might well report insubordination. Frank Kerley wanted above all to continue as a detective and do what he did best. One of the many moral dilemmas he faced. He tried to draw on his grandfather's wisdom, but he was unable to find an answer there. So he was circumspect in his reply. 'I apologize, sir. I did not intend overstepping the mark. It is true – as you will remember Mr Thomson saying – he encourages comment. Sorry, sir, I shall think before speaking in future.'

Buss nodded his acceptance of Frank's apology.

'May I suggest something, sir?'

Buss nodded again.

'That you put pressure on the agents and the captain to insist that the doctors attend to their passengers by way of better food and medications.'

'I shall be pleased to do so, Sergeant. These people have been here long enough causing mischief and making trouble for my men.'

Frank raised his eyebrows questioningly, for he could only have been referring to the upper-decks passengers, the ones putting up at the Royal, but Buss did not enlighten him as to what mischief and trouble those passengers from the *Wangerland* had caused.

The vessel itself appeared as sick and wretched as its below-decks passengers. No wonder it had been damaged in a storm. If its present state was that of a repaired vessel, what had it been like when it sailed from Danzig? Those poor creatures below decks. Who would care to risk life to a tub like that?

That question puzzled Frank Kerley all the way back to London.

Ann Thomson had seen so little of her husband, and he appeared to be having so little sleep or proper meals, that she planned a strategy to make him have at least one evening at home.

Consequently, the Sunday after Hessel's arrest found James in the comfort of his own home, entertaining again, among others, the Granvilles and Colonel and Mrs Henderson. He was under no illusion as to Ann's reason for inviting the chief commissioner: he would not be able to absent himself from the dinner table pleading urgent papers awaiting him, no matter that this was true. Nor was he under any illusion as to why the chief of police should accept Ann's invitation – it was always 'Ann's invitation', her blood being of the very blue kind and not to be refused. Daily, since he had headed the Great Coram Street murder investigation, James had reported formally to the commissioner. The daily facts as they were reported to James himself. Tonight, however, James knew that Commissioner Henderson would want an unofficial briefing. In particular he would want to know why 'E' Division had been so rash as to arrest a respectable clergyman – a German at that, knowing that the queen was still mourning one of that same nationality.

The ladies eventually retired from the table, no doubt to discreetly sympathize with Ann on the dreadful things in which James's work involved him, and hoping to hear some of the more interesting details of a case involving a clergyman and a prostitute. James was assured that they would get nothing out of Ann Martha, even though she had tried to squeeze every last bit of scandal from him.

Still seated at table, Ann's cousin the Honourable

Hammond Proctor-Lazenby opened at once, saving Commissioner Henderson the trouble. 'What's this thing about you arresting a clergyman, James?'

'Landed yourself in something there, old chap. You'll never make anything stick,' added his brother Maurice. 'I mean, the royal household is half German; the country will never stand for it.'

James was able to appear sociable with the aid of the port bottle and a cloud of cigar smoke. He endeavoured to sound amiable. 'The man has only been remanded pending further enquiries. Scotland Yard doesn't give us carte blanche to choose our suspects.'

'But how could you even suspect such a man? A clergyman and a German to boot! Men don't come more respectable than that.'

'What does he look like, James?'

'He fits exactly the description we posted – young, dark, solid.'

'Does he wear his dog-collar when he goes about killing the odd dollymop after matins?' This got a laugh that the women must have heard.

James kept his equilibrium and refrained from what he wished he could say, 'You may as well save your breath to cool your porridge.' Instead he said, 'Why don't you find yourself a seat on the public benches – better yet, one of the reserved seats.'

Maurice said, 'No fear, James, I once tried that. Good God man, the smell of it. All the Lysol in the world cannot disguise the aroma of Mr and Mrs General Public.'

Hammond nodded in agreement. 'I have never been able to understand how a man of your refinement can stand it, day in and day out.'

James worked hard at keeping his good humour, if only for the sake of Lord Granville, who was an old friend, and Colonel Henderson, his superior officer, who might hold James's future in his hands, so he puffed more smoke-rings into the already clouded atmosphere before laughing and slapping Hammond on the shoulder. 'I reckon Mr and Mrs General Public might find this room a bit ripe.'

Good joke. James passed the port.

James Thomson was no fool; he was well aware that his own attitude was unusual to say the least – very unusual in his profession. Society, high and low, was rooted in prejudice. Although he had been nurtured in Smyrna's ex-patriot society, and for a while served Prince Tipo in his palace, his mother's influence had been strong. Bohemian was the current word for such nonconformists. In England they were few and far between. The example of Victoria and Albert had changed two generations. Having conquered such a huge part of the world, British people had become narrow-minded, certain that they were right in everything, examples for the rest of the world to live up to.

He had been glad to see that Josie had a mind of her own. She was problematical because of his own position, but he realized now that the problems were his, not hers. She was intelligent, and brave, and strong enough to see off the Proctor-Lazenbys of this country.

When the last of their friends departed, James went straight to the bedroom. Ann came up looking pleased with herself; he was already in his nightshirt.

'There, my dear,' she said as she stood with her back to him for his help in unpinning her hair. 'Don't you feel the better for an evening in civil company?'

It was over now, and she had arranged the dinner believing that it would do him good. Even so he could not answer her warmly. 'My dear Ann, in spite of what your cousins might think, I do not work among barbarians. Sergeant Kerley is quite as sensitive and intelligent as many who come here to dine.'

'I am sure that you are right, dear, but the Sergeant Kerleys of this world would hardly know how to tackle turbot.'

'Sergeant Kerley might well surprise you, Ann. He often surprises me.'

'Thank you, James, I can manage now.'

'No, let me brush it for you, I always find that very soothing.'

'I know very well that our code of behaviour is not the only one, James, but it is the only one that I know how to deal with.'

'The most alien code must surely have been Hani's when she first came here – you dealt with that wonderfully. *And*, I believe that we may have been the better for having her with us.'

'Absolutely, James. Hani is the most civilized of people.'

'Yet she had been a servant out there. Except for Josie, the woman closest to you, then, is a servant much lower in the pecking order than my Frank Kerley.' She did not reply but gazed into the mirror at the reflection of her own eyes. Moving to more neutral ground, he said, 'I thought that the food was excellent; you know how I love turbot, and the lemon soufflé . . . delicious, light as a feather. You certainly have the flair for planning an original menu.'

'I tried to give you your favourites.'

'Thank you, my dearest, you are my bright flame in a dark world.'

Elbowing him in the stomach, she laughed. 'A dark world, James. It's not at all dark, and spring is just around the corner.'

'Ah, spring. I do look forward to the light days when we can eat and drink alfresco again. I like seeing our friends best in small, informal groups.'

As he lay in bed waiting for sleep to come, he wondered what Kerley would have thought had he been able to spy upon them this evening, but James did not like to speculate further on that. What he had seen of Kerley's private life showed it to be very different. Not worse, and probably not better, but very different. Perhaps that was why they had become such good partners. They came at problems from different directions. Before he fell asleep he wondered whether Kerley had found anything of significance in Ramsgate.

* * *

George Hood summoned Josephine into his office.

'Hessel wants us to buy his story.'

'Confessions of a murderer?'

'No, he is offering a column exposing the conditions under which an arrested person is held.'

'Oh, doesn't he like his conditions, poor thing?'

'Under the law he has not been convicted of a single thing. He is there awaiting a hearing.'

'On suspicion of having slit the throat of a young woman.'

'It is not for us to sit in judgement – Mr Vaughan will do that. In the meantime I am offering you the opportunity of meeting Hessel.'

Josephine was stopped in her tracks. 'Oh, Mr Hood, there is nothing in the world that I should like better at this moment.'

Hood gave a self-satisfied smile. 'You will be no more than a messenger. A contract must be made, so I thought that you could take it to him.'

It was arranged that she would collect the contract and go to Bow Street and meet the solicitor after Hessel's appearance tomorrow.

James knew that from here on he would be bound to his desk, but he did not mind half as much now that he had the stimulating and exacting task of setting up the evidence and depositions for the prosecutor's case at the hearing. It was beginning to come clear that Hessel's entire case would rest upon an alibi, and the prosecution's upon the circumstances in which he was seen with the murdered girl (he still thought of her as that, in spite of it having been confirmed that she was twenty-six years old).

He was at his desk early in the day, wanting to deal with a whole pile of files before his next appearance at the court. First, he had letters, which Kerley had had translated in Ramsgate and brought to Bow Street.

Reading in order of date, James Thomson became increasingly disturbed by what was revealed, not only about the Hessels, but the whole enterprise. Even without suspicion falling upon two of their number, the cabin-passengers on the *Wangerland* were stirring up a hornet's nest. These people were trouble.

Frank Kerley knocked and entered. 'Do you want me for anything, sir?'

'Yes, go back to Kroll's Hotel and question the porters about Hessel's boots. Sit down a moment.' James put down his wire-rimmed spectacles and waved Frank into a chair, where he sat with his ramrod-straight spine pressed against the chair back and his long legs spread out at angles. 'We've had a visit from Mr Mullins.'

'The instructing solicitor?'

James nodded. 'He asked for Wolebe's diary.'

'That's still with the translator.'

'I know, I don't believe that is why he came; he knows that Wolebe's diary won't be relevant to the case. He was letting me know that they are going for an unshakeable alibi.'

'How can they make it unshakeable? Hessel wasn't seen between eleven on Christmas Eve and midday on Christmas Day.'

'He was heard to cough and his boots were outside his door.'

'Those damned boots, sir.'

James smiled behind his straight face. Kerley hadn't even realized he had said that they were 'damned' boots . . . but they *were*. 'I agree.'

Frank continued. 'Hessel said, "I will wear my boots and stand by my friend" when he was persuaded to join the ID parade. Why make a point of telling all and sundry that he would wear his boots? What else would he wear – his carpet slippers? And when I asked Wolebe to be witness to what I was listing to bring away from Hessel's cabin, he said, "Those are the boots he wore in London," indicating the patent-leather boots.'

James followed Kerley's line of thought. 'And the hall porter at the Royal Hotel said, "He took his open-sided boots to London." Is that right?'

'Yes, sir, and the boot-boy said, "I cleaned his sea boots the day after he returned." Alice Douglas said he wore sea boots on the bus.'

'And Daisy, the Wrights' scullery maid, said he carried boots . . . and the maid opposite saw him pull on his boots outside number twelve. Pulling on indicates elastic-sided boots or open-sided boots.'

'*Or* sea boots, sir.'

'Right, Sergeant. Had he been wearing patent-leather, then Alice Douglas would not have called them sea boots.'

'Which were what the Kroll's porter says were put out

for cleaning when he went to bed early on Christmas Eve . . .'

'As early as seven, sir.'

'. . . and on Christmas Day did not get up until one o'clock, when, one assumes, he put on his cleaned boots. Boots, boots, boots.'

'Ah . . . how about this, sir? His alibi stands on the fact that his only pair were seen outside his room door by pretty well everybody, and that they were described as sea boots.'

James nodded. 'Yes . . .'

'But next day a whole lot of them went out to the Crystal Palace and Covent Garden. Glittering venues, both.'

James shoved his glasses back on his face, as if to follow the saga of the boots. 'Wearing his only pair . . . sea boots, Frank? I think not. This was a band of stylish young people, the men were dandies – wouldn't have been seen dead wearing sea boots to Covent Garden.'

'That was my line of thinking, sir.'

'It wouldn't break an alibi on its own, Frank, but it certainly throws doubt upon it. And added to the circumstantial, and eyewitnesses . . .'

'I'll be off to Kroll's Hotel then, sir.'

'It will do no harm, but don't give them any opportunity to say that they are being harassed by us. Mr Mullins has already suggested that Herr Kroll is very important and a man of substance.'

Frank Kerley kept a straight face when he said, 'I am something of a man of substance myself, sir,' ducking his head as he went through the doorway.

*　　*　　*

303

The sun shone brightly as Josephine walked to her office. It was still too early in the year for ideas of spring, but the clear, frosty-blue sky and sunshine was in tune with her mood. Liliana was busy making last-minute decisions about small paintings for her exhibition, which was imminent. 'I wish I could take you with me, Lili.'

'So do I. You must take in every detail of him: his cell, the amount of light – I doubt there's much, what items he has, how they are placed, the condition of the walls; you must fix them in your mind so that you can dictate them to me. I have never painted except from life, but this must be from your mind.'

'I am going to look at Harriet's room later.'

'Never!'

'I asked Mrs Wright what it was like and she's said that I can go there.'

'Take me with you, Jo.'

'I can't do that. It would appear too insensitive. Mrs Wright is very protective of her girls.'

'Your book could have illustrations. How interesting would that be to your readers.' It wasn't a question. Lili, carried away with enthusiasm, was aware that people loved a few illustrations in any factual reading. 'Harriet's room, the bar at the Alhambra Palace, with Tryphena, and then the murderer in his cell.'

'Not the hanging?' Liliana appeared to be considering this. 'No, Lili! I was being facetious.'

'But, yes, Jo. Think how much more dramatic that would be than simply writing "The End".'

'The book won't need that illustration. Everyone has a picture in their mind of the gallows.'

'At least consider it, Jo.'

'Lili!'

'Then at least take me with you to Mrs Wright's.'

Josephine went with Mr Mullins, Hessel's lawyer, into Bow Street station. James and Kerley had both left, so it came to Inspector Cruse to study the papers Josephine carried and question the lawyer until he could find no valid reason to keep them from visiting the prisoner in his cell.

'Five minutes only, sir,' Cruse said authoritatively.

'My client is entitled to confer with me as long as he reasonably wishes and without a jailer present.'

'I know our own rules, sir. I meant the young lady. She does not have your privilege with the prisoner.'

The prisoner Hessel of the Bow Street cells was very different from the Reverend Godfried Hessel of the magistrate's court. There he had been ramrod stiff and had raised an eyebrow superciliously at the court clerk, who had had the audacity to ask him for his plea and to state his name. Even 'Madame Margaret' – Bella – had picked up on that. 'Who the hell does he think he is? The clerk don't have any say in what goes on.'

Here he was an uncombed, dishevelled, nondescript young man, huddled in a grey prison blanket.

Without thinking she remarked, 'It is very chill in here.'

He raised his head and stared straight at her. She might have recoiled from looking into the eyes of the man who

305

had slit Harriet's throat without compunction, but she did not; instead she stared steadily back at him.

A slow smile. 'Yes, Fräulein, perhaps you might mention this to my jailers: the food is for pigs, the walls are damp, and I have asked for reading matter that I have not received, and my clothing has been taken away.'

She spoke up clearly, not intimidated. 'The creature comforts of men such as yourself are no business of mine.' Her stance was challenging, unfeminine.

Hessel looked up at Mullins. 'Why is she here?'

'She—'

'Thank you, Mr Mullins, I am perfectly able to speak for myself. Mr Hessel, you have offered to tell your story to the readers of *The News*?' Making a question of it and waiting for an answer.

'*Ja.*'

'Then here is a contract for you to sign in the presence of your lawyer.' He held out his hand, but she handed the paper to the lawyer. Petty, not wanting to give Harriet's murderer even the slightest courtesy.

'Your name, Fräulein?'

'I am *Miss* Jemima Ferguson.'

Hessel took the document and turned it to where some light came in through the bars of the cell door. 'You see what shall be my first page of Pastor Godfried Hessel's Diary, Fräulein Ferguson. Bad food, no reading material, no warmth, poor bedding, little light. A dog would be better housed. All this I shall write in my daily column.'

'You do understand that, depending on what you

306

write, much of it may not be published until after your trial.'

Again that slow, sly, disturbing smile. 'I shall not go to trial, Fräulein, and be assured I shall write nothing that will give reason for censorship. Your ill-educated and untrained policemen may try to play tricks and bring their so-called evidence, but none of it will stand up against me.'

'You would not be the first one to underestimate them.'

'It is good that you advocate their cause.'

'"Advocate" is not the word you are looking for.' Another petty dig, but petty or not, she relished it. She wished that he would stand because he would be shorter than herself. '"Champion" is a more apt word.'

He didn't take his eyes from hers. She wouldn't be stared down. Or intimidated. She only wished that she could say how much she hated and despised him, but *The News* wanted him to sign up with them, and whatever she might think of that, *The News* was still her paper.

'I am forced to tell you that you are ill-informed about the Metropolitan Police. The truth is that they are estimable men. They are well-trained, relentless, and not ill-educated. One of the detectives who arrested you speaks four languages.' Had she scored a hit there?

He returned his attention to the contract. She doubted if much of what she had said had dented his inflated opinion of himself. Never mind, there would come a day when he would be brought down. Whatever happened, she determined to be there when the judge donned the black cap. '. . . that you be hanged by the neck until you are dead. May your soul rest in peace.' May your soul burn in hell.

He took his time reading each clause. The lawyer tried to bend over to offer help, but Hessel waved him away.

Josephine used every second to examine him. But she could not do it impartially. No matter how objective she tried to be, she felt her scalp growing tight on her head, seeming to draw back her ears. Her teeth were clenched tight. So were her hands, her nails dug into her own flesh. She could scarcely bear to occupy the same space as Harriet's killer.

Yet this would be the only chance she would ever get.

Suddenly he looked up and said in his fluent but accented English. 'What is your concern with me, Fräulein Ferguson?'

Her mouth was dry. 'I am just a representative of *The News* – the kind of thing I deal with on a daily basis.'

You are nothing special. Petty. Satisfying. She would have demeaned him further if she had been able.

He shook his head. 'With *me*. You, pretty fräulein, are curious to see a man who can kill a woman, *ja*?'

'No, no. It is nothing like that. And you are only here on suspicion.' How she managed to say that in such a conversational tone . . .

He smiled a little and shook his head, then returned to reading the contract, leaving her trembling inwardly.

Holding herself together.

At last she had a glimmer of insight into what he was.

He was doing with her what he had done when he had taken no trouble to conceal his identity on Christmas Eve. And again when he had pushed his way into the identification parade when he had no need to. She had seen the determined way he had thrown off his own wife when she had tried to stop him placing his life on the gambling board. Dicing with his own life.

This would not have been the first time he had played for high stakes. It must be in his past. She would find a way to discover it. Where had he been before he joined the Brazilian venture? Mr Hood would surely be able to uncover that.

Writing his signature with a flourish, he handed the contract to her and said to his lawyer, 'I wish to speak privately with Fräulein Ferguson.'

'That is not possible.'

'Make it possible. I am no threat chained to the wall. Tell the jailer,' he ordered.

'I am sure Miss Ferguson has no wish to hear what you have to say, Mr Hessel.'

'You are wrong, my friend, the fräulein does wish so.'

He was so arrogant that her instinct was to turn and give her answer by leaving. The lawyer looked perturbed. 'I don't advise this, Miss Ferguson, even if the jailer agrees.'

'Don't ask him,' Josephine said quietly, 'just wait outside. If the jailer objects, I am sure that you can hold him off for just one minute. One minute, no longer.'

Reluctantly, the man exited from the cell, leaving the door open.

Josephine's inner trembling had ceased. She felt strong and much superior to Hessel, shackled in chains and huddled against the cold and damp in a stale blanket.

'You want to know if I am capable of killing the prostitute.'

'I know without doubt that you are.' If he thought that his sly smile intimidated her, he was wrong. 'Harriet was not a prostitute.'

'Taking a stranger to her room for money is not prostitution?'

'Harriet was a decent woman trying to keep body and soul together and provide for her child.'

'A child?'

'Mr Hessel, I am not here to gossip about Harriet's life. You put an end to it, and I know that.'

'You believe that it was I who killed your friend?'

Why had he called her that?

'No, not *believe* that you murdered my friend – I know that you did it.'

Amazingly, he nodded in agreement, even as he said, 'That cannot be proved.'

'Don't underestimate our police force. You are going to the gallows.'

She often wondered what his expression had been, but she would never know, for she had turned on her heel and strode out.

* * *

As she was making her way up to the police station, she heard the voices of Sergeant Kerley and her uncle James. There was no way of avoiding them. She nodded to Hessel's lawyer and said good afternoon to him.

'Josephine?'

'Uncle James, fancy meeting you here. Sergeant Kerley, very nice to meet you again.'

Her uncle looked somewhat fed up. 'Sergeant, as you are my best detective, you will have discovered that Miss Jemima Ferguson is my niece and ward, Miss Josephine Thomson.'

Sergeant Kerley looked ill-at-ease and went off as soon as he had said something polite.

'In here,' James Thomson ordered.

Again she found herself in the office with 'Superintendent' painted on the door. 'What are you doing here?'

'I am on legitimate business. Your prisoner will be writing a daily column for *The News* and I came with his solicitor so that the contract could be signed.'

'I had heard about that. There is nothing that I can do to stop *The News* paying him money, but they will not be able to publish a word until the hearing and the trial are over.'

'He will not be writing anything about the trial – only a day-to-day diary without comment. *The News* doesn't mind waiting. It has stolen a march on all the others: the murdering devil will write exclusively for us.'

'Oh yes, the "tickle".'

'Guilty or not, Hessel will make a great deal of money out of his writings.'

'And much good may it do him.'

'Uncle James, can you think of no harsher words than that? I told him plainly that he was going to the gallows.'

'Josephine! Did you have to be *The News*'s messenger? Or did you persuade your editor that he would get a Jemima Ferguson article?'

'Neither. Mr Hood knows about the Harriet book, and had the generosity to offer me the chance to . . . to see him face to face. You would never have let me near him.'

'I would not!'

'He did it . . . you know that, I know that.'

'Germans are very good at . . .' He trailed off, realizing that if he said something of the work Hessel's fellow-countrymen were putting in to give the murderer an alibi, then Josie would leap on it. 'I thought that you had come in answer to my note.'

'I haven't received a note, when did you send it?'

'By hand earlier today.'

'And . . . ?'

'I asked if I might talk to you about Harriet.'

Josephine was very taken aback. This was the last thing she had expected from him. 'Yes, of course you may. I shall be very glad of it. What . . . ?'

'Not here. Could we walk to your rooms and talk there?'

'Absolutely! I should love you to come. Of course

312

Liliana is painting away like mad ... an exhibition quite soon; things get a bit slapdash.'

'Josie, I won't be inspecting, just visiting.'

'With luck she will have been baking. Yes. She bakes when she needs to get a new perspective on her work in progress, if that means anything to you. I'm chattering away, aren't I? Nervousness.'

'We would be private there?'

'Of course. We live quite separate lives – except for use of the cooking stove.'

'Separate' must have been hard for her uncle to believe, for when they arrived Liliana, Christine and David were on hands and knees, either painting frames or tacking canvases into them, and the work had spread into the hall and kitchen. Lili leaped to her feet. 'I am *so* sorry, Jo, I had thought to be finished before you came back.'

Normally, Josephine would have waved the apology away and helped out. 'Oh, Lili! I have always told my family what a good thing it was that you came to live here . . . but I can hardly say that now.' She held a hand out indicating her uncle. 'This is—'

David, to the surprise of the three women, leaped to his feet and went towards James, offering his hand. 'Superintendent Thomson! What a pleasure to meet with you again. Josie, you never said that "Thomson of the Met" was your uncle.'

'I don't think I knew that my uncle *was* "Thomson of the Met"!'

Again a surprise as her uncle grasped David's hand

warmly. 'Wilde. I had every intention of asking if we could meet, but at the moment I have no time to spare for charitable work.'

'Of course, the Great Coram Street Murder.' He glanced at Josephine, unsure as to whether he should say anything about them having gone with Bella to the remand hearing.

James felt it incumbent upon himself to explain. 'Mr Wilde and I have spent some time working to raise money for charity. And he has helped me with the work establishing the police orphanage. He is very knowledge-able about how to be charitable without condescension. Which is why we get along together.'

Josephine was very taken aback at how pleased her uncle appeared at seeing David. Perhaps the mutual admiration went some way to explaining why she had seen him at the St Giles night-watch service at New Year.

'Mr Thomson, we are really sorry to have overflowed into Josephine's territory. Come along, Lili, back in your own room.'

All affability, James said, 'Don't trouble yourselves, what I have to say to Josie can be said in any public room in any hotel. Come along, Josie, I'll take you to a very pleasant place in Half-Moon Street.' Nodding politely he said, 'Miss Wilde, Miss . . . ?'

'Derry, Christine Derry. May I put you on the gallery's list, Mr Thomson? You should really see Liliana's work as a collection.'

Josephine would see to it that this would not happen. She did not want her two worlds overlapping any more than they already were. What had happened here today was enough.

As they were leaving, Liliana said, 'Jo, I almost forgot, a policeman called with a note for you. It is on the kitchen mantelshelf.'

In the cab, James Thomson said, 'How do you know Wilde?'

'He's Liliana's brother.'

'Of course . . . and what does he think of his sister's life in Paris?'

She thought that she heard disapproval in the question. 'Probably what you think of mine in London. Liliana might have rooms in the artists' quarter, but that doesn't mean that she lives any differently there than here.'

It was obvious from the greeting by the doorman that her uncle was known at the Half-Moon Hotel. He asked if he might use one of the rooms and be served tea and sandwiches. They were only too happy to oblige. The small smoking room.

'I'm impressed, Uncle James.'

'I solved a small crime. Small, but important. A Dutch master oil painting, worth a great deal of money, disappeared. People might scoff at my meticulous method of keeping records, but I often know just where to enquire when such items are stolen.' A well-laden tray was placed on a low table before them. Josephine, not having eaten for hours, ate her way into the sandwiches.

'The hand-delivered note, Uncle James. Why do you want to talk to me?'

'I want to show you something. But first I must ask you to be sworn to secrecy.'

'Uncle James.'

'I am serious, Josephine. If it were to be known that I have shown you these,' he placed a package on the table, 'I should be reduced to the ranks – or worse.'

'Then why show me?'

'Because you need to see them.' She frowned in puzzlement, but did not respond. 'I have changed my mind about your wish to document the life of Harriet Burton.' She relaxed her frown and raised one eyebrow. 'You know that there is no possibility of you getting any closer to Doctor Hessel than you did this morning. And there is no way that I can help you with anything other than what is available to the general public, to anyone who wants to understand more of the circumstances of the man who killed Harriet Burton, and the kind of man he is. They are not the original letters, but translations. You will not be able to use a word of them.'

'Are they evidence then?'

'No, at least not to his guilt. Josie, if you give me your word that you will never reveal anything of what is contained in them, you may read them.'

'You mean to take away?'

'No, no. The fact that I have not left them under lock and key at the station is enough. No, I will sit here until you know their contents.'

'Very well, Uncle James, you should not need to ask, but I give you the assurance you ask for. No one shall ever hear of them from me.'

Ignoring the jibe. 'Good.' He spread out the bundle of letters on the table. 'They are in date order.'

'Why are you doing this?'

He sipped tea before answering. 'I hardly know, Josie, except that what I read of the book you are writing made me think about how little people know about women like her. Wilde and I and people like us are hard enough put to raise money for orphans. It would be impossible to do likewise for all the Harriet Burtons of this world. There are charities who try to do something for "fallen women", but not very charitably, nor with much understanding. Such women are always seen as architects of their own misfortunes, and until the public's eyes are opened to what lies behind their lives, little will change, and men like Hessel will prey upon them.'

'If you are not able to use the letters in evidence, what will happen to them?'

'Scotland Yard and the Home Office will bury them in their archives, and they will probably never see the light of day again.' He sat back comfortably, lit a cigar and waited for her to read.

The letters, as shown by their dates, had, around the middle of December, flown back and forth. Mrs Hessel accused Dr Franzen, the ship's physician, of neglecting passengers; Mrs Hessel was insulted by Dr Franzen; Reverend Hessel demanded an apology; Franzen hauled the captain before the consul to declare that he had treated between-decks passengers with care and that he had not accused Mrs Hessel of untruthfulness and refused to ask her pardon. The captain was unwilling to be drawn into such disputes and Dr Franzen demanded a higher salary to keep quiet about what was going on aboard the *Wangerland*.

Josephine looked up and raised her eyebrows. 'Blackmail, too . . . nice people.' James hunched his shoulders in reply. 'What do you make of this letter, from a Louis Hermes?'

'Oh, he's the agent.'

'He's asking Hessel to get signatures from "other passengers and intelligent between-decks passengers" to say that there are no problems.'

Taking the letter, he flicked a finger at the page. 'It is all contained in this paragraph. "You know yourself how emigration is visited by hostile attacks and especially that to Brazil. It is our *duty* to do all we can to *keep our backs free against unjustifiable attacks.*" What I have discovered is that this is one of many ships exporting people to the other side of the world in very dubious conditions.'

'So the attacks are not "unjustifiable"?'

'I am afraid that is so.'

'So no honest and self-respecting doctor or clergyman would have anything to do with it.'

'That is my opinion.'

'Can't you use these letters to show that he is not the god-fearing man he is being made out to be?'

James shook his head. 'When the case goes to full trial we would have to call all these people. They would be hostile; we should get nowhere. The letters are only evidence that this is a particularly nasty group of avaricious people without a scruple between them. And, with the exception of the physician, they were all cavorting in London last Christmas.'

'Why do these people do it, Uncle James? I'd have to be in a pretty bad way to leave my country.'

'Many of them sell everything they have to pay for the passage, thinking they are going to the promised land.'

'But the others, Uncle James? Franzen, Wolebe and the Hessels. Are they all running from something?'

James shrugged. 'Avarice? There are wealthy and powerful people behind these colonization enterprises. A mere doctor is no threat to them.'

Josephine neatened the pile of papers and returned them to the original package. 'What a dirty business, Uncle James.'

'True, and whilst we have got one man in the cells for murder, these businessmen get away with many. People die like flies on these emigrant ships.'

'Is there nothing to be done then?'

James shook his head. 'Had the *Wangerland* not hit the Goodwins, we might well have thought that emigrants were going on a brave adventure, to start life in a new land.'

'Thank you for letting me see these. I understand why they are no use to you in Hessel's trial.'

'But they might stimulate interest in a journalist who likes to tilt at windmills – no, that isn't the right analogy. Jemima Ferguson is interested in reality. I thought she might like to look at the scandal of emigration.'

She got up, crossed to where he sat, put her arms

around his neck and kissed him. 'You are a good man, Uncle James'.

He patted her hand. 'I try to be, Josie, but I don't succeed.'

It appeared now that the defence's strategy was to place as much importance on the position and the respectability of Hessel as on his alibi. The hotel records were not to be depended upon.

In an interview with Herr Kroll himself, James saw that they were likely to admit to bad record-keeping. 'Superintendent, you must have like problems with your people. You explain six times how a thing must be done, five times it is done correctly,' he had waved airily at the corrections and errors James was querying, 'on the sixth they forget, or do not take trouble.'

'So these are not alterations to dates and times?'

'No, no, these are corrections made. You understand that at holiday times I am forced to take on extra staff. Kroll's is a most popular establishment for the more refined class of German. I try most hard to obtain servants of the very best calibre, but it is not always possible to obtain Germans. Local people do not always understand my orders. Mistakes are made. I do not suffer this – incompetent servants are dismissed.'

'So, you are saying that there were mistakes made in recording the comings and goings of your guests?'

'Also in the recording of room-services, yes, and what you see are sad attempts to recompense some errors.'

'You are prepared for the honest reputation of Kroll's

Hotel to suffer if you are forced to admit that alterations were made to your records?'

'It must be done. It is more honourable to admit that one's employees have made mistakes than to do otherwise.'

That was when James realized that, although the prosecutor, Mr Poland, would question Hessel's alibi that he did not leave the hotel, the defence's Mr Straight, would raise doubt in magistrate Mr Vaughan's mind. This respectable hotelier had perhaps been over-zealous in presenting correct records – nothing more sinister than that.

Hessel's defence would then rest largely on his character, respectability and being a man of the highest reputation. If Herr Kroll were to take the witness stand, he would be impressive in defence of his countryman.

So, in search of more background to Hessel, on the day prior to the hearing, Frank Kerley went back to Ramsgate to delve further into the life of the cabin passengers during the months following their being stranded.

He did not feel very sanguine that the murder weapon would ever be identified: all of the knives and scalpels discovered in Hessel's chests were clean and polished. But it was necessary to be meticulous, leaving no stone unturned.

Superintendent Buss's enquiries had uncovered something interesting. The young Germans were frequent visitors to Wheeler's, who were dealers and cutlers.

Frank's spirits were raised when he interviewed Mr

George Wheeler. On being shown the artist's impression of the murderer, Wheeler said wearily, 'I know him all right, and the rest of his gang.'

'Gang?'

'I don't mean a gang of villains, but there were always four or five of them who came in here together.'

'Often?'

'Not as you would say *frequently*, but often enough so that I began to feel unsettled when they came into my premises.'

'In what way did they unsettle you?'

'Difficult to say . . . they were boisterous, taking things from cabinets, asking to look at handguns and cutlasses. They would inspect them closely and then proceed to take aim at one another in jest, or swing a cutlass. I tried to point out the foolhardiness of this without putting them off making purchases . . .'

'Did they make purchases?'

'Oh yes. On one occasion one of the men – the one in the drawing – brought in a revolver and asked to have it cleaned and said he wanted to buy cartridges for it.'

'And did he?'

'It's not something we sell at Wheeler's, and when I told him this he said, never mind, he was going to London in a day or two and he could get them there.'

'When was this?'

'I could look it up . . . probably sometime last November.'

'Not December?'

'No. But they did come in again sometime close to

Christmas – there was snow about, so that's when it must have been. A minute, and I'll look it up.' He leafed through pages of a daybook. 'Ah yes, it was December. His name was Mr Hessel, the one who wanted cartridges. He must have got them because he brought the revolver in again to be cleaned. This time he was dressed like a clergyman. He was carrying a dagger at his belt and asked me what I thought of it, and I said that it was a very fine piece.'

'And was it?'

'Oh yes, new I should say. He asked to see similar dagger-knives, which I showed him. He was very much taken by a white-handled dagger-knife and asked the price. I said it was a good blade and not overpriced at five shillings.'

'And did he buy it?'

Wheeler made a wry face. 'He did . . . eventually. He was one of the mean types that's never satisfied unless they can do you down for sixpence. He bought cases of surgical knives, so I let him have it for four-and-six. I remember my brother who was in here at the time, saying, it's a queer sort of vicar carries a dagger and buys cases of surgical knives. I said perhaps he was a surgeon as well as a clergyman, but my brother said, no, the other man was a surgeon, as he had been buying surgical knives as well.'

'You didn't see the "Wanted" posters?'

'No. The other police officer asked me that, but, as I told him, it's not often we leave our workshop, and we live above.'

'Did any women come with the "gang", as you call them.'

'Oh yes. A rather pretty young woman – married, but I couldn't say to which of the young men she was married. She was for ever giving them the benefit of her advice and making gay with them.'

'In what way "making gay"?'

'Like a girl, making flirtatious comments. You must know the kind of thing I mean, Sergeant.'

From Wheeler's, Frank went to the Royal Hotel, and once more questioned some of the servants. Here again, Frank was seeing a similar picture emerging as the one that Wheeler had described. None of the servants said so directly, but they hinted that there was a lot of 'coming and going' among the cabin passengers.

'The clergyman's wife almost always kept to the same room, but some of the men never appeared to settle. Sometimes one or the other would take off and have their bags sent aboard the *Wangerland*.'

'And did this go on from the time they first arrived?'

'Not so much at first. But after a whole party of them went up to London, there was a lot of fidgetiness.'

'Fidgetiness?'

'Mostly with the men.'

'Which men?'

'The captain, Mr Hermes the agent, the ship's surgeon Mr Wolebe (the one who was the first suspect), and the clergyman – who's been arrested and took to London – and his wife. They had spats and arguments. None of them thought to keep their voices down.'

'Do you know why?'

'No, they all spoke in their own language, but there's no mistaking that they were at odds with one another. Which wasn't surprising, seeing how long they were kept hanging about, what with the repairs to the brig taking more and more time. It could be that the agent was at fault.'

'The one, perhaps, they could take it out on?'

The porter who was being questioned nodded. 'The physician sometimes came. He lived in town with his family, but he came here to see the others. There was an occasion when the agent arranged a supper and dance for the cabin passengers, when the doctor and Mr Hessel near came to blows over something Mrs Hessel had said.'

'Did they exchange blows?'

'No. The captain and the agent sorted them out, and the doctor went off flaming with anger.'

'What did you think of them, as a whole?' Frank asked. 'This is just out of interest . . . not to go into a statement.'

'Well, at first, when the surgeon was took away by the police, everyone was saying how shocking and that it was, but then some said they wasn't surprised. There was often a lot of drink taken . . . gambling often . . . the clergyman had let off a revolver from one of the windows and the police was called, the young men – not the captain so much – were always showing off that they was armed one way or another.'

* * *

On the morning of the hearing, as James Thomson had anticipated, a crowd gathered outside the police court long before it was due to open. What with the repeated examinations in the coroner's court, then the Ramsgate hearings following the arrest of Karl Wolebe, then the dramatic arrest of Hessel and the almost daily newspaper coverage for over a month, interest increased greatly. As always when a murder was committed, one might believe from the press that London was awash with blood. True, the city and the river gave up many bodies that had known a violent end, but murder by someone outside the victim's immediate circle was a rare occurrence. So a murder trial like this one was an event arousing intense curiosity.

That morning, a letter had appeared in *The News* berating the police for being so ignorant and uncultured as to have arrested a man of the cloth – shipwrecked, and having been near to death, this respectable man had been arrested on suspicion of having murdered a prostitute. The nation should bow its head in shame . . .

Before he left for the magistrate's court, James ordered Kerley to assemble as many men as were on duty in the station yard.

'Men. We have all read this offensive nonsense in the papers.' Boots shuffled and little snorts of acknowledgement were made.

'Many times in the past the police force has been called ill-educated, badly trained and rough men – or worse, but usually by drunks and regular criminals. I think that the writers of those insulting letters might ask themselves who they would call upon if their homes were burgled, or their wallet stolen or their watch snatched by a foot-pad. Would it be my ill-educated, badly trained and rough men? No . . . you would at once become men of "E" Division, and very pleased they would be to talk to you. Rough men? Do they think that we are rough men when we patrol their streets and keep cat-burglars from entering by way of windows left invitingly open?

'As you know, questions are being asked about the arrest of a distinguished German pastor, "a visitor to our shores". "Outrageous", "ludicrous", it has been said. It is my opinion that we – and the general public – need to think on this. "E" Division and the force at Ramsgate did not hold back from apprehending this distinguished German because of his rank and class. No, there was very good evidence indeed. It was he who was seen with the victim on numerous occasions on the night that she was murdered – to say nothing of his being seen leaving the house of the victim in the early hours.

'We and you have been meticulous in our searches, both here and at Ramsgate. We have taken many dozens of statements. Today, this "visitor to our shores" will again appear before Chief Magistrate Mr Justice Vaughan, to answer to the charge made against him. You have worked long and hard. We have the evidence. We have the man. Do not allow these mean diatribes in the papers concern you. It is only the opinion of the senior officers of "E" Division that should concern you; our opinion of you is a good one.'

With murmurs and the tramping of marching hobnails,

the men who had scoured London from the Haymarket outwards over the last many weeks left to go back to their beats.

Frank's next enquiry was with Captain Wilken, whose statement was simply confined to the going-aground of his ship and her towing into Ramsgate and subsequently to dry-dock in London where she was repaired. When Frank asked what he knew of the sleeping arrangements of Hessel, the captain said, 'He used to sleep at the Royal, but since we came back from London, he's been sleeping on board the greater part of the time.'

'Why do you reckon this was? I mean, his berth on the *Wangerland* is cold and damp and it's January. And not only that, wasn't smallpox supposed to be rife?'

Captain Wilken shrugged his shoulders.

'It's what I was told when I wanted to make a search, you remember? Didn't he ever say why he chose to leave dry and warm quarters for something so uninviting?'

But the captain, even if he knew something, was not saying. He merely spread his hands and shrugged.

Frank, well aware of the absolute necessity to tread most carefully where these touchy foreigners were concerned, retreated. He had no wish for the German consulate to become even more involved than it was. He already felt hemmed about enough, what with the shrewd band of lawyers, barristers and consul officials, to say nothing of the stonewalling alibi being offered by Hessel's fellow countrymen.

He again questioned William Clement about Hessel's

suits, and Mr Hiscock, the owner of the Royal, about the arrangements whereby Hessel and his wife occupied rooms at the Royal, but could get nothing more than he had previously, which was that Hessel always wore the same suit, except sometimes he wore dark trousers, and that when they first arrived they shared room number 17 and on returning from London, Hessel asked for Number 16 for himself and number 15 (for which he did not pay rent) for his trunks. These people would probably be called upon as witnesses when the case went for full trial, so it was vital that nothing was left to chance.

So yet again he went over the statements from Jane Somers and two laundresses who had found the bundle of linen saturated with blood. This bit of evidence might be argued down. The defence could simply ask them whether they had been told where the blood had come from. Mrs Hessel had sent them for washing, had she not? And Mrs Hessel, a young woman caught unprepared for menstruation in a strange place . . . might she have taken her husband's handkerchiefs in emergency? Wouldn't that explain, too, Hessel sleeping apart from her? Perhaps she had miscarried; the laundress had spoken of blood-clots and saturation. But no, she was out and about celebrating . . . Covent Garden theatre, the Crystal Palace. Mrs Hessel was not a woman suffering any kind of female indisposition.

No one statement was sufficient of itself to convict a man of murder, but collectively, and together with the London eyewitnesses pointing to Hessel being the man with the victim, meant sufficient evidence would be stacked against him to convince a jury.

The journey back to London seemed endless to Frank.

For one thing he would again be very late home, and he had hoped that once the hearing started he might see something of his wife more than of late, but he had seven or eight reports to submit, and although he wished to see Elizabeth, he wished more to see Mr Thomson and hear what he had to say about the first day. Elizabeth had started painting again, and this pleased him . . . perhaps not so much pleased him, as made him glad that she was filling spare time exercising her talent, and he therefore need not be too concerned for the long hours of duty, the spoiled meals and late nights. There was nothing to be done about the lot of a policeman's wife: it was an inevitable part of the marriage contract that she must be prepared for disruptions and disappointments. It was true, as she had occasionally pointed out, that he had not been a detective when they married, nor were their lives then circumscribed by Scotland Yard regulations. But Frank liked the companionship of his wife and, in normal circumstances, would have spent time discussing her work and encouraging her.

He looked out of the murky windows at the bleak January landscape, and felt suddenly tired and dejected. It could all fall apart. He had a presentiment that if they were not very careful indeed, the case would be lost. That was unthinkable. He was as sure as he had ever been of any suspect that, clergyman or not, this was the man who had slit Harriet Burton's throat. The prosecution would call her a 'gay woman', a prostitute, a 'woman of the night', a 'woman of low life' – all terms he had himself used at some time in describing a 'dolly-mop'.

He closed his eyes and wished that he could have slept, but this time he was not travelling first class and the compartment was so full that he felt uncomfortable at the space his large body and legs took up. In trying to keep to the space of a man of normal size, his limbs became numb. He hoped the numbness would not turn and seize his muscles with cramp, when he would be forced to leap to his feet and bend the arches of his feet.

Frank Kerley was not to see his super that day as he had hoped. The day in court had proved to be unbelievably exhausting to James, so he had gone home to eat dinner with Ann. That, and hearing first-hand what had gone on that day, pleased her so much that she did not object when he had begged her pardon and, pleading hours of work, gone to sit at his desk in his study, where the hiss of gaslamps and the crackle of a coal fire were the only sounds in the velour-deadened atmosphere.

His notes spread before him, he began to place them in the order in which he would write his report to Colonel Henderson, and for the writing up of his personal journal. Of the two assignments, only one was a duty. The daily entries to his journal were one of his greatest pleasures, whereas police reports were written in a style peculiar only to his profession. Supposedly concise and unambiguous, it was however thought helpful to include such unnecessary niceties as prefacing every address to one's superior with, 'I beg to report that' or, 'I beg to request permission', as though one was a humble petitioner asking a favour rather than doing the work one was engaged to do.

James occasionally indulged in the fanciful thoughts of, 'If I were commissioner of police . . .' and had already subscribed to a list of changes to practice that would make the force more efficient and productive and the men more efficient and content, a thing he knew them not to be at present. And who could blame them? Poorly paid, yet with all of society's troubles thrown at their door; unarmed yet sent on the streets to face whatever violence lay in wait for them; long hours of duty, yet, when things didn't suit it, receiving from society only brickbats. And at the moment, for all the hissing at James's prisoner by the hoi polloi, James also smelt the professional class pack at his back.

Having completed his report, he laid the quarter-bound accountant's book before him. He had a momentary, not-uncommon vision of himself in the future, when he would take up a sheaf of paper and begin writing his autobiography based upon this journal in earnest. He did not deceive himself that he was any great sort of an author, but his material as a Scotland Yard detective would be of interest: he was sure of this from the number of people who were always eager for him to hear the 'inside story'. Even though he was no Dickens, James always tried to give a background to his entries.

'Twenty-ninth of January, Eighteen Seventy-three. There is no doubt of it, I wished many times today that Frank Kerley had been beside me, for over the past four weeks I have seen in him all of those qualities a senior officer looks for in a junior officer, and most of those a man could hope for in a trusted friend. From time to time throughout today I admit to having felt doubts as to the outcome of the Harriet Burton murder case, and I wished that Kerley had been there to give reassurance that my doubts were unfounded and that the man would be put up for a full trial and would go to the gallows for the dreadful deed he has done. But I had sent Frank off to Ramsgate. No doubt Cruse could have gone, but if anyone is to uncover evidence that is firmer than the dozen eyewitnesses to H. and the girl being together on the night she was murdered, then I could trust no one but Frank to try.

'The hearing began with the usual preliminaries. Mr Justice Vaughan, the usual Bow Street Court stipendiary magistrate presided over the hearing. Mr Poland prosecuted, Mr Straight defended. This being a hearing of evidence before bringing the accused to full trial, there was, of course, no jury. Perhaps it was this that has made me feel uneasy, and what I should have liked to have heard Frank Kerley's opinion on. With a jury, one is not relying on the fallibility of a single man, with all his incipient frailty and prejudice. That is not to say that eleven men may not also be frail and biased, but to put such judicious power into a single pair of hands has always seemed to me to be a dangerous thing to do. But I digress.

'In choosing the order in which the witnesses should appear, it was not easy to decide whether to get the greengrocer's boys out of the way early and chance giving a poor opening impression, or to open with Miss Tryphena Douglas, or to have her come last to the witness stand and leave the magistrate with her dignity and assurance in his mind. In the event, as it was necessary to follow the course of the evening of the twenty-fourth in sequence, it was Miss Douglas who appeared first. Another digression, but now to the setting of the scene and the playing-out of the first act.

'Bow Street Court is mostly wooden: wooden floor, doors, forms in the public gallery, wooden pews and seats in the well of the court where sit the main pro-tagonists, a wooden witness stand, and wooden dock in which the prisoner sits upon a wooden chair, and wooden "thrones" upon high where sit the magistrates and county officials, such as the lord sheriff and mem-bers of Parliament associated with the case. Although a magistrate's court does not have the pomp of a court of full hearing with a judge and jury, it is no less a court of procedure, where each taking part must do so in a prescribed manner. Thus, although in this country justice must be seen to be done in the presence of whoever of the passing throng cares to watch the law take its process, these representative overseers too are expected to abide by the rules, and will soon be ejected if there is any unseemly behaviour. (This does not stop a good many of them, if the case looks likely to be entertaining, bringing along small hampers to sustain them, and friends to fight over their seat should they need to leave it for nature's purposes.)

'Today, when I entered, the pungent smell of oranges was already apparent, and mixing with the ever-present haze of dust that seems to hang in the air of Number One Court. And as the lamps are seldom out when the court is in session, they too added to the general confusion of smells that are particular to a police court. My timing was right, for having ascertained that all the witnesses for the prosecution were present in an anteroom and overseen by my men, I took my place in seats on the wing of the courtroom, almost at the moment when the usher called for silence and for all to be upstanding.

'I have been upstanding in that court on many and various occasions for Mr Justice Vaughan, but each time we face one another with an unknown and untried set of circumstances between us. This time, as it seemed to me this morning, the situation was of great seriousness, and I had a feeling that I am sure a soldier must experience as he is about to go into battle. Yet I should not think of bringing a case before Mr Justice Vaughan in such terms, for the battle is not betwixt the two of us, the battle is between the wits of the other two protagonists, Mr Prosecutor and Mr Defence. I can but pray that our Mr Prosecutor has the wit to use my long line of foot soldiers in such formation as to defeat the line of confident German generals and their auxiliaries. (Perhaps that is unfair to those other witnesses for the defence, yet I have felt that the statement by Kroll's night porter is not safe. But he stands by it, as does the maid, who swears she saw Hessel in his bedroom on Christmas morning. She could *not* have done so, unless it was *much* later than she says, or it was *not* on Christmas morning at all. This is a possibility, I must consult Poland on this point. What occasioned the maidservant to remember weeks later that it was this *particular* morning and not another? Herr Kroll is a man of very strong character, who might easily suggest to his underlings that what he tells them is the truth. They remember such and such, and it needs only the hint that yes, it was on Christmas morning that this occurred, or that it was on Christmas Eve that the door was locked, so that . . .'

On this occasion, James not only digressed but fell asleep over his journal. He awoke at three in the morning, cold and cramped, and was forced, feeling quite guilty, to creep in beside Ann.

Tryphena Douglas would never forget the day that had just passed. It was the first time she had ever entered a police court, and it had proved to be quite as frightening as she had supposed it would, but she knew that she had conducted herself well. Even Mr Thomson had taken the trouble to see her outside and tell her how impressed he had been with the way she had given her evidence. Nobody would ever know how terrified she had been. She had been the first of 'their' crowd to be called. She had been shown to a door which, when opened, led directly into the court. It had felt as though everyone in the world was looking at her. Thank the Lord Mr Thomson had seen to it that all the witnesses knew what to expect and to know who was who. 'Remember,' he had said, 'all of you are only doing your public duty. Everyone in the court knows that. There may be times, especially when your word is being questioned, when you may wish that you had never admitted having seen the accused, or to knowing the victim. But remind yourself that it is the job of the defence counsel to question the truth of what you say. Keep in the front of your mind always that there is not a single person in the court of whom you should be afraid. Each one is a person doing his work or his duty. Each one is a human being. Except perhaps one, and it is that one you must think of when you swear to "Tell the truth, the whole truth and nothing but the truth".'

Mr Thomson had been wonderful reassuring, and when it had come to holding the Bible she had not flinched. She had heard her answers echoing clearly around the court. Mr Straight had been the first to question her.

'Give your name.'

'Tryphena Douglas.'

'Miss Douglas, do you work as a barmaid at the Alhambra Palace Theatre?'

'I do.'

'And, in the course of your work, I believe you came to know the woman, Harriet Burton.'

'Yes, sir, she was a singer at the Alhambra, and she came in sometimes for a drink at the bar.'

'Miss Douglas, will you please tell the court what you remember of the evening of the twenty-fourth of December, and the early hours of Christmas Day, the twenty-fifth.'

'Yes sir . . .' And she had gone on to tell what she had already told Mr Thomson and Mr Kerley and the solicitors. Once she had got started, it was, as Mr Thomson had said it would be, quite easy, as long as she kept thinking that there was nobody here she need feel scared of.

Except him in the dock, and she had not looked at him. Not until Mr Straight had asked, 'And is that man here today?'

'Yes, sir.'

'Will you please point to him?'

Tryphena Douglas would not ever forget the absolute silence there had been whilst she was giving her evidence, and the way it was broken when she pointed to the man who had been in the bar and then on the bus going home. When she had seen him then, she had thought what a mean beggar he was, trying to get out of buying Harriet a drink, and counting over his pennies in the way the mean ones do. And then again on the bus, Harriet had had to prompt him to buy the tickets. Being mean wasn't a crime – if it was, half the chaps who came into the bar would be in clink – but killing a nice, kind girl like Harriet was. She hoped he'd swing for it.

George Flack's experience was a bit more intimidating than Tryphena's. He knew that he was a lowly kind of cove in the eyes of toffs, but he had never seen any reason to be ashamed of that. He knew his cockney accent amused gents. They'd get a good laugh late at night shouting, 'Apples a pound, pears!' as they went off home, stumbling about with a basket of fruit as a peace offering for their mothers, or for some other women who scared the trousers off them. He knew people like them said people like him were common. Well, of course he was common – working men was six a penny. But they thought he was inferior, which he wasn't. He was as proud a man as any of them, and he knew what he knew and nobody would stop him saying so. If they got a laugh off of him, then that wasn't no more than happened most days of the week – it was part of his stock in trade. This appearance wouldn't do his shop no harm, no more than his name in the paper had already done.

Mr Kerley had said to him not to go telling his story to every ear'ole who would come and try and get it off him. 'When it's over, George, if the press offers you a quid for your story, then take it, but until the court, just keep it to yourself. That way you won't find yourself telling a different story in court from the one you've told me.' And George hadn't. He had admitted to any customer who asked that he was *that* costermonger, and joked with them that if they wanted to see the whole show, they'd have to buy a ticket.

And today had been the whole show. He had taken the oath without too much hard work, and he had told his story simple and plain as he had told Mr Kerley.

How he had known her for years, and how that night she had come to his stall and bought some apples; how there was this bloke with her who wouldn't buy her a few peaches or a pineapple when she asked him. George had not commented upon the meanness, but he thought he had put it in his voice when he answered. A couple of peaches wouldn't have hurt him.

After he was told he could stand down, he had gone outside for a bit of a blow. The barmaid Tryphena was there and said he'd done all right. 'I liked the way you said, "That's him! That's the one." I wondered if you'd say for certain, he's got up a lot smarter than he was on that night, didn't you think?'

'I saw through all that. I picked him out. When I went down to Ramsgate for the ID parade, that friend of his was there. A'nt you seen him sitting there in court? Well, you just have a look when you go back in, he's about the same stamp, same colouring, but that's not what you go on, is it? You go on their faces, and how they stands, how they walks. I picked him out at once, no trouble. They must think we're daft. I'll tell you sommat that an't very bright . . . him chancing it like that. ID parades is just voluntary. What made him take a gamble like that? If he hadn't done that, who'd a been any the wiser?'

'Perhaps he's a gambling man.'

'With the chance he might end up being charged when he knows we'd seen him?'

She had smiled, and George had made himself a

promise to go and have a drink up the old Alhambra one day. She said, 'Perhaps he's like a lot of others, who think that because people like you and me have to work for our living, that we wouldn't have the nerve to speak up. A lot of people don't, you know, Mr Flack. They touch their caps and curtsey and think that a person born with a silver spoon in their mouth is a superior sort of being.'

George wouldn't have minded telling her that he thought that if there was a superior sort of being, then she herself was one. But she might of got the wrong end of the stick, and they had all got on pretty well together on these trips they'd all been obliged to take. Mr Thomson's people.

'I hope he stands trial and swings for it.'

With that, William Stalker appeared. The waiter from the Cavour restaurant had gone through a similar ordeal. He lit up a cigarillo that gave off a pungent smell. 'Well, people,' he said, 'I should like to stay, but I'm on duty soon as I get back. I suppose the next time we do our act it will be before a judge in full fig.'

As they parted, Tryphena stunned the two men by asking, 'You think it will get that far?'

'Why not?' George Flack asked. 'A whole parade of Mr Thomson's people, one after the other, pointing to him and saying, "That's the man who was with her," and then Mrs Wright who saw him, and the girl who watched him putting on his boots . . . He'll stand trial all right, Miss Tryphena, don't you lose no sleep on that score.'

And neither did Tryphena lose sleep on it, because she returned to court and heard depositions read giving

341

evidence of blood on washing sent to the washerwoman, and a whole bottle of turps being used up when he got back from London. Until today, Tryphena had not realized that there were so many of Mr Thomson's people; she had only met those with whom she had travelled to and from Ramsgate.

The next morning, the second day of the hearing before Mr Justice Vaughan, Frank presented himself before the night-duty men had signed off. 'Gawd, Francis, didn't you go to bed?' This particular desk sergeant never tired of what he thought was the joke of using Frank's correct name, a name Frank had felt too milksop, so had rejected when he became five years old and started school. His grandfather, who had been mother and father during Frank's formative years, had not himself minded being named Francis, but had agreed to the small boy's whim and thereafter had never once forgotten to call his grandson Frank.

'Bed? What's bed? A copper who sits on his backside all night might know that, buggered if I do!' and strode off down the passage to place his reports of his previous day's enquiries at Ramsgate on the super's desk. He knocked and went straight in, only to find that, early as he was, James Thomson was at work before him.

'Sorry, sir. I didn't expect you'd be in. It's just the reports. You all right, sir?'

'Thank you, Sergeant, I'm well enough – considering.'

'It's just that you look like you could do with a good night's sleep.'

'I expect we could all do with that, Frank. How about you?'

'Four hours, out like a log. It does me.' It certainly looked as though it did, for Frank was not only closely shaved and his fair hair shining with soft soap and health, but he had a spring about him that was indefinable except that it showed. Only Frank and Elizabeth knew from what spirited and joyful sort of encounter in the very early hours that healthy glow sprang. James thought, as he often did on seeing Frank early in the morning: the man looks as though he's ready to leap on his horse and ride off to market. 'How did yesterday go, sir, if you don't mind my asking?'

The super only barely hesitated before answering, but Frank noticed. Damn it all, the last thing he could do with was for the super to have lost his assurance. 'They did us proud, Frank. Only Oscar Philippe crumbled. I don't know why, he just looked quickly round the court and said he wasn't certain that he could point out the man who had dined at the Cavour.

'That's only one. And Miss Alice?'

'She said the same as always.'

'I'm glad she did, sir. If she wasn't absolutely sure, then she had to say, or Mr Straight could have torn her evidence to shreds. How was our star?'

'Miss Tryphena? As you would expect. I should have liked to put her up last, and left them all with that air of confidence. She pointed directly at Hessel and said her, "That is the man" piece. Then George Flack, he was excellent, too. "That's him!" he said. "I was never surer of anything in my life." Caused a nice little stir amongst the German contingency.'

'Well, that all sounds pretty satisfactory to me, sir. I don't think we have any need to worry.'

Don't ever underestimate Kerley.

'Are we worrying?'

'I'm sorry, sir, I didn't mean we were actually expecting the worst . . . a manner of speaking, sir, that's all.'

The super sat back and waved Frank into the other chair. 'If we had a single piece of hard evidence, something we could take in our hands and hold up in court . . . How did you fare with the knives?'

'If we could just get him on the stand . . . nothing to do with the knives that we can use, but he did buy a new one when he returned from London. If we could get him on the stand and put questions as to his character. He's presented as a man of the cloth and a man of the highest reputation, greatly wronged by us but, as the man who sold him a dagger said, "It's a queer vicar that fires off a revolver from a hotel window and goes about armed like a brigand" – and, I'd add, who has a friend like Mr Wolebe who hasn't got a very savoury character.' His superintendent nodded thoughtfully but made no reply. 'Have you read the stuff in the papers, sir?'

'No, but I know what they are saying, Frank. It is all the work of the usual ragtag journalists and those readers who haven't a thought, and nothing better to do with their time but to pull something or somebody down. Suggest to the men that they tear the paper in squares and use it for a more suitable purpose than reading it.'

The super's face was so straight when he said this that Frank didn't know whether he was supposed to laugh, but he did anyway.

'Listen, Frank, I've had a thought. It may not be worth much, but we must leave no stone unturned . . . I was writing up my journal last evening, when a couple of things crossed my mind about this alibi. Christmas Eve . . . Hessel went to bed early, his boots were outside his door, he wasn't seen until next morning.'

'Right, sir, but he was heard to cough.'

'The night porter's statement. He locked up the hotel for the night, accompanied by Kroll, as is said to be his custom. Right? The hotel is shut up for the night. Ergo, even if Mr Hessel had managed to get out, he could not have got back in to be in bed when the maid served his late breakfast. Why?'

'Because he would have had to rouse the night porter and the night porter was not aroused, sir—' Frank gave an almost imperceptible whistle – 'except that Mr Wolebe said in his first statement that he had been out on the town and had picked up loose women and gone home with them and had not returned to Kroll's until the early hours.'

James Thomson nodded.

Frank Kerley was gazing into his own mind as he sorted through the train of thought his superintendent had had a couple of hours to ponder. 'Wolebe came back, found the door locked, and kicked up all hell, according to the staff. So, who's to say that whilst that racket is going on, and they're getting him to his room, they didn't leave the door unlocked, letting our dear clergyman sneak in unobserved?'

'Even if this did not happen, Frank, the story about locking up for the night and there being no chance of getting back in is thrown into doubt. It's not too full of holes, you think?'

'No, sir, it's not as bad as going to sea in a colander. I reckon it's worth another go at.'

'I am not pinning any hopes on it, Frank, but if we could show that there is a crack in the alibi they are suggesting is cast iron, and make sure the magistrate sends the case for trial . . .'

'If you don't mind my asking, sir, is that the way your mind is working? Do you believe that Mr Vaughan might *not* send him on?'

'Oh, no, Kerley, not at all. He's bound to send him on, the circumstantial is too strong to ignore, no matter how strong the alibi is. As I see it, the one balances the other, and justice would not be seen to be done if the decision was made in a magistrate's court rather than before a judge and jury.'

'So what now, sir?'

'I am going back to Kroll's Hotel and shall ask to look at the books again, and see whether I can question Kroll and that night porter. I shall not have a warrant, so he will be quite within his rights to refuse to show me the books, so I shall have to ask him in a friendly way, a favour.

James could not read Kerley's expression exactly, but he thought it was saying, Well, you can but try. Which was very much his own thoughts as he left Bow Street Station.

Mrs Hessel was putting up at Kroll's Hotel for the period of her husband's trial, and, having the keys to the Hessel trunks still in his possession, James Thomson used the return of these as his reason for calling there.

'Whilst I am here, I would very much like to have a word with your night porter – the one who locked up on the night in question.'

'That is not possible, officer. I am under the instruction of Mr Mullins.'

'I am aware of Mr Mullins, and I do not propose to do anything, but I should like to see those members of your staff who made statements to my officers.'

'I regret not, sir.'

'Then perhaps the rooms occupied by the Ramsgate party. Merely where they are situated if they are let?'

'No, Superintendent.' Kroll's manner was adamant, and James wished that he had a warrant. 'I cannot possibly allow you to view all those rooms.'

'The Hessel rooms then?'

'I cannot do that.'

'Are they occupied?'

'That is not to do with the matter. You must bring a searching document and I must see my solicitor.'

'Mr Kroll, you are not the man standing trial. Why should you need to consult your solicitor?'

Kroll went tight-lipped but did not accede to James's request.

'I can show you nothing, sir, nothing . . . it may be highly irregular.'

'Mr Kroll, I am a senior and experienced Scotland Yard detective. I trust you are not suggesting that I would do anything irregular?'

'I did not mean irregular. Only that . . . I am sorry for this. Officer, I must be in court ready to give evidence for the good doctor.'

'I think, Mr Kroll, that you should talk to Mr Mullins about that. You will be giving evidence on oath to the *court*, in the person of Mr Justice Vaughan. In a trial that may end with a man forfeiting his life, there is no place for witnesses to be "for" the accused or "against" the police.'

Kroll's pomposity was brushing off on James; he heard himself speaking with the same arrogance, and was ashamed, but not sufficiently to stop himself. 'This is not a game, Kroll. When I gave evidence yesterday as to what I saw in the bedroom of the murdered woman, I spoke only as to what *I saw* . . . nothing personal against Mr Hessel – only in so far as he happens to be the man in the dock. Obviously he was arrested because investigations showed him to be the man who spent time with the young woman, but there is nothing personal between myself and Hessel, which is how it should be with you. In this country we go to court – without prejudice – to try to discover the truth. I am sure that is what you want, too: the truth.'

'I do, of course. And I know the truth. It is that Dr Hessel, a fellow countryman of mine, is accused of a crime that if it could be true brings shame on the name of Germany. But this is a good man, an honourable man.'

'Then for you to let me see your books a second time can only help us both get at the truth. I merely wish to see the guest list, the barman's accounts, dates of arrivals and departures. Books are not people to be influenced by me; they answer for themselves.'

But James Thomson came away empty-handed and angry, feeling cast down by the man's arrogance and self-assurance – and chagrined by his own lapse.

Frank Kerley needed that doubt set up by the super to be quelled, and thought he knew how to do it. As Mrs Wright's scullery maid Daisy was not to be called as a witness, Frank got permission from Mrs Wright to take her to see inside the court. Before doing so, he took her to a pie shop and fed her an eel pie and sweet tea. When he thought of his own daughter, well set-up and educated, he'd have liked to be able to do the same for every little girl. Daisy, if she wasn't lucky enough to find herself a decent admirer soon, stood a fair chance of ending up traipsing the Haymarket as Harriet Burton had ended up doing.

With one reassuring hand upon her shoulder, he stood beside Daisy, behind the public benches where one could see the entire court. At first she seemed unable to take her eyes from the grand figure of Mr Justice Vaughan in his wig and robe, then, after about five minutes, during which all attention was upon Wolebe who was giving evidence, he felt Daisy stiffen and look up at him. He squatted so that she could whisper. 'Mr Kerley, you see that man in that kind of box?' She inclined her head discreetly towards the well of the courtroom.

'Which box, the one where the man is speaking from?'

'No, the other one, with the railings round it. Well, the man in there is the one I seen. His hair wasn't brushed and he could ha' done with a shave, but he's the one I seen.'

The super was wrong, Daisy would have made a good witness. The super had said that they would be open to the accusation of scraping the barrel to put the scullery maid on the witness stand. Too late now. He had overstepped the mark there by taking her into court whilst the hearing was going on. But still, he went out assured that they did have the right man.

On the first day of the hearing, Josephine was in Danzig.

The day before, Mr Hood had summoned Josephine to his office. 'Shut the door, Miss Ferguson. Sit down.' He handed her a letter. 'Read this. It arrived this morning.'

Josephine read.

In how far Dr Hessel now undergoing Examination for murder is guilty of that act the examination will soon show, but we think it to be our duty to give a short history of the accused and his wife. It may not bear as a direct proof upon the act but it will show to some extent their former conduct.

Dr Hessel was for about two or three years

350

employed as a Reformed Preacher at the New Peter's Church, the last year of which he also kept a Boys' School to increase his income, the salary for his pastoral duties not being sufficient to keep up his position in society.

By his good address and gentlemanly appearance, he introduced himself into the best society. This could only be of short duration, as he and his wife contracted debts which only could be recovered by legal proceedings. To this we add his profligate and spendthrift conduct, he used to be drunk late at night and early in the morning, which can be proved by his servants and used to borrow money wherever he could. This brought him of course so low that he could not pay his rent and, not having any more articles of worth to pledge, he saw himself obliged to give in his resignation to the College to search for better luck in a foreign country (Baharia).

His resignation was willingly granted as all his behaviour and conduct was fully known and the College granted him his request, the substantial assistance in the sum of 180 thalers to pay small debts of honour. Which he did not pay.

To complete his disgraceful career during the last days of his stay here, he gave a dinner to his boon companions from which he and his wife disappeared and then left them to pay the expenses to his memory.

All that what he and his wife possessed was

principally borrowed, the smallest part of which was paid by cheques so that in all he leaves now a debt of several thousand thalers.

To the truthfulness of these statements which Dr Hessel cannot deny, we refer you to the Senioren College of this reformed parish and also to the Royal Court of Public Examination here.

Signed, Many of the betrayed believers of Dr Hessel.

'Well?'

'A policeman I know once told me that murder is not often a first offence, that there may well have been other minor offences and some while before.'

George Hood nodded. 'I would agree. An early tendency to criminality that is not stopped will escalate.'

'What will you do with the letter, Mr Hood?'

'For the moment, nothing . . . at least until you have been to Danzig.'

He waited for her response, and when she said nothing, he continued. 'And talked to the "Senioren College", whoever they may be, and visited the Royal Court of Public Examination in Danzig.'

'I don't speak German.'

'*The News* has interpreters. We will provide you with one.'

'Could I take my own interpreter? I have a friend who has several languages.'

'As long as the fees aren't too high.'

'Just pay for the boat ticket and a hotel.'

'All right. But there's no time to lose. The hearing is already under way.'

'Thank you, Mr Hood, but why me? Why not one of *The News*'s Young Lions?'

'Because we are publishing Hessel's memoirs, remember? I can't have *The News* riding two horses. In any case, I think this should be yours to deal with. Confirm the information, come back with some statements to back up this letter, and we shall have something substantial to pass on to the police.' He stretched and laughed, hugely pleased. 'Good, isn't it?'

'Just hope that it isn't too good to be true.'

'You know that it's not.'

Josephine nodded. The impression that she had formed of Hessel when she had taken the contract to him in his cell would be vindicated.

'Will you allow *me* to take our findings to the police?'

'I expect you to make a dramatic scene, and later write an article, "My part in the downfall of a killer". Right?'

'Right, Mr Hood.'

Josephine and her 'interpreter', David, had spent an intensive two days, with scarcely any sleep and precious little food.

Now they were eagerly awaiting their landing back in England. Seated side by side in a small cabin, David helped Josephine assemble their notes. The college from which Hessel had resigned under a cloud, and from where the anonymous letter had originated, had given them a statement. Several of his past colleagues had

353

relinquished their anononymity. Several of the men she had interviewed had spoken quite good English, so she could have managed without David's interpretations, except that it was David rather than herself they chose to speak to. In any language it was easy to hear that indignation – his behaviour still rankled; there was embarrassment, too, at having been duped by the Hessels. Very soon, the instigators of the letter to *The News* rattled off any number of misdemeanours, large and small, committed by the Reverend and Mrs Hessel. Profligacy, dishonesty, arrogance, false pride, deception, drunkenness. Mrs Hessel was extravagant, and a flirtatious troublemaker.

'David . . . did you get the impression that they think that Harriet was not the first woman to be killed by him?'

David thought for a few moments. 'Could be. They certainly went into detail about his firearms and carrying knives.'

'Which may be the prime reason for the letter.'

'Not just character assassination out of pique? I think that you may be right, Jo.'

He had slipped so easily into calling her Jo, as Liliana did, that she hardly noticed the first time it happened. Now, she liked that he used her familiar name.

'Did you pick that up, that they believed him to be capable of murder?'

'I don't know, Jo. I may speak German well enough, but I can't get the nuances, the nudges and winks.'

'Never mind the nudges and winks, I wouldn't have stood a chance without you. But I tell you one thing,

I am determined to learn some languages – I felt an ignoramus. I am sure I must have been standing around with my jaw dropping whilst you induced those people to open up about Hessel.'

'They hardly needed persuasion, Jo.'

'True. Even though I don't speak German, I couldn't fail to recognize their animosity.'

'My impression was that they presumed that he was guilty.'

Josephine tapped the sheaf of papers containing the statements they had gathered. 'And this will help see to it that he doesn't get away with putting on a front of religious respectability.'

A silence fell between them, warm, thoughtful and not fraught with the need to say anything. Just the swish as the prow of the ship cut through the sea.

Eventually, David said, 'Jo.' A moment, then a deep breath, 'Jo, I have made a decision, an important one, and I should like to have your opinion.' Another moment of pause. 'I have decided to give up the church.'

'And you want my opinion on that? David, I can't give it. I've heard you speaking to your congregation. You give them hope, they have great affection for you. Where else in London do the likes of Harriet go when they're in trouble? The homes for fallen women such as my aunt and her friends establish? "Young Father David" – people call you that because we all need someone to speak to who isn't judgemental.'

'Sorry, Jo, but you are reading more into me than there is.'

355

'No, I'm not. You're a good man, David. My Uncle James is another . . . and his Sergeant Kerley. But you're too thin on the ground for London to lose one of you.'

Again, as on the Norfolk train, he captured and held her hand between both of his. 'I can do very little as a clergyman. Look at me now, cast out because I speak out, speak the truth. Our prisons are full of people who have no business being there. The disgusting conditions in orphanages; even more disgusting are the stews and alleyways. Children are born there, grow up, and die there. And frequently they die early and violently.'

'I know that, David, I know, which is why you must not give up speaking out, and it is why *I* want to become a columnist people respect in a newspaper that people can trust to tell the truth.'

He squeezed her hand as he laughed, 'Dear Jo, you know how to make life difficult for yourself.'

'Not difficult, David; exciting, worthwhile, gratifying: a life worth living.'

'But you think that preaching and having the virtuous newspaper owners always on my back is a life worth living for me?'

'You do more than that, David. You help people no one else wants to help.'

'Powerless, Jo. What I do is put a little ointment on ulcers that are never going to heal, that's all. And now that God has left me, I can't even say that I do it in His name.'

'Ah. So what you said at New Year was not taken amiss by the *Telegraph*.'

'I hadn't realized it at the time, but yes, I now think that this is the only life we have, and what we don't do on earth will never get done.'

Josephine fell silent. This was probably the first time he had ever put his thoughts into words. Had he told Liliana about his loss of faith, she would not have been able to contain herself; Liliana had opinions on everything and she wouldn't have waited a minute before telling Jo what she thought about her brother.

'You're very quiet, Jo. Are you shocked?'

'No, no, of course I'm not shocked. But it does put a different slant on the opinion you asked for.'

'Well?'

'Do you remember me saying to you, not particularly seriously at the time, that you should go into politics?'

'I remember. That was what started me thinking. You are right, politics is the only way to change conditions.'

Arrival time was only twenty minutes away. Once they arrived in London, the intimacy they were experiencing would be gone. 'Now that I know what is in your mind, I can give you my opinion – you should stand for Parliament.'

'Thank you, Jo, you're a good friend.'

'And you, David, I could never have succeeded in Danzig without you.'

'You would have found someone ... your Mrs Fisher?'

'Perhaps.' Then, looking directly into his eyes and

smiling, she added, 'but I find you much better company.'

Holding her gaze for a moment, he said, 'If I do try to find a parliamentary seat . . . well, um . . .'

'Come along, David, it's not like you to be lost for words.'

'To become a member of Parliament, a man is required to have a wife. Bachelors are suspect. Do you think that you might marry me, Jo?'

'Oh.' How foolish of her not to have suspected that the hand-holding was more than flirtation. And she had allowed it. Enjoyed it.

He let her hand go. 'You are not going to say "yes" are you, Jo?'

Now she took his hand. 'It is not that I don't want to say "yes", David. I like you enormously, I love being in your company, but my situation is not like yours: members of Parliament need to be married, newspaper reporters – female ones at any rate – need to be spinsters.'

Silence returned, not as warm as before. 'Would you have married me had I stayed with the Church?'

'That has nothing to do with it. It is Jemima Ferguson who can't marry you. She is conceited enough to believe that she can become an equal to any male reporter. Jemima Ferguson cannot be anyone's wife.'

'We can remain friends?'

'I should be devastated if we did not. You and I are an integral part of our rebellious group – all talk, of course, but not if you were to stand for Parliament. With us, you might even have the basis of a new political party – one with a conscience.'

Now they were back in England, back in the real world.

'Shall you mind if I come with you to Bow Street, Jo?'

'Of course not. I expect you to . . . without you, all *The News* would have is an anonymous letter.'

'You *are* going to hand it over to your uncle?'

'Of course. With these statements, the police will have no trouble. Uncle James will send men to Danzig, I'm sure. No stone unturned with Uncle James.'

'Do you know how long the magistrate's hearing will take?'

Josephine shrugged. 'I would think not more than another day or two. But the full trial won't take place for weeks and weeks. Once the police have the letter, though, they will be able to make a lot more enquiries than we were able to. The British consul in Danzig will smooth the way for them.'

What happened next, in London, was something remarkable.

Something so extraordinary and so inexplicable that it was likely to puzzle people generations in the future when, delving in to old public records and archives, they would read the reports of Mr Justice Vaughan's words, and wonder whether British justice lived up to its reputation. They might conclude that justice was not blind, but prejudiced.

* * *

Josephine and David disembarked and at once took a cab to Bow Street magistrate's court, where she thought that she might find her uncle. The public gallery was full. Some uniformed policemen were gathered just inside the courtroom. Josephine saw Sergeant Kerley's head above the rest and, standing with him, her uncle. She and David pushed their way towards them.

'Josie,' he whispered, 'what are you doing here?'

Answering in a whisper close to his ear, '*The News* received an anonymous letter about the Hessels, and sent me to see what I could find out. David and I are just returned from Danzig – you won't believe what we have discovered.'

He took the letter, scanned it briefly, then handed it to Sergeant Kerley.

Suddenly, Josephine realized that something dramatic was happening. The silence surrounding Justice Vaughan's voice was electric. 'What is happening?'

'Justice Vaughan is summing up.'

'The hearing's over?'

'Stopped. He heard the prosecution witnesses. Then all the defence witnesses gave alibi evidence, and the hearing was over. Listen.'

'And so, to the evidence given by other witnesses. Herr Kroll, a German of the highest reputation, has given evidence as to the accused's alibi over the crucial hours when the murder of Harriet Burton took place. The respected surgeon Karl Wolebe and other professional fellow-countrymen spoke as to the accused's character and told the court of their high regard for the accused. Mr Wolebe told of the accused's selfless and Christian action in presenting himself at the identification proceedings when Herr Wolebe himself had been wrongly arrested on suspicion of being the murderer of Harriet Burton.

'To my mind it has been conclusively shown that Doctor Henryk James Godfried Hessel was not the companion of the murdered woman.'

Josephine watched as colour drained from her uncle's face, and Sergeant Kerley's face became suffused with angry blood. Both were grim-faced and tight-lipped. Josephine reached for David's hand and gripped it tightly. *Not* the companion? Conclusively shown? How could that be, when so many people had identified him as the man who had been out and about with Harriet on Christmas Eve? When he had been seen to go up to Harriet's room and to leave the house in the early hours of Christmas Day? The puzzled frown on David's face was as deep as her own.

Mr Justice Vaughan had the attention of the entire court as he continued.

'As to the evidence presented by the prosecution. This did – at first – undoubtedly point to Doctor Hessel as having been in the company of that unfortunate woman, and therefore the police were perfectly justified in taking the course of action they did.

'This case has been most fully investigated here, and the witnesses on both sides have been subject to a close and searching cross-examination, and I am satisfied that

361

the witnesses who have identified *Doctor Hessel* as the companion of the deceased ... are ... *entirely ... in error ...*'

The hearing was all but over, the crucial statements had been made.

'It is therefore my duty, and a duty that I discharge with great satisfaction to myself, to state that the prisoner is released. As far as I can see, I say that he leaves this court without suspicion.'

The following day every newspaper had columns and editorials and letters around the Hessel Case. And *The News* started to serialize 'Doctor Hessel's Story In His Own Words'.

At the breakfast table, Frank Kerley attacked the pages of newsprint. 'Listen, Lizzy: "Mrs Hessel, racked by torturing anxiety, scarcely ate or slept during her husband's imprisonment, and now that the tension of the strain is over, the revulsion is leaving the poor lady's nervous system in a sadly depressed and shattered condition. It is hoped, nevertheless, that Mrs Hessel will have sufficiently recovered to render it possible that in a week's time her husband and herself can leave England by steamer for Baharia, where they will arrive before the fated *Wangerland*.'

'The sooner they are out of the country and it's all forgotten, the better, Frank, if you ask me.' Elizabeth tried to be neutral and careful about what she said, for Frank was undoubtedly not himself.

The one bit of brightness had been yesterday, before the hearing had collapsed, when he had come home pleased as punch with the news that his super had put him forward for a commendation and a reward.

'Of course,' he explained, 'Colonel Henderson could never agree to putting the super's report forward for the reward, but the words in the super's report are better than guineas, Lizzy.'

Elizabeth herself could not see why the commissioner could not put Frank forward: going aboard a plague ship is as brave as facing a pistol. But that's how they were in the police force. If he had actually got smallpox he might have been rewarded, or if the case hadn't collapsed like that. She felt real pain for Frank, and knew that he felt pain himself. He was a very professional policeman, seldom brought his work home with him, never let all that dreadful stuff he had to do affect his relationship with herself and Frances.

But this case seemed to have got to him right from the start.

One night in bed he had said to her, 'This is a Them and Us case, Lizzy. It's like it was when I was a kid back home, the lord of the manor couldn't ever do no wrong. You could put a monkey in a silk shirt and people would believe him before they'd believe a working man in a fustian jacket.'

Josephine went next day to see George Hood. 'You should have handed the letter over to the police as soon as it arrived.'

363

'It would have made no difference. His supporters are "Germans of the highest reputation" – isn't that what Justice Vaughan called them? With the queen mourning the German of the highest reputation of all, the riff-raff of the London streets hadn't a chance of being believed.'

Josephine believed that he was probably right in that.

'What did Superintendent Thomson say when you gave him the letter and the statement?'

'Nothing. He read it and so did his sergeant. Small comfort to know that they were right when he and his wife are out there being feted. Some of his fellow-countrymen living in England have started a subscription.'

George Hood nodded. 'The queen has contributed thirty pounds and the prime minister has made a large donation. I've heard that he is going to make an apology on behalf of the people of Britain.'

'Not on my behalf!'

Liliana read aloud from one of the many newspapers that littered the kitchen table. '"The Sailing of the *Wangerland*. Mrs Hessel's ordeal has rendered her unfit to continue the journey to Brazil at present and she will remain in London until she has rested . . .".'

Josephine snatched the page, crushed it into a ball and threw it at the wall. David picked it up, and sat crushing it into an even harder ball.

'Where were they last night?' Liliana asked. 'Dining at Windsor Castle?'

'Or with Mr Gladstone.'

'Of course, Mr Gladstone is very interested in the plight of prostitutes. He might ask the good doctor about his unique method of clearing the streets of harlots.'

'Lili!' David remonstrated.

'I know ... sorry, a very coarse joke. At least Mr Gladstone does show some concern for "fallen women".'

'The trouble with people who have the power to change things for the better is that they are not *people*, they are *men* ... I'm sorry, David, I don't include you ...'

Liliana said, 'I should stop there before you get yourself in deeper.'

David said, 'A day will come when you will have a say in the country's affairs.'

'Do you mean Jo personally, or women generally?'

'Jo will get her say long before women as a whole do.'

By the time the petals of blossom and spring flowers in London parks had fallen, and the summer of 1873 had bloomed with new fabrics and fashions, the Great Coram Street Murder was all but forgotten. The enthusiasm that book publishers had shown for Josephine's *Life of a Country Girl*, paying her a decent sum of money for its rights, waned. It would be published, but perhaps at a more favourable time.

George Hood let her fume about the capriciousness of publishers. 'Favourable? When would that be, do you think?'

'Do you want me to agree, or tell you what I think?'

'Tell me.'

'Very well, a favourable time will be when there is a similar case of murder. When the murder of another young prostitute is headline news.'

'I didn't write Harriet's story for sensation, I wrote it so that people would become more enlightened about how poor women exist in London, how easy it is for a respectable girl to have to resort to the streets.'

'Of course, but your publishers needed to have your murderer found guilty and hanged. Have they suggested that as a possible denouement?' Josephine didn't answer. 'Of course they did, and you, my dear Miss Ferguson, are determined to be the purist.'

'Don't you see, Mr Hood, my *Country Girl* can't have a satisfactory conclusion – her killer got away scot-free!'

'As I see it, you have two choices: you can insist that your book is published without it ending in a trial and execution, or you can insist that it tells the truth.'

'You think that is a choice?'

George Hood shrugged his shoulders. 'For you? No.'

'The *Country Girl* has not turned out to be what I first intended, a kind of biography told in story fashion. When Justice Vaughan said that he believed the well-off and educated, and that the rest were "entirely mistaken" – *all* of them? *all* mistaken? – my book became a kind of exposé of prejudice.'

'And injustice. Don't forget injustice, Miss Ferguson.'

'Are you laughing at me?'

'Of course not, but where your book is concerned I

think that you are blind to what I thought we agreed upon when you joined *The News*. "Tickle", Miss Ferguson. Have you forgotten why our readership increases daily?'

Josephine fell silent. She had come here believing that she would have an ally in her editor. 'What should I do then?'

'Well, you have already seen that Harriet Burton's life would be more interesting to people in the form of a novel, so write a fictitious conclusion.'

'What?'

'Anything. The truth of your story is in Harriet's life . . . and death.'

'A trial scene?'

'Why not? You could have the accused face all those people who never appeared at the Bow Street hearing, the ones not even the police knew of until the anonymous letter.'

'The Danzig people?'

'Of course. *The News* might start a whispering campaign. "Is this book a true account of what happened?" And put questions in the Personal advertisement columns.'

Jo burst out laughing. 'Oh yes, Mr Hood. What "tickle"!'

Christine Derry put on a splendid show of Liliana's work, the central piece of which was a large canvas entitled "Working Woman", depicting Tryphena Douglas as a kind of proud empress of her glittering bar. As the group of friends walked through the warm streets towards Boot Street. David put a hand on Jo's arm. 'There's something I want to ask you before we get to the Dining Rooms.'

Oh Lord, he's going to ask me to marry him again. Which he was, but not in so straightforward a manner as that.

'I've decided to leave the Church entirely.'

'I can't say that I am surprised.'

'Yes, well, I thought more about our conversation on the boat. I have been approached by some Liberal people and their financiers. They have asked me to allow my name to be proposed for a seat that has become vacant in the West Country – Cornwall, actually.'

'David, that's wonderful – you agreed, I hope.'

'I said that I was interested – very interested, but . . .'

'No buts. Grab the opportunity with both hands. You were born to be a politician.'

'I am so pleased that you think it the right thing. I thought that the other right thing would be for us to be married?

Irritation niggled her. The right thing? Not, I love you to distraction, Jo.

'No response, Jo? You would be a wonderful wife for any politician. Together, we could make such changes in society. This is the time for change, Jo.' He squeezed her hand eagerly. 'I see us in high office.'

Pulling her arm away she said tightly. 'I'm afraid that I don't, David.'

'Jo. I thought we had similar ideas about society, about changing things for the better, a more equal society, the poor better cared for.'

'And you believe that a marriage could thrive on that? Where does love come in, David? Anywhere? Or just after ambition?'

'Love goes without saying. I love you because of all those things I have discovered about you.'

'I am sure that you will find someone who likes the idea – but not me. I should have thought you had realized by now that I am lead violinist, not second fiddle.'

'I am very disappointed, Jo.'

'Don't be, David. Ask Christine, she'd make a much more suitable politician's wife than me.' Did that sound like pique? She hoped not. 'In any case, I have been asked if I would like to join the staff of *The Post* – it's a New York daily paper.' She did not mention that she had sought the position herself. She had sent off a collection of her pieces, and related her part in obtaining the Hessel contract for *The News*.

'You intend going to America alone?'

'I hope that Hani will come too.'

Her almond-shaped eyes almost closed with smiles and tears, Hani said, 'America? Of course I go. MistaJame feel better if I am with you.' She giggled and clasped Jo's hands. 'Oh 'osie, what fun . . . what adventure. There are maybe more Eastern people than in London.'

'You think you might find a husband.'

'I do not, silly gir', but who knows?'

'So you will come?'

'I come . . . of course. This time when you leave home, I take care of you.'

369

'Hani, no! It will be a rule of the house that you understand that I am a grown-up woman.'

'Of course, 'osie. I not tell you what to do.'

Josephine gave Hani a brief hug. 'I don't believe you, but I am so glad that you will come. Right . . . such fun, such adventures.'

On her last evening, before leaving for Southampton, from where she and Hani would leave for New York, James and Ann Martha took Josephine to dine out at one of Ann's favourite restaurants – splendid, of course.

They were seated in a lounge drinking post-prandial brandy and coffee, when James produced an envelope which he passed across the table to Josephine. 'I could have let you see this before your book was published, but in the end decided not to in case it might prove too much of a temptation.'

Taking the strangely folded document from the envelope, she read.

1873

British Consulate – Danzig
Consular No. 8 Confidential.
By post
copy to The Queen. Mr Gladstone. The Home Office.
Confidential information relative to Dr Hessel
To The Right Honble. The Earl of Granville KG, Foreign Office.

My Lord

In compliance with Viscount Enfield's instructions as conveyed to me in His Lordship's Despatch marked No. 1 Consular Confidential, dated 11th instant, but which did not reach me until the 20th instant, on the subject of Doctor Hessel, I have the honour to report to Your Lordship as follows:–

Unfortunately the person who is the object of Your Lordship's enquiries, and who has acquired lately such notoriety, did not leave Danzig with that high character with which he has been credited by his friends and supporters in his misfortune in London.

Dr Hessel came to Danzig from a Parish in the Rhenish Provinces, and was attached here to a Reformed Church, and not as has been erroneously stated to one of the Lutheran Communion, though he may have been originally ordained a Lutheran Minister, of this I cannot be certain.

It is correctly stated in the anonymous letter, that besides his clerical duties at the Church of St Peter, in this town, he was also employed in tuition in a private School, and that by his insinuating manner he gained a favourable admittance into Society at this place.

His connection with the private School of Dr Weiss was suddenly broken off in the Autumn of 1871, and I understand that the cause of it has been ascribed to some money transactions of

Dr Hessel's, but I cannot speak with any degree of certainty on this delicate subject as I am not willing to give my enquiries that openness which might ensure a more complete result, nor am I authorized, by Your Lordship's Instructions, to proceed otherwise.

As far as I am able to ascertain anything further about Dr Hessel, a certain irregularity in his habits ascribed to him, and this with increasing pecuniary difficulties assigned as the cause of the cessation of his clerical duties here, and of his determination to leave Europe for the Brazilian Empire.

I am not in a position to establish with any degree of accuracy the extent to which these charges may be proved, but from a variety of sources to which I have referred with the greatest possible caution, I have arrived at the painful conclusion that there must be some foundation for them, and that the description of Dr Hessel contained in the anonymous letter which I beg leave to return as instructed, cannot be considered as altogether incorrect.

Should Her Majesty's Secretary of State for the Home Department deem further enquiries necessary, I think that it would be requisite to make them through the Prussian Police Authorities, as the only means of establishing accurate data.

The charge of having feted his friends on the day of his departure, and of having left by the train without taking leave of them, or having paid the Bill, is currently believed against Dr Hessel at Danzig liabilities he left behind him may be exaggerated, but I am assured by my own Lawyer Mr Marting that he has succeeded in obtaining a payment of twenty odd pounds for one of his clients from Dr Hessel through the intervention of the German Consul General in London.

I have the honour to remain with the greatest of respect, My Lord, Your Lordship's most obedient, humble servant, W. White

'Thank you for letting me see this, Uncle James. What will happen to it now?'

'It will be secreted away in the deep vaults where other embarrassing and sensitive documents are buried.'

'This makes me even more certain that I am making the right decision to start life in a country where there is no queen sitting heavily on people – and "humble servant". What does that mean, Uncle James?'

'Josephine, you know that is not to be taken literally. I am certain that this man is not one bit humble, quite the reverse.'

'I don't want to be a "subject", I want to be a "citizen".'

Ann Martha said, 'Josephine, you make it appear that this is not a free country.'

James's eyes asked Josephine to forgive Ann Martha her unenlightened views.

'Things will change, Josie.'

'Perhaps, Uncle James, but I can't wait that long.'

Author's Note

My interest in the Great Coram Street Murder started when, researching for another book, I came upon a reference to it quite by chance. The victim's name, being Burton – Harriet/Clara Burton – was the spark that ignited my interest. Then, in a short piece in a collection, there was the comment by an author who, like me, had been intrigued by the story (but abandoned it), that 'it is now known that the murderer got away with it.'

That author's widow generously gave me her husband's research, which didn't give a clue as to why he had come to that conclusion. Now I was hooked, so I spoke to my 'ace' researcher, Elizabeth, who knows her way about the dustier parts of London's archives.

Soon, she had unearthed very many documents, and produced a blizzard of photocopies, police reports, victim antecedents, witness statements, career records of the two detectives, even a photograph of Superintendent Thomson, his will, and a photo of the house in Great Coram Street. In addition there were many column inches of newspaper reports, and a letter from Scotland Yard's Black Museum relating to the clue of the bitten apple found at the scene of the crime. Then there were the long, long love-letters from a Willie Kirby – who one must suspect of stringing Harriet along.

Perhaps most intriguing of all is a confidential Foreign Office report on the suspect, a Clergyman of the Highest Reputation. This was from the British Consulate in Danzig to Earl Granville at the Foreign Office. He passed it on to Queen Victoria and the prime minister to read. Too late! The bird had been released and flown.

One can only speculate on the speed with which this hot potato was passed around. What to do? Obvious, bury it. And so it remained buried until my researcher Elizabeth discovered it. It was the one piece of evidence I needed to justify writing this book, which is not only about the murder of a woman and the man who got away with it, but also about prejudice and injustice. Nothing's new.

The more Elizabeth found, the more interesting became the story of the murder of Harriet Burton.

Chequebook journalism being nothing new, the accused man's 'Story in His Own Words' appeared. Readers' letters, then as now the 'Why-oh-why?' brigade, wanting somebody at whom to hurl abuse, chose to denigrate, insult and berate the police – so ignorant and insensitive that they had arrested a 'Clergyman of the highest reputation'. Add to this that the clergyman accused of killing an actress in her own bedroom was a fellow-countryman of the widowed queen's dead husband, it was enough to ignite the flames of outrage.

After the clergyman was released, donations were called for and money poured in – the queen herself gave £30, a large sum then, and the prime minister was another contributor. A subscription dinner was arranged. A message of abject apology on behalf of the nation was inscribed on a silver dish, which was presented to the young man and his pretty wife before they sailed away to the other side of the world.

Recently, I engaged a profiler to look at this 'cold case murderer' using the same up-to-date methods as would a present-day murder team. The profiler's report confirms what I had come to believe. Godfried Hessel was a psychopath. He enjoyed the 'buzz', such as when he let off a fire-arm from his hotel window. He believed that he was unassailable as, for example, when he forced himself into the ID parade and made no attempt to keep from being seen with Harriet on Christmas Eve. He killed Harriet Burton because he felt like it at the time.

Now, of course, I itch to know what happened to Harriet Burton's killer. Did he continue his journey to Bahai in Brazil? Did he kill again?